GRACE LIVINGSTON HILL

The City of Fire

Time of the Singing of Birds

The Gold Shoe

JUMBO READER II

BARBOUR

ISBN 1-56865-127-9

The
City of Fire

Chapter 1

Sabbath Valley lay like a green jewel cupped in the hand of the surrounding mountains with the morning sun serene upon it picking out the clean smooth streets, the white houses with their green blinds, the maples with their clear-cut leaves, the cozy brick schoolhouse wide-winged and friendly, the vine-clad stone church, and the little stone bungalow with low spreading roof that was the parsonage. The word manse had not yet reached the atmosphere. There were no affectations in Sabbath Valley.

Billy Gaston, two miles away and a few degrees up the mountainside, standing on the little station platform at Pleasant View, waiting for the morning train, looked down upon the beauty at his feet and felt its loveliness blindly. A passing thrill of wonder and devotion fled through his four-teen-year-old soul as he regarded it idly. Down there was home and all his interests and loyalty. His eyes dwelt affec-tionately on the pointing spire and bell tower. He loved those bells, and the one who played them, and under their swelling tones had been awakened new thoughts and lofty purposes. He knew they were lofty. He was not yet alto-gether sure that they were his, but they were there in his mind for him to think about, and there was a strange awe-some lure about their contemplation.

Down the platform was the new freight agent, a thickset, rubber-shod individual with a projecting lower jaw and a lowering countenance. He had lately arrived to assist the regular station agent, who lived in a bit of a shack up the mountain and was a thin sallow creature with sad eyes and no muscles. Pleasant View was absolutely what it stated, a pleasant view and nothing else. The station was a well-weathered box that blended into the mountainside unnoticeably, and did not spoil the view. The agent's cabin was hidden by the trees and did not count. But Pleasant View was important as a station because it stood at the intersection of two lines of threadlike tracks that slipped among the mountains in different directions; one, winding among the trees and about a clear mountain lake, carried guests for the summer to and fro, and great quantities of baggage and freight from afar; the other traveled through long tunnels to the world beyond and linked great cities like jewels on a chain. There were heavy bales and boxes and many trunks to be shifted and it was obvious that the sallow station agent could not do it all. The heavy one had been sent to help him through the rush season.

In five minutes more the train would come from around the mountain and bring a swarm of ladies and children for the hotel at the lake. They would have to be helped off with all their luggage, and on again to the lake train, which would back up two minutes later. This was Billy's harvest time. He could sometimes make as much as fifty cents or even seventy-five if he struck a generous party, just being generally useful, carrying bags and marshaling babies. It was important that Billy should earn something, for it was Saturday and the biggest ball game of the season came off at Monopoly that afternoon. Billy could manage the getting there, it was only ten miles away, but money to spend when he arrived was more than a necessity. Saturday was always a good day at the station.

Billy had slipped into the landscape unseen. His rusty, trusty old bicycle was parked in a thick huckleberry growth just below the grade of the tracks, and Billy himself stood in the shelter of several immense packing boxes piled close to the station. It was a niche just big enough for his wiry young length with the open station window close at his ear. From either end of the platform he was hidden, which was as it should be until he got ready to arrive with the incoming train.

The regular station agent was busy checking a high pile of trunks that had come down on the early lake train from the hotel and had to be transferred to the New York train. He was on the other side of the station and some distance down the platform.

Beyond the packing boxes the heavy one worked with brush and paint marking some barrels. If Billy applied an eye to a crack in his hiding place he could watch every stroke of the fat black brush, and see the muscles in the swarthy cheeks move as the man mouthed a big black cigar. But Billy was not interested in the new freight agent, and remained in his retreat, watching the brilliant sunshine shimmer over the blue-green haze of spruce and pine that furred the way down to the valley. He basked in it like a cat blinking its content. The rails were beginning to hum softly, and it would not be long till the train arrived.

Suddenly Billy was aware of a shadow looming.

The heavy one had laid down his brush and was stealing swiftly, furtively to the door of the station with a weather eye to the agent on his knees beside a big trunk writing something on a check. Billy drew back like a turtle to his shell and listened. The rail was beginning to sing decidedly now and the telephone inside the grated window suddenly set up a furious ringing. Billy's eye came round the corner of the window, scanned the empty platform, glimpsed the office desk inside and the weighty figure holding the receiver, then vanished enough to be out of sight, leaving only a wide curious ear to listen:

"That you, Sam? Yep. Nobody about. Train's coming. Hustle up. Anything doing? You *don't say!* Some big guy? *Say,* that's good news at last! Get on the other wire and hold it. I'll come as quick as the train's gone. S'long!"

Billy cocked a curious eye like a flash into the window
and back again, ducking behind the boxes just in time to
miss the heavy one coming out with an excited air, and a feverish eye on the track where the train was coming into view
around the curve.

In a moment all was stir and confusion, seven women
wanting attention at once, and imperious men of the world
crying out against railroad regulations. Billy hustled everywhere, transferring bags and suitcases with incredible rapid-
ity to the other train, which arrived promptly, securing a
double seat for the fat woman with the canary, and the poo-
dle in a big basket, depositing the baggage of a pretty lady
on the shady side, making himself generally useful to the
opulent-looking man with the jeweled rings; and back again
for another lot. A whole dollar and fifteen cents jingled in
his grimy pocket as the trains finally moved off in their separate directions and the peace of Pleasant Valley settled down
monotonously once more.

Billy gave a hurried glance about him. The station agent
was busy with another batch of trunks, but the heavy one
was nowhere to be seen. He gave a quick glance through the
grated window where the telegraph instrument was clicking
away sleepily, but no one was there. Then a stir among the
pines below the track attracted his attention, and stepping to
the edge of the bank he caught a glimpse of a broad dusty
back lumbering hurriedly down among the branches.

With a flirt of his eye back to the absorbed station agent
Billy was off down the mountain after the heavy one, walking stealthily as any cat, pausing in alert attention, listening,
peering out eerily whenever he came to a break in the undergrowth. Like a young mole burrowing he wove his way
under branches the larger man must have turned aside, and
so his going was as silent as the air. Now and then he could
hear the crash of a broken branch, or the crackle of a twig,
or the rolling of a stone set free by a heavy foot, but he went

on like a cat, like a little wood shadow, till suddenly he felt
he was almost upon his prey. Then he paused and listened.
The man was kneeling just below him. He could hear the
labored breathing. There was a curious sound of metal and
wood, of a key turning in a lock. Billy drew himself softly
into a group of cypress and held his breath. Softly he parted
the foliage and peered. The man was down upon his knees
before a rough box, holding something in his hand which he
put to his ear. Billy could not quite see what it was. And now
the man began to talk into the box. Billy ducked and listened:

"Hello, Sam! You there! Couldn't come any quicker, lots
of passengers. Lots of freight. What's doing, anyhow?"

Billy could hear a faint murmur of words, now and then
one guttural burst out and became distinct, and gradually
enough words pieced themselves together to become intelli-
gible.

". . . Rich guy! High-power machine. . . . Great catch. . . .
Tonight! . . . Got a bet on to get there by sunrise. . . . Can't
miss him!"

Billy lay there puzzled. It sounded shady, but what was
the line anyway? Then the man spoke.

"Sounds easy, Sammy, but how we goin' to kidnap a man
in a high-power machine? Wreck it of course, but he might
get killed and where would be the reward? Besides, he's
likely to be a good shot—"

The voice from the ground again growing clearer:

"Put something across the road that he'll have to get out
and move, like a fallen tree, or one of you lie in the road beside a car as if you was hurt. I'm sending Shorty and Link.
They'll get there about eight o'clock. Beat him to it by an
hour anyway, maybe more. Now it's up to you to look after
details. Get anyone you want to help till Shorty and Link
get there, and pay 'em so in case anything gets them, or
they're late. I'll keep you wise from time to time how the guy
gets on. I've got my men on the watch along the line."

"I'd like t' know who I'd get in this godforsaken place!" growled the heavy one. "Not a soul in miles except the agent, and *he'd* run right out and telegraph for the state constab. Say, Sammy, who is this guy anyway? Is there enough in it to pay for the risk? You know kidnapping ain't any juvenile demeanor. I didn't promise no such stuff as this when I said I'd take a hand over here. Now just a common little holdup ain't so bad. That could happen on any lonely mountain road. But this here kidnapping, you never can tell how its going to turn out. Might be murder before you got through, especially if Link is along. *You know Link!*"

"That's all right, Pat, you needn't worry. This'll go through slick as a whistle, and a million in it if we work it right. The house is all ready—you know where—and never a soul in all the world would suspect. It's far enough away and yet not too far. You'll make enough out of this to retire for life if you want to, Pat, and no mistake. All you've got to do is to handle it right, and you know your business."

"Who'd you say he was?"

"Shafton, Laurence Shafton, son of the big Shafton, you know Shafton and Gates."

A heavy whistle blended with the whispering pines.

"You don't say? How much family?"

"Mother living, got separate fortune in her own right. Father just dotes on him. Uncle has a big estate on Long Island, plenty more millions there. I think a million is real modest of us to ask, don't you?"

"Where's he goin' to? What makes you think he'll come this way 'stead of the valley road?"

" 'Cause he's just started, got all the directions for the way, went over it carefully with his valet. Valet gave me the tip you understand, and has to be in on the rake-off. It's his part to keep close to the family, see? Guy's goin' down to Beechwood to a house party, got a bet on that he'll make it before daylight. He's bound to pass your mountain soon after midnight, see? Are you goin' to do your part, or ain't you? Or have I got to get a new agent down there? And say! I want a message on this wire as soon as the job is completed. Now, you understand? Can you pull it off?"

It was some time after the key clicked in the lock and the bulky form of the freight agent lumbered up through the pines again before Billy stirred. Then he wriggled around through the undergrowth until he found himself in front of the innocent-looking little box covered over with dried grass and branches. He examined it all very carefully, pried underneath with his jackknife, discovered the spot where the wire connected, speculated as to where it tapped the main line, prospected a bit about the place and then on hands and knees wormed himself through the thick growth of the mountain till he came out to the huckleberry clump, and recovering his bicycle walked innocently up to the station as if it were the first time that day and inquired of the surly freight man whether a box had come for his mother.

In the first place Billy hadn't any mother, only an aunt who went out washing and had hard times to keep a decent place for Billy to sleep and eat, and she never had a box come by freight in her life. But the burly one did not know that. Just what Billy Gaston did it for, perhaps he did not quite know himself, save that the lure of hanging round a mystery was always great. Moreover it gave him deep joy to know that he knew something about this man that the man did not know he knew. It was always good to know things. It was always wise to keep your mouth shut about them when you knew them. Those were the two most prominent planks in Billy Gaston's present platform and he stood upon them firmly.

The burly one gave Billy a brief and gruff negative to his query and went on painting barrel labels. He was thinking of other matters, but Billy still hung around. He had a hunch that he might be going to make merchandise in some way of the knowledge that he had gained, so he hung around, silently, observantly, leaning on old rusty trusty.

The man looked up and frowned suspiciously:

"I told you NO!" he snapped threateningly. "What you standin' there for?"

Billy regarded him amusedly as from a superior height.

"Don't happen to know of any odd jobs I could get," he finally condescended.

"Where would you expect a job around this dump?" sneered the man with an eloquent wave toward the majestic mountain. "Busy little hive right here now, ain't it?"

He subsided and Billy, slowly, thoughtfully, mounted his wheel and rode around the station, with the air of one who enjoys the scenery. The third time he rounded the curve by the freight agent the man looked up with a speculative squint and eyed the boy. The fourth time he called out, straightening up and laying down his brush.

"Say, kid, do you know how to keep yer mouth shut?"

The boy regarded him with infinite contempt.

"Well, that depends!" he said at last. "If anybody'd make it worth my while."

The man looked at him narrowly, the tone was at once so casual and yet so full of possible meaning. The keenest searching revealed nothing in the immobile face of the boy. A cunning grew in the eyes of the man.

"How would a five look to you?"

"Not enough," said the boy promptly. "I need twenty-five."

"Well, ten then."

The boy rode off down the platform and circled the station again while the man stood puzzled, half troubled, and watched him:

"I'll make it fifteen. What you want, the earth with a gold fence around it?"

"I said I needed twenty-five," said Billy doggedly, lowering his eyes to cover the glitter of coming triumph.

The thick one stood squinting off at the distant mountain thoughtfully, then he turned and eyed Billy again.

"How'm I gonta know you're efficient?" he challenged.

"Guess you'c'n take me er leave me," came back the boy quickly. "Course if you've got plenty help—"

The man gave him a quick bitter glance. The kid was sharp. He knew there was no one else. Besides, how much had he overheard? Had he been around when the station telephone rang? Kids like that were deep. You could always count on them to do a thing well if they undertook it.

"Well, mebbe I'll try you. You gotta be on hand t'night at eight o'clock sharp. It's mebbe an all-night job, but you may be through by midnight."

"What doing?"

"Nothing much. Just lay in the road with your wheel by your side and act like you had a fall an' was hurt. I wanta stop a man who's in a hurry, see?"

Billy regarded him coolly.

"Any shooting?"

"Oh, no!" said the other. "Just a little evening up of cash. You see that man's got some money that oughtta be mine by good rights, and I wantta get it."

"*I* see!" said Billy nonchalantly. "An' whatcha gonta do if he don't come across?"

The man gave him a scared look.

"Oh, nothin' sinful, son; just give him a rest fer a few days where he won't see his friends, until he gets ready to see it the way I do."

"H'm!" said Billy, narrowing his gray eyes to two slits. "An' how much did ya say ya paid down?"

The man looked up angrily.

"I don't say I pay nothing down. If you do the work right you get the cash, t'night, a round twenty-five, and it's twenty bucks more'n you deserve. Why off in this deserted place you ought ta be glad to get twenty-five cents fer doin' nothin' but lay in the road."

The boy with one foot on the pedal mounted sideways and slid along the platform slowly, indifferently.

"Guess I gotta date t'night," he called over his shoulder as he swung the other leg over the crossbar.

The heavy man made a dive after him and caught him by the arm.

"Look here, kid, I ain't in no mood to be toyed with," he said gruffly. "You said you wanted a job an' I'm being square with you. Just to show I'm being square here's five down."

Billy looked at the ragged green bill with a slight lift of his shoulders.

"Make it ten down and it's a go," he said at last with a take-it-or-leave-it air. "I hadn't oughtta let you off'n less'n half, such a shady job as this looks, but make it a ten an' I'll close with ya. If ya don't like it ask the station agent to help ya. I guess he wouldn't object. He's right here handy, too. I live off quite a piece."

But the man had pulled out another five and was crowding the bills upon him. He had seen a light in that boy's eye that was dangerous. What was five in a case of a million anyway?

Billy received the boodle as if it had been chewing gum or a soiled handkerchief, and stuffed it indifferently into his already bulging pocket in a crumple as if it were not worth the effort.

"A'rright. I'll be here!" he declared, and mounting his wheel with an air of finality, sailed away down the platform, curved off the high step with a bump into the road and coasted down the road below the tunnel toward Monopoly, leaving Sabbath Valley glistening in the sunshine off to the right. With all that money in his pocket what was the use of going back to Sabbath Valley for his lunch and making his trip a good two miles farther? He would beat the baseball team to it.

The thick one stood disconsolately, his grimy cap in his

hand and scratched his dusty head of curls in a troubled way.

"Gosh!" he said wrathfully. "The little devil! Now I don't know what he'll do. I wonder— But what else could I do?"

Chapter 2

Over in Sabbath Valley quiet sweetness brooded, broken now and again by the bell-like sound of childish laughter here and there. The birds were holding high carnival in the trees, and the bees humming drowsy little tunes to pretend they were not working.

Most of the men were away at work, some in Monopoly or Economy, whither they went in the early morning in their tin lizzies to a little store or a country bank, or a dusty law office; some in the fields of the fertile valley; and others off behind the thick willow fringe where lurked the home industries of tanning and canning and knitting, with a plush mill higher up the slope behind a group of alders and beeches, its ugly stone chimneys picturesque against the mountains, but doing its best to spoil the little stream at its feet with all colors of the rainbow, at intervals dyeing its bright waters.

The minister sat in his study with his window open across the lawn between the parsonage and the church, a lovely velvet view with the old graveyard beyond and the wooded hill behind. He was faintly aware of the shouting of the birds in glad carnival in the trees, and the busy droning of the bees, as he wrote an article on modern atheism for a magazine in the distant world; but more keenly alive to the song on the lips of his child, but lately returned from college life in one of the great universities for women. He smiled as he wrote, and a light came in his deep thoughtful eyes. She had gone and come, and she was still unspoiled, mentally, physically or spiritually. That was a great deal to have kept out of life in these days of unbelief. He had been almost afraid to hope that she would come back the same.

In the cool sitting room his wife was moving about, putting the house in order for the day, and he knew that on her lips also was the smile of the same content as well as if he were looking at her beloved face.

On the front veranda Marilyn Severn swept the rugs and sang her happy song. She was glad, glad to be home again, and her soul bubbled over with the joy of it. There was happiness in the curve of her red lips, in the softly rounded freshness of her cheek and brow, in the eyes that held dancing lights like stars, and in every gleaming tendril of her wonderful bright hair that burst forth from under the naive little sweeping cap that sat on her head like a crown. She was small, lithe, graceful, and she vibrated joy, health, eagerness in every glance of her eye, every motion of her lovely hands.

Down the street suddenly sounded a car. Not the rattling, cheap affairs that were commonly used in those parts for hard work and dress affairs, with a tramp snuffle and bark as they bounced along beneath the maples like house dogs that knew their business and made as much noise about it as they could; but a car with a purr like a soft petted cat by the fire, yet a power behind the purr that might have belonged to a lion if the need for power arose. It stole down the street like a thing of the world, well oiled and perfect in its way, and not needing to make any clatter about its going. The very quietness of it made the minister look up, sent the minister's wife to raise the shade of the sitting room window, and caused the girl to look up from her task.

The morning flooded her face, the song was stayed, a great light came into her eyes.

The man who was driving the car had the air of not expecting to stop at the parsonage. Even when he saw the girl on the porch he held to his way, and something hard and cold and infinitely sad settled down over his face. It even looked as though he did not intend to recognize her, or perhaps wasn't sure whether she would recognize him. There was a moment's breathless suspense and the car slid just the fraction past the gate in the hedge, without a sign of stopping, only a lifting of a correct looking straw hat that somehow seemed a bit out of place in Sabbath Valley. But Lynn left no doubt in his mind whether she would recognize him. She dropped her broom and sped down the path, and the car came to an abrupt halt, only a hairbreadth past the gate— but still—that hairbreadth.

"Oh, Mark, I'm so glad to see you!" she cried genuinely with her hand out in welcome. "They said you were not at home."

The boy's voice—he had been a boy when she left him, though now he looked strangely hard and old like a man of the world—was husky as he answered gravely, swinging himself down on the walk beside her:

"I just got in late last night. How are you, Lynn? You're looking fine."

He took her offered hand, and clasped it for a brief instant in a warm strong pressure, but dropped it again and there was a quick cold withdrawing of his eyes that she did not understand. The old Mark Carter would never have looked at her coolly, impersonally like that. What was it, was he shy of her after the long separation? Four years was a long time, of course, but there had been occasional letters. He had always been away when she was at home, and she had been home very little between her school years. There had been summer sessions twice and once Father and Mother had come to her and they had taken a wonderful trip together. But always there had seemed to be Mark Carter, her old friend and playmate, in the background. Now, suddenly he seemed to be removed to indefinite distances. It was as if she were looking at a picture that purported to be her friend, yet seemed a travesty, like one wearing a mask. She stood in the sunlight looking at him, in her quaint little cap and a long white enveloping house apron, and she seemed to him like a haloed saint. Something like worship shone in his eyes, but he kept the mask down, and looked at her with the eyes of a stranger while he talked, and smiled a stiff conventional smile. But a look of anguish grew in his young face, like the sorrow of something primeval, such as a great rock in a desert.

The minister had forgotten his article and was watching them through the window, the tall handsome youth, his head bared with the glint of the sun on his short-cropped gold curls making one think of a young prince, yet a prince bound under a spell and frozen in a block of ice. He was handsome as Adonis, every feature perfect, and striking in its manly beauty, yet there was nothing feminine about him. The minister was conscious of all this as he watched—this boy whom he had seen grow up, and this girl of his heart. A great still question came into the father's look as he watched.

The minister was conscious of Lynn's mother standing in the doorway just behind him, although she had made no noise in entering. And at once she knew he was aware of her presence.

"Isn't that Mark Carter?" she asked just above a breath.

He nodded.

"And she doesn't know! You haven't told her?"

The minister shook his head.

"He will tell her. See, he is telling her now!"

The mother drew a shade nearer.

"But how do you know? See, she is doing the talking. You think he will tell her? *What* will he tell her, Graham?"

"Oh, he will not tell her in words, but every atom of his being is telling her now. Can't you see? He is telling her that he is no longer worthy to be her equal. He is telling her that something has gone wrong."

"Graham, what do you *think* is the matter with him? Do you think he is—BAD?" She lifted frightened eyes to his as she dropped into her low chair that always stood conveniently near his desk.

A wordless sorrow overspread the minister's face, yet there was something valiant in his eyes.

"No, I can't think that. I must believe in him in spite of everything. It looks to me somehow as if he was trying to be bad and couldn't."

"Well, but—Graham, isn't that the same thing? If he wants to be?"

The minister shook his head.

"He doesn't want to be. But he has some purpose in it. He is doing it—perhaps—well—it might be for *her* sake you know."

The mother looked perplexed, and hesitated, then shook her head.

"That would be—preposterous! How could he hurt her so—if he cared. It must be—he does not care!"

"He cares!" said the man.

"Then how do you explain it?"

"I don't explain it."

"Are you going to let it go on?"

"What can be done?"

"I'd do something."

"No, Mary. That's something he's got to work out himself. If he isn't big enough to get over his pride. His self-consciousness. His—whatever he calls it—If he isn't big enough—Then he isn't *big* enough!" The man sighed with a faraway patient look. The woman stirred uneasily.

"Graham," she said suddenly lifting her eyes in troubled question, "when your cousin Eugenie was here, you remember, she talked about it one day. She said we had no right to let Lynn become so attached to a mere country boy who would grow up a boor. She said he had no education, no breeding, no family, and that Lynn had the right to the best social advantages to be had in the world. She said Lynn was a natural born aristocrat, and that we had a great responsibility bringing up a child with a face like hers, and a mind like hers, and an inheritance like hers, in this little antiquated country place. She said it was one thing for you with your culture and your fine education and your years of travel and experience, to hide yourself here if you choose for a few years, pleasing yourself at playing with souls and up-lifting a little corner of the universe while you were writing a great book; but it was quite another for us to allow our gifted young daughter to know no other life. And especially she harped on Lynn's friendship with Mark. She called him a hobbledehoy, said his mother was 'common,' and that coming from a home like that, he would never amount to anything or have an education. He would always be com-mon and loaferish, and it wouldn't make any difference if he did, he would never be cultured no matter how much edu-cation he had. He was not in her *class.* She kept saying that over. She said a lot of things, and always ended up with that. And finally she said that we were perfectly crazy, both of us. That she supposed Lynn thought she was Christianizing the boy or something, but it was dangerous business, and we ought to be warned. And Graham, *I'm afraid Mark heard it!* He was just coming up on the porch as she finished and I'm almost sure he heard it!"

The eyes of the minister gave a startled flicker and then grew comprehending. "I wondered why he gave up college after he had worked so hard to get in."

"But, Graham! Surely, if he had heard he would have wanted to show her that she was wrong."

"No, Mary. He is not built that way. It's his one big fault. Always to be what he thinks people have labeled him, or to seem to be. To be that in defiance, knowing in his heart he really isn't that at all. It's a curious psychological study. It makes me think of nothing else but when the prince of the power of the air wanted to be God. Mark wants to be a young God. When he finds he's not taken that way he makes himself look like the devil in defiance. Don't you remember, Mary, how when Bob Bliss broke that memorial window in the church and said it was Mark did it, how Mark stood

looking defiantly from one to another of us to see if we
would believe it, and when he found the elders were all
against him and had begun to get ready for punishment, he
lifted his fine young shoulders, and folded his arms, and just
bowed in acquiescence, as if to say yes, he had done it?
Don't you remember, Mary? He nearly broke my heart that
day, the hurt look in his eyes; the game, mistaken, little
devil! He was only ten, and yet for four long months he bore
the blame in the eyes of the whole village for breaking that
window, till Bob told the truth and cleared him. Not because he wanted to save Bob Bliss, for everybody knew he
was a little scamp, and needed punishment, but because he
was *hurt*—hurt way down into the soul of him to think anybody had *thought* he would want to break the window we
had all worked so hard to buy. And he actually broke three
cellar windows in that vacant store by the post office, yes,
and paid for them, just to keep up his character and give us
some reason for our belief against him."

The wife with a cloud of anxiety in her eyes, and disapproval in her voice, answered slowly:

"That's a bad trait, Graham. I can't understand it. It is
something wrong in his nature."

"Yes, Mary, it is sin, original sin, but it comes at him from
a different direction from most of us, that's all. It comes
through sensitiveness. It is his reaction to a deep and mortal
hurt. Some men would be stimulated to finer action by criticism, he is stimulated to defy, and he does not know that he
is trying to defy God and all the laws of the universe. Someday he will find it out, and know that only through humility
can he make good."

"But he is letting all his opportunities go by."

"I'm not so sure. You can't tell what he may be doing out
in the world where he is gone."

"But they say he is very wild."

"They were always saying things about him when he was
here, and most of them were not true. You and I knew him,

Mary. Was there ever a finer young soul on earth than he with his clear true eyes, his eager tender heart, his brave fearlessness and strength. I can not think he has sold his soul to sin—not yet. It may be. It may be that only in the far country will he realize it is God he wants and be ready to say, 'I have sinned' and 'I will arise.' "

"But, Graham, I should think that just because you believe in him you could talk to him."

"No, Mary. I can't probe into the depths of that sensitive soul and dig out his confidence. He would never give it that way. It is a matter between himself and God."

"But Lynn—"

"Lynn has God too, my dear. We must not forget that. Life is not all for this world, either. Thank God Lynn believes that!"

The mother sighed with troubled eyes, and rose. The purring of the engine was heard. Lynn would be coming in. They watched the young man swing his car out into the road and glide away like a comet with a wild sophisticated snort of his engine that sent him so far away in a flash. They watched the girl standing where he had left her, a stricken look upon her face, and saw her turn slowly back to the house with eyes down—troubled. The mother moved away. The father bent his head upon his hand with closed eyes. The girl came back to her work, but the song on her lips had died. She worked silently with a far look in her eyes, trying to fathom it.

The eyes of her father and mother followed her tenderly all that day, and it was as if the souls of the three had clasped hands, and understood, so mistily they smiled at one another.

Billy Gaston, refreshed by a couple of chocolate fudge sundaes, a banana whip, and a lemon ice-cream soda, was seated on the bench with the heroes of the day at the Monopoly baseball grounds. He wore his most nonchalant air, chewed gum with his usual vigor, shouted himself hoarse at the proper places, and made casual grown-up responses to the condescension of the team, wrapping them tenderly in ancient sweaters when they were disabled, and watching every move of the game with a practiced eye and an immobile countenance. But though to the eyes of the small fry on the grass at his feet he was as self-sufficient as ever, somehow he kept having strange qualms, and his mind kept reverting to the swart fat face of Pat at the junction, as it ducked behind the cypress and talked into the crude telephone on the mountain. Somehow he couldn't forget the gloat in his eye as he spoke of the "rich guy." More and more uneasy he grew, more sure that the expedition to which he was pledged was not strictly "on the square."

Not that Billy Gaston was afraid. The thrill of excitement burned along his veins and filled him with a fine elation whenever he thought of the great adventure, and he gave his pocket a protective slap where the ten bucks still reposed intact. He felt well pleased with himself to have made sure of those. Whatever happened he had that, and if the man wasn't on the square Pat deserved to lose that much. Not that Billy Gaston meant to turn yellow after promising, but there was no telling whether the rest of the twenty-five would be forthcoming or not. He fell to calculating its worth in terms of new sweaters and baseball bats. If worse came to worst he could threaten to expose Pat and his scheme.

During the first and second innings these reflections soothed his soul and made him sit immovable with jaws grinding in rhythmic harmony with the day. But at the beginning of the third inning one of the boys from his Sunday school class strolled by and flung himself full length on the grass at his feet where he could see his profile just as he had seen it on Sunday while he was listening to the story that the teacher always told to introduce the lesson. He could see the blue of Lynn Severn's eyes as she told it, and strangely enough portions of the tale came floating back in trailing mist across the dusty baseball diamond and obscured the sight of Sloppy Hedrick sliding to his base. It was a tale of one, Judas, who betrayed his best Friend with a kiss. It came with strange illogical persistence, and seemed curiously incongruous with the sweet air of summer blowing over the hard young faces and dusty diamond. What had Judas to do with a baseball game, or with Billy Gaston and what he meant to do on the mountain that night? And earn good money! Ah! That was it. Make good money! But who was he betraying he would like to know? Well if it wasn't on the square perhaps he was betraying that same *One*— Aw— Rats! He wasn't under anybody's thumb and Judas lived centuries ago. He wasn't doing any harm helping a man do something he wasn't supposed to know what. Hang it all! Where was Mark Carter anyway? Somehow Cart always seemed to set a fella straight. He was like Miss Lynn. He saw through things you hadn't even told him about. But this was a man's affair, not a woman's.

Of course there was another side to it. He *could* give some of the money to Aunt Saxon to buy coal—instead of the sweater—well, maybe it would do both. And he *could* give some to that fund for the Chinese mission, Miss Lynn was getting up in the class. He would stop on the way back and give her a whole dollar. He sat, chin in hand, gazing out on the field, quite satisfied with himself, and suddenly someone back by the plate struck a fine clean ball with a click and threw the bat with a resounding ring on the hard ground as he made for a home run. Billy started and looked keenly at the bat, for somehow the ring of it as it fell sounded curiously like the tinkle of silver. Who said thirty pieces of silver? Billy threw a furtive look about and a cold perspiration broke out on his forehead. Strange that old Bible story had to stick itself in. He could see the grieving in the Master's eyes as Judas gave Him that kiss. She had made the story real. She could do that, and made the boy long somehow to make it up to that betrayed Master, and he couldn't get away from the feeling that he was falling short. Of course, old Pat had *said* the man had money *belonging* to *him,* and you had to go mostly by what folks *said,* but it did look shady.

The game seemed slow after that. The two captains were wrangling over some point of rule, and the umpire was trying to pacify them both. Billy arose with well feigned languor and remarked, "Well, I gotta beat it. Guess we're gonta win all right. So long!" and lounged away to his wheel.

He purchased another soda at the drugstore to get one of his fives changed into ones, one of which he stowed away in his breast pocket, while the remainder was stuffed in his trousers after the manner of a man. He bent low over his handlebars, chewing rhythmically and pedaled away rapidly in the direction of Sabbath Valley.

Chapter 3

The bells of the little stone church were playing tender melodies as he shot briskly down the maple-lined street at a breakneck pace, and the sun was just hovering on the rim of the mountains. The bells often played at sunset, especially Saturday evenings, when Marilyn Severn was at home, and the village loved to hear them. Billy wouldn't have owned it, but he loved to hear those bells play better than anything else in his young life, and he generally managed to be around when they were being played. He loved to watch the slim young fingers manipulating the glad sounds. A genius who had come to the quiet hill village to die of an incurable disease had trained her and had left the wonderful little pipe organ with its fine chime of bells attached as his memorial to the peace the village had given him in his last days. Something of his skill and yearning had fallen upon the young girl whom he had taught. Billy always felt as if an angel had come and was ringing the bells of heaven when Marilyn sat at the organ playing the bells.

This night a ray of the setting sun slanting through the memorial window on her bronze-gold hair gave her the look of Saint Cecilia sitting there in the dimness of the church. Billy sidled into a backseat still chewing and watched her. He could almost see a halo in yellow-gold sun dust circling above her hair. Then a sudden revulsion came with the thought of that guy Judas and the possibility that he and the old fellow had much in common. But bah! He would go to the mountain just to prove to himself that there was nothing crooked in it.

The music was tender that night and Billy felt a strange constriction in his throat. But you never would have

guessed, as Lynn Severn turned at the end of her melody to
search the dimness for the presence she felt had entered, that
he had been under any stress of emotion, the way he grinned
at her and sidled up the aisle.

"Yeah, we won awright," in answer to her question. "Red
Rodge and Sloppy had 'em beat from the start. Those other
guys can't play ball anyway."

Then quite casually he brought forth the dollar from his
breast pocket.

"Fer the Chinese fund," he stated indifferently.

The look in her face was beautiful to see, almost as if
there were tears behind the sapphire lights in her eyes.

"Billy! All this?"

He felt as if she had knighted him. He turned red and hot
with shame and pleasure.

"Aw, that ain't much. I earned sommore too, fer m'yant."
He twisted his cap around on his other hand roughly and
then blurted out the last thing he had meant to say:

"Miss Lynn, it ain't wrong to do a thing you don't know
ain't wrong, is it?"

Marilyn looked at him keenly and laughed.

"It generally is, Billy, if you think it *might* be. Don't ever
try to fool your conscience, Billy, it's too smart for that."

He grinned sheepishly and then quite irrelevantly remarked:

"I saw Cart last night."

But she seemed to understand the connection and nodded
gravely:

"Yes, I saw him a moment this morning. He said he might
come back again this evening."

The boy grunted contentedly and watched the warm color
of her cheek under the glow of the ruddy sunset. She always
seemed to him a little bit unearthly in the starriness of her
beauty. Of course he never put it to himself that way. In fact
he never put it at all. It was just a fact in his life. He had two
idols whom he worshiped from afar, two idols who under-

stood him equally well and were understood by him, and for whom he would have gladly laid down his young life. This girl was one, and Mark Carter was the other. It was the sorrow of his young life that Mark Carter had left Sabbath Valley indefinitely. The stories that floated back of his career made no difference to Billy. He adored him but the more in his fierce young soul, and gloried in his hero's need of faithful friends. He would not have owned it to himself, perhaps, but he had spoken of Mark just to find out if this other idol believed those tales and was affected by them. He drew a sigh of deep content as he heard the steady voice and knew that she was still the young man's friend.

They passed out of the church silently together and parted in the glow of red that seemed flooding the quiet village like a painting. She went across the stretch of lawn to the low spreading veranda where her mother sat talking with her father. Some crude idea of her beauty and grace stole through his soul, but he only said to himself:

"How—kind of—*little* she is!" and then made a dash for his rusty old wheel lying flat at the side of the church step. He gathered it up and wheeled it around the side of the church to the old graveyard, threading his way among the graves and sitting down on a broad flat stone where he had often thought out his problems of life. The shadow of the church cut off the glow of sunset and made it seem silent and dark. Ahead of him the valley lay. Across at the right it stretched toward the junction, and he could see the evening train just puffing in with a wee wisp of white misty smoke trailing against the mountain green. The people for the hotels would be swarming off, for it was Saturday night. The fat one would be there rolling trunks across and the station agent would presently close up. It would be dark over there at eight o'clock. The mountains loomed silently, purpling and steep and hazy already with sleep.

To the left lay the road that curved up to the forks where one went across to the highway and at right angles the highway went straight across the ridge in front of him and sloped down to the spot where the fat one expected him to play his part at eight o'clock tonight. The highway was the way down which the "rich guy" was expected to come speeding in a high-power car from New York, and had to be stopped and relieved of money that "did not belong to him."

Billy thought it all over. Somehow things seemed different now. He had by some queer psychological process of his own, brought Lynn Severn's mind and Mark Carter's mind together to bear upon the matter and gained a new perspective. He was pretty well satisfied in his own soul that the thing he had set out to do was not on the level. It began to be pretty plain to him that that rich guy might be in the way of getting hurt or perhaps still worse, and he had no wish to be tangled up in a mess like that. At the same time he did not often get a chance to make twenty-five dollars, and he had no mind to give it up. It was not in his unyellow soul to go back on his word without refunding the money, and a dollar of it was already spent to the Chinese fund, to say nothing of sundaes and sodas and whips. So he sat and studied the mountain ahead of him.

Suddenly, as the sun, which had been for a long time slipping down behind the mountains at his back, finally disappeared, his face cleared. He had found a solution.

He sprang up from the cold stone, where his fingers had been mechanically feeling out the familiar letters of the inscription: "Blessed are the dead—" and catching up the prone wheel, strode upon it and dashed down the darkening street toward the little cottage near the willows belonging to his Aunt Saxon. He was whistling as he went, for he was happy. He had found a way to keep his cake and eat it too. It would not have been Billy if he had not found a way out.

Aunt Saxon turned a drawn and anxious face away from the window at his approach and drew a sigh of momentary relief. This bringing up boys was a terrible ordeal. But thanks be this immediate terror was past and her sister's orphaned child still lived! She hurried to the stove where the waiting supper gave forth a pleasant odor.

"Been down to the game at M'nop'ly," he explained happily as he flung breezily into the kitchen and dashed his cap on a chair. "Gee! That ham smells good! Say, Saxy, whadya do with that can of black paint I left on the doorstep last Saturday?"

"It's in a wooden box in the corner of the shed, Willie," answered his aunt. "Come to supper now. It'll all get cold. I've been waiting most an hour."

"Oh, hang it! I don't s'pose you know where the brush is—Yes, I'm coming. Oh, here 'tis!"

He ate ravenously and briefly. His aunt watched him with a kind of breathless terror waiting for the inevitable remark at the close: "Well, I gotta beat it! I gotta date with the fellas!"

She had ceased to argue. She merely looked distressed. It seemed a part of his masculinity that was inevitable.

At the door he was visited with an unusual thoughtfulness. He stuck his head back in the room to say:

"Oh, yes, Saxy, I *might* not be home till morning. I *might* stay all night some place."

He was going without further explanation, but her dismay as she murmured pathetically:

"But tomorrow is the Sabbath, Willie!" halted him once more.

"Oh, I'll be home time fer Sunday school," he promised gaily, and was off down the road in the darkness, his old wheel squeaking rheumatically with each revolution growing fainter and fainter in the night.

But Billy did not take the road to the junction in his rapid flight. Instead he climbed the left-hand mountain road that met the forks and led to the great highway. Slower and slower the old wheel went, Billy puffing and bending low, till finally he had to dismount and put a drop of oil in a well known spot which his finger found in the dark, from the lit-

tle can he carried in his pocket for such a time of need. He
did not care to proclaim his coming as he crept up the rough
steep way. And once when a tin lizzie swept down upon
him, he ducked and dropped into the fringe of alders at the
wayside until it was past. Was that, could it have been Cart?
It didn't look like Cart's car, but it was very dark, and the
man had not dimmed his lights. It was blinding. He hoped it
was Cart, and that he had gone to the parsonage. Somehow
he liked to think of those two together. It made his own view
of life seem stronger. So he slunk quietly up to the fork
where the highway swept down round a curve, and turned to
go down across the ridge. Here was the spot where the rich
guy would presently come. He looked the ground over, with
his bike safely hidden below road level. With a sturdy set of
satisfaction to his shoulders, and a twinkle of fun in his eye,
he began to burrow into the undergrowth and find branches,
a fallen log, stones, anything, and drag them up across the
great state highway till he had a complete barricade.

There had come a silverness in the sky over the next eastern mountain, and he could see the better what he was
doing. Now and again he stopped cautiously and listened,
his heart beating high with fear lest after all the rich guy
might arrive before he was ready for him. When the ob-
struction was finished the got out a large piece of cardboard
which had been fastened to the handlebars of his wheel, and
from a box also fastened on behind his saddle he produced
his can of paint and a brush. The moon was beginning to
show off at his right, and gave a faint luminous gleam, as he
daubed his letters in crudely.

DETOUR to SABBATH VALLEY
Rode flooded. Brige down.

His card was large, but so were his letters. Nevertheless in
spite of their irregularity he got them all on, and fastened
the card firmly to the most obvious spot in the barricade.

Then with a wicked gleam of mischief in his eye he looked off down the highway across the ridge to where some two miles away one Pat must be awaiting his coming, and gave a single mocking gesture common to boys of his age. Springing on his wheel he coasted down the humps and into the darkness again.

He reflected as he rode that no harm could possibly be done. The road inspector would not be along for a couple of days. It would simply mean that a number of cars would go around by the way of Sabbath Valley for a day or so. It might break up a little of the quiet of the Sabbath day at home, but Billy did not feel that that would permanently injure Sabbath Valley for home purposes, and he felt sure that no one could possibly ever detect his hand in the matter.

The road at the forks led four ways, highway, coming from New York and the great Northeast, running north and south, and the crossroad coming from Economy and running through Sabbath Valley to Monopoly. He had made the detour below the crossroad, so that people coming from Economy would find no hindrance to their progress. He felt great satisfaction in the whole matter. And now there remained but to do his part and get his money. He thought he saw a way to make sure of that money, and his conscience had no qualms for extracting it from so crooked a thief as Pat.

The clock on the church tower at Sabbath Valley was finishing the last stroke of eleven when Billy came slickly up the slope of the road from Sabbath Valley, and arrived on the station platform nonchalantly.

By the light of the moon he could dimly see Pat standing uneasily off by the tracks, and the heads of two men down below in the bushes near the lower end of the highway where it crossed the tracks and swept on south between two mountains.

Pat held his watch in his hand and looked very ugly, but nothing fazed Billy. He didn't have to carry this thing out if he didn't want to, and the man knew he knew too much to be ugly to him.

"There you are, you young whippersnapper you!" was Pat's greeting. "What kinduva time is this 'ere to be coming along to your expensive job? I said *eight!*"

"Oh," said Billy with a shrug and jumped to his wheel again, "then I guess I'll be going back. Good night!"

"Here! Wait up there, you young devil! You come mighty nigh dishing the whole outfit, but now you're here, you'll earn your ten bucks I was fool enough to give you, but nothing more, do you hear that?" and the man leered into his freckled young face with an ugly gun in his hand.

Billy eyed the gun calmly. He had seen guns before. Moreover he didn't believe the man had the nerve to shoot. He wasn't quite so sure of the two dark shadows in the bushes below, but it was well to be on the safe side.

"Keep yer shirt on," said Billy impertinently, "and save yer powder. You don't want the whole nation to know about this little affair of ours do you, *Pat?*"

The wide one glared.

"Well, you better not have anything like shooting going on, fer I've got some friends back here a little way waiting to joy ride back with me when my work's over. They might get funny if they heard a gun and come too soon."

"You little devil, you! I mighta known you'd give it away!" he began, but he lowered the gun perceptibly. "Every little skunk like you is yella—yella as the devil—"

But Pat did not finish his sentence, for Billy, with a blaze in his eyes like the lamps of a tiger, and a fierce young cat-like leap flew at the flabby creature, wrenched the gun out of his astonished hand, and before he could make any outcry held it tantalizingly in his face. Billy had never had any experience before with bullies and bandits except in his dreams; but he had played football, and tackled every team in the valley, and he had no fear of anything. Moreover, he had spent long hours boxing and wrestling with Mark Carter, and he was hard as nails and wiry as a cat. The fat one was completely in his hands. Of course those other two down across the tracks might have made trouble if Pat had cried out, but they were too far away to see or hear the silent scuffle on the platform. But Billy was taking no chances.

"Now, keep on yer shirt, Pat, and don't make no outcry. My friends can get here's easy as yours, so just take it quiet. All you gotta do is take that remark back you just uttered. I ain't yella, and you gotta say so. Then you hand over those fifteen bones, and I'm yer man."

It was incredible that Pat should have succumbed, but he did. he was none too sure of his friends in the bu the time was getting short and he was in a h n the highway. Also he had no mind interrupted. At any rate with a courage he put his hand in e bills.

s you're okay. Any- th zi. Now, sonny, put th I—got an- other." He et with a grin, but Bi

"That's all right, You don't need two. N

Pat edged away from the eye. The moon was coming up darkness. There was a determine shoulders, a lithe alertness about his b in his eye. Pat was really a coward. Besides, nervous. The hidden telephone had called him already. He could hear even now in imagination aint click in the moss. The last message had said that the car had passed the state line and would soon be coming to the last point of communication. After that it was the mountain highway straight to Pleasant View, nothing to hinder. It was not a time to waste in discussion. Pat dropped to an ingratiating whine.

"Come along then, kid. Yes, bring your wheel. We'll want it. Down this way, just over the tracks, so, see? We want you to fall off that there wheel an' sprawl in the road like you had caught yer wheel on the track an' it had skidded, see? Try her now, and just lay there like you was off your feed."

Billy slung himself across his wheel, gave a cursory glance at the landscape, took a running slide over the tracks with a swift pedal or two and slumped in a heap, lying motionless as the dead. He couldn't have done it more effectively if he had practiced for a week. Pat caught his breath and stooped over anxiously. He didn't want a death at the start. He wouldn't care to be responsible for a concussion of the brain or anything like that. Besides, he couldn't waste time fooling with a fool kid when the real thing might be along any minute. He glanced anxiously up the broad white ribbon of a road that gleamed now in the moonlight, and then pulling out his pocket flash, flooded it swiftly over Billy's upturned freckled face that lay there still as death without the flicker of an eyelash. The man was panic-stricken. He stooped lower, put out a tentative finger, turned his flash full in the boy's face again, and was just about to call to his helpers for aid when Billy opened a large eye and solemnly winked.

Pat shut off his flash quickly, stuck it in his pocket, backed off with a low relieved, "All right, kid, you'll do. I guess you're all right after all, now you jest lay—" and slid away down the slope into the cypress clump.

Billy with upturned face eyed the moon and winked again, as if to a friend up there in the sky. He was thinking of the detour two miles up the road.

It was very pleasant lying there in the cool moonlight with the evening breeze blowing his rough hair and playing over his freckles, and with the knowledge of those twenty-four bucks safely buttoned inside his sweater, and that neat little gun in his pocket where he could easily close his fingers about it. The only thing he regretted was that for conscience' sake he had had to put up that detour. It would have been so much more exciting than to have put up this all-night camouflage and wait here till dawn for a guy that wasn't coming at all. He began to think about the guy and wonder if he would take the detour to Sabbath Valley, or turn back, or perhaps try Economy. That would be disappointing. He would stand no chance of even hearing what he was like. Now if he went through Sabbath Valley, Red or Sloppy or Rube would be sure to sight a strange car, particularly if it was a *high-power* racer or something of that sort, and they could discuss it, and he might be able to find out a few points about this unknown whom he was so nobly delivering for conscience' sake—or Lynn Severn's—from an unknown fate. Of course he wouldn't let the fellows know he knew anything about the guy.

He had lain there fifteen minutes and was beginning to grow drowsy after his full day in the open air. If it were not for the joke of the thing he couldn't keep awake.

Pat stole out from the weeds at the slope of the road and whispered sepulchraly:

"That's all right, kid, jest you lay there and hold that pose. You couldn't do better. Yer wheel finishes the blockade. Nobody couldn't get by if he tried. That's the kid! 'Clare if I don't give you another five bucks t'morrer if you carry this thing through. Don't you get cold feet now!"

Billy uttered a guttural of contempt in his throat and Pat slid away to hiding once more. The distant bells struck the midnight hour. Billy thrilled with their sweetness, with the fact that they belonged to him, that he had sat that very evening watching those white fingers among the keys, manipulating them. He thought of the glint on her hair—the halo of dusty gold in the sunshine above—the light in her eyes—the glow of her cheek—her delicate profile against the memorial window—the glint of her hair—it came back, not in those words, but the vision of it—what was it like? Oh—of course. Cart's hair. The same color. They were alike, those two, and yet very different. When he had grown a man he would like to be like Cart. Cart was kind and always understood when you were not feeling right. Cart smoothed the way for people in trouble—old women and animals, and well—girls sometimes. He had seen him do it. Other people didn't always understand, but he did. Cart always had a reason. It took men to understand men. That thought had a good sound to the boy on his back in the moonlight. Although he felt somewhat a fool lying there waiting in the road when all the time there was that detour. It would have been more a man's job if there hadn't had to be that detour, but he couldn't run risks with strange guys, and men who carried guns, not even for—well, thirty pieces of silver! But hark! What was that?

There seemed to be a singing along the ground. Was he losing his nerve lying here so long? No, there it was again! It couldn't be possible that he could hear so far as two miles up that road. It was hard and smooth macadam of course, that highway, but it couldn't be that—what was it they called it—vibrations?—would reach so far! It must be. He would ask Cart about that.

The humming continued and grew more distinct, followed by a sort of throbbing roar that seemed coming toward him and yet was still very far away. It must be a car at the detour. In a moment it would turn down the bumpy road toward Sabbath Valley, and very likely some of those old broken whiskey bottles along the way would puncture a tire and the guy would take till morning getting anywhere. Perhaps he could even get away in time to come up innocently enough and help him out. A guy like that might not know how to patch a puncture.

But the sound was distinctly coming on. Billy opened one eye, then the other, and hastily scanned the sky in either direction for an airplane, but the sky was as clear as crystal without a speck, and the sound was distinctly drawing nearer.

A voice from the roadside hurtled sharply across:

"Hist! There! He's coming! Lay still! Remember you get five more bucks if you pull this off!"

A cold chill crept down Billy's back on tiny needle-pointed fringe of feet like a centipede. There was a sudden constriction in his throat and a leaden weight on each eye. He could not have opened them if he had tried, for a great white light stabbed across them and seemed to be holding them down for inspection. The thing he had wanted to have happen had come, and he was frightened; frightened cold clear to the soul of him—not at the thing that was about to come, but at the fact that he had broken faith with himself after all; broken faith with the haloed girl at the organ in the golden light; broken faith—for thirty pieces of silver! In that awful moment he was keenly conscious of the fact that when he got the other five there would be just thirty dollars for the whole! Thirty pieces of silver and the judgment day already coming on!

Chapter 4

Lynn Severn was restless as she sat on the porch in the cool dark evening and heard unheeding the small village sounds that stole to her ears. The laughter of two children playing hide-and-seek behind the bushes across the way; the call of their mother summoning them to bed. The tinkle of a piano down the street; the whine of a Victrola in another home; the cry of a baby in pain; the murmur of talk on the porch next door; the slamming of a door; the creak of a gate; footsteps going down the brick pavement; the swinging to and fro of a hammock holding happy lovers under the rose pergola at Joneses'. She could identify them all, and found her heart was listening for another sound, a smooth running car that purred, coming down the street. But it did not come!

By and by she slipped out and into the church, opening one window to let in the moonlight, and unlocking the organ by the sense of feeling. Her fingers strayed along the keys in tender wandering melodies, but she did not pull the stop that controlled the bells. She would have liked to play those bells and call through them to Mark across the mountains, where he might be riding, call to tell him that she was waiting, call to ask him why he was so strangely aloof, so silent, and pale in his dignity; what had come between them, old friends of the years? She felt she could say with the bells what her lips could never speak. But the bells would cry her trouble to the villagers also, and she could not let *them* hear. So she played soft melodies of trust and hope and patience, until her father came to find her, and linking his arm in hers walked back with her through the moonlight, not asking anything, only seeming to understand her mood. He was that way always. He could understand without being told.

Somehow she felt it and was comforted. He was that way with everybody. It was what made him so beloved in his parish, which comprised the whole valley, that and his great sincerity and courage. But always his sense of understanding seemed keenest with this flower-faced girl of his. He seemed to have gone ahead of her always to see that all was right— or wrong—and then walked with her to be sure she did not stumble or miss her way. He never attempted to reason her out of herself, nor to minimize her trials, but was just there, a stronghold when she needed it. She looked up with a smile and slipped her hand in his. She understood his perfect sympathy, as if his own past youth were touching hers and making her know that whatever it was she had to face she would come through. He was like a symbol of God's strength to her. Somehow the weight was lifted from her heart. They lingered on the piazza together in the moonlight a few minutes, speaking quietly of the morrow and its duties, then they went into the wide pleasant living room, and sat down, mother and daughter near together, while the father read a portion:

"He that dwelleth in the secret place of the most High shall abide under the shadow of the Almighty.

"I will say of the Lord, He is my refuge and my fortress; my God; in him will I trust.

"Surely he shall deliver thee from the snare of the fowler, and from the noisome pestilence.

"He shall cover thee with his feathers, and under his wings shalt thou trust."

The words seemed to fill the room with a sweet peace, and to draw the hearts of the listeners as a voice that is dear draws and soothes after a day of separation and turmoil and distress.

They knelt and the minister's voice spoke familiarly to the Unseen Presence, giving thanks for mercies received, mentioning little throbbing personalities that belonged to them as a family and as individuals, reminding one of what it must have been in the days before sin had come and Adam walked and talked with God in the cool of the evening, and received instruction and strengthening straight from the Source. One listening would instinctively have felt that here was the secret of the great strength of Lynn Severn's life; the reason why neither college nor the world had been able to lure her one iota from her great and simple faith which she had brought with her from her valley home and taken back again unsullied. This family altar was the heart of her home, and had brought her so near to God that she *knew* what she had believed and could not be shaken from it by any flippant words from lovely or wise lips that only knew the theory of her belief and nothing of its spirit and tried to argue it away with a fine phrase and a laugh.

So Lynn went up to her little white chamber that looked out upon the quiet hills, knelt awhile beside the white bed in the moonlight, then lay down and slept.

Out among the hills on the long smooth road in the white moonlight there shot a car like a living thing gone crazy, blaring a whiter light than the moonlight down the way, roaring and thundering as only a costly and well-groomed beast of a machine can roar and thunder when it is driven by hot blood and a mad desire, stimulated by frequent applications from a handy flask, and a will that has never known a curb.

He knew it was a mad thing he was doing, rushing across space through the dark at the beck of a woman's smile, a woman who was another man's wife, but a woman who had set on fire a whole circle of men of which he was a part. He was riding against all caution to win a bet, riding against time to get there before two other men who were riding as hard from other directions to win the woman who belonged to an absent husband, win her and run away with her if he could. It was the culmination of a year of extravagances, the last cry in sensations, and the telephone wires had been hot with daring, wild allurement, and mad threat in several directions since late the night before.

The woman was in a great summer hotel where extravagances of all sorts were in vogue, and it had been her latest game to call with her lutelike voice over the phone to three of her men friends who had wooed her the strongest, daring them all to come to her at once, promising to fly with the one who reached her first, but if none reached her before morning dawned she remained as she was and laughed at them all.

Laurence Shafton had closed with the challenge at once and given orders for his car to be ready to start in ten minutes. From a southern city about an equal distance from the lady, one Percy Emerson, of the Wellington Emersons, started about the same time, leaving a trail of telegrams and phone messages to be sent after his departure. The third man, Mortimer McMarter, a hot-headed, hot-blooded Scot, had started with the rest, for the lady knew her lovers well, and not one would refuse; but he was lying dead at a wayside inn with his car a heap of litter outside from having collided with a truck that was minding its own business and giving plenty of room to any sane man. This one was not sane. But of this happening not even the lady knew as yet, for Mortimer McMarter was not one to leave tales behind him when he went out of life, and the servants who had sent his messages were far away.

The clock in the car showed nearly twelve and the way was long ahead. But he would make it before the dawn. He must. He stepped on the accelerator and shot round a curve. A dizzy precipice yawned at his side. He took another pull at the flask he carried and shot on wildly through the night. Then suddenly he ground on his brakes, the machine twisted and snarled like an angry beast and came to a stand almost into the arms of a barricade across the road. The young man hurled out an oath, and leaned forward to look, his eyes almost too bloodshot and blurred to read:

DETOUR to SABBATH VALLEY

He laughed aloud. "Sabbath Valley!" He swore and laughed again, then looked down the way the rude arrow pointed, "Well, I like that! Sabbath Valley. That'll be a good joke to tell, but I'll make it yet or land in hell!" He started his car and twisted it round to the rougher road, feeling the grind of the broken glass that strewed the way. Billy had done his work thoroughly, and anticipated well what would happen. But those tires were costly affairs. They did not yield to the first cut that came, and the expensive car built for racing on roads as smooth as glass bumped and jogged down into the ruts and started toward Sabbath Valley, with the driver pulling again at his almost empty flask, and swaying giddily in his seat. Half a mile farther down the mountain, the car gave a gasp, like the flitting soul of a dying lion, and came with sudden grinding brakes to a dead stop in the heart of a deep wood.

Five minutes later another car, with a soft purring engine came up to the crossroads from Economy, slowed just a fraction as it crossed the highway, the driver looking keenly at the barricade, then stopping his car with a sudden jerk and swinging out. He turned a pocket flash on the big cardboard Billy had erected, its daubed letters still wet and blurring into the pasteboard. He looked a bit quizzical over the statement, "RODE FLOODED, BRIGE DOWN," because he happened to know there was no bridge and nothing to flood the road for several miles ahead. He examined the barricade carefully, even down to the broken glass in the road, then deliberately, swiftly, with his foot kicked away the glass, cleared a width for his car, and jumping in backed up, turned and started slowly down the condemned road to investigate. Something was wrong down the highway, and the sooner it was set right the better. There was one thing, he wished he had his gun with him, but then— And he swung on down for two miles, going faster and faster, seeing nothing but white still road, and quiet sleeping trees, with looming mountains against the sky everywhere. Then, suddenly, across the way in the blare of his lights a white face flashed into view, and a body, lying full across the road, with a bicycle flung to one side completing the block. He brought his car to a quick stand and jumped out, but before he could take one step or even stoop, someone caught him from behind, and something big and dark and smothering was flung over his head. A heavy blow seemed to send him whirling, whirling down into infinite space, with a long tongue of living fire leaping up to greet him.

"Beat it, kid, and keep yer face shut!" hissed Pat into Billy's ear, at the same time stuffing a bill into his hand.

Billy had just sense enough left to follow the assisting kick and roll himself out of the road, with a snatch at his machine which pulled it down out of sight. He had a secret feeling that he was yellow after all in spite of his efforts, letting a guy get taken this way without even a chance to put up a fight. Where was that gun? He reached his hand into his pocket and was steadied by the feeling of the cold steel. Then he knew that the men were in the car and about to start. They had dumped the owner into the backseat and were going to carry him off somewhere. What were they going to do? He must find out. He was responsible. He hadn't meant to let anything like this happen. If everything wasn't going to be on the square he might have to get into it yet. He must stick around and see.

The men were having a whispered consultation over the car. They were not used to that kind, but a car was a car. They tried to start it with nervous glances down the road. It jerked and hissed and complained but began to obey. The wheels were beginning to move. In a flash it would be gone!

Billy scrambled noiselessly up the bank behind the car, his move well covered by the noise of the engine. With a quick survey of the situation he tucked himself hastily into the spare tire on the back, just as the car gave a lurch and shot forward down across the tracks. He had all he could do to maintain his position and worm himself into a firmer holding for the first minute or two, and when he began to realize what he was doing he found his heart beating like a young trip-hammer. He slid a groping hand into his pocket once more for reassurance. If anything really happened he had the gun.

But his heart was heavy. Things had not gone right. He had planned to carry this thing through as a large joke, and here he was mixed up in a crooked deal if ever there was one. The worst of it was he wasn't out of it yet. He wished he knew whose car this was and where they were bound for. How about the license tag? Gripping his unstable seat he swayed forward and tried to see it just below him. In the dim light it looked like a New York license. It must be the guy they were after all right—they had telephoned about a New York man—yet—*Cart* had a New York license on his car! He was living in New York now—and there must be lots of other guys!

A kind of sickening thud seemed to drop through his mind down to the pit of his stomach as he tried to think it out. His eyes peered into the night watching every familiar landmark—there was the old pine where they always turned off to go fishing; and yes, they were turning *away* from Economy Road. Yes, they were going through Hackett's Pass. A chill crept through his thin old sweater as the damp breath of ferns and rocks struck against his face. His eyes shone grim and hard in the night, suddenly grown old and stern. This was the kind of thing you read about in novels. In spite of pricks of conscience his spirits rose. It was great to be in it if it had to be. The consciousness of Sabbath Valley bathed in peaceful moonlight, all asleep, of the minister and his daughter, and Aunt Saxon, fell away; even the memory of bells that called to righteousness—he was out in the night on a wild ride and his soul thrilled to the measure of it. He fairly exulted as he reflected that he might be called upon to do some great deed of valor—in fact he felt he *must* do a great deed of valor to retrieve his self-respect after having made that balk about the detour. How did that guy get around the detour anyway? *Some guy!*

Hackett's Pass was far behind and the moon was going low when the car stopped for a moment and a hurried consultation took place inside. Billy couldn't hear all that was said, but he gathered that time was short and the conspirators must be back at a certain place before morning. They seemed somehow to have missed a trail that was to have cut the distance greatly. Billy clung breathlessly to his cramped position and waited. He hoped they wouldn't get out and try to find the way, for then some of them might see him, and he was so stiff he was sure he would bungle getting out of the way. But after a breathless moment the car started on more slowly, and finally turned down a steep rough place, scarcely a trail, into the deeper woods. For a long time they went along, slower and slower, into the blackness of night it seemed. There was no moon, and the men had turned off the lights. There was nothing but a pocket flash which one of them carried, and turned on now and again to show them the way. The engine, too, was muffled and went snuffing along through the night like a blind thing that had been gagged. Billy began to wonder if he would ever find his legs useful again. Sharp pains shot through his joints, and he became aware of sleep dropping upon his straining eyes like a sickening cloud. Yet he must keep awake.

He squirmed about and changed his position, staring into the darkness and wondering if this journey was ever to end. Now they were bumping down a bank, and slopping through water, not very deep, a small mountain stream on one of the levels. He tried to think where it must be, but was puzzled. They seemed to have traveled part of the way in curves. Twice they stopped and backed up and seemed to be returning on their tracks. They crossed and recrossed the little stream, and the driver was cursing, and insisting on more light. At last they began climbing again and the boy drew a breath of relief. He could tell better where he was on the heights. He began to think of morning and Sabbath Valley bathed in its Sabbath peace, with the bells chiming a call to worship—and *he not there!* Aunt Saxon would be *crazy!* She would bawl him out! *He should worry!* And she would weep, pink weak tears from her old thin eyes, that seemed to have never done much else but weep. The thought turned and twisted in his soul like an ugly curved knife and made him angry. Tears always made him angry. And Miss Lynn—she would watch for him! He had promised to be there! And she would not understand—and there would come that grieved look in her eyes. She would think—Oh, she would think he did not *want* to come, and did not *mean* to keep his promise, and things like that—and she would have to think them! He couldn't help it, could he? He *had* to come along, didn't he?

In the midst of his miserable reflections the car stopped dead on a level place, and with a cold perspiration on his forehead Billy peered around him. They must have reached the top of a ridge, for the sky was visible with the morning star pinned against a luminous black. Against it a blacker shape was visible, half hid in trees, a building of some sort, solid, substantial, but deserted.

The men were getting out of the car. Billy gripped the gun and dropped silently to the ground, sliding as stealthily into the shadows of the trees as if he had been a snake.

Pat stepped heavily to the ground and began to give directions in a low growl. Billy crouched and listened.

"Let's get him shifted quick! We gotta beat it outta here! Link, it's up to you an' Shorty to get this car over the state line before light, an' you'll have to run me back to the crossing first, so I can be at the station in time for the early train. That'll be *going some!*"

"Well, I guess *anyhow not,*" said Link sullenly. "Whadda ya think we are? Fools? Run you back to the crossing in a pig's eye. You'll foot it back if you get there, er come with us. We ain't gonna get caught with this car on our hands. What we gonta do with it anyhow, when we get crost the state line?"

"Why, you run it into the field off behind that row of alders. Sam's got a man on the lookout. They'll have that little old car so she won't recognize her best friend before you can count three, so you should worry. And you'll run me back or you won't get the dough. See? *I'll* see to that. Sam said I wasn't to run no risks fer not bein' back in time. Now, shift that guy's feet out on my shoulder. Handle him quick. Nope, he won't wake up fer two hours yet. I give him plenty of dope. Got them bracelets tight on his feet? All right now. He's some hefty bird, ain't he?"

They moved away in the direction of the building, carrying a long dark shape between them, and Billy breathless in the bushes, watched, turning rapid plans in his mind. Here he was in the midst of an automobile getaway! Many the time he had gone with Mark and the chief of police on a still hunt for car thieves, but this time he was of the party. His loyal young heart boiled hot with rage, and he determined to do what he could single-handed to stem the tide of crime. Just what he was going to do he was undetermined. One thing was certain, he must get the number of that license tag. He looked toward the house.

The group had paused with their burden at the door and Pat had turned on his pocket flashlight for just an instant as they fumbled with an ancient lock. In that instant the whole front of the old stone house was lit up clearly, and Billy gasped. The *haunted house!* The house on the far mountain where a man had murdered his brother and then hanged himself. It had stood empty and closed for years, ever since

Billy could remember, and was shunned and regarded with awe, and pointed out by hunters as a local point of interest.

Billy regarded with contempt the superstition that hung around the place, but he gasped when he saw where he was, for they must have come twenty miles round about and it was at least ten across the mountains by the shortcut. Ten miles from home, and he had to foot it! If he had only brought old trusty! No telling now whether he would ever see it again. But what were bicycles at such a time as this?

The flash had gone out and the house was in darkness again, but he could hear the grating of a rusty hinge as the door opened, and faint footfalls of rubbered feet shuffled on a dusty floor. Now was his time! He darted out to the back of the car, and stooping down with his face close to the license, holding his old cap in one hand to shelter it drew out his own pocket flash and turned it on the sign, registering the number clearly on his alert young mind. The flashlight was on its last breath of battery, and blinked asthmatically, winking out into a thread of red as the boy pressed it eagerly for one more look. He had been so intent that he had not heard the rubbered feet till they were almost upon him, and he had barely time to spring back into the bushes.

"Hist! What was that?" whispered Pat, and the three stopped motionless in their tracks. Billy held his breath and touched the cold steel in his pocket. Of course there was always the gun, but what was one gun against three?

Chapter 5

The whistle of the cannery at Sabbath Valley blew a relief blast five minutes ahead of midnight in deference to the church chimes, and the night shift which had been working overtime on account of a consignment of tomatoes that would not keep till Monday, poured joyously out into the road and scattered to their various homes.

The outmost of these homegoers, Tom McMertrie and Jim Rafferty, who lived at the other extreme of the village, came upon a crippled car, coughing and crawling toward them in front of the graveyard. Its driver, much sobered by lack of stimulant, and frequent necessity for getting out and pushing his car over hard bits of road, called to them noisily.

The two workmen, pleasant of mood, ready for a joke, not altogether averse to helping if this proved to be the right guy, halted and stepped into the road just to look the poor noble car over. It was the lure of the fine machine.

"Met with an accident?" Jim remarked affably, as if it were something to enjoy.

"Had toire thrubble?" added Tom, punching the collapsed tires.

The questions seemed to anger the driver who demanded loftily:

"Where's your garage?"

"Garage? Oh, we haven't any garage," said Jim pleasantly, with a mute twinkle in his Irish eye.

"No garage? Haven't any garage! What town is this—if you call it a town?"

"Why, mon, this is Sawbeth Volley! Shorely ye've heard of Sawbeth Volley!"

"No, I never heard of it!" said the stranger contemptuously, "but from what I've seen of it so far I should say it ought to be called Hell's Pit! Well, what do you do when you want your car fixed?"

"Well, we don't hoppen to hove a cyar," said Tom with a meditative air, stooping to examine the spokes of a wheel. "Boot, ef we hod, mon, I'm thenkin' we'd *fix* it!"

Jim gave a flicker of a chuckle in his throat, but kept his outward gravity. The stranger eyed the two malevolently, helplessly, and began once more, holding his rage with a cold voice.

"Well, how much do you want to fix my car?" he asked, thrusting his hand into his pocket and bringing out an affluent wallet.

The men straightened up and eyed him coldly. Jim turned indifferently away and stepped back to the sidewalk. Tom lifted his chin and replied kindly:

"Why, mon, it's the *Sawbeth,* didn't ye know? I'm s'proised at ye! It's the Sawbeth, an' this is Sawbeth Volley! We don't wurruk on the Sawbeth day in Sawbeth Volley. Whist! Hear thot, mon?"

He lifted his hand and from the stone belfry nearby came the solemn tone of the chime, pealing out a full round of melody, and then tolling solemnly twelve slow strokes. There was something almost uncanny about it that held the stranger still, as if an unseen presence with a convincing voice had been invoked. The young man sat under the spell till the full complement of the ringing was finished, the workman with his hand up holding attention, and Jim Rafferty quietly enjoying it all from the curbstone.

When the last sweet resonance had died out, the Scotchman's hand went slowly down, and the stranger burst forth with an oath:

"Well, can you tell me where I can go to get fixed up? I've wasted enough time already."

"I should say from whut I've seen of ye, mon, that yer roight in thot statement, and if I was to advoise I'd say go right up to the parson. His loight's still burnin' in the windo next beyant the tchurtch, so ye'll not be disturbin' him. Not that he'd moind. He'll fix ye up ef anybody cun; though I'm doubtin' yer in a bad wy, only wy ye tak it. Good night to ye, the windo wi' the loight, mon, roight next beyant the tchurtch!"

The car began its coughing and spluttering, and slowly jerked itself into motion, its driver going angrily on his unthankful way. The two workmen watching him with amused expressions, waited in the shadow of a tree till the car came to a stop again in front of the parsonage, and a tall young fellow got out and looked toward the lighted window.

"Oh, boy! He's going in!" gasped Jim, slapping his companion silently on the back. "Whatt'll Mr. Severn think, Tommy?"

"It'll do the fresh laddie gude," quoth Tom, a trifle abashed but ready to stand by his guns. "I'm thenkin' he's one of them what feels they owns the airth, an' is bound to step on all worms of the dust whut comes in thur wy. But, Jim, mon, we better be steppin' on, fer tomorra's the Sawbeth ya ken, an' it wuddent be gude for our souls if the parson shud cum out to investigate." Chuckling away into the silent street they disappeared, while Laurence Shafton stalked angrily up the little path and pounded loudly on the quaint knocker of the parsonage.

The minister was on his knees, beside his desk, praying for the soul of the wandering lad who had been dear to him for years. He had finished his preparation for the coming day, and his heart was full of a great longing. As he poured out his desire he forgot the hour and his need for rest. It was often in such companionship he forgot all else. He was that kind of a man.

But he came to his feet on the instant with the knock, and was ready to go out on any errand of mercy that was needing him. It was not an unusual thing for a knock to come interrupting his midnight devotions. Sometimes the call would be to go far out on the mountain to someone who was in distress, or dying.

The minister swung the door wide and peered into the night pleasantly almost as if to welcome an unexpected guest. In the sudden flood of the porch light his face was illumined, and behind him the pretty living room gave a sweet homely setting. The stranger stood for an instant blinking, half astonished; then the memory of his rendezvous at break of day brought back his irritation at the delay.

"Are you Parsons?" he demanded, just as if "Parsons" were at fault that he had not been on hand before.

"Parsons?" said Mr. Severn reflectively. "I don't recall anyone of that name hereabouts. Perhaps you are on the wrong road. There is a Parsons at Monopoly."

"Parsons is the name. Aren't you Parsons? A couple of men down the road said you were, and that you could fix me up. They said right next the church and that your light was still burning." The visitor's tone was belligerent.

Severn's face cleared with a smile.

"Oh, they must have said 'Parson,' they often call me that. Come in. What can I do for you?"

The young man eyed him coldly and made no move to enter.

"Parson or Parsons, it makes no difference does it? Mr. Parson, if you're so particular then, come out and look at my car. It seems to be in bad shape, and be quick about it. I've got over two hundred miles to make before daybreak, so get a hustle on. I'll pay you well if you don't waste any time."

A queer look descended upon the minister in twinkles of amusement around his eyes and lips much like the smile that Tom McMertrie had worn, only there was not a rag of hurt pride about it. With entire pleasantness he said:

"Just wait a moment till I get a light."

As he turned to go Shafton called after him:

"Oh, by the way, got anything to drink? I'm thirsty as the devil."

Severn turned, instant hospitality in his face.

"What will you have? Water or milk? Plenty of both."

He smiled and Shafton looked at him in haughty amazement.

"Man! I said I wanted something to *drink!*" he thundered. "But don't stand there all night doddering. I've got to get started!"

A slight lifting of the chin, a trifle of steel in the kind eyes, a shade of coolness in the voice, as the clear comprehension of heaven had sifted the visitor, and the minister said, almost sternly:

"Oh, I see," and disappeared through a swinging door into the pantry.

It was about this time that Lynn Severn awoke to near consciousness and wondered what kind of noisy guest her father had now.

The minister was gone some time and the guest grew impatient, stamping up and down the piazza and kicking a porch rocker out of his path. He looked at his watch and frowned, wondering how near he was to the end of his detour, and then he started in pursuit of his man, tramping through the Severn house as if it were a public garage, and almost running into the minister as he swung the door open. Severn was approaching with a lighted lantern in one hand and a plate of brown bread and butter, with a cup of steaming coffee in his other hand.

Laurence Shafton stopped abruptly, a curse on his lips, but something, either the genial face of the minister, or the aroma of the coffee, silenced him. And indeed there was something about Graham Severn that was worth looking at. Tall and well built, with a face at once strong and sweet, and with a certain luminousness about it that almost seemed like transparency to let the spirit shine through, although there was nothing frail about his well-cut features.

Laurence Shafton, looking into the frank kind eyes of the minister suddenly became aware that this man had taken a great deal of trouble for him. He hadn't brought any liquor, probably because he did not know enough of the world to understand what it was he wanted, or because he was playing a joke. As he looked into those eyes and noted with his half-befuddled senses the twinkle playing at the corners he was not quite sure but the joke was on himself. But, however it was, the coffee smelled good and he took it and blundered out a brief "Thanks."

Eating his brown bread and butter, the like of which had never entered his pampered lips before, and taking great swoops of the hot strong coffee, he followed this strange new kind of a man out to the car in the moonlight, paying little heed to the careful examination that ensued, being so accustomed to ordering all his needs supplied and finding them forthcoming without delay.

Finally the minister straightened up:

"I'm afraid you won't go many miles tonight. You've burned out your bearings!"

"Hell!" remarked the young gentleman pausing before the last swallow of coffee.

"Oh, you won't find it so bad as that, I imagine," answered the steady voice of the minister. "I can give you a bed and take care of you over tomorrow, and perhaps Sandy McPherson can fix you up Monday, although I doubt it. He'd have to make new bearings, or you'd have to send for some to the factory."

But Laurence Shafton did not wait to hear the suggestions. He stormed up and down the sidewalk in front of the parsonage and let forth such a stream of choice language as had not been heard in that locality in many a long year. The minister's voice, cool, stern, commanding, broke in upon his ravings.

"I think that will be about all, sir!"

Laurence Shafton stopped and stared at the minister's

lifted hand, not because he was overawed, simply because never before in the whole of his twenty-four years had any-one dared lift voice to him in a tone of command or reproof. He could not believe his ears, and his anger rose hotly. He opened his mouth to tell this insignificant person who he was and where to get off, and a few other common arguments of gentlemen of his class, but the minister had a surprising height as he stood in the moonlight, and there was that something strange and spiritual about him that seemed to meet the intention and disarm it. His jaw dropped, and he could not utter the words he had been about to speak. This was insufferable! But there was that raised hand. It seemed like someone not of this world quite. He wasn't afraid, because it wasn't in him to be afraid. That was his pose, not afraid of those he considered his inferiors, and he did not consider that anyone was his superior. But somehow this was something new in his experience. A man like this! It was almost as if his mere being there demanded a certain homage. It was queer. The young man passed a hand over his hot forehead and tried to think. Then the minister's voice went calmly on. It was almost as if he had not said that other at all. Perhaps he had not. Perhaps he dreamed it or imagined it. Perhaps he had been taking too much liquor and this was one of the symptoms! Yet there still ringing in his ears—well his soul anyway—were those quiet words, "That will be about all, sir!" Sternly. As if he had a *right* to speak that way to *him!* To Laurence Shafton, son of the great Wilson J. Shafton, of New York! He looked up at the man again and found a sort of respect for him dawning in himself. It was queer, but the man was—well, interesting. What was this he was saying?

"I am sorry"—just as if he had never rebuked him at all, "I am sorry that there seems to be no other way. If I had a car I would take you to the nearest railway station, but there are no trains tonight, not even twenty miles away, until six in the morning. There are only four cars owned in the village.

Two are gone off on a summer trip, the third is out of commission being repaired, and the fourth belongs to the doctor, who happens to be away on the mountain tonight attending a dying man. You see how it is."

The young man opened his mouth to curse once more, and strangely enough closed it again. Somehow cursing seemed to have lost its force.

"There is just one chance," went on the minister thoughtfully, "that a young man who was visiting his mother today may still be here. I can call up and find out. He would take you I know."

Almost humbly the great man's son followed the minister back to the house and listened anxiously while he called a number on the telephone.

"Is that you, Mrs. Carter? I'm sorry if I have disturbed you. What? You hadn't gone to bed yet? Oh, waiting for Mark? Then he isn't there? That's what I called up for. There is someone here in trouble, needing to be taken to Monopoly. I was sure Mark would help him out if possible. Yes, please, if he comes soon, ask him to call me. Just leave a note for him, can't you? I wouldn't sit up. Mark will take good care of himself. Yes, of course, that's the mother of it. Well, good night, Mrs. Carter."

The young man strode angrily out to the door, muttering—but no words were distinct. He wanted to be away from the compelling calmness of those eyes that seemed to search him through. He dashed out the screen door, letting it slam behind him, and down the steps, intending to *make* his car go on at all odds until he reached another town somewhere. It had gone so far, it could go on a little farther perhaps. This country fellow did not know about cars, how should he?

And then somewhere right on the top step he made a false step and slipped, or was it his blindness of rage? He caught at the vines with frantic hands, but as if they laughed at him they slipped from his grasp. His feet clattered against

the step trying for footing, but he was too near the edge, and
he went down straight into a little rocky nook where ferns
and violets were growing, and a sharp jagged rock stuck up
and hit him viciously as he slid and struggled for a firm
footing again. Then an ugly twist of his ankle, and he lay in
a humiliating heap in the shadow of the vines on the lawn,
crying out and beginning to curse with the pain that gripped
him in sharp teeth, and stung through his whole excitable
inflamed being.

The minister was there almost at once, bending over him.
Somehow he felt as if he were in the power of somebody
greater than he had ever met before. It was almost like
meeting God out on the road somewhere. The minister
stooped and picked him up, lightly, as if he had been a
feather, and carried him like a baby, thrown partly over his
shoulder; up the steps, and into that blasted house again.
Into the bright light that sickened him and made the pain
leap up and bring a mighty faintness.

He laid him almost tenderly upon a soft couch, and
straightened the pillows about him, seeming to know just
how every bone felt, and how every nerve quivered, and
then he asked a few questions in a quiet voice. "What happened? Was it your ankle? Here? Or *here?* All right. Just be
patient a minute, I'll have you all fixed up. This was my job
over in France, you know. No, don't move. It won't hurt
long. It was right here you said. Now, wait till I get my bottle of lotion."

He was back in an instant with bandages, and bottle, and
seemed to know just how to get off a shoe with the least
trouble.

An hour later the scion of a great New York family lay
sleeping in the minister's study, the old couch made up with
cool sheets, and the swollen ankle comfortably bandaged
with cool wet cloths. Outside in the moonlight the crippled
car stood alone, and Sabbath Valley slept, while the bells
chimed out a single solemn stroke.

Chapter 6

Billy was doing some rapid thinking while he stood motionless in the bushes. It seemed a half hour, but in reality it was but a few seconds before he heard a low whistle. The men piled rapidly into the car with furtive looks on either side into the dark.

Billy gave a wavering glance toward the looming house in the darkness where the motionless figure had been left. Was it a dead man lying there alone, or was he only doped? But what could he do in the dark without tools or flash? He decided to stick with the machine, for he had no desire to foot it home, and anyway, with his bicycle he would be far more independent. Besides, there was the perfectly good automobile to think about. If the man was dead he couldn't be any deader. If he was only doped it would be some time before he came to, and before these keepers could get back he would have time to do something. Billy never doubted his responsibility in the matter. It was only a question of expediency. If he could just get these guys with the goods on them, he would be perfectly satisfied.

He made a dash for his seat at the back while the car was turning, and they were off at a brisk pace down the mountain, not waiting this time to double on their tracks, but splashing through the creek only once and on up to the road again.

Like an uneasy fever in his veins meantime, went and came a vision of that limp inert figure of the man being carried into the haunted house as it stood out in the flare of the flashlight, one arm hanging heavily. What did that hand and arm remind him of? Oh—h! The time when Mark was knocked cold at the Thanksgiving Day football game last

year. Mark's hand and arm had looked like that—he had
held his fingers like that—when they picked him up. Mark
had the baseball hand! Of course that rich guy might have
been an athlete too, they were sometimes. And of course
Mark was right now at home and in bed, where Billy wished
he was also, but somehow the memory of that still, dark,
knocked-cold attitude, and that hanging hand and arm
would not leave him. He frowned in the dark and wished
this business was over. Mark was the only living soul Billy
felt he could ever tell about this night's escapade, and he
wasn't sure he could tell him, but he knew if he did that
Mark would understand.

Billy watched anxiously for a streak of light in the east,
but none had come as yet. The moon had left the earth
darker than darkness when it went.

He tried to think what he should do. His bicycle was lying
in the bushes and he ought to get it before daylight. If they
went near the station he would drop off and pick it up. Then
he would scuttle through the woods and get to the crossroads, and beat it down to the Blue Duck Tavern. That was
the only place open all night where he could telephone. He
didn't like to go to the Blue Duck Tavern on account of his
aunt. She had once made him promise most solemnly,
bringing in something about his dead mother, that he would
never go to the Blue Duck Tavern. But this was a case of necessity, and dead mothers, if they cared at all, ought to understand. He had a deep underlying faith in the principle of
what a mother—at any rate a dead mother—would be like.
And anyhow, this wasn't the kind of *going* to the tavern his
aunt had meant. He was keeping the spirit of the promise if
not the letter. In his code the spirit meant much more than
the letter—at least on this occasion. There were often times
when he rigidly adhered to the letter and let the spirit take
care of itself, but this was not one.

But if, on the other hand they did not take Pat all the way
back to the crossing by the station it would be even better

for him, for the road on which they now were passed within a quarter of a mile of the Blue Duck Tavern, and he could easily beat the car to the state line, by dropping off and running.

But suddenly and without warning it became apparent that Pat was to be let out to walk to the station crossing, and Billy had only a second to decide what to do, while Pat lumbered swearing down from the car. If he got off now he would have to wait till Pat was far ahead before he dared go after his wheel, and he would lose so much time there would be no use in trying to save the car. On the other hand if he stayed on the car he was liable to be seen by Pat, and perhaps caught. However, this seemed the only possible way to keep the car from destruction and loss, so he wriggled himself into his seat more firmly, tucked his legs painfully up under him, covered his face with his cap, and hid his hands in his pockets.

"You've plenty of time," raged Pat. "You've only a little five-mile-run left. It's a good half hour before light. You're a pair of cowards, that's whut ye are, and so I'll tell Sam. If I get fired fer not being there fer the early milk train, there'll be no more fat jobs fer youse. Now be sure ye do as you're told. Leave the car in the first field beyond the woods after ye cross the state line, lift yer flashlight and wink three times, count three slow, and wink three times more. *Then beat it!* And doncha ferget to go feed that guy! We don't want he should die on us."

The engine began to mutter. Pat with a farewell string of oaths rolled off down the road, too sleepy to look behind, and Billy held his breath and ducked low till the rolling Pat was one with the deep gray of the morning.

The first streak of light was beginning to show in the east, and the all-night revelers at the Blue Duck were in the last stages of going home after a more than usually exciting season, when Billy like the hardened promise-breaker he felt himself to be, boldly slid in at the door and disappeared inside the telephone booth behind the last row of tables in the corner. For leave it to a boy, even though he be not a frequenter of a place, to know where everything needful is to be found!

He had to wait several minutes to get the chief of police in Economy, and while he waited two gaunt habitues of the tavern slid into seats at the table to the left of the booth, ordered drinks, and began to discuss something in a low tone. Billy paid no heed till he happened to hear his friend's name:

"Yep, I seen Mark come in with Cherry early in the evening. He set right over there and gotter some drink. The girl was mad because he wouldn't get her what she wanted to drink. I happened to be settin' directly in front and I heard her gassin' about it. She tossed her head and made her eyes look little and ugly like a pig, and once she got up to go, and he grabbed her hands and made her set down; and just set there fer sometime alookin' at her hard an' holdin' her han's and chewin' the rag at her. I don't know what all they was sayin', fer he talked mighty low, an' Ike called me to take a hand in the game over tother side the room, so I didn't know no more till I see him an' Cherry beatin' it out the side door, an' Dolphin standin' over acrost by the desk lampin' 'em with his ugly look, an' pretty quick, Dolph he slid out the other door an' was gone quite some time. When he come back Cherry was with him, laughin' and makin' eyes, and vampin' away like she always does, an' him an' her danced a lot after that—"

A voice on the end of the wire broke in upon this amazing conversation, and Billy with difficulty adjusted his jaded mind to the matter in hand:

" 'Zis the chief? Say, Chief, a coupla guys stole a machine—Holes-Mowbrays—license number 6362656-W— Got that? New York tag. They're on their way over to the state line beyond the crossroads. They're gonta run her in the field just beyond the woods, you know. They're gonta give a flashlight signal to their pal, three winks, count three slow, and three winks more, and then beat it. Then some guy is gonta wreck the machine. It's up to you and your men to hold the machine till I get the owner there. He don't know it's pinched yet, but I know where to find him, an' he'll have the license and can identify it. Where'll I find you? Station house? 'Conomy? Sure! I'll be there soon's I get 'im. What's that? I? Oh, I'm just a kid that happened to get wise. My name? Oh, rats! That don't cut any ice now! You get on yer job! They must be almost there by now. I gotta beat it! Gub-bye!"

Billy was all there even if he had been up all night. He hung up with a click, for he was anxious to hear what the men were saying. They had finished their glasses and were preparing to leave. The old one was gabbling on in a quer-ulous gossipy tone:

"Well, it'll go hard with Mark Carter if the man dies. Everybody knows he was here, and unless he can prove an alibi—"

They were crawling reluctantly out of their haunts now, and Billy could catch but one more sentence:

"Well, I'm sorry fer his ma. I used to go to school with Mrs. Carter when we were kids."

They were gone out and the room suddenly showed empty. The waiter was fastening the shutters. In a moment more he would be locked in. Billy made a silent dash among the tables and slid out the door while the waiter's back was turned. The two men were ambling slowly down the road to-ward Economy. Billy started on a dead run. His rubber-soled shoes made no echo and he was too light on his feet to make a thud. He disappeared into the grayness like a spirit. He had more cause than ever now for hurry. Mark! Mark! His beloved Mark Carter! What must he do about it? Must he tell Mark? Or did Mark perhaps know? What had hap-pened anyway? There had evidently been a shooting. That Cherry Fenner was mixed up in it. Billy knew her only by sight. She always grinned at him and said: "Hello, Billee!" in her pretty dimpled way. He didn't care for her himself. He had accepted her as a part of life, a necessary evil. She wore her hair queer, and had very short tight skirts, and high heels. She painted her face and vamped, but that was her affair. He had heretofore tolerated her because she seemed in some way to be under Mark Carter's recent protection. Therefore he had growled "Ello!" grimly whenever she accosted him and let it go at that. If it had come to a showdown he would have stood up for her because he knew that Mark would, that was all. Mark knew his own business. Far be it from Billy to criticize his hero's reasons. Perhaps it was one of Mark's weaknesses. It was up to him.

But this was a different matter. This involved Mark's honor. It was up to him to find Mark!

Billy did not take the highroad down from his detour. He cut across below the crossroads, over rough ground, among the underbrush, and parting the low growing trees, was lost in the gloom of the woods. But he knew every inch of ground within twenty miles around, and darkness did not take away his sense of direction. He crashed along among the branches, making steady headway toward the spot where he had left his bicycle, puffing and panting, his face streaked with dirt, his eyes bleared and haggard, his whole lithe young body straining forward and fighting against the dire weariness that was upon him, for it was not often that he stayed up all night. Aunt Saxon saw to that much at least.

The sky was growing rosy now, and he could hear the rumbling of the milk train. It was late. Pat would not lose his job this time, for he must have had plenty of time to get back to the station. Billy wormed himself under cover as the train approached, and bided his time. Cautiously, peering from behind the huckleberry growth, he watched Pat slamming the milk cans around. He could see his bicycle lying like a dark skeleton of a thing against the gravel bank. It was lucky he got there before day, for Pat would have been sure to see it, and it might have given him an idea that Billy had gone with the automobile.

The milk train came suddenly in sight through the tunnel, like a lighted thread going through a needle. It rumbled up to the station. There was a rattling of milk cans, empty ones being put on, full cans being put off, grumbling of Pat at the train hands, loud retorts of the train hands. The engine puffed and wheezed like a fat old lady going upstairs and stopping on every landing to rest. Then slamming of car doors, a whistle, the snort of the engine as it took up its way again out toward the rosy sky, its headlight weird like a sick candle against the dawn, its taillight winking with a leer and mocking at the mountains as it clattered away like a row of gray ducks lifting webbed feet and flinging back space to the station.

Pat rolled the loaded truck to the other platform ready for the lake train at seven, and went in to a much needed rest. He slammed the door with a finality that gave Billy relief. The boy waited a moment more in the gathering dawn, and then made a dash for the open, salvaging his bicycle, and diving back into the undergrowth.

For a quarter of a mile he and the wheel like two comrades raced under branches, and threaded their way between trees. Then he came out into the highroad and mounting his wheel rode into the world just as the sun shot up and touched the day with wonder.

He rode into the silent sleeping village of Sabbath Valley just as the bells from the church chimed out gently, as bells should do on a Sabbath morning when people are at rest, One! Two! Three! Four! Five!

Sabbath Valley looked great as he pedaled silently down the street. Even the old squeak of the back wheel seemed to be holding its breath for the occasion.

He coasted past the church and down the gentle incline in front of the parsonage and Joneses, and the Littles and Browns, and Gibsons. Like a shadow of the night passing he slid past the Fowlers and Tiptons and Duncannons, and fastened his eyes on the little white fence with the white-pillared gate where Mrs. Carter lived. Was that a light in the kitchen window? And the barn that Mark used for his garage when he was at home, was the door open? He couldn't quite see for the syringa bush hid it from the road. With a furtive glance up and down the street he wheeled in at the driveway, and rode up under the shadow of the green-shuttered white house.

He dismounted silently, stealthily, rested his wheel against the trunk of a cherry tree, and with keen eyes for every window, glanced up to the open one above which he knew belonged to Mark's room. Strong grimy fingers went to his lips and a low cautious whistle, more like a birdcall issued forth, musical as any wild note.

The white muslin curtains wavered back and forth in the summer breeze, and for a moment he thought a head was about to appear for a soft stirring noise had seemed to move within the house somewhere, but the curtains swayed on and no Mark appeared. Then he suddenly was aware of a white face confronting him at the downstairs window directly opposite to him, white and scared and—was it accusing? And suddenly he began to tremble. Not all the events of the night had made him tremble, but now he trembled, it was Mark's mother, and she had pink rims to her eyes, and little damp crimples around her mouth and eyes for all the world like Aunt Saxon's. She looked—she looked exactly as though she had not slept all night. Her nose was thin and red, and her eyes had that awful blue that eyes get that have been much washed with tears. The soft waves of her hair drooped thinly, and the coil behind showed more threads of silver than of brown in the morning sun that shot through the branches of the cherry tree. She had a frightened look, as if Billy had brought some awful news, or as if it was his fault, he could not tell which, and he began to feel that choking sensation and that goneness in the pit of his stomach that Aunt Saxon always gave him when she looked frightened at something he had done or was going to do. Added to this was that sudden premonition, and a memory of that drooping still figure in the dark up on the mountain.

Mrs. Carter sat down the candle on a shelf and raised the window:

"Is that you, Billy?" she asked, and there were tears in her voice.

Billy had a brief appalling revelation of mothers the world over. Did all mothers—women—act like that when they were *fools?* Fools is what he called them in his mind. Yet in spite of himself and his rage and trembling he felt a sudden tenderness for this crumply, tired, ghastly little pink-rimmed mother, apprehensive of the worst as was plain to see. Billy recalled like a flash the old man at the Blue Duck saying, "I'm sorry for his ma. I used to go to school with her." He looked at the faded face with the pink rims and trembling lips and had a vision of a brown-haired little girl at a desk, and old Si Appleby, a teasing boy in the desk opposite. It came over him that someday he would be an old man somewhere telling how he went to school— And then he asked:

"Where's Mark? Up yet?"

She shook her head apprehensively, withholdingly.

Billy had a thought that perhaps someone had beat him to it with news from the Blue Duck, but he put it from him. There were tears in her eyes and one was straggling down between the crimples of her cheeks where it looked as if she had lain on the folds of her handkerchief all night. There came a new tenderness in his voice. This was *Mark's* mother, and this was the way she felt. Well, of course it was silly, but she was Mark's *mother*.

"Man up the mountain had n'accident. I thought Mark ud he'p. He always does," explained Billy awkwardly with a feeling that he ought to account for his early visit.

"Yes, of course, Mark would like to help!" purred his mother comforted at the very thought of everyday life and Mark going about as usual. "But," and the apprehension flew into her eyes again, "he isn't home. Billy, he hasn't come home at all last night! I'm frightened to death! I've sat up all night! I can't think what's happened! There's so many holdups and Mark will carry his money loose in his trousers' pocket!"

Billy blanched but lied beautifully up to the occasion even as he would have liked to have somebody lie for him to Aunt Saxon:

"Aw! That's nothing! Doncha worry. He tol' me he might have t'stay down t'Unity all night. There's a fella down there that likes him a lot, an' they had somekinduva blowout in their church last night. He mightuv had ta take some girl home out of town, ya know, and stayed over with the fella."

Mrs. Carter's face relaxed a shade:

"Yes, I've tried to think that!"

"Well, doncha worry, Mizz Carter, I'll lookim up fer ya, I know 'bout where he might be."

"Oh, thank you, Billy," her face wreathed in wavering smiles brought another thought of school days and life and how queer it was that grown folks had been children sometime and children had to be grown folks.

"Billy, Mark likes you very much. I'm sure he won't mind your knowing that I'm worried, but you know how boys don't like to have their mothers worry, so you needn't say anything to Mark that I said I was worried, need you? You understand, Billy. I'm not *really* worried, you know. Mark was always a good boy."

"Aw, sure!" said Billy was a knowing wink. "He's a prince! You leave it t'me, Mizz Carter!"

"Thank you, Billy. I'll do something for you sometime. But how's it come you're up so early? You haven't had your breakfast yet have you?"

She eyed his weary young face with a motherly anxiety:

"Naw, I didn't have no time to stop fer breakfast." Billy spoke importantly. "Got this call about the sick guy and had to beat it. Say, you don't happen to know Mark's license number, do you? It might help a lot, savin' time 'f'I could tell his car at sight. Save stoppin' to ast."

"Well, now, I don't really—" said the woman ruminatively. "Let me see. There was six and six, there were a lot of sixes if I remember—"

"Oh, well, it don't matter—" Billy grasped his wheel and prepared to leave.

"Wait, Billy, you must have something to eat—"

"Aw, naw, I can't wait! Gotta beat it! Might miss 'im!"

"Well, just a bite. Here, I'll get you some cookies!"

She vanished, and he realized for the first time that he was hungry. Cookies sounded good.

She returned with a brimming glass of milk and a plate of cookies. She stuffed the cookies in his pockets, while he drank the milk.

"Say," said he after a long sweet draught of the foaming milk, "ya, ain't got enny more you cud spare fer that sick guy, have ya? Wait, I'll save this. Got a bottle?"

"Indeed you won't, Billy Gaston. You just drink that every drop. I'll get you another bottle to take with you. I got extra last night 'count of Mark being home, and then he didn't drink it. He always likes a drink of milk last thing before he goes to bed."

She vanished and returned with a quart of milk cold off the ice. She wrapped it well with newspapers, and Billy packed it safely into the little basket on his wheel. Then he bethought him of another need.

"Say, m'y I go inta the g'rage an' get a screwdriver? Screw loose on m'wheel."

She nodded and he vanished into the open barn door. Well, he knew where Mark kept his tools. He picked out a small pointed saw, a neat little auger, and a file and stowed them hurriedly under the milk bottle. Thus reinforced without and within, he mounted his faithful steed and sped away to the hills.

The morning sun had shot up several degrees during his delay, and Sabbath Valley lay like a thing newborn in its glory. On the belfry a purple dove sat glistening, green and gold ripples on her neck, turning her head proudly from side to side as Billy rode by, and when he topped the first hill across the valley the bells rang out six sweet strokes as if to remind him that Sunday school was not far off and he must hurry back. But Billy was trying to think how he should get into that locked house, and wondering whether the kidnappers would have returned to feed their captive yet. He realized that he must be wary, although his instinct told him that they would wait for dark, besides, he had hopes that they might have been pinched.

Nevertheless he approached the old house cautiously, skirting the mountain to avoid Pleasant Valley, and walking a mile or two through thick undergrowth, sometimes with difficulty propelling the faithful machine.

Arrived in sight he studied the surroundings carefully, harbored his wheel where it would not be discovered and was yet easily available, and after reconnoitering stole out of covert.

The house stood gaunt and grim against the smiling morning, its shuttered windows giving an expression of blindness or the repellant mask of death. A dead house, that was what it was. Its doors and windows closed on the tragedy that had been enacted within its massive stone walls. It seemed more like a fortress than a house where warm human faces had once looked forth, and where laughter and pleasant words had once sounded out. To pass it had always stirred a sense of mystery and weirdness. To approach it thus with the intention of entering to find that still limp figure of a man gave a most overpowering sense of awe. Billy looked up with wide eyes, the deep shadows under them standing out in the clear light of the morning and giving him a strangely old aspect as if he had jumped over at least ten years during the night. Warily he circled the house, keeping close to the shrubbery at first and listening as a squirrel might have done, then gradually drawing nearer. He noticed that the downstairs shutters were solid iron with a little half-moon peephole at the top. Those upstairs were solid below and fitted with slats above, but the slats were closed on all the front windows, and all but two of the back ones, which were turned upward so that one could not see the glass. The doors, both back and front, were locked, and unshakable, of solid oak and very thick. A Yale lock with a new look gave all entrance at the front an impossible look. The back door was equally impregnable unless he set to work with his auger and saw and took out a heavy oak panel.

He got down to the ground and began to examine the cellar windows. They seemed to be fitted with iron bars set into the solid masonry. He went all around the house and found each one unshakable, until he reached the last at the back. There he found a bit of stone cracked and loosened, and it gave him an idea. He set to work with his few tools and finally succeeded in loosening one rusted bar. He was much hindered in his work by the necessity of keeping a constant watch out, and by his attempts to be quiet. There was no telling when Link and Shorty might come to feed their captive and he must not be discovered.

It was slow work picking away at the stone, filing away at the rusty iron, but the bars were so close together that three must be removed before he could hope to crawl through, and even then he might be able to get no further than the cellar. The guy that fixed this house up for a prison knew what he was about.

Faintly across the mountains came the echo of bells, or were they in the boy's own soul? He worked away in the hot sun, the perspiration rolling down his weary dirty face, and sometimes his soul fainted within him. Bells and the sweet quiet church with the pleasant daily faces about and the hum of Sunday school beginning! How far away that all seemed to him now as he filed and picked, and sweated, and kept up a strange something in his soul half yearning, half fierce dread, that might have been like praying, only the burden of its yearning seemed to be expressed in but a single word, "Mark! Mark!"

At last the third bar came loose and with a great sigh that was almost like a sob, the boy tore it out and cleared the way. Then carefully gathering his effects, tools, milk bottle, and cap together, he let them down into the dungeonlike blackness of the cellar, and crept in after them, taking the precaution to set up in place the iron bars once more and leave no trace of his entrance.

Pausing cautiously to listen he ventured to strike a match, mentally belaboring himself at the wasteful way in which he had always used his flashlight which was now so much needed and out of commission. The cellar was large, running under the whole house, with heavy rafters and looming coal pits. A scurrying rat started a few lumps of coal in the slide, and a cobwebby rope hung ominously from one cross beam, giving him a passing shudder. It seemed as if the spirit of the past had arisen to challenge his entrance thus. He took a few steps forward toward a dim staircase he sighted at the farther end, and then a sudden noise sent his heart beating fast. He extinguished the match and stood in the darkness listening with straining ears. That was surely a step he heard on the floor above!

Chapter 7

Laurence Shafton awoke late to the sound of church bells come alive and singing hymn tunes. There was something strangely unreal in the sound, in the utter stillness of the background of Sabbath Valley atmosphere that made him think, almost, just for an instant, that he had stumbled somehow into the wrong end of the other world, and come into the fields of the blessed. Not that he had any very definite idea about what the fields of the blessed would look like or what would be going on there, but there was something still and holy between the voices of the bells that fairly compelled his jaded young soul to sit up and listen.

But at the first attempt to sit up a very sharp, very decided twinge of pain caught him, and brought an assorted list of words which he kept for such occasions to his lips. Then he looked around and tried to take in the situation. It was almost as if he had been caught out of his own world and dropped into another universe, so different was everything here, and so little did he remember the happenings of the night before. He had had trouble with his car, something infernal that had prevented his going farther—he recalled having to get out and push the thing along the road, and then two loutish men who made game of him and sent him here to get his car fixed. There had been a man, a different sort of man who gave him bread and butter instead of wine—he remembered that—and he had failed to get his car fixed, but how the deuce did he get landed on this couch with a world of books about him and a thin muslin curtain blowing into the room, and fanning the petals of a lovely rose in a long-stemmed clear glass vase? Did he try to start and have a smashup? No, he remembered going down the steps with the intention of starting, but stay! Now it was coming to him. He fell off the porch! He must have had a jag on or he never would have fallen. He did things to his ankle in falling. He remembered the gentle giant picking him up as if he had been a baby and putting him here, but where was *here?* Ah! Now he remembered! He was on his way to Opal Verrons's. A bet. An elopement for the prize! Great stakes. He had lost of course. What a fool! If it hadn't been for his ankle he might have got to a trolley car or train somehow and made a garage. Money would have taken him there in time. He was vexed that he had lost. It would have been great fun, and he had the name of always winning when he set out to do so. But then, perhaps it was just as well—Verrons was a good fellow as men went—he liked him, and he was plain out and out fond of Opal just at present. It would have been a dirty shame to play the trick behind his back. Still, if Opal wanted to run away with him it was up to him to run of course. Opal was rare sport and he couldn't stand the idea of smart aleck McMarter, or that conceited Percy Emerson getting there first. He wondered which had won. It made his fury rise to think of either, and he had promised the lady neither of them should. What was she thinking of him by now that he had sent her no word of his delay? That was inexcusable. He must attend to it at once.

He glanced around the pleasant room. Yes, there on the desk was a telephone! Could he get to it? He sat up and painfully edged his way over to the desk.

> Safely through another week,
> God has brought us on our way—

chimed the bells,

> Let us now a blessing seek,
> Waiting in His courts today—

But Laurie Shafton had never sung those words in his life and had no idea what the bells were seeking to get across to him. He took down the receiver and called for Long Distance.

O day of rest and gladness!

pealed out the bells joyously,

O day of joy and light!
O balm of care and sadness,
Most beautiful, most bright—!

But it meant nothing to Laurie Shafton seeking a hotel in a fashionable resort. And when he finally got his number it was only Opal's maid who answered.

"Yes, Mrs. Verrons was up. She was out walking on the beach with a gentleman. No, it was not Mr. Emerson, nor yet Mr. McMarter. Neither of those gentlemen had arrived. No, it was not Mr. Verrons. He had just telegraphed that he would not be at the hotel until tomorrow night. Yes, she would tell Mrs. Verrons that he had met with an accident. Mrs. Verrons would be very sorry. Number one-W Sabbath Valley. Yes, she would write it down. What? Oh! The gentleman Mrs. Verrons was walking with? No, it was not anybody that had been stopping at the hotel for long, it was a new gentleman who had just come the night before. She hadn't heard his name yet. Yes, she would be sure to tell Mrs. Verrons at once when she came in, and Mrs. Verrons would be likely to call him up!"

He hung up the receiver and looked around the room discontentedly. A stinging twinge of his ankle added to his discomfort. He gave an angry snarl and pushed the wavering curtain aside, wishing those everlasting bells would stop their banging.

Across the velvet stretch of lawn the stone church nestled among the trees, with a background of mountains, and a studding of white gravestones beyond its wide front steps. It was astonishingly beautiful, and startlingly close for a church. He had not been so near to a church except for a wedding in all his young life. Dandy place for a wedding that would be, canopy over the broad walk from the street, charming architecture, he liked the line of the arched belfry and the slender spire above. The rough stone fitted well into the scenery. The church seemed to be a thing of the ages placed there by Nature. His mind trained to detect a sense of beauty in garments, rugs, pictures, and women, appreciated the picture on which he was gazing. Where was this anyway? Surely not the place with the absurd name that he remembered now on the mountain detour. Sabbath Valley! How ridiculous! It must be the home of some wealthy estate, and yet there seemed a rustic loveliness about it that scarcely established that theory.

The bells had ceased. He heard the roll of a deep throated organ skillfully played.

And now, his attention was suddenly attracted to the open window of the church where framed in English ivy a lovely girl sat at the organ. She was dressed in white with hair of gold, and a golden window somewhere back of her across the church, made a background of beaten gold against which her delicate profile was set like some young saint. Her white fingers moved among the keys, and gradually he came to realize that it was she who had been playing the bells.

He stared and stared, filled with admiration, thrilled with this new experience in his blasé existence. Who would have expected to find a beauty like that in a little out-of-the-way place like this? His theory of a great estate and a rich man's daughter with a fad for music instantly came to the front. What a lucky happening that he should have broken down close to this church. He would find out who the girl was and work it to get invited up to her house. Perhaps he was a fortunate loser of his bet after all.

As he watched the girl playing, gradually the music entered his consciousness. He was fond of music, and had heard the best of the world of course. This was meltingly lovely. The girl had fine appreciation and much expression, even when the medium of her melody was clumsy things like bells. She had seemed to make them glad as they pealed out their melodies. He had not known bells could sound like happy children, or like birds.

His meditations were interrupted by a tap on the door, followed by the entrance of his host bearing a tray:

"Good morning," he said pleasantly, "I see you're up. How is the sprain? Better? Would you like me to dress it again?"

He came over to the desk and set down the tray on which was beautifully brown buttered toast, eggs and coffee:

"I've brought you just a bite. It's so late you won't want much, for we have dinner immediately after church. I suppose you wouldn't feel like going over to the service?"

"Service?" the young man drawled almost insolently.

"Yes, service is at eleven. Would you care to go over? I could assist you."

"Naw, I shouldn't care to go," he answered rudely, "I'm pulling out of here as soon as I can get that machine of mine running. By the way, I've been dong some telephoning"—he slung a ten-dollar note on the desk. "I didn't ask how much it was, guess that'll cover it. Now, help me to the big chair and I'll sample your breakfast."

The minister picked up the young man easily and placed him in the big chair before the guest realized what he was doing, and then turned and took the ten-dollar bill between his thumb and finger and flipped it down in the young man's lap.

"Keep it," he said briefly. "It's of no consequence."

"But it was long distance," explained the guest loftily. "It'll be quite a sum. I talked overtime."

"No matter," said the minister pulling out a drawer of the desk and gathering a few papers and his Bible. "Now, would you like me to look at that ankle before I go, or will you wait for the doctor? He's likely to be back before long, and I've left a call for him."

"I'll wait for the doctor," the young man's tone approached the insolent note again, "and, by the way, I wish you'd send for a mechanic. I've got to get that car running."

"I'm sorry," said Severn, "I'm afraid you'll have to wait. The only one in this region that would be at all likely to help you out with those bearings is Carter. He has a car, or had one, of that make. He might happen to have some bearings, but it is not at all likely. Or, he could tow you ten miles to Monopoly. But Carter is not at home yet."

The young man fairly frothed at the mouth:

"Do you mean to tell me that there is no one can mend a broken machine around this forsaken dump? Where's your nearest garage? Send for a man to come at once. I'm willing to pay anything," he flourished a handful of bills.

The minister looked at his watch anxiously:

"I'm sorry," he said again. "I've got to go to the service now. There is a garage at Monopoly and their number is ninety-seven-M. You can phone them if you are not satisfied. I tried them quite early this morning while you were still sleeping, but there was nothing doing. The truth is the people around this region are a little prejudiced against working seven days out of the week, although they will help a man out in a case like yours when they can, but it seems the repairman, the only one who knows about bearings, has gone fifty miles in another direction to a funeral and won't be back till tomorrow morning. Now, if you're quite comfortable I'll have to leave you for a little while. It is time for my service to begin."

The young man looked at his host with astonishment. He

was not used to being treated in this offhand way. He could
hardly believe his ears. Throw back his money and lay down
the law that way!

"Wait!" he thundered as the door was about to close upon
the departing minister.

Severn turned and regarded his guest quietly, questioningly:

"Who's that girl over there in the window playing the
organ?" He pulled the curtain aside and revealed a glimpse
of the white and gold saint framed in the ivy. Severn gave a
swift cold glance at the insolent youth and then answered
with a slightly haughty note in his courteous voice, albeit a
quiver of amusement on his lip:

"That is my daughter."

Laurence Shafton dropped the curtain and turned to stare
at his host, but the minister had closed the door and was already on his way to church. Then the youth pulled back the
curtain again and regarded the lady. The man's daughter!
And playing like that!

The rich notes of the organ were rolling out into the summer day, a wonderful theme from an old master, grandly
played. Yes, she could play. She had been well taught. And
the looks of her! She was wonderful at this distance. Were
these then wealthy people perhaps summering in this quiet
resort? He glanced about at the simple furnishings. That was
a good rug at his feet, worn in places, but soft in tone and
unmistakably of the Orient. The desk was of fumed oak,
somewhat massive and dignified with a touch of hand carving. The chairs were of the same dark oak with leather cushions, and the couch so covered by his bed drapery that he
could not see it, but he remembered its comfort. There was
nothing showy or expensive looking but everything simple
and good. One or two fine old pictures on the wall gave evidence of good taste. The only luxury seemed books, rows
and rows of them behind glass doors in cases built into the
wall. They lined each space between windows and doors,

and in several spots reached to the ceiling. He decided that these people must have had money and lost it. These things were old and had perhaps been inherited. But the girl! She teased his curiosity. She seemed of a type entirely new, and most attractive. Well, here was good luck again! He would stay till church was out and see what she might be like at nearer view. It might amuse him to play the invalid for a day or two and investigate her. Meantime, he must call up that garage and see what could be done for the car. If he could get it patched up by noon he might take the girl out for a spin in the afternoon. One could judge a girl much better getting her off by herself that way. He didn't seem to relish the memory of that father's smile and haughty tone as he said "My daughter." Probably was all kinds of fussy about her. But if the girl had any pep at all she surely would enjoy getting away from oversight for a few hours. He hoped Opal would call before they got back from their service. It might be awkward talking with them all around.

But the organ was suddenly drowned in a burst of song:

Glory be to the Father, and to the Son, and to the Holy Ghost, As it was in the beginning, is now and ever shall be—world without end, Amen!

Somehow the words struck him with a strange awe, they were so distinct, and almost in the room with him. He looked about half feeling that the room was filled with people, and felt curiously alone. There was an atmosphere in the little house of everybody being gone to church. They had all gone and left him alone. It amused him. He wondered about this odd family who seemed to be under the domination of a church service. They had left him a stranger alone in their house. The doors and windows were all open. How did they know but he was a burglar?

Someone was talking now. It sounded like the voice of his host. It might be a prayer. How peculiar! He must be a preacher. Yet he had been sent to him to fix his car. He did not look like a laboring man. He looked as if he might be— well almost anything—even a gentleman. But if he was a clergyman, why, that of course explained the ascetic type, the nunlike profile of the girl, the skilled musician. Clergymen were apt to educate their children, even without much money. The girl would probably be a prude and bore, but there was a chance that she might be a princess in disguise and need a prince to show her a good time. He would take the chance at least until after dinner.

So he ate his delicate toast, and drank his delicious coffee, and wished he had asked that quiet man to have his flask filled at the drugstore before he went to his old service, but consoled himself with numerous cigarettes, while he watched the face of the musician, and listened idly to the music.

It was plain that the young organist was also the choir leader, for her expressive face was turned toward the singers, and her lovely head kept time. Now and then a motion of the hand seemed to give a direction or warning. And the choir too sang with great sweetness and expression. They were well trained. But what a bore such a life must be to a girl. Still, if she had never known anything else! Well, he would like to see her at closer range. He lit another cigarette and studied her profile as she slipped out of the organ bench and settled herself nearer the window. He could hear the man's voice reading now. Some of the words drew his idle attention:

"All the ways of a man are clean in his own eyes; but the Lord weigheth the spirits."

Curious sentence that! It caught in his brain. It seemed rather true. From the Bible probably, of course, though he was not very familiar with that volume, never having been obliged to go to Sunday school in his childhood days. But was it true? Were all a man's ways clean in his own eyes?

Take, for instance, his own ways? He always did about as he pleased, and he had never asked himself whether his ways were clean or not. He hadn't particularly cared. He supposed some people would think they were not—but in his own eyes, well—was he clean? Take for instance this expedition of his? Running a race to get another man's wife—an alleged friend's wife, too? It did seem rather despicable when one thought of it after the jag was off. But then one was not quite responsible for what one did with a jag on, and what the deuce did the Lord have to do with it anyway? How could the Lord weigh the spirit? That meant of course that He saw through all subterfuges. Well, what of it?

Another sentence caught his ear:

"When a man's ways please the Lord, he maketh even his enemies to be at peace with him."

How odd, the Lord—if there was a Lord, he had never thought much about it—but how odd, if there was a Lord for Him to care about a man's ways. If he were Lord he wouldn't care, he'd only want them to keep out of his way. He would probably crush them like ants, if he were Lord. But the Lord—taking any notice of men's ways, and being pleased by them and looking out to protect them from enemies! It certainly was quaint—a quaint idea! He glanced again at the reverent face of the girl, the down-drooped eyes, the lovely sensitive mouth. Quaint, that was the word for her, quaint and unusual. He certainly was going to enjoy meeting her.

"Ting-aling-ling-ling!" burst out the telephone bell on the desk. He frowned and dropped the curtain. Was that Opal? He hobbled to the desk painfully, half annoyed that she had called him from the contemplation of this novel scene, not so sure that he would bother to call up that garage yet. Let it go till he had sampled the girl.

He took down the receiver and Opal's voice greeted him, mockingly, tauntingly from his own world. The little ivy-leaved church with its Saint Cecilia at the organ, and its strange weird message about a God that cared for man's ways, dropped away like a dream that was past.

When he hung up the receiver and turned back to his couch again the girl had closed the window. It annoyed him. He did not know how his giddy badinage had clashed in upon the last words of the sermon.

It seemed a long time after the closing hymn before the little throng melted away down the maple-lined street. The young man watched them curiously from behind his curtain, finding only food for amusement in most of them. And then came the minister, lingering to talk to one here and there, and his wife—it was undoubtedly his wife, even the hare-brained Laurie knew her, in the gray organdy, with the white at her neck, and the soft white hat. She had a pleasant light in her eyes, and one saw at once that she was a lady. There was a grace about her that made the girl seem possible. And lastly, came the girl.

She stepped from the church door in her white dress and simple white hat, white even to her little shoes, and correct in every way, he could see that. She was no country gawk! She came forth lightly into the sunshine which caught her hair in golden tendrils around her face as if it loved to hide therein, and she was immediately surrounded by half a dozen urchins. One had brought her some lilies, great white starry things with golden hearts, and she gathered them into her arms as if she loved them, and smiled at the boys. One could see how they adored her. She lingered talking to them, and laid her hand on one boy's shoulder, he walking like a knight beside her trying to act as if he did not know her hand was there. His head was drooped, but he lifted it with a grin at last and gave her a nod which seemed to make her glad, for her face broke forth in another smile:

"Well, don't forget, tonight," she called as they turned to go, "and remember to tell Billy!"

Then she came trippingly across the grass, a song on her lips. Some girl! Say! She certainly was a stunner!

Chapter 8

Opal Verrons was small and slight with large childlike eyes that could look like a baby's, but that could hold the very devil on occasions. The eyes were dark and lustrous with long curling black lashes framing them in a face that might have been modeled for an angel, so round the curves, so enchanting the lips, so lofty the white brow. Angelé Potocka had no lovelier set to her head, no more limpal fire in her eye, than had Opal Verrons. Indeed her lovers often called her the Fire Opal. The only difference was that Angelé Potocka developed her brains, of which she had plenty, while Opal Verrons had placed her entire care upon developing her lovely little body, though she too had plenty of brains on occasion.

And she knew how to dress! So simply, so slightly sometimes, so perfectly to give a setting—the right setting—to her little self. She wore her heavy dark hair bobbed, and it curled about her small head exquisitely, giving her the look of a Raphael cherub or a boy page in the court of King Arthur. With a flat band of silver olive leaves about her brow, and the soft hair waving out below, nothing more was necessary for a costume save a brief drapery of silver spangled cloth with a strap of jewels and a wisp of black malines for a scarf. She was always startling and lovely even in her simplest costume. Many people turned to watch her in a simple dark blue serge made like a child's girded with a delicate arrangement of medallions and chains of white metal, her dark rough woollen stockings rolled girlishly below white dimpled knees, and her feet shod in flat-soled white buckskin shoes. She was young enough to get away with it, the older women said cattishly as they watched her stroll

away to the beach with a new man each day, and noted her
artless grace and indifferent pose. That she had a burly millionaire husband who still was under her spell and watched
her jealously only made her more interesting, and they pi-
tied her for being tied to a man twice her age and bulky as a
bale of cotton. She who could dance like a sylph and was
light on her little feet as a thistledown. Though wise ones
sometimes said that Opal had her young eyes wide open
when she married Ed Verrons, and she had him right under
her little pink well manicured thumb. And some said she
was not nearly so young as she looked.

Her hands were the weakest point in Opal Verron's whole
outfit. Not that they were unlovely in form or ungraceful.
They were so small they hardly seemed like hands, so unde-
veloped, so useless, with the dimpling of a baby's, yet the
sharp nails of a little beast. They were so plump and well
cared for they were fairly sleek, and had an old wise air
about them as she patted her puffy curls daintily with a motion all her own that showed her lovely rounded arm, and
every needle-pointed, shell-tinted fingernail, sleek and
puffy, and never used, not even for a bit of embroidery or
knitting. She couldn't, you know, with those sharp transparent little nails, they might break. They were like her little
sharp teeth that always reminded one of a mouse's teeth,
and made one shudder at how sharp they would be should
she ever decide to bite.

But her smile was like the mixing of all smiles, a baby's,
woman of the world, a grieved child's, a spirit who had put
aside all moral purpose. Perhaps, like mixed drinks it was
for that reason but the more intoxicating. And because she
did not hide her charms and was lavish with her smiles,
there were more poor victims about her little feet than about
any other woman at the shore that summer. Men talked
about her in the smoking rooms and billiard rooms and
compared her to vamps of other seasons, and decided she
had left them all in the shade. She was a perfect production

of the modern age, more perfect than others because she
knew how to do the boldest things with that cherubic air
that bereft sin of its natural ugliness and made it beautiful
and delicious, as if degradation had suddenly become an
exalted thing, like some of the old rites in a pagan temple,
and she a lovely priestess. And when each new folly was
over there was she with her innocent baby air, and her pure
childlike face that looked dreamily out from its frame of little girl hair, and seemed not to have been soiled at all. And
so men who played her games lost their sense of sin and fell
that much lower than those who sin and know it and are
afraid to look themselves in the face. When a man loses his
sense of shame of being among the pigs, he is in a far country indeed.

But Opal Verrons sauntering forth to the hotel piazza in
company with three of her quondam admirers suddenly lost
her luxurious air of nestling content. The hotel clerk handed
her two telegrams as she passed the desk. She tore them
open carelessly, but her eyes grew wide with horror as she
read.

Percy Emerson had been arrested. He had run over a
woman and a baby and both were in a hospital in a critical
condition. He would be held without bail until it was seen
whether they lived.

She drew in her breath with a frightened gasp and bit at
her red lip with her little sharp teeth. A pretty child with
floating curls and dainty apparel ran laughing across her
way, its hand outstretched to a tiny white dog that was
dancing after her, and Opal gave a sharp cry and tore the
telegram into small bits. But when she opened the second
message her face paled under its delicate rouge as she read:
"Mortimer McMarter killed in an accident when his car collided with a truck. His body lies at Saybrook Inn. We find
your address on his person, with a request to let you know if
anything happens to him. What do you wish done with the
body?"

Those who watched her face as she read say that it took on an ashen color and she looked years older. Her real spirit seemed to be looking forth from those wide limpid eyes for an instant, the spirit of a coward who had been fooling the world; the spirit of a lost soul who had grown old in sin; the spirit of a soul who had stepped over the bounds and sinned beyond her depth.

She looked about upon them all, stricken, appalled—not sorry but just afraid—and not for her friends, but for *herself!* And then she gave a horrid little lost laugh and dropping the telegram as if it had burned her, she flung out her voice upon them with a blaze in her big eyes and a snarl in her lute voice:

"Well, I wasn't to blame was I? They all were grown men, weren't they? It was up to them. *I'm* going to get out of here! This is an *awful* place!"

She gave a shudder and turning swiftly fled to the elevator, catching it just as the door was being shut, and they saw her rising behind the black and gold grating and waving a mocking little white hand at them as they watched her amazed. Then one of them stooped and picked up the telegram. And while they still stood at the doorway wondering someone pointed to a brilliant blue car that was sliding down the avenue across the beach road.

"She has gone!" they said looking at one another strangely. Did she really care then?

The dinner at Sabbath Valley parsonage was a good one. It was quite different from any dinner Laurie Shafton had ever eaten before. It had a taste that he hadn't imagined just plain chicken and mashed potatoes and bread and butter and coffee and cherry pie could have. Those were things he seldom picked out from a menu, and he met them as something new and delicious, prepared in this wonderful country way.

Also the atmosphere was queer and interesting.

The minister had helped him into the dining room, a cheery room with a bay window looking toward the church and a window box of nasturtiums in which the bees hummed and buzzed.

The girl came in and acknowledged the casual introduction of her father with a quite sophisticated nod and sat down across from him. And there was a *prayer* at the beginning of the meal! Just as he was about to say something graceful to the girl, there was a *prayer*. It was almost embarrassing. He had never seen one before like this. At a boarding school once he had experienced a thing they called grace which consisted in standing behind their chairs while the entire assembled hungry multitude repeated a poem of a religious nature. He remembered they used to spend their time making up parodies on it—one ran something about "this same old fish upon my plate," and rhymed with "hate." He stared at the lovely bowed hair of the girl across the table while it was going on, and got ready a remark calculated to draw her smiles, but the girl lifted eyes that seemed so far away he felt as though she did not see him, and he contented himself with replying to his host's question something about the part of the chicken he liked best. It was a strange home to him, it seemed so intimate. Even the chicken seemed to be a detail of their life together, perhaps because there was only one chicken, and one breast. Where he dwelt there were countless breasts, and everybody had a whole breast if he wanted it, or a whole chicken for the matter of that. Here they had to stop and ask what others liked before they chose for themselves. This analysis went through his mind while he sat waiting for his plate and wondering over the little things they were talking about. Mrs. Severn said Miss Saxon had been crying all through church, and she told her Billy had been away all night. She was awfully worried about his going with that baseball team.

A fleeting shadow passed over the girl's face:

"Billy promised me he would be there today," she said

thoughtfully. "Something must have happened. I don't think Billy was with the baseball team—" then her eyes traveled away out the window to the distant hills, she didn't seem to see Laurence Shafton at all. It was a new experience for him. He was fairly good-looking and knew it.

Who the deuce was this Billy? And what did she care about Miss Saxon crying? Did she care so much for Billy already? Would it be worth his while to make her uncare?

"Mrs. Carter wasn't out," said Mrs. Severn as she poured coffee. "I hope she's not having more trouble with her neuralgia."

The minister suddenly looked up from his carving:

"Did Mark come back yesterday, Marilyn?"

The girl drew a quick breath and brought back her eyes from the hills, but she did not look at the young man:

"No, Father, he didn't come."

Who the deuce was *Mark?* Of course there would be several, but there was always *one.* Billy and Mark! It was growing interesting.

But Billy and Mark were not mentioned again, though a deep gravity seemed to have settled into the eyes of the family since their names had come up. Laurie decided to speak of the weather and the roads:

"Glorious weather we're having," he chirped out condescendingly, "but you certainly have the limit for roads. What's the matter with the highway? Had a detour right in the best part of the road. Bridge down, it said, road flooded! Made the deuce of a time for me!"

"Bridge?" remarked Marilyn looking up thoughtfully.

"Flood?" echoed the minister sharply.

"Yes. About two miles back where the highway crosses this valley. Put me in some fix. Had a bet on you know. Date with a lady. Staked a lot of money on winning, too. Hard luck." Then he looked across at Marilyn's attentive face. Ah! He was getting her at last! More on that line.

"But it'll not be all loss," he added gallantly with a gesture of admiration toward her. "You see, I didn't have any idea I was going to meet *you.*"

But Marilyn's eyes were regarding him soberly, steadily, analytically, without an answering smile. It was as if she did not like what he had said—if indeed she had heard it at all—as if she were offended at it. Then the eyes took on an impersonal look and wandered thoughtfully to the mountains in the distance. Laurie felt his cheeks burn. He felt almost embarrassed again, like during the prayer. Didn't the girl know he was paying her a compliment? Or was she such a prude that she thought him presuming on so slight an acquaintance? Her father was speaking:

"I don't quite understand," he said thoughtfully. "There is no bridge within ten miles, and nothing to flood the road but the creek, which never was known to overflow its banks more than a few feet at most. The highway is far above the valley. You must have been a bit turned around."

The young man laughed lightly:

"Well, perhaps I had a jag on. I'm not surprised. I'd been driving for hours and had to drink to keep my nerve till morning. There were some dandy spilling places around those mountain curves. One doesn't care to look out and see when one is driving at top speed."

Heavens! What had he said now? The girl's eyes came round to look him over again and went through to his soul like a lightning flash and away again, and there was actually scorn on her lips. He must take another line. He couldn't understand this haughty country beauty in the least.

"I certainly did enjoy your music," he flashed forth with a little of his own natural gaiety in his voice that made him so universal a favorite.

The girl turned gravely toward him and surveyed him once more as if she were surprised and perhaps had not done him justice. She looked like one who would always be willing to do one justice. He felt encouraged:

"If it hadn't been for this blamed foot of mine I'd have

hobbled over to the—service. I was sorry not to hear the music closer."

"There is another service this evening," she said pleasantly. "Perhaps Father can help you over. It is a rather good organ for so small a one." She was trying to be polite to him. It put him on his mettle. It made him remember how rude he had been to her father the night before.

"Delightful organ, I'm sure," he returned, "but it was the organist that I noticed. One doesn't often hear such playing even on a good organ."

"Oh, I've been well taught," said the girl without self-consciousness. "But the children are to sing this evening. You'll like to hear the children, I'm sure. They are doing fairly well now."

"Charmed, I'm sure," he said, with added flattery of his eyes which she did not take at all because she was passing her mother's plate for more gravy. How odd not to have a servant pass it!

"You come from New York?" the host hazarded.

"Yes," drawled the youth. "Shafton's my name, Laurence Shafton, son of William J., of Shafton and Gates, you know," he added impressively.

The host was polite but unimpressed. It was almost as though he had never heard of William J. Shafton the multi-millionaire. Or was it? Dash the man, he had such a way with him of acting as though he knew everything and *nothing* impressed him; as though he was just as good as the next one! As though his father was something even greater than a millionaire! He didn't seem to be in the least like Laurie's idea of a clergyman. He couldn't seem to get anywhere with him.

The talk drifted on at the table, ebbing and flowing about the two ladies as the tide touches a rising strand and runs away. The girl and her mother answered his questions with direct steady gaze, and polite phrases, but they did not gush nor have the attitude of taking him eagerly into their circle as he was accustomed to being taken in wherever he went. Nothing he said seemed to reach further than kindly hospitality. When that was fulfilled they were done and went back to their own interests.

Marilyn did not seem to consider the young man a guest of hers in any sense personally. After the dinner she moved quietly out to the porch and seated herself in a far chair with a leather-bound book, perhaps a Bible, or prayer book. He wasn't very familiar with such things. She took a little gold pencil from a chain about her neck and made notes on a bit of paper from what she read, and she joined not at all in the conversation unless she was spoken to, and then her thoughts seemed to be elsewhere. It was maddening.

Once when a tough-looking little urchin went by with a grin she flew down off the porch to the gate to talk with him; she stood there sometime in earnest converse. What could a girl like that find to say to a mere kid? When she came back there was a look of trouble in her eyes, and by and by her father asked if Harry had seen *Billy,* and she shook her head with a cloud on her brow. It must be *Billy* then. Billy was the one! Well, dash him! If he couldn't go one better than Billy he would see! Anyhow, Billy didn't have a sprained ankle, and a place in the family! A girl like that was worth a few days' invalidism. His ankle didn't hurt much since the minister had dressed it again. He believed he could get up and walk if he liked, but he did not mean to. He meant to stay here a few days and conquer this young beauty. It was likely only her way of vamping a man, anyway, and a mighty tantalizing one at that. Well, he would show her! And he would show Billy, too, whoever Billy was! A girl like that! Why, a girl like that with a face like that would grace any gathering, any home! He had the fineness of taste to realize that after he got done playing around with Opal and women like her, this would be a lady anyone would be proud to settle down to. And why not? If he chose to fall in love with a country nobody, why couldn't he? What was the use of being Laurie

Shafton, son of the great William J. Shafton, if he couldn't marry whom he would? Shafton would be enough to bring any girl up to par in any society in the universe. So Laurie Shafton set himself busily to be agreeable.

And presently his opportunity arrived. Mrs. Severn had gone in the house to take a nap, and the minister had been called away to see a sick man. The girl continued to study her little book:

"I wish you would come and amuse me," he said in the voice of an interesting invalid.

The girl looked up and smiled absently:

"I'm sorry," she said, "but I have to go to my Sunday school class in a few minutes, and I was just getting my lesson ready. Would you like me to get you something to read?"

"No," he answered crossly. He was not used to being crossed in any desire by a lady, "I want you to talk to me. Bother the Sunday school! Give them a vacation today and let them go fishing. They'll be delighted, I'm sure. You have a wonderful foot. Do you know it? You must be a good dancer. Haven't you a Victrola here? We might dance if only my foot weren't out of commission."

"I don't dance, Mr. Shafton, and it is the Sabbath," she smiled indulgently with her eyes on her book.

"Why don't you dance? I could teach you easily. And what has the Sabbath got to do with it?"

"But I don't care to dance. It doesn't appeal to me in the least. And the Sabbath has everything to do with it. If I did dance I would not do it today."

"But why?" he asked in genuine wonder.

"Because this is the day set apart for enjoying God and not enjoying ourselves."

He stared.

"You certainly are the most extraordinary young woman I ever met," he said admiringly. "Did no one ever tell you that you are very beautiful?"

She gave him the benefit of her beautiful eyes then in a cold amused glance:

"Among my friends, Mr. Shafton, it is not considered good form to say such things to a lady of slight acquaintance." She rose and gathered up her book and hat that lay on the floor beside her chair, and drew herself up till she seemed almost regal.

Laurie Shafton stumbled to his feet. He was ashamed. He felt almost as he had felt once when he was caught with a jag on being rude to a friend of his mother's:

"I beg your pardon," he said gracefully, "I hope you will believe me, I meant no harm."

"It is no matter," said the girl graciously, "only I do not like it. Now you must excuse me. I see my class are gathering."

She put the hat on carelessly, with a push and a pat and slipped past him down the steps and across the lawn. Her dress brushed against his foot as she went and it seemed like the touch of something ethereal. He never had felt such an experience before.

She walked swiftly to a group of boys, ugly, uncomely, overgrown kids, the same who had followed her after church, and met them with eagerness. He felt a jealous chagrin as he watched them follow her into the church, an anger that she dared to trample upon him that way, a fierce desire to get away and quaff the cup of admiration at the hand of some of his own friends, or to quaff some cup, *any* cup, for he was thirsty, thirsty, *thirsty,* and this was a dry and barren land. If he did stay and try to win this haughty country beauty he would have to find a secret source of supply somewhere or he never would be able to live through it.

The Sunday school hour wore away while he was planning how to revenge himself, but she did not return. She lingered for a long time on the church steps talking with those everlasting kids again, and after they were gone she went back into the church and began to play low sweet music.

It was growing late. Long red beams slanted down the village street across the lawn, lingered and went out. A single ruby burned on one of the memorial windows like a lamp, and went purple and then gray. It was growing dusk, and that girl played on! Dash it all! Why didn't she quit? It was wonderful music, but he wanted to talk to her. If he hobbled slowly could he get across that lawn? He decided to try. And then, just as he rose and steadied himself by the porch pillar, down the street in a whirl of dust and noisy claxon there came a great blue car and drew up sharp in front of the door, while a lutelike voice shouted gaily: "Laurie, Laurie Shafton, is that you?"

Chapter 9

After Billy had listened a long time he took a single step to relieve his cramped toes, which were numb with the tensity of his strained position. Stealthily as he could he moved his shoe, but it seemed to grind loudly upon the cement floor of the cellar, and he stopped frozen in tensity again to listen. After a second he heard a low growl as if someone outside the house were speaking. Then all was still. After a time he heard the steps again, cautiously, walking over his head, and his spine seemed to rise right up and lift him, as he stood trembling. He wasn't a bit superstitious, Billy wasn't. He knew there was no such thing as a ghost, and he wasn't going to be fooled by any noises whatsoever, but anybody would admit it was an unpleasant position to be in, pinned in a dark unfamiliar cellar without a flashlight, and steps coming overhead, where only a dead man or a doped man was supposed to be. He cast one swift glance back at the cobwebby window through which he had so recently arrived, and longed to be back again, out in the open with the bells, the good bells sounding a call in his ears. If he were out wouldn't he run? Wouldn't he even leave his old bicycle to any fate and *run?* But, no! He couldn't! He would have to come back inevitably. Whoever was upstairs in that house alone and in peril he must save. Suppose—His heart gave a great dry sob within him and he turned away from the dusty exit that looked so little now and so inadequate for sudden flight.

The steps went on overhead shuffling a little louder, as they seemed further off. They were climbing the stair he believed. They wore rubber heels! *Link* had worn rubber heels! And Shorty's shoes were covered with old overshoes! Had

101

they come back, perhaps to hide from their pursuers? His heart sank. If that were so he must get out somehow and go after the police, but that should be his last resort. He didn't want to get anyone else in this scrape until he knew exactly what sort of a scrape it was. It wasn't square to anybody— not square to the doped man, not square to himself, not even square to Pat and the other two, and—yes, he must own it— not square to *Cart*. That was his first consideration, Cart! He must find Cart. But first he must find out somehow who that man was that had been kidnapped.

It seemed an age that he waited there in the cellar and everything so still. Once he heard a door far up open, and little shuffling noises, and by and by he could not stand it any longer. Getting down softly on all fours, he crept slowly, noiselessly over to the cellar stairs, and began climbing, stopping at every step to listen. His efforts were much hampered by the milk bottle which kept dragging down to one side and threatening to hit against the steps. But he felt that milk was essential to his mission. He dared not go without it. The tools were in his other pocket. They too kept catching in his sleeve as he moved cautiously. At last he drew himself to the top step. There was a crack of light under the door. Suppose it should be locked? He could saw out a panel, but that would make a noise, and he still had the feeling that someone was in that house. A cellar was not a nice place in which to be trapped. One bottle of milk wouldn't keep him alive very long. The haunted house was a great way from anywhere. Even the bells couldn't call him from there, once anybody chose to fasten him in the cellar, and find the loose window and fasten it up!

Such thoughts poured a torrent of hot fire through his brain while his cold fingers gripped the doorknob, and slowly, fiercely, compellingly, made it turn in its socket till its rusty old spring whined in complaint, and then he held his breath to listen again. It seemed an age before he dared put any weight upon that unlatched door to see if it would

move, and then he did it so cautiously that he was not sure it
was opening till a ray of light from a high little window shot
into his eyes and blinded him. He held the knob like a vise,
and it was another age before he dared slowly release the
spring and relax his hand. Then he looked around. He
found himself in a kind of narrow butler's pantry with a
swinging door opposite him into the room at the back, and a
narrow passage leading around the corner next the door. He
peeked cautiously, blinkingly round the doorjamb and saw
the lower step of what must be back stairs. There were no
back stairs in Aunt Saxon's house, but before his mother
died Billy Gaston had lived in the city where they always
had back stairs. That door before him likely led to the dining room. He took a careful step, pushed the swing door half
an inch and satisfied himself that was the kitchen at the
back. No one there. Another step or two gave him the same
assurance about the dining room and no one there. He surveyed the distance to the foot of the back stairs. It seemed
long. What he was afraid of was that light space at the foot
of those stairs. He was almost sure there was a hall straight
through to the front door, and he had a hunch that that front
door was open. If he passed the steps and anyone was there
they would see him, and yet he wanted to get up those stairs
now, right away, before anything happened. It was too still
up there to suit him. With trembling fingers he untied his
shoestrings, and slipped off his shoes, knotting the strings together and slinging the shoes around his neck. He was taking no chances. He gripped the revolver with one hand and
stole out cautiously. When he reached the end of the dining
room wall he applied an eye toward the opening of light,
and behold it was as he had suspected, a hall leading straight
through to the front door, and Shorty, with his full length
profile cut clear against the morning, standing on the upper
step keeping lookout! He dodged back and caught his
breath, then made a noiseless dart toward those stairs. If
Shorty heard, or if he turned and saw anything he must have

thought it was the reported ghost walking, so silently and like a breath passed Billy up the stair. But when he was come to the top, he held his breath again, for now he could distinctly hear steps walking about in the room close at hand, and peering up he saw the door was open partway. He paused again to reconnoiter and his heart set up an intolerable pounding in his breast.

He could dimly make out the back of a chair, and further against a patch of light where the back window must be he could see the footboard of a bed, the head of which must be against the opposite wall. The door was open about a third of the way. There was a key in the lock. Did that mean that they locked the man in? It would be a great thing to get hold of that key!

A moan in the direction of the bed startled him, and prodded his weary mind. He gave a quick silent spring across in front of the door and flattened himself against the wall. He knew he had made a slight noise in his going, and he felt the stillness in the room behind the half open door. Link had heard him. It was a long time before he dared stir again.

Link seemed to lay down something on the floor that sounded like a dish and started toward the door. Billy felt the blood fly to the top of his head. If Link came out he was caught. Where could he fly? Not downstairs. Shorty was there, with a gun of course. Would it do to snap that door shut and lock Link in with the prisoner? No telling what he might do, and Shorty would come if there was an outcry. He waited in an agony of suspense, but Link did not come out yet. Instead he tiptoed back to the bed again, and seemed to be arranging some things out of a basket on a little stand by the bed. Billy applied an eye to the crack of the door and got a brief glimpse. Then cautiously he put out his stubby fingers and grasped that key, firmly, gently; turning, slipping, little by little, till he had it safe in his possession. Several times he thought Link turned and looked toward the door.

Once he almost dropped the key as he was about to set it free from the lock, but his anxious fingers were true to their trust, and the key was at last drawn back and safely slid into Billy's pocket. Then he looked around for a place to hide. There were rooms on the front, and a door was open. He could slide in there and hide. It was dark, and there might be a closet. He cast one eye through the door crack and beheld in the dim light Link bending over the inert figure on the bed with a cup and spoon in his hand. Perhaps they were giving him more dope! If he only could stop it somehow! The man was doped enough, sleeping all that time! But now was the time for him and the key to make an exit.

Slowly, cautiously he backed away from the door, down the hall and into the next open door, groping his silent way toward a little half-moon in the shutter. He made a quick calculation, glanced about, did some sleight of hand with the door till it swung noiselessly shut, and then slipping back to the window he examined the catches. There was a pane of glass gone, but it was not in the right place. If he only could manage to slide the sash down. He turned the catch and applied a pressure to the upper sash, but like most upper sashes it would not budge. If he strained harder he might be able to move it but that would make a noise and spoil his purpose. He looked wildly round the room, with a feeling that something must help him, and suddenly he discovered that the upper sash of the other window was pulled all the way down, and a sweet breath of wild grape blossoms was being wafted to his heated forehead. With a quick move he placed himself under this window, which he realized must be almost over Shorty's head. It was but the work of an instant to grasp Pat's gun and stick its nose well through the little half-moon of an opening in the shutter, pointed straight over Shorty's head into the woods, and pull the trigger.

The report went rolling, reverberating down the valley from hill to hill like a whole barrage it seemed to Billy; and perhaps to Shorty waiting for his pard below, but at any rate before the echoes had ceased to roll Shorty was no longer on the doorstep. He had vanished and was far away, breaking through the underbrush, stumbling, and cutting himself, getting up to stumble again, he hurled himself away from that haunted spot. Ghosts were nothing to Shorty. He could match himself against a spirit any day, but ghosts that could shoot were another matter, and he made good his going without hesitation or needless waiting for his partner in crime. He was never quite sure where that shot came from, whether from high heaven or down beneath the earth.

As for Link, if he was giving more dope, he did not finish. He dropped a cup in his hurry and darted like a winged thing to the head of the stairs, where he took the flight at a slide and disappeared into the woods without waiting for locks or keys or any such things.

"He seems a little nervous," grinned Billy, who had climbed to the window seat with one eye applied to the half-moon, watching his victims take their hurried leave. And lest they should dare to watch and return before he was ready for them he sent another shot into the blue sky, ricocheting along the hills; and still another, grimly, after an interval.

Then swiftly turning he stole down the front stairs and took the key from the lock, shut the door, pushing a big bolt on the inside. With a hasty examination of the lower floor that satisfied him that he was safely ensconced in his stronghold and would not be open to immediate interruption he hurried upstairs again.

His first act was to open a window and throw back the shutters. The morning sunlight leaped in like a friend, and a bird in a tree caroled out gladly. Something in Billy's heart burst into a tear. A tear! Bah! He brushed it away with his grimy hand and went over to the bed, rolling the inert figure toward him till the face was in plain view. A sudden fit of trembling took possession of him and he dropped nervelessly beside the bed with his hands outstretched and uttered a sob ending in a single syllable.

"*Cart!*"

For there on the bed still as the dead lay Mark Carter, his beloved idol, and *he had helped to put him there!*

Thirty pieces of silver! And his dearest friend dead, perhaps! A Judas! All his life he would be a Judas. He knew now why Judas hanged himself. If Cart was dead he would have to hang himself! Here in this house of death he must hang himself, like Judas, poor fool. And he would fling that blood money back. Only, *Cart must not be dead!* It would be hell forever for Billy if Cart was dead. He *could not stand it!*

Billy sprang to his feet with tears raining down his cheeks, but his tired dirty face looked beautiful in its anxiety. He tore open Mark Carter's coat and vest, wrenched away collar, necktie, and shirt, and laid his face against the breast. It was warm! He struggled closer and put his ear to the heart. It was beating!

He shook him gently and called,

"Cart! Cart! Oh, *boy!*" with sobs choking in his throat. And all the while the little bird was singing in a tree enough to split his feathered throat, and the sweet air full of wild grape was rushing into the long closed room and driving out the musty air.

Billy laid Mark down gently on the dusty pillow and opened another window. He stumbled over the cup and spoon, and a bottle fell from the table and broke sending out a pungent odor. But Billy crept close to his friend once more and began rubbing his hands and forehead and crooning to him as he had once done to his dog when he suffered from a broken leg. Nobody would have known Billy just then, as he stood crooning over Mark.

Water! He looked around. A broken pitcher stood on the table half filled. He tasted it dubiously. It was water, luke warm, but water! He soused a towel he found on the washstand into it and slopped it over Mark's face. He went through all the maneuvers they use on the football field when a man is knocked out, and then he bethought him of the milk. Milk was an antidote for poisons. If he could get some down him!

Carefully he rinsed out a glass he found on the bureau and poured some milk in it, crept on the bed and lifted Mark's head in his arms, put the glass to his lips, and begged and pled, and finally succeeded in prying the lips and getting a few drops down. Such joy as thrilled him when Mark finally swallowed. But it was a long time, and Billy began to think he must go for the doctor, leave his friend here at the mercy of who would come and go after all. He had hoped he might keep his shame, and Mark's capture from everybody, but what was that verse the teacher had taught them once awhile ago? "Be sure your sin will find you out." That was true. He couldn't let Mark die. He must go for the doctor. Doc would come, and he would keep his mouth shut, but Doc would *know,* and Billy liked Doc. Well, he would have to get him! Mark would hate it so, too, but Billy would have to!

It was just then that Mark drew a long deep breath of the sweet air, sighed, and drew another. Billy pressed the glass to his lips and Mark opened his eyes, saw the boy, smiled, and said in a weak voice:

"Hullo, Billy, old boy, got knocked out, didn't I?" Then he closed his eyes and seemed to go away again. But Billy, with wildly beating heart poured some more milk and came closer:

"Drink this, Cart. It's good. Drink it. We gotta get them dirty bums, Cart! Hurry up an' drink it!"

Billy understood his friend. Mark opened his eyes and roused a little. Presently he drank some more, nearly a whole glassful and Billy took heart of hope.

"Do ya think ya could get up now, Cart, ef I he'ped ya?" he asked anxiously. "We gotta get after those guys ur they'll make a getaway."

"Sure!" said Mark rousing again. "Go to it, kid. I'm with you," and he tried to sit up. But his head reeled and he fell back. Billy's heart sank. He must get him out of this house before the two keepers returned, perhaps with Pat or some other partner in their crime. Patiently he began again, and gradually by degrees he propped Mark up, fed him more milk, and urged him to rise; fairly lifted him with his loving strength, across the room, and finally, inch by inch down the stairs and out the back door.

Billy felt a great thrill when he heard that door shut behind him and knew his friend was out in the open again under God's sky. Nothing ever quite discouraged Billy when he was out of doors. But it was a work of time to get Mark across the clearing and down in the undergrowth out of sight of the house, where the old bicycle lay. Once there Billy felt like holding a Thanksgiving service. But Mark was very white and lay back on the grass looking wholly unlike himself.

"Say, Cart," said Billy after a brief silence of thought, "I gotta get you on my machine. We gotta get down to Unity an' phone."

"All right, old man, just as you say," murmured Mark too dizzy to care.

So Billy with infinite tenderness, and much straining of his young muscles got Mark up and managed to put him astride the wheel; but it was tough going and slow, over rough places, among undergrowth, and sometimes Billy had to stop for breath as he walked and pushed and held his friend.

But Mark was coming to his own again, and by the time they reached a road he was able to keep his balance, and know what he was doing. It was high noon before they reached Unity and betook themselves to the drugstore. While Mark asked for medicine Billy hied him to a telephone booth. His heart was beating wildly. He feared him much that Mark's car was gone.

But the chief's voice answered him after a little waiting, and he explained:

"Say, I'm the kid that phoned you early this morning. Didya get that car aw'right?" Billy held his breath, his jaded eyes dropped shut with anxiety and weariness. But the chief's voice answered promptly, "Yes, we got yer car all right, but didn't get the men. They beat it when they heard us coming. What sort of men were they, do you know?"

"Aw, that's aw'right, Chief, I'll tell ya when I gi'down there. Can't tell ya over the phone. Say, I'm Billy, Billy Gaston. You know me. Over to Sab'th Valley. Yes. You seen me play on the team. Sure. Well, say, Chief, I'm here in Unity with the guy that owns the car. Mark Carter. You know him. Sure! Mark! Well, he's all in, an' he wants his car to get home. He's been up all night and he ain't fit to walk. He wants me to come over and bring his car back to Unity fer him. I got my bike here. See? Now, I ain't got a license of course, but I c'd bring his along. That be aw'right, Chief, just over to Unity? Aw'right, Chief? Thank ya, Chief. Yas, I'm comin' right away. S'long!"

Billy saw Mark comfortably resting on a couch in the back room of the drugstore, where an old pal of his was clerk, and then stopping only for an invigorating gulp or two of a chocolate ice cream soda, he climbed on his old wheel and pedaled on his happy way to Economy. The winds touched him pleasantly as he passed, the sunshine had a queer reddish look to his feverish eyes, and the birds seemed to be singing in the top of his head, but he was happy. He might go to sleep on the way and roll off his wheel, but he should worry! Mark was safe. He had almost sold him for thirty pieces of silver, but God had somehow been good to him and Mark was alive. Now he would serve him all the rest of his life—Mark or God—it seemed all one to him now somehow, so long had he idealized his friend, so mixed were his ideas of theology.

But Billy did not go to sleep nor fall off his wheel, and in due time he arrived in Economy and satisfied the chief's curiosity with vague answers, a vivid description of Link and Shorty, and the suggestion that they might be found somewhere near the haunted house on Stark Mountain. He had heard them talking about going there, he said. He got away without a mention of the real happening at Pleasant View or a hint that he had had anything to do with the stealing of the car. Billy somehow was gifted that way. He could shut his mouth always just in time, and grin and give a turn to the subject that entirely changed the current of thought, so he kept his own counsel. Not for his own protection would he have kept back any necessary information, but for Mark's sake. Yes—for Mark's sake! Mark would not want it to be known.

It was in the early evening, and the sky was still touched by the afterglow of sunset, beneath the evening star, as Mark and Billy in the reclaimed car, finally started from Unity for home.

In both their hearts was the thought of the bells that would be ringing now in Sabbath Valley for the evening service, and of the one who would be playing them, and each was trying to frame some excuse that would explain his absence to her without really explaining *anything*.

And about this time the minister came forth from the parsonage, much vexed in spirit by the appearance of the outlandish lady in her outlandish car. She seemed to be insisting on remaining at the parsonage as if it were a common hostelry, and he and his wife had much perplexity to know just what to do. And now as he issued quietly forth from a side door he could hear her lutelike voice laughing from his front porch, and looking back furtively he saw to his horror that the lady, as well as the gentleman, was smoking a cigarette!

He paused and tried to think just what would be the best way to meet this situation, and while he hesitated his senior elder, a man of narrow vision, hard judgments, yet staunch sincerity, approached him. The minister had grown to expect something unpleasant whenever this man sought him out, and tonight he shrank from the ordeal; but anything was better than to have him see the visitor upon his front steps, so Severn turned and hurried toward him cordially:

"Good evening, Harricutt. It's been a good day, hasn't it?" he said grasping the wiry old hand:

"Not so pleasant as you'd think, Mr. Severn," responded the hard old voice harshly. "I've come on very unpleasant business. Very unpleasant indeed; but the standard of the church must be kept up, and we must act at once in this matter! It is most serious, most serious! I've just called a meeting of the session to be held after church, and I've sent out for this *Mark Carter* to be present. He must answer for himself the things that are being said about him, or his name must be stricken from our church roll. Do you know what they are saying about him, Brother Severn? Do you know what he's done?"

But the arrow had entered the soul of the minister and his voice was too unsteady to respond, so the senior elder proceeded:

"He has been keeping company with a young woman of dissolute character, and he has been to a place of public amusement with her and been seen drinking with her. He affects dance halls, and is known to live a worldly life. It is time he was cast out from our midst and become anathema. And now, it is quite possible he may be tried for murder! Have you heard what happened last night, Mr. Severn? Did you know that Mark Carter, a member of *our church,* tried to *kill a man* down at the Blue Duck Tavern, and for jealousy about a girl of loose character? And now, Brother Severn, what are we going to do about it?"

Said the minister, answering quietly, calmly:

"Brother Harricutt, we are not going to do anything about it just now. We are going into the church to worship God.

We will wait at least until Mark Carter comes back and see what he has to say for himself."

And about that minute, Mark, now thoroughly restored and driving steadily along the road, turned to Billy and said quietly with a twinkle in his eye:

"Kid, what made you put up that detour?"

Chapter 10

The service that evening had been one of peculiar tenderness. The minister prayed so earnestly for the graces of forgiveness, loving kindness, and tender mercy, that several in the congregation began to wonder who had been hard on his neighbor now. It was almost uncanny sometimes how that minister spotted out the faults and petty differences in his flock. Many examined their own hearts fearfully during the prayer, but at its close the face of the senior elder was stern and severe as ever as he lifted his hymnbook and began to turn the leaves to the place.

Then the organ swelled forth joyously:

> Give to the winds thy fears,
>   Trust and be undismayed,
> God hears thy prayers and counts thy tears
>   God shall lift up thy head.

Elder Harricutt would much rather it had been "God the All Terrible." His lips were pursed for battle. He knew the minister was going to be softhearted again, and it would fall to his lot to uphold the spotless righteousness of the church. That had been his attitude ever since he became a Christian. He had always been trying to find a flaw in Mr. Severn's theology, but much to his astonishment and perhaps disappointment, he had never yet been able to find a point on which they disagreed theologically, when it came right down to old-fashioned religion, but he was always expecting that the next sermon would be the one wherein the minister had broken loose from the old dyed-in-the-wool creeds and joined himself to the new and advanced thinkers, than whom, in his opinion, there were no lower on the face of God's

114

earth. And yet in spite of it all he loved the minister, and was his strong admirer and loyal adherent, self-appointed mentor though he felt himself to be.

Over on the other side of the church Elder Duncannon, tall, gaunt, hairy, with kind gray eyes and a large mouth, reminding slightly of Abraham Lincoln, sang earnestly, through steel-bowed spectacles adjusted far out on the end of his nose. Behind him Lemuel Tipton, also an elder, sandy, with cherry lips, apple cheeks, and a fringe of grizzled red hair under his chin, sang with his head thrown back, looking like a big robin. The minister knew he could depend on those two. He scanned his audience. The elders were all present. Gibson. He had a narrow forehead, nearsighted eyes, and an inclination to take the opposite side from the minister. His lips were thin, and he pursed them often, and believed in efficiency and discipline. He would undoubtedly go with Harricutt. Jones, the short fat one who owned the plush mills and hated boys. He had taken sides against Mark about the memorial window. No hope from him! Fowler, small, thin, gray, with a retreating chin, had once lived next to Mrs. Carter and had a difference about some hens that strayed away to lay. Harricutt likely had him all primed. Jones, Gibson, Harricutt—three against three. Joyce's vote would decide it. Joyce was a new man, owner of the canneries. He was a great stickler for proprieties, yet he seemed to feel that a minister's word was law—Well— *God* was still above!

The benediction held a tenderness that fairly compelled the waiting congregation to attend with their hearts.

* * * * * * * *

"Let's go over there and hear that girl play," suggested Laurie suddenly. "Church is out and we'll make her play the bells. They're simply *great*. She's some *player!*"

Opal leaned back in her chair and regarded him through

the fringes of her eyelashes, laughing a silvery peal that shivered into the reverence of the benediction like a shower of icicles going down the back. Marilyn heard and blended the Amen into the full organ to break the shock as the startled congregation moved restlessly, with half unclosed eyes. Elder Harricutt heard, shut his eyes tighter, and pressed severe lips together with resistance. This doubtless was that woman they called Cherry. That irreverent Mark Carter must be close at hand. And on the rose-vined porch Laurence Shafton felt the sting of the laugh and drew himself together:

"Oh, Laurie, Laurie!" she mocked, "you might as well be dead at Saybrook Inn or imprisoned for killing a family as fall in love with that girl. She isn't at all your kind. How would you look singing psalms? But come on, I'm game! I can see how she'll hate me. Can you walk?"

They sauntered slowly over to the church in the fragrant darkness, he leaning on a cane he had found by the door. The kindly, curious people coming out eyed them interestedly, looking toward the two cars in front of the parsonage, and wondered. It was a neighborhood where everybody took a kindly interest in everybody else, and the minister belonged to them all. Nothing went on at his house that they did not just love and dote on.

"Seems to me that girl has an awful low-necked dress for Sunday night," said Mrs. Little to Mrs. Jones as they walked slowly down the street. "Did you catch the flash of those diamonds on her neck and fingers?"

"Yes," said Mrs. Jones contemptuously, "paint on her face too, thick as piecrust. I saw her come. She drove her own car and her dresses were up to her knees, and such stockings! With stripes like lace in them! And little slippers with heels like knitting needles! I declare, I don't know what this generation is coming to! I'm glad my Nancy never wanted to go away to boarding school. They say it's terrible, the boldness of young girls nowadays."

"Well, if you'd ask me, *I'd* say she wasn't so very *young!*" declared Mrs. Little. "The light from the church door was full in her face when I was coming down the steps, and she looked as if she'd cut her eyeteeth sometime past."

"She had short hair," said Mrs. Jones, "for she pulled off her hat and ran her fingers through it just like a boy. I was cutting bread at the pantry window when she drove up and I couldn't help seeing her."

"Oh, when my sister was up in New York this spring she said she saw several old gray-haired women with bobbed hair. She said it was something terrible to see how the world had run to foolishness."

"Well, I don'no as it's wicked to bob your hair," said Mrs. Jones. "I suppose it does save some time taking care of it if you have curly hair, and it looks good on you, but mercy! It attracts so much attention. Well, I'm glad we don't live in New York! I declare, every time I come to church and hear Mr. Severn preach I just want to thank God that my lines are cast in Sabbath Valley. But speaking of going to boarding school, it didn't hurt Marilyn Severn to go. She's just as sweet and unspoiled as when she went away."

"Oh, *her!* You *couldn't* spoil her. She's all *spirit.* She's got both her father's and mother's souls mixed up in her and you couldn't get a better combination. I declare I often wonder the devil lets two such good people live. I suppose he doesn't mind as long's he can confine 'em to a little place among the hills. But, my soul! If those two visitors didn't need a sermon tonight I never saw folks that did. Do you know, when that man came last night in a broken-down car he swore so he woke us all up, all around the neighborhood. If it had been anybody else in town but Mr. Severn he'd been driven out or tarred and feathered. Well, good night. I guess you aren't afraid to walk the rest of the way alone."

Back in the church Marilyn had lingered at the organ, partly because she dreaded going back to the house while the two strangers were there, partly because it was only at the organ that she could seem to let her soul give voice to the cry of its longing. All day she had prayed while going quietly about her Sabbath duties. All day she steadily held herself to the tasks that were usually her joy and delight, though sometimes it seemed that she could not go on with them. Billy and Mark! Where were they? What had their absence to do with one another? Somehow it comforted her a little to think of them *both* away, and then again it disquieted her. Perhaps, oh, perhaps Mark had really changed as people said he had. Perhaps he had taken Billy to a baseball game somewhere. In New York or many other places that would not seem an unusual thing, she knew, not so much out of the way. Even church members were lenient about these things in the great world. It would not be strange if Mark had grown lax. But here in Sabbath Valley public opinion on the keeping of the Sabbath day was so strong that it meant a great deal. It amounted to public disgrace to disregard the ordinary rules of Sabbath; for in Sabbath Valley working and playing were alike laid aside for the entire twenty-four hours, the housewives prepared their dinner the day before, an unusually good one always, with some delectable dessert that would keep on ice, and everything as in the olden time was prepared in the home for a real keeping of a day of rest and enjoyment of the Lord. Even the children had special pastimes that belonged to that day only, and Marilyn Severn still cherished a box of wonderful stone blocks that had been her most precious possessions as a child, and had been used for Sabbath amusement. With these blocks she built temples, laid out cities, went through mimic battles of the Bible until every story lived as real as if she had been there. There were three tiny blocks, one a quarter of a cube which she always called Saul, and two half the size that were David and Jonathan. So vivid and so happy were those Sunday afternoons with Mother and Father and the blocks. Sabbath devoted to the pursuance of heavenly things had meant real joy to Marilyn. The calm and quiet of it were delight. It had been the hardest thing about her years in the world that there seemed to be so little Sabbath there. Only by going to her own room and fencing herself away from her friends, could she get any semblance of what had been so dear to her, that feeling of leisure to talk to and think about Christ, her dearest Friend. I grant she was an unusual girl. There is now and then an unusual girl. We do not always hear about them. They are not always beautiful nor gifted. It chanced that Marilyn was all three.

So she sat and played at her dear organ, playing sweet and tender hymns. Played gentle, pleading, throbbing themes that almost spoke their words out, as she saw Elder Harricutt leading his file of elders into the session room which was just behind the organ. She knew that in all probability there was to be a time of trial for her father, and that some poor soul would be mauled over and ground up in the mill of criticism, or else some of her father's dearest plans were to be held up for an unsympathetic discussion. She thanked God for the strong homely face of Elder Duncannon as he stalked behind the rest with a look of uplift on his worn countenance, and she played on softly through another hymn, until suddenly somehow, she became aware that the two strangers on the parsonage porch had left their rockers and were coming slowly across the lawn. The woman's hard silvery laugh rang out and jabbed into the tender hymn she was playing, and she stopped short in the middle of a phrase, as if the poor thing had been killed instantly. The organ seemed to hold its breath, and the sudden silence almost made the little church tremble.

She sat tense, listening, her fingers spread toward the stops to push them in and close the organ and be gone before they arrived if they contemplated coming in, for she had no mind to talk to them just now. Then coldly, harshly out from the cessation of great sound came Elder Harricutt's voice:

"But, Brother Severn, supposing that it turns out that Mark Carter is a murderer! You surely would not approve of keeping his name on the church roll then, would you? It seems to me that in order to keep the garments of the bride of Christ clean from soil we should anticipate such a happening and show the world that we recognize the character of this young man, and that we do not countenance such doings as he has been guilty of. Now, last night, it is positively stated that he and this person they call Cherry Fenning were at the Blue Duck!"

Crash! The bells!

Lynn had heard so much through the open session-room door, had turned a quick frightened glance and caught the glimpse of two people coming slowly in at the open door of the church peering at her, had made one quick motion which released the bells, and dashed into the first notes that came to her mind, the old hymn "Rock of Ages, Cleft for Me, Let Me Hide Myself in Thee!" But instead of playing it tenderly, grandly, as she usually did, with all the sweetness of the years in which saints and sinners have sung it and found refuge and comfort in its noble lines, she plunged into it with a mad rush as if a soul in mortal peril were rushing to the refuge before the gates should be forever closed, or before the enemy should snatch it from the haven. The first note boomed forth so sharply, so suddenly, that Elder Harricutt jumped visibly from his chair, and his gossipy little details were drowned in the great tone that struck. Behind his hand, the troubled minister smiled in spite of his worries, to think of the brave young soul behind those bells defending her own.

Down the aisle just under the tower Opal Verrons paused for an instant, startled, thinking of prison walls, and of the dead man lying at Saybrook Inn that night. Suddenly the words of the telegram flashed across her: "What disposition do you want made of the body?" The body! The *body!* Oh! Her eyes grew wide with horror. She ought to answer that telegram and give them his home address. But why should she? What had she to do with him now? Dead. He was *dead*. He had passed to another world. She shuddered. She looked around and shrank back toward Shafton, but Laurie was rapt in the vision of Saint Cecilia seated at the organ under the single electric light that the janitor had left burning over her head. She resembled a saint with a halo more than ever, and his easily excited senses were off chasing this new flower of fancy.

Behind the organ pipes the session sat with the reputation of a man in their ruthless fingers, tossing it back and forth, and deliberating upon their own damning phrases, while the minister sat with stern white face, and sought to hold them from taking an action that might brand a human soul forever. Marilyn needed no more than those harsh words to know that her friend of the years was being weighed in the balance.

Many a Sabbath afternoon in his childhood had Mark Carter spent with her playing the stone block play of David and Jonathan, and then eaten bread and milk and apple-sauce and sponge cake with her and heard the evening prayers and songs and said good night with a sweet look of the heavenly Father's child on his handsome little face. Many a time as an older boy had he sung hymns with her and listened to her read the Bible, and talked it over with her afterward. He had not been like that when she went away. Could he so have changed? And Cherry Fenning! The little girl who had been but ten years old when she went away to college, Cherry a precocious little daughter of a tailor in Economy, who came over to take music lessons from her. Cherry at the Blue Duck! And with Mark! Could it be true? It could not be true! Not in the sense that Mr. Harricutt was trying to make out. Mark might have been there, but never to do wrong. The Blue Duck was a dance hall where liquor was sold on the quiet, and where unspeakable things happened every little while. Oh, it was outrageous!

Her fingers made the bells crash out her horror and disgust, and her appeal to a higher power to right this dreadful wrong. And then a hopeless sick feeling came over her, a whirling dizzy sensation as if she were going to faint, although she never fainted. She longed to drop down upon the keys and wail her heart out, but she might not. Those awful words or more like them were going on behind the organ there, and the door was open—or even if the door was not open they could be heard, for the room behind the organ was only screened by a heavy curtain! Those two strangers must not hear! At all costs they must not hear a thing like this! They did not know Mark Carter of course, but at any rate they must not hear! It was like having him exposed in the public square for insult. So she played on, growing steadier, and more controlled. If only she could know the rest! Or if only she might steal away then, and lie down and bear it alone for a little! So this was what had given her father such a white drawn look during his sermon! She had seen that hard old man go across the lawn to meet him, and this was what he was bringing her father to bear!

But the music itself and the words of the grand old hymns she was playing gradually crept into her soul and helped her, so that when the lame stranger made at last his slow progress up to the choirloft and stood beside her she was able to be coolly polite and explain briefly to him how the organ controlled the action of the bells.

He listened to her, standing in open admiration, his handsome careless face with its unmistakable look of self-indulgence was lighted up with genuine admiration for the beautiful girl who could play so well, and could talk equally well about her instrument, quite as if it were nothing at all out of the ordinary run of things that she were doing.

Opal, sitting in the front pew, where she had dropped to wait till her escort should be satisfied, watched him at first discontentedly, turning her eyes to the girl, half wondering, half sneering, till all at once she perceived that the girl was not hearing the hot words of admiration poured upon her, was not impressed in the least by the man, did not even seem to know who he was—or care. How strange. What a very strange girl! And really a beautiful girl, too, she saw, now that her natural jealousy was for the moment averted. How extremely amusing. Laurie Shafton interested in a girl who didn't care a row of pins about him. What a shouting joke! She must take it back to his friends at the shore, who would kid him unmercifully about it. The thing had never been known in his life before. Perhaps, too, she would amuse herself a little, just as a pastime, by opening the eyes of this village maiden to the opportunity she was missing. Why not? Just on the verge of his departure perhaps.

And now, with tender touch, the music grew softer and dropped into the sorrowful melody:

> The mistakes of my life have been many,
>   The sins of my heart have been more,
> But I come as He has bidden,
>   And enter the open door,
> I know I am weak and sinful,
>   It comes to me more and more
> But since the dear Saviour has bid me come in
>   I'll enter the open door.

It was one of the songs they used to sing together, Mark and she, on Sunday afternoons just as the sun was dropping behind the western mountain, and Marilyn played it till the bells seemed to echo out a heart's repentance, and a great forgiveness to one far, far away.

At its first note the song was recognized by Mark Carter as he drove along through the night and it thrilled him to his sad sick soul. It was as if she had spoken to him, had swept his heartstrings with her white fingers, had given him her sweet wistful smile, and was calling to him through the dark. As they came in sight of the church Billy pulled his cap a little lower and tried to keep the choke out of his throat.

Somehow, the long hours without sleep or food, the toil, the anxiety, the reaction, had suddenly culminated in a great desire to cry. Yes, *cry* just like a baby! Why, even when he was a baby he didn't cry, and now here was this sickening gag in his throat, this smarting in his eyelids, this sinking feeling. He cast an eye at Cart. Why, Cart looked that way too. Cart was feeling it also. Then he wasn't ashamed. He gulped and smudged his dirty hand across his smarting eyes, and got a long streak of wet on the back of his hand which he hastily dried on the side of his sweater, and so they sat, two still dark figures traveling along quietly through the night, for Carter had shut off the engine and let the natural incline of the road carry them down almost in front of the church.

When they reached the church they saw a figure standing with a lifted hand. The janitor, ordered by Harricutt to keep a watch.

The car stopped at once.

"Mark, they're wantin' ye in there," he said with a flirt of his thumb over his shoulder and a furtive glance behind. "Keep yer eyes peeled, fer old Cutter-up is bossin' the job, an' *you know him!*"

Billy sat up and took notice.

Mark got out with a grave old look upon his face, and started up the walk. Billy made a move to follow, hesitated, drew back, held himself in readiness, and watched, all his boy instincts and prejudices keen on the trail again.

And so to the old sad song of his mistakes and sins Mark entered the door of the sessions room where once he and Marilyn had gone one happy summer morning to meet the session and confess their faith in Christ.

As he had passed the window by the organ loft he gave one look up where Lynn's face was framed in the ivy of the window under the light. He drank in the sight hungrily. But the next instant he caught the vision of the young stranger standing with admiring eyes, saw Marilyn turn and look up and answer him, but could not see how far away and sad her eyes.

And with this shadow upon his heart he passed in to that waiting group of hard critical men, with the white-faced minister in their midst, and stood to meet their challenge.

Chapter 11

The janitor had gone in to put the church in order for the night and hover about to find out what was going on in the session room. He never told but he liked to know. The moon had gone under a cloud. Billy slipped out of the car, and slid up the side path like a wraith, his tired legs seeming to gather new vigor with the need. He gave a glance of content up to the window. He was glad the bells were ringing, and that *she* was there. He wished she knew what peril their friend had been in last night, and how he was rescued and safe.

And then *he* sighted the stranger!

Who was that guy! Some sissy, that was sure! Aw, *gee!*

He slid into the shadow out of sight and flattened himself against the wall with an attentive ear to the door of the session room. He raised himself by chinning up to the window ledge and got a bird's-eye view of the situation at a glance. Aw, gee! That old crab! He wished the bells would stop. That sissy in there with *her,* and all these here with Cart, and no telling what's up next? Aw, *gee!* Life was jest one— He slumped his back to the wall and faced the parsonage. Say, what were those two cars over there in front of the parsonage? *Say!* That must be the guy, the rich guy! Aw, gee! In there with *her!* If he only hadn't put up that detour! Pat knew what he was about after all, a little sissy guy like that— *Aw, gee!* But *two* cars! What did two cars mean?

And over on the parsonage piazza, at the far end in the shelter of the vines sat Aunt Saxon in the dark crying. Beside her was Mrs. Severn with her hand on the woman's shoulder talking in her gentle steady voice. Everybody loved the minister's wife just as much as they loved the minister:

126

"Yes, he went away on his wheel last night just after dark," she sobbed. "Yes! he came home after the baseball game, and he made a great fuss gettin' some paint and brushes and contrapshions fixed on his old bicycle, and then he went off. Oh, he usually goes off awhile every night. I can't seem to stop him. I've tried everything short of lockin' him out. I reckon if I did he'd never come back, an' I can't seem to bring myself to lock out my sister's baby!"

"Of course not!" said Mrs. Severn tenderly.

"Well, he stuck his head back in the door this time, an' he said mebbe he wouldn't be back till mornin', but he'd be back all right for Sunday school. That's one thing, Mrs. Severn," she lifted her tearstained face, "that's one thing he does like—his Sunday school. Billy does, and I'm that glad! Sometimes I just sit down an' cry about it I'm so glad. You know awhile back when Miss Lynn was off to college that Mr. Harricutt had the boys' class, an' I couldn't get him to go anyhow. Why, once I offered to pay him so he could save fer a baseball bat if he'd go, but do you know he said he'd rather go without baseball bats fer ever than go listen to that old—Well, Mrs. Severn, I won't repeat what he said. It wasn't respectful, not to an elder, you know. But Miss Lynn, why he just worships, an' anything she says he does. But that's one thing worries me, Mrs. Severn, he *didn't come back for her even!* He said he'd be back fer Sunday school, an' he hasn't come back yet!"

"Who does he go with most, Miss Saxon? Let's try to think where he might be. Perhaps we could call up someone and find out where he is."

"Well, I tell you," wailed the aunt, "that's just it. There's just one person he likes as well, or mebbe better'n Miss Mary Lynn, an' that's Mark Carter! Mrs. Severn, I'm just afraid he's gone off with Mark Carter!" she lowered her voice to a sepulchral whisper, "and, Mrs. Severn, they do say that Mark is real *wild!*"

Mrs. Severn sat up a little straighter and put a trifle of assurance into her voice, or was it aloofness?

"Oh, Miss Saxon!" she said earnestly. "I don't think you ought to feel that way about Mark. I've known him since he was a mere baby, and I've always loved him. I don't believe Mark will ever do Billy any harm. He's a boy with a strong character. He may do things that people don't understand, but I'd trust him to the limit!"

She was speaking eagerly, earnestly, in the words that her husband had used to her a few days before, and she knew as she said it that she believed it was all true. It gave her a great comfort to know that she believed it was true. She loved Mark almost as though he were her own.

Miss Saxon looked up with a sigh and mopped her pink wet face:

"Well, I certainly am relieved to hear you say that! Billy thinks the sun rises and sets in Cart, as he calls him. I guess if Cart should call him he'd go to the ends of the earth with him. I know *I* couldn't stop him. But you see, Mrs. Severn, I oughtn't to have to bring up children, especially boys. Billy always was headstrong, and he's getting worse every day."

"I'm sure you do your best, Miss Saxon, and I'm sure Billy will turn out a fine man someday. My Lynn thinks a great deal of him. She feels he's growing very thoughtful and manly."

"Does she now?" the tired pink face was lifted damply with a ray of cheer.

Then the telephone bell rang. Mrs. Severn rose and excused herself to answer it:

"Yes? Yes, Mrs. Carter. Mrs. Severn is speaking. Is anything the matter? Your voice sounds troubled. Oh, Mrs. Carter! I'm so sorry, but I'm sure you can trust Mark. He's a man, you know, and he's always been an unusually dependable boy, especially to us who know him well. He'll come back all right. What? Oh, Mrs. *Carter!* No, I haven't heard any such reports, but I'm sure they're just gossip. You know how people will talk. What do you say? They phoned you from Economy? Who? The police? They asked for Mark? Well, I wouldn't let that worry you. Mark always was helpful to the police in finding people, or going with them after a lost car, you know. I wouldn't worry. Who? Billy? Billy Gaston? Oh, you saw Billy this morning? Well, that's good. His aunt has worried all day about him. I'll tell her. Who? A sick man on the mountain? Well, now Mrs. Carter, don't you know Mark always was doing things for people in trouble? He'll come home safely, but of course we'll just turn the earth upside down to find him for we are not going to let you and Miss Saxon worry any longer. Just you wait till Mr. Severn gets back. He's in a session meeting and it oughtn't to last long, it was just a special meeting called hurriedly. He'll come right over as soon as it's out and see what he can do to help. Yes, of course he will. No, don't bother to thank me. He would want to of course. Good-bye!"

She came hopefully out to the piazza to Miss Saxon. But just at that instant Billy's aunt jumped to her feet, her eyes large with excitement, and pointed toward the open session door, where framed against the light stood Mark Carter, straight and tall facing the circle of men, and behind him, out in the dark, with only his swaggy old sweater shoulder and the visor of his floppy old cap showing around the doorjamb lurked Billy.

"There! There!" whispered Mrs. Severn, patting her shoulder. "I told you he'd come back all right. Now, don't you worry about it, and don't you scold him. Just go home and get him some supper. He'll be likely very hungry, and then get him to go right to bed. Wait till tomorrow to settle up. Miss Saxon, it's always better, then we have clearer judgment and are not nearly so likely to lose our tempers and say the wrong thing."

The bells had stopped ringing, and Marilyn had closed the organ and drawn the window shut. The two strangers were trailing slowly across the lawn, the lady laughing loudly. Miss Saxon eyed them with the kind of fascination a wild rabbit has for a strange dog, pressed the hand of the minister's wife with a fervent little squeeze, and scurried away into the dark street. Marilyn lingered silently on the front steps after the janitor had locked the door inside and gone back to the session room.

In the session room Mark Carter, white with the experiences of the night and day, yet alert, stern, questioning, stood looking from one man to another, keenly, uncompromisingly. This was a man whom any would notice in a crowd. Character, physical perfection, strength of will all combined to make him stand out from other men. And over it all, like a fire from within there played an overwhelming sadness that had a transparent kind of refining effect, as if a spirit dwelt there who by sheer force of will went on in the face of utter hopelessness.

The stillness in the session room was tense as the self-appointed jury faced their victim and tried to look him down; then slowly recognized something that made them uneasy, and one by one each pair of eyes save two, were vanquished and turned embarrassedly away, or sought the pattern of the mossy carpet.

Those two pairs of eyes that were friendly Mark found out at once, and it was as if he embraced them with his own. His friends—Duncannon and the minister! He shot a grateful glance at them and faced the others down, but opened not his lips.

At last Harricutt, his chief accuser, mustered up his sharp little eyes again from under the overhanging eaves of rough gray brow, and shot out a disagreeable underlip:

"We have sent for you, here, tonight, Mark Carter," he began slowly, impressively, raising a loose-jointed long forefinger accusingly, as he gained courage, "to inquire concerning the incriminating reports that are in circulation with regard to your character."

Mark turned his hard eyes toward the elder, and seemed

to congeal into something inflexible, impenetrable, as if he had suddenly let down a cold sheet iron door between his soul and them, against which the words, like shot or pebbles, rattled sharp and unharming and fell in a shower at the feet of the speaker. There was something about his bearing that became a prince or president, and always made a faultfinder feel small and inadequate. The minister felt his heart throb with a thrill of pride in the boy as he stood there just with his presence hurling back the suspicions that had meant to undo him. His stern young face was like a mask of something that had once been beautiful with life, whose utter sorrow and hopelessness pierced one at the sight. And so he stood and looked at Elder Harricutt, who shot him one glance and then looking down began to fiddle with his watch chain, halting in his speech:

"They say—" he began again with a hiss, as he lifted his eyes, strong in the consciousness that he was not alone in his accusation—"They *say—!* "

"Please leave what they say out of the question, Mr. Harricutt. What do *you* say?" Mark's voice was cold, incisive, there was nothing quailing in his tone.

"Young man, we can't leave what they say out of the question! It plays a very important part in the reputation of the Church of Christ of which you are an unworthy part," shot back the hard old man. "We are here to know what you have to say concerning the things that are being said openly about you."

"A man does not always know what is being said about him, Mr. Harricutt." Still that hard cold voice, still indifferent to the main issue, and ready to fight it.

"A man ought to!" snapped Harricutt impatiently.

Suddenly, without warning, the mask lifted, the curve of the lips drew up at the left corner revealing the row of even white teeth, and a twinkle at the corners of the gray, thoughtful eyes, giving in a flash a vision of the merry mischief-loving boy he had been, and his whole countenance was lit. Mark was never so attractive as when smiling. It brought out the lovingness of his eyes, and took away the hard oldness of his finely cut features.

"Mr. Harricutt, I have often wondered if *you* knew, all that people say about *you?*"

"*WHAT?*"

There was sudden stir in the session room. The elders moved their chairs with a swishing sound, cleared their throats hastily, and put sudden hands up to hide furtive smiles. Elder Duncannon grinned broadly, there was a twinkle in even the minister's eyes, and outside the door Billy manfully stifled a snicker. Elder Harricutt shot his angry little eyes around in the mirthful atmosphere, starting at Mark's quizzical smile, and going around the uneasy group of men, back to Mark again. But the smile was gone! One could hardly be sure it had been there at all. Mark was hard cold steel again, a blank wall, impenetrable. There was no sign that the young man intended to repeat the mocking offense.

"Young man! This is no time for levity!" he roared forth menacingly. "You are on the verge of being arrested for murder! Did you know it?"

The minister watching, thought he saw a quiver go through the steady eyes, a slight contracting of the pupil, a hardening of the sensitive mouth, that was all. The boy stood unflinching, and spoke with steady lips:

"I did not."

"Well, you are!" reiterated the elder. "And even if the man doesn't die, there is plenty else. Answer me this question. It's no use beating around the bush. Where were you at three o'clock this morning?"

The answer came without hesitation, steadily, frankly:

"On Stark Mountain, as nearly as I can make out."

Billy held his breath and wondered what was coming next. He caught his hands on the window ledge and chinned himself again, his eyes and the fringe of his disheveled brown hair appearing above the windowsill, but the startled session was not looking out the window just then. Mr. Harricutt looked slightly put out. Stark Mountain had nothing to do with this matter, and the young man was probably trying to prove an alibi. He sat up jerkily and placed his elbows on the chair arms, touching the tips of his long bony fingers, fitting them together carefully and speaking in aggravated detached syllables in rhythm with the movement of his fingers.

"Young—man! An—swer me! *Ware*—you—or ware you—*not*—at—the—Blue— Duck— Tavern—last—evening?"

Blue and red lights seemed to flicker in the cold steel eyes of the young man.

"I *was!*"

"A—hemmm!" The elder glanced around triumphantly, and went on with the examination:

"Well—young *man!* Ware you—or—ware you *not*—accompanied—by a young wumman—of—notorious—I may say—infamous character? In other words—a young girl—commonly called— Cherry? Cherry Fenning I believe is her whole name. Ware you with her?"

Mark's face was set, his eyes were glaring. The minister felt that if Harricutt had dared look up he would almost be afraid, now.

But after an instant's hesitation when it almost looked as if Mark were struggling with desire to administer corporal punishment to the little old bigot, he lifted his head defiantly and replied in hard tones as before:

"I *was!*"

"There!" said Elder Harricutt, wetting his lips and smiling fiendishly around the group. "There! Didn't I tell you?"

"May I inquire," asked Mark startlingly, "what business of yours it is?"

Harricutt bristled.

"What business? What *business?*" he repeated severely.

"Why, this business, young man. Your name is on our church roll as a member in good and regular standing! For sometime past you have been dragging the name of our Lord and Saviour in the dust of dishonor by your goings on. It is our responsibility as elders of this church to see that this goes on no longer."

"I see!" said Mark. "I haven't heard from any of the other elders on the subject, but assuming that you are all of one mind—" he swept the room with his glance, omitting the stricken faces of the minister and Mr. Duncannon, "I will relieve you of further responsibility in the matter by asking you to strike my name from the roll at once."

He was turning, his look of white still scorn fell upon them like fire that scorches. Outside the door Billy, forgetful that he might be seen, was peering in, his brows down in deep scowls, his lower jaw protruded, his grimy fists clenched. A fraction of a second longer and Billy would butt into the session like some mad young goat. Respect for the session? Not he! They were bullying his idol, Cart, who had already gone through death and still lived! They should see! Aw, gee!

But a diversion occurred just in the nick of time. It was Joyce, the new member, the owner of the canneries, who had just built a new house with electric appliances, and owned the best car in town. He was a stickler for proprieties, but he was a great admirer of the minister, and he had been watching Mr. Severn's face. Also, he had watched Mark's.

"Now, now, *now,* young brother!" he said soothingly, rising in his nice pleasant gentlemanly way. "Don't be hasty! This can all be adjusted I am sure if we fully understand one another. I am a comparative stranger here I know, but I would suggest taking this thing quietly and giving Mr. Carter a chance to explain himself. You must own, Brother Carter, that we had some reason to be anxious. You know, the Bible tells us to avoid even the appearance of evil."

Mark turned with perfect courtesy to this new voice:

"The Bible also tells us not to judge one another!" he replied quickly. "Mr. Joyce, you are a stranger here, but I am not. They have known me since childhood. Also there are some items that might be of interest to you. Cherry Fenning five years ago was a little girl in this Sunday school. She stood up in that pulpit out there one Children's Sunday and sang in a sweet little voice, 'Jesus loves me this I know, for the Bible tells me so.' She was an innocent little child then, and everybody praised her. Now, because she has been talked about you are all ready to condemn her. And who is going to help her? I tell you if that is the kind of Christ you have, and the kind of Bible you are following I want no more of it, and I am ready to have my name taken off the roll at once."

Harricutt rose in his excitement pointing his long flapping forefinger:

"You see, gentlemen, you see! He defies us! He goes farther! He defies his God!"

Suddenly the minister rose with uplifted hand, and the voice that never failed to command attention, spoke:

"Let us pray!"

With sudden startled indrawing of breath, and half obedient bowing of the heads, the elders paused, standing or sitting as they were, and Mark with high defiant head stood looking straight at his old friend.

"Oh, God, our Father, Oh, Jesus Christ our Saviour," prayed the minister in a voice that showed he felt the Presence near, "save us in this trying moment from committing further sin. Give us Thy wisdom, and Thy lovingkindness. Show us that only he that is without sin among us may cast the first stone. Put Thy love about us all. We are *all* Thy children. Amen."

Into the silence that followed this prayer his voice continued quietly:

"I will ask Mr. Harricutt to take the chair for a moment. I would like to make a motion."

The elders looked abashed.

"Why—I—" began Harricutt, and then saw there was nothing else for him to do, and stepped excitedly over to the minister's seat behind the table, and sank reluctantly down, trying to think how he could best make use of his present position to further his side of the question.

The minister was still standing, seeming to hold within his gaze the eyes of everyone in the room including Mark.

"I wish to make a motion," said the minister. "I move that we have a rising vote, expressing our utmost confidence in Mr. Carter, and leaving it to his discretion to explain his conduct or not as he pleases! I have known this dear young brother since he was a boy, and I would trust him always, anywhere, with anything!"

A wonderful shiny look of startled wonder, and deep joy came into the eyes of the young man, followed by a stabbing cloud of anguish, and then the hard controlled face once more, with the exception of a certain tenderness as he looked toward the minister.

"Mr. Duncannon, will you second my motion?" finished Severn.

The long gaunt dark elder was on his feet instantly:

"Sure, Brother Severn, I second that motion. If you hadn't got ahead of me I'd have firsted it myself. I know Mark. He's *all right!*" and he put out a hairy hand and grasped Mark's young strong fingers, that gripped his warmly.

Harricutt was on his feet, tapping on the table with his pencil: "I think this motion is out of order," he cried excitedly. But no one listened, and the minister said calmly, "Will the chair put the question?"

Baffled, angry, bitter, the old stickler went through the hated words: "It is moved and seconded that we express our confidence—"

"Utmost confidence, Brother Harricutt—" broke in the minister's voice. The red came up in the elder's face, but he choked out the words "utmost confidence," on through the whole motion, and by the time it was out four elders were on their feet, Duncannon and Joyce first, thank God, Gibson, more slowly, Fowler pulled up by the strong wiry hand of Duncannon who sat next him.

"Stop!" suddenly spoke Mark's clear incisive voice, "I cannot let you do this. I deeply appreciate the confidence of Mr. Severn and Mr. Duncannon," he paused looking straight into the eyes of the new elder and added—"and Mr. Joyce, who does not know me. But I am not worthy of so deep a trust. I ask you to remove my name from your church roll that in future my actions shall not be your responsibility!" With that he gave one lingering tender look toward the minister, pressed hard the hairy hand of the old Scotch elder, and went out of the room before anyone realized he was going.

Billy, with a gasp, and a look after his beloved idol, hesitated, then pulled himself together and made a dash into the session room, like a catapult landing straight in the spot where Mark had stood, but ignoring all the rest he looked up at the minister and spoke rapidly:

"Mr. Severn, please, sir. Mark was with me last night from twelve o'clock on. Me an' him passed the Pleasant View station in a car going over to Stark Mountain, just as the bells was ringing over here fer midnight, cause I counted 'em, and Mark was over to Stark Mountain till most noon today, and I come home with him!"

The minister's face was blazing with glory, and old Duncannon patted Billy on the shoulder, and beamed, but Harricutt arose with menace in his eye and advanced on the young intruder. However, before anyone could do anything about it a strong firm hand reached out from the doorway and plucked Billy by the collar:

"That'll do, kid. Keep your mouth shut and don't say another word!" It was Mark and he promptly removed Billy from the picture.

"I move we adjourn," said Elder Duncannon, but the minister did not even wait for the motion to be seconded. He followed Mark out into the moonlight, and drew him, Billy and all, across the lawn toward the parsonage, one arm thrown lovingly across Mark's shoulder. He had forgotten entirely the two guests parked on the piazza smoking cigarettes!

Chapter 12

As the shades of evening had drawn down two figures that had been lurking all day in the fastnesses of Lone Valley over beyond the state highway, stole forth and crept stealthily under cover to Stark Mountain.

A long time they lingered in the edge of the woods till the dark was velvet black around them, before the moon arose. Then slowly, cautiously they drew near the haunted house, observing it long and silently from every possible angle, till satisfied that no enemy was about. Yet taking no chances even then, the taller one crept forth from shelter while the other watched. So stealthily he went that even his companion heard no stir.

It was some ten minutes that Shorty waited there in the bushes scarcely daring to breathe, while Link painfully quiet, inch by inch encircled the house, and listened, trying the front door first and finding it fast; softly testing the cellar windows one by one, beginning from the eastern end, going toward the front first, and so missing the window by which Billy had entered. A hundred times his operation was halted by the sound of a rat scuttling across the floor, or racketing in the wall, but the hollow echoes assured him over and over again that the house was not occupied, at least not by anyone awake and in his senses. Link had been in the business so long that he "felt" when there was an enemy near. That was what vexed him now. He had felt that morning that someone was near, but he had laid it to nerves and the reported ghost, and had not heeded his trained faculties. He was back now doubly alert to discover the cause and make good his failure in the morning. He had undertaken to look after this guy and see this job through and there was big

139

money in it. He was heavily armed and prepared for any reasonable surprise. He meant to get this matter straight before morning. So, feeling his way along in the blackness, listening, halting at every moment with bated breath, he came at last to the back door, and drawing himself up to the steps, took the knob in his hand and turned it. To his surprise it yielded to his touch, and the door came open. And yet it was some seconds of tense listening before he let himself down to the ground again, and with his hand in the grass let out a tiny winking flashlight, no more than a firefly would flicker, and out again.

This was answered by a wink from the bushes, as if the same firefly or its mate might be glowing, and after an instant another wink from the ground near the house. Slowly Shorty arrived without noise, his big bulk muffling in fat the muscles of velvet. It was incredible how light his step could be—*professionally*. It was as if he had been wafted there like down. Silently still and without communication the two drifted into the open door, sent a searching glowworm ahead into the crannies of the dusty, musty kitchen, surprising a mouse that had stolen forth domestically. The door being shut and fastened cautiously, the key in Link's pocket, they drifted through the swing door, as air might have circulated, identifying the mouse's scuttle, the rattle of a rat among the loose coal in the cellar bin, the throaty chirp of a cricket outside in the grass, and drifting on.

Thus they searched the lower floor, even as Billy had done, though more thoroughly, and mounted to the landing above, here they divided. Shorty at watch in the hall, while Link went to the front rooms first and seached each hastily, not omitting closets, ending at the back room where the prisoner had been.

"He's gone!" said Link in a hoarse whisper, speaking for the first time after a hasty scanning of the shadowy place.

Shorty took the precaution to turn the key of the door

leading to the third story before he entered to investigate.

"Do you think it was him fired that shot?"

Link shook his head.

"Couldn't! I had him lifted up in my arms and was just handing him some more dope when the sound come. It seemed it was out front. It must a been somebody in the front room. Sure! That guy never coulda got them bracelets off hisself. Looka here! Them was filed off!" They stood with the flashlight between them examining the handcuffs, and then turned their attention to the rest of the room, studying the bed and floors carefully for any traces of the possible assistant to the runaway but finding none. Then they went in the front room again, and this time discovered the lowered window and the little half-moon aperture in the shutter.

"How do you figger it?" asked Shorty turning a ghastly face toward Link in the plaided darkness of the flashlight.

"Pat!" said Link laconically.

"Pat?"

"Pat. He's yella! I told Sam, but he would have him! I ain't sure but Sam's yella! I think I'm about done with this outfit!"

"But Pat? What would he do it for?"

"Goin' to run the whole game hisself, perhaps, or then again he might be in with Sam, so they won't have to divvy up. He could say we hadn't kept our contrac', you know, runnin' away like that."

"We ain't to blame. How'd we know it want the police? We had a mighty close shave over that state line this A.M."

"Well, that's what he could say, an' refuse to divvy up. But b'lieve me, Shorty! Nobody's goin' to do me dirty like that! Somebody's been doing us dirty, you and me, and it's good and right we beat 'em to it."

"Yes, but how ya goin' to do it?"

"I ain't sure yet, but I'm goin' to do it. The first thing, Shorty, is fer us to get outta here mighty good an' quick. Ef anybody's watchin' round, we better not be here. We'll fade away. See?"

Without flash or noise they faded, going cautiously out by the front door this time and disappearing into the dark of the woods just as the horizon over Lone Valley began to show luminous in the path of the oncoming moon.

They walked several miles, stealthily, and a mile or two more naturally, before they ventured on a word, and then Shorty impatiently:

"I don't see what you can do. Whattirya goin' ta do?"

"Don't get excited. Shorty, I see my way out," said Link affably. "I didn't come off here half-cocked. I investigated before I took on the job."

"Whaddaya mean?"

"Well, I just looked up the parties in the blue book before I come off. Didn't have much time, but I just looked 'em up. Great thing that blue book. Gives ya lots of information. Then I got another thing, a magazine I always buy and keep on hand. It's called *The House Lovely,* an' it has all these grand gentlemen's places, put down in pictures, with plans and everything. It's real handy when you wantta find out how to visit 'em sort of intimate like, and it kind of broadens yer mind. It's a real pity you never learned to read, Shorty. There's nothing like it fer getting valuable information. I read a lot and I always remember anything that's worth-while."

"I don't see how that's doin' us any good now," growled Shorty.

"Don't get hasty, Shorty, I'm comin' to it. You see these here Shaftons have been on my mind fer some while back. I make it a point to know about guys like that. I read the so-ciety columns and keep posted about little details. It pays, Shorty. Now see! I happen to know that these here Shaftons have several summer homes, one in the mountains, one at the seashore, one up at an island out in the ocean, and a farm down in Jersey, where they go at Christmas fer the holidays sometimes. Well, just now I happen to know Mrs. Shafton—that's this guy's mother, is down at the Jersey house all alone with the servants. Real handy fer our purposes, ain't it? Not so far we can't get there by mornin' if we half try, and the old man is off out West on a business trip."

"What you gonta do?" asked Shorty.

"Well, I haven't exactly got it all doped out yet, but I reckon our business is with the old lady. Let's beat it as fast as we can to a trolley and dope it out as we go. You see this here old woman is nuts on her son, and she's lousy with money and don't care how she spends it, so her baby boy is pleased. Now, I figger if we could come off with five thousand apiece, you'n I we'd be doin' a good night's work and no mistake. Whaddayou say?"

"Sure thing," grumped Shorty unbelievingly.

"You see," continued Link, "we're in bad, this guy escaping and all, and like as not Pat swiping all the boodle and layin' the blame onto us. You can't tell what might happen with Pat an' Sam, the dirty devils. They might even let it come to a trial and testify against us. Sam has it in fer me an' you this long time, 'count of that last pretty little safe blowout that didn't materialize. See?"

Shorty growled gloomily.

"Now on the other hand if we can step in before it is too late, or before the news of his havin' escaped gets to his fond parents, and get in our little work, we might at least make expenses out of it and beat it out of the country fer a while. I been thinkin' of South America fer my health fer some time past. How 'bout you?"

"Suits me. But how you gonta work it?"

"Well, you see I know a little bit about wimmen. An' I seen this woman oncet. If she was one of these here newfangled political kind you couldn't do nothin' with her, she'd be onta you in no time an' have you up before the supreme court 'fore she goddone, but this here woman is one o' them old-fashioned, useless kind that's afraid of everything and cries easy, and gets scairt at her shadder. I seen her on the boardwalk once with her husband, took notice to her, thought I might need it sometime. She has gray hair but she ain't never growed up. She was ridin' in a wheeled chair, an' him walkin' beside her an' a man behind pushin' her, an' a maid comin' along with a fur coat. She never done a thing fer herself, not even think, an' that's the kind you can put anything over on from a teaparty to a blizzard without her suspectin' a thing. Shorty, I'm gonta make up to Mrs. Shafton an' see what I can get out of her. But we gotta get a trolley line down to Unity an' catch that evenin' train. See?"

About half past ten that night, with the moon at full sail, Shorty and Link, keeping the shady side of the street, slunk into a little obscure, and as yet unsuppressed saloon in a back street in a dirty little manufacturing city not many miles from Unity. Just off the side entrance was a back hall in which lurked a dark smelly little telephone booth under a staircase, too far removed from the noisy crowd that frequented the place to be heard. Here Link took instant refuge with Shorty bulking largely in front of the door, smoking a thin black twisted cigar, and looking anything but happy. He had figured greatly on getting his share of a million, and now at a single shot he had let it go through his fingers. There were reasons why he needed that part of a million at once.

Link had all sorts of nerve. He called up the Shafton home in New Jersey and jollied the maid, calling her girlie, and saying he was in the employ of young Laurie Shafton and had a special private message from the young man to his mother. It was not long before a peevish elderly voice in his ear said:

"Well? Mrs. Shafton at the phone."

And Link sailed in:

"Mrs. Shafton, I got a message from your son, a very private message. He said, would you please send your maid out of the room first before I told you?"

She seemed annoyed and hesitant at this, but finally complied:

"Now, Mrs. Shafton, you don't need to get worried at what I'm tellin' you. Your son ain't dead, nor nothing like that, you know, but he's just met with a little accident. No, now, wait a minute till I tell you. You don't need to get excited ner nothing. If you just keep calm an' do as I tell you it'll all come out right in the end—"

He could tell by her voice that she was much excited and that so far his scheme was working well. If he could only pull the rest off! He winked one eye jauntily at Shorty who was standing wide-mouthed, bulging-eyed listening, and went on.

"No, he didn't have no collision, ma'am, he just got kidnapped, you see. And not wanting to get found out, natchelly the kidnappers give him a little dope to keep his mouth shut fer a while. What's that? Who'm I? Well, now, Mrs. Shafton, that's tellin', ain't it? I wouldn't want to go so far as that 'thout I was sure of your cooperation. What's that? You'll reward me? Oh, thanks, that's what I was figering about. You see, I'm in rather of a hole myself. That's what. You see, much against my will I was one of the kidnappers myself, ma'am. Yes, ma'am, much against my will! You see I'm a farmer's son myself, good an' honest and respectable. Never had nothin' to do with such doin's in my life, my word of honor, lady. But I come to town just to look around an' have a bit of fun an' I got in with a bad lot, an' they pract'cally *compelled* me to assist 'em in this here kidnappin'. Oh, I didn't do nothin', jest helped to carry him— Oh, ma'am, it ain't that bad. He's still livin' an' he'll be awwright if you just he'p me to get him away 'thout their knowin'. Yes, ma'am. I'm honest. I'm offerin' to help you. You see, when I see him layin' there on the bed— Oh, yes, he's on a bed, I ain't sayin' how comfortable it is, but it's a bed, an' he ain't sufferin' now—but of course if they don't get what they want they may put him to the torture jest to get more outta you all—No, ma'am, don't scream that way ur I'll have to hang up. This is on the qt you know. What? You don't understand? Why, I was sayin' you mustn't let a soul know what's happened. Not a *soul.* If it should get out an' his kidnappers should find it out they'd kill him easy as a fly an' no mistake. You gotta go slow on this. Yes, lady, they're desperate characters, *I'm sayin' it!* An' the sooner you get your son outta their han's the better fer his future, lady, fer even if he should escape after they'd been found out they'd probably lame him fer life or put out his eyes or some little old thing like that, so you see, lady, you gotta talk low an' take care you don't let on to no one. If you should turn yella it ud be all up with little Laurie an' no mistake, so keep yer mouth shet an' do as I tell ye, and I'll help ye out. Yes, as I was sayin' when I seen little Laurie layin' there so still an' white, my conscience—There, there, lady, don't you take on—as I was sayin' my conscience troubled me, an' I says, I'm agonta get this fella free! So I figgered out a way. You see, lady, there's two of us, me'n another feller set to watch 'im, an' feed him dope if he tries to wake up, an' when I get feelin' worried about it I says to the other fella I was agonta tell his folks, an' he says he'll shoot me, but I keeps on tellin' him how sinful 'twas to make a poor mother suffer—I gotta mother myself, ma'am! Yes, ma'am, a good old mother, an' she taught me to be honest, so I says to thother fella, I says what'll you take an' git out, an' he says ten thousand dollars, an' I says, awwright, I'll get it fer ya, an' so now, lady, 'f I was you I'd pay it right down quick 'fore he changes his mind. Cause the other fellas they was goin' to ast a million, an' kill 'im if you didn't fall fer it right to oncet. No, ma'am, I don't want nothin' fer myself. I just want to go back to the old farm with a clean conscience. What? Oh, yes, I want the money right away, that is before mornin'. If we can't get him out before mornin' it ain't no use, fer the other fellas is comin' back an' move him an' we can't do nothin'. What? Where is he? I couldn't really say,

lady, it wouldn't be allowed, an' my mate he's outside the
telephone booth with a loaded revolver holdin' it up to my
head, and he's listenin' an' ef I give anythin' away he'd
shoot me on the spot. So where would your nice lookin' son
be then? Mrs. Shafton, hadn't you better— That's right,
lady, I knew you'd thank me, an', yes, now I'll tell you what
to do. First place, how much money ya got in the house? No,
that's not 'nough. That wouldn't do a mite of good, it
wouldn't be a drop in the bucket. Ain't ya got any bonds, ur
jewels, or papers? Yes, that's the talk! Now yer shoutin'—
Yes, lady, that would do. No—not that. You gotta have
something that he can't get caught with. I know you're loosin' a lot lady, but you got lots left, and what's money an'
jewels compared to your only son, ma'am? Why, think how
he used to look when he wore little white dresses an' used to
come to have his head kissed when he fell down! Wasn't he
sweet, lady, and he had a pair of little blue shoes, didn't he?
I thought so. Say, lady, you'r the right sort! I knowed you
must be to be a mother of such a handsome son. Now, lady,
could you hustle those things together you spoke of an' any
more you may happen to come on, and just put 'em in a little box er basket, and tie a string on 'em an' let 'em down
outta yer winda? It's all I'll ask. Let 'em down outta yer
winda. Then you turn out the lights and turn 'em on again
three times real quick, out an' in, an' that'll be the signal.
An' after ten minutes you look out yer front winda an' off as
fur as ye can see an' I'll flash a signal light to ya jest to let ya
know it's all right. An' I'll promise you on my word of honor
that you'll hear your own son's voice over the telephone
good an' early tomorrow mornin' an' no mistake. But, lady,
ye mustn't turn yella an' holler ner nothin or we'll fling yer
jewels an' paper back in yer yard an' let yer son die. We ain't
goin' to run no chances ye know. You ain't got no dogs,
have ye? And which side is yer room on? The front? Yes, an'
which is the easiest way to get to the house without comin'
near the servants' quarters? To the right? Yes, I see. An'

you'll play straight? All right, lady. Your son's as good as home now. I'll give you just one hour by the clock to get yer stuff together, but mind ya, if ya weaken an' try to put the p'lice onto me, I got a way to signal my pal, an' he'll have that boy o' yours shot within five minutes after you call fer help. Understand? Oh, yes, I know, lady, you wouldn't do no such a thing, but my pal he made me say that. He's a desperate man, lady, an' there ain't no use toyin' with him. All right. One hour. It's just quarter to 'leven. Good-bye!"

Link came lounging out of the booth mopping his wet forehead:

"She fell fer it all right," he said jerking a wan smile, but he looked as though the last of his own nerve had gone into the telephone receiver. "She wanted to put in an extra check, but I told her we'd be generous and let it go at what she could find without her name on it. Gosh, what fools some wommen are! I thought I got her number all right, a whimperin' fool! A whimperin' little old fool! Now, Shorty, all we gotta do is collect the boodle. It's up to you to watch outside the hedge. I'm takin' all the risks this time m'self, an' I'm goin' to ferret my way under that there madam's winder. You stay outside and gimme the signal. Ef you get cold feet an' leave me in the lurch you don't get no dividends. See?"

Chapter 13

Billy, with that fine inner sense that some boys have, perceived that there was deep emotion of a silent sort between the minister and Mark, and he drifted away from them unnoticed, back toward the car.

"Billy!" whispered Lynn, rising from the upper step in the shadow of the church.

The boy turned with a quick silent stride and was beside her:

"I couldn't help it, Miss Lynn, I really couldn't—There was something very important—Cart— That is—Cart needed me! I knew you'd understand."

"Yes, Billy, I understand. Somehow I knew you were with Mark. It's good to have a friend like you, Billy!" She smiled wanly.

Billy looked up half proud, half ashamed:

"It's nothin'!" said Billy. "I just had to. Cart—well, I had to."

"I know, Billy— Mark needed you. And, Billy, if there's any trouble—any—any—that is if Mark ever needs you, you'll stick by him I know."

"Sure!" said Billy looking up with a sudden searching glance. "Sure, I'll stick by him!"

"And if there's anything—anything that ought to be done—why—I mean anything *we* could do—Billy—you'll let us know?"

"Sure, I will!" There was utmost comprehension in the firm young voice. Billy kicked his heel softly into the grass by the walk, looking down embarrassedly. He half started on toward the car and then turning back he said suddenly, "Why doncha go see Cherry, Miss Lynn?"

"Cherry?" she said startled, her face growing white in the darkness.

The boy nodded, stuffing his hands deep into his pockets and regarding her with sudden boldness. He opened his lips as if he would speak further, then thought better of it and closed them again firmly, dropping his eyes as if he were done with the topic. There was a bit of silence, then Lynn said gravely:

"Perhaps I will," and, "thank you, Billy."

Billy felt as though the balm of Gilead had suddenly been poured over his tired heart.

"G'night!" he murmured, feeling that he had put his troubles into capable hands that would care for them as he would himself.

There had been no word spoken between the minister and Mark as they went together toward the parsonage, but there had seemed to each to be a great clearing of the clouds between them, and a tender love springing anew, with warm understanding and sympathy. Mark felt himself a boy again, with the minister's arm across his shoulder, and a strong yearning to confide in this understanding friend swept over him. If there had been a quiet place with no one about just then there is no telling what might have happened to change the story from that point on, but their silent intercourse was rudely interrupted by the voice of Laurie Shafton breaking in:

"Oh, I say, Mr. Severn, who did you say that man was that could fix cars? I'd like to call him up and see if he doesn't happen to have some bearings now. He surely must have returned by this time, hasn't he? I'd like to take these girls for a spin. The moon is perfectly gorgeous. We could go in the lady's car, only it is smaller and I thought I'd ask your daughter to go along."

"Oh!" said the minister suddenly brought back into the world of trivial things. "Why, *this* is Mr. Carter, Mr. Shafton. He can speak for himself."

Mark stood with lifted head and his princely look regarding the interloper with cold eyes. He acknowledged the introduction almost haughtily, and listened to the story of the burnt out bearings without a change of countenance, then said gravely:

"I think I can fix you up in the morning."

"Not tonight?" asked the spoiled Laurie with a frown of displeasure.

"Not tonight," said Mark with a finality that somehow forbade even a Shafton from further parley.

Opal had regarded Mark from the vine-covered porch as he stood with bared head in the moonlight and clattered down on her tiny patent leather pumps to be introduced. She came and stood hanging pertly on Laurie Shafton's arm as if he were her private property, with her large limpid eyes fixed upon the stranger, this prince of a man that had suddenly turned up in this funny little country dump.

She put her giddy little tongue into the conversation, something about how delicious it would be to take a little ride tonight, implying that Mark might go along if he would fix up the car. She was dressed in a slim, clinging frock of some rich Persian gauzy silk stuff, heavy with beads in dull barbaric patterns, and girt with a rope of jet and jade. Her slim white neck rose like a stem from the transparent neckline, and a beaded band about her forehead held the fluffy hair in place about her pretty dark little head. She wore long jade earrings which nearly touched the white shoulders, and gave her the air of an Egyptian princess. She was very gorgeous, and unusual even in the moonlight, and she knew it, yet this strange young man gave her one cold scrutinizing glance and turned away.

"I'll see you again in the morning, Mr. Severn," he said, and wringing the minister's hand silently, he went back across the lawn. The spell was broken and the minister knew it would be of no use to follow. Mark would say no more of his trouble tonight.

It was so that Lynn, coming swiftly from her shadow, with troubled thoughts, came face to face with Mark:

He stopped suddenly as if something had struck him.

"Oh, Mark!" she breathed softly, and put out her hand.

He made a swift motion away from her, and said quickly: "Don't touch me, Marilyn—I am—not—*worthy!*"

Then quickly turning he sprang into his car and started the engine.

The minister stood in the moonlight looking sadly after the wayward boy whom he had loved for years.

Lynn came swiftly toward her father, scarcely seeing the two strangers. She had a feeling that he needed comforting. But the minister, not noticing her approach, had turned, and was hurrying into the house by the side entrance.

"Come on, girls, let's have a little excitement," cried Laurie Shafton gaily. "How about some music? There's a piano in the house, I see, let's boom her up!"

He made a sudden dive and swooped an arm intimately about each girl's waist, starting them violently toward the steps, forgetting the lame ankle that was supposed to make him somewhat helpless.

The sudden unexpected action took Marilyn unware, and before she could get her footing or do anything about it she caught a swift vision of a white face in the passing car. Mark had seen the whole thing! She drew back quickly, indignantly flinging the offending arm from her waist, and hurried after her father; but it was too late to undo the impression that Mark must have had. He had passed by.

Inside the door she stopped short, stamping her white-shod foot with quick anger, her face white with fury, her eyes fairly blazing. If Laurie had seen her now he would scarcely have compared her to a saint. To think that on this day of trouble and perplexity this insolent stranger should dare to intrude and presume! And before Mark!

But a low-spoken word of her mother's reached her from the dining room, turning aside her anger:

"I hate to ask Lynn to take her into her room. Such a brash girl! It seems like a desecration! Lynn's lovely room!"

"She had no right to put herself upon us!" said the father in troubled tones. "She is as far from our daughter as heaven is from the pit. Who is she, anyway?"

"He merely introduced her as his friend Opal."

"Is there nothing else we can do?"

"We might give her our room, but it would take some time to put it in order for a guest. There would be a good many things to move—and it would be rather awkward in the morning, cots in the living room. I suppose Lynn could come in with me and you sleep on a cot!"

"Yes, that's exactly it! Do that. I don't mind."

"I suppose we'll have to," sighed the mother, "for I know Lynn would hate it having a stranger among her pretty intimate things!"

Marilyn sprang up and burst into the dining room:

"Mother! Did you think I was such a spoiled baby that I couldn't be courteous to a stranger even if she was a destestable little vamp? You're not to bother about it anymore. She'll come into my room with me of course. You didn't expect me to sail through life without any sacrifices at all did you, Motherie? Suppose I had gone to Africa as I almost did last year? Don't you fancy there'd have been some things harder than sharing my twin beds with a disagreeable stranger? Besides, remember those angels unaware that the Bible talks about. I guess this is up to me, so put away your frets and come on in. It's time we had worship and ended this day. But I guess those two self-imposed boarders of ours need a little religion first. Come on!"

She dropped a kiss on each forehead lightly and fled into the other room.

"What a girl she is!" said her father tenderly putting his hand gently on the spot she had kissed. "A great blessing in our home! Dear child!"

The mother said nothing, but her eyes were filled with a great content.

Marilyn, throwing aside her hat and appearing in the front door called pleasantly to the two outside:

"Well, I'm ready for the music. You can come in when you wish."

They sauntered in presently, but Marilyn was already at the piano playing softly a bit from the Angel Chorus, a snatch of Handel's Largo, a Chopin Nocturne, one of Mendelssohn's songs without words. The two came in hilariously, the young man pretending to lean heavily on the girl, and finding much occasion to hold her hands, a performance to which she seemed to be not at all averse. They came and stood beside the piano.

"Now," said Opal gaily, when Marilyn came to the end of another Nocturne: "That's enough gloom. Give us a little jazz and Laurie and I'll dance awhile."

Marilyn let her hands fall with a soft crash on the keys and looked up. Then her face broke up into a smile, as if she had put aside an unpleasant thought and determined to be friendly :

"I'm sorry," she said firmly, "we don't play jazz, my piano and I. I never learned to love it, and besides I'm tired. I've been playing all day, you know. You will excuse anything more I'm sure. And it's getting late for Sabbath Valley. Did you have any plans for tonight?"

Opal stared, but Marilyn stared back pleasantly, and Laurie watched them both.

"Why, no, not exactly," drawled Opal. "I thought Laurie would be hospitable enough to look me up a place. Where is your best hotel? Is it possible at all?"

"We haven't a sign of a hotel," said Marilyn smiling.

"Oh, horrors, nothing but a boardinghouse I suppose. Is it far away?"

"Not even a boardinghouse."

"Oh heavens! Well, where do you stop then?"

"We don't stop, we live," said Marilyn smiling. "I'm afraid the only thing you can do unless you decide to go back home tonight is to share my room with me—I have twin beds, you know, and can make you quite comfortable. I often have a college friend to stay with me for a few weeks."

Opal stared round-eyed. This was a college girl then, hidden away in a hole like this. Not even an extra spare room in the house!

"Oh, my gracious!" she responded bluntly. "I'm not used to rooming with someone, but it's very kind of you I'm sure."

Marilyn's cheeks grew red and her eyes flashed but she whirled back to her keyboard and began to play, this time a sweet old hymn, and while she was playing and before the two strangers had thought of anything to say, Mr. Severn came in with the Book in his hand, followed by his wife, who drew a small rocker and sat down beside him.

Marilyn paused and the minister opened his Bible and looked around on them:

"I hope you'll join us in our evening worship," he said pleasantly to the two guests, and then while they still stared he began to read: "Let not your heart be troubled: ye believe in God, believe also in me," on through the beautiful chapter.

It was as Greek to the strangers, who heard and did not comprehend, and they looked about amazed on this little family with dreamy eyes all listening as if it meant great treasures to them. It was as if they saw the Severns for the first time and realized them as individuals, as a force in the world, something complete in itself, a family that was not doing the things they did, not having the things considered essential to life, nor trying to go after any of the things that life had to offer, but living their own beautiful lives in their own way without regard to the world, and actually enjoying it! That was the queer part about it. They were not dull nor bored! They were happy! They could get out from an environment like this if they chose, and *they did not*. They *wanted* to stay here. It was incredible!

Laurie got out his cigarette case, selected a cigarette, got out his match box, selected a match, and all but lit it. Then somehow there seemed to be something incongruous about the action and he looked around. No one was seeing him but Opal, and she was laughing at him. He flushed, put back the match and the cigarette, and folded his arms, trying to look at home in this strange new environment. But the girl Marilyn's eyes were far away as if she were drinking strange knowledge at a secret invisible source, and she seemed to have forgotten their presence.

Then the family knelt. How odd! Knelt down, each where he had been sitting, and the minister began to talk to God. It did not impress the visitors as prayer. They involuntarily looked around to see to whom he was talking. Laurie reddened again and dropped his face into his hands. He had met Opal's eyes and she was shaking with mirth, but somehow it affected him rawly. Suddenly he felt impelled to get to his knees. He seemed conspicuous reared up in a chair, and he slid noiselessly to the floor with a wrench of the hurt ankle that caused him to draw his brows in a frown. Opal, left alone in this room full of devout backs, grew suddenly grave. She felt almost afraid. She began to think of Saybrook Inn and the man lying there stark and dead! The man she had danced with but a week before! Dead! And for her! She cringed, and crouched down in her chair, till her beaded frock swept the polished floor in a little tinkley sound that seemed to echo all over the room, and before she knew it her fear of being alone had brought her to her knees. To be like the rest of the world—to be even more alike than anybody else in the world, that had always been her ambition. The motive of her life now brought her on her knees because others were there and she was afraid to sit above lest their God should come walking by and she should see Him and die! She did not know she put it that way to her soul, but she did, in the secret recesses of her inner dwelling.

Before they had scarcely got to their knees and while that awkward hush was yet upon them the room was filled with the soft sound of singing, started by the minister, perhaps, or was it his wife? It was unaccompanied, "Abide with me, Fast falls the eventide, the darkness deepens, Lord with me abide!" Even Laurie joined an erratic high tenor humming in on the last verse, and Opal shuddered as the words were sung, "Hold thou thy cross before my closing eyes, Shine through the dark and point me to the skies." Death was a horrible thing to her. She never wanted to be reminded of death. It was a long, long way off to her. She always drowned the thought in whatever amusement was at hand.

The song died away just in time or Opal might have screamed. She was easily wrought up. And then this strange anomaly of a girl, her young hostess, turned to her with a natural smile just as if nothing extraordinary had been going on and said:

"Now, shall we say good night and go upstairs? I know you must be tired after your long ride, and I know Father has had a hard day and would like to get the house settled for the night."

Opal arose with a wild idea of screaming and running away, but she caught the twinkle of Laurie's eyes and knew he was laughing at her. So she relaxed into her habitual languor, and turning haughtily requested:

"Would you send your maid to the cyar for my bag, please?"

Before anyone could respond the minister stepped to the door with a courteous "Certainly," and presently returned with a great blue leather affair with silver mountings, and himself carried it up the stairs.

At the head of the stairs Marilyn met him, and put her head on his shoulder hiding her face in his coat, and murmured, "Oh, Daddy!"

Severn smoothed her soft hair and murmured gently: "There, there, little girl! Pray! *Pray!* Our Father knows what's best!" but neither of them were referring to the matter of the unwelcome guests.

Mrs. Severn was solicitous about asking if there was anything the guest would like, a glass of milk, or some fruit? And Opal declined curtly, made a little moue at Shafton and followed up the stairs.

"Well!" she said rudely, as she entered the lovely room and stared around, "so this is your room!" Then she walked straight to the wall on the other side of the room where hung a framed photograph of Mark at twelve years old; Mark, with all the promise of his princely bearing already upon him.

"So this is the perfect icicle of a stunning young prince that was down on the lawn, is it? I thought there was some reason for your frantic indifference to men. Is his name Billy or Mark? Laurie said it was either Billy or Mark. He wasn't sure which."

Chapter 14

Mark Carter and Billy as they rode silently down the little street toward Aunt Saxon's cottage did not speak. They did not need to speak, these two. They had utmost confidence in one another, they were both troubled, and had no solution to offer for the difficulty. That was enough to seal any wise mouth. Only at the door as Billy climbed out Mark leaned toward him and said in a low growl:

"You're all right, kid! You're the best friend a man ever had! I appreciate what you did!"

"Aw!" squirmed Billy, pulling down his cap, "that's awright! See you t'morra', Cart! S'long!" And Billy stalked slowly down the street remembering for the first time that he had his aunt yet to reckon with.

With the man's way of taking the bull by the horns he stormed in:

"Aw, gee! I'm tired! Now, I 'spose you'll bawl me out fer a nour, an' I couldn't help it! You always jump on me worst when I ain't to blame!"

Aunt Saxon turned her pink damp face toward the prodigal and broke into a plaintive little smile:

"Why, Willie, is that you? I'm real glad you've come. I've kept supper waiting. We've got cold pressed chicken, and I stirred up some waffles. I thought you'd like something hot."

Billy stared, but the reaction was too much. In order to keep the sudden tears back he roared out crossly:

"Well, I ain't hungry. You hadn't oughtta have waited. Pressed chicken, did ya say? Aw, *gee!* Just when I ain't hungry! Ef that ain't *luck!* An' waffles! You oughtta known better! But bring 'em on. I'll try what I can do," and he flung himself down in his chair at the table and rested a torn

159

elbow on the clean cloth, and his weary head on a grimy hand. And then when she put the food before him, without even suggesting that he go first and wash, he became suddenly conscious of his disheveled condition and went and washed his hands and face *without being sent!* Then he returned and did large justice to the meal, his aunt eyeing furtively with watery smiles, and a sigh of relief now and then. At last she ventured a word by way of conversation:

"How is the man on the mountain?" Billy looked up sharply, startled out of his usual stolidity with which he had learned from early youth to mask all interest or emotion from an officious and curious world.

Miss Saxon smiled:

"Mrs. Carter told me how you and Mark went to help a man on the mountain. It was nice of you, Billy."

"Oh! *That!*" said Billy scornfully, rallying to screen his agitation. "Oh, he's better. He got up and went home. Oh, it wasn't nothing. I just went and helped Cart. Sorry not to get back to Sunday school, Saxy, but I didn't think 'twould take so long."

After that most unusual explanation, conversation languished, while Billy consumed the final waffle, after which he remarked gravely that if she didn't mind he'd go to bed. He paused at the foot of the stair with a new thoughtfulness to ask if she wanted any wood brought in for morning, and she cried all the time she was washing up the few dishes at his consideration of her. Perhaps, as Mrs. Severn had told her, there was going to come a change and Billy was really growing more manly.

Billy, as he made his brief preparation for bed told himself that he couldn't sleep, he had too much to worry about and dope out, but his head had no more than touched the pillow till he was dead to the world. Whatever came on the morrow, whatever had happened the day before, Billy had to sleep it out before he was fit to think. And Billy slept.

But up the street in the Carter house a light burned late in

Mark's window, and Mark himself, his mother soothed and comforted and sent to sleep, sat up in his big leather chair that his mother had given him on the last birthday before he left home, and stared at the wall opposite where hung the picture of a litle girl in a white dress with floating hair and starry eyes. In his face there grew a yearning and a hopelessness that was beyond anything to describe. It was like a face that is suffering pain of fire and studying to be brave, yet burns and suffers and is not consumed. That was the look in Mark Carter's eyes and around his finely chiseled lips. Once, when he was in that mood traveling on a railway carriage, a woman across the aisle had called her husband's attention to him. "Look at that man!" she said. "He looks like a lost soul!"

For a long time he sat and stared at the picture, without a motion of his body, or without even the flicker of an eyelash, as if he were set there to see the panorama of his thoughts pass before him and see them through to the bitter end. His eyes were deep and gray. In boyhood they had held a wistful expectation of enchanting things and doing great deeds of valor. They were eyes that dream, and believe, and are happy even suffering, so faith remain and love be not denied. But faith had been struck a deadly blow in these eyes now, and love had been cast away. The eyes looked old and tired and unbelieving, yet still searching, searching, though seeing dimly, and yet more dim every day, searching for the dreams of childhood and knowing they would never come again. Feeling sure that they might not come again because he had shut the door against them with his own hand, and by his own act cut the bridge on which they might have crossed from heaven to him.

A chastened face, humbled by suffering when alone, but proud and unyielding still before others. Mark Carter looking over his past knew just where he had started down this road of pain, just where he had made the first mistake, sinned the first sin, chosen pride instead of humility, the devil instead of God. And tonight Mark Carter sat and faced the immediate future and saw what was before him. As if a painted map lay out there on the wall before him, he saw the fire through which he must pass, and the way it would scorch the faces of those he loved, and his soul cried out in anguish at the sight. Back, back over his past life he tramped again and again. Days when he and Lynn and her father and mother had gone off on little excursions, with a lunch and a dog and a book, and all the world of nature as their playground. A little thought, a trifling word that had been spoken, some bit of beauty at which they looked, an ant they watched struggling with a crumb too heavy for it, a cluster of golden leaves or the scarlet berries of the squaw vine among the moss. How the memories made his heart ache as he thought them out of the past.

And the books they had read aloud, sometimes the minister, sometimes his wife doing the reading, but always he was counted into the little circle as if they were a family. He had come to look upon them as his second father and mother. His own father he had never known.

His eyes sought the bookcase near at hand. There they were, some of them birthday gifts and Christmases, and he had liked nothing better than a new book which he always carried over to be read in the company. Oh, those years! How the books marked their going! Even way back in his little boyhood! *Hans Brinker or the Silver Skates.* He touched its worn blue back and silver letters scarcely discernible *The Call of the Wild.* How he had thrilled to the sorrows of that dog! And how many life lessons had been wrapped up in the creature's experience! How had he drifted so far away from it all? How could he have done it? No one had pushed him, he had gone himself. He knew the very moment when after days of agony he had made the awful decision, scarcely believing himself that he meant to stick by it; hoping against hope that some great miracle would come to pass that should change it all and put him back where he longed to be! How he had prayed and prayed in his childish faith and agony for the miracle, and—*it had not come!* God had gone back on him. He had not kept His promises! And then he had deliberately given up his faith. He could think back over all the days and weeks that led up to this. Just after the time when he had been so happy; had felt that he was growing up, and understanding so many of the great problems of life. The future looked rosy before him, because he felt that he was beginning to grasp wisdom and the sweetness of things. How little he had known of his own foolishness and sinfulness!

It was just after they had finished reading and discussing Dante's *Vision*. What a wonderful man Mr. Severn was that he had taken two children and guided them through that beautiful, fearful, wonderful story! How it had impressed him then, and stayed with him all these awful months and days since he had trodden the same fiery way!

He reached his hand out for the book, bound in dull blue cloth, the symbol of its serious import. He had not opened the book since they finished it and Mr. Severn had handed it over to him and told him to keep it, as he had another copy. He opened the book as if it had been the coffin of his beloved, and there between the dusty pages lay a bit of blue ribbon, creased with the pages, and jagged on the edges because it had been cut with a jackknife. And lying smooth upon it in a golden curve a wisp of a yellow curl, just a section of one of Marilyn's, the day she put her hair up, and did away with the curls! He had cut the ribbon from the end of a great bow that held the curls at the back of her head, and then he had laughingly insisted on a piece of the curl, and they had made a great time collecting the right amount of hair, for Marilyn insisted it must not make a rough spot for her to brush. Then he had laid it in the book, the finished book, and shut it away carefully, and gone home, and the next day—the very next day, the thing had happened!

He turned the leaves sadly:

> In midway of this our mortal life,
> I found me in a gloomy wood, astray
> Gone from the path direct.

It startled him, so well it fitted with his mood. It was himself, and yet he could remember well how he had felt for the writer when he heard it first. Terrible to sit here tonight and know it was himself all the time the tale had been about! He turned a page or two and out from the text there stood a line:

> All hope abandon, ye who enter here.

That was the matter with himself. He had abandoned all hope. Over the leaf his eye ran down the page:

> This miserable fate
> Suffer the wretched souls of those who lived
> Without praise or blame, with that ill band
> Of angels mixed, who nor rebellious proved
> Nor yet were true to God, but for themselves
> Were only.

How well he remembered the minister's little comments as he read. How the sermons had impressed themselves upon his heart as he listened, and yet here he was, himself, in hell! He turned over the pages again quickly unable to get away from the picture that grew in his mind, the vermilion towers and minarets, the crags and peaks, the "little brook, whose crimson'd wave, yet lifts my hair with horror," he could see it all as if he had lived there many years. Strange he had not thought before of the likeness of his life to this. He read again:

> O Tuscan! thou who through the city of fire
> Alive art passing.

Yes, that was it. A City of Fire. He dwelt in a City of Fire! Hell! There was a hell on earth today and mortals entered it and dwelt there. He lived in that City of Fire continually now. He expected to live there forever. He had sinned against God and his better self, and had begun his eternal life on earth. It was too late ever to turn back. "All Hope abandon, ye who enter here." He had read it and defied it. He had entered knowing what he was about, and thinking, poor fool that he was, that he was doing a wise and noble thing for the sake of another.

Over in the little parsonage, the white-souled girl was walking in an earthly heaven. Ah! There was nothing, *nothing* they had in common now anymore. She lived in the City of Hope and he in the City of Fire.

He flung out the book from him and dropped his face into his hands crying softly under this breath, "Oh, Lynn, Lynn—Marilyn!"

Chapter 15

For one instant Lynn stood against the closed door, flaming with anger, her eyes flashing fire as they well knew how to flash at times. Then suddenly her lips set close in a fine control, the fire died out of her eyes, she drew a deep breath, and a quick whimsical smile lighted up her face, which nevertheless did not look in the least like one subdued:

"You know, I could get very angry at that if I chose and we'd have all kinds of a disagreeable time, but I think it would be a little pleasanter for us both if you would cut that out, don't you?" She said it in a cool little voice that sounded like one in entire command of the situation, and Opal turned around and stared at her admiringly. Then she laughed one of her wild silvery laughs that made them say she had a lutelike voice, and sauntered over toward her hostess:

"You certainly are a strange girl!" she commented. "I suppose it would be better to be friends, inasmuch as we're to be roommates. Will you smoke with me?" and out from the depths of a beaded affair that was a part of her frock and yet looked more like a bag than a pocket, she drew forth a gold cigarette case and held it out.

Marilyn controlled the growing contempt in her face and answered with spirit:

"No, I don't smoke. And you won't smoke either—*not in here!* I'm sorry to seem inhospitable, but we don't do things like that around here, and if you have to smoke you'll have to go outdoors."

"Oh, really?" Opal arched her already permanently arched, plucked brows and laughed again. "Well, you cer-

166

tainly have lots of pep. I believe I'm going to like you. Let's sit down and you tell me about yourself."

"Why don't *you* tell me about *yourself?*" hedged Marilyn relaxing into a chair and leaving the deep leather one for her guest. "I'm really a very simple affair, just a country girl very glad to get home after four years at college. There's nothing complex and nothing to tell, I assure you."

"You're entirely too sophisticated for all that simplicity," declared Opal. "I suppose it's college that has given you so much poise. But why aren't you impressed with Laurie? Simply *everybody* is impressed with Laurie! I don't believe you even know who he is!"

Lynn laughed:

"How should I? And what difference would it make anyway? As for being impressed, he gave me the impression of a very badly spoiled boy out trying to have his own way, and making a great fuss because he couldn't get it."

"And you didn't know that his father is William J. Shafton, the multimillionaire?" Opal brought the words out like little sharp points that seemed to glitter affluently as she spoke them.

"No," said Marilyn, "I didn't know. But it doesn't matter. We hadn't anything better to offer him than we've given, and I don't know why I should have been impressed by that. A man is what he is, isn't he? Not what his father is. He isn't your—*brother*—is he? I was over at the church when you arrived and didn't hear the introductions. I didn't even get your name."

Opal laughed uproariously as if the subject were overwhelmingly amusing.

"No," she said recovering, "I'm just Opal. Fire Opal they call me sometimes, and Opalescence. That's Laurie's name for me, although lately he's taken to calling me effervescence. No, he's not my brother, little simple lady, he's just one of my friends. Now don't look shocked. I'm a naughty

married lady run off on a spree for a little fun." Marilyn regarded her thoughtfully:

"Now stop looking at me with those solemn eyes! Tell me
what you were thinking about me! I'd lots rather hear it. It
would be something original, I'm sure. You're nothing if not
original!"

"I was just wondering why," said Marilyn still thoughtfully.

"Why what?"

"*Why*. Why you did it. Why you wanted to be that kind of
a married woman when the real kind is so much more beautiful and satisfactory."

"What do you know about it?" blazed Opal. "You've
never been married, have you?"

"My mother has had such a wonderful life with my father—and my father with my mother!"

Opal stared at her amazed for an instant, then shrugged
her shoulders lightly:

"Oh, *that!*" she said and laughed disagreeably. "If one
wants to be a saint, perhaps, but there aren't many *men*-
saints I can tell you! You haven't seen my husband or you
wouldn't talk like that! Imagine living a saintly life with Ed
Verrons! But, my dear, wait till you're married! You won't
talk that rubbish anymore!"

"I shall never marry unless I can," said Lynn decidedly.
"It would be terrible to marry someone I could not love and
trust!"

"Oh, love!" said Opal contemptuously. "You can love
anyone you want to for a little while. Love doesn't last. It's
just a play you soon get tired to death of. But if that's the
way you feel don't pin your trust and your love as you call it
to that princely icicle we saw down on the lawn. He's seen
more of the world than you know. I saw it in his eyes. There!
Now don't set your eyes to blazing again. I won't mention
him anymore tonight. And don't worry about me, I'm going
to be good and run back tomorrow morning in time to meet

my dear old hubby in the evening when he gets back from a week's fishing in the Adirondacks, and he'll never guess what a frolic I've had. But you certainly amuse me with your indifference. Wait till Laurie gets in some of his work on you. I can see he's crazy already about you, and if I don't decide to carry him off with me in the morning I'll miss my guess if he doesn't show you how altogether charming the son of William J. Shafton can be. He never failed to have a girl fall for him yet, not one that he *went* after, and he's been after a good many girls, I can tell you."

Lynn arose suddenly, her chin a bit high, a light of determination in her eyes. She felt herself growing angry again:

"Come and look at my view of the moon on the valley," she said suddenly, pulling aside the soft scrim curtain and letting in a flood of moonlight. "Here, I'll turn out the light so you can see better. Isn't that beautiful?"

She switched off the lights and the stranger drew near apathetically, gazing out into the beauty of the moonlight as it touched the houses half hidden in the trees and vines, and flooded the valley stretching far away to the feet of the tall dark mountains.

"I hate mountains!" shuddered Opal. "They make me afraid! I almost ran over a precipice when I was coming here yesterday. If I have to go back that same way I shall take Laurie, or if he won't go I'll cajole that stunning prince of yours if you don't mind. I loathe being alone. That's why I ran down here to see Laurie!"

But Lynn had switched on the lights and turned from the window. Her face was cold and her voice hard:

"Suppose we go to bed," she said. "Will you have the bed next the window or the door? And what shall I get for you? Have you everything? See, here is the bathroom. Father and Mother had it built for me for my birthday. And the furniture is some of mother's grandmother's. They had it done over for me."

"It's really a dandy room!" said Opal admiringly. "I

hadn't expected to find anything like this," she added without seeming to know she was patronizing. "You are the only child, aren't you? Your father and mother just dote on you too. That must be nice. We had a whole houseful at home, three girls and two boys, and after Father lost his money and had to go to a sanitarium we had frightful times, never any money to buy anything, the girls always fighting over who should have silk stockings, and Mother crying every night when we learned to smoke. Of course Mother was old-fashioned. I hated to have her weeping around all the time, but all our set smoked and what could I do? So I just took the first good chance to get married and got out of it all. And Ed isn't so bad. Lots of men are worse. And he gives me all the money I want. One thing the girls don't have to fight over silk stockings and silk petticoats anymore. I send them all they want. And I manage to get my good times in now and then too. But tell me, what in the world do you do in this sleepy little town? Don't you get bored to death? I should think you'd get your father to move to the city. There must be plenty of churches where a good-looking minister like your father could get a much bigger salary than out in the country like this. When I get back to New York I'll send for you to visit me and show you a real good time. I suppose you've never been to cabarets and eaten theater suppers, and seen a real New York good time. Why, last winter I had an affair that was talked of in the papers for days. I had the whole lower floor decorated as a wood, you know, with real trees set up, and mossy banks, and a brook running through it all. It took days for the plumbers to get the fittings in, and then they put stones in the bottom, and gold fish, and planted violets on the banks and all kinds of ferns and lilies of the valley, everywhere there were flowers blossoming so the guests could pick as many as they wanted. The stream was deep enough to float little canoes, and they stopped in grottoes for champagne, and when they came to a shallow place they had to get out and take off their shoes and stockings and wade in the brook. On the opposite bank a maid was waiting with towels. The ladies sat down on the bank and their escorts had to wipe their feet and help them on with their shoes and stockings again, and you ought to have heard the shouts of laughter! It certainly was a great time! Upstairs in the ballroom we had garden walks all about, with all kinds of flowers growing, and real birds flying around, and the walls were simply covered with American beauty roses and wonderful climbers, in such bowers that the air was heavy with perfume. The flowers alone cost thousands—What's the matter? Did you hear something fall? You startled me, jumping up like that! You're nervous aren't you? Don't you think music makes people nervous?"

Marilyn smiled pathetically, and dropped back to the edge of her bed:

"Pardon me," she said, "I was just in one of my tempers again. I get them a lot but I'm trying to control them. I happened to think of the little babies I saw in the tenement districts when I was in New York last. Did you ever go there? They wear one little garment, and totter around in the cold street trying to play, with no stockings, and shoes out at the toes. Sometimes they haven't enough to eat, and their mothers are so wretchedly poor and sorrowful!"

"Mercy!" shuddered Opal. "How morbid you are! What ever did you go to a place like that for? I always keep as far away from unpleasant things as I can. I cross the street if I see a blind beggar ahead. I just loathe misery! But however did you happen to think of them when I was telling you about my beautiful ballroom decorations?"

Lynn twinkled:

"I guess you wouldn't understand me," she said slowly, "but I was thinking of all the good those thousands of dollars would have done if they had been spent on babies and not on flowers."

"Gracious!" said Opal. "I *hate* babies! Ed is crazy about them, and would like to have the house full, but I gave him to understand what I thought about that before we were married."

"I *love* babies," said Marilyn. "They want me to go this fall and do some work in that settlement, and I'm considering it. If it only weren't for leaving Father and Mother again—but I do love the babies and the little children. I want to gather them all and do so many things for them. You know they are all God's babies, and it seems pitiful for them to have to be in such a dreadful world as some of them have!"

"Oh, *God!*" shuddered Opal quite openly now. "Don't talk about God! *I hate* God! He's just killed one of my best men friends! I wish you wouldn't talk about God!"

Marilyn looked at her sadly, contemplatively, and then twitched her mouth into a little smile:

"We're not getting on very well, are we? I don't like your costly entertainments, and you don't like my best Friend! I'm sorry. I must seem a little prude to you I'm afraid, but really, God is not what you think. You wouldn't hate Him, you would love Him—if you *knew* Him."

"Fancy knowing *God*—as you would your other friends! How *dreadful!* Let's go to bed!"

Opal began to get out her lovely brushes and toilet paraphernalia and Lynn let down her wonderful golden mane and began to brush it, looking exquisite in a little blue dimity kimono delicately edged with Valenciennes. Opal made herself radiant in a rose-chiffon and old-point negligee and went through numerous gyrations relating to the complexion, complaining meanwhile of the lack of a maid.

But after the lights were out, and Lynn kneeling silently by her bed in the moonlight, Opal lay on the other bed and watched her wonderingly, and when a few minutes later, Marilyn rose softly and crept into bed as quietly as possible lest she disturb her guest, Opal spoke:

"I wonder what you would do if a man—the man you liked best in all the world—had got killed doing something

to please you. It makes you go *crazy* when you think of it—
someone you've danced with lying dead that way all alone. I
wonder what *you'd do!*"

Lynn brought her mind back from her own sorrows and
prayers with a jerk to the problem of this strange guest. She
did not answer for a moment, then she said very slowly:

"I think—I don't know— but I *think* I should go right to
God and ask Him what to do. I think nobody else could
show what ought to be done. There wouldn't be anything
else to do!"

"Oh, *murder!*" said Opal turning over in bed quickly, and
hiding her face in the pillow, and there was in the end of her
breath just the suggestion of a shriek of fear.

But far, far into the night Marilyn lay on her sleepless pillow, her heart crying out to God: "Oh, save Mark! Take care
of Mark! Show him the way back again!"

Afar in the great city a message stole on a wire through
the night, and presently the great presses were hot with its
import, printing thousands and thousands of extras for early
morning consumption, with headlines in enormous letters
across the front page:

LAURENCE SHAFTON, SON OF WILLIAM J. SHAF-
TON, KIDNAPPED!

Mrs. Shafton is lying in nervous collapse as the result of
threats from kidnappers who boldly called her up on the
phone and demanded a king's ransom, threatening death to
the son if the plot was revealed before ten o'clock this
morning. The faithful mother gathered her treasures which
included the famous Shafton emeralds, and a string of
pearls worth a hundred thousand dollars, and let them
down from her window as directed, and then fainted,
knowing nothing more till her maid hearing her fall, rushed
into the room and found her unconscious. When roused
she became hysterical and told what had happened. Then
remembering the threat of death for telling ahead of time
she became crazy with grief, and it was almost impossible
to soothe her. The maid called her family physician, ex-

plaining all she knew, and the matter was at once put into the hands of capable detectives who are doing all they know how to locate the missing son, who has been gone only since Saturday evening; and also to find the missing jewels and other property, and it is hoped that before evening the young man will be found.

Meantime, Laurence Shafton slept soundly and late in the minister's study, and knew nothing of the turmoil and sorrow of his doting family.

Chapter 16

Though Mark had scarcely slept at all the night before he was on hand long before the city-bred youth was awake, taking apart the big machine that stood in front of the parsonage. Like a skillful physician he tested its various valves and compartments, went over its engine carefully, and came at last to the seat of the trouble which the minister had diagnosed the night before.

Lynn with dark circles under her eyes had wakened early and slipped down to the kitchen to help her mother and the little maid of all work who lived down the street and was a member of the Sunday school and an important part of the family. It was Naomi who discovered the young mechanic at the front door. There was not much that Naomi did not see. She announced his presence to Marilyn as she was filling the saltcellars for breakfast. Marilyn looked up startled, and met her mother's eyes full of comfort and reassurance. Somehow when Mark came quietly about in that helpful way of his it was impossible not to have the old confidence in him, the old assurance that all would soon be right, the old explanation that Mark was always doing something quietly for others and never taking care for himself. Marilyn let her lips relax into a smile and went about less heavy of heart. Surely, surely, somehow, Mark would clear himself of these awful things that were being said about him. Surely the day would bring forth a revelation. And Mark's action last night when he refused to speak with her, refused to let her touch his arm, and called himself unworthy was all for her sake; all because he did not want her name sullied with a breath of the scandal that belonged to him. Mark would be that way. He would protect her always, even though he did not belong to her, even though he were not her friend.

She was almost cheerful again, when at last the dallying guests appeared for a late breakfast. Mark was still working at the car, filing something with long steady grinding noises. She had seen him twice from the window, but she did not venture out. Mark had not wished her to speak to him, she would not go against his wish—at least not now—not until the guests were out of the way. That awful girl should have no further opportunity to say things to her about Mark. She would keep out of his way until they were gone. Oh, pray that the car would be fixed and they pass on their way at once! Later, if there were opportunity, she would find a way to tell Mark that he should not refuse her friendship. What was friendship if it could not stand the strain of falsehood and gossip, and even scandal if necessary? She was not ashamed to let Mark know she would be his friend forever. There was nothing unmaidenly in that. Mark would understand her. Mark had always understood her. And so she cheered her heavy heart through the breakfast hour, and the foolish jesting of the two that sounded to her anxious ears, in the language of Scripture, like the "crackling of thorns under a pot."

But at last they finished the breakfast and shoved their chairs back to go and look at the car. Mr. Severn and his wife had eaten long ago and gone about their early morning duties, and it had been Marilyn's duty to do the honors for the guests, so she drew a sigh of relief, and, evading Laurie's proffered arm slid into the pantry and let them go alone.

But when she glanced through the dining room window a few minutes later as she passed removing the dishes from the table, she saw Mark upon his knees beside the car, looking up with his winning smile and talking to Opal, who stood close beside him all attention, with her little boy attitude, and a wide childlike look in her big effective eyes. Something big and terrible seemed to seize Marilyn's heart with a viselike grip, and be choking her breath in her throat. She turned quickly, gathered up her pile of dishes and hurried into the pantry, her face white and set, and her eyes stinging with proud unshed tears.

A few minutes later, dressed in brown riding clothes exquisitely tailored, and a soft brown felt hat, she might have been seen hurrying through the back fence, if anybody had been looking that way, across the Joneses' lot to the little green stable that housed a riding horse that was hers to ride whenever she chose. She had left word with Naomi that she was going to Economy and would be back in time for lunch, and she hoped in her heart that when she returned both of their guests would have departed. It was perhaps a bit shabby of her to leave it all on her mother this way, but Mother would understand, and very likely be glad.

So Lynn mounted her little brown horse and rode by a circuitous way, across the creek, and out around the town to avoid passing her own home, and was presently on her way up to the crossroads down which Laurie Shafton had come in the dark midnight.

As she crossed the highway, she noticed the detour, and paused an instant to study the peculiar sign, and the partly cleared way around. And while she stood wondering a car came swiftly up from the Economy way past the Blue Duck Tavern. The driver bowed and smiled and she perceived it was the chief of police from Economy, a former resident of Sabbath Valley, and very much respected in the community, and with him in the front seat was another uniformed policeman!

With a sudden constriction at her heart Marilyn bowed and rode on. Was he going to Sabbath Valley? Was there truth in the rumor that Mark was in trouble? She looked back to see if he had turned down the highway, but he halted the car with its nose pointed Sabbath Valleyward and got out to examine the detour on the highway. She rode slowly and turned around several times, but as long as she was in sight his car remained standing pointed toward the valley.

Chapter 17

Billy awoke to the light of day with the sound of a strange car going by. The road through Sabbath Valley was not much frequented, and Billy knew every car that usually traveled that way. They were mostly Economy and Monopoly people, and as there happened to be a mountain trolley between the two towns higher up making a circuit to touch at Brooktown, people seldom came this way. Therefore at the unusual sound Billy was on the alert at once. One movement brought him upright with his feet upon the floor blinking toward his window, a second carried him to shelter behind the curtain where he could see the stranger go by.

Billy had reduced the science of dressing to a fine degree. He could climb into the limited number of summer garments in less time than any boy in the community, and when he saw that the car had halted just above the house and that the driver was interviewing Jim Rafferty, he reached for a handful of garments, and began to climb, keeping one eye out the window for developments. Was that or was it not the chief's car out there? If it was what did it want?

Billy was in socks, trousers, and shirt by the time the car began to puff again for starting, and he stove his feet into his old shoes and dove downstairs three steps at a stride and out the door where he suddenly became a casual observer of the day.

"Hullo, Billy! That you?" accosted the chief driving slowly down the street. "Say, Billy, you haven't seen Mark Carter, have you? They said he had gone down to the blacksmith's to get something fixed for a car. I thought perhaps you'd seen him go by."

Billy shook his head lazily:

"Nope," he said, "I've been busy this morning. He mighta gone by."

"Well, I'll just drive down and see!" The car started on and turned into the lane that led to the blacksmith shop.

Billy dove into the house, made short work of his ablutions, gave his hair a brief lick with the brush, collected his cap and sweater, bolted the plate of breakfast Aunt Saxon had left on the back of the stove when she went away for her regular Monday's wash, and was ready behind the lilac bush with old trusty, down on his knees oiling her a bit, when the chief drove back with Mark Carter in the backseat looking strangely white and haughty, but talking affably with the chief.

His heart sank. Somehow he knew something was wrong with Mark. Mark was in his old clothes with several pieces of iron in his hand as if he hadn't taken time to lay them down. Billy remained in hiding and watched while the chief's car stopped at Carter's and Mark got out. The car waited several minutes, and then Mark came out with his good clothes on and his best hat, and got into the car and they drove off, Mark looking stern and white. Billy shot out from his hiding and mounting his steed flew down the road, keeping well behind the maples and hedges, and when the chief's car stopped in front of the parsonage he dismounted and stepped inside Joneses' drive to listen. Mark got out, sprang up the steps, touched the bell, and said to someone who appeared at the door, "Mr. Shafton, I'm sorry, but I'll not be able to get those bearings fixed up today. The blacksmith doesn't seem to have anything that will do. I find I have to go over to Economy on business, and I'll look around there and see if anybody has any. I expect to be back by twelve o'clock, and will you tell the lady that I will be ready to start at half past if that will suit her. I am sure we shall have plenty of time to get *her* to Beechwood by five or sooner. If anything occurs to keep me from going I'll tele-

phone you in an hour, so that she can make other arrangements. Thank you, Mr. Shafton. Sorry I couldn't fix you up
right away, but I'll look after the lady for you." Mark hurried back to the car again and they drove off.

Billy escorted the department of justice distantly, as far as
the crossing at the highway, from which eminence he
watched until he saw that they stopped at the Blue Duck
Tavern for a few minutes, after which they went on toward
Economy; then he inspected the recent clearing of his detour, obviously by the chief, and hurried down the highway
toward the railroad crossing at Pleasant View. It was almost
train time, and he had a hunch that there might be something interesting around that hidden telephone. If he only
had had more time he might have arranged to tap the wire
and listen in without having to go so near, but he must do
the best he could.

When he reached a point on the highway where Pleasant
View station was easily discernible he dismounted, parked
his wheel among the huckleberries, and slid into the green of
the valley. Stealing cautiously to the scene of the Saturday
night holdup he finally succeeded in locating the hidden
telephone, and creeping into a well-screened spot not far
away arranged himself comfortably to wait till the trains
came. He argued that Pat would likely come down to report
or get orders about the same time as before, and so in the
stillness of the morning he lay on the ground and waited. He
could hear a song sparrow high up on the telegraph wire,
sing out its wild sweet lonely strain: sweet—sweetsweet-
sweet—sweetsweet—sweetsweet—and a hum of bees in the
wild grape that trailed over the sassafras trees. Beside him a
little wood spider stole noiselessly on her busy way. But his
heart was heavy with new burdens and he could not take his
usual rhapsodic joy in the things of Nature. What was happening to Mark and what could he do about it? Perhaps
Mark would have been better off if he had left him in the old
house on Stark Mountain. The chief couldn't have found

him then and the kidnappers would have kept him safe for a good many days till they got some money. But there wouldn't have *been* any money! For Mark wasn't the right man! And the kidnappers would have found it out pretty soon and *what* would they have done to Mark? Killed him perhaps so they wouldn't get into any more trouble! There was no telling! And time would have gone on and nobody would have known what had become of Mark. And the murder trial—if it was really a murder—would come off and they couldn't find Mark, and of course they would think Mark had killed the man and then run away. And Mark would never be able to come home again! No, he was glad Mark was out and safe and free from dope. At least Mark would know what to do to save himself. Or would he? Billy suddenly had his doubts. Would Mark take care of himself, just himself, or not? Mark was always looking after other people, but he had somehow always let people say and do what they would with him. Aw, gee! Now Mark wouldn't let them locate a thing like a murder on him, would he? And there was Miss Lynn! And Mark's mother! Mark oughtta think of them. Well, maybe he wouldn't realize how much they did care. Billy had a sudden revelation that maybe that was half the matter, Mark didn't know how much any of them cared. Back in his mind there was an uncomfortable memory of Aunt Saxon's pink damp features and anxious eyes and a possible application of the same principle to his own life, as in the case of Judas. But he wasn't considering himself now. There might come a time when he would have to change his tactics with regard to Aunt Saxon somewhat. She certainly had been a good sport last night. But this wasn't the time to consider that. He had a great deal more important matters to think of now. He had to find out how he could make it perfectly plain to the world that Mark Carter had not shot a man after twelve o'clock Saturday night at the Blue Duck Tavern. And as yet he didn't see any way without incriminating himself as a kidnapper. This cut deep because in the strict sense of the word he was not a kidnapper, because he hadn't meant to be a kidnapper. He had only meant to play a joke on the kidnappers, and at worst his only really intended fault had been the putting up of that detour on the highway. But he had an uncomfortable conviction that he wouldn't be able to make the chief and the constable, and some of those people over at Economy courthouse see it that way. As matters stood he was safe if he kept his mouth shut. Nobody knew but Mark, and he didn't know the details. Besides, Mark would never tell. Mark would even go to trial for murder before he would let himself out by telling on Billy. Billy knew that as well as he knew that the old mountain on whose feet he lay stretched now would stand up there for ages and always keep his secret for him. Mark was that way. That was why it made it worse for Billy. Judas again! Billy was surprised to find how much Judas blood there seemed to be in him. He lay there and despised himself without being able to help himself out or think of anything he could do. And then quite suddenly as he was going over the whole circumstance from the time he first listened to Pat's message into the moss of the mountain, until now, the name Shafton came to him. Laurence Shafton. Shafton, son of William J., of Gates and Shafton. Those were the words the telephone had squeaked out quite plainly. And Shafton. Mr. Shafton. That was the name Mark had called the guy with the car at the parsonage. Mr. Shafton. The same guy, of course. Bah! What a mess he had made of it all! Got Mark kidnapped, landed that sissy guy on the Severns for no knowing how long, and perhaps helped to tangle Mark up in a murder case. Aw, gee! There's the train! What could he do? That rich guy! Well, there wasn't anything to that. He would get out as soon as Mark got his car fixed up and never know he had been kidnapped. And what was he, Billy, waiting here for anyway? Just a chance! Just to see whether Pat and Sam had found out yet that their quarry had vanished. Just to wonder what had become of Link and Shorty.

The trains came and went, and the hush settled down once more at the station. From where he lay, hidden under a ledge, with a thick growth of laurel and sumac between him and the world, Billy could not see the station platform, and had no means of telling whether Pat was about or not.

He had lain still a long time and was beginning to think that his trip had been in vain, when he heard a soft crackling of the twigs above him, a heavy tread crashing through the bushes, a puffing snorting breath from the porpoiselike Pat, and he held his own breath and lay very still. Suppose Pat should take a new trail and discover his hiding place? His heart pounded with great dull thuds. But Pat slid heavily down to the little clearing below him, fumbled a moment with his key, and then in a gruff guarded voice called:

"Hullo! Hullo! Sam? That you? Yes, aw'right! Yes, aw'right! How's things? What? Hell's to pay? Whaddaya mean hell? Ain't you gonta put it over? After all my trouble you ain't a gonta let that million slip through? What? Oh! Who? The valet? He's beat it, has he? Whaddaya mean? *He* took 'em. *He* took the pearls an' diamonds? Well, em'ruls then! What's tha diffrunce? *We* ain't gottum have we? Oh, bonds too! Well, whattya gonta do about it? Move him? What, the rich guy? Move him where? *Why?* We ain'ta gonta run no more risks. Link an' Shorty are sore 'za pup, when they come. I don't think they'll stan' for it. Well, where'll ya move him? Who? Shorty? Oh, Link? Both? Well, I ain't seen 'em. I tol' 'em to keep good an' far away from me. I don't build on loosin' this job just now, see? What? It's in the papers a'ready? You don't say! Well, who you figger done that? That valet? Well, where's the harm? Can't you work it all the better? We got the guy, ain't we? *He* ain't gottim that's certain. We c'n deliver the goods, so we get the reward. How much reward they offerin? You don't say!

Well, I should say, get in yer work soon 'fore we get caught.
Aw'right! I'm with ya. Well, s'long! I'll be down here at nine
sharp. Take a trip to China with ya next week ef ya pull it
off. Aw'right! Goobby!" and Pat hung up and puffed his way
up the hill again, leaving Billy drenched with perspiration
and filled with vague plans, and deep anxiety. He had got a
clue but what good was it? How could he work it to the salvation of Mark? He could easily put the sissy over at the
parsonage wise, do him a good turn, save his dad some
money, but what good would that do Mark? Mark needed to
establish an alibi, he could see that with half an eye, but how
would anything Billy knew help that along unless—unless
he told on himself? For a moment a long trail of circumstances that would surely follow such a sacrificial ordinance
appeared before him and burned into his soul, most prominent among them being Aunt Saxon, hard worked and
damp pink-eyed, crying her heart out for the boy she had
tried faithfully to bring up. And Miss Lynn. How sad her
eyes would grow if Billy had to be tried and sentenced to
prison. Not that Billy was afraid to go to prison, in fact the
thought of it as an experience was rather exhilarating than
not, but he was afraid to have those two know he had gone,
afraid of their eyes, their sad eyes! Yes, and he was afraid of
the thought of his own ingratitude, for down deep in his
heart he could see a long line of things Aunt Saxon had
done for him that she hadn't been obliged to do. Going
without a new winter coat to get him an overcoat. His old
one was warm, but his arms were out of it too far and he
wouldn't wear it. Sitting up nights the time he drank swamp
water and had the fever! That was fierce! How he did rag
her! And how patiently she bore it! The scare she had when
the dog bit him! As if a little dog bite was anything! Doggone it, why were women such fools!

And now this! Billy sat up with a jerk and shook himself
free from the dead moss and leaves, wending his way sulkily
across to where he had left his wheel, and pondering, pon-

dering. Shafton! There ought to be something there to work on, but there wasn't!

Meantime Marilyn rode hard down the way to Economy, not slowing her pony till they reached the outskirts of Economy. Her mind was in such a tumult that she felt as if she were being whirled on with circumstances without having a will to choose one thing from another. Mark! The unwelcome guests! Mark and Opal! Mark and Cherry! *Cherry!* The chief of police! Mark! And yes, Cherry! She was on her way to see *Cherry!* But what was she going to do when she got there, and how was she to excuse her strange visit after almost five years since she had seen the child? If there was truth in the rumor that she was connected with a shooting affair at the Blue Duck, and especially if there was truth in the charge that Mark had been going with her, would it not seem strange—perhaps be misconstrued by Cherry? By her family? They had all known of her own intimacy with Mark in the past. She shrank from the idea. Yet Marilyn Severn had not been brought up to regard public opinion when it was a question of doing something that ought to be done. The only question was, was it really something that ought to be done or was she letting Billy influence her unduly? Billy was shrewd. He knew Mark. He knew a lot more than he ever told. What did Billy know? How she wished she had asked her father's advice before coming, and yet, if she had, he might have been unduly influenced by dreading to have her put herself in the position of prying into the matter.

As she rode and pondered she came near to the little house on the village street where Cherry lived, a house set out plumb with the sidewalk, and a little gate at the side to go round to the back door where the family lived, the front room being the tailor shop. As she drew near she looked up and was sure she saw Cherry in a short narrow skirt and an old middy blouse scurrying through the gate to the back door, and her heart thumped so hard she was almost tempted to ride on to the store first before making her call. But something in her that always held her to a task until it was completed forced her to dismount and knock at the door.

It seemed long to wait with her heart thumping so, and why did it thump? She found herself praying, "Oh, God, show me what to say!" and then the door was open a crack and a sharp wizened face with a striking resemblance to Cherry's bold little beauty, was thrust at her. It must be Cherry's mother. Of course it was!

"Mr. Fenner ain't in the shop!" said the woman. "He can't do nothin today. He's sick!"

Marilyn smiled:

"But I wanted to see Cherry," she said. "Aren't you her mother? Don't you remember me? I'm Marilyn Severn, her old music teacher. Is Cherry in?"

A frightened look passed over the woman's face as she scanned the sweet face before her, and then a wily expression darted into her eyes:

"Oh," she said with a forced smirk, "yes, Miss Marilyn. Excuse me fer not recognizing you. You've grown a lot. Why, no, Cherry ain't at home this morning. She'll be awful sorry not to see you. She thought a lot of you, she did. She got on so well with you in her music too. I says to her the other day, I says, Cherry, I hear Miss Marilyn is home again, you'll have to take up yer music again, and she says yes, she guessed she would. She'll be around someday to see you. Sorry I can't ask you in, but Mr. Fenner's pretty sick. Oh, just the grip, I guess. He'll soon be all right."

She began to realize that the woman was in a hurry to get rid of her and she hastened away, relieved yet puzzled at the whole affair. She rode down into the village mechanically and bought a spool of silk and the coffee strainer which had been her legitimate errand to the village, and turning back had scarcely passed the last house before she saw the chief's car coming toward her, and Mark, his face white and haggard, looking out from the backseat. He drew back as he recognized her, and tried to hide, and she rode on with only a passing bow which comprehended the whole car; but she was aware of Mark's eyes upon her, steadily, watching her. She would have known he was watching her from the darkness of the backseat if her own eyes had been shut. What was it all about and what were they doing to Mark?

Chapter 18

The last house in the village on the road to Economy was the Harricutt's. It was built of gray cement blocks that the elder had taken for a bad debt, and had neither vine nor blossom to soften its grimness. Its windows were supplied with green holland shades, and its front yard was efficiently manned with plum trees and a peach, while the backyard was given over to vegetables. Elder Harricutt walked to Economy every day to his office in the Economy bank. He said it kept him in good condition physically. His wife was small and prim with little quick prying eyes and a false front that had a tendency to go askew. She wore bonnets with strings and her false teeth didn't quite fit; they clicked as she talked. She kept a watch over the road at all times and very little ever got by her unnoticed.

In wholesome contrast next door was the trim little white cottage where Tom McMertrie and his mother Christie lived, smothered in vines and ablaze with geraniums all down the front walk. And below that, almost facing the graveyard was a little green shingled bungalow. Mary Rafferty kept her yard aglow with phlox, verbenas, and pansies, and reveled in vines and flowering shrubs.

These two women were wonderful friends, though forty years marched between them. Mary's hair was black as a crow's wing above her great pansy-blue eyes with their long curling lashes, while Christie's hair was sandy-silver and her tongue full of brrrs. They had opposite pantry windows on the neighboring sides of their houses, where they often talked of a morning while Christie molded her sweet loaves of bread or mixed scones and Mary made tarts and pies and cake for Jim's supper. Somehow without much being said about it they had formed a combination against their hard little knot of a neighbor behind the holland shades.

The first house on the side street that ran at right angles to the main thoroughfare, just below Rafferty's, was Duncannon's. A picket fence at the side let into the vegetable gardens of the three, and the quiet little Mrs. Duncannon with the rippley brown hair and soft brown eyes often slipped through and made a morning call under cover of the kindly pole beans that hid her entrances and exits perfectly from any green holland-shaded windows that might be open that way. Jane Duncannon formed a third in this little combination.

On the Monday morning following the session meeting Mary Rafferty and Christie McMertrie were at their respective pantry windows flinging together some toothsome delicacies for the evening meal, that all might move smoothly during the busy day.

A neat line of flopping clothes glimmered in each backyard over the trim green that stretched across in front of the back door, and the irons were on in both kitchens preparing for a finish as soon as a piece should show signs of drying.

"Hev ye haird whut the extra session meetin' was called for, Mary?" asked the older woman looking up from her mixing bowl. "Tom went to the mill to tak the place of the noight watchman. His feyther's dyin' ye ken, and Tom's not come by yet. I thot ye might hev haird."

Mary lifted her eyes with troubled glance:

"Not yet," she said, "but I'm thinking of running over to Duncannon's as soon as I get these pies in the oven. The clothes won't be dry for a while, an' I'll take my pan of peas to shell. She'll know of course. Maybe it's nothing much— but Jim said they held up Mark Carter and made him come in. It was ten minutes of ten before he got away! You don't suppose anybody's taken the gossip to the session do you?"

"There's one we know well would be full cawpable of the same," affirmed Christie patting her biscuits into place and tucking the bread cloth deftly over them, "but I'd be sorry to see a meenister an' a session as wud be held up by one poor whimperin' little elder of the like of him."

"Mr. Severn won't, I'm sure o' that!" said Mary trustingly, "but there comes Mrs. Duncannon now. I'll run over and see what's in the wind."

Mrs. Duncannon had grown a smile on her gentle face that was like as two peas to her husband's wide kindly grin, but there was no smile on her face this morning as she greeted her two friends, and dropped into a chair by the door of Christie's immaculate kitchen, and her soft brown eyes were snapping: She had an air of carrying kindly mysterious explosives:

"Did ye hear that the old ferret held up Mark Carter last night and as good as called him a murderer in the face of the whole session?" she asked breathlessly.

"And whut said our meenister to thot?" inquired Christie.

Jane Duncannon flashed her a twinkle of appreciation:

"He just clapped the senior elder in the chair as neat as a pin in a pincushion an' moved an expression of confidence, *utmost* confidence was the word!"

"Mmmmmmmm! I thot as much!" commented Christie. "The blessed mon!"

"Oh, I'm so glad!" sighed Mary Rafferty sinking into a chair. "Jim thinks the sun rises and sets in Mark Carter. They were kids together you know. He says people don't know Mark. And he said if they turned Mark down at the church now, if they didn't stand by him in his trouble, he had no more use for their religion!"

"Don't you believe it, Mary Rafferty! Jim Rafferty loves the very ground the meenister walks on!"

"What was that?" exclaimed Jane Duncannon running to the side window. "A strange car! Mary, come here! Is that the chief of police from Economy?"

Mary darted to the window followed by the elder woman:

"Yes, it is!" she exclaimed drawing back aghast. "You

don't suppose he's going to Carter's? He *wouldn't* do that would he?"

"He huz to do his dooty, doesn't he?" mused Christie. "But thot's not sayin' he *loikes* it, child!"

"Well, he might find a way not to frighten his mother!"

Mrs. Duncannon stretched her neck to see if he was really stopping at the parsonage, and Christie murmured: "Perhaps he will."

The little group lingered a moment, till Mary bethought her of her pies in the oven and the three drifted thriftily back to their morning tasks, albeit with mind and heart down in the village.

Presently on the glad morning air sounded again the chug chug of the motor, bringing them sharply back to their windows. Yes, there was the chief's car again. And Mark Carter with white haggard face sat in the backseat! Apprehension flew to the soul of each loyal woman.

But before the sound of the chief's motor bearing Mark Carter Economyward had passed out of hearing, Jane Duncannon in a neat brown dress with a little round brown-ribboned hat set trimly on her rippley hair, and a little round basket on her arm covered daintily with a white napkin, was nipping out her tidy front gate between the sunflowers and asters and tripping down Maple Street as if it had been on her mind to go ever since Saturday night.

Even before Mary Rafferty had turned from her Nottingham laced parlor window and gone with swift steps to her kitchen door Christie McMertrie stood on her back step with her sunbonnet on and a glass of jelly wrapped in tissue paper in her hand:

"She's glimpsed 'em," she whispered briefly, with a nod toward the holland shades, "an' she's up in her side bedroom puttin' on her Sunday bunnit. She'll be oot the door in another two meenits, the little black crow! If we bide in the fields we can mak Carters' back stoop afore she gets much past the tchurch!"

Mary Rafferty caught up her pan of peas, dashed them into a basket that hung on the wall by the door, and bareheaded as she was hastened out through the garden after her friend for all the world as if she were going to pick more peas. Down the green lane between the bean poles they hurried through the picket gate, pushing aside the big gray Duncannon cat who basked in the sun under a pink hollyhock with a Duncannon smile on its gray whiskers like the rest of the family.

"Jane! Jane Duncannon!" called Christie McMertrie. But the hollow echoes in the tidy kitchen flung back emptily, and the plate of steaming cinnamon buns on the white scrubbed table spoke as plainly as words could have done that no one was at home.

"She's gone!"

The two hurried around the house, through the front gate, across the street with a quick glance up and down to be sure that the Petrie babies playing horse in the next yard were their only observers, and then ducking under the bars of the fence they scuttled down a slope, crossed a trickle of a brook that hurried creekward, and up the opposite bank. Behind Little's barn they paused to glance back. Someone was coming out the Harricutt door, someone wearing a bonnet and a black veil. They hurried on. There were two more fences separating the meadows. Mary went over and Christie between. They made quick work of the rest of the way and crept panting through the hedge at the back of Carter's just as Jane Duncannon swung open the little gate in front with a glimpse back up the street in triumph and a breath of relief that she had won. By only so much as a lift of her lashes and a lighting of her soft brown eyes did she recognize and incorproate the other two in her errand, and together the three entered the Carter house by the side entrance, with a neighborly tap and a call: "Miz Carter, you home?"

Quick nervous steps overhead, a muffled voice calling catchily, "Yes, I'm coming, just set down, won't you?" and they dropped into three dining room chairs and drew breath, mopping their warm faces with their handkerchiefs and trying to adjust their minds to the next move.

Their hostess gave them no time to prepare a program. She came hurriedly downstairs, obviously anxious, openly with every nerve on the qui vive, and they saw at once that she had been crying. Her hair was damp about her forehead as if from hasty ablution. She looked from one to another of her callers with a frightened glance that went beyond them as if looking for others to come, as she paused in the doorway puzzled.

"This is a s'prise party, Miz Carter," began Jane Duncannon laughing. "We all brought our work along and can't stay but a minute, but we got an idea an' couldn't keep it till Ladies' Aid. You got a minute to spare? Go get your knitting and set down. *Now!* It's Miz'Severn's birthday next Sat'day an' we thought 'twould be nice to get her a present. What do you think about it?"

Mrs. Carter who had stood tensely in the doorway, her fingers whitely gripping the woodwork, her face growing whiter every minute, suddenly relaxed with relief in every line of her body, and bloomed into a smile:

"Oh, why, *is* it? Of course! What'll it be? Why couldn't we finish that sunburst bed quilt we started last year while she was away? If we all get at it I think we could finish. There's some real fast quilters in the Aid. Wait, till I get my apples to pare. I promised Mark I'd have applesauce for lunch!"

A quick glance went from eye to eye and a look of relief settled down on the little company. She *expected Mark home for lunch* then!

They were in full tide of talk about the quilting pattern when a knock came on the front door, and Mary Rafferty jumped up and ran to open it. They heard the Harricutt voice, clear, sharp, incisive:

"I came to sympathize—!" And then as Mary swung her face into the sunlight the voice came suddenly up as against a stone wall with a gasp and "Oh, it's *you!* Where's Mrs. Carter? I wish to see Mrs. Carter."

"She's right back in the dining room, Mrs. Harricutt. Come on back. We're talking over how to celebrate Miz Severn's birthday. Do you like a straight quilting or diamond, Miz Harricutt. It's for the sunburst coverlet, you know!"

"The sunburst coverlet!" exclaimed Mrs. Harricutt irately, as though somehow it were an indecent subject at such a time as this, but she followed Mary back to the dining room with a sniff of curiosity. She fairly gasped when she saw Mrs. Carter with her small sensitive face bright with smiles:

"Just take that chair by the window, Mrs. Harricutt," she said affably, "and *excuse me* fer not getting up. I've got to get these apples on the fire, for I promised Mark some applesauce for lunch, and he likes it stone cold."

Mrs. Harricutt pricked up her ears:

"Oh, Mark is coming home for *lunch* then!" Her voice was cold, sharp, like a steel knife dipped in lemon juice. There was a bit of a curl on the tip of it that made one wince as it went through the soul. Little Mrs. Carter flushed painfully under her sensitive skin, up to the roots of her light hair. She had been pretty in her girlhood, and Mark had her coloring in a stronger way.

"Oh, yes, he's coming home for lunch," she answered brightly, glad of this much assurance. "And he has to have it early because he has to drive that strange young woman from the parsonage back somewhere down in New Jersey. She came alone by herself yesterday, but the mountain passes sort of scairt her, and she asked Mark to drive back with her."

"Oh!" There was a challenge in the tone that called the red to Mrs. Carter's cheek again, but Christie McMertrie's soft burring tongue slid in smoothly:

"What wad ye think o' the briar pattern around the edge? I know it's some worruk, but it's a bonnie border to lie under, an' it's not so tedious whan there's plenty o' folks to tak a hand."

They carried the topic along with a whirl then and Mrs. Harricutt had no more chance to harry her hostess. Then suddenly Mary arose in a panic:

"I left my pies in the oven!" she cried. "They'll be burned to a crisp. I must go. Miz Harricutt, are you going along now? I'll walk with you. I want to ask you how you made that plum jam you gave me a taste of the other day. Jim thinks it is something rare, and I'll have to be making some or he'll never be satisfied, that is if you don't mind—" And before Mrs. Carter realized what was happening Mary had marshaled the Harricutt vulture down the street, and was questioning eagerly about measures of sugar and plums and lemon peel and nuts.

"Now," said Christie setting down her jelly glass that she had been holding all this time, "we'll be ganging awa. There's a bit jar of raspberry jam for the laddie with the bright smile, an' you think it over and run up and say which pattern you think is bonniest."

"It was just beautiful of you all to come," said little Mrs. Carter looking from one to another in painful gratitude— "why it's been just *dear* for you to run in this way."

"Yes, a regular party!" said Jane Duncannon squeezing her hand with understanding. "See, Mary has left her peas. You'd best put them on to boil for Mark. He'll be coming back pretty soon. Come, Christie, wumman, it's time we was back at our worruk!" and they hurried through the hedge and across the meadows to their homes once more, but as they entered the Duncannon gate they marked Billy Gaston, head down, pedaling along over on Maple Street, his jaws keeping rhythmic time with his feet.

One hour later the smooth chug of a car that was not altogether unfamiliar to their ears brought those four women eagerly to their respective windows, and as the old clock chimed the hour of noon they beheld Mark Carter driving calmly down the street toward his own home in his own car. *His own car!* And Billy Gaston lounging lazily by his side chewing rhythmically.

Mark's car! Mark! Billy! *Ah, Billy!* Three of them mused with a note of triumph in their eyes.

And Mrs. Harricutt as she rolled her Sunday bonnet strings mused:

"Now, how in the world did that Mark Carter get his own car down to Economy when he went up with the chief? He had it down here this morning, I know, for I saw him riding round. And that little imp of a Billy! I wonder why he always tags him round! Miss Saxon ought to be warned about that! I'll have to do it! But how in the world did Mark get his car?"

Billy enjoyed his lunch that day, a bit of cold chicken and bread, two juicy red-cheeked apples, and an unknown quantity of sugary doughnuts from the stone crock in the pantry. He sat on the side step munching the last doughnut he felt he could possibly swallow. Mark was home and all was well. Himself had seen the impressive glance that passed between Mark and the chief at parting. The chief trusted Mark that was plain. Billy felt reassured. He reflected that that guy Judas had been precipitate about hanging himself. If he had only waited and *done* a little something about it there might have been a different ending to the story. It was sort of up to Judas anyway, having been the cause of the trouble.

With this virtuous conclusion Billy wiped the sugar from his mouth, mounted his wheel and went forth to browse in familiar and much neglected pastures.

He eyed the Carter house as he slid by. Mrs. Carter was placidly shaking out the tablecloth on the side porch. Mark had eaten his applesauce and gone. He passed Brown's, Todd's, Bateses' chasing a white hen that had somehow escaped her confines, but in front of Joneses' he suddenly

became aware of the blue car that stood in front of the parsonage. It had come to life and was throbbing. It was back-
ing toward him and going to turn around. On the sidewalk
leaning on a cane stood the obnoxious stranger for whose
presence in Sabbath Valley he, Billy Gaston, was responsible. He lounged at ease with a smile on his ugly mug and
acted as if he lived there! There was nothing about his appearance to suggest *his* near departure. His disabled car still
stood silent and helpless beside the curb. Aw, *gee!*

Billy swerved to the other side of the road to avoid the
blue car at a hairbreadth, but as it turned he looked up impudently to behold the strange girl with the flour on her face
and the green baseball bats in her ears smiling up into the
face of Mark Carter, who was driving. Billy nearly fell off
his wheel and under the car, but recovered his balance in
time to swerve out of the way without apparently having
been observed by either Mark or the lady, and shot like a
streak down the road. Beyond the church he drew a wide
curve and turned in at the graveyard, casting a quick furtive
eye toward the parsonage, where he was glad not to discover
even the flutter of a garment to show that Lynn Severn was
about. That guy was there, but Miss Lynn was not chasing
him. That was as it should be. He breathed a sigh from his
heavy heart and stole sadly back to the old mossy stone
where so many of his life problems had been thought out.
Still, that guy *was there! He* had the advantage! And Mark
and that lady! Bah! He sat down to meditate on Judas and
his sins. It seemed that life was just about as disappointing
as it could be! His rough young hand leaned hard against
the grimy old stone till the half worn lettering hurt his flesh
and he shifted his position and lifted his hand. There on the
palm were the quaint old letters, imprinted in the flesh,
"Blessed are the dead—" Gosh yes! *Weren't* they? Judas had
been right after all. "Aw, gee!" he said aloud. "Whatta fool I
bin!" He glanced down at the stone as he rubbed the imprint
from the fleshy part of his hand. The rest of the text caught

his eye. "Blessed are the dead that die in the Lord!" There was a catch in that of course. It wasn't blessed if you didn't *die in the Lord*. "In the Lord" meant that you didn't do anything Judaslike. He understood. The people who didn't die in the Lord weren't blessed. They didn't go to heaven, whatever heaven was. They went to *hell*. Heaven had never seemed very attractive to Billy when he thought of it casually, and he had taken it generally for granted that he being a boy was naturally destined for the other place. In fact until he knew Lynn Severn he had always told himself calmly that he *expected* to go to hell sometime, it had seemed the manly thing to do. Most men to his mind were preparing for hell. It seemed the masculine place of final destiny. Heaven was for women. He had ventured some of this philosophy on his aunt once in a particularly strenuous time when she had told him that he couldn't expect the reward of the righteous if he continued in his present ways, but she had been so horrified, and wept so long and bitterly that he hadn't ever had the nerve to try it again. And since Marilyn Severn had been his teacher he had known days when he would almost be willing to go to heaven—for her sake. He had also suspected, at times, that Mr. Severn was fully as much of a man as Mark Carter, although Mark was *his own,* and if Mark decided to go to hell Billy felt there could be no other destiny for himself.

But now, face-to-face with realities, Billy suddenly began to realize what hell was going to be like. Billy felt hell surrounding him. Flames could not beat the reproach that now flared him in the face and stung him to the quick with his own sinfulness. He, Billy Gaston, captain of the Sabbath Valley baseball team, prospective captain of the Sabbath Valley football team, champion runner, and high jumper, champion swimmer and boxer of the boys' league of Monopoly County, friend and often tolerated companion of Mark Carter the great, trusted favorite of his beloved and saintly Sunday school teacher, was in *hell!* He could never more hold up his head and walk proud of himself. He was in hell at fourteen for life, and by his own act! And gosh hang it! Hell didn't look so attractive in the near vision stretching out that way through life, and *then some,* as it had before he faced it. He'd rather walk through fire somewhere and stand some chance of getting done with it sometime. "Aw, gee! Gosh! Whatta fool I bin!"

And then he set himself to see just what he had done, while the high walls of sin seemed to rise closer about him, and his face burned with the heat of the pit into which he had put himself.

There was that guy Shafton—sissyman! He had put him in the parsonage along with his beloved teacher! If he only hadn't taken that ten dollars or listened to that devil of a Pat, he wouldn't have put up that detour and Shafton would have gone on his way. What difference if he had got kidnapped? His folks wouldda bailed him out with their old jewels and things. Whaddid anybody want of jewels for anyway? Just nasty little bits of stone and glass! Mark had seen the guy there in church. Mark didn't like it. He knew by the set of Mark's mouth. Of course Mark went with Cherry sometimes, but then that was different! Lynn was—well, Lynn was Miss Marilyn! That was all there was about it.

And, if he hadn't put up that detour, Mark would have gone home that night before twelve and his mother would have known he was home, and likely other people would have seen him, and been able to prove he wasn't out shooting anybody, and then they wouldn't have told all those awful things about him. Of course now Mark was safe, *of course,* but then it wasn't good to have things like that said about Mark. It was fierce to have a thing like that session meeting to remember! He wanted to kill that old ferret of a Harricutt whenever he thought about it. Then he would be a murderer, and be hanged, and he wouldn't care if he did mebbe. *Aw, gee!*

A meadowlark suddenly pierced the sky with its wild

sweet note high in the air somewhere, and Billy wondered with a sick thud of his soul how larks dared to sing in a world like this where one could upset a whole circle of friends by a single little turn of finance that he hadn't meant anything wrong by at all. The bees droned around the honeysuckle that billowed over the little iron fence about a family burying lot, and once Lynn Severn's laugh—not her regular laugh, but a kind of a company polite one—echoed lightly across to his ears and his face dropped into his hands. He almost groaned. Billy Gaston was at the lowest ebb he had ever been in his young life, and his conscience, a thing he hadn't suspected he had, and wouldn't have owned if he had, had risen up within him to accuse him, and there seemed no way on earth to get rid of it. A conscience wasn't a *manly* thing according to his code, yet here he was, he Billy Gaston, with a conscience!

It was ghastly!

Chapter 19

Laurie Shafton had caught Lynn as she came down the stairs with a bit of sewing in her hand to give Naomi a direction from her mother, and had begged her to come out on the porch and talk to him. He pleaded that he was lonesome, and that it was her duty as hostess to amuse him for a while.

Lynn had no relish for talking with the guest. Her heart was too sore to care to talk with anyone. But her innate courtesy, and natural gentleness finally yielded to his pleading, for Laurie had put on a humility that was almost becoming, and made her seem really rude to refuse.

She made him sit down in the hammock at the far end, however, and insisted on herself taking the little rocker quite near the front door. She knew her father would soon be returning from some parish calls and would relieve her, so she settled herself with the bit of linen she was hemstitching and prepared to make the best of it.

"It's a shame my car is out of commission yet," began Laurie settling back in the hammock and by some strange miracle refraining from lighting a cigarette. It wouldn't have entered his head that Lynn would have minded. He didn't know any girls objected to smoking. But this girl interested him strangely. He wasn't at all sure but it was a case of love at first sight. He had always been looking for that to happen to him. He hoped it had. It would be such a delightful experience. He had tried most of the other kinds.

"Yes, it is too bad for you to be held up in your journey this way," sympathized Lynn heartily, "but Father says the blacksmith is going to fix you up by tomorrow he hopes. Those bearings will likely come tonight."

"Oh, but it has been a dandy experience. I'm certainly

glad it happened. Think what I should have missed all my life, not knowing *you!*"

He paused and looked soulfully at Lynn waiting for an appreciative glance from her fully occupied eyes, but Lynn seemed to have missed the point entirely:

"I should think you might have well afforded to lose the experience of being held up in a dull little town that couldn't possibly be of the slightest interest to you," she said dryly, with the obvious idea of making talk.

"Oh, but I think it is charming," he said lightly! "I hadn't an idea there was such a place in the world as this. It's ideal, don't you know, so secluded and absolutely restful. I'm having a dandy time, and you people have been just wonderful to me. I think I shall come back often if you'll let me."

"I can't imagine your enjoying it," said Lynn looking at him keenly. "It must be so utterly apart from your customary life. It must seem quite crude and almost uncivilized to you."

"That's just it, it's so charmingly quaint. I'm bored to death with life as I'm used to it. I'm always seeking for a new sensation, and I seem to have lighted on it here all unexpectedly. I certainly hope my car will be fixed by morning. If it isn't I'll telegraph for my man and have him bring down some bearings in one of the other cars and fix me up. I'm determined to take you around a bit and have you show me the country. I know it would be great under your guidance."

"Thank you," said Lynn coolly, "but I haven't much time for pleasuring just now, and you will be wanting to go on your way—"

He flushed with annoyance. He was not accustomed to being baffled in this way by any girl, but he had sense enough to know that only by patience and humility could he win any notice from her.

"Oh, I shall want to linger a bit and let this doctor finish up this ankle of mine. It isn't fair to go away to another doctor before I'm on my feet again.

He thought she looked annoyed, but she did not answer.

"Did you ever ride in a racer?" he asked suddenly. "I'll teach you to drive. Would you like that?"

"Thank you," she said pleasantly, "but that wouldn't be necessary, I know how to drive."

He almost thought there was a twinkle of mischief in her eye:

"You know how to drive! But you haven't a car! Oh, I suppose that young Carter taught you to drive his," he said with chagrin. He was growing angry. He began to suspect her of playing with him. After all, even if she was engaged to that chap, he had gone off with Opal quite willingly it would appear. Why should he and she not have a little fling?

"No," said Marilyn, "Mr. Carter did not have a car until he went away from Sabbath Valley. I learned while I was in college."

"Oh, you've been to college!" the young man sat up with interest. "I thought there was something too sophisticated about you to have come out of a place like this. You had a car while you were in college I suppose."

Lynn's eyes were dancing:

"Why didn't you say 'dump' like this? That's what your tone said," she laughed, "and only a minute ago you were saying how charming it was. No, I had no car in college, I was—" But he interrupted her eagerly:

"Now, you are misunderstanding me on purpose," he declared in a hurt tone. "I think this is an ideal spot off in the hills this way, the quaintest little utopia in the world, but of course you know you haven't the air of one who had never been out of the hills, and the sweet sheltered atmosphere of this village. Tell me, when and where did you drive a car, and I'll see if I can't give you one better for a joy ride."

Lynn looked up placidly and smiled:

"In New York," she said quietly, "at the beginning of the war, and afterward in France."

Laurie Shafton sat up excitedly, the color flushing into his handsome face:

"Were you in France?" he said admiringly. "Well, I might have known. I saw there was something different about you. Red Cross, I suppose?"

"No," said Lynn, "Salvation Army. My father has been a friend of the commander's all his life. She knew that we believed in all their principles. There were only a very few outsiders, those whom they knew well, allowed to go with them. I was one."

"Well," said Laurie, eyeing her almost embarrassedly, "you girls made a great name for yourselves with your doughnuts and your pies. The only thing I had against you was that you didn't treat us officers always the way we ought to have been treated. But I suppose there were individual exceptions. I went into a hut one night and tried to get some cigarettes and they wouldn't let me have any."

"No, we didn't sell cigarettes," said Lynn with satisfaction. "That wasn't what we were there for. We had a few for the wounded and dying who were used to them and needed them of course, but we didn't sell them."

"And then I tried to get some doughnuts and coffee, but would you believe it, they wouldn't let me have any till all the fellows in line had been served. They said I had to take my turn! They were quite insulting about it! Of course they did good, but they ought to have been made to understand that they couldn't treat United States officers that way!"

"Why not? Were you any better than any of the soldiers?" she asked eyeing him calmly, and somehow he seemed to feel smaller than his normal estimate of himself.

"An *officer?*" he said with a contemptuous haughty light in his eye.

"What is an officer but the servant of his men?" asked Lynn. "Would you *want* to eat before them when they had stood hours in line waiting? They who had all the hard work and none of the honors?"

Laurie's cheeks were flushed and his eyes angry:

"That's rot!" he said rudely. "Where did you get it? The officers were picked from the cream of the land. They represent the great nation. An insult to them is an insult to the nation!"

Lynn began to smile impudently—and her eyes were dancing again.

"I beg your pardon, Mr. Shafton, you must not forget I was there. I knew both officers and men. I admit that some of the officers were princely, fit men to represent a great Christian nation, but some of them again were well—the scum of the earth, rather than the cream. Mr. Shafton, it does not make a man better than his fellows to be an officer, and it does not make him fit to be an officer just because his father is able to buy him a commission."

Laurie flushed angrily again:

"My father did not buy me a commission!" he said indignantly. "I went to a training camp and won it."

"I beg your pardon, Mr. Shafton, I meant nothing personal, but I certainly had no use for an officer who came bustling in on those long lines of weary soul-sick boys just back from the front, and perhaps off again that night, and tried to get ahead of them in line. However, let's talk of something else. Were you ever up around Dead Man's Curve? What division were you in?"

Laurie let his anger die out and answered her questions. For a few minutes they held quite an animated conversation about France and the various phases of the war. Laurie had been in air service. One could see just how handsome he must have looked in his uniform. One would know also that he would be brave and reckless. It was written all over his face and in his very attitude. He showed her his service medal.

"Mark was taken prisoner by the Germans," she said sadly as she handed it back, her eyes dreamy and faraway, then suddenly seeming to realize that she had spoken her thoughts aloud she flushed and hurried on to other experiences during the war, but she talked abstractedly, as one whose thoughts had suddenly been diverted. The young man watched her baffled:

"You seem so aloof," he said all at once watching her as she sewed away on the bit of linen. "You seem almost as if you—well—*despised* me. Excuse me if I say that it's a rather new experience. People in my world don't act that way to me, really they don't. And you don't even know who I am nor anything about me. Do you think that's quite fair?"

Lynn looked at him with suddenly arrested attention:

"I'm sorry," she said, "I didn't mean to be rude. But possibly you've come to the heart of the matter. I am not of your world. You know there's a great deal in not being able to get another's point of view. I hope I haven't done you an injustice. I haven't meant to. But you're wrong in saying I don't know who you are or anything about you. You are the son of William J. Shafton—the only son, isn't that so? Then you are the one I mean. There can't be any mistake. And I do know something about you. In fact I've been very angry at you, and wished I might meet you and tell you what I thought of you."

"You don't say!" said Laurie getting up excitedly and moving over to a chair next to hers regardless of his lame ankle. "This certainly is interesting! What the deuce have I been doing to get myself in your bad graces? I better repent at once before I hear what it is?"

"You are the one who owns the block of warehouses downtown and won't sell at any price to give the little children in all that region a place to get a bit of fresh air, the grass, and a view of the sky. You are the one who won't pull down your old buildings and try new and improved ways of housing the poor around there so that they can grow up decently clean and healthy and have a little chance in this world. Just because you can't have as many apartments and get as much money from your investment you let the little children crowd together in rooms that aren't fit for the pigs to live in, they are so dark and airless, and crowded already. Oh, I know you keep within the law! You just skin through without breaking it, but you won't help a little bit, you won't even let your property help if someone else is willing to take the bother! Oh, I've been so boiling at you ever since I heard your name that I could hardly keep my tongue still, to think of that great beautiful car out there and how much it must have cost, and to hear you speak of one of your other cars as if you had millions of them, and to think of little Carmela living down in the basement room of number eighteen in your block, growing whiter and whiter every day, with her great blue eyes and her soft fine wavy hair, and that hungry eager look in her face. And her mother, sewing, sewing, all day long at the little cellar window, and going blind because you won't put in a bigger one; sewing on coarse dark vests, putting in pockets and buttonholes for a living for her and Carmela, and you grinding her down and running around in cars like that and taking it out of little Carmela, and little Carmela's mother! Oh! How can I help feeling aloof from a person like that?"

Laurie sat up astonished watching her:

"Why, my dear girl!" he exclaimed. "Do you know what you're talking about? Do you realize that it would take a mint of money to do all the fool things that these silly reformers are always putting up to you? My lawyer looks after all those matters. Of course I know nothing about it!"

"Well, you *ought* to know," said Lynn excitedly. "Does the money belong to your lawyer? Isn't it yours to be responsible for? Well, then if you are stealing some of it out of little Carmela and a lot of other little children and their mothers and fathers oughtn't you to know? Is your lawyer going to take the responsibility about it in the kingdom of heaven I should like to know? Can he stand up in the judgment day and exempt you by saying that he had to do the best he could for your property because you required it of him? Excuse me for getting so excited, but I love little Carmela. I went to see her a great deal last winter when I was in New York taking my senior year at the university. And I can't help telling you the truth about it. I don't suppose you'll do anything about it, but at least you ought to know! And *I'm not your dear girl, either!*"

Marilyn rose suddenly from her chair, and stood facing him with blazing eyes and cheeks that were aflame. It was a revelation to the worldly wise young man that a saint so sweet could blossom suddenly into a beautiful and furious woman. It seemed unreal to find this wonderful, unique, excitable young woman with ideas in such a quiet secluded spot of the earth. Decidedly she had ideas.

"Excuse me," he said, and rose also, an almost deprecatory air upon him, "I assure you I meant nothing out of the way, Miss Severn. I certainly respect and honor you. And really, I had no idea of all this about my property. I've never paid much heed to my property except to spend the income of course. It wasn't required of me. I must look into this matter. If I find it as you think—that is if there is no mistake, I will see what I can do to remedy it. In any case we will look after little Carmela. I'll settle some money on her mother, wouldn't that be the best way? I can't think things are as bad as you say—"

"Will you really do something about it?" asked Lynn earnestly. "Will you go up to New York and see for yourself? Will you go around in *every room* of your buildings and get acquainted with those people and find out just what the conditions are?"

"Why—I—" he began uncertainly.

"Oh, I thought you couldn't stand that test! That would be too much bother—You would rather—"

"No, wait! I didn't say I wouldn't. Here! I'll go if you'll go with me and show me what you mean and what you want done. Come. I'll take you at your word. If you really want

all those things come on and show me just what to do. I'm
game. I'll do it. I'll do it whether it needs doing or not, *just
for you.* Will you take me up?"

"Of course," said Lynn quickly, "I'll go with you and
show you. I expect to be in New York next month helping at
the Salvation Home while one of their workers is away on
her vacation. I'll show you all over the district as many times
as you need to go, if it's not too hot for you to come back to
the city so early."

He looked at her sharply. There was a covert sneer in her
last words that angered him, and he was half inclined to refuse the whole thing, but somehow there was something in
this strange new type of girl that fascinated him. Now that
she had the university and the war and the world for a
background, she puzzled and fascinated him more than
ever. Half surprised at his own interest he bowed with a new
kind of dignity over his habitual light manner:

"I shall be delighted, Miss Severn. It will not be too hot
for me if it is not too hot for you. I shall be at your service,
and I hope you will discover that there is one officer who
knows how to obey."

She looked at him half surprised, half troubled and then
answered simply:

"Thank you. I'm afraid I've done you an injustice. I'm
afraid I didn't think you would be game enough to do it. I
hope I haven't been too rude. But you see I feel deeply about
it and sometimes I forget myself."

"I am sure I deserve all you have said," said Laurie as
gravely as his light nature could manage, "but there is one
thing that puzzles me deeply. I wish you would enlighten
me. All this won't do *you* any good. It isn't for *you* at all.
Why do you care?"

Marilyn brought her lovely eyes to dwell on his face for a
moment thoughtfully, a shy beautiful tenderness softening
every line of her eager young face:

"It's because—" she began diffidently. "It's because they all are God's children—and I love *Him* better than anything else in life!"

The swift color made her face lovely as she spoke, and with the words she turned away and went quickly into the house. The young man looked after her and dared not follow. He had never had a shock like that in his life. Girls had talked about everything under heaven to him at one time or another, but they had never mentioned God except profanely.

Marilyn went swiftly up to her room and knelt down by her bed, burying her hot cheeks in the cool pillow and tried to pray. She was glad, glad that she had spoken for her poor city children, glad that there was a prospect of help perhaps; but beside and beyond it all her heart was crying out for another matter that was namelessly tugging away at the very foundations of her soul. Why, oh, *why* had Mark gone away with that girl? He must have seen what she was! He must have known that it was unnecessary! He must have known how it would hurt his friends, and that the man she came to see could have gone as well as he and better. Why did he go? She would not, she could not believe anything wrong of Mark. Yet *why did he go?*

Chapter 20

Billy had no appetite for the nice supper that Aunt Saxon had ready when he came dejectedly home that night. He had passed the parsonage and seen through the dining room window that the rich guy was sitting at the supper table opposite Marilyn laughing and talking with her and his soul was sick within him. That was his doing! Nobody else but himself to blame!

Aunt Saxon had apple dumplings with plenty of "goo," black with cinnamon just the way he loved it, but he only minced at the first helping and scarcely tasted the second. He chopped a great many kindling after supper, and filled the woodbox, and thoughtfully wound the clock. Then instead of going out with his usual "I gotta beat it!" he sat languidly on the doorstep in the dusk, and when she anxiously questioned if he were sick he said crossly:

"Aw, gee! Can't ya let a fella *alone! I'm all in, can't ya see* it? I'm gonta *bed!"* and knowing he had said the most alarming thing in the whole category he slammed upstairs to his own room and flung himself across his bed.

Aunt Saxon filled with vague fears crept softly up after him, tapping at his locked door:

"Willie, what is the matter? Just tell Auntie where the pain is and I'll get you some medicine that will fix you all up by morning. I'll get you a hot water bag—!"

"DON'T WANT NO HOT WATER BAGS!" roared the sore-hearted Billy. "Can't ya lemme *alone?"*

Silence a moment while Aunt Saxon pondered tearfully and sighfully, then:

"Willie, is it the toothache?"

"NooooOH!" roared Billy.

211

A pause, then:

"Billy, you've had a fall off that wheel and hurt yer head or cut yer knee, I know, I've always thought you'd do that, that old wheel! You oughtta have a new one. But I'll bring the arnica and bathe it. And we'll paint it with iodine— where was it, Willie? Yer knee?"

Billy's shoes came to the floor with a bang:

"Aw, gee! Can't ya keep yer mouth shut an' let a fella have a little sleep. It ain't *nowhere!* It ain't *nothin'* an' I didn't have no fall an' I don't want no new bicycle. D'ye hear? I don't want nothin' 'cept just to be let alone. I wantta go ta sleep. Ain't I ben tellin' ya fer the last half hour? It ain't *sinful* fer a fella to wantta take a little sleep is it when he's been up half the night before taking care of a fella on the mountain? But if I ain't allowed, why then I'll get up an' go out somewheres. I know plenty of places where they'll lemme sleep—"

"Oh, *Wil-lee!*" sobbed Aunt Saxon. "That's all right, dear! Just you lie right down in your bed and take a good sleep. I didn't understand. Auntie didn't understand. All right, Willie. I'll keep it real still. Now you lie down, won't you? You will, won't you? You'll really lie down and sleep, won't you, Willie?"

"Didn't I say I would?" snapped Willie shamedly, and subsided on his bed again while Aunt Saxon stole painfully, noiselessly over the creak in the stair, closed the house for the night and crept tearfully to her own bed, where she lay for hours silently wiping the steady trickle of hopeless tears. Oh, Willie, Willie! And she had had such hopes!

But Billy lay staring wide-eyed at the open square of his window that showed the little village nestling among the trees dotted here and there with friendly winking lights, the great looming mountains in the distance, and Stark Mountain, farthest and blackest of them all. He shut his eyes and tried to blot it out, but it seeed to loom through his very eyelids and mock him. He seemed to see Mark, his idol, carried between those other three dark figures into the blackness of that haunted house. He seemed to see him lying helpless, bound, on the musty bed in the deserted room, Mark, his beloved Mark. Mark, who had carried him on his shoulder as a tiny child, who had ridden him on his back, and taught him to swim and pitch ball and box. Mark, who let him go where even the big boys were not allowed to accompany him, and who never told on him or treated him mean nor went back on him in any way! Mark! *He* had been the means of putting Mark in that helpless position, while circumstances which he was now quite sure the devil had been specially preparing, wove a tangled maze about the young man's feet from which there seemed no way of extrication.

Billy shut his eyes and tried to sleep but sleep would not come. He began to doubt if he would ever sleep again. He lay listening to the evening noises of the village. He heard Jim Rafferty's voice going by to the night shift, and Tom McMertrie. They were laughing softly and once he thought he heard the name "Old Haircut." The Tully baby across the street had colic and cried like murder. Murder! *Murder!* Now why did he have to think of *that* word of all words? Murder? Well, it was crying like it wanted to murder somebody. He wished he was a baby himself so he could cry. He'd cry harder'n that. Little's dog was barking again. He'd been barking all day long. It was probably at that strange guy at the parsonage. Little's dog never did like strangers. That creak was Barneses' gate with the iron weight hitched on the chain to make it shut, and somebody laughed away up the street! There went the clock, nine o'clock! Gee! Was *that* all? He thought it must be about three in the morning! And then he must have dozed off for a little, for when he woke with a start it was very still and dark, as if the moon had gone away, had been and gone again, and he heard a cautious little mouse gnawing at the baseboard in his room, gnawing and stopping and gnawing again, then whisking over the lath like fingers running a scale on the piano. He had watched Miss Lynn do it once on the organ.

He opened his eyes and looked hard at the window. The dim outline of Stark Mountain off in the distance began to grow into form, and what was that? A speck of light? It must be his eyes. He rubbed them sleepily and looked again. Yes, a light. Alert at once with the alertness that comes to all boys at the sound of a fire bell or some such alarm, he slid from his bed noiselessly and stole to the window. It was gone! Ah, gee! He had been asleep and dreamed it. No, there it was again, or was it?

Blackness all before his eyes, with a luminous sky dimly about the irregular mountaintop fringed with trees. This was foolish. He felt chilly and crept back to bed, but could not keep his eyes from the dark spot against the sky. He tried to close the lids and go to sleep, but they insisted on flying open and watching. And then came what he had been watching for. Three winks, and stop, three winks, stop, and one long flash. Then all was dark. And though he watched till the church clock struck three he saw no more.

But the old torment came back. Mark and Cherry and Lynn. The guy at the parsonage and the girl with the floured face and baseball bats in her ears! Aw, gee! He must have a fever! It was hours since the clock had struck three. It must be nearly four, and then it would soon be light and he could get up. There seemed to be a light somewhere down the street through the trees. Not the street lamp either. Somebody sick likely. Hark! What was that? He wished he hadn't undressed. He sat up in bed and listened. The purr of a car! Someone was stealing Mark's car! Mark was away and everybody knew it. Nobody in Sabbath Valley would steal, except, perhaps over at the plush mill. There were new people there—Was that Mark's car? *Some car!*

With a motion like a cat he sprang into the necessary garment which nestled limply on the floor by the bed, and was at the window in a trice. A drop like a cat to the shed roof,

down the rain waterspout to the ground, a stealthy step to
the back shed where old trusty leaned, and he was away
down the road a speck in the dark, and just in time to see the
dim black vision of a car speeding with muffled engine down
the road toward the church. It was too dark to say it was
Mark's car. He had no way but to follow.

Panting and puffing, pedaling with all his might, straining
his eyes to see through the dark the car that was flying along
without lights, his hair sticking endwise, his sleepy hungry
face peering wanly through the dark, he plodded after. Over
the highway! He slowed down and wasn't quite sure till he
heard the chug of the engine ahead, and a few seconds later
a red light bloomed out behind and he drew a new breath
and pedaled on again, his heart throbbing wildly, the collar
of his pajamas sticking up wildly like his hair, and one pajama leg showing whitely below his trouser like a tattered
banner. The pedals cut his bare feet, and he shivered though
he was drenched with perspiration, but he leaned far over
his handlebars and pedaled on.

Down past the Blue Duck Tavern, and on into the village
of Economy the car went, not rapidly now as though it were
running away, but slower, and steadier like a car on legitimate business and gravely with a necessary object in view.
Billy's heart began to quake. Not for nothing had he learned
to read by signs and actions at the feet of the master Mark.
An inner well-developed sense began to tell him the truth.

The car stopped in front of the chief's house, and a horn
sounded softly once. Billy dismounted hastily and vanished
into the shadows. A light appeared in the upper window of
the house and all was still. Presently the light upstairs went
out, the front door opened showing a dimmer light farther
in, and showing the outline of the chief in flannel shirt and
trousers. He came down the walk and spoke with the man in
the car, and the car started again and turned in at the chief's
driveway, going back to the garage.

Billy left his wheel against a hedge and hiked noiselessly

after, slinking behind the garage door till the driver came out. *It was Mark!*

He went down the drive, met the chief at the gate and they went silently down the dark street, their rubber heels making no noise on the pavement. Economy was asleep and no wiser, but Billy's heart was breaking. He watched the two and followed afar till they turned down the side street which he feared. He stole after and saw them enter the brick building that harbored the county jail. He waited with shaking limbs and bleeding heart, waited, hoping, fearing, dreading, but not for long. The chief came out alone! It was as he had feared.

Then as if the very devil himself pursued him, Billy turned and fled, retrieving his bicycle and whirled away noiselessly down the road, caring not where he was going, ready to hang himself, wild with despair and self-condemnation.

The dark lay over the valley like a velvet mantle black and soft with white wreaths of mist like a lady's veil flung aside and blown to the breeze, but Billy saw naught but red winking lights and a jail, grim and red in the midnight, and his friend's white face passing in beneath the arched door. The bang of that door as it shut was echoing in his soul.

He passed the Fenner cottage. There were lights and moving about, but he paid no heed. He passed the Blue Duck Tavern, and saw the light in the kitchen where the cook was beginning the day's work just as the rest of the house had been given over to sleep. There was the smell of bacon on the air. Someone was going away on the milk train likely. He thought it out dully as he passed with the sick reeling motion of a rider whose life has suddenly grown worthless to him. Over bottles and nails, and bumping over humps old trusty carried him, down the hill to Sabbath Valley, past the graveyard where the old stones peered eerily up from the dark mounds like wakened curious sleepers, past the church in the gray of the morning with a pinkness in the sky behind. Lynn lying in a sleepless bed listening to every sound for Mark's car to return, and recognizing Billy's back wheel squeak. On down the familiar street, glad of the thick maples to hide him, hunching up the pajama leg that would wave below in the rapidly increasing light, not looking toward the Carters', plodding on, old trusty on the back porch; shinning up the waterspout, tiptoeing over the shed roof, a quick spring in his own window and he was safe on his bed again staring at the red morning light shining weirdly, cheerily on his wall and the rooster crowing lustily below his window. Drat that rooster! What did it want to make that noise for? Wasn't there a rooster in that Bible story? Oh, no, that was Peter perhaps. He turned hastily from the subject and gave his attention to his toilet. Aunt Saxon was squeaking past his door, stopping to listen:

"Willie?"

"Well." In a low growl, not encouragingly.

"Oh, Willie, you up? You better?"

"Nothin' the matter with me."

"Oh—"

"Breakfast ready?"

"Oh, yes, Willie! I'm so glad you're feeling better." She squeaked on down the stairs sniffing as if from recent tears! Doggone those tears! Those everlasting tears! Why didn't a woman know! Now, what did he have to do next? Do! Yes, he must do something. He couldn't just sit here, could he? What about Stark Mountain and the winking light? What about that sissy guy making up to Miss Lynn? If only Mark were here now he would tell him everything. Yes, he would. Mark would understand. But Mark was in that unspeakable place! Would Mark find a way to get out? He felt convinced he could, but *would* he? From the set of his shoulders Billy had a strong conviction that Mark would not. Mark seemed to be going there for a purpose. Would the purpose be complete during the day sometime and would Mark return? Billy must do something before night. He wished it might be to smash the face of that guy Shafton. Assuredly he must do something. But first he must eat his breakfast. He didn't want to, but he had to. Aunt Saxon would raise a riot if he didn't. Well, there was ham. He could smell it. Ham for breakfast. Aw, gee! Saxy was getting extravagant. Somehow pretty soon if he didn't hang himself he must find a way to brighten up Saxy and pay her back for all those pink tears.

And over on Stark Mountain as the morning dawned a heavy foot climbed the haunted stairs and a bloodshot eye framed itself at the little half-moon in the front window that looked out over Lone Valley toward Economy, and down over Sabbath Valley toward Monopoly commanding a strategic position in the whole wild lovely region.

Down in the cellar where the rats had hitherto held sway a soft chip, chip, chipping sound went steadily forward hour by hour, with spaces between and chip, chip, chipping again, a new kind of rat burrowing into the earth, over close to the edge of the long deserted scanty coal pile. While up under the dusty beams in a dark corner various old parcels were stowed away awaiting a later burial. From the peephole where the eye commanded the situation a small black speck went whirling along the road to Monopoly which might be a boy on a bicycle, but no one came toward Stark Mountain on that bright sunny morning to disturb the quiet worker in the dark cellar.

Billy was on his way to Monopoly, his aunt appeased for the time being, with the distinct purpose of buying the morning paper. Not that he was given to literature, or perused the daily news as a habit, but an idea had struck him. There might be a way of finding out about Mark without letting anyone know how he was finding out. It might be in the paper. Down at Monopoly no one would notice if he bought a county paper, and he could stop in the woods and read it.

But when he reached the newsstand he saw a pile of New

York papers lying right in front, and the great black headlines caught his eye:

FATE OF LAURENCE SHAFTON
STILL UNKNOWN

Son of multimillionaire of New York City who was kidnapped on Saturday night on his way from New York to a
weekend house party at Beechwood, N.J., not yet heard
from. No clew to his whereabouts. Detectives out with
bloodhounds searching country. Mother in a state of collapse. It is feared the bandits have fulfilled their threats and
killed him. Father frantically offering any reward for news
of son!

Billy read no further. He clapped down a nickel and
stuffed the paper indifferently into his pocket, almost forgetting in his disgust to purchase the county news. "Aw,
gee!" he said to himself. "More o' that Judas stuff. I gotta get
rid o' them thirty pieces!"

He stepped back and bought a county paper, stood idly
looking over its pages a moment with the letters swimming
before his eyes, at last discovering the column where the
Economy "murder" was discussed, and without reading it
stuffed it in the pocket on the other side and rode away into
the sunlight. Murder! It was called murder! Then Dolph
must be dead! The plot thickened! Dead! Murder! Who
killed him? Surely he wasn't responsible for that at least! He
was out on the road with Mark when it happened. *He* hadn't
done anything which in the remotest way had to do with the
killing, he thanked his lucky stars for that. And Mark. But
who did it? Cherry? She might be a reason for what Mark
did last night.

At a turn in the road where a little grove began he got off
his wheel and seeking a sheltered spot dropped down under
a tree to read his papers. His quick eye searched through the
county paper first for the sensational account of the murder,

and a gray look settled over his pug countenance as he read. So might a mother have regarded her child in deep trouble, or a lover his beloved. Billy's spirit was bowed to the depths. When he had devoured every word he flung the paper aside wrathfully, and sat up with a kind of hopeless gesture of his hard young hands. "Aw, gee!" he said aloud, and suddenly he felt a great wet blob rolling down his freckled cheek. He smashed it across into his hair with a quick slash of his dirty hand as if it had been a mosquito annoying him, and lest the other eye might be meditating a like trick he gave that a vicious dab and hauled out the other paper, more as a matter of form than because he had a deep interest in it. All through the description of those wonderful Shafton jewels, and the mystery that surrounded the disappearance of the popular young man, Billy could see the word murder dancing like little black devils in and out among the letters. The paragraph about Mrs. Shafton's collapse held him briefly:

"Aw, gee!" he could see pink tears everywhere. He supposed he ought to do something about that. For all the world like Aunt Saxon! He seemed to sense her youth through the printed words as he had once sensed Mrs. Carter's. He saw her back in school, pretty and little. Rich women were always pretty and little to his mind, pretty and little and helpless and always crying. It was then that the thought was born that made him look off to the hills and ponder with drawn brows and anxious mien. He took it back to his home with him and sat moodily staring at the lilac bushes, and gave Aunt Saxon another bad day wondering what had come to Willie. She would actually have been glad to hear him say: "I gotta beat it! I gotta date with tha fellas!"

That evening the rumor crept back to Sabbath Valley from who knows where that Dolph was dead and Mark Carter had run away!

Chapter 21

Tuesday morning Lynn slipped down to Carter's with a little cake she had made all white frosting and sprinkles of nuts. Her face was white but brave with a smile, and she said her mother wanted to know how Mrs. Carter's neuralgia was getting on.

But Mrs. Carter was the only one in the village perhaps who had not heard the rumor, and she was gracious and pleased and said she wished Mark was home, he loved nut cake so much.

"You knew he was called back to New York suddenly last night didn't you?" she said. "He felt real sorry to leave so soon, but his partner wired him there was something he must see to himself, and he just took his car and went right away as soon as he got back from taking that girl home. He hoped he'd get back again soon though. Say, who was that girl? Wasn't she kind of nervy to ask Mark to take her home? Seems somehow girls are getting a little forward these days. I know you'd never do a thing like that with a perfect stranger, Marilyn."

The girl only stayed a few minutes, and went home with a braver heart. At least Mark was protecting his mother. He had not changed entirely. He wouldn't let her suffer! But what was he doing? Oughtn't he to be told what rumors were going around about him? But how could it be done? Her father? Perhaps. She shrank from that, Mark had so withdrawn from them, he might take it as an interference. Billy? Ah, yes, Billy!

But Billy did not appear anywhere, and when she got back she found that Shafton's car had been finished and was ready to drive, and he wanted her to take a little spin with

221

him to try it, he said. He warily invited her mother to go
along, for he saw by her face that she was going to decline,
and the mother watching her daughter's white face said:
"Yes, Marilyn, we will go. It will do you good. You have
been housed up here ever since you came home." And there
was nothing for the girl to do but succumb or seem exceedingly rude. She was not by nature rude, so she went.

As they drove by the Saxon cottage Billy was just coming
out, and he stared glumly at the three and hardly ackowl-
edged Marilyn's greeting. He stared after them scowling.

"Hell!" said Billy aloud, regardless of Aunt Saxon at the
front window. "Yes! *Hell!*" and he realized the meaning of
his epithet far better than the young man he was staring
after had the first night he had used it in Sabbath Valley.

"What was that you said, Willie?" called Aunt Saxon's
anxious voice.

"Aw, nothing!" said Billy, and slammed out the gate, his
wheel by his side. *Now!* Something had to be done. He
couldn't have *that* going on. He was hurt at Mrs. Severn. She
ought to take better care of her daughter! In sullen despair
he mounted and rode away to work out his problem. It was
certain he couldn't do anything with Saxy sniveling round.
And *something had to be done!*

Billy managed to get around the country quite a little that
morning. He rode up to Economy and learned that Mr.
Fenner, the tailor, was sick, had been taken two nights ago,
was delirious and had to have two men to hold him down.
He thought everybody was an enemy and tried to choke
them all. He rode past the jail but saw nothing though he
circled the block three times. The chief stood out in front
talking with three strange men. Billy sized them up for detectives. When there was nothing further to be gained in
Economy he turned his steed toward Pleasant Valley and
took in a little underground telephone communication between a very badly scared Pat and a very angry Sam at some
unknown point at the end of the wire. It was then, lying

hidden in the thick undergrowth, that a possible solution of his difficulties occurred to him, a form of noble self-sacrifice that might in part do penance for his guilt. Folded safely in his inner pocket was the thirty pieces of silver, the blood money, the price of Mark Carter's freedom and good name. If he had not taken that he might have fixed this Pat so he would be a witness to Mark's alibi. But according to the code he had been taught it would not be honorable to squeal on somebody whose money he had taken. It wasn't square. It wasn't honorable. It was yella, and yella he would not be if the sky fell. It was all the religion he had as yet, not to be yella. It stood for all the fineness of his soul. But he had reasoned within himself that if in some way he could get that money back to Pat, then he would be free from obligation. Then he could somehow manage to put Pat where he would have to tell the right thing to save Mark. Just how it could be done he wasn't sure, but that was another question.

When Pat had trundled away to the train he rolled himself out from ambush and went on his way across Lone Valley by a little tree-shaded path he knew that cut straight over to Stark Mountain.

Not a ripple of a leaf showed above him as he passed straight up the mountain to the old house, for the watchful eye looking out to see. Billy was a great deal like an Indian in his goings and comings, and Billy was wary. Had he not seen the winking light? Billy was taking no chances. Smoothly folded in his hip pocket he carried a leaf of the New York paper wherein was offered a large reward for information concerning jewels and bonds and other property taken from the Shafton country home on pretense of setting free the son. Also there was a stupendous reward offered for information concerning the son, and Billy's big thought as he crept along under the trees with all the stealth of a wild thing, was that here was another thirty pieces of silver multiplied many times, and *he wasn't going to take it!* He *could,* but he *wouldn't!* He was going to give these folks the information they wanted, but he wasn't going to get the benefit of it. That was going to be his punishment. He had been in hell long enough, and he was going to try to pull himself out of it by his good works. And he would do it in such a way that there wouldn't be any chance of the reward being pressed upon him. He would just fix it so that nobody would particularly know he had anything to do with the clews. That was Billy all over. He never did a thing halfway. But first he must find out if there was anybody about the old house. He couldn't get away from those three winks he had seen.

So, feeling almost relieved for a moment, Billy left his wheel on guard and crept around to his usual approach at the back before he came out in the open. And then he crept cautiously to the cellar window where he had first entered the house. He gripped Pat's old gun with one hand in his pocket, and slid along like a young snake, taking precaution not to appear before the cellar window lest his shadow should fall inside. He flattened himself at last upon the grass a noticeless heap of gray khaki trousers and brown flannel shirt close against the house. One would have to lean far out of a window to see him, and there he lay and listened a while. And presently from the depths beyond that grated window he heard a little scratch, scratch, scratch, tap, tap, tap, scratch, tap, scratch, tap, steadily, on for sometime like his heartbeats, till he wasn't sure he was hearing it at all, and thought it might be the blood pounding through his ears, so strange and uncanny it seemed. Then, all at once there came a puff, as if a long breath had been drawn, like one lifting a heavy weight and then a dull thud. A brief silence and more scratching in soft earth now.

He listened for perhaps an hour, and once a footstep grated on the cement floor, and coals rattled down as if they were disturbed. Once too a soft chirrup from up above like the call of a wood bird, only strangely human and the sounds in the cellar ceased altogether, till another weird note sounded and they began again.

When he was satisfied with his investigations he began slowly to back away from his position, lifting each atom of muscle slowly one at a time till his going must have been something like the motion picture of a bud unfolding, and yet as silent as the flower grows he faded away from that cellar window back into the green and no one was the wiser. An hour later the watchful eye at the little half-moon opening in the shutter might have seen a little black speck like a spider whizzing along on the highroad and turning down toward Sabbath Valley, but it never would have looked as if it came from Stark Mountain, for it was headed straight from Lone Valley. Billy was going home to get cleaned up and make a visit to the parsonage. If that guy was still there he'd see how quick he would leave! If there wasn't one way to make him go there was another, and Billy felt that he held the trick.

But as fate would have it Billy did not have to get cleaned up, for Miss Severn stood on the front porch looking off toward the mountains with that wistful expression of hers that made him want to laugh and cry and run errands for her anywhere just to serve her and make her smile, and she waved her hand at Billy, and ran down to the gate to speak to him.

"Billy, I want to ask you—If you were to see Mark Carter—of course you mightn't, but then you might—you'll let him know that we are of course his friends, and that anything he wants done, if he'll just let us know—"

"Sure!" said Billy lighting off his wheel with a downward glance at his dirty self, all leaves and dust and grime. "Sure, he'd know that anyhow."

"Well, Billy, I know he would, but I mean, I thought perhaps you might find something we *could do,* something maybe without letting him know. He's very proud about asking any help, you know, and he wouldn't want to bother us. You may discover something he—needs—or wants done—while—he is away—and maybe we could help him out, Father or Mother or I. You'll remember, won't you, Billy?"

"Sure!" said Billy again feeling the warm glow of her friendliness and loyalty to Mark, and digging his toes into the turf embarrassedly. Then he looked up casually as he was about to leave:

"Say is there a guy here named Shafton? Man from n'Yark?"

"Why, yes," said Lynn looking at him curiously. "Did you want to see him?"

"Well, if he's round I might. I got a message for him."

She looked at him keenly:

"You haven't *seen* Mark today, have you, Billy?"

"Aw, naw, 'taint from him," he grinned reassuringly. "He's away just now. But I might see him soon, ya know, ur hear from him."

Lynn's face cleared. "Yes, of course. His mother told me he was suddenly called back to New York."

"Yep. That's right!" said Billy as if he knew all about it, and pulled off his old cap with a glorious wave as she turned to call the stranger.

Billy dropped his wheel at the curb and approached the steps as he saw Shafton coming slowly out leaning on a cane. He rustled the folded newspaper out from his pocket with one hand and shook it open as only a boy's sleight of hand can do, wafting it in front of the astonished Laurie, and saying with an impudent swag:

"Say, z'your name Shafton? Well, *see that?* Why don't you beat it home? Your ma is about t'croke, an' yer dad has put up about all his dough, an' you better rustle back to where you come from an' tell 'em not to b'leeve all the bunk that's handed out to 'em! Good night! They must need a nurse!"

Laurie paused in the act of lighting one of his interminable cigarettes with which he supplied the lack of a stronger stimulant, and stared at the boy curiously, then stared at the paper he held in his hand with the flaring headlines, and reaching out his hand for it began to laugh:

"Well, upon my word, kid, where'd you get this? If that isn't a joke! I wonder if Opal's seen it. Miss Severn, come here! See what a joke! I'm kidnapped! Did you ever hear the like? Look at the flowery sentences. It's almost like reading one's own obituary, isn't it?"

Marilyn, glancing over his shoulder at the headlines, took in the import of it instantly. "I should think you'd want to telephone your mother at once. How she must have suffered!" she said.

Laurie somewhat sobered agreed that it would be a good idea:

"The mater's a good old scout," he said lightly. "She's always helping me out of scrapes, but this is one too many to give up her emeralds, the Shafton emeralds! Gosh but Dad will be mad about them! And, oh, say, call that boy back will you? I want to give him a dollar!"

But Billy had faded down the road with mortal indignation in his breast. To think of giving up a ten-thousand-dollar reward and having a dollar flung at you! It seemed to measure the very depth of the shame to which he had descended.

The Severns came a few paces out of their indifference to this self-imposed guest and gathered around the sheet of newspaper while Laurie held an intensive conversation with his family beginning with several servants who were too excited at first to identify his voice.

But at last he hung up the receiver and turned toward them:

"Well, I guess there's nothing for it but for me to pull out. The mater doesn't think she'll be satisfied till she has her hands on me. Besides, I've got to get things started about those jewels. Dad and Mother are too excited to know what they're about. I declare, it's like being dead and seeing how they feel about it."

There was a boyish eager look about the young man's face that made him for the first time seem rather lovable, Mrs. Severn thought. The mother in her rose to appreciation. Lynn was so glad that he was going away that she was almost friendly during lunch. And when the young man was about to depart he went to Mr. Severn's study and wrote a check for five hundred dollars:

"Just in appreciation of your kindness," he said as he held it out to the minister.

The minister looked amused but did not offer to take it:

"That's all right," he said pleasantly, "we don't keep boarders you know. You were welcome to what we could give you."

"But, my dear sir, I couldn't think of not remunerating you," declared Laurie.

"And I couldn't think of taking it," smiled the minister.

"Well, then take it for your poor people," he insisted.

"From what Lynn tells me you have more of those than we have," answered the minister.

The young man looked annoyed:

"Well, then take it for something for your church, another bell or something, anything you're interested in."

"I can give you an address of a young missionary out West who is having a hard time of it, and has a very needy parish," said the minister taking out his fountain pen and writing the address on a card, "but I should prefer that you would send it to him yourself. He wouldn't take it from me, but if you'd send it he'll write and tell you what he does with it, and he'll tell me too, so it will give pleasure all around. He's a game young chap, and he's given his life. You couldn't help but like him."

Laurie had to be content with this, though he felt annoyed at having to write a letter to a missionary. He felt he shouldn't know how to address him.

"I'll send it tonight when I get home," he declared, "or no,

I'll send it now," and he sat down at the minister's desk, and scribbled a note. It read: "Your friend Severn won't take anything himself for kindness to me, so he's letting me send you this for your work. Here's wishing you good luck." This he signed and handed to the minister with a relieved air as if to say: "There! That's that!"

"You see," said Laurie getting up and taking his hat again, "I want to come back here again and see your daughter. I may as well tell you I'm crazy about your daughter."

"I see," said the minister gravely, albeit with a twinkle in his eye. "The fact is I'm somewhat crazy about her myself. But in all kindness I may as well tell you that you'll be wasting your time. She isn't your kind, you know."

"Oh, well," said Laurie with an assured shrug, "that's all right if I don't mind, isn't it?"

"Well, no," said the minister smiling broadly now, "you forget that she might mind, you know."

"I don't get you," said Laurie looking puzzled as he fitted on his immaculate driving glove. "She might mind, what do you mean?"

"I mean that my daughter minds very much indeed whether her men friends ask in a certain tone of voice for something to *drink* at midnight, and use language such as you used when you first arrived here, smoke continual cigarettes, and have friends like the young woman who visited you last Sunday."

"Oh, I see!" laughed Laurie thoroughly amused. "Well, after all, one doesn't have to keep on doing all those things, you know—if it were worth one's while to change them."

"I'm afraid," said the minister still amused, "that it would have to be worth your while to change before she would even consider you as a possibility. She happens to have a few ideas about what it takes to make a man, her ideal man, you know."

Laurie smiled gaily:

"Perhaps I can change those ideas."

"Help yourself, young man. You'll find it a task, I assure you."

"Well, I'm coming back anyway."

"We shall welcome you," said the minister politely, but not at all gladly, and Laurie departed without his usual complacency, assuring the minister that he had found Sabbath Valley the garden spot of the world and meant to return soon and often.

Billy watched him from the graveyard enclosure whither he had retired to write a letter, and he made a face and wasted a gesture of defiance after his departing car. So much Billy felt he had accomplished toward reparation. He was now attempting a third act.

On the smooth end of the old stone he had a newspaper spread, and upon that a sheet of letter paper which he had extracted from Aunt Saxon's ancient box in the old secretary in the corner of the kitchen. Kneeling beside the stone he carefully inscribed the following words:

Yoors to cummand,
 B. Gaston.

He folded the paper with his smudgy fingers, and stuffed it into a soiled envelope on which he wrote Mark's name, and as he had seen Lynn write down in the corner of a note that he had taken to Monopoly for her, "Kindness of Billy," so he wrote "Kindnus of Cheef." Then he mounted his wheel and rode to Economy. After some apparently aimless riding he brought up at the back of the chief's garage where he applied a canny eye to a crack and ascertained just how many and what cars were inside. He then rode straight to the bank where he was pretty sure the chief would be standing near the steps at this hour. Waiting a time of leisure he handed him the envelope:

"Say, Chief, c'n I trouble you to d'liver that?"

The chief looked at the envelope and then at Billy and opened his lips to speak, but Billy forestalled him:

"I know you don't know where he is at all now, Chief, o'course, but I just thought you might happen to meet up with him sometime soon. That's all right, Chief. Thank ya." Billy ended with a knowing wink.

The chief turned the envelope over, noted that it was unsealed, grinned back and put it in his pocket. They had been good friends, these two, for several years, ever since Billy had been caught bearing the penalty for another boy's misdemeanor.

"That's all right, Billy," said the chief affably, "I won't forget it—if I see him! Seen anything more of those automobile thieves?"

"Nope," said Billy sadly, "but I gotta line on 'em. 'f'I find anythin' more I'll callyaup!"

"Do!" said the chief cordially, and the interview was closed.

Billy bought some cakes at the bakery with ten cents he had earned running an errand from the grocery that morning, and departed on important business. He had definitely decided to give up his thirty pieces of silver. No more blood money for him. His world was upside down and all he loved were suffering, and all because he had been mercenary. The only way to put things right was to get rid of any gain that might accrue to himself. Then he would be in a position to do something. And Pat was his first object now. He meant to give back the money to Pat! He had thought it all out, and he meant to waste no time in getting things straight.

He went to the Economy Post Office and on the back of a circular that he found in the wastebasket he wrote another note:

Pat. This is blood money an' I can't kep it. I didunt no when I undertuk the job wot kind of a job it was. Thers only one way fur yoo to kep yur hid saf, an that is to tel the trooth abot wot hapuned. If yoo ar wiling to tel the trooth put a leter heer sayin so. If yoo dont I am havin' you watshed an you will los yoor job an likely be hanged. We are arumd so be keerful. Ths ain't yella. This is rite.

THE KID.

It was a long job and he was tired when it was finished, for his days at school had been full of so many other things besides lessons that literary efforts were always strenuous for him. When he had finished he went out and carried three parcels for the meat market, receiving in return thirty cents, which exactly made up the sum he had spent from his tainted money. With this wrapped bunglingly in his note he proceeded to ambush near Pleasant Valley. He had other fish to fry, but not till dark. Meantime, if that underground telephone was being used at other times in the day he wanted to know it.

He placed the note and money obviously before the little hidden telephone from which he had cleared the leaves and rubbish that hid it, and then retired to cover where he settled himself comfortably. He knew Pat would be busy till the two evening trains had arrived, after that if he did not come there would likely be no calls before morning again, and he could go on his way. With a pleasant snack of sugar cookies and cream puffs he lay back and closed his eyes, glad of this brief respite from his life of care and perplexity. Of course he couldn't get away from his thoughts, but what a pleasant place this was, with the scent of sassafras and wintergreen all around him, and the meadowlark high in the air somewhere. There were bees in the wild honeysuckle not far away. He could hear their lazy drone. It would be nice to be a bee and fly, fly away from everything. Did bees care about things? Did they have troubles, and love folks and lose 'em? When a bee died did the other bees care? Aw, gee! Mark in—j—*No!* He wouldn't say it! Mark was in New York! Yes, of course he was. It would all come right someday. He would catch those crooks and put 'em in jail—no, first he'd use 'em to clear Mark. When he got done here he was going up to watch the old house and find out about that noise, and he'd see whether Link and Shorty, would put anything more over! Link and Shorty and Pat, and that sissy Shafton and Sam, whoever Sam was! They were all his enemies! If Mark were only here how they would go to that old haunted house together and work this thing out. He ought to have told Mark everything. Fool! Just to save his own hide! Just to keep Mark from blaming him! Well, he was done saving himself or getting ill-gotten gains. Him for honesty for the rest of his life.

The bees droned on and the lark grew fainter and fainter. Billy's eyes drooped closer shut, his long curling lashes lay on his freckled cheeks the way they lay sometimes when Aunt Saxon came to watch him. That adorable sweep of lash that all mothers of boys know, that air of dignity and innocence that makes you forget the day and its doings and undoings and think only, this is a man child, a wonderful creature of God, beloved and strong, a gift of heaven, a wonder in daytime, a creature to be afraid of sometimes, but weak in sleep, *adorable!*

Billy slept.

The afternoon train lumbered in with two freight cars behind, and a lot of crates and boxes to manipulate, but Billy slept. The five o'clock train slid in and the evening express with its toll of guests for the lake hotel who hustled off wearily, cheerily, and on to the little lake train that stood with an expectant insolent air like a necessary evil waiting for a tip. The two trains champed and puffed and finally scampered away, leaving echoes all along the valley, and a red stream of sun down the track behind them from a sky aflame in the west preparing for a brilliant sunset. The red fingers of the sun touched the freckles on Billy's cheek lightly as if to warn him that the time had come. The shutters slammed on at the little station. The agent climbed the hill to his shack among the pines. Pat came out the door and stood on the platform looking down the valley, waiting for the agent to get out of sight.

And Billy slept on!

Chapter 22

Three days later a pall hung over Sabbath Valley. The coroner's inquest had brought in a verdict of murder, and the day of the hearing had been set. Mark Carter was to be tried for murder—was *wanted* for murder as Elder Harricutt put it. It was out now and everybody knew it but Mrs. Carter, who went serenely on her way getting her regular letters from Mark postmarked New York and telling of little happenings that were vague but pleasant and sounded so like Mark, so comforting and sonlike. So strangely tender and comforting and more in detail than Mark's letters had been wont to be. She thought to herself that he was growing up at last. He spoke of a time when he and she would have a nice home together somewhere, some new place where he would get into business and make a lot of money. Would she like that? And once he told her he was afraid he hadn't been a very good son to her, but sometime he would try to make it up to her, and she cried over that letter for sheer joy. But all the rest of the town knew that Mark was supected of murder, and most of them thought he had run away and nobody could find him. The county papers hinted that there were to be strange revelations when the time of the trial came, but nothing definite seemed to come out from day to day more than had been said at first, and there was a strange lack of any mention of Mark in connection with it after the first day.

Lynn Severn went about the house quiet and white, her face looking like an angel's prayer, one continual petition, but she was sweet and patient, and ready to do anything for anybody. Work seemed to be her only respite from the gnawing horror of her thoughts. To know that the whole village believed that Mark, her lifelong playmate, had been guilty of a crime so heinous was so appalling that sometimes she just stood at the window and laughed out into the sunshine at the crazy idea of it. It simply could not be. Mark, who had always been so gentle and tender for every living thing, so chivalrous, so ready to help! To think of Mark killing anyone! And yet, they might have needed killing. At least, of course she didn't mean that, but there were circumstances under which she could imagine almost anyone doing a deed—well what was the use, there was no way to excuse or explain a thing she didn't understand, and she could just do nothing but not believe any of it until she knew. She would trust in God, and yes, she would trust in Mark as she always had done, at least until she had his own word that he was not trustable. That haughty withdrawing of himself on Sunday night and his "I am not worthy" meant nothing to her now when it came trailing across her consciousness. It only seemed one more proof of his tender conscience, his care for her reputation. He had known then what they were saying about him, he must have known the day before that there was something that put him in a position so that he felt it was not good for her reputation to be his friend. He had withdrawn to protect her. That was the way she explained it to her heart, while yet beneath it all was the deep down hurt that he had not trusted her, and let her be his friend in trouble as well as when all was well.

She had written him a little note, not too intimate, just as a sister might have written, expressing her deep trust, and her sincere desire to stand by and help in any time of need. In it she begged him to think her worthy of sharing his trouble as she used to share his happiness, and to know always that she was his friend whatever came. She had read it over and over to be sure she was not overstepping her womanly right to say these things, and had prayed about it a great deal. But when it came to sending it she did not know his New York address. He had been strangely silent during the last few months and had not written her. She did not want to ask his mother. So she planned to find it out through Billy. But Billy did not come. It had been two days since Billy had been around, or was it three? She was standing at the window looking down the road toward the Saxon cottage and wondered if she wanted to go down and hunt for Billy when she saw Miss Saxon coming up the street and turning in at the gate, and her face looked wan and crumpled like an old rose that had been crushed and left on the parlor floor all night.

She turned from the window and hurried down:

"Miss Marilyn," Aunt Saxon greeted her with a gush of tears, "I don't know what to do. Billy's away! He hasn't been home for three days and three nights! His bed ain't been touched. He never did that before except that last time when he stayed out to help Mark Carter that time on the mountain with that sick man, and I can't think what's the matter. I went to Miz Carter's, but she ain't seen him, and she says Mark's up to his business in New York, so Billy can't be with him, and I just know he's kilt, Miss Marilyn. I just know he's kilt. I dreamt of a shroud night before last and I can't help thinkin' he's *kilt!*" and the tears poured down the tired little face pitifully.

Marilyn drew her tenderly into the house and made her sit down by the cool window, brought a palm leaf fan and a footstool, and told Naomi to make some iced orangeade. Then she called her mother and went and sat down by the poor little creature who now that somebody else was going to do something about it had subsided into her chair with relief born of exhaustion. She had not slept for three nights and two of those days she had washed all day.

"Now, Miss Saxon, dear, you're not to worry," said the girl taking the fan, and waving it gently back and forth, touching the work-worn hand tenderly with her other hand. "Billy is not dead, I'm sure! Oh, I'm quite sure! I think somehow it would be hard to kill Billy. He has ways of keeping alive that most of us don't enjoy. He is strong and young and sharp as a needle. No one can put anything over on Billy, and I have somehow a feeling, Miss Saxon, that Billy is off somewhere doing something very important for somebody. He is that way, you know. He does nice unusual things that nobody else would think of doing, and I just expect you'll find out someday that Billy has been doing one of those. There's that man on the mountain, for instance. He might be still very sick, and it would be just like Billy to stay and see to him. Maybe there isn't anybody else around to do it, and now that Mark has gone he would feel responsible about it. Of course he ought to have told you before he went, but he wouldn't likely have expected to stay long, and then boys don't think. They don't realize how hard it is not to understand!"

"Thas'so, Miss Marilyn," sniffed Miss Saxon. "He don't hardly ever think. But he mighta phomed."

"Well, it isn't likely they have phones on the mountain, and you haven't any, have you? How could he?"

"He mighta phomed to you."

"Yes, he might, but you know how boys are, he wouldn't want to bother anybody. And if the man was in a lonely cabin somewhere he couldn't get to a phone."

"Thas'so too. Oh, Miss Marilyn, you always do think up comfort. You're just like your ma and pa. But Billy, he's been so kinda peaked lately, so sorta gentle, and then again sorta crazy like, just like his mother useta be 'fore her husband left her. I couldn't help worryin'."

"Well, now Miss Saxon, I'll inquire around all I can without rousing any suspicion. You know Billy would hate that."

"Oh, I know he would," flushed the little woman nervously.

"So I'll just ask the boys if they know where he is and where they saw him last, and don't you worry. I'll tell them I have a message for him, you know, and you just stop crying and rest easy and don't tell a soul yet till I look around. Here comes Mother. She'll help you better than I can."

Mrs. Severn in a cool white dimity came quietly into the room, bringing a restful calm with her, and while Lynn was out on her errand of mercy she slipped a strong arm around the other woman's waist and had her down on her knees in the alcove behind the curtains, and had committed the whole matter to a loving heavenly Father—Billy, and the tired little Aunt, and all the little details of life that harrow so on a burdened soul—and somehow when they rose the day was cooler, and life looked more possible to poor Aunt Saxon.

Presently came Lynn, brightly. She had seen the boys. They had met Billy in Economy day before yesterday. He had said he had a job, he didn't know how long it would last, and he might not be able to come to baseball practice. He told them who to put in his place till he got back.

"There, now, Miss Saxon, you go home and lie down and take a good sleep. You've put this whole thing in the hands of the Lord, now don't take it out again. Just trust Him. Billy'll come back safe and sound, and there'll be some good reason for it," said Mrs. Severn. And Aunt Saxon, smiling wistfully, shyly apologetic for her foolishness, greatly cheered and comforted, went. But Lynn went up to her little white room and prayed earnestly, adding Billy to her prayer for Mark. Where was Billy Gaston?

When Miss Saxon went home she found a letter in the letter box out by the gate addressed to Billy. This set her heart to palpitating again and she almost lost her faith in prayer and took to her own worries once more. But she carried the letter in and held it up to the window, trying her best to make out anything written therein. She justified this to her conscience by saying that it might give a clew to Billy's whereabouts. Billy never got letters. Maybe, it might be from his long lost father, though they had all reason to believe him dead. Or maybe—Oh, what if Albert Gaston had come back and kidnapped Billy! The thought was too awful. She dropped right down in the kitchen where she stood by the old patchwork rocking chair that always stood handy in the window when she wanted to peel potatoes, and prayed: "Oh, God, don't let it be! Don't bring that bad man back to this world again! Take care of my Billy and bring him back to me, Amen!" Over and over again she prayed, and it seemed to comfort her. Then she rose, and put the teakettle on and carefully steamed open the letter. She had not lost all hope when she took time to steam it open in place of tearing it, for she was still worse afraid that Billy might return and scold her for meddling with his precious letter, than she was afraid he would not return. While the steam was gathering she tried to justify herself in Billy's eyes for opening it at all. After her prayer it seemed a sort of desecration. So the kettle had almost boiled away before she mustered courage to hold the envelope over the steam, and while she did this she noticed for the first time significantly that the postmark was New York. Perhaps it was from Mark. Then Billy was not with Mark! But perhaps the letter would tell.

So she opened the flap very carefully, and pulled out the single sheet of paper, stepping nearer the window to read it in the late afternoon light. It read: "Dear Kid, shut your mouth and saw wood. Buddy." That was all.

Aunt Saxon lifted frightened eyes and stared at the lilac bush outside the window, the waterspout where Billy often shinned up and down, the old apple tree that he would climb before he was large enough to be trusted, and then she read the letter again. But it meant nothing to her. It seemed a horrible riddle. She took a pencil and a scrap of paper and quickly transcribed the mysterious words, omitting not even the punctuation, and then hurriedly returned the letter to its envelope, clapped the flap down and held it tight. When it was dry she put the letter up in plain sight on the top of the old secretary where Billy could find it at once when he came in. She was taking no chances on Billy finding her opening his mail. It never had happened before, because Billy never had had a letter before, except notices about baseball and athletic association, but she meant it never should happen. She knew instinctively that if it ever did she would lose Billy, if not immediately, then surely eventually, for Billy resented above all things interference. Then Aunt Saxon sat down to study the transcription. But after a long and thorough perusal she folded it carefully and pinned it in her bosom. But she went more cheerily down to the market to get something for supper. Billy might come any time now. His letter was here, and he would surely come home to get his letter.

Down at the store she met Marilyn, who told her she looked better already, and the poor soul, never able to hold her tongue, had to tell the girl about the letter.

"He's had a letter," she said brightening, "about a job I guess. It was there when I got back. It's sawing wood. The letter doesn't have any head. It just says about sawing wood. I 'spose that's where he is, but he ought to have let me know. He was afraid I'd make a fuss about it, I always do. I'm afraid of those big saws they use. He's so careless. But he was set on a grown-up job. I couldn't get him to paste labels on cans at the factory, he said it was too much of a kid game."

"Oh," said Marilyn, wondering. "Sawing wood. Well, that's where he is of course, and it's good healthy work. I wouldn't worry. Billy is pretty careful, I think. He'll take care of himself."

But to herself on the way home she said: "How queer for Billy to go off sawing wood just now! It doesn't seem like him. They can't be so hard up. There must be something behind it all. I hope I didn't start anything asking him to stick by Mark! Oh, *where* is Mark?"

That afternoon Marilyn took a horseback ride, and touched all the points she knew where there might be likely

to be woodsawing going on, but no Billy was on the job anywhere.

As she rode home through Economy she saw Mrs. Fenner
scuttling down a side street from the jail, and hurrying into
her own side gate like a little frightened lizard.

Marilyn came back home heartsick and sad, and took refuge in the church and her bells. At least she could call to
Billy across the hills somewhere by playing the songs he
loved the best. And perhaps their echoes would somehow
cross the miles to Mark too, by that strange mysterious
power that spirit can reach to spirit across space or years or
even estrangement, and draw the thoughts irresistibly. So
she sat at the organ and played her heart out, ringing all the
old sweet songs that Mark used to love when the bells first
were new and she was learning to play them; "Highland
Laddie," "Bonnie Bonnie Warld," "Mavourneen," "Ken-
tucky Home," songs that she had kept fresh in her heart and
sometimes played for Billy now and then. And then the old
hymns. Did they echo far enough to reach him where he had
gone, Mark sitting alone in his inferno? Billy holding his
breath and trying to find a way out of his? Did they hear
those bells calling?

> O God, our help in ages past,
> Our hope for years to come!
> Our refuge from the stormy blast,
> And our eternal home!

The soul of the girl in the little dusky church went up in a
prayer with the bells.

> Before the hills in order stood,
> Or earth received her frame,
> From everlasting Thou art God!
> A thousand years the same!

Every mortal in the village knew the words, and in
kitchens now, preparing savory suppers, or down in the

mills and factories, or out on the street coming home, they were humming them, or repeating them over in their hearts. The bells did not ring the melody alone. The message was well known and came to every heart. Mark and Billy knew them too. Perhaps by telepathy the tune would travel to their minds and bring their words along:

> Under the shadow of Thy wings
> Thy saints have dwelt secure,
> Sufficient is Thine arm alone,
> And Thy defense is sure!

The bells ceased ringing and the vibration slowly died away, hill answering to hill, in waves of softly fading sound, while the people went to their suppers with a light of blessing and uplift on their faces. But in the darkened church, Marilyn, with her fingers on the keys and her face down upon her hands was praying, praying that God would shelter Mark and Billy.

Chapter 23

High in the tree over Billy's head a little chipmunk whisked with a nut in his mouth. He selected a comfortable rocking branch, unfurled his tail for a wind shield at his back, and sat up to his supper table as it were with the nut in his two hands. Something unusual caught his attention as he was about to attack the nutshell, and he cocked his little striped head around, up, and down, and took in Billy. Then a squirrel smile overspread his furry face and a twinkle seemed to come in his eye. With a wink down toward Billy he went to work. Crack, crack, crack! The shell was open. Crack! And a large section fell, whirling spinning down, straight down. The squirrel paused in his nibbling and cocked an eye again with that mischievous twinkle as if he enjoyed the joke, watching the light bit of shell in its swift descent, plump on the end of Billy's nose. It couldn't have hit straighter if Chippie had been pitcher for the Sabbath Valley baseball team.

Billy opened his eyes with a start and a scowl, and there before him, glaring like a wild beast, thick lips agap showing gnarled yellow teeth, wicked eyes, red glittering and murderous, was Pat, ugly, formidable, and threatening!

"Come outta there you little varmint you!" roared Pat. "Come out and I'll skin the nasty yella hide off'n ya. I gotcha good and hard now right where I wantcha an' ye won't—"

Bang! Click! BANG!

Billy had been lying among the thick undergrowth, flat on his back, his left arm flung above his head, but his right arm was thrust out from his body under a thick clump of laurel, and his right hand held the gun ready for any emergency

244

when he inadvertently went to sleep. The gun was pointed down the valley along the ground and his fingers wrapped knowingly, lovingly around the weapon. He had so long wanted to own one of his own. That gun was not included in the blood money and was not to be returned. It was a perquisite of war.

Billy was all there always, and even awakening suddenly from much needed sleep he was on the job. One glance at Pat's devilish face and his fingers automatically pulled the trigger. The report roared out along the valley like a volley from a regiment.

Billy hardly felt the rebound of the weapon before he realized that Patrick was no more between his vision and the sun's last rays. Patrick was legging it down the valley with all the strength he had left, and taking no time to look back. Billy had presence of mind to let off another volley before he rose to investigate; but there was nothing left of Pat but a ruffled path in the undergrowth and a waving branch or two he had turned aside in his going. So that was that! Doggone it, why did he have to go to sleep? If he had only been ready he could have managed this affair so much better for his own ends. He wanted a heart-to-heart talk with Pat while he had him good and frightened, and now it was too late. He must get back to the other job. He shinned up a tree and observed the broad shoulders of Pat wallowing up the bank over by the railroad. He was going back to the station. It was as well. He might see him again tomorrow perhaps, for Pat he must have as evidence. And besides, Pat might read the note and conclude to come back and answer it.

Billy parted the bushes to see if Pat had taken the money and note with him, and lo, here was the rude mountain telephone box wide open with the bunch of keys in the lock just as Pat must have left it when he discovered the paper and money, or perhaps Pat had been going to report to Sam what had happened, who knew? You see Billy knew nothing of his little red and brown striped partner up in the tree who had dropped a nut to warn him of danger, and did not realize that Chippie had also startled Pat, and set him looking among the bushes for the sources of the sound.

But Billy knew how to take advantage of a situation if he didn't know what made it, and in a trice he was down on his knees with the crude receiver in his hands. It was too late to ride down to the Blue Duck and telephone, but here was a telephone come to him, and now was a chance to try if it was a telephone at all, or only a private wire run secretly. He waited breathless with the long hum of wires in his ears, and then a quick click and "Number please." Billy could hardly command his voice but he murmured "Economy thirteen" in a low growl, his hard young hands shaking with excitement. "Your letter please!" Billy looked wildly at the rough box but could see no sign of number. "Why, it's the station, doncha know? What's thamatterwithya?" His spirits were rising. "Jay" stated the operator patiently. "Well, jay then," said Billy, "WhaddoIcare?" "Just-a-minute-please," and suddenly the chief's voice boomed out reassuringly. Billy cast a furtive eye back of him in the dusk and fell to his business with relief.

"Say, Chief, that you? This's Bill! Say, Chief, I wantcha he'p right away pretty quick! Got a line on those guys! You bring three men an' ge'down on the Lone Valley Road below Stark Mountain an' keep yer eye peeled t'ward the hanted house. Savvy? Yes, old hanted house, you know. You wait there till I signal. Yes, flash! Listen, one wink if you go to right, two come up straight, and three to the left. If it's only one repeated several times, you spread all round. Yep. I'm goin' up there right now. No, Chief, I wouldn't call ye f'I didn't think t'was pretty sure. Yep! I think they'll come out soon's it gets real dark. Yep, I think they ben there all day. I ain't sure, but I think. You won't fail me, will you, Chief? No, sure! I'll stick by. Be sure to bring three men, there's two of 'em, I ain't rightly sure but three. I jus' stirred another up. Whatssay? No, I'm 'lone! Aw, I'm awright! Sure.

I'll be careful. Whatssay? Where? Oh' I'm at a hole in the ground. Yes, down below Pleasant Valley station. Some telephone! I'll show it to you t'morra! S'long, Chief, I gotta go! It's gettin' dark, goobbye!"

Billy gave hurried glances about and rustled under the branches like a snake over to where old trusty lay. In ten minutes more he was worming his way up the side of Stark Mountain, while Pat was fortifying himself well within the little station, behind tables and desks for the night, and scanning the valley from the dusty windowpanes.

Billy parked his wheel in its usual place and continued up the hill to the opening at the back, then stood long listening. Once he thought he heard something drop inside the kitchen door, but no sound followed it and he concluded it had been a rat. Halfway between himself and the back door something gleamed faintly in the starlight. He didn't remember to have seen anything there before. He stole cautiously over, moving so slowly that he could not even hear himself. He paused beside the gleam and examined. It was an empty flask still redolent. Ummm! Booze! Billy wasn't surprised. Of course they would try to get something to while away their seclusion until they dared venture forth with their booty. He continued his cautious passage toward the house and then began to encircle it, keeping close to the wall and feeling his way along, for the moon would be late and small that night and he must work entirely by starlight. It was his intention after going around the house to enter and reconnoiter in his stocking feet. As he neared the front of the house he dropped both hands to his sweater pockets, the revolver in his right hand with its two precious cartridges, the flashlight which he had taken care to renew in Economy in his left hand, fingers ready to use either instantly. He turned the corner and stole on toward the front door, still noiseless as a mouse would go, his rubber sneakers touching like velvet in the grass.

He was only two feet from the front stoop when he became aware of danger, something, a familiar scent, a breathlessness, and then a sudden stir. A dark thing ahead and the feeling of something coming behind. Billy as if a football signal had been given, grew calm and alert. Instantly both arms flashed up, and down the mountain shot two long yellow winks of light, and simultaneously two sharp reports of a gun, followed almost instantly by another shot, more sinister in sound, and Billy's right arm dropped limply by his side, while a sick wave of pain passed over him.

But he could not stop for that. He remembered the day when Mark had been coaching the football team and had told them that they must not stop for *anything* when they were in action. If they thought their legs were broken, or they were mortally wounded and dying, they must not even think of it. Football was the one thing, and they were to forget they were dead and go ahead with every whiff of punch there was in them, blind or lame, or dead even, because when they were playing, football was the only thing that counted. And if they were sick or wounded or bleeding let the wound or the sickness take care of itself. *They* were *playing football!* So Billy felt now.

He hurled himself viciously at the dark shadow ahead, which he mentally registered as Link because he seemed long to tackle, and then kicked behind at the thing that came after, and struggled manfully with a throttling hand on his throat till a wad of vile cloth was forced into his mouth—and just as he had a half nelson on Shorty, too! If he could have got Shorty down and stood on him he might have beaten off Link until Chief got there. Where was Chief? Where was the gun? Where was he? His head was swimming. Was it his head he had hit against the wall, or did he bang Shorty's? How it resounded! There were winding stairs in his head and he seemed to be climbing them, up, up, up, till he dropped in a heap on the floor, a hard floor all dust, and the dust came into his nostrils. He was choking with that rag! Why couldn't he pull it out? What was cutting his wrists when he tried to raise his hand? And what was that queer pain in his shoulder?

There were shouts outside. How did he get inside? Was that more shooting? Perhaps he had found his gun after all. Perhaps he was shooting the men before the chief got there, and that was bad, because he didn't feel competent to judge about a thing as serious as shooting with that dirty rag in his mouth. He must get rid of it somehow. Doggone it! He had somehow got his hands all tangled up in cords, and he must get them out no matter if they did cut. He had to give the chief a signal.

He struggled again with all his might, and something somewhere gave way. He wasn't sure what, but he seemed to be sinking down, perhaps downstairs or down the mountain, somehow so it was down where the chief—where Mark! The light in his brain went out and he lay as one dead in the great dusty front bedroom where a man who had sinned, hanged himself once because he couldn't bear his conscience any longer.

And outside in the front door yard five men struggled in the dark, with curses, and shots, and twice one almost escaped, for Link was desperate, having a record behind him that would be enough for ten men to run away from.

But after the two were bound and secured in the car down at the foot of the mountain, the chief lingered, and looking up said in a low tone to one of his men: "I wonder where that boy is!"

"Oh, he's all right," said his assistant easily, "he's off on another piece of business by this time, Chief. He likes to seem mysterious. It's just his way. Say, Chief, we gotta get back if we wantta meet that train down at Unity t'night."

That was true too, and most important, so the chief with a worried glance toward the dark mountain turned his car and hurried his captives away. Now that they were where he could get a glance at them in the dim light of the car, he felt

pretty sure they were a couple of "birds" he had been looking for for quite a while. If that was so he must reward Billy
somehow. That boy was a little wonder. He would make a
detective someday. It wouldn't be a bad idea to take him on
in a quiet sort of way and train him. He might be a great
help. He mustn't forget this night's work. And what was that
the kid had said about a secret underground wire? He must
look into it as soon as this murder trial was off the docket.
That murder trial worried him. He didn't like the turn
things were taking.

Chapter 24

In the gray of the morning Billy came to himself and stared around in the stuffy grimness everywhere. The gag was still in his mouth. He put up his hand involuntarily and pulled it out, and then remembered that his hands had been tied. Then he must have succeeded in breaking the cord! The other hand was still encumbered and his feet were tied together, but it happened that the well hand was the freed one, and so after a hard struggle he succeeded in getting out of the tangle of knots and upon his feet. He worked cautiously because he wasn't sure how much of what he remembered was dream and how much was reality. The two men might be in the house yet, very likely were, asleep somewhere. He must steal down and get away before they awoke.

There was something warm and sticky on the floor and it had got on his clothes, but he took no notice of it at first. He wondered what that sick pain in his shoulder was, but he had not time to stop and see now or even to think about it. He must call the chief before the men were awake. So he managed to get upon his feet and steady himself against the wall, for he felt dizzy and faint when he tried to walk. But he managed to get into the hall, and peer into each room, and more and more as he went he felt he was alone in the house. Then he had failed and the men were gone! Aw, gee! Pat too! What a fool he had been, thinking he could manage the affair! He ought to have taken the chief into his confidence and let him come along. Aw, gee!

Down in the kitchen he found a pail of water and a cup. He drank thirstily. His head felt hot and the veins in his neck throbbed. There seemed to be a lump on his forehead. He bathed his face and head. How good it felt! Then he found a whiskey bottle on the table half full. This after carefully smelling he poured over his bruised wrists, sopping it on his head and forehead, and finally pouring some down his shoulder that pained so, and all that he did was done blindly, like one in a dream; just an involuntary searching for means to go on and fulfill his purpose.

After another drink of water he seemed to be able to think more clearly. That tapping in the cellar yesterday! What had that been? He must look and see. Yes, that was really what he had come about. Perhaps the men were down there yet hidden away. He opened the cellar door and listened. Doggone it, where was that gun of his? But the flashlight! Yes, the flashlight!

He shot the light ahead of him as he went down, moving as in a dream, but keeping true to type, cautious, careful, stealthy. At last he was down. No one there! He turned the little flash into every nook and cranny, not excepting the ledges above the cellar wall whereon the floor beams rested. Once he came on a tin box long and flat and new looking. It seemed strange to meet it here. There was no dust upon it. He poked it down with his torch and it sprawled open at his feet. Papers, long folded papers printed with writing in between, like bonds or deeds or something. He stooped and waved the flash above them and caught the name Shafton in one. It was an insurance paper, house and furniture. He felt too stupid to quite understand, but it grew into his consciousness that these were the things he was looking for. He gathered them up, stuffing them carefully inside his blouse. They would be safe there. Then he turned to go upstairs, but stumbled over a pile of coal out in the floor and fell. It gave him a sick sensation to fall. It almost seemed that he couldn't get up again, but now he had found the papers he must. He crawled to his knees, and felt around, then turned his light on. This was strange! A heap of coal out in the middle of the floor, almost a foot from the rest! A rusty shovel lay beside it, a chisel, and a big stone. Ah! The tapping! He got up forgetting his pain and began to kick away the coal, turning the flashlight down. Yes, there was a crack in the cement, a loose piece. He could almost lift it with his foot. He pried at it with the toe of his shoe, and then lifted it with much effort out of the way. It was quite a big piece, more than a foot in diameter! The ground was soft underneath as if it had been recently worked over. He stooped and plunged the fingers of his good hand in and felt around, laying the light on the floor so it would shed a glare over the spot where he worked. He could feel down several inches. There seemed to be something soft like cloth or leather. He pulled at it and finally brought it up. A leather bag girt about with a thong of leather. He picked the knot and turned the flash in. It sent forth a million green lights. There seemed also to be a rope of white glistening things that reminded him of Saxy's tears. That brought a pang. Saxy would be crying! He must remember that and do something about it. He must have been away a long time and perhaps those men would be coming back. But it wouldn't do to leave these things here. They were the Shafton jewels. What anybody wanted of a lot of shiny little stones like that and a rope of tears! But then if they did they did, and they were theirs and they oughtta have 'em. This was the thing he had come to do. Get those jewels and papers back! Make up as far as he could for what he had done! And he must do it now quick before he got sick. He felt he was getting sick and he mustn't think about it or he would turn into Aunt Saxon. That was the queerest thing, back in his mind he felt this *was* Aunt Saxon down here in the haunted cellar playing with green stones and ropes of tears, and he must hurry quick before she found him and told him he couldn't finish what he had to do.

He did the work thoroughly, feeling down in the hole again, but found nothing more. Then he stuffed the bag inside his blouse and buttoned up his sweater with his well hand and somehow got up the stairs. The arm pained him a lot, and he found his sweater was wet. So he took his hand-kerchief and tied it tight around the place that hurt the most, holding one end in his teeth to make the knot firm.

The sun blinded him as he stumbled down the back steps and went to get his wheel, but somehow he managed it, plunging through the brakes and tangles, and back to the road.

It ran in his brain where the Shaftons lived out in the country on the Jersey Shore. He had a mental picture in the back of his mind how to get there. He knew that when he struck the highroad there was nothing to do but keep straight on till he crossed the state line and then he would find it somehow, although it was miles away. If he had been himself he would have known it was an impossible journey in his present condition, but he wasn't thinking of impossi-bilities. He had to do it, didn't he? He, Billy, had set out to make reparation for the confusion he had wrought in his small world, and he meant to do so, though all hell should rise against him. Hell! That was it. He could see the flames in hot little spots where the morning sun struck. He could hear the bells striking the hour in the world he used to know that was not for him anymore. He zigzagged along the road in a crazy way, and strange to say he met nobody he knew, for it was early. Ten minutes after he passed the crossroads Elder Harricutt went across the highway toward Economy to his day's work, and he would have loved to have seen Billy, and his rusty old wheel, staggering along in that crazy way and smelling of whiskey like a whole moonshiner, fairly reeking with whiskey as he joggled down the road, and a queer little tinkle now and then just inside his blouse as if he carried loaded dice. Oh, he would have loved to have caught Billy shooting crap!

But he was too late, and Billy swam on, the sun growing hotter on his aching head, the light more blinding to his bloodshot eyes, the lump bigger and bluer on his grimy forehead.

About ten o'clock a car came by, slowed down, the driver watching Billy, though Billy took no note of him. Billy was looking on the ground dreaming he was searching for the state line. He had a crazy notion it oughtta be there somewhere.

The man in the car stopped and called to him:

"How about putting your wheel in the backseat and letting me give you a lift? You look pretty tired."

Billy lifted bleared eyes and stopped pedaling, almost falling off his wheel, but recovering himself with a wrench of pain and sliding off.

"Awwright!" said Billy. "Thanks!"

"You look all in, son," said the man kindly.

"Yep," said Billy laconically, " 'yam! Been up all night. Care f'I sleep?"

"Help yourself," said the man, giving a lift with the wheel, and putting it in behind.

Billy curled down in the backseat without further ceremony.

"Where are you going, son?"

Billy named the country seat of the Shaftons, having no idea how far away it was. The man gave a whistle.

"What! On that wheel? Well, go to sleep, son. I'm going there myself, so don't worry. I'll wake you up when you get there."

So Billy slept through the first long journey he had taken since he came to live with Aunt Saxon, slept profoundly with an oblivion that almost amounted to coma. Sometimes the man, looking back, was tempted to stop and see if the boy was yet alive, but a light touch on the hot forehead showed him that life was not extinct, and they whirled on.

Three hours later Billy was awakened by a sharp shake of his sore shoulder and a stinging pain that shot through him like fire. Fire! Fire! He was on fire! That was how he felt as he opened his eyes and glared at the stranger:

"Aw, lookout there, whatterya doin'?" he blazed.

"Whadda ya think I am? A football? Don't touch me. I'll get out. This the place? Thanks fer tha ride, I was all in. Say, d'ya know a guy by the name of Shafton?"

"Shafton?" asked the man astonished. "Are you going to Shafton's?"

"Sure," said Billy, "anything wrong about that? Where does he hang out?" The look of Billy, and more than all the smell of him made it quite apparent to the casual observer that he had been drinking, and the man eyed him compassionately. Poor little fool! He's beginning young. What on earth does he want at Shafton's?

"I 'spose you've come down after the reward," grinned the man. "I could have saved you the trouble if you'd told me. The kidnapped son has got home. They are not in need of further information."

Billy gave him a superior leer with one eye closed:

"You may not know all there is to know about that," he said impudently, "where did you say he lived?"

The man shrugged his shoulders indifferently.

"Suit yourself," he said, "I doubt if they'll see you. They have had nothing but a stream of vagrants for two days and they're about sick of it. They live on the next estate and the gateway is right around that corner."

"I ain't no vagrant," glared Billy, and limped away with old trusty under his left arm.

No one molested him as he walked in the arched and ivied gateway, for the gatekeeper was off on a little private errand of his own at a place where prohibition had not yet penetrated. Billy felt too heavy and dizzy to mount his wheel, but he leaned on the saddle as he walked and tried to get things straight in his head. He oughtn t to have gone to sleep, that's what he oughtn't. But this job would soon be over and then he would hike it for home. Gee! Wouldn't home feel good! And Aunt Saxon would bathe his head with witch hazel and make cold things for him to drink! Aw, gee!

The pedigreed dogs of which the place boasted a number

came suddenly down upon him in a great flare of noise, but dogs were always his friends, why should he worry? A pity he couldn't stop to make friends with them just now. Some dogs! Here, pup! Gee! What a dog to own! The dogs whined and fawned upon him. Pedigree or no pedigree, rags and whiskey and dirt notwithstanding, they knew a man when they saw one, and Billy hadn't batted an eyelid when they tried their worst tramp barks on him. They wagged their silky tails and tumbled over each other to get first place to him, and so escorted proudly he dropped old trusty by a clump of imported rhododendrons and limped up the marble steps to the wide vistas of circular piazzas that stretched to seemingly infinite distances, and wondered if he should ever find the front door.

An imposing butler appeared with a silver tray, and stood aghast.

"Shafton live here?" inquired Billy trying to look businesslike. "Like to see him er the missus a minute," he added as the frowning vision bowed. The butler politely but firmly told him that the master and mistress had other business and no desire to see him. The young gentleman had come home, and the reward had been withdrawn. If it was about the reward he had come he could go down to the village and find the detective. The house people didn't want to interview any more callers.

"Well, say," said Billy disgusted, "after I've come all this way too! You go tell 'er I've brought her jewels! You go tell 'er I've *gottum here!*"

The butler opened the door a little wider: he suggested that seeing was believing.

"Not on yer tintype!" snapped Billy. "I show 'em to nobody an' I give 'em to nobody but the owner! Where's the young fella? He knows me. Tell 'im I brang his ma's string o' beads an' things."

Billy was weary. His head was spinning round. His temper was rising.

"Aw, you make me tired! Get out of my way!" He lowered his head and made a football dive with his head in the region of the dignified butler's stomach, and before that dignitary had recovered his poise Billy with two collies joyously escorting him, stood blinking in wonder over the great beautiful living room, for all the world as pretty as the church at home, only stranger, with things around that he couldn't make out the use of.

"Where'ur they at? Where are the folks?" he shouted back to the butler who was coming after him with menace in his eye.

"What is the matter, Morris? What is all this noise about?" came a lady's voice in pettish tones from up above somewhere. "Didn't I tell you that I wouldn't see another one of those dreadful people today?"

Billy located her smooth old childish face at once and strode to the foot of the stairs peering up at the lady, white with pain from his contact with the butler, but alert now to the task before him:

"Say, Miz Shaf't'n, I got yer jools, would ya mind takin' 'em right now? 'Cause I'm all in an' I wantta get home."

His head was going around now like a merry-go-round, but he steadied himself by the bannister:

"Why, what do you mean?" asked the lady descending a step or two, a vision of marcelled white hair, violet and lace negligee, and well preserved features. "You've got them *there?* Let me see them."

"He's been drinking, Sarah, can't you smell it?" said a man's voice higher up, "Come away and let Morris deal with him. Really, Sarah, we'll have to go away if this keeps up."

"Say, you guy up there, just shut yer trap a minute won't ya! Here, Miz Shaf't'n, are these here yours?"

Billy struggled with the neck of his blouse and brought forth the leather bag, gripped the knot fiercely in his teeth, ran his fingers in the bag as he held it in his mouth, his lamed arm hanging at his side, and drew forth the magnificent pearls.

"William! My pearls!" shrieked the lady.

The gentleman came down incredulous, and looked over her shoulder.

"I believe they are, Sarah," he said.

Billy leered feverishly up at him, and produced a sheaf of papers, seemingly burrowing somewhere in his internal regions to bring them forth.

"And here, d'these b'long?"

The master of the house gripped them.

"Sarah! The bonds! And the South American shares!" They were too busy to notice Billy who stood swaying by the newel post, his duty done now, the dogs grouped about him.

"Say, c'n I get me a drink?" he asked of the butler, who hovered near uncertain what to be doing now that the tide was turned:

The lady looked up.

"Morris!"

He scarcely heard the lady's words but almost immediately a tall slim glass of frosty drink, that smelled of wild grapes, tasted of oranges, and cooled him down to the soul again, was put into his hand and he gulped it greedily.

"Where did you say you found these, young man?" The gentleman eyed him sternly, and Billy's old spirit flamed up:

"I didn't say," said Billy.

"But you know we've got to have all the evidence before we can give the reward!"

"Aw, cut it out! I don't want no reward. Wouldn't take it if you give it to me! I just wanta get home. Say, you gotta telephone?"

"Why certainly." This was the most astonishing burglar!

"Well, where is't? Lemme call long distance on it? I ain't got the tin now, but I'll pay ya when I git back home!"

"Why, the idea! Take him to the telephone, Morris. Right there! This one—"

But Billy had sighted one on a mahogany desk near at hand and he toppled to the edge of the chair that stood before it. He took down the receiver in a shaky hand, calling long distance.

"This Long Distance? Well, gimme Economy thirteen."

The Shaftons for the instant were busy looking over the papers, identifying each jewel, wondering if any were missing. They did not notice Billy till a gruff young voice rang out with a pathetic tremble in it: "That you, Chief? This is Billy. Say, c'n I bother you to phone to Miss Severn an' ast her to tell m'yant I'm aw'wright? Yes, tell her I'll be home soon now, an' I'll explain. And, Chief, I'm mighty sorry those two guys got away, but I couldn't help it. We'll get 'em yet. Hope you didn't wait long. Tell you more when I see ya. S'long—"

The boyish voice trailed off into silence as the receiver fell with a crash to the polished desk, and Billy slipped off the chair and lay in a huddled heap on the costly rug.

"Oh, mercy!" cried the lady. "Is he drunk or what?"

"Come away, Sarah, let Morris deal—"

"But he's sick, I believe, William. Look how white he is. I believe he is dead! William, he may have come a long way in the heat! He may have had a sunstroke! Morris, send for a doctor quick! And—call the ambulance too! You better telephone the hospital. We can't have him here! William, look here, what's this on his sleeve? Blood? Oh, *William!* And we didn't give him any reward!"

And so, while the days hastened on Billy lay between clean white sheets on a bed of pain in a private ward of a wonderful memorial hospital put up by the Shaftons in honor of a child that died. Tossing and moaning, and dreaming of unquenchable fire, always trying to climb out of the hot crater that held him, and never getting quite to the top, always knowing there was something he must do, yet never quite finding out what it was. And back in Sabbath

Valley Aunt Saxon prayed and cried and waited and took heart of cheer from the message the chief had sent to Lynn. And quietly the day approached for the trial of Mark Carter, but his mother did not yet know.

Chapter 25

Mrs. Gibson, the wife of the comparatively new elder of the Sabbath Valley church was a semi-invalid. That is she wasn't able to do her own work and kept "help." The help was a lady of ample proportions whose husband had died and whose fortunes were depleted. She consented to assist Mrs. Gibson provided she were considered one of the family, and she presented a continual front of offense so that the favored family must walk most circumspectly if they would not have her retire to her room with hurt feelings and leave them to shift for themselves.

On the morning of the trial she settled herself at her side of the breakfast table, after a number of excursions to the kitchen for things she had forgotten, the cream, the coffee, and the brown bread, of which Mr. Gibson was very fond. She was prepared to enjoy her own breakfast. Mr. Gibson generally managed to bolt his while these excursions of memory were being carried on and escape the morning news, but Mrs. Gibson, well knowing which side her bread was buttered, and not knowing where she could get another housekeeper, usually managed to sit it out.

"Well, this is a great day for Sabbath Valley," said Mrs. Frost mournfully, spreading an ample slice of bread deep with butter, and balancing it on the uplifted fingers of one hand while she stirred the remainder of the cream into her coffee with one of the best silver spoons. She was wide and bulgy and her chair always seemed inadequate when she settled thus for nourishment.

"A great day," she repeated sadly, taking an audible sip of her coffee.

"A great day?" repeated little Mrs. Gibson with a puzzled air, quickly recalling her abstracted thoughts.

"Yes. Nobody ever thought anybody in Sabbath Valley would ever be tried for murder!"

"Oh!" said Mrs. Gibson sharply, drawing back her chair as if she were in a hurry and rolling up her napkin quickly.

"Yes, poor Mark Carter! I remember his sweet little face and his long yellow curls and his baby smile as if it were yesterday!" narrowing her eyes and harrowing her voice, "I wonder if his poor mother knows yet."

"I should hope not!" said Mrs. Gibson rising precipitately and wandering over to the window where hung a gilded canary cage. "Mrs. Frost, did you remember to give the canary some seed and fresh water?"

"Yes, I b'lieve so," responded the fat lady, "but you can't keep her from knowing it always. Whatt'll you do when he's *hung?* Don't you think it would be easier for her to get used to it little by little?"

"Mrs. Frost, if you were a dog would you rather have your tail cut off all at once, or little by little?" said Mrs. Gibson mischievously.

"I shouldn't like to have it cut off at all I'm quite sure," said Mrs. Frost frostily.

"Well, perhaps Mrs. Carter might feel that way too," said the lady bending over a rose geranium and pinching a leaf to smell.

"I don't understand you," said Mrs. Frost from her coffee cup. "Oh, you mean that perhaps Mark may not be convicted? Why, my dear lady, there isn't a chance at all, not a chance in the world for Mark, and while I'm real sorry I can't say I'd approve. Think of how he's carried on, going with that little huzzy of a Cherry. Mrs. Harricutt says she saw him have her out riding in his automobile one day!"

"Oh, *Mrs. Harricutt!*" said Mrs. Gibson impatiently. "Mrs. Frost, let's find something pleasanter to talk about.

It's a wonderful morning. The air's like wine. I wonder if I couldn't take a little walk. I mean to ask the doctor."

"My dear woman," said Frost patronizingly, "you can't get away from the unpleasant things in this world by just not talking about them!"

"It seems not," said the Gibson lady patiently, and wandered out on the porch.

Down the street Marilyn lingered by her mother's chair:

"Are you—going to Economy today, Mother?"

"Yes, dear, your father and I are both going. Did you—think you ought—wanted to—go, dear?"

"Oh, I should *hate it!*" cried Lynn flinging out her hands with a terrible little gesture of despair, "but I wanted to go just to stand by Mark. I shall be there anyway, wherever I am. I shall see everything and feel everything in my heart I know. But in the night it came to me that someone ought to stay with Mrs. Carter!"

"Yes, dear! I had hoped you would think of that. I didn't want to mention it because I wanted you to follow your own heart's leading, but I think she needs you. If you could keep her from finding out until it was over—"

"But suppose—"

"Yes, dear, it is possible. I've thought of that, and if it comes there will be a way I'm sure, but until it does—*then* suppose—"

"Yes, Mother, I'll go and make her have one happy day first anyway. If any of those old vultures come around I'll play the piano or scream all the while they are there and keep them from telling her a thing!"

"I think, dear, the old vultures will all be in Economy today."

"All except Mrs. Frost, Mother dear. She can't get away. But she can always run across the street to borrow a cup of soda."

So Lynn knelt for a moment in her quiet room, then came down, kissed her mother and father with a face of brave serenity, and went down the maple-shaded street with her silk workbag in her hand. And none too soon. As she tapped at the door of the Carter house she saw Mrs. Frost ambling purposefully out of the Gibson gate with a teacup in her hand.

"Oh, hurry upstairs and stay there a minute till I get rid of Mrs. Frost," Lynn whispered smiling as her hostess let her in. "I've come to spend the day with you, and she'll stay till she's told you all the news and there won't be any left for me."

Mrs. Carter, greatly delighted with Lynn's company, hurried obediently up the stairs and Lynn met the interloper, supplied her with the cup of salt she had come for this time, said Mrs. Carter was upstairs making the beds and she wouldn't bother her to come down—*beds,* mind you, as if Mark was at home of course—and Mrs. Frost went back across the street puzzled and baffled and resolved to come back later for an egg after that forward young daughter of the minister was gone.

Lynn locked the front door and ran upstairs. She tolled her hostess up to the attic to show her some ancient gowns and poke bonnets that she hadn't seen since she was a little girl in which she and Mark used to dress up and play history stories.

Half the morning she kept her up there looking at garments long folded away, whose wearers had slept in the church yard many years; trinkets of other days, quaint old pictures, photographs and daguerreotypes, and a beautiful curl of Mark's:

"Marilyn, I'm going to give that to you," the mother said as she saw the shining thing lying in the girl's hand. "There's no one living to care for it after I'm gone, and you will keep it I know till you're sure there's no one would want it I— mean—"

"I understand what you mean," said Marilyn, "I will keep it and love it—for you—and for him. And if there is ever

anybody else that—deserves it—why I'll give it to them!"
Then they both laughed to hide the tears behind the unspoken thoughts, and the mother added a little stubbed shoe and a sheer muslin cap, all delicate embroidery and hemstitching:

"They go together," she said simply, and Lynn wrapped them all carefully in a bit of tissue paper and laid them in her silk bag. As she turned away she held it close to her heart while the mother closed the shutters. She shuddered to think of the place where Mark was sitting now, being tried for his life. Her heart flew over the road, entered the court, and stood close by his side, with her hand on his shoulder, and then slipped it in his. She wondered if he knew that she was praying, praying, praying for him and standing by him, taking the burden of what would have been his mother's grief if she had known, as well as the heavy burden of her own sorrow.

The air of the courtroom was heavy for the place was crowded. Almost everybody from Sabbath Valley that could come was there, for a great many people loved Mark Carter, and this seemed a time when somehow they must stand by him. People came that liked him and some that did not like him, but more that liked him and kept hoping against hope that he would not be indicted.

The hum of voices suddenly ceased as the prisoner was led in and a breath of awe passed over the place. For until that minute no one was quite sure that Mark Carter would appear. It had been rumored again and again that he had run away. Yet here he was, walking tall and straight, his fine head held high as had been his wont. "For all the world like he walked when he was usher at Mary Anne's wedding," whispered Mrs. Hulse, from Unity.

The minister and his wife kept their eyes down after the first glimpse of the white face. It seemed a desecration to look at a face that had suffered as that one had. Yet the expression upon it now was more as if it had been set for a certain purpose for this day, and did not mean to change whatever came. A hopeless, sad, persistent look, yet strong withal and with a hint of something fine and high behind it.

He did not look around as he sat down, merely nodded to a few close to him whom he recognized. A number pressed close as he passed, and touched him, as if they would impress upon him their loyalty, and it was noticeable that these were mostly of a humble class, workingmen, boys, and a few old women, people to whom he had been kind.

Mrs. Severn wrote a little note and sent it up to him, with the message, "Lynn is with your mother." Just that. No name signed. But his eyes sought hers at once and seemed to light, and soon, without any apparent movement on his part a card came back to her bearing the words: "I thank you." But he did not look that way again all day it seemed. His bearing was quiet, sad, aloof, one might almost have said disinterested.

Mark's lawyer was one whom he had picked out of the gutter and literally forced to stop drinking and get back on his job. He was a man of fine mind and deep gratitude, and was having a frantic time with his client, for Mark simply wouldn't talk:

"I wasn't there, I was on Stark Mountain, I am not guilty," he persisted, "and that is all I have to say."

"But, my dear friend, don't you realize that mere statements unadorned and uncorroborated won't get you anywhere in court?"

"All right, don't try to defend me then. Let the thing go as it will. That is all I have to say." And from this decision no one had been able to shake him. His lawyer was nearly crazy. He had raked the county for witnesses. He had dug into the annals of that night in every possible direction. He had unearthed things that it seemed no living being would have thought of, and yet he had not found the one thing of

which he was in search, positive evidence that Mark Carter
had been elsewhere and otherwise employed at the time of
the shooting.

"Don't bother so much about it, Tony," said Mark once
when they were talking it over, or the lawyer was talking it
over and Mark was listening. "It doesn't matter. Nothing
matters anymore!" and his voice was weary as if all hope
had vanished from him.

Anthony Drew looked at him in despair:

"Sometimes I almost think you *want* to die," he said. "Do
you think I shall let you go when you pulled me back from
worse than death? No, Mark, old man, we're going to pull
you through somehow, though I don't know how. If I were a
praying man I'd say that this was the time to pray. Mark,
what's become of that kid you used to think so much of, that
was always tagging after you? Billy—was that his name?"

A wan smile flitted across Mark's face, and a stiff little
drawing of the old twinkle about eyes and lips:

"I think he'll turn up sometime."

The lawyer eyed him keenly:

"Mark, I believe you've got something up your sleeve. I
believe that kid knows something and you won't let him tell.
Where is he?"

"I don't know, Tony" and Mark looked at him straight
with clear eyes, and the lawyer knew he was telling the
truth.

Just at the last day Anthony Drew found out about the
session meeting. But from Mark he got no further statement
than the first one. Mark would not talk. An ordinary lawyer,
one that had not been saved himself, would have given up
the defense as hopeless. Anthony simply wouldn't let Mark
go undefended. If there were no evidence he would make
some somehow, and so he worked hoping against hope up to
the very last minute. He stood now, tall, anxious, a fine face,
though showing the marks of wreck behind him, dark hair

silvered at the edges, fine deep lines about his eyes and
brows, looking over the assembled throng with nervous hurrying eyes. At last he seemed to find what he wanted and
came quickly down to where the minister sat in an obscure
corner, whispering a few words with him. They went out together for a few minutes and when they came back the minister was grave and thoughtful. He himself had scoured the
country round about quietly for Billy, and he was deeply
puzzled. He had promised to tell what he knew.

The business of the day went forward in the usual way
with all the red tape, the cool formalities, as if some trifling
matter were at stake, and those who loved Mark sat with
aching hearts and waited. The Severns in their corner sat for
the most part with bended heads and praying hearts. The
witnesses for the prosecution were most of them companions
of the dead man, those who had drunk and caroused with
him, frequenters of the Blue Duck, and they were herded together, an evil-looking crowd, but with erect heads and defiant attitude, the air of having donned unaccustomed
garments of righteousness for the occasion, and making a
great deal of it because for once everyone must see that they
were in the right. They were fairly loudmouthed in their
boasting about it.

There was the little old wizened up fellow that had been
sitting with the drinks outside the booth the night Billy telephoned. There were the serving men who had waited on
Mark and Cherry. There was the proprietor of the Blue
Duck himself, who testified that Mark had often been there
with Cherry, though always early in the evening. Once he
had caught him outside the window looking in at the dancers as late as two o'clock at night, the same window from
which the shot was fired that brought Dolph to his death.
They testified that Mark had been seen with Cherry much of
late driving in his car, and that she had often been in deep
converse as if having a hot argument about something.

The feeling was tense in the courtroom. Tears were in many eyes, hopeless tears in the eyes of those who had loved the boy for years.

But the grilling order marched on, and witness after witness came, adding another and another little touch to the gradually rising structure that would shut Mark Carter away from the world that loved him and that he loved forever.

Cherry was called, a flaunting bit of a child with bobbed golden hair and the air of a bold young seraph, her white face bravely painted, her cherry lips cherrier even than the cherry for which she had been named. She wore a silk coat reaching to the bottom of her frock, which was shorter than the shortest, and daring little high-heeled, many strapped shoes with a myriad of bright buckles. Her hat was an insolent affair of cherry red. She made a blinding bit of color in the dreary courtroom. She appeared half frightened, half defiant. Her sharp little face seemed to have lost its round curves and childlike sweetness. She testified that she had been with Mark on the night of the shooting, but that he had taken her home early and she had seen no more of him that night. She admitted that she had returned later to the Blue Duck Tavern with Dolph and had danced late and eaten supper with him afterwards, and that it was while they were eating that the shot was fired and Dolph fell over on the table. No, she didn't see any face at the window. She had covered her face with her hands and screamed. She guessed she fainted. Questioned further she admitted that she had had an argument with Mark earlier in the evening, but she didn't remember what it was about. They often argued. Yes, Dolph was jealous of Mark and tried to stop her going with him. Yes, Mark had tried to stop her going with Dolph too, but he never acted jealous—On and on through the sorry little details of Cherry's career. The courtroom vultures receiving it avidly, the more refined part of the company with distaste and disgust. Mark sat with stern white face looking straight at Cherry all the time she was on the stand as if he dared her to say other than the truth. When she happened to look that way she gave a giggling little shudder and half turned her shoulder away, avoiding his eyes. But when she was done she had said nothing against Mark, and nothing to clear him either.

The sharp unscrupulous lawyer who acted for the prosecution had secured some fellows "of the baser sort" who testified that they had seen Mark Carter buying a gun, that they had seen him creep softly to the window, peer into the room, and take aim. They had been on their way home, had seen Mark steal along in a very suspicious manner and had followed him to find out what it meant. There were three of them, fellows whom Mark had refused to play against on a County team because they were what is called "dirty" players. There had been hot words between Mark and them once when one of them had kicked a man in the face with spiked shoes who was just about to make a goal. Mark had succeeded in winning the umpire to his point of view and the others had lost their game and incidentally some money, and they had a grudge against him. Moreover there was money in this testimony for the Blue Duck Tavern could not afford to have its habitues in the public eye, and preferred to place the blame on a man who belonged more to the conservative crowd. The Blue Duck had never quite approved of Mark, because though he came and went he never drank, and he sometimes prevented others from doing so. This was unprofitable to them. So matters stood when the noon hour came and court adjourned for lunch.

Chapter 26

And while the long morning dragged itself away in Economy listening to a tale of shame, over on the bright Jersey coast the waves washed lazily on a silver strand reflecting the blueness of the September sky, and soft breezes hovered around the classsic little hospital building that stood in a grove of imported palms, and lifted its white columns picturesquely like some old Greek temple.

There was nothing in the life he was living now to remind Billy of either hell or Sabbath Valley, yet for long days and weeks he had struggled through flames in a deep dark pit lighted only by lurid glare and his soul had well nigh gone out under the torture. Once the doctors and nurses had stood around and waited for his last breath. This was a marked case. The Shaftons were deeply interested in it. The boy had mysteriously brought back all their valuable papers and jewels that had been stolen from them, and they were anxious to put him on his feet again. It went sadly against the comfortable self-complacent grain of a Shafton to feel himself under such mortal obligation to anyone.

But Billy was tougher than anyone knew, and one night after he had made the usual climb through the hot coals on his bare knees to the top of the pit, and come to the place where he always fell back, he held on a little tighter and set his teeth a little harder, and suddenly, with a long hard pull that took every atom of strength in his wasted young body, he went over the top. Over the top and out into the clean open country where he could feel the sea breeze on his hot forehead and know that it was good. He was out of hell and he was cooling off. The first step in the awful night that began that night in the old haunted house on the mountain had been won.

For three days he lay thus, cooling off and resting. He was fed and cared for but he took no cognizance of it except to smile weakly. Swallowing things was like breathing. You had to do it and you didn't think about it. The fourth day he began to know the nurses apart, and to realize he was feeling better. As yet the past lay like a blur of pain on his mind, and he hadn't a care about anything save just to lie and know that it was good to smell the salt, and see the shimmer of blue from the window. At times when he slept the sound of bells in old hymns came to him like a dream and he smiled. But on the fifth morning he lifted his light head uncertainly and looked out of the window. Gee! That was pretty! And he dropped back and slept again. When he awoke there was a real meal for him. No more slops. Soup, and potato and bit of bread and butter. Gee! It tasted good! He slept again and it was morning, or was it the same morning? He didn't know. He tried to figure back and decided he had been in that hospital about three days, but when the next morning dawned and he felt the life creeping back into his veins he began to be uncertain. He asked the nurse how soon he could get up and get dressed. She smiled in a superior way and said the doctor hadn't said. It would likely be some time yet, he had been pretty sick. He told her sharply he couldn't spare much more time, and asked her where his clothes were.

She laughed and said:

"Oh, put away. You'll have some new clothes when you get well. I heard Mrs. Shafton talking about it this morning when she was in the office. She's coming to see you pretty soon, and they mean to do a lot for you. You brought back her jewels, didn't you? Well, I guess you'll get your reward all right."

Billy looked at her blanky. Reward! Gosh! Was that reward going to meet him again?

"Say," said he frowning, "I want my own clothes. I don't want any new ones. I want my own! Say, I got some stuff in my pockets I don't wantta have monkeyed with!"

"All right," she said cheerily, "they're put away safe. You can have them when you're well." But when he asked her suddenly what day it was she said vaguely "Tuesday," and went away. He was so tired then he went to sleep again and slept till they brought his dinner, a big one, chicken and fixings and jelly, and a dish of ice cream! Oh, gee! And then he went to sleep again. But in the morning—how many days was it then? He woke to sudden consciousness of what he had to do and to sudden suspicion of the time. Billy was coming back to his own. His wilyness had returned. He smiled at the nurse ravishingly and asked for a newspaper, but when she brought it he pretended to be asleep, so she laid it down and went away softly. But he nabbed that paper with a weak hand as soon as her back was turned and read the date! His heart fell down with a dull thud. The third! This was the day of the trial! It couldn't be! He read again. Was it really the day of the trial? The paper that had the court program had been in his trousers pocket. He must have it at once. Perhaps he had made a mistake. Oh, gee! What it was to be helpless! Why, he was weaker than Aunt Saxon!

He called the nurse crossly. She bustled in and told him the doctor had just said he might sit up tomorrow if he kept on without a temperature for twenty-four hours longer. But he paid no heed to her. He demanded his clothes with a young roar of a voice that made her open her eyes. Billy had heretofore been the meekest of meek patients. She was getting the voice and manner now that he generally retained for family use. He told her there was something in the pocket he must see right away, and he made such a fuss about it that she was afraid he would bring up his temperature again and finally agreed to get the clothes if he would lie real still and rest afterward. Billy dropped his head back on the pillow and solemnly said: "Aw'wright!" He had visions of going to court in blue and white striped pajamas. It could be done, but he didn't relish it. Still, if he had to—

The nurse brought his jacket and trousers. The sweater was awfully dirty she said, but she was finally prevailed upon to bring that too, and Billy obediently lay down with closed eyes and his arm stretched out comfortingly over the bundles. The nurse hovered round till he seemed to be asleep and then slipped out for a moment, and the instant her white skirt had vanished from the doorway Billy was alert. He fumbled the bundles open with nervous fingers and searched eagerly for the bit of paper. Yes, there it was and the date the third of September. Aw, gee!

He flung back the neatly tucked sheets, poked a slim white foot that didn't look like his at all into a trouser leg, paused for breath and dove the other in, struggled into his jacket and lay down again quickly under the sheet. Was that the nurse?

He had to admit that he felt queer, but it would soon pass off, and anyhow if it killed him he had to go. Aw, bah! What was a little sickness anyhow? If he stayed in the hospital any longer they'd make a baby out of him!

The nurse had not returned. He could hear the soft plunk, plunk of her rubber heels on the marble steps. She was going downstairs. Now was his time! Of course he had no shoes and stockings, but what was a little thing like that? He grasped the bundle of sweater tightly and slid out of bed. His feet felt quite inadequate. In fact he began to doubt their identity. They didn't seem to be there at all when he stood on them, but he was not to be foiled by feet. If they meant to stick by him they'd gotta obey him.

Slowly, cautiously, with his head swimming lightly on ahead of him and a queer gasp of emptiness in the region of his chest that seemed to need a great deal of breath, he managed a passage to the door, looked down the long white corridor with its open doors and cheerful voices, saw a pair of stairs to the right quite nearby, and with his steadying hands on the cool white wall slid along the short space to the top step. It seemed an undertaking to get down that first step, but when that was accomplished he was out of sight and he sat down and slid slowly the rest of the way, wondering why he felt so rotten.

At the foot of the long stairs there was a door, and strange it was made so heavy! He wondered a nurse could swing it open, just a mere girl! But he managed it at last, almost winded, and stumbled out on the portico that gave to the sea, a wide blue stretch before him. He stopped, startled, as if he had unexpectedly sighted the heavenly strand, and gazed blinking at the stretch of blue with the wide white shore and the boom of an organ following the lapping of each white crested wave. Those palm trees certainly made it look queer like Saxy's Pilgrim's Progress picture book. Then the panic for home and his business came upon him and he slid weakly down the shallow white steps, and crunched his white feet on the gravel wincing. He had just taken to the grass at the edge and was managing better than he had hoped when a neat little coupe rounded the curve of the drive, and his favorite doctor came swinging up to the steps, eyeing him keenly. Billy started to run, and fell in a crumpled heap, white and scared and crying real tears, weak, pink tears!

"Why, Billy! What are you doing here?" The stern loving voice of his favorite doctor hung over him like a knife that was going to cut him off forever from life and light and forgiveness and all that he counted dear.

But Billy stopped crying.

"Nothin," he said, "I just come out fer a walk!"

The doctor smiled.

"But I didn't tell you you might, Billy boy!"

"Had to," said Billy.

"Well, you'll find you'll have to go back again, Billy.

Come!" and the doctor stooped his broad strong shoulders
to pick up the boy. But Billy beat him off weakly:

"Say, now, Doc, wait a minute," he pleaded. "It's jus' this
way. I simply *gotta* get back home t'day. I'm a very 'mpor-
tant witness in a murder case, see? My bes' friend in the
world is bein' tried fer life, an' he ain't guilty, an' I'm the
only one that knows it fer sure, an' can prove it, an' I gotta
be there. Why, Doc, the trial's *going on now* an' I ain't there!
It ud drive me crazy to go back an' lay in that soft bed like a
reg'lar sissy, an' know he's going to be condemned. I put it
to you, Doc, as man to man, would you stand fer a thing like
that?"

"But, Billy, suppose it should be the end of you!"

"I sh'd worry, Doc! Ef I c'n get there in time an' say what
I want I ain't carin' fer anythin' more in life, I tell ye. Say,
Doc, you wouldn't stop me, would ya? Ef you did I'd get
thar anyhow *someway!*"

The earnestness of the eager young face, wan in its illness,
the light of love in the big gray eyes, went to the doctor's
heart. He gave the boy a troubled look.

"Where is it you want to go, Billy?"

"Economy, Doc. It ain't far, only two or three hours' ride.
I c'n get a jitney somewheres I guess ta take me. I'll pay up
ez soon as I get home. I got thirty dollars in the bank my
own self."

"Economy!" said the doctor. "Impossible, Billy, it would
kill you!"

"Then I'm goin' anyhow. Good-bye, Doc!" and he darted
away from the astonished doctor and ran a rod or so before
the doctor caught up with him and seized him firmly by his
well shoulder:

"Billy, look here!" said the doctor. "If it's as bad as that
I'll take you!"

"Oh, would ya, Doc? Would ya? I'll never forget it, Doc!"

"There now, Billy, never mind, son, you save your

strength and let me manage this thing the right way. Couldn't I telephone and have them hold up things a few days? That can be done, you know."

"Nothin' doing, Doc, there's them that would hurry it up all the more if they thought I was comin' back. You get in, Doc, and start her up. I c'n drive myself if you'll lend me the m'chine. P'raps you ain't got time to go off 'ith me like this."

"That's all right, Billy. You and I are going on a little excursion. But first I've got to tell the nurse, or there'll be all kinds of a time. Here, you sit in the machine." The doctor picked him up and put him in and ran up the steps. Billy sat dizzily watching and wondering if he hadn't better make his escape. Perhaps the doc was just fooling him, but in a moment back he came again, with a nurse trailing behind with blankets and a bottle.

"We're going to get another car, son, this one's no good for such a trip. We'll fix it so you can lie down and save your strength for when you get there. No—son—I don't mean the ambulance," as he saw the alarm in Billy's face, "just a nice big car. That's all right, here she comes!"

The big touring car came round from the back almost immediately, and the backseat was heaped with pillows and blankets and Billy tenderly placed among them where he was glad enough to lie down—and close his eyes. It had been rather strenuous. The nurse went back for his shoes, bringing a bottle of milk and his medicine. The doctor got in the front seat and started.

"Now, son," he said, "you rest. You'll need every bit of strength when you get there if we're going to carry this thing through. You just leave this thing to me and I'll get you there in plenty of time. Don't you worry."

Billy with a smile of heavenly bliss over his newly bleached freckles settled back with dreamy eyes and watched the sea as they were passing swiftly by it, his lashes drooping lower and lower over his thin young cheeks. The doctor glancing back anxiously caught that look the mothers

see in the young imps when they are asleep, and a tenderness came into his heart for the staunch loyal little sinner.

Doctor Norris was a good scout. If he had got a soft snap
of a job in that Shafton hospital, it was good practice of
course, and a step to really big things where he wouldn't be
dependent upon rich people's whims, but still he was a good
scout. He had not forgotten the days of the grasshopper, and
Billy had made a great appeal to his heart. He looked at his
watch, chose his roads, and put his machine at high speed.
The sea receded, the Jersey pines whirled monotonously by,
and by and by the hills began to crop up. Off against the
horizon Stark Mountain loomed, veiled with a purple haze,
and around another curve Economy appeared, startlingly
out of place with its smug red brick walks and its gingerbread porches and plastered tile bungalows. Then without
warning Billy sat up. How long had that young scamp been
awake? Had he slept at all? He was like a man, grave and
stern with business before him. The doctor almost felt shy
about giving him his medicine.

"Son, you must drink that milk," he said firmly. "Nothing
doing unless you drink that!" Billy drank it.

"Now where?" asked the doctor as they entered the straggling dirty little town.

"That red brick building down the next block," pointed
Billy, his face white with excitement, his eyes burning like
two dark blue coals.

The big car drew up at the curb, and no one there to notice, for everybody was inside. The place was jammed to the
door.

Cherry had come back late after lunch, her hat awry and
signs of tears on her painted face. Her eyes were more obviously frightened and she whispered a message which was
taken up to Mark. Mark lifted a haggard face to hear it,
asked a question, bowed his head, and continued listening to
the cross-examination of a man who said he had heard him
threaten to kill Dolph the week before the murder down at

Hagg's Mills. When the witness was dismissed Mark whispered a word to his lawyer, the lawyer spoke to the judge and the judge announced that the prisoner wished to speak. Every eye was turned toward Mark as he rose and gave a sweeping glance around the room, his eyes lingering for just a shadow of an instant wistfully on the faces of the minister and his wife, then on again as if they had seen no one, and round to the judge's face.

It was just at this instant that Billy burst into the room and wedged his way fiercely between elbows, using his old football methods, head down and elbows out, and stood a moment breathless, taking it all in.

Then Mark spoke:

"Your Honor, I wish to plead guilty to the charge!"

A great sigh like a sob broke over the hush in the courtroom and many people half rose to their feet as if in protest, but Billy made a dive up the aisle, self and sickness forgotten, regardless of courts or law or anything, and stood between the judge and Mark:

"It ain't so, an' I can prove it!" he shouted at the top of his lungs.

The prosecuting attorney rose to a point of order like a bulldog snapping at his prey, the sergeant at arms rushed around like corn popping off in a corn popper, but Anthony Drew whispered a word to the judge, and after order was restored Billy was called to the witness stand to tell his story.

Doctor Norris standing squeezed at the back of the room looking for his quondam patient, recognized with a thrill the new Billy standing unafraid before all these people and speaking out his story in a clear direct way. Billy had etherealized during his illness. If Aunt Saxon had been there—she was washing for Gibsons that day and having her troubles with Mrs. Frost—she would scarcely have known him. His features had grown delicate and there was something strong and sweet about his mouth that surely never had been there before. But the same old forceful boy speech wherewith he had subdued enemies on the athletic field, bullied Aunt Saxon, and put one over on Pat at the station, was still his own. He told the truth briefly and to the point, not omitting his own wrongdoing in every particular, and he swayed that crowd as a great orator might have been proud to sway a congregation. They laughed till they cried and cried till they laughed again at Billy's quaint phrases, and they enjoyed the detour—Oh, how they enjoyed that detour! Even the judge had twinkles in his eyes.

For the first time since the trial began Mark was sitting up proudly, a warm look of vivid interest in his face, the cold mask gone. His eyes dwelt upon Billy with a look almost fatherly, at least brotherly. It was a startling contrast to what he had been all day. This was a different man.

Suddenly from the corner of the prosecution the low growl which had been gradually rising like a young storm, broke, and the prosecuting attorney arose and lifted his voice above all others:

"I protest, Your Honor, against this witness. He has mentioned no less than five different lies which he has told, and has narrated a number of episodes in which he deliberately broke the law. Is it or is it not a misdemeanor for anyone to meddle with our highroads in the manner that has just been described? By his own confession this young man is disqualified for a witness! By his own confession he is a lawbreaker and a liar!"

"Aw, gee!" broke forth Billy furiously. "Didn't I tell ya I come here to tell the truth n' get it off'n my chest?"

Someone put a strong hand on Billy and silenced him, and someone else rose to protest against the protestor, and the air grew tense with excitement once more.

The prosecution declared that Billy was in league with Mark, that everybody knew he trailed him everywhere, therefore his testimony was worthless. He was probably bribed; there was nothing, absolutely nothing in the story the boy had told to prove anything.

Billy was growing whiter and angrier, his eyes flashing, his fists clenched. His testimony was not going to be accepted after all! It had been vain to bear the shame himself. Nothing, *nothing* that he could do would blot out the trouble because he had unfitted himself to blot it out. It had to be a witness who told the truth who would be believed. It had to be one with a good record to take away the shame! That was something like what Miss Marilyn said in Sunday school once, that only Jesus Christ could take the place of a sinner and make it right about our sinning because He had never sinned. It had sounded like rot when she said it, but he began to understand what she meant now. Yes, that was it. Only God's Son could do that and he, Billy Gaston, had tried to do it himself!

The courtroom seemed to be very dark now. His head was whirling away and getting beyond his control, When he looked up he seemed to see it on the other side of the room. He did not recognize the two men in handcuffs that the chief was bringing into the room. He did not hear what the judge was saying. He had slumped in a little heap on the witness stand with his eyes closed, and his hands groping together. He thought that he was praying to God's Son to come and help Mark because he had failed. *He* wasn't good enough and he *had failed!*

The doctor had come with a bound up the aisle and was kneeling with Billy in his arms. Mark was leaning over the rail with a white anxious face. The minister was trying to make a way through the crowd, and the sergeant at arms was pushing the crowd back, and making a space about the unconscious boy. Someone opened a window. The chief and one of his men brought a cot. There was a pillow from the car, and there was that medicine again—bringing him back—just as he thought he had made God hear— Oh, *why* did they bother him?

Suddenly down by the door a diversion occurred. Someone had entered with wild burning eyes dressed in a curious assortment of garments. They were trying to put him out, but he persisted.

The word was brought up: "Someone has a very important piece of evidence which he wishes to present."

Billy's gray eyes opened as the man mounted to the witness stand. He was lying on the cot at one side and his gaze rested on the new witness, dazedly at first, and then with growing comprehension. Old Ike Fenner, the tailor, Cherry Fenner's father! Mark was looking at Billy and had not noticed.

But the man began to speak in a high shrill voice:

"I came to say that I'm the man that killed Dolph Haskins! Mark Carter had nothin' to do with it. I done it! I *meant* to kill him because he ruined the life of my little girl. *My baby!*"

There was a sudden catch in his voice like a great sob, and he clutched at the rail as if he were going to fall, but he went on, his eyes burning like coals:

"I shot him with Tom Petrie's gun that I found atop o' the door, an' I put it back where I found it. You take my fingerprints and compare 'em with the marks on the gun an' the windersill. You ask Sandy Robison! He seen me do it. You ask Cherry! She seen me too. She was facin' the winder eatin' her supper with that devil, and I shot him and she seen me! *I* did it—"

His voice trailed off. He swayed and got down from the stand, groping his way as if he could not see. The crowd gave way with a curious shudder looking into his wild burning eyes as he passed. A girl's scream back by the door rang through the court. The man moaned, put out his hands and fell forward. Kindly hands reached to catch him. The doctor left Billy and came to help.

They carried him outside and laid him on the grass in front of the courthouse. The doctor used every restorative he had with him. Men hurried to the drugstore. They tried everything, but all to no avail. Ike Fenner the tailor was dead! He had gone to stand before a higher court!

When it was all over, the fingerprints and the red tape, and the case had been dismissed, Mark came to Billy where he was lying in the big car waiting, with his eyes closed to keep back weak tears that would slip out now and then. He knelt beside the boy and touched his hand, the hand that looked so thin and weak and so little like Billy's:

"Kid," he said gently, "kid, you've been a wonder! It was really you that saved me, buddy! *My buddy!*"

Billy's tears welled over at the tone, the words, the proud intimate name, but he shook his head slowly, sadly.

"No," he said, "no, it wasn't me. I tried, but I wasn't fit! It had to be *Him.* I didn't understand! They wouldn't believe me. But *He* came as soon as I ast!"

Mark looked at the doctor.

"Is he wandering a little?" he asked in a low tone:

"I shouldn't wonder. He's been through enough to make anyone wander. Here, son take this."

Billy smiled and obediently accepted his medicine. Mark held his hand all the way home. He knew that Mark didn't understand but he was too tired to tell him now. Sometime he would explain. Or perhaps Miss Lynn would explain it for him. He was going home, home to Saxy and Sabbath Valley and the bells, and Mark was free! He hadn't saved him, but Mark was free!

It was like a royal passage through the village as they came into Sabbath Valley, for everybody came out to wave at Mark and Billy. Even Mrs. Harricutt watched grimly from behind her holland shades. But Billy was too weak to notice much, except to sense it distantly, and Mark would only lift his hat and bow gravely, quietly, as if it didn't matter, just as he used to do when they carried him round on their shoulders after a football game, and he tried to get down and hide. Why did Mark still have that sad look in his eyes? Billy was too tired to think it out. He was glad when they reached Aunt Saxon's door and Mark picked him up as he used to do when he was just a little kid, and carried him up to his room. Carried him up and undressed him, while Saxy heard the story from the doctor's lips, and laughed and cried and laughed again. The nervy little kid! He would always be a little kid to Saxy, no matter what he did.

He turned over in his own bed, *his bed,* and smelled the sweet breath of the honeysuckle coming in at the window, heard the thrushes singing their evening song up the street. The sea had been great, but, oh, you Sabbath Valley! Out there was the waterspout, and someday he would be strong enough to shin down it, and up it again. He would play football this fall, and run Mark's car! Mark, grave, gentle, quiet, sitting beside him till he got asleep, and his mother not knowing, down the street, and Miss Lynn—

"Mark—you'll tell Miss Marilyn about it all?" He opened his eyes to murmur lazily, and Mark promised still gravely.

He shut his eyes and drifted away. What was that the chief had told him down at Economy in the car? Something about three strange detectives stepping off the train one day and nabbing Pat? And Pat was up at Sing Sing finishing his term. Was that straight or only a dream? And anyhow he didn't care. He was home again, home—*and forgiven!*

Night settled sweetly down upon Sabbath Valley, hiding the brilliant autumn tinting of the street. Lynn had made a maple nut cake and set the table for two before she left the Carters', for her mother had slipped out of the courtroom and telephoned her, and a fire was blazing in the little parlor with the lace curtains and asters in every vase all gala for the returning son. The mother and son sat long before the fire, talking, pleasant converse, about the time when Mark would send for her to come and live with him, but not a word was said about the day. He saw that his friends had helped to save his mother this one great sorrow that she could not have borne, and he was grateful.

Marilyn, up at the parsonage, with a great thankfulness upon her, went about with smiling face. The burden seemed to have lifted and she was glad.

But that night at midnight there came the doctor from Economy driving hard and stopping at the parsonage. Cherry Fenner was dying and wanted to see Miss Marilyn. Would she come?

Chapter 27

Cherry's little bedroom under the roof was bright with the confusion of cheap finery scattered everywhere and swept aside at the sudden entrance of the death angel. A neighbor had done her best to push away the crude implements of complexion that were littering the cheap oak bureau top, and the doctor's case and bottles and glasses crowded out the giddy little accessories of beauty that Cherry had collected. Two chairs piled high with draggled finery, soiled work aprons, and dresses made a forlorn and miscellaneous disorder in one corner, and the closet door sagged open with visions of more clothing hung many deep upon the few hooks.

Mrs. Fenner stood at the head of the bed wringing her hands and moaning uncontrolledly, and Cherry, little Cherry, lay whitely against the pillow, the color all gone from her ghastly pretty little face, that had lately hid its ravished health and beauty behind a camouflage of paint. There were deep dark circles under the limpid eyes that now were full of mortal pain, and pitiful lines around the cherry mouth that had been wont to laugh so saucily.

The doctor stood by the window with the attitude of grave waiting. The helpful neighbor lingered in the doorway, holding her elbows and taking minute note of Marilyn's dress. This might be a sad time, but one had to live afterward, and it wasn't every day you got to see a simple little frock with an air like the one the minister's daughter wore. She studied it from neck to hem and couldn't see what in the world there was about it anyway to make her look so dressed up. Not a scratch of trimming, not even a collar, and yet she could look like that! Mercy! Was that what education and going to college did for folks?

The light of a single unshaded electric bulb shone startlingly down to the bed, making plain the shadow of death even to an inexperienced eye.

Marilyn knelt beside the bed and took Cherry's cold little hand in her own warm one. The waxen eyelids fluttered open, and a dart of something between fright and pain went over her weird little face.

"Can I do anything for you, Cherry?" Marilyn's voice was tender, pitiful.

"It's *too late,*" whispered the girl in a fierce little whisper. "Send 'em out— I—wantta— tell—you—someth—" The voice trailed away weakly. The doctor stepped over and gave her a spoonful of something, motioned her mother and the neighbor away, tiptoeing out himself and closing the door. The mother was sobbing wildly. The doctor's voice could be heard quieting her coldly:

The girl on the bed frowned and gathered effort to speak:

"Mark Carter—didn't mean no harm—goin'—with me!" she broke out, her breath coming in grasps. "He was tryin'—to stop me—goin'—with—*Dolph!*" The eyes closed wearily. The lips were white as chalk. She seemed to have stopped breathing!

"It's all right—Cherry—" Marilyn breathed softly. "It's all right—I understand! Don't think any more about it!"

The eyes opened fiercely again, a faint determination shadowed round the little mouth:

"You gotta know!" she broke forth again with effort. "He was good to me—when I was a little kid, and when he found I was in trouble—" the breath came pitifully in gasps— "he—offered—to—*marry me!*"

Marilyn's fingers trembled but she held the little cold hand warmly and tried to keep back the tears that trembled in her eyes.

"He—didn't—*want to—*! He—just—*done it to be kind!*

But I—couldn't—see—it— That's—what—we—*argued*—"
Her voice grew fainter again. Marilyn with gentle controlled
voice pressed the little cold hand again:

"Never mind, Cherry dear—it's all right!"

"Cherry's eyes opened with renewed effort, anxiously:

"You won't—blame—Mark? He never—did—nothin'—
wrong!" He's—*your*—friend!"

"No, Cherry! It's all right!"

The girl seemed to have lost consciousness again, and
Marilyn wondered if she ought not to call the doctor, but
suddenly Cherry screamed out:

"There he is again! He's *come for me!* Oh—I'm—a—
gon'ta—*die!* An' I'm *afrrrr-aid!*"

Cherry clutched at Marilyn's arm, and looked up with far
off gaze in which terror seemed frozen.

The minister's daughter leaned farther over and gathered
the fragile form of the sick girl in her arms tenderly, speaking in a soothing voice:

"Listen, Cherry. Don't be afraid. Jesus is here. He'll go
with you!"

"But I'm afraid of Jesus!" the sharp little voice pierced out
with a shudder. "I haven't been—*good!*"

"Then tell Him you are sorry. You *are* sorry, aren't you?"

"Oh, *yes!*" the weak voice moaned. "I—never—*meant*—
no—harm! I only—wanted—a little—good time!"

The eyes had closed again and she was almost gone. The
doctor had come in and he now gave her another spoonful
of medicine. Marilyn knew the time was short.

"Listen, Cherry, say these words after me!" Cherry's eyes
opened again and fastened on her face, eagerly:

"Jesus, I'm sorry!"

"Jesus—I'm—sor-ry!" repeated the weak voice in almost
a whisper.

"Please forgive me," said Marilyn slowly, distinctly.

"Please—for—give—" the slow voice repeated.

"And save me."

"—save—" the voice was scarcely audible.

The doctor came and stood close by the bed, looking down keenly, but Cherry roused once more and looked at them, her sharp little voice stabbing out into the silence piercingly,

"Is that—*all?*"

"That is all," said Marilyn with a ring in her voice, "Jesus died to take care of all the rest! You can just rest on Him!"

"Oh-h!" The agony went out of the pinched little face, a half smile dawned and she sank into rest.

As Marilyn went home in the dawn with the morning star beginning to pale, and the birds at their early worship, something in her own heart was singing too. Above the feeling of awe over standing at the brink of the river and seeing a little soul go wavering out, above even the wonder that she had been called to point the way, there sang in her soul a song of jubilation that Mark was exonerated from shame and disgrace. Whatever others thought, whatever she personally would always have believed, it still was great that God had given her this to make her know that her inner vision about it had been right. Perhaps sometime, in the days that were to come, Mark would tell her about it, but there was time enough for that. Mark would perhaps come to see her this morning. She somehow felt sure that at least he would come to say he was glad she had stayed with his mother. It was like Mark to do that. He never let any little thing that was done for him or his pass unnoticed.

But the morning passed and Mark did not come. The only place that Mark went was to see Billy.

"Billy, old man," he said, sitting down by the edge of the bed where Billy was drowsing the early morning away, just feeling the bed, and sensing Saxy down there making chicken broth, and knowing that the young robins in the apple tree under the window were grown up and flown away. "Billy, I can't keep my promise to you after all. I've got to go away. Sorry, kid, but she'll come to see you and I want you to tell her for me all about it. I'm not forgetting it, kid, either, and you'll know, all the rest of my life, *you and I are buddies!* Savvy, kid?"

Billy looked at Mark with big understanding eyes. There was sadness and hunger and great self-control in that still white face that he worshiped so devotedly. All was not well with his hero yet. It came to him vaguely that perhaps Mark too had even yet something to learn, the kind of thing that was only learned by going through fire. He struggled for words to express himself, but all he could find were:

"I say, Mark, why'n't'tya get it off'n yer chest? It's *great!*"

Perhaps there wouldn't have been another human in Sabbath Valley, except perhaps it might have been Marilyn who would have understood that by this low growled suggestion Billy was offering confession of sin as a remedy for his friend's ailment of soul, but Mark looked at him keenly, almost tenderly for a long minute, and shook his head, his face taking on a grayer, more hopeless look as he said:

"I can't, kid. It's *too late!*"

Billy closed his eyes for a moment. He felt it wasn't quite square to see into his friend's soul that way when he was off his guard, but he understood. He had passed that way himself. It came to him that nothing he could say would make any difference. He would have liked to tell of his own experience in the courtroom and how he had suddenly known that all his efforts to right his wrong had been failures, that there was only One who could do it, but there were no words in a boy's vocabulary to say a thing like that. It sounded unreal. It had to be *felt,* and he found his heart kept saying over and over as he lay there waiting with closed eyes for Mark to speak: "Oh, God! Why'n'tchoo show him Yerself? Why'n'tchoo show him Yerself?" He wondered if Miss Lynn couldn't have shown Mark if he had only gone and talked it over with her. But Mark said it was too late. "Well, Why'n'tchoo show him Yerself, then? Why'n'tchoo show him Yerself, God—*please!*"

Mark got up with a long sigh:

"Well, s'long, kid, till I see you again. And I won't forget, kid, you know I won't forget! And, kid, I'm leaving my gun with you. I know you'll take good care of it and not let it do any damage. You might need it you know to take care of your Aunt or— or— Miss Severn—or!"

"Sure!" said Billy with shining eyes clasping the weapon that had been Mark's proud possession for several years. "Aw, gee! Ya hadn't oughtta give me this! You might need it yourself."

"No, kid, I'd rather feel that you have it. I want to leave someone here to kind of take my place—watching—you know. There'll be times—"

"Sure!" said Billy, a kind of glory overspreading his thin eager face. "*Aw, gee! Mark!*"

And long after Mark had gone, and the sound of his purring engine had died away in the distance, Billy lay back with the weapon clasped to his heart, and a weird kind of rhythm repeating itself over and over somewhere in his spirit: "Why'n'tchoo show him Yerself, God? Why'n'tchoo show him Yerself? You will! I'll bet You *will!* yet!"

And was that anything like the prayer of faith translated into theological language?

Aunt Saxon went up tiptoe with the broth and thought he was asleep and tiptoed down again to keep it warm awhile. But Billy lay there and felt like Elisha after the mantle of the prophet Elijah had fallen upon him. It gave him a grand solemn feeling, God and he were somehow taking Mark's place till Mark got ready to come back and do it himself. He was to take care of Sabbath Valley as far as in him lay, but more particularly of Miss Marilyn Severn.

And then suddenly, without warning, Miss Marilyn herself went away, to New York she said, for a few weeks, she wasn't sure just how long. But there was something sad in her voice as she said it, and something pathetic about the look she wore that made him sure she was not going to the part of New York where Mark Carter lived.

Billy accepted it with a sigh. Things were getting pretty dry around Sabbath Valley for him. He didn't seem to get his pep back as fast as he had expected. For one thing he worried a good deal, and for another the doctor wouldn't let him play baseball nor ride a bicycle yet for quite awhile. He had to go around and act just like a "gurrull!" Aw, gee! Sometimes he was even glad to have Mary Little come across the street with her picture puzzles and stay with him awhile. She was real good company. He hadn't ever dreamed before that girls could be as interesting. Of course, Miss Marilyn had to be a girl once, but then she was Miss Marilyn. That was different.

Then too, Billy hadn't quite forgotten that first morning that Saxy got her arms around him and cried over him glad tears, bright sweet tears that wet his face and made him feel like crying happy tears too. And the sudden surprising desire he felt to hug her with his well arm, and how she fell over on the bed and got to laughing because he pulled her hair down in his awkwardness, and pulled her collar crooked. Aw, gee! She was just Aunt Saxy and he had been rotten to her a lot of times. But now it was different. Somehow Saxy and he were more pals, or was it that he was the man now taking care of Saxy and not the little boy being taken care of himself? Somehow during those weeks he had been gone Saxy had cried out the pink tears, and was growing smiles, and home was kinda nice after all. But he missed the bells. And nights before he got into bed he got to kneeling down regularly, and saying softly inside his heart: "Aw, gee, God, please why'n'tcha make Mark understand, an' why'n'tcha bring 'em both home?"

Chapter 28

Marilyn had not been in New York but a week before she met Opal. She was waiting to cross Fifth Avenue, and someone leaned out of a big limousine that paused for the congestion in traffic and cried:

"Why, if that isn't Miss Severn from Sabbath Valley. Get in please, I want to see you."

And Lynn, much against her will, was persuaded to get in, more because she was holding up traffic than because the woman in the limousine insisted:

"I'll take you where you want to go," she said in answer to Lynn's protests, and they rolled away up the great avenue with the moving throng.

"I'm dying to know what it is you're making Laurie Shafton do," said Opal eagerly. "I never saw him so much interested in anything in my life. Or is it you he's interested in? Why, he can't talk of anything else, and he's almost stopped going to the Club or any of the house parties. Everybody thinks he's perfectly crazy. He won't drink anymore either. He's made himself quite *notorious.* I believe I heard someone say the other day they hadn't even seen him smoking for a whole week. You certainly are a wonder."

"You're quite mistaken," said Lynn, much amused, "I had nothing to do with Mr. Shafton's present interest, except as I happened to be the one to introduce him to it. I haven't seen him but twice since I came to New York, and then only to take him around among my babies at the settlement and once over to the Orphans' Home, where I've been helping out while an old friend of mine with whom I worked in France is away with her sick sister."

"For mercy sake! You don't mean that Laurie consented

to go among the poor? I heard he'd given a lot of money to fix up some buildings, but then all the best men are doing things like that now. It's quite the fad. But to go himself and see the wretched little things. Ugh! I don't see how he could. He must be quite crazy about you I'm sure if he did all that for you."

"Oh, he seemed to want to see them," said Lynn lightly, "and he suggested many of the improvements that he is making himself. They tell me he has proved a great helper, he is on hand at all hours superintending the building himself, and everybody is delighted with him!"

"Mmmm!" commented Opal looking at Marilyn through the fringes of her eyes. "You really are a wonder. And now that you are in New York I'm going to introduce you to our crowd. When can you come? Let's see. Tomorrow is Sunday. Will you spend the evening with me tomorrow? I'll certainly show you a good time. We're going to motor to—"

But Lynn was shaking her head decidedly:

"I couldn't possibly spare a minute, thank you. I'm only out on an errand now. I'm needed every instant at the home!"

"For mercy sake! Hire someone to take your place then. I want you. You'll be quite a sensation, I assure you. Don't worry about clothes, if you haven't anything along. You can wear one of my evening dresses. We're almost of a size."

"No," said Lynn smiling. "It simply isn't possible. And anyway, don't you remember Sabbath Valley? I don't go out to play Sunday nights, you know."

"Oh, but this is New York! You can't bring Sabbath Valley notions into New York."

Lynn smiled again:

"You can if they are a part of you," she said. "Come in and see how nicely I'm fixed."

Opal looked up at the beautiful building before which they were stopping.

"Why, where is this?" she asked astonished, "I thought you were down in the slums somewhere."

"This is a home for little orphan children kept up by the Salvation Army. Come in a minute and see it."

Following a whim of curiosity Opal came in, and was led down a long hall to a great room where were a hundred tiny children sitting on little chairs in a big circle playing kindergarten games. The children were dressed in neat pretty frocks such as any beloved children would wear, with bright hair ribbons and neckties, and each with an individuality of its own. The room was sunny and bright, with a great playhouse at one end, with real windows and furniture in it and all sorts of toboggan slides and swings and kiddy cars and everything to delight the soul of a child. On a wide space between two windows painted on the plaster in soft wonderful coloring blended into the gray tint of the wall, there glowed a life-size painting of the Christ surrounded by little children, climbing upon His knees and listening to Him as He smiled and talked to them.

Opal paused in the doorway and looked at the picture first, shyly, shamedly, as though it were no place for her to enter, then curiously at the little children, with a kind of wistful yearning, as if here were something she had missed of her own fault. Lynn called out a charming baby and made her shake hands and bow and say a few lisping smiling words. Opal turned to Lynn with a strangely subdued look and spoke in a moved tone:

"I guess you're right," she said, "you wouldn't fit at my company. You're different! But some day I'm coming after you and bring you home all by yourself for a little while. I want to find out what it is you have that I need."

Then she turned with swift steps and went down the hall and out the door to her waiting limousine, and Lynn smiled wonderingly as she saw her whirled away into the world again.

Lynn had not seen Mark.

Laurie Shafton had called upon her many times since those two trips they had taken around the settlements and looking over his condemned property, but she had been busy, or out somewhere on her errands of mercy, so that Laurie had got very little satisfaction for his trouble.

But Mark had seen Lynn once, just once, and that the first time she had gone with Laurie Shafton, as they were getting out of his car in front of one of his buildings. Mark had slipped into a doorway out of sight and watched them, and after they passed into the building had gone on, his face whiter and sadder than before. That was all.

Marilyn was to spend only a month in New York, as at first planned, but the month lengthened into six weeks before the friend whose place she was taking was able to return, and two days before Marilyn was expecting to start home there came a telephone message from her mother:

"Lynn, dear, Mrs. Carter is very low, dying, we think, and we must find Mark at once! There is not a minute to lose if he wants to see her alive. It is a serious condition brought on by excitement. Mrs. Harricutt went there to call yesterday while everybody else was at Ladies' Aid. And Lynn, *she told her about Mark!* Now, Lynn, can you get somebody to go with you and find Mark right away? Get him to come home at once? Here is the last address he gave, but they have no telephone and we dare not wait for a telegram. See what you can do quickly!"

It was four o'clock in the afternoon when this message came. Lynn put on a uniform of dark blue serge and a poke bonnet that was at her disposal whenever she had need of protection, and hurried out.

She found the address after some trouble, but was told that the young gentleman was out. No one seemed to know when he would return.

Two or three other lodgers gathered curiously, one suggesting a restaurant where he might be found, another a club where he sometimes went and a third laughed and called out from halfway up the stairs:

"You'll find him at the cabaret around the corner by ten o'clock tonight if you don't find him sooner. He's always there when he's in town."

Sick at heart Lynn went on her way trying carefully each place that had been suggested but finding no trace of him. She met with only deference for her uniform wherever she went, and without the slightest fear she traveled through streets at night that she would scarcely have liked to pass alone in the daytime in her ordinary garb. But all the time her heart was praying that she might find Mark before it was too late. She tried every little clue that was given her, hoping against hope that she would not have to search for her old friend in a cabaret such as she knew that place around the corner must be. But it was almost ten o'clock and she had not found Mark. She went back to the first address once more, but he had not come, and so she finally turned her steps toward the cabaret.

Sadly, with her heart beating wildly, hoping, yet fearing to find him, she paused just inside the doors and looked around, trying to get used to the glare and blare, the jazz and the smoke, and the strange lax garb, and to differentiate the individuals from the crowd.

Food and drink, smoke and song, wine and dance, flesh and odd perfumes! Her soul sank within her, and she turned bewildered to a servitor at the door.

"I wonder, is there any way to find a special person here? I have a very important message."

The man bent his head deferentially as though to one from another world, "Who did you want, Miss?"

"Mr. Mark Carter," said Marilyn, feeling the color rise in her cheeks at letting even this waiter see that she expected to find Mark Carter here.

The man looked up puzzled. He was rather new at the place. He summoned another passing one of his kind:

"Carter, Carter?" the man said thoughtfully. "Oh, yes, he's the guy that never drinks! He's over there at the table in the far corner with the little dancer lady—" The waiter pointed and Lynn looked. "Would you like me to call him, Miss?" Lynn reflected quickly. Perhaps he might try to evade her. She must run no risks.

"Thank you, I will go to him," she said, and straight through the maze of candle-lighted tables, and whirling dancers, in her quiet holy garb, she threaded her way hastily, as one might have walked over quicksands, with her eye fixed upon Mark.

She came and stood beside him before he looked up and saw her, and then he lifted his eyes from the face of the girl with whom he was talking, and rose suddenly to his feet, his face gone white as death, his eyes dark with disapproval and humiliation.

"Marilyn!" His voice was shaking. He knew her instantly in spite of poke bonnet and uniform. She was the one thought present with him all the while, perhaps for years wherever he had been. But he did not look glad to see her. Instead it was as if his soul shrank shamedly from her clear eyes as she looked at him.

Marilyn had not known what she was going to say to him when she found him. She did not stop to think now.

"Mark, your mother wants you. She is dying! You must come quick or she will be gone!"

Afterward she repeated over the words to herself again and again as one might do penance, blaming herself that she had not softened it, made it more easy for him to bear. Yet at the time it seemed the only thing there was to say, at such a time, in such a place. But at the stricken look upon his face her heart grew tender. "Come," she said compassionately. "We will go!"

They went out into the night and it was as if they had suddenly changed places, as if she were the protector and he the led. She guided him the quickest way. There was only a chance that they might catch the midnight train, but there was that chance. Into the subway she dived, he following, and breathless, they brought up at the Pennsylvania Station at their train gate as it was being closed, and hurried through.

All through that agonized night they spoke but few words, those two who had been so much to one another through long happy years.

"But you are not going too?" he spoke suddenly roused from his daze as the train started.

"Yes, I am going too, of course, Mark," she said.

He bowed his head and almost groaned:

"I am not worthy, Marilyn!"

"That—has nothing to do with it!" said Marilyn sadly. "It never will have anything to do with it! It never did!"

Mark looked at her, with harrowed eyes, and dropped his gaze. So he sat, hour after hour, as the train rushed along through the night. And Marilyn, with head slightly bent and meek face, beneath the poke bonnet with its crimson band, was praying as she rode. Praying in other words the prayer that Billy murmured beside his bed every night.

But Billy was not lying in his bed that night, sleeping the sleep of the just. He was up and on the job. He was sitting in the Carter kitchen keeping up the fires, making a cup of tea for the nurse and the doctor, running the endless little errands, up to the parsonage for another hot water bag, down to the drugstore for more aromatic spirits of ammonia, fixing a newspaper shade to dull the light in the hall, and praying, all the time praying: "Oh, God, ain'tcha gonta leave her stay till Mark gets here? Ain'tch gonta send Mark quick? You know best I 'spose, but ain'tch *gonta?*" And then, "Aw, gee! I wisht Miss Lynn was here!"

In the chill before the dawning the two stepped down

from the train at a little flag station three miles from Sabbath Valley on the upper road that ran along the ridge. They had prevailed upon the conductor to let them off there. Mark had roused enough for that. And now that they were out in the open country he seemed to come to himself. He took care of Lynn, making her take his arm, guiding her into the smooth places, helping her over rough places. He asked a few questions too. How did she know of his mother's condition? How long had she been this way? Had she any idea that his mother's heart was affected? Did she have a shock?

Lynn did not tell all she knew. It was hard enough without that. He need not know that it was the knowledge of his disgrace that had brought her to the brink of death.

So, walking and talking almost as in the old days, they passed into Sabbath Valley and down the street, and Christie McMertrie listening perhaps for this very thing, crept from her bed in her long flannel nightgown, and big ruffled nightcap, and looked out the window to see them go by. "Bless them!" she breathed and crept back to her bed again. She had nursed all day, and all the night before, and would have been there too tonight, only Mary Rafferty took things in her own hands and had her go to bed, herself taking charge. Mrs. Duncannon was there too. There really was no need of her, but Christie could not sleep, and after they passed she rose and dressed and slipped down the street with a hot porridge that had been cooking on the stove all night, and the makings of a good breakfast in her basket on her arm.

Mark Carter reached home in time to take his mother in his arms and bid her good-bye. That was all. She roused at his voice and touch, and reached out her little pretty hands toward him. He took her in his big strong arms and held her, kissed her with tender lips and she drew a beautiful smile of perfect content and slipped away, with the graying golden hair straying out over Mark's sleeve to the pillow in a long curl, and a quiver of her last smile on the pretty curve of her lips, as if this was all that she had waited for, the little pretty girl that had gone to school so long ago with golden hair and a smile. Billy, standing awed in the doorway whither he had come to say there was more hot water ready, caught the vision of her face, remembered those school days, and felt a strange constriction in his throat. Some day Saxy would have to go like that, and would show the little girl in her face too, and he maybe would have to hold her so and think of how cross he had been. Aw, gee! Whattaqueer thing life was anyhow! Well, hadn't his prayer been answered? Didn't Mark get here in time? Well, anyhow it was likely better for Mrs. Carter to go. But it was rotten for Mark. Aw, gee! *Mark!* Was *this* the way he had to learn it? Aw, gee! Well, God would have to show him. *He* couldn't dope it out anyhow.

During the days that followed Mark hardly stirred from the side of the pretty little clay that had been his mother except when they forced him for a little while. An hour before the service he knelt alone beside the casket, and the door opened and Marilyn came softly in, closing it behind her. She walked over to Mark and laid her hand on his hand that rested over his mother's among the flowers, and she knelt beside him and spoke softly:

"Oh, God, help Mark to find the light!"

Then the soul of Mark Carter was shaken to the depths and suddenly his self-control which had been so great was broken. His strong shoulders began to shake with sobs, silent, hard sobs of a man who knows he has sinned, and tears, scalding tears from the depths of his self-contained nature.

Marilyn reached her arm out across his shoulders as a mother would try to protect a child, and lifted her face against his, wet with tears, and kissed him on his forehead. Then she left him and went quietly out.

"Well," said Mrs. Harricutt with satisfaction as she walked home after the funeral with Christie McMertrie,

"I'm glad to see that Mark Carter has a little proper feeling at last. If he'd showed it sooner his ma mighta ben in the land of the living yet."

Christie's stern face grew sterner as she set her teeth and bit her tongue before replying. Then she said with more brrrr than usual in her speech:

"Martha Harricutt, there's na land that's sa livin' as tha land where Mark Carter's mither has ganged tae, but there's them that has mair blame to bear fer her gaein' than her bonny big son, I'm thinkin', an' there's them in this town that agrees with me too, I know full well."

Down in front of the parsonage the minister had his arm around Mark Carter's shoulders and was urging him:

"Son, come in. We want you. Mother wants you, I want you. Marilyn wants you. Come, son, come!"

But Mark steadily refused, his eyes downcast, his face sad, withdrawn:

"Mr. Severn, I'll come tomorrow. I can't come tonight. I must go home and think!"

"And you will promise me you will not leave without coming, Mark?" asked the minister sadly when he saw that it was no use.

"Yes, I will promise!" Mark wrung the minister's hand in a warm grip that said many things he could not speak, and then he passed on to his lonely home. But it was not entirely empty. Billy was there, humbly, silently, with dog-true eyes, and a grown-up patient look on his tired young face. He had the coffeepot on the stove and hot sausages cooking on the stove, and a lot of Saxy's doughnuts and a pie on the table. Billy stayed all night with Mark. He knew Saxy would understand.

Chapter 29

In the middle of the night the fire bell rang out wildly. Three minutes later Mark and Billy were flying down the street, with Tom McMertrie and Jim Rafferty close after and a host of other tried and true, with the minister on the other side of the street. The fire company of Sabbath Valley held a proud record, and the minister was an active member of it.

The fire was up in the plush mill and had already spread to a row of shackley tenements that the owners of the mills had put up to house the foreign labor that they had put in. They called them apartment houses, but they were so much on the order of the city tenements of several years back that it made Lynn's heart ache when she went there to see a little sick child one day. Right in the midst of God's trees and mountains, a man *for money* had built a deathtrap, tall, and grim and dark, with small rooms and tiny windows, built it with timbers too small for safety, and windows too few for ventilation, and here an increasing number of families were herded, in spite of the complaints of the town.

"I ben thenkin' it would coom," said Tom as he took long strides. "It's the apartmints fer sure, Jimmy. We better beat it. There'll be only a meenit er so to get the children oot, before the whole thing's smoke!"

They were all there, the doctor, the blacksmith, the postmaster, the men from the mills, and the banks, and the stores. Economy heard the bells—for Marilyn had hurried to the church and added the fire chime to the call—and came over with their little chemical engine. Monopoly heard and hurried their brand-new hook and ladder up the valley road, but the fire had been eating long in the heart of the plush mill and laughed at their puny streams of water forced

up from the creek below, laughed at the chemicals flung in
its face like drops of rain on a sizzling red-hot stove. It
licked its lips over the edge of the cliff on which it was built,
and cracked its jaws as it devoured the mill, window by
window, section by section, leaping across with an angry red
tongue to the first tall building by its side.

The fire had worked cunningly, for it had crept out of
sight to the lower floors all along the row, and unseen, unknown, had bitten a hold on each of those doomed buildings
till when the men arrived it went roaring ghoulishly up the
high narrow stairs cutting off all escape from above, and
making entrance below impossible. Up at the windows the
doomed people stood, crying, praying, wringing their hands,
and some losing their heads and trying to jump out.

The firemen were brave, and worked wonders. They flung
up ladders in the face of the flames. They risked their lives
every step they took, and brought out one after another,
working steadily, grimly, rapidly. And none were braver
among them all than Mark Carter and the minister, each
working on the very top of a tall treacherous ladder, in the
face of constant danger, bringing out one after another until
the last.

The next house to the mill had caved in, and Mark had
come down just in time with an old woman who was bedrid-
den and had been forgotten. The workers had paused an instant as the horrible sound of falling timbers rent through
the other noises of that horrible night, and then hurried to
increase their vigilance. There were people in the top floor
of the next house and it would go next. Then the word went
forth that no more must go up the ladder. The roof was
about to fall in, and a young mother shrieked, "My baby!
My baby! She's up in the bed. I thought Bob had her, but he
couldn't get up!" Mark Carter looked at her sharply.
"Which window?" he asked, and was up the ladder before
detaining hands could reach him, and Billy, sliding under
the arm of the fire chief, swung up just behind.

The crowd watched breathless as they mounted round after round, Aunt Saxon standing with a shawl over her head and gasping aloud, "Oh, *Willie!*" and then standing still in fear and pride, the tears streaming down a smiling countenance on which the red glare of the fire shone. The ladder was set crazily against the flaming window and swayed with their weight. Every step seemed as if it would topple the building, yet the ladder held, and Mark sprang through the blazing window out of sight. It seemed an eternity till he returned bringing a tiny bundle with him, and handing it out to Billy waiting below.

The boy received as it had been a holy honor, that little bundle of humanity handed through the fire, and came solemnly down amid the breathless gaze of the crowd, but when they looked to the top again Mark had disappeared!

A murmur of horror went round the throng, for the flames were licking and snapping, and the roof seemed to vibrate and quiver like a human thing. Then before anyone could stop him or even saw what he was going to do, the minister sprang forward up the ladder like a cat, two rounds at a time—three! He dashed through the fire and was gone!

For an instant it seemed that the people would go mad with the horror of it. *Those two!* Even the fire chief paused and seemed petrified. It was Billy who sensed the thing to do.

"Getcher canvas man? Are ya' asleep?"

And instantly a great piece of canvas was spread and lifted. But the building tottered, the flames ate on, and the window seemed entirely enveloped. The moment lasted too long for the hearts that waited. A groan rent the air. Then suddenly a breath seemed to part the flames and they saw the minister coming forward with Mark in his arms!

It was just at this instant that Lynn came flying down the street. She had kept the bells going till she knew all the help had come from a distance, and now she was coming to see if there was anything else for her to do. There before her she saw her father standing in that awful setting of fire, with Mark limp and lifeless in his arms! Then the flames licked up and covered the opening once more. *Oh, God!* Were they *both gone?*

Only for an instant more the suspense lasted, and then the cataclysm of fire came. The roof fell carrying with it the floors as it went, down, down, down, shuddering like a human thing as it went, the rain of fire pouring up and around in great blistering flakes and scorching the onlookers and lighting their livid faces as they stood transfixed with horror at the sight.

The canvas fluttered uselessly down and fire showered thick upon it. Timbers and beams crumbled like paper things and were no more. The whole flimsy structure had caved in!

Paralyzed with terror and sorrow the firemen stood gazing, and suddenly a boy's voice rang out: "Aw, gee! Git to work there! Whatterya doin'? Playin' dominoes? Turn that hose over there! That's where they fell. Say, you, Jim, get that fire hook and lift that beam! *Aw, gee!* Ya ain't gonta let 'em *die*, are ya? *Them two!*"

Billy had seized a heavy hose and was turning it on a central spot and Jim Rafferty caught the idea and turned his stream that way, and into the fire went the brave men, one and another, instantly, cheerfully, devotedly, the men who loved the two men in there. Dead or alive they should be got out if it killed them all. They would all die together. The fire chief stood close to Billy, and shouted his directions, and Billy worked with the tallest of them, black, hoarse and weary.

It seemed ages. It was hours. It was a miracle! But they got those two men out alive! Blackened and bruised and broken, burned almost beyond recognition, but they were alive. They found them lying close to the front wall, their faces together, Mark's body covered by the minister's.

Tender hands brought them forth and carried them gently

on stretchers out from the circle of danger and noise and smoke. Eagerly they were ministered to, with oil and old linen and stimulants. There were doctors from Economy and one from Monopoly besides the Sabbath Valley doctor, who was like a brother to the minister and had known Mark since he was born. They worked as if their lives depended upon it, till all that loving skill could do was done.

Billy, his eyelashes and brows gone, half his hair singed off, one eye swollen shut and great blisters on his hands and arms, sat huddled and shivering on the ground between the two stretchers. The fire was still going on but he was "all in." The only thing left he could do was to bow his bruised face on his trembling knees and pray:

"Oh, God, ain't You gonta let 'em live—*please!"*

They carried Mark to the Saxon cottage and laid him on Billy's bed. There was no lack of nurses. Aunt Saxon and Christie McMertrie, the Duncannons and Mary Rafferty, Jim too, and Tom. It seemed that everybody claimed the honors. The minister was across the street in the Little house. They dared not move him farther. Of the two the case of the minister was the most hopeless. He had borne the burden of the fall. He had been struck by the falling timbers, his body had been a cover for the younger man. In every way the minister had not saved himself.

The days that followed were full of anxiety. There were a few others more or less injured in the fire, for there had been fearless work, and no one had spared himself. But the two who hung at the point of death for so long were laid on the hearts of the people, because they were dear to almost everyone.

Little neighborhood prayer meetings sprang up quietly here and there, beginning at Duncannons. The neighbor on either side would come in and they would just drop down and pray for the minister, and for "that other dear brave brother." Then the Littles heard of it and called in a few friends. One night when both sufferers were at the crisis and there seemed little hope for the minister, Christie McMertrie called in the Raffertys and they were just on the point of kneeling down when Mrs. Harricutt came to the door. She had been crying. She said she and her husband hadn't slept a wink the night before, they were so anxious for the minister. Christie looked at her severely, but remembering the commands about loving and forgiving, relented:

"Wull, then, come on ben an' pray. Tom, you go call her husband! This is na time fer holdin' grudges. But mind, wumman, if ye coom heer to pray ye must pray with as *mooch fervor* for the healin' o' *Mark Carter* as ye do fer the meenister! He's beloved of the Lord too, an' the meenister nigh give his life for him."

And Mrs. Harricutt put up her apron to her eyes and entered the little haircloth parlor, while Tom, with a wry face went after the elder. The elder proved that underneath all his narrowness and prejudice he had a grain of the real truth, for he prayed with fervor that the Lord would cleanse their hearts from all prejudice and open their minds to see with heavenly vision that they might have power in prayer for the healing of the two men.

So, through the whole little village breaches were healed, and a more loving feeling prevailed because the bond of anxiety and love held them all together and drew them nearer to their God.

At last the day came when Mark, struggling up out of the fiery pit of pain, was able to remember.

Pain, fire, flame, choking gases, smoke, remorse, despair! It was all vague at first, but out of it came the memory slowly. There had been a fire. He had gone back up the ladder after Mrs. Blimm's baby. He remembered groping for the child in the smoke-filled room, and bringing it blindly through the hall and back to the window where the ladder was, but that room had all been in flames. He had wished for a wet cloth across his face. He could feel again the licking of the fire as he passed the doorway. A great weight had been on his chest. His heart seemed bursting. His head had reeled, and he had come to the window just in time. Someone had taken the child—was it Billy? or he would have fallen. He *did* fall. The memory pieced itself out bit by bit. He remembered thinking that he had entered the City of Fire literally at last, "the minarets" already he seemed to descry "gleaming vermilion as if they from the fire had issued." It was curious how those old words from Dante had clung in his memory. "Eternal fire that inward burns." He thought he was feeling now in his body what his soul had experienced for long months past. It was the natural ending, the thing he had known he was coming to all along, the road of remorse and despair. A fire that goes no more out! And this would last forever now! Then, someone, some strong arm had lifted him—God's air swept in—and for an instant there seemed hope. But only that little breath of respite and there came a cry like myriads of lost souls. They were falling, falling, down through fire, with fire above, below, around, everywhere. Down, down—an abysmal eternity of fire, till his seared soul writhed from his tortured body, and stood aside looking on at himself.

There, there he lay, the Mark Carter that had started with life so fair, friends, prospects, so proud that he was a man, that he could conquer and be brave—so blest with opening life, and heaven's high call! And then—in one day—he had sinned and lost it all, and there he lay, a white upturned face. That was himself, lying there with face illumined by the fire, and men would call him dead! But he would not be dead! He would be living on with that inward fire, gnawing at his vitals, telling him continually what he might have been, and showing him what high heaven was that he had had, and lost. He saw it now. He had deliberately thrown away that heaven that had been his. He saw that hell because he made it so, it was not God that put him there, but he had chosen there to go. And still the fire burned on and scorched his poor soul back into the body to be tortured more. The long weeks upon that bed seemed like an infinite space of burning rosy, oily flames poured upward from a lake of fire, down through which he had been falling in constant and increasing agony.

And now at last he seemed to be flung upon this peaceful shore where things were cool and soothing for a brief respite, that he might look off at where he had been floating on that molten lake of fire, and understand it all before he was flung back. And it was all so very real. With his eyes still closed he could hear the rushing of the flames that still seemed ascending in columns out a little way from shore, he could see through his eyelids the rosy hue of livid waters— of course it was all a hallucination, and he was coming to himself, but he had a feeling that when he was fully awake it would be even more terrible than now. Two grim figures, Remorse and Despair, seemed waiting at either hand above his bed to companion him again when he could get more strength to recognize them. And so he lay thus between life and death, and faced what he had done. Hours and hours he faced it, when they knew not if he was conscious yet, going over and over again those sins which he knew had been the beginning of all his walk away from Hope. On through the night and into the next morning he lay thus, sometimes drowsing, but most of the time alert and silent.

It was a bright and sparkling morning. There was a tang of winter in the air. The leaves were gone from the apple trees at the window and the bare branches tapped against the waterspout like children playing with a rattle. A dog barked joyously, and a boy on the street shouted out to another—*Oh, to be a boy once more!* And suddenly Mark knew Billy was sitting there. He opened his eyes and smiled: There were bandages around his face, but he smiled stiffly, and Billy knew he was smiling.

"Kid," he said hoarsely from out the bandages, "this is God's world." It seemed to be a great thought that he had been all this time grasping, and had to utter.

"Sure!" said Billy in a low happy growl.

A long time after this, it might have been the next day, he wasn't sure, or perhaps only a few minutes, he came at another truth:

"Kid, you can't get away from God—even when you try."

"I'll say not," said Billy.

"But—when you've sinned—" speculatively.

"You gotta get it off yer chest."

"You mean—confess?"

"Sure thing. Miss Lynn tells us in Sunday school about a fella in the Bible got downta eatin' with the pigs in a far country, an' when he come to himself he thought about his father's servants, an' he said 'I'll get up and beat it home an' say I'm sorry!' "

"I know," said Mark, and was still the rest of the day. But the next morning he asked the doctor how soon he might get up. This was the first real indication that Mark was on the mend, and the doctor smiled with satisfaction. He meant to take off some of the bandages that morning.

That afternoon with his head unswathed, Mark began to ask questions. Before that he had seemed to take everything for granted:

"Billy, where's the minister?" For Billy had never left his idol's side except when Aunt Saxon needed him to help.

"Oh, he's up to tha parsonage," responded Billy carelessly.

"But why hasn't he been to see me, kid?"

"Why—he—hasn't been feelin' very good." Billy's voice was brisk as if it wasn't a matter of much moment.

Mark turned his thoughtful gray eyes steadily on Billy:

"Now, look here, kid, I'm well, and there's no further need to camouflage. Billy, is the minister dead?"

"Not on yer tintype, he ain't dead!"

"Well, is he hurt?"

"Well, some," Billy admitted cheerfully.

"Kid, look me in the eye."

Billy raised a saucy eye as well masked as Mark's own could be on occasion.

"Kid, how much is he hurt! *Tell me the truth!* If you don't I'll get right up and go and see."

"I'll tell the world, you won't!" said Billy rising lazily and taking a gentle menacing step toward the bed.

"Kid!"

"Well—he's some hurt—but he's getting along fine now. He'll be aw'wright."

"How'd he get hurt?"

"Oh, the fire, same's you."

"How?" insisted Mark.

"Oh, he went up again after a fella when it was too late—"

"Billy, was it me?"

"Ugh huh!" nodded Billy.

Mark was so still that Billy was frightened. When he looked up worried he saw that a great tear had escaped out from under the lashes which were growing nicely now, and had rolled down Mark's cheek. *Mark crying!*

In consternation Billy knelt beside the bed:

"Aw, gee! Mark, now don't you feel like that. He's gettin' all right now they hope, an' gee! He was *great!* You oughtta seen him!"

"Tell me about it," said Mark huskily.

"He just ran up that there ladder when it was shaking like a leaf, an' the wall beginning to buckle under it, an' he picked you up. Fer a minute there the flames kinda blew back, and we seen ya both, and then the roof caved, an' you all went down. But when we gotcha out he was layin' right atop of ya, 'ith his arms spread out, trying t'cover ya! Gee, it was *great!* Everybody was just as still, like he was preachin'!"

After a long time Mark said:

"Billy, did you ever hear the words, 'Greater love hath no man than this, that a man lay down his life for his friend'?"

"Yep," said Billy, "that's in the Bible I think, if 'taint in Shakespeare. Miss Lynn said it over last Sunday. She says a lot of things from Shakespeare sometimes, and I kinda get'em mixed."

But Mark did not talk anymore that day. He had a great deal to think about.

But so did Billy, for looking out the window in the direction of the parsonage he had sighted the big Shafton car stopping before the door that morning. "Aw, gee!" he said. "That sissy guy again? Now, how'm I gonta get rid of him this time? Gee! Just when Mark's gettin' well too! If life ain't just *one thing after another!*"

Chapter 30

It was a bright frosty morning in the edge of winter when at last they let Mark go to see the minister, and Billy took care that no hint of the Shafton car should reach his knowledge. Slowly, gravely he escorted Mark down the street and up the parsonage steps.

The minister was lying on a couch in the living room and there was a low chair drawn up nearby with a book open at the place, and a bit of fluffy sewing on the low table beside it. Mark looked hungrily about for the owner of the gold thimble, but there was no sign of either Mrs. Severn or Marilyn about.

There was a bandage over the minister's eyes. They hadn't told Mark about that yet.

The minister held out a groping hand with his old sweet smile and hearty welcoming voice:

"Well, son, you've come at last! Beat me to it, didn't you? I'm glad. That was fair. Young blood, you know."

Mark knelt down by the couch with his old friend's hand held fast: Billy had faded into the landscape out on the front steps somewhere, and was even now settling down for an extended wait. If this interview went well he might hope to get a little rest and catch up on sports sometime soon. It all depended on this.

Mark put up his other hand and touched the bandage:

"Father!" he said. "Father!" and broke down "Father, I have sinned—" he said brokenly.

The minister's arm went lovingly up across the young man's shoulders:

"Son, have you told your heavenly Father that?" he asked gently.

315

"I've tried," said Mark. "I'm not sure that He heard."

"Oh, He *heard*," said the minister with a ring of joy in his voice. "While you were a great way off He came to meet you, son."

"You don't know yet," said Mark lifting a white sad face.

"If you've told Him I'll trust you, son. It's up to you whether you tell me or not."

"It is your right to know, sir. I want you to know. I cannot rest again until you do."

"Then tell." The minister's hand folded down tenderly over the boy's, and so kneeling beside the couch Mark told his story:

"I must begin by telling you that I have always loved Marilyn."

"I know," said the minister, with a pressure on the hand he covered.

"One day I heard someone telling Mrs. Severn that I was not good enough for her."

"I know," said the minister again.

"You know?" said Mark in surprise.

"Yes, go on."

"I went away and thought it over. I felt as if I would die. I was mad and hurt clear through, but after I thought it over I saw that all she had said was true. I wasn't good enough. There was a great deal of pride mixed with it all of course, I've seen that since, but I wasn't good enough. Nobody was. Lynn is *wonderful!* But I was just a common, insignificant nobody, not fit to be her mate. I knew it! I could see just how things were going too. I saw you didn't realize it, you nor Mrs. Severn. I knew Marilyn cared, but I thought she didn't realize it either, and I saw it was up to me. If she wasn't to have to suffer by being parted from me when she grew older, I must teach her not to care before she knew she cared. For days I turned it over in my mind. Many nights I lay awake all night or walked out on the hills, threshing it all over again. And I saw another thing. I saw that if it was so hard for me then when I was not much more than a kid it would be harder for her if I let her grow up caring, and then we had to be parted, so I decided to make the break. The day I made the decision I went off in the hills and stayed all day thinking it out. And then I looked up in the sky and told God I was done with Him. I had prayed and prayed that He would make a way out of this trouble for me, and He hadn't done anything about it, and I felt that He was against me too. So when I had done that I felt utterly reckless. I didn't care what happened to me, and I decided to go to the bad as fast as I could. I felt it would be the best way too to make Marilyn get over being fond of me. So I went down to Monopoly that night and looked up a fellow that had been coaching the teams for a while and was put out by the association because he was rotten. He had always made a fuss over me, wanted to make a big player out of me, and I knew he would be glad to see me.

"He was. He took me out to supper that night and gave me liquor to drink. You know I had never touched a drop. Never had intended to as long as I lived. But when he offered it to me I took it down as if I had been used to it. I didn't care. I wanted to do all the wrong I could.

"I drank again and again, and I must have got pretty drunk. I remember the crowd laughed at me a great deal. And they brought some girls around. It makes me sick to think of it now. We went to a place and danced. I didn't know how, but I danced anyway. And there was more drinking. I don't remember things very distinctly. I did whatever the coach said, and he had been going a pretty good pace himself. That night—" His voice choked with shame and it seemed as though he could not go on—but the minister's clasp was steady and the boy gathered courage and went on— "That night—we—went—to a house of shame!"

He dropped his head and groaned. The minister did not attempt to break the pause that followed. He knew the struggle that was going on in the bitterness of the young man's soul. He maintained that steady handclasp:

"In the morning—when I came to myself—" he went on, "I knew what I had done. I had cut myself off forever from all that made life worthwhile. I would never be worthy again to even speak to you all whom I loved so much. I would never be able to look myself in the face again even. I was ashamed. I had given up God and love, and everything worthwhile.

"That was when I went away to New York. Mother tried to stop me, but I would go. I tried when I got to New York to plunge into a wild life, but it didn't attract me. I had to force myself. Besides, I had resolved that whatever came, wherever I went I would not drink and I would *keep clean*. I thought that by so doing I might in time at least win back my self-respect. Later I conceived the idea of trying to save others from a life of shame. I did succeed in helping some to better ways I think, both men and girls. But I only won a worse reputation at home for it, and I'm not sure I did much good. I only know I walked in hell from morning to night, and in time I came to dwell among lost souls. It seemed the only place that I belonged.

"You remember when you read us Dante 'Thou who through the City of Fire alive art passing'? You used to preach in church about beginning the eternal life now, and making a little heaven below, I'm sure that is as true of hell. I began my eternal life five years ago, but it was in hell, and I shall go on living in that fire of torture forever, apart from all I love. I tried to get out by doing good to others, but it was of no avail. I thought never to tell you this, but something made me, after you—you gave your life for me!"

"And had you forgotten," said the minister tenderly, "that the blood of Jesus Christ His Son cleanseth us from all sin? And that He said, 'Come now and let us reason together: though your sins be as scarlet they shall be as white as snow'?"

"I gave up all right to that when I gave up God on the mountain."

"But God did not give up you," said the minister. "Do you think a true father would cast out a child because it got angry and shook its fist in his face? You will find Him again when you search for Him with all your heart. You have told Him you were sorry, and He has promised to forgive. You can't save yourself, but He can save you. Now, son, go and tell Marilyn everything."

"Do you mean it—*Father?*"

"I mean it—*Son.* The doctor is coming by and by to take off these bandages, and I want the first thing that my eyes rest upon after my dear wife's face, to be the faces of you two. My beloved children.

Sabbath Valley lay tucked warm and white beneath a blanket of snow. All the week it had been coming down, down, in great white flakes of especially sorted sizes, filling the air mightily with winter clean and deep. Here in the fastnesses of the hills it seemed that the treasure troves of the sky had been opened to make all beautiful and quiet while winter passed that way. Lone Valley was almost obliterated, pierced with sharp pine trees in bunches here and there, like a flock of pins in a pincushion, and the hills rose gently on either side like a vast amphitheater done in white and peopled thick with trees in heavy white furs.

The highway was almost impassable for a day or two, but the state snowplow passed over as soon as the snow stopped falling, and left a white pavement with white walls either side. The tunnel through the mountains was only a black dot in the vast whiteness, and Pleasant View Station wore a heavy cap of snow dripping down in lavish fringes edged with icicles. The agent's little shanty up the mountain was buried out of sight behind a snowdrift and had to be dug out from the back, and no lake train ran anymore. The express was five hours late. Stark Mountain loomed white against the sky. And over in Sabbath Valley the night it stopped snowing all the villagers were out shoveling their walks and calling glad nothings back and forth as they flung the white stardust from their shovels, and little children came out with rubber boots and warm leggings and wallowed in the beauty. The milkman got out an old sleigh and strung a line of bells around his horse. The boys and girls hurried up the mountain to their slide with homemade sleds and laughing voices, and the moon came up looking sweetly from a sudden clearing sky.

Over in the church the windows shone with light, and the bells were ringing out the old sweet songs the villagers loved. Marilyn was at the organ and Mark by her side. In the body of the church willing hands were working, setting up the tall hemlocks that Tom and Jim had brought in from the mountain, till the little church was fragrant and literally lined with lacey beauty, reminding one of ancient worship in the woods. Holly wreaths were hanging in the windows everywhere, and ropes of ground pine and laurel festooned from every pillar and corner and peak of roof.

Laurie Shafton had sent a great coffer of wonderful roses, and the country girls were handling them with awe, banking them round the pulpit, and trailing them over the rail of the little choirloft, wonderful roses from another world, the world that Marilyn Severn might have married into if she had chosen. And there sat Marilyn as indifferent as if they were dandelions, praising the *trees* that had been set up, delighting in their slender tops that rose like miniature spires all round the wall, drawing in the sweetness of their winter spicy breath, and never saying a word about the roses. "Roses? Oh, yes, they look all right, girls, just put them wherever you fancy. I'll be suited. But aren't those trees too beautiful for words?"

When the work was done they trooped out noisily into the moonlight, bright like day only with a beauty that was almost unearthly in its radiance. The others went on down the street calling gay words back and forth, but Mark and Marilyn lingered, bearing a wreath of laurel, and stepping deep into the whiteness went over to the white piled mound where they had laid Mrs. Carter's body to rest and Mark stooped down and pressed the wreath down into the snow upon the top:

"Dear little Mother," he said brokenly, "she loved pretty things and I meant to give her so many of them sometime to make up—"

"But she'll be glad—" said Marilyn softly. "We loved each other very much!"

"Yes, she'll be glad!" he answered. "She often tried to find out why I never went to the parsonage anymore. Poor little mother! That was her deepest disappointment! Yes, she'll be glad!"

When morning came it seemed as though the very glory of God was spread forth on Sabbath Valley for display. There it lay, a shining gem of a little white town, in the white velvet cup of the valley, dazzling and resplendent, the hills rising round about reflecting more brightness and etched with fringes of fine branches each burdened with a line of heavy furry white. Against the clear blue sky the bell tower rose, and from its arches the bells rang forth a wedding song. Marilyn in her white robes, with a long white veil of rare old lace handed down through the generations, falling down the back and fastened about her forehead, and with a slim little rope of pearls, also an heirloom, was ringing her own wedding bells, with Mark by her side, while the villagers gathered outside the door waiting for the wedding march to begin before they came in.

The minister and his wife stood back in his little study behind the pulpit, watching their two with loving eyes, and down by the front door stood Billy in a new suit with his hair very wet and licked back from an almost crimson countenance, waiting the word to fling open the door and let the congregation in.

"*Tum,* diddy*dum*—Diddy*dum*—diddy*dum*—Diddy*dum*—diddy*dum*—Diddy*dum*—*dum*—*dum*—Dum—Dum—Dum!" began the organ and Billy flung the portals wide and stood aside on the steps to let the throng pass in, his eyes shining as if they would say, "Aw, gee! Ain't this great?"

And just at that moment, wallowing through the snow, with the air of having come from the North Pole there arrived a great car and drew up to the door, and Laurie Shafton jumped anxiously out and flung open the door for his passengers.

"Aw, gee! That fish! Whadde wantta come here for? The great *chump!* Don't he knew he ain't *in it?*"

Billy watched in lofty scorn from his high step and decided to hurry in and not have to show any honors to that sissy guy.

Then out from the car issued Opal, done in furs from brow to shoe and looking eagerly about her, and following her a big handsome sporty man almost twice her age, looking curiously interested, as if he had come to a shrine to worship, Opal's husband. Billy stared, and then remembering that the wedding march was almost over and that he might be missing something:

"Aw, gee! Whadduw I care? He ain't little apples now, anyhow. He couldn'ta bought her with *barrels* of roses, an' he knows it too, the poor stiff. He must be a pretty good scout after all, takin' his medicine straight!"

Then Billy slid in and the quiet little ceremony began.

The organ hushed into nothing. Marilyn arose, took Mark's arm, and together they stepped down and stood in front of the minister, who had come down the steps of the pulpit and was awaiting them, with Marilyn's mother sitting only a step away on the front seat.

It was all so quiet and homey, without fuss or marching or any such thing, and when the ceremony was over the bride and groom turned about in front of the bank of hemlock and roses and their friends swarmed up to congratulate them. Then everybody went into the parsonage, where the ladies of the church had prepared a real country wedding breakfast with Christmas turkey and fixings for a foundation and going on from that. It wasn't every day in the year that Sabbath Valley got its minister's daughter married, and what if the parsonage *was* small and only fifty could sit down at once, everybody was patient, and it was all the more fun!

The three guests from out of town, self-imposed, looked on with wonder and interest. It was a revelation. Marilyn looked up and found big Ed Verrons frankly staring at her, a puzzled pleased expression on his large coarse face. She was half annoyed and wondered why they had come to spoil this perfect day. Then suddenly the big man stepped across the little living room and spoke:

"Mrs. Carter, we came over today because Opal said you had something that would help us begin over again and make life more of a success. I want to thank you for having this chance to see a little bit of heaven on earth before I die."

Later, when the city guests were fed and comforted perhaps, and had climbed back into the big car, Billy stood on the front porch with a third helping of ice cream and watched them back, and turn, and wallow away into the deep white world, and his heart was touched with pity:

"Aw, gee! The poor fish! I 'spose it *is* hard lines! And then it was sorta my faultchu know," and he turned with a joyful sigh that they were gone, and went in to look again at Mary Louise Little, and see what it was about her in that new blue challis that made her look so sorta nice today.

The Gold Shoe

Chapter 1

Anastasia Endicott shivered and drew her velvet evening wrap closer about her shoulders, as she sat forward in the Pullman chair and tried to look through the snow-blotched window at her side.

The train seemed to be crawling, like a baffled invalid that gained a few inches and then stopped to cough. It had been going on that way for an hour, and did not seem to be getting anywhere. It was outrageous, such service! A ride only thirty-five miles taking all this time! What would her friends think of her? They would be waiting in their car at the station, and in such a storm!

But surely the train must be almost there!

She glanced down anxiously at the little trifle of platinum and diamonds on her wrist that stood for a time piece, and then out the baffling window again; but no friendly light outside illumined the blanket of snow that covered the glass, and she shivered again.

How cold it was!

She leaned down and touched the heat pipes that ran along under the window, and drew back with a shudder. They were cold as stone. The heat had gone out! How unpardonable in the railroad company to let a thing like that happen on such a cold stormy night!

She leaned forward and summoned the official who was passing rapidly through the car, speaking in a tone of accusation as if the fault belonged to him personally.

"Yes, Miss," he said, "fire's out. She's broke. We're trying to patch her up, but we can't make much headway. Something wrong with her connections. This ain't the only car is cold, Miss; the whole train is in the same fix."

She felt the lack of sympathy in his cold blue eyes as he started on again. She resented his suggestion that others were suffering. What had that to do with her?

"When are we going to get to Stonington?" she asked sharply. "We've been an hour and a quarter already from the city and this

3

train is scheduled to do it in fifty-five minutes."

"Not on a night like this, Miss," said the brakeman. "Schedules ain't in it. The snow plow is ahead of us, and it's stuck in a drift high as a house. We got twelve men out there shoveling an' the wind blowin' forty knots a minute."

"But I'm going to a dance!" said the girl stupidly. "I shall be late!" Her voice was most impatient. "And I'm freezing!" she added and shivered again visibly.

The brakeman grinned.

"Better have yer dance in here then an' keep warm!" he advised. "There's a man in the next car goin' to his dyin' child!" His tone was significant, and he passed out of the car and slammed the door. She was alone in the parlor car. The only other occupant had gone out to help with the shoveling. She drew her velvets closer and shuddered back into the plush of the chair, drawing her feet up and tucking one under her to get it warm. Then she remembered her delicate dance frock and put it quickly down again.

Dying child! What did he want to tell her that for? How horrid of him when he knew she was going to a dance. A dance and a dying child did not fit together. Oh, how cold it was! Why had she not brought her fur coat? But she had counted on driving back in the Lymans' limousine with her friend Adrienne, and there were always plenty of fur robes in the Lymans' car. She had not dreamed of being cold. She had come to the station in a taxi from her overheated home; there had been heat in the taxi. The parlor car was always warm enough in her experience and she felt ill-used that it had suddenly failed her. She was expecting to be met at her journey's end by a heated limousine and conveyed to the country house some five miles from the station, where the dance was to be held. There really had been no need for a fur coat, for her evening wrap was lined with rich silk and warmly interlined.

She glanced helplessly about her. She had no hand baggage save a delicate beaded bag containing her compact, handkerchief, and gloves. She had arrived home from a trip to Washington but that afternoon, to find awaiting her this invitation to a dance at a friend's magnificent country estate; had telephoned her friend Adrienne Lyman who was also an invited guest and arranged to return with her, and her friends; had dressed hurriedly, been driven to this train just in time and here she was! Shivering! Snow banks on every side!

It began to occur to her that the return trip might not be so easy even in Adrienne's big limousine. Why, if a great iron train on a railroad track found it difficult going, how could an automobile manage? But then, railroads were different of course. Railroads had drifts on them. They went out in the country through queer places where there were winds that blew a lot and made a very little snow seem much. Of course a track got clogged up sooner than just a road where cars were going back and forth all the time. And the road between Stonington and the city was a main highway, with a great deal of traffic. Of course there wouldn't be any trouble in getting home.

She took her delicate handkerchief and mopped away at the window pane, breathing on the glass, trying to melt the clogging feathers and see through to the storm, but everything seemed a blot of impenetrable whiteness.

She settled back disconsolately into her cold chair and felt more like crying than she had since she was a child and broke her doll. To think that she, Tasha Endicott, should be caught in a fix like this! And then, just as she was in despair the brakeman came back through the car, slamming the door after him and stamping off snow from his feet. He gave her a familiar grin as he passed her, and lurched on out at the other end, slamming that door too. She felt a helpless fury rise within her. The impertinence! For a man like that to presume to grin at her in that leering triumphant way! He ought to be reported and discharged. She would tell her father about it. He should be discharged!

She got up and tried to walk up and down the aisle, stamping her gold slippered feet impatiently, trying to bring back life into them. It would be awful if she got her feet frost bitten. How could she dance? It was very painful to have frost bitten feet!

Then, without warning, the train gave a great lurch which sent her in a little rustling heap of rose color and gold in the aisle.

Angry and disheveled she arose quickly, for a sudden draft of air told her that someone had opened the door; and looking anxiously she saw the grinning brakeman with a lantern in his hand, standing in the open door, a twinkle of merriment in his eyes.

More furious than ever she essayed to be seated, with dignity, but just at that instant the train gave another tremendous lurch that precipitated her into her chair in a hurry and completely robbed the act of all dignity. In fact one gold slipper flew off in the aisle and she had to catch herself with inglorious haste to keep from sliding back onto the floor again.

She did not look up at the brakeman again, but when she had rescued and donned her slipper she felt that the door was closed and she was alone. Also, she realized that the train was moving once more slowly, creaking, but steadily with a pause now and then, and a lurch, but moving.

They had gone perhaps a hundred yards or more when the train slowed down and stopped with something of its old decision, and the door opened and the brakeman called out:

"Stonington! Stoooooo-ning-toooon! All out for Stonington!"

Tasha arose hastily, excitedly, and made her shaky way down the aisle. She seemed somehow weak in the knees, and trembling. Perhaps it was the fall, or her anger. She came to the platform, and the obnoxious brakeman with his lantern stood on the bottom step looking as if he meant to assist her.

She stiffened and threw her shoulders back.

"Is this really Stonington?" she asked sharply, trying to peer into the blear of blanket whiteness that constituted the air. It had not been snowing like this in town when she started. At least she had not noticed that it was so thick.

"Yep!" answered the brakeman. "Jump, an' I'll put you over where the snow ain't so deep."

Tasha drew back.

"Where is the porter?" she asked haughtily.

"Out shovelin'!" said the brakeman. "Better jump quick ef you wanta git off. We ain't stoppin' long!"

Tasha advanced to the steps and looked down into the sea of whiteness, then drew back again"

"Why, this is outrageous!" she said crisply. "The railroad company has no right to stop in a place like this. Where is the platform? I'd rather go to the other end of the car."

"Say, Miss, ef you don't git off here you git carried to Elkins station. We're only 'commodation this far, and then we're 'xpress. You sure you wanta git off at Stonington?"

"I certainly do!" she said freezingly. "But I want you to go and get the porter for me!"

A snort from the engine and a slight lurch of the train broke upon the conversation.

"Nothin' doin'!" said the brakeman. "Either you git off ur you don't!"

He gave a quick glance around, peering beyond the station into the white darkness.

"Say, Miss, is anyone meeting you? Because this station is closed for the night."

"There certainly is someone meeting me," said Tasha, still haughtily.

The brakeman cast another uncertain glance about, and saw a tiny spark of light wavering toward them several rods away.

"Oh, all right then!" he said with a relieved tone, "here you go! We ain't got any more time for fooling!" and to her horror he caught her in his burly arm like a bundle of baggage and swung her across the steps and far out over the billows of whiteness, setting her down under what seemed like a great shadow, in comparative shelter, where only a few of the stinging snowflakes cut into her unprotected face, and bit her lips and her eyes. And then he was gone, clinging to the lower step of the car, his lantern swinging out into the white storm, signaling to some force in the impenetrable whiteness beyond. She saw him moving slowly away from her, leaving her in sudden awful loneliness.

It had all happened so quickly that she had not realized. The chill of the snow on her silken ankles seemed to enfold her as if she were in the grasp of a new and awful power. She realized that she was standing almost knee keep in snow, and she tried to take a step out of it, but nowhere was there a shallower place to put her foot.

In new horror she cried out and tried to run toward the train that was slipping past her now with its lighted windows, the very window where her breath a few minutes before had melted a black circle on the pane, was leering mockingly down upon her now like a bright eye, and her soul suddenly knew how safe and warm she had been inside and how fearfully perilous was her present position. She cried again and waved her arms toward the brakeman whose lantern was giving its final swing, as he jerked himself in out of the storm, but her voice was flung back upon the blanket stillness and frightened her the more.

The tears were running down her cheeks and freezing as they fell, but she did not know it. She was stung to sudden panic and began to run after the train, but she fell in the first attempt and lay there helpless for a moment, her bare hands plunging elbow deep into the heavy snow, her face even going down into its smothering chill. Snow inside her flimsy inadequate garments, snow round her throat like icy fingers, snow in her eyes and her mouth and her hair, smothering icy snow!

One of her little gold slippers, the loose one that had come off before, came off again and was lost in the whiteness. The snow bit into the little gold silk foot that felt in vain for its covering.

Tasha cried aloud and knew not what she said as she sobbed, but it seemed to come to her dimly through it all that there was no one by to help her and she must help herself. She had never had to help herself in any trying situation before, but now she must. There had always been servants, or persons whose business it was to care for her, close at hand, in any predicament before. Now she was alone! It was somebody's fault of course that she was, and they should suffer for it when she got home, but now she must take care of herself. Home! Would she ever be home again? A fear gripped her! Snow killed people sometimes. They froze to death in it. Even now she could feel it would be easier to lie still and sink, sink, and forget it all. She was so cold! Oh, how her feet hurt! She wouldn't be able to dance to-night! But that didn't matter! Oh, why didn't the chauffeur come after her? He must have seen her get off. Was he waiting around the other side of the station?

She looked up and the dark shadow of a snow draped building loomed above her. She must get up and find that slipper. She must get around to the other side of the station quickly before the chauffeur decided she hadn't come and went home without her. She must! She must!

She called as she struggled to her feet:

"Hello! Hello! I'm here! Wait! Wait! I'm coming!" But the wind caught her voice and flung it back into her own ears, and the snow flung a blanket over the echo too so that she knew she had not been heard.

At last she got to her feet again, her poor insensate feet, and then with a mighty resolve, she clutched around in the snow with her bare hands until she came upon the little slipper. She drew it to her breast and hugged it with her bead purse as if it were moving slowly, with difficulty, toward the station till she almost fell against the stone wall, and her feet came unexpectedly upon shallower going. She stood for an instant to get her breath, leaning against the wall, and finding that the wind here did not swoop and search her quite so violently, as out by the tracks. Perhaps if she could get around to the other side it might be even more sheltered. Oh, why did they close stations in places like this! If she could only get inside the door!

But when she reached the other side of the building and came unexpectedly in contact with a latch she found it would not open. She stood within the doorway, braced against it, one little gold slipper and her bead bag still pressed against her breast, one little icy foot drawn up against her cold cold knee. The other icy foot was trying to balance on a tiny gold spike of a heel, and one slender arm was frantically clutching the big bronze knob of the closed door for support as she tried to peer into the blank whiteness beyond.

But nowhere could she see a sign of a car! It was all a level whiteness, earth and air and sky, all full of whirling whiteness, stinging and snatching and biting at her, and how long could she hold out?

Suddenly out of the terrible white darkness before her a light danced, glared and danced away again, like a new menace. Was it the headlight of a car? It did not seem large enough for that and yet as she looked, there it was again, still larger, glaring into her eyes like some beast of prey. She shook off the new fear that took hold of her. Of course it was the car which was to have come for her, and she must make them know where she was.

She lifted up her voice and shouted:

"Here! Here! Here I am!"

The wind flung her words down her throat. They could not get by the blanket that hung between her and all human kind. It was silly! It was a nightmare! She must rouse herself and make them hear or they would go away again and leave her here all night. She doubted not she was in the first stages of freezing, else why could she not get her words across to that stupid chauffeur? She must!

Down went the little cold gold chiffon-stockinged foot, into the feathery snow, almost comforted from the bitter cold above, and she caught her breath and called again:

"Heee-rrr!-"

But she stopped suddenly as a tall dark figure loomed above her and one bright eye stared into her face, a great burning eye that seemed to be looking down into her very soul.

Chapter 2

"Why, what's all this?" said a great voice just above her. It wasn't the brakeman come back—Or was it? A great gust of wind came hurricaning round the corner of the station and filled her mouth and her eyes with stifling flakes, and she was almost strangled. Then the hurricane and the snow seemed suddenly shut out. It grew more luminous about her, and the big voice was shouting through the storm over her head.

"Are you waiting for the train? How ever did you get here? It's outrageous to close the station on a night like this!"

She was aware of a pair of kindly eyes shrouded in snow, bushy white eyebrows, cheeks plastered with flakes; eyelashes, too, fringed white. The rest was covered with a woolen scarf bound firmly about head and neck. But the sight of another human being suddenly broke her down. Even if it had been the impertinent brakeman she couldn't have helped it.

"Oh, I'm soooo-ccc-ooo-llldddd!" she chattered, more tears flowing over the icicles on her face, "I can't find the ca-ca-ca-rrr-r!" she babbled feebly.

"What car?" asked the apparition, glancing keenly about the white distance.

"The Framstead c-c-arrrr!" answered Tasha trying to keep her teeth from chattering. "They promised to be here when the train came in!" There was a wail in the end of her words.

"Framstead!" said the man in a startled tone. "They can't get down from Framstead's to-night! The bridge is down and the other road is impassable! It drifted twelve feet at least!"

"Oh! What shall I do-o-o-oo!" cried Tasha in terror. "I'm freezing! My feet are dead now. I ca-ca-can't feel them anymore at all. How l-l-l-long does it t-t-t-ake to fr-f-f-reeze?"

"You poor kid!" said the man stooping to lift her in his snowy arms, and feeling with one hand for her feet. "You poor little kid!

11

No wonder! Why—you haven't but one shoe—! Well that settles it! We'll have to get inside here somehow at once. Just wait a minute and I'll get this door open!

He set her down again in the snow, but she was not conscious of feeling any colder. It seemed that she was numb all over except for the sharp point of hurt where the cold was still aching and stinging. She felt as if she were come to the end of life in a terrible way. She gave a pitiful thought back to the gayety that had been hers but a few short hours before, and wondered that her butterfly existence had been so short. But it didn't seem to matter any more; the cold was so terrible, as if it had her by the throat and were putting her out like a candle flame being snuffed.

She heard a crash of glass in the dark, and then saw the imp of light go flashing again and presently she was picked up and carried inside the little box of a station.

She felt the cessation of the storm, and the dry warm air of a room that had at least recently known fire, and then she was put down in the darkness on a wooden seat.

"Now," said the man, as he seemed to be moving about a few feet from her, "we've got to get you warm first. Whoever let you out a night like this with so few clothes on?"

Tasha giggled hysterically. She had forgotten her haughtiness. In this warm darkness with the roar of the storm shut away, she could no longer hold her pride.

"Haven't you any baggage with you?" asked the man's voice. He seemed to be shaking some heavy garment on the other side of the room. A spatter of snow reached viciously and hit her cheek. The room was a very small one.

"No," she said in answer to his question. "No," almost stupidly, "I am going to a dance!"

Then he came over to where she was sitting in the dark, and almost roughly lifted her to wrap a great rough garment about her. "It must be his overcoat," she thought to herself, and tried to protest.

"You'll nnnn-eee-ddd it!" she chattered.

"Not as much as you do!" he said shortly. "Now, what can we do about these feet?"

"They are dead!" she said, and shivered in the roughness of the overcoat. "It won't matter."

The man stepped out the door and brought in a bag. He set it down on the floor and flashed his torch into it, searching for something. She watched him apathetically. The snow had melted from his features now, though they were still well swathed in brown woolen scarf. "Not entirely dead yet," he answered as he laid the flash down on the floor and came toward her with something dark in his hand. He reached for her unslippered foot and began to rub it, finally tearing away the little rag of gold silk chiffon stocking and chafing the foot with his big warm hands from which he had taken the heavy woolen mittens that now lay on the floor beside the flash light.

She watched him as if it were a sort of moving picture in which she had no part, but most surprisingly the foot began to feel alive again, and to prickle under the chafing. And when he had it quite dry and warm again he drew on a long thick woolen stocking, that came well up to her little cold knee.

"My mother insisted on my taking these golf stockings with me tonight," he meditated, "and now I'm glad I brought them."

Tasha did not say anything. She was wondering how she would look going through life with only one foot. One foot had come alive but the other was stone dead. And she was so cold all over in spite of the great rough overcoat that she felt as if she were made of ice with a hot fire inside of it.

"Now!" said the man, "that's better. Do you begin to feel a little more comfortable?" and he began his ministrations toward the other foot.

She did not see the look on his face as he unbuttoned and laid down the other little gold slipper, a mixture of awe and contempt upon him. He went on silently chafing the cold little foot till it too responded to treatment and came alive.

"Now," said he, "I suppose you'd like me to telephone to Framstead's. They'll be wondering what has become of you. We'll see whether I can pick the lock of the inner office and get to the telephone. What name shall I say?"

"Endicott," said Tasha stupidly, "Miss Endicott." Somehow the dance no longer seemed real. She was getting a little warm again in spots, and longed only to get somewhere to lie down to rest. She felt as if she had been battling against wild beasts.

There was a sound of some little metal instrument trying to force a lock. An interval of silence and the dancing flash light; more metal grinding against resisting locks, then the shudder of a thick door against a great forceful shoulder. Presently the man returned to her. "Well, it's no use. I think there is a big bolt or bar to that door. Anyhow I can't budge it. I suppose they have to be extra careful for they keep a safe in there I think, and it is rather lonely around here." "Oh, what shall I do? Shall I have to stay in this awful place all night? Are you going away?" she asked in sudden fright.

"No, you can't stay here," he said decidedly. "I'll have to take you home to Mother. There's no other house nearer where you could stay. I'll have time to take you back before my train gets here." He turned the flash light on his wrist watch now, and she could see his face studying the dial anxiously, then he lifted his wrist and listened. "What train did you come on?" he asked suddenly. "Did you come up from the city?"

"Yes, on the six-five. But my train was late. We just got in. I had not been here but a few minutes when you came, though it seemed like hours it was so cold."

She shuddered at the memory, and realized that a slight sense of warmth was really stealing over her.

"Why?" she asked suddenly. "Is there a train back now? Oh, are you going to the city? I must go too. I can't stay here alone, since there is no way to get to Framstead's."

"No," he said gravely, "I'm not going to the city; I'm going up the road about fifty miles where I'm supposed to preach to-morrow. There is no train back to the city that stops at this station to-night. The only down train is an express and you have to go five miles up the road to get it. But I was thinking. If your train was as late as that, the next train will be still later. I shall have plenty of time to get back, but we can't lose a minute talking about it. I'll take you to Mother, but you'll have to do just as I say and be quick about it!"

Tasha had no time to resent this dictatorial speech, for he came over, picked her up summarily, and slung her over his shoulder as if she had been a bag of meal.

"Excuse me," he said as she gasped. "It isn't very pleasant but it's the only way, and I simply must get that train."

She tried to struggle, to protest, to say she could not let him take so much trouble, but he strode to the door, and was out before she had finished a sentence.

"Your bag!" she called. "Stop! You must not leave your bag!"

"It's all right till I get back!" he shouted over his shoulder. "Lie still, can't you, and put your arm around my neck, that way. Now, keep your face down and you won't get the worst of the blast."

He plunged off the platform, and wallowed for a moment till he found the solid path, dancing the flash light ahead of him weirdly through the storm.

The girl gasped, and hid her face perforce on the broad shoulder that held her. The touch of the rough wool made her conscious that she was wearing this man's overcoat, and that he was unprotected himself. She tried to say something about this, but her words were flung back into the soft plush cold of the storm, and caught away into space. She made a feeble effort to reach the top button of the coat and show him that she wished to take it off, but he shouted back, "Lie still, can't you?" and struggled on.

And it was a struggle, she could see. Slender though she was and lightly clothed, yet wrapped in that great heavy overcoat she made a burden that was by no means easily carried through such going.

As her eyes came accustomed to the strange white darkness, she could peer out occasionally, and catch a glimpse of the depth of the drifts through which he had to wade. Up to his knees, above his knees sometimes. Once when he almost lost his footing and very nearly went down with her, she saw he had to lift her high above his head to keep her above the snow.

And the way seemed interminable.

He had said it was the nearest house, but how far away it seemed! Occasionally she thought of his train, and thought she heard the roar of its coming. But the darkness kept on being thick and white and impenetrable, and the little firefly of light danced on and made no impression except to illumine a step at a time.

It strangely did not enter her head to be afraid, even though she could not see the man who was carrying her, had never really got a view of his face, yet she knew she could trust him. It occurred to her that perhaps she was being kidnapped. Perhaps he might have seen the flash of her jewels at throat and wrist. but she dismissed that as foolish. If he had wanted her jewels it would have been easy to overpower her and take them, even to have killed her. There was no one by to see, and the snow would have covered all tracks by morning. No, she was strangely at peace, almost even interested, as she hung there over his shoulder, her arms clasped around his neck, trying to help all she could in the struggle he was having to take her to safety and warmth.

She was by no means warm even now, for the wind swooped around and roared down the neck of the overcoat, and even the thick golf stockings seemed but flimsy protection. But the feeling of the strength that bore her, helped her to bear the deadly cold that swirled about her and chilled her to the heart; and when it grew too awful she could hide her face entirely and breathe through the thick rough wool of his coat, to gain a moment's respite from the agony of breathing in the cold.

It seemed a space set apart in her lifetime never to be forgotten, that journey through the storm on the shoulder of an unknown man. She was growing drowsy with the cold and excitement, and had ceased to wonder if it would never end, when she felt him turn sharply from the road, a pace or two, then up some snow-muffled steps to a porch, and stamp, and knock at the door.

"It's I, Mother, open the door please! I can't get at my key!" he called. She roused and noticed that he was panting. How hard it must have been for him! And he was in a hurry. It came to her that the minister of their fashionable church in the city, which they attended semi-occassionally, would never have attempted a thing like this, would not have been able physically to carry it out if he had. Then hurrying footsteps interrupted her thoughts and a flood of light broke over the little porch, and blinded her eyes.

"Oh, my laddie!" she heard a sweet voice exclaim, "and what have you got? Did you lose your train?"

"No, Mother, the train is late but I found this alone in the snow at the station, and brought her to you. Take care of her please, till the storm is over or I get back, for now I must hurry."

He turned to the girl and began unbuttoning the great coat, blinking his eyes that still were blinded from coming into the light.

"I'll have to have my coat now, if you please," he said pleasantly, "and I hope I wasn't over rough with you. I hope you'll not suffer from the exposure."

The coat fell away and she looked up and tried to say the conventional thing—what was the conventional thing for such a time as this?—but she could only blink and give a sorry little smile. Then her velvet wrap slipped back, and fell away around her feet, and she stood there in the bright little cottage room in her rosy silk and tulle dance frock, like some lovely draggled flower plucked out of its garden.

The young man stepped back and looked at her for an instant with a drawing in of his breath, for she was lovely. Her delicate makeup was a wreck, with the storm and her crying, her wisps of coral tulle were trailing limply about her feet, her hair was tousled and falling about her face, yet she was lovely, and he looked.

His mother too, looked, and was filled with dismay.

"But—Thurly!—" she gasped, and the word brought him to his senses.

He turned, picked up the coat from the floor, and swung into it with a single motion, buttoning it high around his chin which was still swathed in the brown woolen scarf.

"But Mother, I must go!" he said, "I've got an instant to waste. The lady will explain!" and he stooped and kissed his mother's forehead. "I'm all right, Mother! There's nothing to worry about."

"But, Thurly! The storm! It's so terrible! Just give it up and telegraph them it's impossible!" she pleaded, following him to the door. "Do, Thurly, do! For my sake!"

"But, Mother, you know we had all that out on our knees awhile back. You know I must go, dearest. Now away to the lady, for she's well nigh frozen and needs a hot drink at once, and warm blankets or she'll be ill!"

He smiled and was gone, and the mother stood for an instant watching him down the white path vanishing into the white darkness, till even the little twinkle of the flash light was invisible. Then the mother turned and shut the door and came back to her strange and unexpected guest.

Chapter 3

Thurly Macdonald's mother was small and frail and gentle. Her sweet old face had grown lovely with age, like a well bred rose, with nevertheless a ruggedness about it that spoke of autumn frosts, and weathered winds, and a strong green vital stem.

She stood and faced this exotic girl that her son had suddenly thrust upon her, and her keen, farseeing eyes read much in the one glance with which she swept her very soul, before she set to work to care for her.

The glance gave due tribute to the visitor's loveliness, to the exquisite texture and vivid coloring of her attire, but it went farther and seemed to analyze her character in one brief flash. Tasha felt suddenly unduly clothed. She shivered and tried to draw her cloak up from the floor.

"But we must get you warm at once!" said her hostess, flinging open a closet door, and drawing out a thick warm plaid shawl, so old and soft that it gave pleasure to the touch.

She wrapped it around the girl and tucked her up on the couch:

"Why, you poor little lassie," she said in a sudden tenderness. "You're all of a tremble! Wait, I'll get some blankets and a hot water bag. We'll soon have you warm."

She hurried into the kitchen and set the hot water running, then upstairs and came down with her arms full of big soft blankets. It was incredible how fast a little old lady could move, and how much she could accomplish in a brief moment.

"We'll just lift this off!" she said crisply as she came back to the girl who was struggling to control the shaking chill which had seized her as the warmth of the room began to penetrate her senses.

She seemed to know just how to get off the wisp of rose silk and tulle, even though its intricacies must have been strange to her, and she did not gasp at the brief silk trifles that were revealed beneath, though their brevity must have shocked her. With just a few motions

19

she had the girl arrayed in a long, warm flannelette nightgown, one of the old fashioned kind with long sleeves and a high neck. It was probably the first of its kind the girl had ever seen, and certainly the first she had ever worn; but she shuddered into its folds gratefully, and was glad of the big blankets that were tucked close about her. With a hot water bag at her feet and another against her back she presently began to feel a sense of delicious warmth, and the great shudders which had shaken her began to relax. But it was not until the cup of hot tea was given her that she really began to feel comfortably warm once more.

"Now," said Mrs. Macdonald eyeing her keenly, "you'll be wanting something more substantial. When did you eat last?"

"Oh," said the girl trembling, "why, I was going to dinner, a dinner dance it was. It was to have been at eight thirty. It must be more than that now." She dropped her head back wearily and snuggled into the blankets. "But don't bother. I'm not the least bit hungry. I had lunch on the train coming up from the South. I'd rather have another cup of that nice tea."

Mrs. Macdonald gave her another searching look and vanished into the kitchen, whence she returned in an incredibly short space of time with a tempting tray.

"Thurly and I had an oyster stew for supper tonight, just for a treat," she said as she drew a small table to the side of the couch and put the tray upon it. "This hot broth will keep you from taking a cold."

The girl saw a sprigged china bowl the steaming fragrance of whose contents made her know suddenly that she was hungry. There was a plate of delicately browned buttered toast, a tiny mound of ruby jelly, some crisp hearts of celery, and the cup of tea. She sat up almost briskly and did full justice to it, still enveloped in her blankets.

"I didn't know I was so hungry," she said gratefully. "But I'm sorry I have made you so much trouble. I really ought to get in touch with my home and have the chauffeur come for me—"

"But, my dear!" said Mrs. Macdonald glancing significantly toward the window. "No chauffeur could get through the drifts tonight. This is a blizzard, you know. I have sore anxiety over my son going out in this terrible storm. I tried hard to keep him from attempting it, but now I see it was the Lord's will, for he tells me you would have perished if someone had not helped you."

"Oh!" said the girl, a kind of gray horror filling her face. "Yes, it was awful!" and she shivered at the memory. "Yes, I really didn't know what to do. The snow went inside my clothes, and my slipper came off—"

"You poor little dear—!"

But Anastasia Endicott was not accustomed to pity from anyone, not since her long gone baby days, and the sound of this gentle voice calling her a poor little dear brought a rush of quite involuntary tears. She could not understand such weakness in herself. She considered herself to be quite "hard boiled."

"I don't know why I'm doing this," she said, trying to pass it off with a laugh, and mopping her eyes like a little girl with her pink flannelette sleeve.

"There, there, little dear," said Mrs. Macdonald, "you're all fagged out with the storm. Thurly said it was terrible! Here, let me get you a nice warm wash rage and wash your face. Then you'll feel better!" She came with a soft wet cloth and a towel that smelled of lavender, and washed the girl's face and wiped it as if she had been a little child. A soothed sense of love and care swept over the young thing that filled her with a strange yearning for something she had never known.

"Now, finish your soup, darling, and we'll get you to bed," said the elder woman comfortably.

And Tasha obediently did as she was told.

"It's a great pity we can't telephone your folks. Our telephone seems to be out of order," said her hostess. "Will your mother worry about you? Will the Framstead people send her word you have not arrived?"

The girl laughed, a hard, sharp little laugh full of a bitter mirth that did not belong in the elder woman's world. She looked at the girl startled, with the same doubt and trouble in her eyes that had been there when she first viewed the lovely little made-up face, and the drabbled rosy finery.

"Lucia worry about me?" she mocked. "Not so you'd know it. She never concerns herself in the least about me!"

Then she saw the shocked sadness in the face of her hostess and explained:

"I haven't any real mother you know. Lucia's only a step. At least I guess that's what you'd call her. Dad's been divorced twice, and Lucia's the second mistake, though she's not quite so bad as Clarice was. She was impossible. My first mother married an army officer and she's stationed in India. I haven't seen her since I was four years old. Dad hated her so for the way she went away that he got the court to fix it so I couldn't go to her till I'm of age. But I'm not keen about her. I doubt if she remembers me any more. I'll be of age next summer, but I don't think I shall bother with her. Why should I? She went off and left me, didn't she? And India really never attracted me much. I'd rather stick with Dad."

Mrs. Macdonald had lowered her eyes as at something indecent and began slowly going about the room dusting the furniture with her best pocket handkerchief in an absent-minded, careful way, not realizing what she was doing.

"Oh, my dear!" said Mrs. Macdonald, brushing away something like a tear from the corner of her eye, as Tasha wound up her tale. "Oh, my little lost lamb!"

The girl looked at her half perplexed. Here seemed to be something sweet offered her which she did not quite understand.

"Oh, it's all right," she said carelessly. "Lucia isn't half bad. She lets me alone and I let her alone. We get on finely. The only thing I can't stand is when she borrows my car without asking me, but Dad has stopped that now. He told her he'd get her a new town car if she'd let mine alone."

There was silence in the room while the girl finished the last bite of toast and jelly, and drank her tea. Thurly's mother was working thoughtfully with the books between the book ends on the little mahogany center table, changing them elaborately, the blue one next the gold and brown, the red leather cover against the green leather; and then back again, studying them, as if their arrangement mattered. At last she lifted her sweet eyes to the girl and smiled.

"I wonder?" she said. But she did not say what she wondered. The girl felt as if she would like to know, as if it might be something that mattered.

Then the elder woman turned briskly, sweeping all other considerations aside.

"We must get you to bed!" she said. "You've been through a great strain, and got a terrible chill. You must get tucked up all nice and warm and sleep it off. We'll talk about it in the morning."

A great blast of wind swept round the house, and a little visible drift of snow peppered in around the edges of the front window. The girl saw the mother glance toward the front windows, with a quick anxious frown. Suddenly she realized that her rescuer was out there in the storm again, and there came a pull at her heart at the thought of breathing that cold cold air, and breasting those drifts that long way back to the station. Where was he now? Had he reached the train in time, and was he riding safely to some other place? For what?

She voiced her thought.

"Why did your son go out again? He ought not to have gone!" She drew her brows and looked anxiously toward the window.

"He had to go, lassie. He was on the Lord's errand. The Father will care for him."

There was something beautiful and trustful in the woman's face, a kind of silver radiance. The girl looked at her wonderingly, and said: "Oh, is his father out there? What is he doing? What can anybody do in such a storm as this?"

"He rides upon the wings of the storm," was the astonishing answer. The girl looked and the silver radiance was still there. The woman was not crazy for she had a lovely smile in her eyes, one who talks in tender enigmas.

"If his father is out there why doesn't he come in?" persisted the girl impatiently. She did not like enigmas. They baffled her.

The woman turned from the window and gave her a sweet full look, the silver radiance changing to a golden smile.

"He is here, my child. I mean the Father, God!"

The girl stared. She did not sneer as she might have done at another time. She did not mock and say there was no God, as she had often felt in her heart. There was something in the woman's look that prevented any such thought. It was a great bright assurance. She had spoken with the conviction of one who has seen with her own eyes.

"Now, we will go up to the little room upstairs, dearie. Can you walk? I should have made Thurly carry you aloft before he left, only he had so little time, poor laddie."

"Oh, I can walk!" cried Tasha and essayed to spring up, but found her knees strangely weak, and a great inertia upon her.

"It's queer!" she said, catching hold of a chair shakily. "I feel as if I hadn't any power to move! I shouldn't have made much of a show at that dance, even if I'd got there. I didn't imagine just getting cold could make a person feel this way."

"There's a mighty power in cold," said Mrs. Macdonald, slipping her arm around the girl and helping her up the stairs. "You know the Bible says: 'Who can stand against His cold?'"

"Does it?" asked the girl coldly. "How queer! I never read the Bible. It's such a big book. I never thought it would be interesting." "Oh, but it is, dearie. It has a many hidden treasures. You ought to take a dip into it and see. After you've had a good sleep I'll show you a few."

Tasha yawned and dropped down upon the bed gratefully. It had seemed quite a journey up those stairs.

The little white room was cheery with a border of roses at the top of the wall, and roses on the little white painted set of furniture. The bed had a white starched valance clean and crisp, and a gay patch-work quilt dimpled with infinitesimal stitches in intricate pattern, and when it was turned back there were soft white blankets with pink bindings. There was a little rocking chair with a pink flannel cushion, and a small lamp on the dressing bureau with a pink crepe-paper shade, that shed a rose light on the white linen cover. There were quaint hooked and braided rugs on the floor, soft and warm, and a few pictures about the walls. One was merely a text beautifully lettered and framed: "WITH GOD ALL THINGS ARE POSSIBLE." What a strange thing to put on a wall! But there was a lovely painting of sunset on a summer evening, and a water color of a shepherd on a hillside with his sheep; and across the room over the white painted desk was a photograph of a young giant in football regalia. There was a haunting familiarity in the eyes that looked out laughing from the picture that caught her gaze.

Tasha wondered at the little room, so simple, with its white ruffled curtains against the white snow covered windows, yet so restful. Then she lay down on the soft bed, let her hostess tuck the pink and white blankets around her, and pull up the patchwork quilt, and somehow she felt more like sleeping than she had felt for months. What a quaint sweet place she had fallen upon! How did it come to be hidden away so near to the rushing world of excitement.

"Now, lassie, we'll just have a bit of prayer," said Mrs. Macdonald, as simply as she had brought the cup of tea, and kneeling down beside the astonished girl she spoke as to One close beside her:

"Now Father we thank Thee that Thou has brought this stray lamb safe in out of the storm, and we commend her to Thy care and keeping. Give her sweet refreshing sleep, grant new strength for the morrow, and may she know what it is to be a child of the Heavenly Father. We ask it for Christ's sake. Amen."

Gentle lips pressed a kiss lightly on the girl's forehead, and then the light was snapped off.

"Now, lassie, I'll be in the next room and I'll hear you in case you call. I'll just close the door to, but not tight. Then you'll not be disturbed by the light in the hall. And don't hesitate to call me if you don't feel well or you want anything. I don't mind being disturbed. Now, are you sure you're warm? Well, we dare not open so much as a crack of the window tonight, or the storm would fling in, but there's air enough for the night creeping in with every gust through the cracks, so good night, little girl, and pleasant sleep."

She tiptoed out and closed the door all but an inch. Tasha wondered why she did not feel like laughing. Such a quaint mother, and such an unexpected thing to do, yet her throat was full of tears rather than laughter.

Tasha lay there with her eyes wide open and thought of the contrast between this place and the Framstead ballroom where she had expected to be this evening. Just about now she would have been

dancing with Barry Thurston or with the dark Duke boy who had
followed her trail so constantly of late; and one or the other of them
would have been drinking too much, perhaps both. Here in this white
quiet peace it was impossible to think of the gaiety and excitement of
Framstead going on now. She thought of the storm, and shuddered.
She heard the wind, and again felt it searching her inadequate garments and biting at her flesh, searching to the very spirit of her. She
saw the great white splotches of snow that plunked against the window pane in the light of that one bright crack from the door. She
closed her eyes to shut it all out, and there as if printed on her eye-
balls she saw those dark letters in the gold frame, "WITH GOD
ALL THINGS ARE POSSIBLE" just as if she were reading them
again in the light. She wondered anew what they meant. That couldn't
be true of course. There must be things God couldn't do. God couldn't
bring back her childhood and giver her a home and a mother. And if
God had been able to do anything why did He let her have such a
rotten time?

That young football giant, over there in the photograph on the wall?
Was he the son of the house who had brought her home? She wished
she had got a better glimpse of his face. Would she ever see him
again? Would he get back before she had to leave in the morning?

What a home he had! She felt a brief passing envy. How his
mother loved him! What would it be to live in a home like this one?
Would she have been contented if she had been born here, and never
known anything else? Or would she have longed to get out into the
world, and go to dances at Framstead, and spend winters in Palm
Beach and summers in Europe, or at the shore?

Queer, that mother! But nice! How soft her lips had been! And
that strange prayer, like talking to someone. "Father!" just as if she
knew God intimately!

But the warm dark, the lavender-scented blankets, the soft bed,
with the wind and cold noisily tearing about outside, were doing
their work, and she was growing drowsy. What a sweet quite haven
she had found. But in the morning she must get out.

She would have to have clothes, too. She couldn't wear those
rose-colored rags in the daytime, and her evening cloak would not do

even to wear home. She would phone to Adrienne to send her some clothes the first thing in the morning. For of course the telephone would be repaired by that time, and Adrienne would send her car, or perhaps it would be better to phone her maid and have Dad's chauffeur bring her things and take her home. He would rave, of course, but still what did that matter? It would be far better not to have the crowd know where she had adventured this night. They would make no end of fun, and somehow she did not care to have this adventure desecrated. These were simple, sweet, wonderful people and she had seen a kind of life to-night that she had never dreamed existed in the world. Think of a man driving himself out a second time into a storm like this because he had promised to preach somewhere? What was preaching! And then, so curious a thing is the mind, Tasha had to follow him out through the storm, struggle with him back to that station and wait for the train. As she drifted off to sleep she was listening, listening for the sound of a whistle against the wind, a whistle that did not come.

Chapter 4

Thurly Macdonald's mother, downstairs, after a long sorrowful look through a spot she had melted on the window pane, was down upon her knees keeping vigil with her child.

Not for nothing was she born a Thurly, daughter of distinguished Scotch preacher, bred in the faith, trained to pray as naturally as to breathe. It was her refuge at all times in any care or anxiety.

And Thurly Macdonald was out in the wild storm.

Twice he stumbled and fell on his way back to the station, once he ran blindly against a tree when his flash light gave out and he essayed to get on without renewing the battery from those in his pocket. He was almost stunned for several minutes as he stood leaning against the encrusted trunk of the tree and tried to get his bearings. He finally succeeded in refilling his torch, by holding it under his coat. Then he lost his glove in the snow, and found it at least after his hands were wet and almost frozen.

Back at last to the station he went at once to the track side and examined the snowfall carefully. No, it had not been disturbed since he went back to the house, he was sure of that. The snow lay smooth and thick across the roadbed. There had been no train through there since the girl had arrived. It was therefore yet to come. And likely it would not come through until the snow-plow came back and cleared the track. That might be some time. He would have to wait. He would not dare go back to the house lest he had miscalculated, however, and might miss a train that brought a snow-plow of its own. It was unbelievable that there would be no further train to-night, for there must be many residents of these suburbs who were still in the city and the Railroad Company would surely run a late train, perhaps along toward midnight. Yes, he must sit down and bide his time.

He was well wrapped up. His mother had seen to that, although his two falls, and his search for his glove had not added to his warmth. The snow had managed to penetrate inside his garments and leave an

icy dampness which brought little shivers down his spine. Nevertheless, Thurly Macdonald was not one to worry about a little thing like
that. He would go inside that station and tramp up and down until he
was all in a glow and the wet places had dried. He would not take
cold. Besides, he felt sure his mother had put a few extra warm
things in his big grip. He could stuff them under the wet places if he
felt there was danger of his catching cold. And for the rest, he was
on his Father's business, and would be cared for.

He groped his way into the station, gave a hasty survey of the
contents of his bag which his mother always packed for him, and
found an extra pair of woolen socks and a warm bath robe. He decided to put on the woolen socks instead of the damp ones he was
wearing at present. When he had done this a pleasant sense of warmth
stole over his numbed feet. He began to hum an old hymn that his
mother loved to sing:

> "From every stormy wind that blows,
>   From every swelling tide of woes,
> There is a calm, a sure retreat,
>   'Tis found beneath the mercy seat—"

His voice trailed into a whistle and he stood up, pulling on his
gloves again.

Ugh! It was cold! He decided to throw the bath robe around him.
It could be easily hustled into his grip if the train came. He must
keep on the alert, for a train might very well steal up without being
heard in the wildness of the storm. One could hear nothing but the
roar of the wind. He must be ready to signal them to stop, for it
might be that on such a night the engineer would not think it worth
while to stop at a little station like Stonington, unless he carried passengers who wanted to get off there. Things were not going by schedule of course. But he must husband his flash light, for he might have
a long wait and it would be his only means of signaling to the train.

As he stooped to snap his grip shut his light fell upon a small gleaming object that gave back the light in a hundred delicate facets.
Startled, he went over to it, and picked it up. A little gold slipper,

with a gleaming side of flashing white stones on the strap! The girl's lost slipper!

He had almost forgotten the girl in his own struggle with the elements, and his anxiety to get to his appointment in time. Now the memory of it all rushed back upon him with a thrill of wonder as he stood and held that frail gold foot covering, and studied it carefully, forgetful of his wasting battery. How curious it was, how intricately, yet fragilely formed! A bright spike of a heel, a tiny pointed shelter for a lovely foot, a few gilded straps and a cluster of sparkling stones! That was called a shoe! And that girl had stepped out into this awful storm shod in a trifle like this!

His face grew stern as he stood in the shadowed station, the flash light in one hand and the little gold slipper in the other.

The wind swooped down upon the solid little building and boomed along its trig tight roof in vain, but the sound startled the young man, and reminded him that he must save his flash light.

He snapped it off quickly and put it in his pocket where he could reach it instantly. But the little gold shoe he held in his bare hand as he paced to and fro, thinking about the girl, and how cold she must have been. Thinking of the chill of those little frozen feet in their silken covering when he rubbed them into life again and swathed them in his heavy golf stockings.

He was glad he had had them with him, glad his mother put them into his bag. He would be grateful for them now himself, for his feet were getting numb. He sat down to rest himself, and kept on thinking about those little cold feet, and his own grew colder. He got up and began to pace the floor again, and became aware that his hands were bare and cold. He had forgotten to put on his gloves again.

The little slipper was in his way and he stuffed it into the breast of his coat while he dived into his big coat pocket and got out his warm woolen gloves. He laughed to himself about that slipper as he drew on his gloves. Suppose the train should suddenly come, and he have to run for it, with the slipper inside his coat, and suppose the slipper fell out in the train! What a laugh the conductor would have on him! And the other passengers if there were any on a night like this! A golden slipper in the breast of a young minister's coat! Suppose some of his fellow classmatès should hear of it! He of all fellows in the class, to carry a golden slipper in his breast! He who had always fought shy of girls! Who had no use for the modern girl! Who had never had time nor money to hunt up a girl who was not modern. Who had scarcely any faith that there were any left that were worth hunting for! Carrying around a gold slipper in his coat! He laughed aloud at himself, and then hushed again. it was as if he had been rude to the girl who so short an hour ago had sat in this very room with him; whom he had rescued from what might have been an awful death of a bright young thing that God had made.

Awe came upon him. After all, these girls that he had despised and shunned were living souls for whom Christ had died. And probably not for nothing had he been left to meet this special one in the storm and carry her home to his mother.

Ah! His mother! A satisfaction filled his heart. His mother would know what to do. His mother would help the pretty child if she needed help. She had started to a dance, but God had turned her aside by a few snow flakes and sent her to his mother! Well, all would be well. He thought of her as he had seen her with the coats slipped off and the rose petal frock billowing about her, a lovely child! A strange thrill filled his breast. The touch of the little gold shoe became magnetic. For an instant a beautiful fleeting vision filled his mind. Ah! She was lovely! He was glad that she was with his mother! She was a child of the world, and not for his admiration, of course, but he was glad that such a lovely young soul could come into contact with his mother even for an hour.

He would probably never see her again, but mayhap some day she would come home to God, led by his mother's touch, his mother's prayers. And he would have been the humble instrument to bring her to such a leading! A strange gladness filled his soul, and grew as he thought about it! It would be a great thing to lead a lovely soul like that to God!

But what should he do with the shoe? Keep it of course somehow, and take it back home. The girl would be gone Monday morning when he got back, but his mother would have found out her address, and anyhow, if she had not he could send it up to Framstead and say

he had found it in the station, and that it belonged to the young woman
who had come on the evening train in the storm.

Yet he walked several times back and forth in the station with that
little gold show in the breast of his coat, as if he hated to put it out in
the cold again; as if keeping it warm were somehow keeping the girl
warm too, and undoing some of the cold she had suffered.

Then his clear mind got the upper hand.

"Fool!" he said. "What are you dreaming about? Fool!" He
turned on the light, went to his bag and thrust that little warm gold
slipper down beneath his heavy flannelette pajamas at the very bottom of the bag, put his Scofield Bible on the very top, and snapped
the bag shut with a click.

"There!" said he aloud. "That's the end of that incident. Now, I'll
think of my sermon. This is a splendid place to preach!" and so he
went walking up and down, preaching aloud to the storm, shouting
out thunderous sentences against worldliness, uttering tender pleadings for repentance, growing eloquent at times. Till suddenly he
realized that he was really preaching to that girl, calling to her from
the side of God's children, to give up her frivolous life as typified by
those trifling dance slippers, and come where joy and peace and safety
abounded. His voice was yearning and tender, and he seemed to be
looking into her blue eyes. He stopped, astounded.

"This is most extraordinary!" he said to himself sternly. "My mind
must have been affected by the storm. I must have hit my head on
that tree harder than I knew! I never had such a foolish obsession
before!"

So he buttoned his coat to the chin and went out in the storm to
investigate the tracks once more, but the snow was coming with just
as driving a force, and the wind was slanting the drifts on the road
bed, till one never would have known there had been a track there, or
that a train had ever gone through that part of the country. He soon
came back to his refuge, and began his pacing again, and this time he
fortified his mind with repeating scripture. Chapter after chapter,
verse after verse, but somehow he always seemed to be repeating it
to that little girl. The memory of her shivering form upon his shoulder, and the feel of her small arms about his neck seemed wonder-

fully sweet and dependent to him. Till suddenly he came to a stand still, and lifted his eyes up.

"God!" he said aloud, "what do you want me to do about this?"

Then straightway he fell upon his knees beside the bench where Tasha had sat while he ministered to her, and began to pray. For a burden seemed to be laid upon his soul for this girl, and he must not be afraid of it.

If Tasha in her warm pink blankets could have heard that prayer for her young straying soul, what would she have thought! Tasha, millions of miles away from this young man's world, Tasha, an utter stranger strayed into his home for the night! And Thurly Macdonald was upon his knees in a lonely cold station, praying for her as if his very life depended upon the answer to that prayer.

It was after one o'clock when Thurly finally rose from his knees and went out to view the storm, and this time he decided there would be no train any more that night and he would go home. He had prayed till the burden had left his soul, and he was suddenly weary with a great heaviness.

The road to his home was almost impassable, but he managed it, though it took him a good hour, and the little flash had spent itself down to a mere pale wisp when he finally stumbled up the steps of the cottage and fumbled for his latch key.

But he did not need the key. His mother was at the door before he could unbutton his coat with his still fingers. There was light and warmth and a glad welcome.

Marget Macdonald was fully dressed, and there was coffee hot on the back of the stove.

"I watched and I listened for the train," she explained when her son reproved her for having sat up. "I hied me up to the little loft where I can always see the light of the evening train when you go, and I was sure it would at least show a bit luminous through the storm, even if I could not hear the rush of it. But no train went by. I said I would not undress till I heard the train go by."

"Mother! Mother!" he said as he kissed her tenderly. "There's never such a mother as you are the world over, I'm sure!"

She helped him unwind the woolen scarf that was frozen round his chin; she helped him unbuckle the great galoshes, for his fingers were still stiff with the cold. She lugged his wet overcoat out to the shed, chafed his hands, passed her rose-petal soft little fingers over his cold face, till it glowed, and she kissed him and murmured; "Ah, my laddie! God has brought ye safe through the storm!"

And then while he was drinking his coffee, and eating the bit of hot toast she had made he asked her quite casually:

"How's your guest?"

Marget had been waiting for the question. It would have seemed significant to her whether it came or not. Such bits of lovely flesh and blood do not drop down upon a quiet household like theirs without making a notable stir. For years Marget had been dreading and waiting for the time when the first girl should take hold upon the notice of her son. And now it had come! It could not help but come. She had been casting the thought of it upon her Burden Bearer during the long hours of her waiting. She had waited anxiously for the moment when the recognition of this should come between them.

Yet she took it calmly and answered with a smile:

"Oh, she's sleeping quite sweetly, and seemingly no bit the worse for her chilling."

"That's good!" he answered with a relieved ring to his voice. "Mother, I've been thinking. Perhaps God sent her—" his voice trailed off perplexedly—"for—something—you know—" he finished lamely.

"No doubt in the least, laddie!" said his mother, trying to make her voice sound hearty. "But, laddie—she's a bit thing of the world, you know."

"She's all that!" agreed Thurly earnestly, looking deeply into the dregs of his coffee cup, and then, lifting serious eyes as if he were stating something quite new and original: "Yes, she's all that!" and there was something like a sigh in the end of his words.

Marget thought of it long after Thurly was asleep, that "bit sigh" as she called it to herself, "more like a sough in the summer trees! Ah! Laddie! laddie! I knew it had tae come some time, but it's sore against my will that it comes this way. Nevertheless the Lord has ways, and it's not for me to question."

She thought of it again the next afternoon when she slipped up to "redd" up the rooms, and opened Thurly's bag to put away his things in the closet again.

Tasha had slept late, and the mother had let Thurly sleep as long as he would. They had merged breakfast into a midday meal about which they had lingered pleasantly, though it was but a "picked up" dinner. Just a meat pie out of some bits of meat of last week which Marget had though plenty for herself when her boy was away over Sunday. But the bits of meat snuggled beneath the most delicate flaky crust that could be imagined, and the potatoes were baked to that perfection of turn that made even the skins a delicacy. There were stewed tomatoes and crisp coleslaw, with apple sauce and cookies for dessert, and it all tasted perfectly wonderful to Tasha who never in her life had eaten real "home" cooking before.

So, they had lingered around the table, and finally all helped with the dishes. At last while the two young people were looking over some college photographs of Thurly's, Marget slipped up to the rooms, for it was not her way to leave them untidy far into the evening.

It did not take long for the guest room to be put right. It meant only the making of the bed, which evidently it had never occurred to the guest to do, and the hanging up of the various garments which had been brought out for the girl to choose a dinner costume from.

Marget smiled as she hung up her various offerings to think how the girl had picked the unlikeliest one of her things she had brought, an old black silk wrapper. She had slipped it on, with a pin here and pucker there, and strung an old Roman ribbon around her waist and made a frock of it. There she was downstairs now, sitting beside Thurly on the couch, looking over those foolish football pictures, and "havering" with Thurly as if she had know him always, just because she once met the sister of one of Thurly's fraternity brothers. It made her a bit uneasy to have them sitting so in friendly converse, the two heads together over the book, the gold one and the brown. She must hurry and get back to them. Nothing really alarming could happen with her right there in the room with them. Though of course falling in love was a strange thing and had ways of its own, and to have Thurly lose his heart to a girl of the world who would

string his scalp to her pretty little waist and go her dancing way, was
not to be prevented by just sitting in the room with him. Marget
sighed as she went with swift steps to Thurly's room.

Thurly always made his own bed. She had taught him that when
he was a little boy, and he had kept it up to save her work. There was
not much to do save to unpack the bag, put the things away, and the
bag on the shelf against the time when he had to go and preach again.
Even that could wait until the next day. She hesitated and almost
turned to go down, then her thrifty soul turned her back to the bag. It
would take but a minute and be so much more tidy when Thurly
came up at night.

She hung up the dressing gown as she called it, though Thurly had
tried to teach her it was now called a bath robe, and she put away the
comb and the brush, and the sermons on his desk. Then she reached
in for the pajamas and came against something hard and sharp and
lumpy. Turning the flannelette back, curious, she came upon the
little gold slipper!

For a full minute she stood and looked at that slipper, lying on the
bottom of the bag—*hidden* under the pajamas! What did it mean?
That Thurly was treasuring it, and did not mean her to see it? She
readily understood that he must have found it somewhere at the station when he went back, and had probably picked it up in the first
place to restore it. But in that case why was it not on top in plain
sight, tumbled in anyway, and not put carefully down at the bottom,
as if he were ashamed of it?

Ah, laddie, laddie! Was it too late? Had it happened then before
she was aware, before even *he* was aware?

She put out her hand to take the little gaudy shoe, thumb and finger, as if it were something not nice to handle, something she hated
that she would like to fling away, and then she drew back, and looked
again. No, she could not do that. She could not ruthlessly pull out
what Thurly had taken pains to cover. There had always been respect between them toward what each had done or wanted done,
even when he was a mere baby. She had never thrown out even his
toads and his pebbles from his pocket without asking his leave, or
rather reasoning with him to show him that a pocket was not a proper

place for mud and toads, and preparing a better place for them.

But this was something different. She could not go down and say, "Thurly, lad, perhaps you've forgotten it, but you've a lady's yellow slipper in under your night things, and that's not a suitable place for a lady's slipper. Won't you go up and bring it down to the lady? Perhaps she would rather wear her own than the flat-heeled black ones of mine she's wearing now."

No, she could not shame her son. She could not even call him out and tell him privately what she had found, because she must wait for her son to tell her about that slipper if he wanted her to know. She had come to the place where she must not go ahead of him. She must go behind. And she must not let him even know that she had found it.

Softly she laid back the pajamas over the slipper, giving a quick glance to the hook on the inside closet door to make sure had worn his old ones without unpacking his bag last night, and not just put these clean ones back this morning to hide the slipper from her. Softly she tiptoed over to the bureau and the desk for the brush and comb, the black leather cover that held his sermons, and put them all back just as she had found them. Then she shut the bag quietly, and went out of her son's room without looking back.

But she did not go down to the little parlor where her son sat with the woman of the world. Instead she went into her own little bedroom, and shutting the door and locking it, she knelt beside her plump white bed. And there she poured out her heart to the One who knoweth all things, and seeth the end from the beginning.

Chapter 5

The storm raged on, with no sign of letting up.

The two young people in Marget Macdonald's little parlor were getting acquainted without realizing it, over the book of college photographs which Tasha had found on the under part of the little stand. Idly she had reached from the low chair in which she had seated herself after the unusual task of wiping dishes, and pulled it toward her turning over the pages, with little idea of being amused, till she suddenly came upon a face which she knew.

"Why! Isn't that Jerry Fisher?" she exclaimed. "This one with the football in his hand? Do you know Jerry?"

"I sure do!" was the hearty response, as Thurly came over to her side and looked over her shoulder. "I roomed with Jerry for two semesters at college!"

That was the beginning. At once her respect for the young minister went up several degrees. He couldn't be such a prune if Jerry had him for a roommate. Jerry was a perfect scream.

"I had his sister down at the shore with me last summer all the season. She's some peach, Betty Fisher. Do you know her!"

"No," said Thurly with sudden reserve in his voice. "That is, I met her once I believe, she came down for the game. Jerry is some kid!"

He did not add that he had not cared to more than meet Betty Fisher, that she was not a type of girl he admired.

But Tasha did not notice the reserve in his voice! She was only glad to find some common topic of conversation.

"He must be!" she said eagerly. "Betty used to be really nuts about him. She had her room at school all plastered over with his photographs, and she used to be always raving about him. I imagine he must have been pretty speedy!"

Well, he wasn't exactly slow," said Thurly gravely, remembering several serious scrapes that Jerry had got into. Thurly had had to help him out of them or see him expelled. Tasha turned over the pages and discovered more pictures.

"Why, that is yourself, isn't it? Really! Why, you were captain, weren't you?"

Thurly nodded gravely, watching her vivacious little face trying to study her possible background. Betty Fisher and her ilk would be just about what this girl admired, likely. Oh, she was far from being his kind of girl. Why had she dropped down upon them in this intimate way, when he could not get away, and must stay by and attempt to entertain her! His natural shy reserve that had been forgotten over the old college pictures, returned upon him, and he stepped back and glanced out of the window into the still fine whiteness of the blizzard.

"Yes, I was captain," he said coldly, and deliberately walked over to the couch on the opposite side of the room and sat down stiffly.

But Tasha was interested.

"Why, isn't that perfectly gorgeous! You captain! What year? You don't mean it! Why, that must have been the year they beat Yale! Macdonald! Why, surely, I remember! I was at that game myself. My friend Adrienne Lyman and I went up with Dad! And you were that Macdonald! Why, you were the whole team that day! I watched you with the greatest admiration, and rooted for you till I was hoarse, but I never dreamed you would some day save me from freezing to death! It's quite like a fairy tale to think I should have come upon you when I stopped out of that cold tomb of a train into the snow. No wonder you carried me off as easily as if I had been a feather. I heard a lot about how strong you were at that game. Simply everybody was raving about you on every side!"

Thurly was almost embarrassed. He watched her as she talked, her eyes all a sparkle, her face vivid with interest, and felt a sudden warmth around his heart again, but almost immediately despised himself for it. Here he was falling for a girl merely because she admired his football of other days. She probably had no higher standards for any man than merely to see him play football better than the next one. Yet she was a lovely little thing. Even in his mother's old black silk wrapper, she had an innate grace and charm about her that made him want to watch her.

"And who is this man?" she asked suddenly as she turned another page, and springing up she brought the book with her and sat down beside him on the couch.

So, together, the brown head and the gold one, Marget found them bending over more pictures and talking like old friends, when an hour later she came down, a chastened look about her lips, a peace within her eyes.

The two looked up smiling and Marget summoned a smile. Her face was one that radiated love, and Tasha felt it like a sudden sunbeam. She looked around the homely cozy room with almost wistful eyes and thought how happy those two seemed together. What was it that had made them happy, with so seemingly little of all the things that other people had to have to make them happy?"

"Thurly, I'm wondering if the young lady doesn't sing?" said Marget, in a sudden silence that followed her entrance, "it's about our hour for a little sing you know."

"Sing?" said Tasha graciously, "sure, let's sing! What do you know? Have you heard the prune song? Of course you have. It's on all the radios now. Let's sing that. It's been ringing in my head all the morning and I'd like to get it out of my system."

"I'm afraid I'm not acquainted with it," said Thurly, casting a startled look at his mother.

"It goes like this," said Tasha, trilling out:

"No matter how young a prune may be,
It's very often stewed—"

Her voice was young and fresh and the words rang out clearly. Thurly smiled gravely.

"No, I don't think I've happened to hear it," he said. "I'm not up on those songs since I left college, I'm afraid, and perhaps you won't like our kind, but I'm thinking this little mother of mine will be disappointed if we don't give her two or three of her favorites. Would you mind trying some of ours? We've some books that will help. Mother, where have you put the hymn books?"

A great light came into Marget's eyes at that. Her boy knew a way to carry off a situation! "Wise as a serpent, harmless as a dove," her glad heart murmured to itself, as she went to the little book shelf and hunted out three books.

"Get your fiddle, Thurly, lad, and we'll have a fine sing. The young lady has a blithesome voice, and I'm thinking we can have real music the day!"

Tasha accepted the hymn book meekly and watched the young man as he opened the worn old violin case and took out his instrument lovingly. So he was a musician too, as well as a football player—and preacher! What a combination! But then most of the college fellows could play something if it was only a mouth organ, and likely he didn't really play much!

But the first touch of the bow to the strings made her certain that he could. Such rich sweetness, such tender melody, wailed from the strings, that she sat and watched him in amazement.

"Is that the one you want first, Mother?" he asked stopping his bow suddenly. "It's number fifty-six, I think. Mother always likes to sing that when there's a storm.

The mother smiled tenderly at the gentle note in her boy's voice.

"It seems so cozy like and comforting when it's all noise and bluster outside," she explained apologetically to the visitor.

And then they sang, and Tasha, wondering, opened her book to the number and followed the words, humming along with the triumphant tenderness of the violin, the sweet quaver of the old lady's voice, and the splendid baritone of the young man:

> "From every stormy wind that blows,
>   From every swelling tide of woes,
> There is a calm, a sure retreat,
>   'Tis found beneath the mercy seat."

Tasha had seldom gone to church in her young life, only occasionally to Sunday School; if she had ever heard this hymn before she had taken no note of it. She sat and read the strange mysterious words over while the other two sang them. She wondered what it was all about.

At the fourth verse she trilled clearly:

> "Ah, whither could we flee for aid,
> When tempted, desolate, dismayed,
> Or how the hosts of hell defeat.
> Had suffering saints no mercy seat."

The words were still more puzzling. What could a mercy seat be, and why did saints have to suffer? It was all entirely out of her line, but she sang on:

> "There, there on eagle wings we soar,
> And sense and sin molest no more,
> And Heaven comes down our souls to greet,
> And glory crowns the mercy seat."

It was all mystic and beautiful, whatever it meant. Probably it was just like all religion, kind of sweet and mysterious and full of imagination. Tasha didn't see much in it, yet somehow as she sang that line "Heaven comes down our souls to meet" she got a curious kind of thrill of spirit from it, and wondered. Nothing like this had ever touched her life before. She had never believed anything because she was utterly ignorant of anything to believe. She knew of all religions only as a kind of cult that people affected, she had always supposed, because of some underlying fear or some weakness. Yet neither of these two people looked as if they had a fear or weakness. Even the old mother wore a look of strength and character about her firm sweet chin that belied fears, or weaknesses, and the young man's record in football was enough to free him from any question in that line, even if she could not see the outline of his strong keen face, with its flashing eyes, and lips that could be stern upon occasion. No, there was no weakness here, no superstition or fear. Yet why, *why* did this sort of thing appeal to them? Was it merely tradition that they were living out?

But a glance at each of their faces as they sang the closing verse belied that. They meant it all with their whole souls, and they looked as if they could live it to the death.

> "O may my hand forget her skill,
> My tongue be silent, cold and still,
> This throbbing heart forget to beat,
> If I forget the mercy seat!"

The words had seemed too dreadful to the girl to take upon her own lips. Not that she was superstitious, but it sounded like a challenge to all the evil powers of the universe, and she shuddered involuntarily and turned her eyes toward the white window panes and remembered last night. It came to her that she might have been lying "silent and cold and still" down under the snow by the railroad, if this young man had not found her and brought her to this retreat. And what was this mercy seat they talked about? She had no idea and she would not ask for anything, but she was glad when the song was ended and they fluttered the leaves on to another.

The night was fast closing in around them again, and the room was growing dusky. Thurly had made a fire of logs in the tiny fireplace and the flame gave a rosy tinge to the white shawl of the old lady, and glowed like sheen upon her silver hair.

They sang other songs"

> "Oh, God, our help in ages past,
> Our hope for years to come,
> Our shelter form the stormy blast,
> And our eternal home,
> Under the shadow of Thy wings,
> Thy saints shall rest secure—"

There it was again, "saints." Well, as she watched these two in the gloaming, sitting there singing, they looked like saints. That is they looked as she should imagine saints might look, though she had never thought of strength in connection with sainthood before. Saints in her parlance were always spoken of with a sneer, as something too weak to be bad enough to have a good time.

It presently grew too dark to see any more hymns, and then Thurly played on, melody after melody. They were all unfamiliar to Tasha, but from the fact that his mother sometimes quavered out a few words to the accompaniment, she surmised that they were more hymn tunes, and she marveled how they loved them! She had never known before that hymn tunes could be so tender and touching. She had supposed they were all gloomy and lugubrious.

But finally Thurly put down his violin, and the mother said:

"Put on the lights, laddie dear, and let's have our worship now, before we have our tea. It's so pleasant with the sound of the music lingering in the room. It'll seem more like the Sabbath day. I hate to stay away from church on the Lord's day, but the Lord Himself has shut us in this time."

Thurly had turned on the lights before she finished speaking, and Tasha's eyes met those of the old lady as she spoke, and marveled again at the strange things she was saying. It was as if she talked another language; the parlance of an entirely different world. How strange it was that people could all live on an earth together, and yet each one live a different life! How different for example was the life of these two, from any that she knew. Why, take Lucia, for example, or Dad, they would not know what it was all about! And they would laugh and mock! She knew they would! She would have laughed too, before she had come so close to this mother and son, but now she resented the thought that her friends would laugh at the two who had been so wonderful to her.

But what was this worship they were going to have? She was getting a little bit fed up on religion. Still they were so sweet about it, and it was interesting to see a young man like that, who had really been quite a notable character in the athletic world, just sit down and be interested in religion. It was queer—queer, but intriguing. He certainly was good-looking, too. There was no denying that.

They gave her a Bible, with soft old leather covers, the place all found for her, and she discovered they were about to read, and that she was to take her turn reading.

She had always boasted that she could be equal to any occasion that might arise, but somehow this performance was exceedingly embarrassing to her, and she stumbled over the simplest words as she read her first turn.

It was the story of the man born blind, and she found it interesting. She had not known that there were stories in the Bible. The mother made quaint remarks now and then about the "laddie" and his healing, and once or twice Thurly told what the Greek word was in a certain phrase, and just what significance it had in this particular setting.

Tasha listened and wondered, and felt that here was a third side to this versatile young man. He seemed to be a scholar. Moreover, and strangest of all, he seemed to take for honest fact the story he was reading, and talked about the Healer as if he were intimate with Him! It was all strange.

And they did the oddest thing! The mother and son got up from their seats and knelt down, both of them, quite simply as if it were their common practice. Tasha sat there feeling dumb and foolish, till in self-defense she too slipped down, silently, and knelt beside the couch.

Thurly was praying for her, she discovered, earnestly, kindly; he called her "the young stranger whom Thou has sent as our guest today." He asked strange mysterious blessings upon her which warmed her heart though she could not understand them, and they brought a great sense of loneliness to her, and of longing for something she did not have, though she did not know what it was.

And then quite as sharply there came to her the realization of how her friends would mock and scream with laughter if they could see her now, shut up in a little cottage home, arrayed in an old woman's black silk wrapper and flat-soled slippers, kneeling beside a hair cloth sofa being prayed for! And the revulsion almost set her giggling!

But there were tears in her eyes as she got to her feet at the close, and she went swiftly to the white blank window to hide them.

Thurly had gone at once down cellar to see to the furnace and the mother had bustled happily out to the kitchen. As Marget passed her she gave Tasha a smile and a little loving pat on her hand.

Tasha was almost afraid to go out to the dining room, though she was vigorously hungry, and the smell of hot coffee and something spicy and sweet drew her mightily.

But when she took her seat she found them both bright-faced and happy. The grace the young minister asked was so sincere that the girl forgot to be impatient over another dose of religion.

"They just live in it, like sunshine!" she thought to herself as she watched them. "It is not put on. It is real!"

It was a simple little supper, yet it tasted wonderfully good to this girl. A round bright pan of baked beans, piping hot from the oven where they had been all the afternoon. Delicate home made bread, brown and white, the like of which she had never eaten before, and sweet country butter. Sweet baked apples and cream, with little caraway cookies for dessert.

She would have laughed but a day before at such a menu, but she ate, and enjoyed it, and knew suddenly that she was having a good time. There was a half wish upon her that she might just stay here always and live this strange peaceful life with them, and get away from all the restlessness and fever of her own world. Only of course she couldn't. Of course it would bore her to death if she had to.

And even now she was feverish and restless from the lack of things to which she had been accustomed. She had not smoked a cigarette for more than twenty-four hours, nor tasted any stimulant stronger than coffee and tea, and her nerves were beginning to cry out against such treatment.

When at last the evening was over, Marget Macdonald went up with the girl, saw that her bed was turned down, and filled the hot water bag for her feet, for the wind was searching its way round the window cracks, swirling in at every crevice, and promised another wild night. Marget kissed her good night, called her "my dear," said she hoped she would sleep sweetly, and went down stairs.

Tasha opened the door after she had gone, and stood in the little hall listening. Thurly had gone down to the cellar again. She could hear him rattling the furnace.

With a quick stealthy step she crossed the hall into what she thought must be the young man's room. The desire for a cigarette had come over her so overwhelmingly that she was willing to go to any length to get one. There would be some in his room somewhere of course, and he would not notice if one or two were gone.

She listened for an instant at the door to make sure no one was coming up, and then snapped on the light from the button beside the door for it was scarcely light enough from the hall to find anything in a strange room.

She gave a quick glance about; at the bureau and table, not a sign of a pipe, or a tobacco jar, nor a pack of cigarettes anywhere! Only a Bible open as if it had been read lately, and left reluctantly.

She turned impatiently to search on the closet shelf. Perhaps his mother was too neat to have anything like that around.

But she almost fell over the open-mouthed bag, standing in the middle of the floor where Marget Macdonald had left it.

Ah! There would be some in his bag, of course.

She could hear the cellar door being shut with a bang, and Thurly and his mother talking down stairs. She must hurry!

She stooped over the bag and looked in. The sermon case didn't mean a thing to her. She lifted the hair brush, and felt. There seemed to be something hard beneath the other things. She lifted the folded garment, and stared! There lay her own gold slipper, its gleaming side of stones twinkling almost wickedly up at her! She dropped the things into the bag and started back, and turning met Thurly face to face!

Chapter 6

His face was stern! It frightened her. What right had he to look at her like that? It seemed to undo all the beauty of the day that they had spent together.

Her face was flaming, and for once her old pert self knew not how to explain. It suddenly seemed that she had committed some unpardonable offense. It made her feel angry to feel so. Who was he to look at her like that?

"I'm dying for a smoke!" she said, assuming her old hard-boiled attitude, and laughing with a sharpness that startled even herself. "I thought maybe you had left some cigarettes about, but I see you haven't!"

He just looked at her, opened his lips as if to speak, and looked again. That look went with her for many a day. She could not quite analyze it. It was stern, it was sorrowful, it even had a tinge of disgust in it; and yet there was an almost infinite yearning about it, as though he would, if he could, save her from the thing that had happened, and put her back in his estimation where she had been but a few moments before. Oh, there was no mistaking it, she had fallen in his estimation! She knew that from the minute she saw him standing there in the door.

It seemed eons that she stood there being looked through by those keen, tender, true eyes of his. Then he spoke, very quietly.

"I do not use them."

He stepped aside as if she had made a motion to pass, and she heard footsteps on the stairs. His mother was coming. She suddenly sensed that he would not want his mother to know she had been in his room. Would not want her to know she had been searching for a smoke.

Her cheeks flamed red, and her knees were trembling. For an instant she was tempted to defy him. To defy his mother. To stand there and laugh at them both! It was nothing she had done. She had been twice as indiscreet every day of her life without thinking of it. In her world no one would have dreamed of taking exception to her action. These people were a pair of old hypocrites!

Then suddenly his look upon her seemed like the eyes of the God they had been reading about and praying to, and she went swiftly past him into her room and closed the door, standing against it. She was trembling in every fiber, her eyes flashing, furious with the young man for his condemnation of her. Furious with his mother for the condemnation she would have given if she had known.

She flung herself upon the bed at last and cried silently in a fury of rage at her own situation; cried finally at herself for having caused that look in those pleasant eyes that had been so friendly all the afternoon. Cried out that she was she, and born into a world she could not understand, with always this great longing for something that could not be attained.

The other rooms were silent and dark a long time before Tasha roused herself to put out the light, undressing in the dark, and creeping in shivering to the grateful touch of the hot water bag, and the enfolding blankets.

Yet she did not sleep, even in the warm comfortable bed. She could not get away from the memory of those fine incredulous eyes as they looked her through. In vain did she turn over and tell herself that the young preacher was nothing to her. On the morrow she would be gone and never likely see him again. In vain did she call him a country boy, and a prig. The eyes looked steadily at her through the dark with that surprised contempt. And now she could not tell whether it was more for the fact that she wanted to smoke, or that she was willing to steal into a man's room to get his cigarettes, or whether it was because he had found her searching through his property.

Suddenly came the memory of the little gold slipper! In her confusion she had forgotten that he might have seen it, and known that she had found it. Then she turned back to the memory of his look again, but could find no answer to her question. If he disliked her finding him out, he disliked her still more for the smoking. The icy way in which he had said, "I do not use them" told her that. Prig! Conceited ape! Coward! He was a sissy! Even if he was a preacher, he needn't

think he was better than all creation. It was sissy for a man not to
smoke! Sissy! Sissy!

She said it over under the bedclothes, and set her small white teeth
in the blanket to emphasize the thought. Yet even as she said it she
knew there was nothing sissy about that man. The man that had
become famous by reason of his athletic prowess could never by
called a sissy. She could see him now as she had seen him three
years ago, running the length of the field, brushing aside all oppo-
nents, dodging, sliding, almost miraculously eluding his pursuers—
no, he was no sissy. And the man who had carried her through that
storm, taken off his own coat, and with her on his shoulder struggled
through the snow in a blinding sleet to bring her to warmth and safety;
and then struggled back again so unnecessarily just to fulfill some
little appointment in a church somewhere, and waited far into the
night in hope of a train before he came home to shelter! No, he was
no coward.

Yes, and the man who could play such heavenly music, and then
kneel down in front of a girl like herself and pray! No, she had to
acknowledge that he was no hypocrite and no coward. Not any of
the things she had tried to call him! She had a suspicion that perhaps
the hardest for him to do of all those things she had named to herself,
had been that prayer with her, an alien, present. For she sensed her
own difference, and began to understand that the difference was not
against him, but to her discredit. He was a strong man, a superman
perhaps, and all the things she had thought herself before this night
seemed to dwindle into nothing.

Tasha did not like to acknowledge this to herself. She fought against
it. She loathed herself for letting such an idea pass through her mind.
But it was there! And so were the eyes that had looked her through
and scorned her. Yet he had protected her name in his mother's eyes
by stepping aside and making her know that she must go quickly to
her own room and shut the door. Oh, she loathed him for that! She
would never forgive him for it! And yet she was glad somehow
underneath it all that he had done so, that the sweet old mother had
not seen anything by which to judge her ill.

Then the restless outcry of her nerves for soothing came upon her,

and it seemed that she would sell her very soul for some drug to quiet
the anguish she was in. Oh, for a good stiff drink from Barry's flask,
or one of the Framstead highballs! Oh, for anything to still this fever
and give her sleep! At one time she thought with longing for the cold
bitter sleet of the outside world and wished she might plunge from
the window into the snow and never be seen again! Her nerves were
getting beyond her control, yet she could not, or would not, cry out
and call for help. Even a cup of tea or coffee would have helped, if
she only could creep down stairs and get it, but of course she would
be heard. Even a drink of water would be wonderful. Was there any
left in the glass Mrs. Macdonald had brought to her last night?

She stole to the bureau and groped in the dark. Yes, there was half
a glass. She drank it eagerly and crept shivering back to bed, but not
to sleep. For now, suddenly, the gold slipper took command and had
its innings. Should she demand that slipper in the morning? It was
hers. He had no right to be carrying it in his grip. How did it come
there anyway? Its mate was even now under the edge of the bed. It
must have dropped off in the snow. She remembered now, her foot
had been without one when he found her. All after that was confusion. Had he rubbed her feet? Yes, and put on warm soft woolen
stockings that had felt so wonderful! But how did he come to have
that slipper under his things in his bag? If it had been on the top it
would not have seemed strange, but to have hidden it that way it
almost looked as if he wanted to keep it perhaps, just as the men
were always trying to get one's handkerchiefs and gloves for a col-
lection. But it did not seem as if he was like that. She found she did
not want to think he was. It would show a weakness, it would show
that after all he was human, just like everybody else, and had his
weak points. And—she gasped at the truth as she began to see it.
She did not *want* to find him human. She wanted to think there was
one man on earth that was different; that was strong, and fine and
true and dependable; whose eye was clear, and whose heart was true.
It was the kind of thing she had always mocked at, but she really
wanted it, after all; one true fine man that one could adore, that one
could really look up to and not despise.

Well, and if he was thinking to keep her slipper sentimentally and not let her know he had it, he would find he was mistaken. She was a woman of the world, whether he was a man of the world or not, and she would fling out upon him and ask for her slipper that he had hidden—and then her eyelids trailed down upon her cheeks, and she suddenly seemed to be caught in great strong arms and lifted over whirling, drifting snow banks, and carried miles and miles to safety, on a warm broad shoulder, held close, with a great sense of safety upon her.

She was asleep and the matter of the golden slipper had not been settled.

Sometime in the night the wind grew stronger, more steady, less turbulent, and the wild falling sleet and hail against the window pane ceased. When the morning dawned the sun shone out in radiance over a new white world shining in startling unearthly beauty. It was so still and white and deep that it almost frightened one to look, as if this mortal had suddenly put on immortality unaware and were gazing through an unexpectedly open gate into another world.

Tasha slept late, after her vigil, and there were soft dark rings under her lovely eyes when she came down to breakfast.

The girl looked round half fearfully as she came into the pleasant breakfast room where the sun shone broad across one end of the table and caught the modest silver and glass, transforming it into prisms of beauty against the fine worn linen of the cloth.

There was no one in the room but the mother, however, and she need not have feared. It was plain the son had been a true knight and said nothing to his mother about her escapade of the night before. Well, she was grateful for that, but she dreaded his coming down, and kept looking around nervously at the least little sound.

Marget greeted her with a smile.

"Well, the storm's o'er at last, lassie," she aid, as she brought in a plate of hot biscuit, and a smoking platter of ham omelet. "I'm thinking you'll soon be leaving us, and we'll be sad to have you go. It's been a cozy Sabbath with you here, and we've fitted very well together. It will be pleasant if you can find time from your friends to come visit us again sometime. We'll be like old friends, now, I hope. Perhaps sometime when you have a spare day, you'll come and bide with me when my laddie's away. He's preaching hither an yon this winter, and not expecting to take a regular charge till next summer, while he finishes the course of study he's taking in the city. But there are some week ends when he had to go quite far to fill some other body's place, and I'd be pleased for company if you'd care to come." The girl was deeply embarrassed over this invitation. She scarcely knew how to answer and found herself accepting almost eagerly, though it was the last thing she wanted to do, and she had no intention whatever of keeping her engagement.

Marget passed her a china dish of delectably fried potatoes, and smiled again at her. Marget too had spent many wakeful hours that night. The gold slipper and the girl's eyes had kept her awake. That and the look in her lad's face. The lad was smitten at last, she thought, and who was this lassie the Lord had let come into their home in the storm? Was she a temptation to be dealt with, or a poor stray lamb to be comforted and shown the way home? Marget had laid her burden down at the mercy seat, and come away with a smile, and now she was calm enough, slipper or no slipper, to note the faint blue lines under the beautiful tempestuous eyes, and reach out in sympathy.

She noted, too, the quick nervous glance now and again toward the stair, and sought to set her guest at rest on that point.

"Thurly's gone out at break of day to shovel,: she said quite casually, and noted how the slender shoulders relaxed, and the girl began to eat as if she were really enjoying her breakfast and not just toying with her fork.

"Oh," said Tasha, blooming into a smile. "Shoveling? Does he have to do that?"

"Everybody will have to shovel, my dear. The snow has got the upper hand. It's been a big blizzard, and we're verra fortunate that it's o'er, and has done no great damage. There'll be some that will be suffering from the cold, however, and even from hunger too, and perhaps some have perished in the storm. We'll not be knowing till the day is well up and the paper men have been able to gather the news."

"Oh!" said Tasha, quite stricken at the thought. "I would have perished, I'm quite sure I would, if it had not been for your son—"

"Well, dearie, the Lord was thinking on you, and brought him in good time, and we're all thankful for that. But, lassie, do you know you've not told us your name? And we can't have you going as you came and leaving nothing but your pretty memory behind."

The girl grew grave at once, as if she were suddenly confronted with her old self in the midst of these new surroundings.

"I'm Tasha Endicott," she said with a little shrug. "You've maybe seen my name in the papers, but I'm not much, really. Beside you people I'm absolutely the froth of the earth!" She laughed a little gay laugh without any merriment in it. A laugh that prepared her to slip away back to her own world again.

"Tasha!" exclaimed the older woman gravely, looking deep into the girl's eyes. "I've never heard the name—" and she looked almost troubled at the idea. "But that'll never be your right name I'm sure, dear! What was your baptismal name?"

"Oh, no," laughed the girl, "I'm really Anastasia, after a stuffy old grandmother years and years ago, but everybody calls me Tasha, and it really fits me much better than the other. I couldn't possibly live up to Anastasia."

"Did you ever look up its meaning?" asked Marget interestedly. "I like to look up names, don't you? Shall we look it up in Thurly's dictionary? There's often a great dea in a name."

Marget moved softly over to a little stand in the window where a worn dictionary lay beside a Bible. She turned the pages slowly, as if she were familiar with them, and Tasha watched her, wondering why she felt so drawn to this curious old woman, who was not beautiful nor yet nobly clad, but had the true grace of gentility in her every movement. Tasha did not really use the word gentility in her thoughts, because she had not been brought up to think in terms of real gentility. Her standards had been money and style rather than the finer virtues.

Marget looked up with a thoughtful light in her eyes:

"I didn't find the name itself here," she said disappointedly, "not as a name; but the word is here, down in the small added words below the line. That'll mean that the word used that way is a bit antiquated, you know. But still the meaning will be there. 'Anastasia,' it says, and it has a bonny meaning, 'convalescence' it says, 'return to health.' That'll be a good thought to carry in a name, will it no?"

Tasha watched her thoughtfully, wonderingly, as she closed the book and laid it back beneath the Bible. Afterward this incident was to come back to her with a new meaning one day.

Chapter 7

It was nearly noon when the telephone tinkled at last showing that the line was open again. Thurly was on the wire to say he would not be back to lunch. They had found the Widow Frailey was entirely snowed under, and were still at work digging her out. They had been able to reach her door and found that she was all right, but here was still a lot of digging to make her place habitable, and not all the men could stay that afternoon.

Marget turned back to her guest, her heart at rest. She was not anxious that Thurly should return to the society of this attractive girl. She had put the matter of the gold slipper into the hands of her Father, but perhaps this was the way He was going to handle it.

As she hung up the receiver and turned around there was Tasha standing beside her.

"May I telephone home, please?" she said. "It is certainly high time I relieved you of my presence, though I have had a lovely time."

There was a wistfulness in her tone that pricked the soul of the good woman, and forgetting her fears she said impulsively:

"It's been nothing but pleasure, my dear, to have you with us. You made a bonnie spot in the storm, and I hope you'll soon come again." And then she recalled her fears and a sudden panic came upon her to think what she had done, so that she turned away and began hurriedly to wipe a fleck of dust from the telephone table with her gingham apron.

It was almost dark, at that, when the big Endicott limousine floundered slowly through the half broken road and stopped before the cottage. The snow-plow had been by, and a hardy car or two, but the road was still well nigh impassable on the side streets. The Macdonald street was a side street.

Tasha's maid came breezing in with French epithets about the storm that created an entirely raw atmosphere, and Marget set her lips and went meekly on with what she was doing. The maid was one who put all but the wealthy on a plane so far beneath her that they were not even in the same world.

She hurried up to the room her mistress had occupied, and began to unpack the things she had brought, casting a contemptuous look at the soft black silk that Tasha was wearing, and taking command as if she owned the place. She stripped off the offending silk and flung Lady Macdonald's garments on the floor in a corner as if they were cast away forever. Then she set about arraying the young woman in a soft coral wool frock with a dashing blouse of coral and cream and brown with a glint of silver in the gaudy weave.

Marget brought the drabbled rose silk, and patted it lovingly out on the bed.

"I doubt not it'll need some reconstructing," she said sadly. "A pity! Such a pretty little dress! You looked like a flower in it."

Tasha smiled in appreciate, a quick glad light in her eyes. What was it in this plain old woman that made her seem like nobility? Why was it she was glad to have had her commendation?

Quite unlike her usual thoughtless self, she went and picked up the borrowed clothes from the corner, and smoothed them out carefully laying them in a neat pile on the bed.

"I don't know what I should have done without these," she said gently, patting them as they lay together.

Marie, the maid, gave a contemptuous glance that slithered like a knife past Marget's consciousness. Marie sniffed significantly.

"I wish I had had something more fitting—" said Marget with a gentle dignity, looking toward her black silk wrapper deprecatingly.

The maid was giving attention to the party frock on the bed. "It's scarcely worth bothering with, Miss Tasha," she said haughtily. "You'll not wear it again. We might as well leave it—!"

"No!" said Tasha quickly. "Don't leave it around in their way. Besides, I want it. I—mean to keep it!"

"Yes, dear! Keep it! It's too pretty. You can do something with it sometime I'm sure. I'd like to see you in it once more."

"Oh, very well," said Marie frigidly, and folded the poor drabbled rose petals as carefully as if they had just come from the store.

"I don't see your other slipper," said Marie, pausing in her rapid ministrations.

Marget felt her heart give a jerk and go on again. Ought she—? No, she could not say she knew where it was. She could not bring it forth from her son's bag. What should she do? Was it honest—? Honorable? But—she was not supposed to know where it was. And what would Thurly think if he found it gone? Could she make it seem natural that she had been unpacking his bag and had taken it for granted that he had found the slipper in the snow, as doubtless he had, and had restored it to its owner? Could she bridge that way of knowing where it was hidden, and make it right with Thurly without seeing her fear in her eyes?

But while she hesitated the calm voice of Tasha answered as she turned swiftly and went toward the head of the stairs:

"I lost it off in the snow, Marie. Never mind. Come, it is getting late! We should be gone!"

Marget had not seen the sudden paling of Tasha's cheek, the quick-drawn breath before she spoke. Marget was wondering even yet if she ought not to go into her son's room and get that slipper from its hiding place. But how could she do it now, since no one knew that she knew it was there?

The cold hard voice of Marie broke in with a cutting glance at Marget that almost seemed like suspicion, as if it were all her fault.

"It's a pity, Miss Tasha. Those were your diamond slides."

"Oh—!" breathed Marget, paling. "They'll—maybe be found!" She pronounced it "foond" and made it like a croon.

"It doesn't matter," said Tasha sharply, feeling the blood sting her cheeks, and lowering her eyes as she hurried down the stairs.

Marie brushed past the hostess rudely with the suit case she had brought and hurried after her mistress. Marget lingered with a helpless glance toward her son's door, and a bewildered idea even yet of doing something about the slipper, then hurried down after them.

"Take it out to the car, Marie!" Tasha was saying as she held the door open and motioned to her maid. "I'll be out in a minute."

Then she closed the door abruptly and turned toward Marget, the look almost of a child on her face, a child who was sorry to leave.

"You've been so nice," she said simply, coming toward Marget with her hand out for good bye. "I don't seem to be able to thank you enough!"

"My dear!" said Marget, suddenly folding her arms about the astonished girl. "My dear!" and kissed her tenderly on her warm young lips.

Tasha had never had a caress like that. It thrilled her. It was like what she thought a mother's kiss would be, and for an instant she yielded herself to it warmly, eagerly, then drew back almost embarrassed, speaking quickly to hide her confusion.

"You'll thank you son for me, too—" she said. "He was—wonderful—!"

There had been a stamping at the front door, and now the two turned at the breath of cold air that blew upon them, and there stood Thurly! How much had he heard? Had there been too great fervor in her voice? Tasha's cheeks flamed like to the color of her coral dress, and she stood there in her confusion before him, beautiful in her bright frock and little close coral hat, as she had been in the rose petals Saturday night.

The young man, tall and brawny in old gray trousers and sweater, with a gray woolen scarf still bound around his neck, thick leather mittens on his hands, snow still caked all over his garments, his face ruddy and tired, and his hair sticking out rampantly, stood and looked at her, severity and wistfulness mingled in his gaze.

She was lovely! Oh, yes, she was lovely!

Tasha rallied first.

"I'm glad you came before I had to leave," she said with a gay little laugh that somehow sounded almost near to tears.

He took her hand gravely. He did not smile. Somehow his mother wished he would smile. It would have meant less. She was thinking of the slipper. Ought she to remind him? Would it embarrass him? It would be so easy to say right now, "She has lost her slipper" and then he would remember and say, "Why, yes, of course! I found that slipper. I forgot to mention it, I will get it," and then it would all be over and straightened out and she would never have to think of it any more. And yet, somehow, she did not say it. Was she afraid Thurly was wanting to keep that slipper? Was she afraid—of what? But of course it would not be honest to keep it. She must tell him at once. He was helping Tasha on with the rich brown fur coat. He was going to take her out to the car.

She opened her lips.

"She has lost her slipper, Thurly!" but the sound was faint and tentative as if she were trying out her voice. The wind had swished in the door as they opened it, and they did not hear her. Thurly had gone ahead with his snow shovel as she were a princess. She went and stood in the door herself, shivering, and called again, aimlessly, foolishly, "She has lost her slipper, Thurly, her gold slipper!" But neither of them heard, and she felt like a fool standing there. The engine of the car had started. It would be impossible to make them hear now. What a fool she had been! Now it was out of her hands.

"Oh, God! I ought to have said it," she murmured. "What a fool I've been. But please fix it right somehow!"

The car plunged over a drift and wallowed away around the corner into the more broken highway, and Tasha waved a small gloved hand out the window as the lights of the car vanished.

Tasha was gone back into her own world again.

Marget felt a choking in her throat, a smarting of something like tears in her eyes. Why?

Out there in the dusk, big and strong, stood Thurly. His shoulders took a tired sag, and the loosened scarf swung grotesquely about his face. He was staring blankly toward the corner round which the car had gone. The sound of its expensive engine was even now out of hearing. So she had come, and so she had gone! Like a disquieting dream. How beautiful she was! How little her hand had been as it lay in his after he had pulled off his wet mitten. Hers seemed like a baby's hand. He hadn't wanted to let it go.

It is safe to say that Thurly had forgotten all about the little slipper. He came in at last when it had grown suddenly dark around him. His mother hurried from the window where she had been furtively watching him, and stirred the open fire which she had kept going all day. She had Thurly's slippers on the hearth, and his big warm dressing gown lying over the deep chair he loved. The coffee was bubbling in the kitchen and sending forth a delicious aroma. Marget bustled about self-consciously to make everything seem quite natural.

"Don't bother to go up the stairs, laddie," she called, as Thurly stamped the snow off and came into the living room. "Just sit ye down by the fire and I'll bring you a cup of coffee before you do another thing. You must be wearied to death and half starved."

"I must get off these wet things first, Mother," said Thurly in a voice that sounded strangely tired and old. "I think if you don't mind, I'll just get a bath while I'm up. I'm stiff with the shoveling and I think it will help."

But what Thurly did when he went up stairs was to stand at the door of the guest room for several long minutes, and stare at the vacant room. It had a storm-tossed look for a room in his mother's house, neat as it yet was. There was a scrap of paper on the floor that Marie had dropped when she unwrapped her lady's garments. There was a bit of white box on the bureau lined with white velvet that had held the coral beads my lady wore about her throat. There was a length of string on the floor dropped from the suit case, and a large pink shred of tulle under the bed. Thurly noted with a pan his mother's silk robe, and the bright scarf folded together on the chair, but he went deliberately and picked up the piece of rose tulle and crushed it in his hand.

Even when he went at last to his own room he did not immediately set about divesting himself of his wet garments. He stood a long time just where he had stood the night before when he caught the girl hunting in his bag for cigarettes! Then he sighed and, stooping, opened his bag, with a strange unreasoning desire to see what she had seen when she looked in. He ran his hand down among his possessions, and came sharp against the jeweled buckle of the little shoe. Then he remembered! He had hidden the gold slipper under this things. Had she found it? Did she know he had it there?

When he came upon her she had been standing still, looking down at something beneath the clothes her hand was holding away. Did she know it was her slipper? What did she think of him for having it there and not giving it back to her?

He lifted the foolish little shoe and held it in his big hand. Such a tiny thing, so inadequate, it seemed, to carry anyone through the world.

A bauble for a dance! Just a little light dancing girl! How pretty she had looked in that pink party gown! Yes, how pretty just now in the other flaming dress that set off her beauty so fittingly, and the rich fur coat! He sighed. She was a girl of the world. Of course she was pretty. Well, what of it? He had seen pretty girls before, plenty of them, perhaps girls prettier than she was. She was positively not a person for his thoughts to linger about. She was essentially worldly. If he had now known that before last night he certainly knew it now. The diamonds twinkled wickedly, and shot a prism into his eyes. He set the little shoe sharply on his bureau, and began to fumble with the button of the heavy woolen shirt he had worn all day.

His mother's footsteps padded softly here and there below and paused at the foot of the stairs.

"Thurly, almost ready?" she called anxiously. Thurly started and picked up the little shoe sharply again. Thunder! What was he going to do with that shoe?

Did his mother get the girl's address? A pang went through him as he remembered that he did not even know her name. But Mother never forgot such things. She would have the address. It was going to be awkward to ask for it—but he could manage that. He would tell her how he had found the shoe and forgotten it. Then he would send it by mail. That would be best of course. By mail. Would he have to write a letter? No. Yes. What might the girl think? That he had meant to keep the shoe? Had she seen it already? Well, perhaps she thought he was keeping it for some sentimental reason. He must not under any consideration let her think that. He would just send it back by mail if Mother had the address, and let her think what she pleased. That was it—let her think what she pleased. She was nothing to him!

"Laddie, are you ready? I don't hear the water running. There's plenty of hot water, you know."

Thurly started and jabbed the shoe back into his bag under the pajamas again. He couldn't stop now to decide. Mother would think it queer.

"I'll be ready soon!" he shouted.

He dashed into the bathroom and started the hot water, rapidly disrobing. It occurred to him that in case his mother had not been provident enough to get the girl's address he could telephone to Framstead. They would know what young woman had been missing from their dance. Or would they? There might have been more than one missing on such a night as that. Still he could probably get some clue. But the idea of bringing Framstead into the problem was distasteful to him.

He was absorbed and silent when he came down, and Marget was self-conscious too, and so for the first time in their lives there seemed to be a cloud between mother and son, which each was too distrait to break. But when the supper things were put away, and it came time for evening worship Marget hovered near her boy, and putting a timid hand on his shoulder said:

"Laddie, ye'll be praying for the bonnie guest that's gone, the night. Laddie, I think she needs it sairly."

A light came into Thurly's eyes, and he answered heartily, "Yes, Mother—we'll *pray!*" and so they knelt.

But it was by that fervent eager prayer that Marget knew that the little gold shoe had some way got entangled with her lad's heart strings, and she could only pray the more, that the Lord's will might be done; but oh, that her laddie might be spared making any mistakes in the things of this world!

Chapter 8

It was three days later that Thurly made his decision. The shoe had to go back, and the manly thing to do was to take it. He had decided also that in any case, shoe or no shoe, it was only decent to call and see if the lady had suffered any damages from her exposure in the storm.

Thurly had arrived at his decision after hours of argument with himself. Now he was all contempt for the girl who had dared to enter a man's room and search for cigarettes, again he was all tenderness for the fairy-like little person he had carried on his shoulder through the storm. The matter was getting on his nerves and obtruding itself between him and his work. He felt that it must be finished up, cleared out of his system, and forgotten. He finally faced himself in the glass and realized that some inner weakness in himself actually longed to see that girl again! All that he acknowledged was probably true about her, yet he desired more than he could understand in himself, to see her once more. He finally arrived at the decision that to go and see her in her natural setting would probably be the best antidote for his foolishness that could be had.

So he came down to breakfast the next morning and asked his mother in the most casual manner if she happened to know the address of their late guest.

Marget faced about from the stove where she was dishing up the oatmeal porridge and tried to be casual too, but there was that in her tone that made her answer seem momentous.

"Oh, yes. She's Miss Anastasia Endicott, and I found her father's name in the paper this morning. It's the same I know for it mentioned her as having been a debutante last winter, and it called her by the name she said they all used, so I was sure."

The son's eyes were veiled as he asked huskily:

"What was the name?"

The way his mother said "Tasha" gave it a pagan sound, and Thurly sat looking down at the coffee he was stirring and considered it with a queer sinking in his heart. Of course! That would be she. He might have known it would be some loud dashing name like that—yet—she was so small and delicate—so lovely—!

He was suddenly roused to realize that his mother was watching him and that her face was anxious. He looked up and tried to laugh. "Queer name, isn't it? Sounds kind of heathen. Well, I'm glad you know who she is. You see, I found her shoe."

"Yes," said Marget without interrogation in her voice.

"It's got to be returned, I suppose," said Thurly, and suddenly realized that a personal call was utterly superfluous. He paused.

"Yes," stated Marget. "I told her it would likely be found."

Another pause.

"You—would like *me*—" she hesitated. "You want me to sent it to her of course," she finished blithely as if that were a sudden solution of the difficulty she had not thought of before.

"Why—would you—Mother?" said Thurly, the sun suddenly gone blank— "You—don't—think—. It won't be necessary for me to take it in person?"

Marget's voice trembled a little as she answered.

"Why, no—no, Thurly, not unless—why, no, I shouldn't see how that would be expected at all. She's not a personal friend, of course," she finished briskly.

"Of course," said Thurly colorlessly.

"I'll write her a note," said Marget happily. "I'll say you found her shoe near the station. You did find it near the station, didn't you, laddie?"

"Yes, I found it in—near—that is it was really in the station. It was dark, you know. I ran across it."

"Well, it isn't necessary, I'll just say you found it. And oh, was the buckle on it? The maid said it was real diamonds. I hope that isn't lost."

"It's there!" said Thurly crisply. "I'll get it."

He brought the slipper down and Marget held it in her hand, the diamonds sparkling gloriously in the morning sun.

"Now isn't that a pretty little trick!" said Marget, gayly twinkling the gems back and forth in the sun. "It looks just as if it belonged to her, doesn't it?"

Marget was so happy to have this slipper out from between her lad and herself that she forgot she was admiring the girl to him. The sudden light in his eyes brought her sharp understanding, and the diamonds smote her so that she had to close her eyes. Then a new thought stung into her consciousness.

"Laddie, I don't know as it's safe after all to send diamonds through the mail. Someone might steal them. I'm afraid I'd always be uneasy lest she never got them. I wouldn't like to be responsible for them, sending them that way. Do you think perhaps we ought to take them in?"

The sun leaped up again in the day and Thurly smiled broadly.

"Well, perhaps—" he said cheerfully. "Yes, I suppose that would be the careful, kindly thing to do," he added and rising suddenly with a hand full of dishes he made his way to the kitchen with them, as was his custom after meals, whistling gayly, like his old happy self.

Meanwhile, Tasha Endicott, as the limousine wallowed slowly cityward, had a strange impression that she was passing back into life again after a temporary aberration. She questioned her maid eagerly as to what had happened during her absence. Was the storm terrible in the city? The maid was voluble in her description of conditions.

"Mrs. Endicott got quite angry about the storm," she said. "It hindered guests from arriving. Something went wrong, too, with the heating plant and the fire was out for several hours. Mrs. Endicott was furious with Talbot and dismissed him. It was found afterward that snow had fallen down the chimney in great quantities and stopped the draft."

Marie did not express a word of blame toward Mrs. Endicott, but Tasha knew there was veiled indignation behind the maid's formal words. Marie had been fond of Talbot. And it had not been Talbot's fault. But that was Lucia! She had to take out any annoyance or discomfort on someone else, usually the servants. Tasha stared out of the car window for several seconds thinking. She was sorry to have Talbot go. He was the last one of the old servants who had been with the family since Tasha was a child. But it had been inevitable. Lucia never had liked him and was only seeking a good cause of complaint before she got rid of him. Now what would Dad say? Would he make a stand and send for Talbot? If he did there would be a storm in the house again that might last for days.

Tasha flung the thought aside and turned back to Marie.

"Is Dad home?" she asked, her tone dismissing the other bit of information without comment.

"No, Miss Tasha." He is *not*. I believe they said he was gone to New York," said Marie, her tone answering her mistress' very thought. Marie had a great way of carrying on conversations this way without actually saying anything disrespectful or presuming. It was impossible to reprove her for anything she had said. Tasha let this go by without comment also.

"There was company," volunteered Marie with a knowing twinkle and lifting of her chin. All day Sunday!"

Tasha turned a quick glance and swept the maid's furtive face.

"The—same—one?" she asked casually, trying not to sound annoyed.

"Yes, Mr. Clancy!" There was so much understanding of Tasha's own annoyance in the simple answer that Tasha changed the subject with dignity.

"Is there much mail?"

"Oh, yes, a quantity," assented the maid eagerly. "Many invitations. It's going to be quite the gayest season yet, judging by the way it begins. Yes, and there are boxes of flowers. I've kept them fresh. Orchids from Mr. Barry, and violets and roses—"

But Tasha was not listening. She was visioning a cozy room, that she had seen that very morning, with white muslin curtains at the windows, and a potted geranium on a little stand near the snow-covered panes, cheerfully blooming, a spot of scarlet color; she was remembering a sweet-faced old lady fussing tenderly among the leaves, removing a withered bit of bloom, hovering over the great scarlet blossoms as if they were her children, beaming at them with a smile almost as warm as the sun. Somehow orchids and hot house hybrids paled in contrast; there was something so vivid and friendly

in the wholesome scarlet geranium. They would not fit into the exquisite simplicity of the home where she had been staying. She tried
to picture the orchids arriving and being set within one of the stately
old vases painted with shepherdesses and little white lambs. They
would seem strangely out of place. But the violets would fit. They
would nestle in the quaint glass bowl that had held the quince pre-
serve. They would fill the whole little sweet house with the subtle
fragrance. they would tone their purpose to the homespun, and not
flaunt themselves nor seem out of place. Yes, she would send some
violets to Thurly Macdonald's mother! That was a pleasant thought.
She could sometimes send pleasant gifts to the woman who had tucked
her in bed, called her lassie, and prayed for her as if she were a little
stray lamb. Her eyes grew misty with the memory.

"There's talk of Palm Beach," insinuated Marie, watching her mistress furtively.

"There would be," said Tasha indifferently.

"Oh, but Miss Tasha, you oughtn't to take it like that!" said the
maid vivaciously. "It's going to be grand this year. Dorset went
down with Madame and the children from next door, and he says
there are so many improvements you wouldn't know the place, and
that simply everyone is going to be there. You've got so much to
make it nice for yourself. All the young men just crazy for you, and
your father just building the new villa and all. Dorset says it is
sweet. He says there's nothing can touch it anywhere in that locality."

"Yes, I suppose there'll be a thrill in that. Did my things come
from New York yet? I hope you unpacked. Those transparent velvets crush so easily, and the green one is the prettiest I ever saw. I
couldn't duplicate it if it got spoiled."

"Yes, Miss Tasha, they're all hanging up under their covers, and
there's not a crease on one. They were well packed."

But Tasha was not listening. She was hearing a sweet little old
voice saying, "It's such a pretty dress! You look like a flower in it.
I'd like to see you in it again—" Why was it that she could not get
her thoughts away from that plain little house, and that plain little
woman, and her strong disconcerting son?

Tasha, arrived at length, entered the stately mansion they called her home, and passed through the more formal rooms. She did not enter the more intimate library just beyond the stair, though she could hear the murmur of languorous voices, her stepmother's and a male voice she disliked beyond reason. She could see the flicker of fire-light through the doorway on the wall. She stood for an instant, her foot poised on the stair, listening, then with a shrug she slid noise-lessly up to her own apartment.

There was a fire on the hearth here, too, and her own deep chair drawn comfortably near the hearth. A small table was beside the chair, bearing a silver tray with a tea service, a plate of sandwiches, and some bonbons. Her cigarette case lay beside it, just where she had left it when she forgot it in her hurry Saturday night. A soft light fell from beneath silken draperies, and the little shelf beneath the table held the book she had been reading on the train up from Wash-ington. The room was filled with the perfume of exotic flowers. They smiled at her from the period mantel, from table and desk, and carved taboret, bearing the homage of half a dozen different men she knew. Several pounds of costly sweets were lying open handily, their expensive boxes blending with the richness of the room, the firelight flickering over it all. This was hers. All this luxury! And Thurly Macdonald out in the snow dug the Widow Frailey's little cottage back into life again!

The maid came and removed the traveling boots from Tasha's feet, took her wraps and hung them away out of sight, brought the mail, turned the lamp at just the right angle. She had nothing to do but sink into the down cushions of her chair, and amuse herself, while Thurly Macdonald struggled through storms to preach to a lot of common people who probably wouldn't trouble themselves to come out in the snow to hear him! Life was queer!

But here at last were cigarettes! Why worry about it all? She sank into her chair, reached for a cigarette and prepared to light it.

But something arrested her. Her eyes lifted involuntarily and looked toward the corner of the mantel. There, suddenly, he seemed to stand, as if he had come quietly in, just as he had come upon her the evening before. The rich shadows of the lovely room gathered about he vision of him like colored mists, and seemed to conspire to shield him, as he stood there, in her room, his eyes upon her—*accusing* eyes!—just as they had been last night, looking through and through her!

What nonsense! He was not there at all! 'Twas just the lilies in the jade bowl on the mantel against the dusky background of the room that looked like a face! Her nerves were shot to pieces by her late experiences! She would smoke and dispel the illusion.

She lifted her hand again, but once more the arresting illusion! His eyes, looking through her. His voice, after that pointed silence: "I do not use them," his face flaming white contempt!

She dropped her hand once more to the arm of her chair and looked beyond to where a picture of gay dancing nymphs garlanded a young god, and tried to adjust her vision to the familiar objects of the room, differentiating the blossoms one from another, and from their dim background, making them again but flowers; the semblance of a tall form below the face, only the tall carved chair with its velvet upholstery in black and silver!

She laughed out an empty little ripple of triumph as she dispelled the fancy for the second time. She lifted the cigarette to her lips with a defiant gesture, part and parcel of her old flippant self. But again a third time, as if an invisible hand had drawn her hand back, as if a voice had spoken and directed her eyes again to the shadowy corner beyond the mantel, she looked, and still he seemed to stand there. He was searching her through, condemning her with a look that held both sternness and disappointment. Condemning her, and praying for her, and yearning over her. She did not call these things by their names, but she felt them keenly, each one distinctly, in her soul, and she cringed in her chair. The moisture started on her brow and lip, her hand that held the cigarette trembled and dropped to her lap. The cigarette fell upon the floor.

Down in a little heap she crumpled in her chair, with her face hidden in her arms, all unhappy, disgusted with herself; all weak with a kind of moral fright; all angry with herself. Her little hard-boiled self. Why had that young man such power over her? Just because he had saved her life did he mean to hang around her physically, and dominate her? Did he presume to order what she would do? He had not bought her soul by carrying her through the storm that night. He need not think he had! Oh, she would break this power he had over her. She would find a way to make him cringe as he had made her cringe. She would offer him money in return for what he had done for her. He might be holy and self-exalted, but he probably needed money. In fact every room of the little house where he lived cried out that money was scarce. His very garments showed poverty, though they were immaculate, and well cut. They had a hint of threadbare edges here and there. Money would break this power he had over her. Her father was able to pay him a large sum. If he followed her this way she would cast his own contempt back in his face in the form of silver and gold!

She lifted her head and looked toward the mantel defiantly again. The lilies nodded like a white face through the gloom, and the illusion was gone, but the cigarette lay where it had fallen upon the floor. As if to stamp upon him now she had downed him, she spoke aloud:

"I will pay you money for saving my life!" and there was in her voice all the contempt she had seen in his eyes.

"Did you call me?"

It was Marie appearing from the next room. Her keen eyes took in the cigarette upon the floor.

"Yes! Take those cigarettes away!" said Tasha pettishly. "They make me sick!"

Chapter 9

 T he maid came wonderingly, and took up the pack.

"Why, Miss Tasha," she said, examining them, "they are the same ones you always—"

"I know—take them away!"

"Shall I send out for others?"

"No! I do not wish to smoke now. What time is it? Are we dining at home?"

Tasha sat up and gathered a handful of her mail to examine it.

"Dinner is ordered. I fancy Mrs. Endicott is expecting to be at home," said Marie, stooping to pick up the offending cigarette.

"Has Mr. Clancy gone yet?"

"I'm not sure. I think he is still there."

"Find out if he is staying to dinner."

The maid disappeared and in a few minutes came back.

"Mrs. Endicott has ordered the table set for a guest."

"Then you may tell her I am not coming down tonight. I wish to have my dinner sent up. I'm tired."

Marie hesitated.

"I think Mr. Barry Thurston will be in later in the evening," she insinuated. "He seemed upset that you were not here this morning when he called."

"If he comes you may tell him I'm not seeing anyone to-night," said Tasha petulantly, her mood hardening with opposition. It helped her to keep Barry out to-night. It somehow satisfied the angry restlessness in her heart to shut them all out, to punish others as well as the young stranger who had presumed to show her contempt. Oh, he was insufferable!

Tasha sat up and drank a cup of tea thirstily, then opened her mail. There was no thrill there at all. The same round of dances and theater parties, the same bridge clubs, and pageants, and benefits. It was just going to be last winter over again! Bah! And Lucia with her hangers on! Perhaps she would ask Dad to let her go to Europe. Of course Palm Beach and the new house would be a slight break in the monotony, and there were always new things there, new people. But life was terribly tasteless somehow. What had happened? She had not felt that way when she started out for Framstead. It must be that killjoy Sunday. She must do something to get rid of this restlessness.

She took up a book and tried to read, but the book she had been eager over had now become tame, silly, a rehash of vapid doings that seemed without a reason.

She flung herself over to the telephone and called up her friend Adrienne Lyman, and after some delay was answered by a dreary voice.

The dreary voice grew a shade more interested however when she recognized Tasha.

"Oh, is that you, Tasha? You're a peach, you are! What became of you? We telephoned everywhere we knew to let you know the Framstead bus was coming for you, but we couldn't locate you, and then we heard the bridge was down! Where on earth were you, and why didn't you call up? Barry went wild, and then he spent most of the night under the table. Really, Tash, he was disgraceful! Even *I* was ashamed of him. He certainly needed you there to keep him straight. And as for Ducky Duke, he was worse than usual. He and Helena Linton—but I really can't tell it all over the telephone. We had the wildest time. It was some thrill. You ought to have been there. Gloria Framstead simply outdid herself in costume and set the pace, and darling, we danced all night! We simply didn't stop! Think of it! And when morning came and we found we couldn't get home we danced on! We danced all day Sunday by spells, just danced till we dropped somewhere, and then slept a while wherever we were, and then got up and had more cocktails and danced again. In fact we danced most of Sunday night too, and everybody else stayed till Monday morning. Sunday night about midnight we had a masked parade, and Barry Thurston led it with Gloria Framstead. Darling, they marched right up on the table among the supper things and threw cake and wine—Oh, it was wild. They say Mrs. Framstead don't like it, much, but she didn't do a thing about it, and so everybody had a grand time. But darling! I'm *dead*! I'm simply a *fragment*! I've just waked up, been asleep all day, and I'm not in my right mind yet. I've smoked so many cigarettes and drank so many cocktails I simply loathe the thought of food, and I think I shall have to sleep for a week— But darling! Where *were* you? Did you have a frumpy time at home, or were you caught somewhere in the storm? Explain."

And then a strange thing happened to Tasha.

She had intended to have a good laugh with Adrienne over the "quaint" old woman and "frumpy" fanatic of a son who had corralled her for the storm time. She had hoped by trampling on all that was good in her soul toward those who had saved her and entertained her, to dispel the restlessness that their memory caused in her. But as she listened to her friend's account of the Framstead affair she felt a violent reaction, and a keep disgust swept over her. Something froze within her, and she answered coldly:

"Oh, I was staying with friends near Stonington. I was quite all right and had a wonderful time. I couldn't telephone because the wires were down, but I was sure you would understand. Of course you must feel rotten after all that, so I won't keep you now. I just wanted to let you know I'm all right, and see if you were the same. See you soon," and with a very few more words she hung up.

She stared around her luxurious room and wondered what was the matter with her. Wondered why she had hung up so soon, without asking for more details, and then suddenly was confronted with the idea that she actually had felt as if that young giant of an accusing minister were over there by the mantel all the time listening, and she was feeling his accusing eyes upon her back while she talked.

She put her cold hands on her hot cheeks and gave a little shivering sigh, then marched back to her seat by the fire and deliberately turned on a flare of light in the room. This was ridiculous! This was acting like a baby! Perhaps she was going to be sick. She must buck up!

Marie came in with her dinner, and she ate, picking at this and that, and going back over the Sunday dinner they had eaten in the little cottage at Stonington while the storm raged without, and peace reigned within. There was a wistfulness in her eyes as she glanced up fearfully toward the great bunch of pure white lilies, that shone out distinctly now in the flare of light, with no mocking face of contempt to search her soul.

But later, when Marie had drawn her bath and laid out her night things and gone, Tasha snapped off the light and sat a long time in the dusk, with the fire playing softly over the room, and the dusky white lilies on the mantel that looked like a face, just above her. She was thinking just what she should write in a letter of thanks for her visit; thinking what she would send to Mrs. Macdonald for a present. Afterwards when she lay in her bed she thought of how Marget Macdonald's soft hands had tucked her in and how the gentle voice had prayed for her. She had often wondered that anybody could believe in supernatural things. She had laughed at credulous fanatics who had caused the Bible to become a sacred book. Now there stole into her heart a faint wonder if perhaps after all there might be something in it. Since such a woman as Marget Macdonald believed, and had taught such a son as hers to believe, it must not be so silly after all.

Not that Tasha was an intelligent unbeliever. She was entirely too indifferent a pagan for that. She had never troubled her head about such things. In college she had passed over Bible study class as too trivial and stupid for her to bother with, so that modern destructive criticism had not even touched her in passing. She had not been where it was. She had been spending her time in the froth of life too far from such questions to even weigh them and discard them. But somehow the influence of that Sabbath shut in by God's snow and cold, with its atmosphere of prayer and praise, with its Bible words and sweet old hymns, and trustful communion with the Father, had left its touch on her gay soul, as nothing had ever done before. It seemed to fill in a way the great emptiness that had always been in her soul. She thought it was because of the lack of a mother, or anything beloved, save her gay, busy, absent father, who had made up in money what he lacked time to give in love and companionship.

Tasha lay and thought about it all until her thoughts blended into her dreams, and she thought she saw Thurly standing by the door, smiling as he had done, before he found her rummaging in his traveling bag.

Then came dimly the memory of her slipper, and it flashed its way into her dreams and became a sprite that danced over a snow-lit field. She seemed to be struggling waist deep to capture it, and fell down exhausted at last, deeper, deeper, colder and colder, till suddenly she was lifted and borne in strong arms, high above the drifts, to the tune of an old hymn. What were those words? "From every stormy wind that blows!" That was it. She must not let that get away.

Marget Macdonald had taken cold, out on the back steps, trying to melt the ice off the brick walk, with just a little shawl around her shoulders, and her hands cold and wet with snow and salt.

"I'm an old fule," she told her son, with a wistful smile. "I kept telling myself to go in and get a warm coat and a hood, and my rubbers. An now, Thurly, son, ye'll have ta gang by yerself. And I'm thinking perhaps that was the way it was meant onygait. Just take the little gold shoe, and give her my best luve, and ye'll have that off yer mind. It's best not to wait. And she might be needing her shoe. I doubt not there are other dances," and she sighed a trifle sadly.

"And other shoes, Mither mine," said Thurly with a lilt in his voice. "I doubt if she'll miss this one but it's my business to return it anyhow. So here goes."

It is safe to say that never since he faced the vast audience in his High School auditorium to voice his commencement oration had Thurly Macdonald felt so diffident and so utterly inadequate to the situation as he did when he started out with the little gold shoe in a neat package tucked away in the deep pocket of his overcoat.

Clean, shaven, well groomed, clear of eye, with his crisp brown curls brushed smooth, he was as goodly a specimen of young manhood as one would care to look upon, and more than one girl tripping by on her little high heels behind her rouge and lipstick turned and looked wistfully after him. But Thurly was feeling more excited than he had ever felt before a big football game. He was going into an unknown field, and he didn't rightly know the signals.

He stopped outside on the corner and got his bearings for a moment after he had located the number. The great stone mansion loomed ominously, its stately portico guarded by a double portcullis of delicate and intricate iron work. It seemed a daring thing to do to attempt to enter there. He had not quite visioned anything so imposing, and yet her home would be like that. He ought to have known. There would be a butler, with maybe a footman in livery. Thurly Macdonald hated running the gauntlet between lines of liveried servants. Yet his mother's last words had been, "Remember, lad, that ye come of a royal family, and hold your head high. You're a prince and your Father's a King. Look whomsoever ye meet in the eye, and not get tae thinking of yourself!"

How canny his mother was, born and bred among the heather, yet wise to the ways of this world, and knowing the human heart like a book! He gave a little quiet laugh—the one he used to use as he went into battle in the old football days—and stepped through the iron grill into the stately portico.

Thurly Macdonald had been in just as pretentious mansions as the Endicott home many a time, going home with his college friends for week ends, an honored guest anywhere; and occasionally being entertained somewhere for over night when he went to take a great man's pulpit on a sudden call; but never before had a house so overawed him. As he followed the servant through the dimness of a spacious hallway into a formal reception room at one side, he glanced about him and caught his breath. The very chime of the cathedral clock in some dim recess seemed like fairy bells. For was he not in the home of the beautiful girl who had dropped down upon his own humble home in the midst of a storm in a rose-petaled frock, looking too exquisite to be true. This was her world that he saw about him, the nest of luxury where she was bred. The other lovely homes where he had entered had been but beautiful backgrounds for his friends, but this was different. This was where the lovely worldly young woman walked and talked and had her being; it was a fitting background for surely the loveliest creature God had ever put on this earth, even though she was wholly apart from his world. It was good that he should be here and see how she lived. It was good that he should get all ideas of friendship with her out of his head. Here was where the little gold shoe belonged, and he was bringing it home. It never belonged on his bureau, or in his traveling bag. Its jewels were not made to shine in a cottage, but to sparkle on a gay foot upon a palace floor.

So Thurly Macdonald held his head high and remembered his royal birth as he followed the liveried man to the high quiet room and waited.

It was some minutes before the servant returned and Thurly had time to get into tune with the new surroundings. He noted the rich furnishings, rare carvings and articles of vertu scattered lavishly about; a great picture so hung that its figures seemed to be living men and women going about just beyond the next room; a mirror that seemed to reach to heaven and reflect the universe; rugs that caught the sound of a footfall and choked it into silence. And then the man stood before him again.

"Miss Endicott is not in," he said in his cold mechanical voice.

"I will wait," said Thurly with a firm set of his fine lips. "Will it be long before her return?"

The man might have answered "five minutes" in the same tone with which he spoke, but he said:

"Not until Spring, probably. Mrs. Endicott and Miss Endicott have left for Palm Beach. They usually stay until the cold weather is over."

Thurly got to his feet with a sudden sinking of dismay. Gone! Spring! At the least three months, then the cold would be over!

He walked the silent hallways lingeringly, willfully, gave one quick glance back as the great grill opened to let him out, and gravely trod the portico into the sunshine of the wintry day again.

But it was not until he was seated in a bus being carried swiftly toward the station that he remembered that he was still carrying the little gold shoe tucked safely away in his deep overcoat pocket!

Chapter 10

Lucia Endicott, slim, sleek, groomed to the last degree, lolled in her seat in the drawing-room compartment and smoked one cigarette after another as she idly watched her pretty, contemptuous stepdaughter. She had hair like black satin cut sharply and close to her small round head, and her sharp features were somewhat accentuated by the points of hair that lay on her deeply tinted cheeks, and by the sharp lines of the deeply red lips that were startling against the pearly whiteness of her skin. She wore wriggly clanging earrings that seemed to have personalities like serpents, hired to go with her make-up, and her eyes were like two bright black stones that imprisoned something slimy and cruel. She was sitting in the conventional fashionable attitude, with a spine like a new moon, and just the right amount of slim knee showing beneath her brief skirt, surmounting the proper length of silken limb, like two clothesprops crossed and lolling from the clothesline.

She narrowed her eyelids that were thick and white, and just touched with a fashionable amount of blue shadow, and studied Tasha, sitting gloomily opposite, staring out the window, a closed magazine lying unheeded in her lap.

"What's the idea, Tash?" she asked at last, "trying a new pose? You haven't smoked once to-day."

"It doesn't interest me," said Tasha without taking her gaze from the window. "I'm fed up on smoke. Besides, it's a silly thing to do. Did you ever think how senseless it is?"

"You'll never get anywhere on that," advised the stepmother languidly, "it isn't good form. And besides, people don't like you if you don't do as they do."

"There isn't anywhere to get, Lucia darling," moralized Tasha contemptuously, " and why should I want people to like me? I'm bored to death with people liking me now. I don't get the least kick out of it anymore!"

79

"Try something new, angel child! It really is time you got married. Which reminds me. I'd advise you to annex Barry Thurston presently or you may lose him. They tell me he was devoted to Gloria Framstead at the dance you didn't attend. You know you've been out a whole year now, and it doesn't do to let the younger set come in and pick what belongs to you. I've noticed a number of times that Gloria has her eye on Barry, and if she wants him she'll get him!"

"Let her have him!" said Tasha with a shrug, as she remembered Adrienne's account of the Saturday night dance. There was contempt in her eyes and voice, and the other woman narrowed her gaze. "You're foolish!" she said sharply, "you can't count on lasting forever with a man like Barry. He likes to be flattered and Gloria flatters him. You've wiped the earth up with him for months, and he's getting fed up on it, Tash! You can't treat a man that way forever, not when there's a stunning beauty around like Gloria. I know the signs and I tell you Barry Thurston's fed up on being a mat under your feet!"

"And I'm fed up on Barry Thurston!" declared Tasha in a cold voice. "That's one reason I consented to go to Palm Beach just now. He's not the absolutely only man!"

"Don't be silly, Tash! You know Barry Thurston is your best bet. There isn't another man in our crowd can touch him for wealth and position. You could have simply anything you wanted, and go anywhere you liked. And if you got tired of Barry you could live in Europe for a while."

"What the matter, Lucia," said Tasha, sitting up and eyeing her stepmother sharply, "are you getting tired of having me around? Or is it that you want to stage a display wedding with yourself as a loving mother? Speak out and get it off your chest. I can always go to Europe or somewhere else if I'm in the way."

"Infant!" said the other woman lazily, "as if I couldn't give you a word of advice without your going into a fury like that. I simply hate to see you let the best catch of the season go through your fingers, with a flock of little buds just waiting to catch him as he falls. I didn't like to tell you, but I've been hearing things about that dance. You certainly ought to have got there somehow! Strange! I never knew you to give up a thing as easily as that. You surely could have got a taxi to take you around another way if the bridge was down. There is always another road."

"By the way, Tash, you never told me what kind of place you stayed in. Was it a hotel? I asked Marie about it but she didn't seem to have much opinion of it."

"No, it wasn't a hotel. It was a private house near the station."

"Near the station? Stonington? I don't seem to remember any private house nearer than Framstead estate. Do I know the people? Where did you meet them? How did you come to go there?"

"It wasn't an estate, Loo, it was just a small cottage."

"Horrors! A porter's lodge, or some servant's quarters!"

"No they were not servants. They were very nice people, but it was a plain little private house. I met the—them—in the station. It was perfectly obvious that I was storm stayed, for the station was closed and locked and the snow was almost to my waist. They very kindly—took me home!"

"You poor infant! You must have been bored stiff!"

"No, I enjoyed it," said Tasha almost to her own surprise. "There was a dear old lady who seemed like what I used to think a mother would be."

Mrs. Endicott eyed her stepdaughter curiously to see if here was a hidden stab intended in this sentence, but Tasha sat looking idly across the hurrying landscape with dreamy eyes, and nothing vindictive in her expression.

"Was there nobody there but an old lady?" asked Lucia with narrowed eyes and cunning in her voice.

"Oh, the rest of the family were all right—" drawled Tasha, "but the old lady was especially rare. She was a kind I never saw before. I got a good rest."

"It sounds sketchy to me," said Lucia. "Did you have enough to eat?"

"Oh, plenty!" said Tasha, making her lips into a little tight line that Lucia knew meant the girl did not mean to be further communicative.

"Well, if you ask me," she said with a tone of dissatisfaction, "I should say it didn't do you much good. You've been as prickly as a thistle ever since the experience."

"At that I haven't much on you, Loo," Tasha countered. "By the way, is Will Clancy coming down to Palm Beach next week?"

"I'm sure I don't know," snapped Lucia crossly, and turned toward the window to hide the quick color that rolled up under her careful make-up.

After this sudden stab Tasha settled down with a magazine and the conversation languished. But Tasha did not read much, although she duly turned the leaves from time to time. She found herself strangely stirred at the conversation. She found herself resenting her stepmother's attitude toward her rescuers, and her contempt of the little house that had given her haven during the storm, even more than the attempt to pry into her private affairs.

And back of it all there was something else. She was wondering within herself why she did not wish to reveal the fact that there had been a young man in that home, a man both interesting and well known among college people? To have told this would have explained at once to Lucia why she had not been bored. But that would have entailed endless questions. And why, then, on the other hand, was she not willing to hold him up to ridicule as a fanatic? Was it possible that she had respect for the things for which he stood?

Though he had shown contempt for her and her ways, did she yet feel that there had been that in him that she must protect from the scorn of her family?

After a time she closed her magazine and lay back in her chair, pretending to be asleep, but in reality going over her whole experience in the snow storm, detail by detail, and getting a new view of herself as well as a new view of her rescuer. But ever, her meditations came around to the same place, with the young man standing in the door of his room, looking at her with those clear, cold blue eyes, that searched her soul and applied scorn to the wounds.

As she remembered that the hot blood burned in her cheeks and her proud young soul writhed. She felt she would like to go back to his precious home and flaunt all her sins. She would like to smoke a cigarette in his face! Yes, even in the sweet face of his old lady mother! She would rejoice to defy him, and show him that his scorn meant nothing to her! She would like to ride roughshod over his soul as he had by his look ridden over hers, and make him writhe too!

Yet Tasha had not touched a cigarette since the night she saw his face looking at her from the spray of lilies in the dusk.

Then like a ray of light in the dark, there came the memory. "Well, he has my shoe yet, anyway! I can hold that over him any time I like. I wonder what he means to do with it?"

And suddenly she sat up and looked at her wrist watch.

"It's dinner time, Lucia, let's wake up."

So the cloud between the two young women was for the time dispelled.

And about that time Thurly was tramping up the steps of his own home, with a slump of weariness in his shoulders and the little gold shoe still in his pocket.

Marget had hovered near the window all day watching for her boy, and when he did not come on his usual train she brought her sewing and sat close to the window, where she could watch the street and see him as he first turned the corner.

Over and over she imagined the interview between her boy and the girl who had so intruded into their peaceful life and disquieted her heart. There was really not much to be imagined about. The mother had thought of all possibilities. Miss Endicott might be out, or be busy, and send down word that she could not see him; and at that thought Thurly's mother would lift her Scotch chin proudly, and view the girl with a scorn so fine that she might not half have understood it.

Perhaps she would invite Thurly in—and it would likely be that of course, for how could a girl in her senses not wish to be welcoming such a young man as hers? That would be it, of course. She would ask Thurly in, and they would maybe talk over the latest books, and Thurly would recommend one a bit, one that would perhaps help the young woman, for Thurly knew how. They would mayhap talk of music, for the lass had spoken of a great violinist who was soon to visit the city. Marget had read enough of the society notes to know that rich folk invited their friends to sit with them in their boxes at the Academy on great occasions like that, and Marget dreaded the thought that the girl might think to repay her son for his rescue and hospitality by inviting him to a concert with her; dreaded, yet half hoped she would. Marget liked to think of her precious son as being welcome in the grandest boxes in the land, and able to move among the world's people without shame; yet she knew in her heart that herein would lie the danger for him. He loved music, and was not able to afford to hear much.

Yet even as she longed for such pleasure for him, she prayed in her heart, "Oh, Lord, save him! Help him! Guide him! Don't tempt my laddie too strongly! Don't let the world pull him away! She's not for him, I'm sure you think, oh Lord! She's just a worldling sent to try my laddie! Make him strong! Don't let him be led into temptation! All day she had dreamed and prayed, and watched, and when the dusk was coming down he came tramping slowly up the street, with no spring in his walk, and his gaze on the pavement before him; just his stubborn plod that he wore at times when things were all against him and he meant to keep right on anyway. Ah, she knew her laddie! She hurried to open the door, and reached her warm soft arms, with their warm roseleaf touch, around his neck. She took his greeting kiss with her soft lips trembling with her love for him, against the hard ruddy coldness of his cheek, keen from the cold night air.

She waited while he hung up his hat and coat on the little hall rack, for he never would let her wait upon him. Then she saw with a start that he was bringing a package in his hand—the package he had carried away in the morning—and her heart sank for him, for she saw that his face was clouded over, and her mother love sprang at once to the defense. Had the girl been unkind to him? But no, for he would not have brought the package back again. Perhaps her eyes had deceived her. It might be something else he had brought from the city, put up in the same wrappings, or a gift the girl had sent to her. But there was no sparkle in her laddie's eye as there would have been if he bore a pleasant thing like a gift. So she waited for his word.

"It's very cold out," was all he said and laid the little package down on the table, going over to the fire and holding a chilled foot toward the blaze. "It seems to be growing colder all the time!" he added as if he did not know that she was waiting, just waiting, for his account of what had happened in the day, and especially about his visit to the Endicott house.

"But you brought the bit package back again," said Marget when her patience would not hold out any longer, "why did you do that, laddie!"

Thurly mustered a grave smile.

"Yes," he said languidly, "I did. I didn't intend to, but I did it without thinking."

Marget paused on this thought a moment and caught a gleam of hope from it.

Ah, then! If her laddie could forget the little shoe, surely then there was no need for worry about him.

"How about?" she asked perplexed.

"Well, you see, she wasn't there," said Thurly, as if somehow the day had been a disappointment and his thoughts were still heavy with it.

"Not?" said his mother sympathetically. "Weel, could ye na have left the bit shoe? It seems a long way to plod back again."

"Why, you see, Mother, I forgot I had it with me when I came away." Thurly laughed foolishly as if he knew he was showing his keen old mother how he had been upset by the whole matter.

"And was the house so grand then?" she eyed him tenderly, proudly.

"Grand. Yes. It is grand. It is—" he hesitated and said almost tenderly, "it is such a place as she would belong, Mother."

"Yes, it would be, laddie!" sympathized his mother, and neither of them seemed to realize that they were making queer meaningless conversation, for each knew what the other meant.

"They had a serving man, Mother, who rather magnified his office," explained Thurly half sheepishly.

"I see, laddie! And so ye forgot. Well mayhap it's just as weel!" Marget relapsed into the vernacular of her childhood on occasion, when she would be deeply stirred. She brushed the tip of her finger across her misty eyes, and smiled thoughtfully.

"There must be a way to send it safely," she mused, caressing the package. "I'll find a bit box and some cotton and put the pretty trick up safely, and it'll maybe be more dignified to send it, after all! Isn't ther a way to insure it or something, lad?"

"Yes, we can insure it, or register it. Oh, it'll be safe enough I suppose!" And there was that in Thurly's tone that made his mother not so sure after all that Thurly was safely past this rock.

"Well, we'll think about it, lad. Were ye thinking of going again? Perhaps after all—" She eyed him anxiously. If Thurly felt he ought to go, she must not seem to hinder him. "Could ye make it to-morrow morn again? Ye can ill spare anither day from the study I suppose."

"Why, she'll not be home to-morrow, Mother. She's away until Spring the man said, gone to Florida till the cold is over; and I was so surprised that I stupidly carried off the shoe again and didn't realize it till the bus was half way to the station. Of course I didn't just see going back then. The next block after I discovered it one of the professors from the University got in the bus and wanted me to take lunch with him, and go with him afterward to meet a man who is interested in a church, and I've been with him ever since till I ran for my train."

"Well, come now, laddie, the dinner is all but dished. We'd best sit down, and we can talk while we eat."

So the little shoe lay on the parlor table while mother and son went out to dinner.

"And so it was a grand hoose!" mused Marget when they were both served and had begun to eat.

Thurly described as best he could the glories of the Endicott mansion, and Marget sat and watched her son, analyzing his every intonation, the turn of his smile, the lift of a lash, as if her senses were a thermometer that could register the state of his heart.

They spoke no more of the girl that night, though the little shoe remained between them on the table all the evening. But when it came time to go upstairs to bed, Marget lingered.

"You'd best take it up with you, Thurly," she said pointing to the little package as if it were a great responsibility, "we're not used to having diamonds in the house. I feel we should get it to her as soon as possible. She'll be needing the shoe. A bit trick like that must cost something."

"She's plenty of shoes, Mother, don't worry about that! She'd never miss this one if it never reached her at all."

But he said it a bit bitterly, as he picked up the package to carry it up stairs.

Far back on his closet shelf he hid it, and piled Jamieson, Fausset, and Brown's *Critical and Explanatory Commentary on the Bible, Young's Concordance,* and *The Works of Josephus* in front of it, not because he was afraid of his mother's burglars, but because he wished to dispel the bright radiance of the glittering gems that seemed to emanate from even the brown paper parcel of it.

But though the gems were guarded safely by the most orthodox brand of theology, yet there was little sleep that night for either the young minister or his mother. They were trying to decide what to do with that little gold shoe. It seemed such a simple matter, just to send it back, or take it back—which? And then they would go back to the beginning of the argument and have it all over again, both from their point of view and the girl's point of view, and perhaps several other points of view.

The mother, used to yielding her will to the Higher Will, made out to set the whole matter in wiser Hands than her own, and fell asleep at last, but it was not till toward morning that the young man got out of bed and down upon his knees.

"Oh, God. That shoe has to go back! But oh, Father! Save that girl!"

After which prayer, the young man too slept.

It was the next morning that Marget found Tasha's picture in the paper with an account of her migration to Florida, in company with her stepmother. Marget, after a thoughtful look at the pictured face, folded it open upon the breakfast table where Thurly could see it the first thing when he came down.

After he had read it she said in a quiet voice: "I guess, laddie, after all, we'd better let the bit bootie bide until the lassie gets home."

Thurly assented gravely, and by common consent they laid the subject aside.

It was while Thurly still lingered at his late breakfast there came a ring at the door. A messenger boy from one of the great city florists had brought a big box of sweet violets for Mrs. Macdonald from Miss Endicott.

Marget put them in a lovely old pewter bowl that she kept hoarded away on her pantry shelf, and set them on a little parlor table, from whence they promptly filled the house with wondrous fragrance.

Marget stood and looked at them long and buried her sweet old face in their purple depths. After she was gone back to the kitchen to finish her dishes Thurly came and gazed down upon them, drew in a deep breath of their sweetness, flicked one purple blossom from the rest, brought it up to his face for an instant, with closed eyes, and then slipped it away in his vest pocket for further reference, and went his way into the world to his belated work. But Marget spent much time that day, smelling of those flowers, and looking at them, half in awe and fear, and half in a great delight of the beauty which her soul loved.

Chapter 11

Tasha plunged into the gayeties of Palm Beach with a restless energy that made her as usual the center of the gay set. Her followers and her frocks were the talk of the town. Nevertheless her heart was not at rest. It was as if she were ever seeking some great thrill which would satisfy, and drive the fever from her soul.

Perhaps part of her restlessness was due to her having broken her habit of smoking which truly had been heavy upon her. Several times she was on the verge of going back to it, but always there seemed to come that vision of the lilies in the dusk, and as if to prove she could she seemed to dare her soul to keep free from it. Just what her own idea in doing so was she was not sure. Sometimes in the small hours of the night as she crept to her couch she wondered over it, half thinking it was a silly superstition from which she should rid herself. But always the thought of the cool, steady contemptuous glance brought her back to her first decision, and she came to acknowledge to herself that her real reasons was that she might exorcise that glance by one as cool and steady and as clean. "I do not use them." Well, she could say so too, now!

It was after she had come to that point of understanding that the vision came again.

She was standing in a brilliantly lighted room among a lot of other dinner guests, awaiting a late arrival, and the cocktails were being passed. She accepted her glass with her usual grace, and lifted it with a gay word to Barry Thurston who had come down that day and was giving her news of Gloria Framstead.

But as she did so her glance went to the wide doorway opening into the spacious hall, and there, quite distinctly, she seemed to see Thurly Macdonald, standing under the archway, not in evening dress like the other men, but dressed in his fine dark blue serge as he had stood that Sunday night at Stonington. One hand was resting lightly against the door frame, and his eyes were upon her as she lifted the

89

wine glass to her lips. In those eyes was that terrible glance of mingled yearning and disapproval that searched her vapid young soul and turned existence into ashes.

The laughter died on her lips and her eyes took on a frightened look. She forgot her friends all about her, and the gayety that rang through the house. She stood, and stared across the room with paling cheek and lips that wanted to tremble, and slowly, almost mechanically her hand with its glass went down from her lips.

"What's the matter, Tasha!" cried Barry, "you look as though you saw a ghost."

Tasha became suddenly aware of her position and rallied, trying to laugh, and lifting the glass once more. She must get herself in hand. She must swallow the liquor quickly. Perhaps she was going to faint. But involuntarily her gaze went again to the door, and there those eyes seemed now to hold her own, and control her gaze. She could not take her eyes away, though she tried. She knew it was but an illusion, yet it had power over her. Her hand went slowly down again, and her eyes took their stunned look once more.

"Why, Tasha, are you sick?" It was Barry's voice that recalled her again, with real anxiety in it now, and Tasha turned and held out the glass to him.

"No, not sick, Barry, just trying to find a place to set this glass down. Won't you take it for me?"

"But you look white," said Barry. "Why don't you drink it? It's the new cocktail. Haven't you tasted them? We had them up at Framstead after you left. They're great! Just taste it!"

"No to-night, Barry. Take it for me, please. I want to speak to Lucia a minute before we go out to dinner. That's a dear!" and she pressed the glass upon him and slipped away toward the doorway. He saw her presently standing there with her face turned partly away from him, her hand resting lightly against the door frame, a strange smile upon her lips, but she was not talking to Mrs. Endicott who in slight draperies of cloth of gold, and green emerald serpents in her ears and about her neck and wrists, was discoursing eagerly to their host a few feet away. Tasha seemed to be suddenly detached from the company with which she was surrounded, and to be alone in a little world of her own. He could not quite understand it; why let a perfectly good cocktail go to waste? He slipped his own empty glass behind a picture on the mantel, and working his way around into the sun porch he found a secluded spot in which to imbibe Tasha's cocktail.

But to Tasha, standing in that doorway where the vision had stood, with her hand where Thurly Macdonald's hand had seemed to be, there came a thrill that surpassed all the artificial thrills she had ever manufactured for herself. What it all meant she did not stop to question. She might be going mad, or turning sentimental, or about to die; but it was sweet, and she had the consciousness that she had conquered that cold stern look in the young man's eyes, and done something with which he would have been pleased if he had really been there. Her eyes might look back to his now, clean and free. Why, yes of course, he probably didn't use cocktails any more than he used cigarettes. He probably did not approve of women who drank any more than of those who smoked. It was incredible that there was a man like that, but it seemed to be true, and somehow she liked it in him.

Well then, she would not drink cocktails either. She did not stop to ask herself whether it was going to be a hard task to give them up, whether it would bring ridicule upon her, and put her in embarrassing situations. She just registered a resolve that she was done with that, and the firm set of the pretty lips would have told anyone who knew Tasha well that it was of no use to argue with her. She was doing this thing as a challenge to a young man who had affronted her with his eyes, who had charged her with being unfine, unwomanly. That was what his look had meant that night. It was what it had meant to-night as he looked at her from the doorway as she was about to drink.

That it was all a sort of mirage, a figment of her imagination, made no difference. That the young man in all probability would never know of her resolve, would never likely see her again in his life, and if he did would not know what she had done because of him, did not enter into her calculations. She had conquered and set right something in herself to which he had objected, and she felt not only her self-respect rising, but a kind of new joy—or was it just elation? At least it was something precious to keep and turn over in her soul.

Standing thus alone, within that doorway, all in misty white with something sparkling about her throat and in her hair, and that misty look in her eyes, more than one in the gay assemblage looked and called attention to her. "Isn't Tasha lovely to-night?" And Barry emerging from his ambush in search of more cocktails caught a glimpse of her and swore softly to himself, with a vague fear, and murmured:

"I'll gamble there's another man! I'll make her answer me to-morrow. Gloria isn't in it with Tasha, and that's a fact!"

But although he took her out to dinner, and she was gayer than usual, yet Barry got nowhere with her. Tasha was jubilantly, brilliantly floating along in a world all of her own in which Barry had no part.

It took some days for her friends to realize that Tasha was neither drinking nor smoking any more. They thought it was just a whim at first, for she was given to whims and odd doings, but had never been the daringest of the set. Then one and another began to whisper it about, to watch her and question.

It was their laughter and utter contempt for her new fancy that finally riveted her half formed purpose, and made her declare that she was fed up on smoking and drinking, and had decided to cut them out. She was one of those whom opposition makes but the stronger, and so several of them set about arguing the matter with her, and trying to show her that she could not keep that up and hold her position: that it was an impossible situation. One could not go against fashion and custom. It was rude. It was impolite. As if any of them had ever bothered themselves much about good manners in this day and generation! But then perhaps they thought they did, and they certainly were outraged by Tasha's stand, insomuch that she grew quite firm in her laughing statements, and finally declared that if they did not like her as she was she would seek other company.

So she went her way as always, gay, beautiful, gorgeously dressed, entering into all the sports, present at all the functions, notable for her high spirits, yet in her heart strangely restless and weary of it all.

For now that she was entirely sane and sober when the rest were drinking she began to wonder if she too had talked such vapid nonsense at the close of a dinner? Or was it that they were all just a stupid lot and she had not had sense enough to know it before? She began to grow silent as they grew hilarious, and then her stepmother took a hand and remonstrated once more.

"Tasha, you really are acting like a spoiled child. What is it you are trying to put across, anyway? Can't you see that Gloria is just putting it all over you, the way she is leading Barry around by the nose?"

Tasha's answer to the whirl around from the balcony where she was overlooking the sea, watching the white sails dip in the wind, and face her stepmother down with a straight steady look.

"Lucia," she said, "get this. Gloria isn't putting a thing over on me. I'm putting it on her, if there is any putting at all. I sent Gloria off to walk with Barry last night on the beach because I simply couldn't stand their idiocy any longer. They were both of them silly drunk and it made me sick."

"Nonsense?" said Lucia sharply, a bright red spot on either cheek beneath the rouge, "I've seen you in just the same condition!"

Tasha eyed her quizzically.

"I wonder!" she said, "well, I'm glad you told me. You won't seem me that way any longer. And now, Loo, you've given me a good deal of advice, perhaps you'll take a little from me. If I were you I wouldn't be seen with Will Clancy any more. People are beginning to talk and Dad is coming down next week."

"Nonsense!" said Lucia, angrily, "you don't know what you are talking about! Everybody goes around together. I'm not with one any more than another! There's absolutely nothing your father could object to in our friendship."

"Cut it, Loo, you can't put anything over on me. I cut my eye teeth long ago. But I mean what I say. You better watch your step. Dad divorced Marietta for less than you are doing, and you know Will Clancy hasn't enough to keep himself, let alone buying cigarettes and imported gowns for you. You can't get away with it and you'd better take my advice and cut it!"

With which sage advice Tasha walked jauntily across the porch and went up to her room, where she locked her door and flung herself across the bed.

"There, I've done it, but what good'll it do?" she asked herself. "Poor Dad! He's never had half a chance!"

Then quite unexpectedly she burst into tears and hid her face in the pillow. Decidedly Tasha was not herself.

She did not go down to dinner that evening, but had something sent up to her room, and then, arrayed in a simple little blue frock that was as much like a home dress than anything she owned, she slipped out while the rest were at dinner, and walked fast and far.

The smell of the sea was good, the soft perfume of the yellow jessamine, the whisper of the pines, above her among the great southern stars, the silken swish of stiff palmetto leaves outlined against the night sky, the soft black darkness, as she walked away from the brilliant lights and came toward the plainer less populated portion of town all rested her feverish soul. The sea could be heard out here, away from the numberless orchestras, and sounds of luxury.

There were plain little houses, with lights in cozy rooms, and children running in and out the door calling one another. Their voices sounded distant in the clear atmosphere as if they stood beside her. The fragrance of a simple vegetable stew floated out appetizingly, reminding in some subtle way of the Sunday dinner at Macdonald's, and strangely softening her heart toward these unknown dwellers in the humble homes.

She stumbled on, sometimes walking in the sand now, for she had strayed beyond the sidewalks and come to where there were mere paths along the edge of the road.

And now a little light sprang up in a tiny chapel, twinkling feebly, and spreading from window to window, till the whole little frame structure stood like a toy church on a sandy plain, almost isolated save for a group of palmettos and a lofty pine waving gray arms of moss among the stars. Stark and lonely it stood, yet beckoned her as if there were something warm and human and true inside, and a little steeple pointed whitely, with a star twinkling just above the apex.

Tasha to her own surprise began to take her way across a sandy space shredded with coarse grass and wild pea blossoms, and bristling with sand spurs. She got sand spurs on her stockings, all the way up to her knees, and sand inside her small white slippers, but she kept on like a hungry person to a meal.

There was a little street presently that led past the tiny church, and she filed down with a few other stragglers and entered the building, sliding into a back seat and looking about her.

There were about twenty people in the church, and a few more entered as she sat down. A girl somewhat older than herself was at the organ, a plain girl without style, who was turning over the pages of a hymn book. An old man with white hair and a saintly look sat by the table in front of the pulpit, and he presently announced a hymn.

There seemed something familiar in the strains that quavered out from the organ. It was a poor organ, and rather badly played, but the girl kept good time and seemed to enter into her task with spirit. Someone with squeaky shoes came down the aisle and handed Tasha a hymn book open at the place, and then they began to sing:

> "From every stormy wind that blows,
> From every swelling tide of woes,
> There is a calm, a sure retreat,
> 'Tis found beneath the mercy seat."

Why, that was the very hymn they had sung at Stonington that Sunday night, Thurly Macdonald and his mother! Tasha sat remembering every little happening, every turn of a note, the wailing of Thurly's violin, the placid look of his mother's face, the sweet voices blending with the violin, and the way Thurly's hair fell over his forehead when he stooped to pick up her handkerchief that had fallen to the floor. It set her heart a-throbbing.

The little scattered flock in the church were all singing, and Tasha found herself trying to sing goo. They were not all singing on the key. They were not all keeping time. Some dragged fearfully. Some voices quavered and broke. Others were shrill and unmusical, but all were singing with their hearts. One tall thin old lady with a queer combination of ancient fashions in garments, and a hat of the vintage of the *most* Victorian ages perched high on a notably false front was shrilling out a high tenor above all the others, her eyes shut, and her book held upside down, but the words she sang were clear and distinct, though they were off the key.

> "And heaven comes down our souls to greet,
> And glory crowns the mercy seat."

Tasha did not mind the harsh singing, nor the voices off the key. She was back in Stonington singing with the Macdonalds, singing the words this time with a groping yearning to know their meaning. All these people, even the woman with the funny hat and tenor voice seemed to be singing with a meaning, singing with their souls. She wished she knew just what this mercy seat was they were talking about. Why hadn't she asked Mrs. Macdonald? She had wondered then what it was. But she sensed that in some way it was connected with worshipping God.

Quite unconsciously she bowed her head, because her spirit was listening, when the old minister began to pray. He had a voice that was feeble and monotonous, and now and again she would lose several words or a sentence, but she could see that he took the same general tone of intimate converse with an invisible One that Thurly Macdonald had done. It was all strange and mysterious, but it hushed her impatient, wild, young soul, and gave her a thrill to hear them.

They sang another hymn after the prayer, "I need Thee every hour." That was one of the hymns they had sung at Stonington too. Did all religious people use the same hymns, she wondered? Tasha's experience with church had been very slight, mainly confined to being a bridesmaid at weddings, and having to be very conscious of her step and how she managed her train and flowers.

The minister opened an old soft Bible that looked as if it was ready to fall to pieces, and seemed to know itself where to fall open at the right time.

It was not the same scripture that Thurly had read and it meant very little to the devotee of the world. She got but one sentence out of it, and that did not convey a very clear meaning. The droning voice read about a corruptible body and an incorruptible body, and Tasha did not get a thing out of it. But the sentence that stuck and remained for weeks afterward was "Now this I say, brethren, that flesh and blood cannot inherit the kingdom of God."

In a vague way she struggled for a meaning to it, but was glad when they sang another hymn. And then a strange thing took place. The minister asked all who would to pray, and those men and women, sitting right in their hard little benches, bowed their heads in a long silence. Tasha bowed hers too, wondering what was coming to pass next. Then almost in front of her an old woman began in a low quavering voice:

"Oh, our Father, we thank Thee that Thou art a prayer-hearing, and a prayer-answering God. We thank Thee that we can come to Thee in all our need, and that Thou wilt supply us. I thank Thee for the way that Thou did'st answer my prayer this day, and send me that money in my sore distress. I can never thank Thee enough, dear Lord. I will praise Thee while my breath lasts. I thank Thee for the mercy seat where I can come with all my troubles, and where Thou has promised to answer my needs—"

Ah! So that was a mercy seat! A sort of throne where a King sat to grant petitions!

Tasha opened her eyes and looked curiously at the old black bonnet in the seat before her, trembling with the emotion of the little old woman, whose prayer had been so low that Tasha was sure nobody else in the room but herself could have heard the words, unless it might be true that there was a God who heard such pleadings. A mercy seat! And Thurly Macdonald and his mother believed in it, that was sure.

The low thankful voice in front of her had ended in a tiny sob of gratitude, and an old man with a quavering voice took up the sound. Before he was finished a third had begun, and voice after voice took up the low weird cry. Even the young organist prayed a sharp little prayer full of neat pious wishes for her neighbors, and a sparse plea for her own spiritual growth.

Tasha was glad when the closing hymn was announced. She had been almost afraid they would expect her to join in the service. She had glanced furtively toward the door for a way of escape.

After a quiet benediction, something about, "Keep us from falling and present us faultless—" Tasha turned to hurry out, but found the old woman of the rusty black bonnet intercepting her with a black cotton gloved hand held out.

"We're pleased to see you here," she said shyly.

Tasha ignored the hand in the cotton glove. She did not rightly understand such salutation, but she smiled and said thank you.

"Are you staying in the village? went on the woman affably, and Tasha perceived that there was still a tear glistening on her cheek from the prayer time, a tear from that sob that had meant joy.

Tasha assented.

"Oh, then you'll come again perhaps."

"Why, I don't know," said Tasha pondering, "I'm rather busy. I don't get down this end of town very often."

"But you're one of His," the old lady said with a smile. "I know you are or you wouldn't be at prayer meeting. They don't when they ain't."

"Was this a prayer meeting?"

"Why, yes," said the old woman eyeing her curiously. "Didn't you know?"

They had passed out the door together, and the old woman stumbled. Tasha caught her arm and guided her down the steps.

"Thank you, dearie!" she said, "I ain't so keen of eye as I used to be. Sometimes I can't get down those steps alone. My daughter usually comes with me, but o-night she had a sick child and couldn't."

"Which way do you live?" asked Tasha, moved by a sudden kindly impulse, "couldn't I walk home you?"

"Would you, dearie? I'd be wonderfully obliged. I'm most afraid to go alone, and Martha she begged me not to, but I says, 'Martha, the Lord has been so good to us to-day, sending us the money for that operation for the baby, that I wouldn't have the face not to go to meeting and thank Him.'"

"Do you mean," asked Tasha curiously, "that you really had some money sent in answer to prayer?"

"I really did," said the old woman eagerly. "You see we hadn't a cent. We'd spent everything for medicine and doctors, and a big bill at the grocery too, and when the doctor said an operation was the only thing would save Timmy I says to Martha, 'Martha, there's only one thing to do. I'll go ask Father.' So I did. And this morning there come a letter from Kansas City from my Cousin Harriet. Five years ago she borrowed two hundred dollars off us when she was about to lose her place that was mortgaged, and we ain't thought to ever see it again, 'cause Harriet, she ain't forehanded, and the man she married didn't turn out to be much of a business hand neither, but here, didn't she send me a check for the whole thing with interest! And now Timmy can have his operation, and they say he'll walk again! Ain't that grand?"

They had come to the door of one of the very humblest of the humble homes, where a light in an upstairs window showed the room of the little invalid, and the grandmother turned in eager haste to say good night and be back in the sick room again.

Tasha impulsively held out a little purse.

"Here!" she said putting the beaded trifle in the astonished woman's hand, "won't you let me help too? I'd like you to get a little something for Timmy with that. It isn't much but perhaps it will get something to amuse him at least."

And then with the woman's thanks ringing in her ears she fled away toward the lights of town.

A great moon like a burnished plaque had come up in the heavens during the meeting, and flooded the world with almost daylight brilliance, and Tasha flitted along in its radiance like a little white moth, thinking of what she had seen that evening, and wondering what Thurly Macdonald would think if he knew she had been to prayer meeting.

Chapter 12

The little gold shoe remained on the closet shelf, perhaps not forgotten, but hidden. Jamieson, Fausset and Brown, and Young's *Concordance* were forced to come down and assist in preparing a sermon, but Josephus stayed on the job, and so thoroughly protected the small package done up in brown paper, that no one would ever have suspected it contained a valuable diamond buckle.

Then one day there came a letter for Marget from Florida, just a note in a high scrawly hand on queer big expensive paper:

> "Dear Mrs. Macdonald:
> I'm sending you a little trinket, just to remember me by. Please don't think I ever can pay for all you and your son did for me when I was storm-stayed, but I want you to have this just to know how grateful I am.
> Sincerely,
> Anastasia Endicott."

The little trinket proved to be a tiny platinum wrist watch set about with twinkling little diamonds. More diamonds! *Diamonds!* Diamonds for Marget Macdonald! Hitherto diamonds had only meant a gem reserved for the heavenly city. Now she looked at hers in amaze, doubting if it were quite right to enjoy such rare and costly things.

But Thurly's eyes shone, and Thurly told her yes, she must keep it. He put it on her wrist under the cuff of her little gray mohair she was wearing that morning, and showed her how to fasten it, and how to wind it. Without any key. Such a dear little trick! And for her! What would Thurly's father say if he could look down from heaven and see his Marget with a little pretty thing like that on her wrist? Diamonds. Bonnie little trick! Her eyes filled with tears. Her John had always meant to get her a watch, a round gold one with a long chain, and a pocket sewed in her basque to carry it in; that was the kind they wore then. But this was so handy! And so neat and hidden like, right under the sleeve till you needed it, and ready there without undue display to tell the time of day.

She cast a sweet grateful thought to the lovely girl who had sent it, and then she lifted anxious eyes to Thurly's face. How was Thurly taking this? This would be one more thing to make her lad think of the lassie who was so far out of his world. Ah! He must not! What should she do about the watch? Send it back and put the thought out of his mind? But no, she could not do that and hurt the wee young thing. She would have to pray about it. Just ask the Father.

Two hours later there came a telegram from Chicago. One of the Christian workers in a noted organization had been called away by severe illness in his family, and might be gone from his classes for weeks. Could Mr. Macdonald come on at once and fill his place indefinitely until his return?

They talked it over hastily, anxiously.

"If it's the Lord's call you must go, laddie," sighed Marget, sore perplexed, "and no, lad, I'll bide. We couldna tear up the hoose for an uncertainty, and we couldna leave things as they are without somebody here. It's cold weather. The pipe would freeze up and spoil our wee hoose. You go, lad, and I'll bide."

"But I'll not leave you alone, Mother."

"Nonsense, laddie, I'm best by myself. You mind I don't like a stranger butting about telling me what I shall do in my ain."

"I know, Mother, but this time you'll simply have to stand that for a little while if I'm to go. I simply won't leave you alone," and Thurly put on his stubborn Scotch tone that his mother knew meant business.

Marget got up and dusted the parlor table nervously, as was her wont when she was disturbed about anything. Then she looked up.

"Weel, then laddie, we'll fix it. We mustna go against the call of the Lord. I'll just send for Martha. You mind she wrote me she was coming to pay me a visit. Let her come noo."

Marget sighed as she gave her word. Her son knew that she was not greatly fond of this friend and neighbor of her childhood who had married and come to this country to live.

"If you mean that, Mother, I'll get her on the phone and arrange it at once. I've no time to lose if I'm going. I'm afraid it'll be a trial for you, Mother, but I can't leave you alone."

Thurly went to the telephone and arranged everything.

"She says she'll start day after to-morrow morning," he announced with satisfaction. "I'll get Jimmy Fargo to sleep here those two nights. No, Mother, don't say a word. I couldn't rest easy a minute if you were alone. Not in weather like this. There's liable to be another storm you know—"

So Thurly went his way, and with a heavy heart Marget went up to pack his bag, and see that every button was in place, and every sock well mended.

Thurly left on the evening train, and after Marget had made up the cot in the little room off the dining room for the high school boy Jimmy, she felt very forlorn and alone. For the first time in several years Thurly was away, really away, for more than a night or two, and the worst of it was she did not know how long it would be before she might look for him back again. A kind of feeling as if she were bleeding in her heart came over her, but she put it resolutely away.

"It's of the devil," she told herself. "He's just foond of the weak places in me, and he's romping all over my puir soul. I'll away to my Father!" and she hurried upstairs to her trysting place.

At last with peace upon her brow, the peace of an utterly yielded will, she went down stairs and looked about her for something to occupy her hands. This first night was going to be the hardest, and she must keep busy until she was weary enough to sleep.

Then she bethought her of the treasure that was in the house. The little slipper with its diamond buckle. What had Thurly done with it? She had forgotten to ask him. Of course he went away in such a hurry that he never thought. But she ought to know where it was, even if he had hidden it safe from burglars, for in case of fire she would want to rescue it first of anything because it was not her own and she was now responsible for it.

So she trotted over to Thurly's room, and was glad for the chance to be among his things, and work around putting things to rights as usual, just as if he were coming back next morning; meanwhile hunting for the slipper.

It would be in his bureau of course.

She opened all the drawers, but only neat piles of summer clothing were left, and some outworn collars that he considered not good enough to take with him. She got away with one fifteen minutes happily enough going over the summer things and finding a torn buttonhole, a missing button and a small place in the shoulder of a shirt that needed darning. Tomorrow morning she would sit down with her needed and set those right, then they would be off her mind.

But the slipper.

It would be in a drawer of his desk, of course, and she went confidently to the little desk where Thurly wrote his sermons. The drawers were locked. Yes, of course they would be with the diamonds inside. But the key was in the little top door by the cubbyholes. That was careless of him. But he must have intended to give it to her and had forgotten.

She fitted the key in the top drawer and looked in it. Nothing there at all but some bundles of old letters and receipted bills, neatly strapped with rubber bands and labeled. There was correspondence with "Marathon Church," "Hutton's Mills," "Chester," all places where he had preached from time to time. "College." Those would be from his professors and classmates. "University," "The Mission," "Bible School," she knew for what each one stood. She shut the drawer and locked it again.

The next drawer contained sermons. A glance showed that there was not place for hiding diamonds or a little high-heeled shoe.

The bottom drawer had nothing but a pile of writing stationery, a box of envelopes, another of pencils and some old pens. She even opened the box of envelopes and poked them to see if the slipper was hidden in there, but of course it was not. In dismay she turned back to the room.

Then she searched the bed, thoroughly, underneath the pillows and mattress. He might have kept them there for safety, though it was not like Thurly to make much thought of a burglar. But still he might have put it there to be out of the way, and safe. But there was no slipper.

Last, she went to his closet, for all else in the room was open to the causal glance, and no slipper could be hidden there without her being able to see it. She cleared all Thurly's old shoes out and took the little flash light he made her keep by her bed, to look in and be sure a diamond buckle was not hid in some corner; the little slipper was so small. Yet of course that was foolish for it would still be wrapped in its papers. Then she took all Thurly's old coats, and his old flannel bath robe down and looked through their pockets, but no slipper!

She glanced at the shelf above her head. Thurly kept books up there but they were mostly gone. The shelf seemed empty save for an old felt hat that had so much the slump of the way he wore it that it brought the sudden tears to her eyes. But she climbed on a chair and continued her investigations. The left side was the deepest, because the closet went back beyond a niche in the chimney, but she turned the search light deep into it. She moved away Thomas a Kempis, Keith on the Prophecy, and Life of the Early Christian Martyrs, but there was no sign of a little gold slipper belonging to the elite. No little package tied up with string. Only the sturdy red bricks of the chimney and a crumbling chunk of mortar fallen from its crevice. Well, if it were some people she might think Thurly had gone to the trouble of removing a brick and hiding the diamonds in the very edge of the chimney. But Thurly would never do a dramatic thing like that. She knew her boy, and though she searched the chimney keenly with the bright eyes that needed as yet no glasses to see anything less diminutive than print, she turned from that end of the shelf, leaving the early Christian martyrs and Thomas a Kempis where she had found them.

The other end of the shelf seemed to have only one big fat book, "Josephus," for "Cruden" and "Jamieson, Fausset and Brown" had gone to Chicago with Thurly. But Josephus was standing in such a manner, with his gold letters glittering in the flash light, that he seemed to be plumb up against the end of the closet wall.

At that psychological instant the doorbell rang through the house, and with another quick scan of Josephus, Marget climbed nimbly down from her chair, closed the closet door, shut off her flash and went down stairs. There really wasn't any other place to look unless

Thurly had pried up one of the boards of the floor and put the slipper under it, and she was sure her fearless son would never have been as anxious about it as all that.

But the thing which caused her to catch her breath and almost fall as she got down from the chair and hurried down the stairs, was a new idea entirely. Could Thurly have taken that shoe with him? Surely he would not do that. Not even to protect the shoe. Not even to protect her from a burglar getting in and frightening her—though how a burglar would know whether Thurly had the shoe or it was still in the house, she did not stop to reason out. But she was immediately alarmed for Thurly.

True, he had carried that shoe in his bag once before, but there was excuse for that. he had just picked it up, and might have forgotten that he had it after he came into his home. But the fact that it had lain in there once before a day or two; that it had been hidden under his garments as if he wished no one to know he had it, made her more than uneasy, and immediately all her alarms for her precious son returned in full force. If Thurly had taken that shoe with him it must show that he was more than just causally interested in the "bit lassie." He maybe intended to send it to her from Chicago, but how would that look? He surely should have told her what he was doing. Poor bit mannie, he would never think how queer it would look to the lassie that he should carry her shoe off away to Chicago to send it to her, when he should have sent it from home.

So thinking her distracted thoughts she came to the door to let in her young protector, who had arrived early according to arrangement and demanded a place to study his lessons for the day.

Marget established him at the dining-room table under a good light and went her way about the house, doing whatever little things she could find to do, and they were very few for Marget's house was always in the pink of order. But that was more than Marget's thoughts were the night. If it was true as she thought that worriments were but teasings of her enemy the devil, then surely the prince of this world was romping all over the old battle ground with her that night.

As she pottered about in her kitchen, changing the arrangement of some of the dishes to make work for her nervous hands while her

thoughts castigated her, she went back over the night of the storm
when Thurly had brought the wee drabbled lassie into her house.
She forced herself to remember his expression, one of high disapproval and extreme annoyance, as he set her down and told his mother
in the same breath that he must hurry back or he would lose his train.
Certainly up to that moment he was not interested in the little painted
woman of the world.

She went carefully over her first impressions, the messy little face
with the paint all spotted with the weather till she had washed it off.
The dripping rosy gauze in tatters round her little frozen feet, the
naked look of her as she stood from her fur trimmed wrap and seemed
not a whit embarrassed at the slim expanse of bare flesh; the lack of
adequate clothing, showing that modesty was not one of her particular charms. The way she talked of her parents, especially her stepmother, calling her by her first name. The flip little way she had with
words, and the lack of respect she showed for anybody or anything.

And yet as she pondered there grew in her heart the warm pleasant
charm of the lovely child, as she had nestled her in blankets and
folded her in the great old-fashioned gown, several sizes too large
for her. The love that had come to her in spite of everything as she
tucked the little lost lassie in the blankets and kissed her and prayed
for her there beside the bed. Something warm and tender that wanted
to stay in her heart pled for the child, and asked not to be banished.

Yet Marget knew that she must not keep this stranger in her thoughts
even, if it meant danger to her own child. Such a subtle thing is love.
Marget felt that it was the only temptation of the world that she really feared for her strong young consecrated son. Just why she could
not trust the Lord to protect him from this danger as well as all the
others that a wicked world could hold, she never reasoned out with
herself, but surely it was that Marget allowed herself many hours of
misery over the one possibility that her precious son would marry
the wrong woman who would lead him into trouble and temptation.
It had never occurred to her that this attitude argued that perhaps she
was trusting Thurly himself to keep himself from evil, rather than his
Lord. After all it takes a canny soul to read her own heart. Though
Marget Macdonald was cannier than most people, at that.

In due time she got her high-school boy to bed on his cot, and herself to bed in her own room, but not to sleep. There she lay hour after hour, staring blankly at the opposite wall where the electric light in the little street cast shadows of bleak bare branches, waving weirdly; and when she at last fell asleep toward morning it was to dream that there were burglars in the house tearing up all the floor boards to find the little shoe.

But she had the courage to laugh out at her fears and say to herself: "Well, and what a little old fule I am to be sure! As if the Lord couldn't look after that shoe, as well as my Thurly."

So she got up and went about getting some breakfast for her young lodger so that he might get off to school in due time.

She had decided in the watches of the night that she must not mention the matter of the shoe to Thurly in a letter, for if he had carried that shoe off to Chicago with him, he did not want her to know it, and she did not want him to think she had thought he did, in case he had not. In fact she did not want to bring up the matter of the shoe at all.

So once again the little gold shoe became a golden wall between this wonderful woman and her son; and a heavy heart she carried about her work, as she began to prepare for her unwelcome guest.

The guest room had not been in use since Tasha had occupied it. There were things that Marget felt she ought to do to it. She remembered Martha as an indefatigable housekeeper, critical to a fault and she marched to the door of the room and surveyed it with the cold hard look of a stranger just entering. Yes, the paint was a bit dusty, the windows could bear a little shining, and there was that place on the door where the paint had been cleaned so many times it had worn thin and showed the lumber through.

She went to the telephone and ordered a can of white paint that would dry quickly, and a brush. She would remedy the paint. There would be enough to go all around the base board and windows and touch up the two doors.

She took the rugs out on the back porch and flung snow upon them, giving them a good sweeping in it. She made up the bed in her finest linen sheets, and got out the rose blankets with the pink bindings, the same ones that had tucked so tenderly about Tasha when she slept.

She put fresh covers on the bureau and wash stand, rubbed the windows, and did up the two curtains crisply, looping them back with
clean cords from her sewing basket.

And all the while she was doing it, she was searching furtively for
that little gold shoe. Twice she went into Thurly's room and gazed
about her as if somehow the four walls would give forth the secret if
she looked hard enough, but Josephus remained at his post and never
said a word. Josephus was a good warder.

The day passed and the night came. The high school guardian
returned and silently studied his lesson beside the plate of gingerbread that Marget had prepared for him, and another night was lived
through, but still the little gold shoe had not been found, although
Marget had not lost sight of her search for it for a single instant all
day long. She had even gone to the extent of tapping every board in
Thurly's floor, and closet, to make sure he had not hidden it somewhere. She had taken out and searched behind every drawer on the
upper floor. It certainly was perplexing. She wondered if perhaps
she had missed it in her excitement. Perhaps she should begin again
and go over the places she had looked the first night. But the anxiety
and the housecleaning, and her wakefulness of the night before, one
or all, put her to sleep the minute her head touched the pillow, and
when she woke in the morning she felt saner and stronger to bear the
new day.

She got up and prepared a lunch for her night's guardian, thanked
him smilingly for his care, and gave him the money Thurly had left in
an envelope for him, bidding him good bye. Then she set about preparing such a dinner for Martha, as would forestall any criticisms of
her ability as a housekeeper once and for all.

Meanwhile, as a certain Western train hurried on its way toward
Stonington, a surprise was nearing Marget which was destined to fill
her thoughts pretty well to the exclusion of everything else, for a
time at least.

Chapter 13

The night before Martha Robertson was to take the train to visit her old friend Marget Macdonald, she fell down stairs and broke her leg!

Out of the bewilderment and pain of her first oblivion, Martha roused with stern Scotch promptness to attend her duty, and early next morning sent for her niece Hesba Hamilton.

"How'd you like to take my place, Hesby?" she gasped from among the pillows, her thin lined face anxious with her responsibility. She had promised Marget's son to stay with her till he returned.

"It'ud be a nice vacation for you, Hesby," she added anxiously as Hesba hesitated.

"Yes, but you know Aunt," said Hesba turning her round serious eyes toward the sufferer, "I'm right in the midst of my course of study in the training school, and it might put me back a whole year, if I go."

"Oh, no, Hesby," argued the old woman crossly, "You're real bright. You can take your books along. Besides, there's likely just as good a training school put in that city as here, and it's a good thing to see the world a little, especially if you're going off to teach in some college in China or Turkey. You're young yet, you know, and you better see what you get a chance to see."

Hesba considered.

"I might—" she said. "Of course I'd have to ask our dean. I could telephone him," she glanced at her wrist watch. "He's in the office usually at this hour. I'd like to help you out of course if I could. How soon would I have to start?"

"The train leaves at five o'clock," sighed the sufferer, a twinge of pain making her close her eyes and wince. "You'll find the ticket and reservation in my purse in the upper drawer. You can take the hand bag right along. It's all packed ready with everything, money, time table and all, clean handkerchief, and my traveling comb. Just

109

take it. That will save you some time. I'll be so glad to have you go.
I couldn't go back on my word you know. You see Marget and I used
to go to school together back in the old country, and I've always
meant to visit her. But this is just my luck. I'll tell you, Hesby, if I
get better before that son of hers gets home, I'll come on and relieve
you."

"Son?" said Hesba, turning her round shell-rimmed eyes on her
aunt. "Has she got a son? What's he like?"

"I never saw him," said the aunt wearily, "but they say he's a fine
fellow. He's studying to be a preacher. You two ought to know each
other, seeing you are both thinking of being some kind of a missionary some day. He might get back while you're there, too, and take
you round a little. It might turn out to be real pleasant, Hesby."

"Oh, well," said the girl strong mindedly, "I'm not in this life for
pleasure, you know, Aunty. But I'll do my best to help you out at
least till somebody else can be found to stay with your friend. Of
course if I can get transferred to another training school that would
be great. I'll see what I can do."

Hesba went calmly out and in half an hour telephoned she would
go. Methodically she set about her preparations, and by five o'clock
she was seated in the sleeper, rolling eastward, complaisance in her
round gray eyes. This was one of the advantages that had come for
her further education, and she meant to make the most of it. Incidentally of course she would do her duty as it came, no matter how
unpleasant it might be, and do it thoroughly and well.

In due season, in fact earlier than due season for Marget, she arrived in Stonington, an hour before Marget had calculated she could
possibly get there.

Being young, and being early, she missed Jimmy Fargo entirely,
who had promised to meet Martha Robertson's train and convey her
safely in his uncle's Ford to the house.

But Hesba Hamilton was always sufficient to an occasion. She
stared around the station mildly for a moment, surrounded by her
two sensible pieces of baggage, and then she corralled a passing
truck and compelled its driver to convey herself and her two suit
cases to the Macdonald home. The driver agreed that he knew the

house, said he was in the habit of delivering coal and wood there. Nothing daunted the young woman swung her suit cases up to the swarthy youth who was driving, and then climbed up beside him. So she arrived at Marget's door, paid her chauffeur twenty-five cents, and strode up the steps, a suit case in either hand, staring around her interestedly through her shell rimmed gray eyes. She was wearing a thick gray tailored suit, and a tan felt hat that was unbecoming, but it was a matter of the least moment in the world to her. She felt herself to be on a higher plane than most poor mortals. It was virtue and intellect that counted in this world, not the outward show.

Marget went to the door with a dab of flour on her cheek, and a flush from the oven in her face. She thought it was the paper boy with the evening paper, and she wanted to tell him that the paper had not come that morning, and he must be more careful and lay it under the door mat where it would not blow away. She opened the door and there stood Hesba with the two suit cases in her hand.

"Is this Mrs. Macdonald?" asked Hesba. And when Marget assented with a kindly smile, Hesba walked in.

"Well, I've come to stay with you," she announced, setting down her suit cases and looking frankly around. "What room shall I take? I suppose I might as well go right up and get washed before we talk."

"You've—come to—*stay* with me?" said Marget wheeling round from the door which in her astonishment she still held half ajar. "Why, who are you?" There was dignity, a bit of severity in Marget Macdonald's tone, which was wholly lost on the guest.

"Oh, didn't I explain?" Well, you see it's a long story and I thought I might as well get cleaned up and tell it calmly. Why, you see my aunt Martha was to come, and she fell down stairs last night and broke her leg, so she asked me to come in her place. It wasn't very convenient of course, but I managed to arrange it so I could. She didn't like to disappoint you. We didn't telegraph because there really wasn't time, and it seemed a waste of money, as I was coming anyway."

"Fell down stairs!" exclaimed Marget sympathetically, closing the door now and coming over to the girl. "The puir buddy! Now isn't that fearsome! And to think she broke her leg! That's just what

Thurly's always expecting of me to do. It's a sair thing for a buddy at our ages to have to lie abed when we'd rather be round doing our daily stint. But you needn't have bothered to come all this long way to stay with me, my dear. I'm grieved I did not know, and I would have wired ye. Didn't yer Aunt Martha need ye to nurse her?"

"Oh no, she has a trained nurse, and Uncle Geoffrey is there. I shouldn't have been with her in any case. You see I have my training school to attend when I'm home, and that was one reason why I thought I couldn't come when Aunt asked me. I couldn't miss my school. But she suggested I might find another school here, and I talked with my dean. There is one, and he's arranging for me to be transferred, that is if you can spare me during the day, and occasionally in the evenings perhaps—but we can talk all that over afterwards. I'd better get my things off now—"

"Oh, my dear, it's not necessary for anyone to stay with me—not in the least—it was just a whimsy of my son that it would be nice for my old friend to visit me now while he's away for a wee while. But it's all right, Jimmy Fargo will sleep here, and I can bide. You stay over night and get rested a bit, and then you run back to your school, my dear. I'm obliged, but it's not in the least necessary!"

"Oh, that's all right," said Hesba easily, swinging her suit cases a trifle impatiently, "if you'll just show me, is it upstairs I go? I can find my way—" and Hesba moved toward the staircase.

"No, wait!" said Marget desperately, as a strong spicy sweetness suddenly penetrated to the hall from the region of the kitchen. "Excuse me a minute, I've a pie in the oven—!" and she turned to fly to the kitchen.

But Hesba set down her suit cases and kept easy pace in long strides, with her quick little steps.

"Let *me* go," she said, and her voice though loud and distinct enough to be heard as they went, was still calm, as if she had grasped the situation fully, "I always tell my mother she should never leave her oven while she's baking without turning the gas down, even if the house is on fire. They always draw up when you least expect it. Here, let me do this, you'll burn yourself. Shall I take this cloth?"

She had swung into the kitchen at a good pace, and now she seized on Marget's fine white apron with hemstitching across the bottom which she had discarded on a chair as she went to answer the bell. Before Marget could open her mouth to stop her, the girl had flapped open the oven door and seized the rich blackberry pie with the folds of the fine linen apron, bringing it forth from the oven triumphantly.

"There!" she said calmly. "Where shall I set it? Here?" and without more ado she plumped it down on Marget's nice newly covered white oilcloth table, where it promptly stuck to the white surface, and sent up a smell of burnt paint to mingle with the blackberry juice that was dripping down to the bottom of the oven.

"Oh, my dear!" said Marget aghast, "the pie is only just put in. It's juice that has run down a wee bit and is burning, not the pie at all. Here, let me take the apron. It's all sticky." She surveyed her best white apron in dismay.

"But, my dear, you've juice on your dress, and on your shoes. Oh, I shouldn't have let you—" she added politely—as if she could have helped it!

"It's of no consequence," said Hesba, still calm, "I presume it will clean. Boiling water will take out blackberry stain, and the shoes are old ones. You shouldn't fill your pies so full, and then this wouldn't happen. Shall I wash my hands at the sink?"

Hesba was running true to form. It was her habit to ask permission for what she was already doing.

Marget herded her out of the kitchen at last and up to her room, her heart boiling with indignation, as she strove to hide her annoyance, and then she hurried back to her little white kitchen and essayed to undo some of the damage.

She lifted the pie back into the oven with the little patent lifter that hung by her range, grieving at the havoc wrought on her new white oilcloth which was badly scorched and stained, deprecating the sticky pan which would be to clean on the bottom as well as the top from the oilcloth adhering to it. And the "bit pannie" would never be quite so bright again. She moaned to herself as she wiped up the path of juice from the stove to the table, and then dropped her pretty white apron into a pan of boiling water to soak till she had time to try and get the stains out. Such a mess! And all because the poor mistaken stranger had mind to help! Well, she mustn't be too hard on her. Her soul was just being tried a bit more, that was all. She had lived so long alone, and had things her own way, and the bit girl had wanted to be kind.

So Marget soothed herself into calm once more, and went on with her dinner preparations.

Meanwhile, upstairs, the "bit girl" was taking a survey of the new land in which she had come to dwell for a while. She removed her hat and coat and tidied herself briskly. Then before she even hung up her coat in the closet Marget had showed her, she went out into the hall with catlike tread, and made a careful investigation of the rest of the second story, not excluding the store room and linen closet, though she opened their door cautiously, and noiselessly. Then she went back to the guest room and brought her suit cases and her coat and hat into Thurly's room, hanging the coat and hat in the closet, and standing her baggage bedside the bed. She gave the room a careful survey, examined minutely the several pictures of college life on the walls, and especially the picture of Thurly in his football regalia, and then went down stairs, stealing upon Marget in the kitchen so silently that she jumped and almost slopped over the pitcher of cream she was carrying to the dining table.

"Let me take that!" demanded Hesba as if it were her right: "You're tired, I can see, or you wouldn't have jumped. You sit down now and I'll finish getting dinner. By the way, ought I to have dressed for dinner? Aunt thought you did, but I didn't see any use if we're all alone, unless you think I should."

"Dress for dinner?" said Marget perplexed, "why, you are dressed, I'm sure."

"All right if you're satisfied," said Hesba, "I wanted to do the right thing, the first night, anyway. Now, where's your bread box? I'll cut the bread."

But Marget at last roused to the occasion.

"You will not cut the bread, my dear," she said, and looked her guest in the eye with battle, gently shown, "I prefer to cut my own bread, and to get my own dinner. It will please me far better if you will sit in the parlor and rest yourself until I call you."

"Oh, very well," said Hesba coolly, "then if you don't need me just now I'll go up and unpack. I hurried down because I thought I could help, but if you've everything nearly ready why I suppose you would rather finish. However, I'll take over a good part of the work tomorrow."

"No," said Marget smilingly, "no, my girl, you won't take over my work. I never let anyone take over my work. And you'll go in the parlor now, or up the stair, and make yourself contented in any way you like, till I call you."

Greek had met Greek, and Hesba looking into Marget's eyes said, "Oh, very well." Hesba was not a fighter. She was a doer. She usually worked so quickly that one had no time to prevent or to battle. She turned and went upstairs.

Half an hour later when Marget rang the little tea bell that usually summoned Thurly from his study, Hesba came down stairs quite complaisant.

Marget, her face a little red from worry and flurry, presided at her table with dignity. She put all the serving at her own place, and kept a firm hand on things. She kept the lead in the conversation too, asking quick discerning questions that kept the guest busy answering, while they ate.

Hesba talked frankly about herself.

"You know I'm in training for some kind of social service. I've been attending a school, and I'm going to keep up my studies."

"Yes?" said Marget quite interested for a moment. "Yes? It'll maybe be like the school where Thurly was teaching last winter. It's a wonderful school—" and she launched into a description of the curriculum and the teachers, and the good they were doing, that showed she was well acquainted with the facts.

"Oh," said Hesba coolly, "I never heard of it," and then she went on with her own plans. Her teacher was to write her, and get her in touch with the dean of this school in the city near Stonington, a training school just like the one she had been attending.

Marget chided herself that she felt somehow an antipathy toward this girl who was so serious and well informed, and so evidently right minded. A girl who was planning to devote her life to Christian work, even to social service, must be a girl of true worth. And yet she found from the first an aversion to her. Why was it? She was not ill to look upon. Her features were good, her complexion was fair with healthy color in her cheeks, she wore no rouge, and did not deck herself out as if the life of the flesh were all that was worth while; and yet, she could not to save her, like this girl. Why was it? Was it just that she was perverse?

Look how she had loved the bit lassie from the world that had dropped down upon them through the storm! And she was avowedly the world's own, with no attempt to even pretend to be making her life worth while.

Well, it must just be that Marget Macdonald was perverse in her thoughts, loving the world herself and the things of the world. For if this new lassie was the Lord's own treasure, as she was like to be if she was devoting her life to others, why then it just simply must be all wrong that Marget Macdonald didn't love her, and she must get to work, and find our her lovableness.

She suffered her to help with the clearing off of the table, saying nothing when her assistant suggesting putting things in another place than was her custom. It would be easy enough to put them back where they belonged when the guest had gone upstairs, and she must not antagonize her this first night. She must remember that the girl was trying to be kind and help.

They had family worship together. It had worried Marget to think about it, but if this was another child of the kingdom of course she would be in hearty accord.

Hesba seemed indifferently willing, and they read in turn verse about, a portion of the fourth chapter of John, the story of Jesus at the well talking to the woman of Samaria. When they came to the twenty-ninth verse, where the woman of Samaria came to the men and said: "Come see a man, which told me all things that ever I did: is not this the Christ?" Hesba read it and then paused and added:

"You know our professor in Bible says that that is a mistake of course, for Jesus had no means whatever of knowing all that that woman had done, unless of course He might have heard some gossip about her as He passed through the village."

"A mistake!"

Marget Macdonald looked up and something blazed in her soft blue eyes that resembled fire mixed with steel.

"A mistake, did ye say? A mistake in the blessed Buik? Why, now that is strange! A mistake! Why, it cuid na be! Why have ye na heeard how not even one dotting of an 'i' or one crossing of a 't' shall be changed in the Word of the Buik till all be fulfilled? Girlie, ye may be ignorant and therefore not culpable, but ye canna say such like things again the Buik in this hoose. This hoose is a hoose of prayer and faith, and neither I nor my laddie will list to sayings of unbelievers. Yon is atheism, pure and simple, and if ye dinna know better, ye'll mind and keep it to yersel' while yer here!"

"Now, Grandma, don't get excited!" said Hesba soothingly. "I was only telling you the modern view of things. Of course you're old fashioned and like to think of things as you used to know them, and I don't suppose it will hurt you any, but you ought to be broad minded enough to listen to the other side. However, if you don't wish me to—"

"Broad minded!" said Marget Macdonald rising, closing her Bible with a snap, and laying it on the table. "Dinna ye know, poor buddy, where the broad road leads to? 'Wide is the gate and broad is the road that leads to *death,* and many there be that go in thereat—' Lassie, we'll kneel and pray now." And Marget Macdonald knelt and prayed such a prayer for the erring young soul as would have melted a heart of stone.

But Hesba Hamilton was quite unmoved as she rose from her knees. She turned to her hostess, all weak, and tearful with her emotion, and aid quite calmly:

"Grandma, you're very amusing, but don't you thing it's bad for you to get so excited? I think religion is largely self-control, don't you?"

"There's a deal of that needed sometimes," said Marget, and went and dusted off her little table with her best pocket handkerchief.

Having gained the needed control she sought to get rid of her guest.

"Ye'll be weary with the journey," she said kindly, "and I've a bit sponge to set for my bread the morn. So ye'll juist feel free to go to yer bed without waiting for me."

"All right," said Hesba, "I guess I will retire. I like to read a while before I sleep. You needn't bother about waking me in the morning. I always set myself to waken at a certain time. Good night!"

Marget gave a sigh of relief and slipped out to her kitchen pondering how she was to get rid of this unwelcome visitor and send her on her way without hurting either her feelings or those of the woman whose place she was supposed to be taking.

She tiptoed upstairs cautiously, not to waken her guest, but found her precaution unnecessary. Hesba, in a mannish kimono tied about her waist with a cord and tassel was awaiting her in the hall.

"I thought I better tell you," she said, "in case you should want me in the night. I looked about a little and found that this front room which has evidently been your son's room, is much nearer to you, right across the hall from your door, where I could hear you if you moved, so I took the liberty of moving into it. I moved the bed-clothes too, so there's nothing for you to do, and I've been cleaning out the closet and hanging up my clothes, so I'd be ready for living in the morning. I've stacked those pictures of college things in the other room on the bureau, and tomorrow I'll move all the things in the desk drawers for I'll want to study at that desk. Here's a shoe I found on the shelf in the closet behind a book. You might take care of it, or maybe you'll want to throw it away. I opened it to see what on earth was hidden so far back. It's likely some souvenir from a dance your son went to. They collect all sorts of queer souvenirs now. I guess likely he didn't want you to know he had it.

She handed out Tasha's little gold slipper with the gleaming diamond buckle, half hidden by the wrappings.

Marget had been trembling so with anger during this speech that she was ready to fall down the sair, but when the little gold shoe appeared she grasped it with a relief that was almost like a shout of joy, and with it in her hand, as if it had been a sword she stood forth.

"This is the slipper belonging to a friend who was visiting us, and who left in haste leaving one of her shoes behind her. She is getting it when she returns from Florida. Meantime it was hidden away in what we supposed was a safe place from prying eyes, for the diamonds in the buckle are valuable. But girlie, this is my son's room, and no one else occupies it, *ever!* He likes not to have his things disturbed, and you may take your bag and baggage and go back to the room I gave you, or you may go out of this hoose." With which ultimatum Marget walked majestically into Thurly's room, gathered the maiden's garments from the hooks in the closet, in one wide swoop, her brushes from the bureau, and carried them into the guest room dumping them unceremoniously upon the chairs. Then she took her arms full of the pictures and things of Thurly's that had been taken out of his room and brought them back, while her guest stood and watched her, finally saying:

"Oh, very well, if you feel that way about it. I'm sure I thought I was doing the right thing," and picking up her empty suit cases she marched back to the guest room.

Marget had by this time rolled up the bedding for her son's bed, brought it back, and sweeping the few things from the closet went into her son's room and locked the door, leaving her guest to do what she pleased.

Marget, as she worked, swiftly, eagerly, putting back her son's Lares and Penates into their accustomed places, was singing a little paean in her heart. The slipper was found. She had it stuffed safely away in her apron pocket, the dainty little trick! And Thurly hadn't taken it with him at all! Thurly hadn't kept anything from his mother! Thurly was all right! The slipper was found! The slipper was found! It was not stolen, it was not strayed, it was here, here, *here!* Safe! Safe! *Safe!* There was nothing to worry about that little shoe any more. Diamonds and all it was found! And even if it did take a little huzzy of a thing to discover it, the Lord had lifted her worry and set her up above even a girl like this one that had come down upon her determined to manage her. Well, she might try, if she could, and Marget would hold her peace, and stand as much as she could, but there were two things the girl could not touch. She might not speak against God's Word, and she might not enter Thurly Macdonald's room any more.

So Marget locked her son's room door, after all was in order again, and then went across to her own room, and locked *her* door, a thing she had not done since she could ever remember.

But she lay down and slept the sleep of the just, and the little shoe was with her, wrapped soft in a silk handkerchief, and then in cotton wool, and tied with a "bit ribbon," blue like the eyes of its owner, and hid under Marget Macdonald's pillow.

Chapter 14

Marget awoke with a start next morning, with the knowledge that she must have overslept. Dismay came over her as she gradually realized the situation, for she had intended to forestall the visitor and have breakfast all ready when she should wake. Now she would probably find that forward young woman sitting primly in the parlor reading the newspaper, with reproach in her eyes for a housekeeper who rose so late. Her only hope was that the girl might be human enough to be weary herself from her journey.

She jumped out of bed cautiously, and listened. The house seemed to be perfectly quiet. Still, that would be the case if the guest were reading the newspaper. Nevertheless she clung to the hope that she was till asleep, and got dressed in haste and with the utmost quiet, tiptoeing out into the hall cautiously when she was ready.

Hesba's door was wide open, and in dismay Marget noted that the bed was made up most precisely, and the room in absolute order. With mingling emotions she descended the stairs, and looked into the little parlor. But there was no one sitting there. What had the girl found to do? With rising apprehension for her own order of things she hurried into the kitchen, but again order reigned, seemingly as she had left it, save that the dishcloth hung limp and damp on its little rack, instead of stiff and dry as it usually was in the morning. A quick glance around showed a cup and plate out of order on the shelf. Ah! The guest had eaten her breakfast, for there was the coffee pot on the back of the stove, and she had probably made the coffee with cold water instead of boiling water as Marget had always done. They mostly did when they preferred to put in cream afterward, instead of pouring it in the bottom of the cup before pouring the coffee, so that it would better blend.

Then suddenly the old saint began to marvel at her own smallness. What were such things compared to peaceful living. She must not let the enemy blind her with trifles so that she would sin. Better have all the coffee spoiled and take it pleasantly, even if it was her own house and her own coffee, and her own right to have it as she liked, than to soil her soul with fretting and rancor over a trifle.

"Surely He shall deliver thee from the snare of the fowler." If this wan't just like the little snare that bird catcher would set in the grass to trip the unwary bird to his capture, then she did not know scripture, and it was quite plain to her suddenly that she was being tried. After all these years of peaceful quiet living, having her own way, and being respected and tenderly guarded by an adoring son, she was having to be teased and tried by the little trifles of life. She had had many a big trial in her life, like the noisome pestilence in its overwhelming suddenness, and devastating sorrow; but her life had been singularly free from the little annoyances that make up the whole existence, seemingly, of many of God's children.

She must beware. "Your enemy the devil, goeth about like a roaring lion, seeking whom he may devour," but she remembered that he often came in sheep's clothing, or as an angel of light. She decided that as soon as she could occupy her guest contentedly in something for a little while, where she would be out of danger, she would seek the mercy seat, and find strength for the day, for she suddenly felt most inadequate to meet it.

But where was the guest? She couldn't have gone out to survey the back yard for the back door was duly bolted as she had left it the night before.

Going back into the dining room she discovered a note propped up against the sugar bowl, and for an instant her heart leaped with joy. Perhaps the "bit girl" had taken offense at the way she had ordered her back to the guest room last night, and had taken herself home! Although she would always feel ashamed that the exit had been a matter of offense, still it would be a great relief to have her out of the house. It certainly would, and Thurly none the wiser. She could get along perfectly well alone, with Jimmy Fargo nights. And Jimmy would like to stay. She was sure of that. She would put him in the guest room and let him study there evenings, and he wouldn't be a bit of trouble, just a bit pan of gingerbread now and then, or a plate of cookies, to please him.

All this she thought while she was getting out her spectacles and framing them on her nose with excited hands that trembled in their eagerness.

Then she read the note:

"Dear Grandma:",

Marget felt a twinge of dislike at once. She wan't anybody's grandmother yet, certainly not this prim maiden's. But that was an unworthy feeling. The old enemy again! She must put away such ungodliness! She read on:

"I've gone to town to arrange about my school. The coffee pot is on the back of the stove, and there are some fried tomatoes in the warming oven. I'll be back in time to help get dinner.

Hesba"

"The dickens, you will!" said Marget aloud. "I'll make me a pot of soup and have it hot on the back of the stove whenever she comes. I'll make me an apple pie, and some cottage cheese from the jar of soul milk, and that's enough dinner for anybody, for the bread'll be fresh. I've no call to let her ramp all over me in my own hoose, even if this is a trial set for my training. I must keep my identity, and my self-respect. I'm sure the Lord would tell me that!"

So Marget went eagerly and hurriedly about her work. There was a pot of soup stock already in the house, for she always kept all the bits of meat and used every drop of nutriment. She went to the telephone and ordered a piece of meat to make the soup more tasty, and then she set about preparing her vegetables, and making her apple pie and cheese, and while she worked, she planned how she might send that girl away to her home again, without having to be disagreeable about it. It was quite evident that her teaching had been all wrong. It smacked of what Thurly called "modern." She might be right intentioned, and if she only knew the Lord Jesus, it might make all the difference in the world. There was no limit to how the Lord might change a buddy, once He had them.

Then she recalled how easily she had felt about that other lassie that the Lord had sent her there for a purpose. How eager she had been to teach the pretty child, and to pray for her and love her in spite of her paint, and silly clothing, and her being a little pretty world-ling. Was she to do less for this other girl because she was less weak, less appealing, less lovely in her ways?

This really was probably a stronger minded girl, more capable of developing into a fine character, with teaching; more the kind of girl who would make a good mate for Thurly! She winced over that thought. Suppose Thurly was home and she had to worry over that too! Suppose she had to look forward to having her for a daughter-in-law! Ah! then! That would be a trial! And yet she had half toyed with the thought of having a daughter like the other little lassie, so bonnie, and dainty, and graceful.

This girl was not bad looking either. She had nice eyes if she wouldn't stare so much, with that look as if she knew it all and ev-erybody else was all wrong, but she must set them right. As if she had been sent into the world just to set everybody else right!

Ah! But she mustn't think of her that way! It was not Christian. Perhaps she was prejudiced just because of that little incident of the pie right at the start of their acquaintance. They began wrong. That was it. She must be more longsuffering and kindly. Perhaps she would grow to love the girl. For after all a girl who could give up the world, and look forward to a life of sacrifice for other people was not to be despised. She certainly had chosen more wisely than a child of fri-volity, whose only thought was to amuse herself. Yet she was cher-ishing the thought of the girl who had worn that little gold shoe, in spite of all her fears for Thurly. What a mystery was the human heart! Yes, even one's own heart. There were things hid away in the corners of it that one never suspected. But God must see them clearly all the time. One ought to pray without ceasing as the Bible said.

Nevertheless it was not to be thought of that the present incumbent should remain with her during Thurly's absence. It might even open the way to further acquaintance, and force Thurly somehow into her company; and while Marget was ready to submit to the Lord's will if

He had picked out this girl for a future mate for her beloved son, still she did not want it to be her fault, just because she had to be taken care of. And she must find a way, to gently, kindly, pleasantly remove her. "Oh, Lord, please show me how to get rid of the little huzzy!" she prayed with a deep sigh of trouble, and then caught herself in the act and anxiously added, "unless it be Thy will, Oh, Lord, and then give me strength to submit, for ya ken I'm dinna able to bear wi' the nagging, high handed ways of her alone, dear Lord."

Marget reffected that this summary taking of things for granted by Hesba, and going ahead with her school, was going to make it harder. If she only knew the name of the school to which she had gone she would telephone and try to reach her, and tell her not to make any arrangements until they had talked together. Then there wouldn't be anything to undo. But there was nothing she could do about it until the girl came home, so she worked hard and the morning passed rapidly. She scarcely stopped to take a bite herself at noon; till the kettle of soup began to send forth savory odors; two apple pies stood cooling on the pantry shelf, their tops all frosty with powdered sugar, their spicy juices making little appetizing gummy streaks around the crimps; three loaves of perfectly baked white bread browned to a nicety, cooling across their pans on the kitchen table, and a bowl of cottage cheese in the refrigerator.

After she had taken a cup of tea to hearten her up she added a sponge cake to the list of her deeds, and when that was baked and cooling in the pantry, she went up stairs.

Hesba arrived at five o'clock promptly.

Marget had taken the precaution to put the night latch on that she might not be taken unawares. She did not like the feeling that a stranger had stepped into her home, and might walk in on her at almost any moment. If the girl had the ordinary polite ways of a well bred person, it wouldn't be so hard, but she seemed to think that coming here to be a companion constituted her housekeeper, and general reformer, and there must be some way to show her her place while she remained. Marget meant that she should not remain long. Of course she could not just ship her back over night. She must be hospitable, yet she would make it very plain that she was not needed.

Marget went to the door, in another nice white apron, the mate to the one that Hesba had done her best to ruin the night before.

Marget had rested fifteen minutes, even falling into a restful doze, and now she had just finished setting the table, even going so far as to pick a couple of her best geranium blooms and arrange them on the table with a bit of asparagus fern in a tiny crystal vase, for good cheer. She had done this to prove to herself that she was going to be cordial and pleasant to this girl thus thrust upon her.

Hesba walked in with her arm full of books. She had the sharp, worn, alert look of an old blackbird who had been out scratching too long for worms. It was sharper than the quick sharpness of youth, that passes, and leaves the soft smooth contours again. It was almost careworn, in one so young.

"I'm late!" stated Hesba, as she laid down her books on the table and began to take off her strong sensible fabric gloves. "Your trains don't run on schedule. I waited fully three quarters of an hour for the train gate to open. They made some excuse about trouble on the road, but it really is inexcusable I think on a big road like this one. However, I've planned what I can get in a hurry. I'm used to thinking up quick make shifts, and I'll have dinner ready on time. Have you got any parsley?"

"Parsley?" smiled Marget, gazing placidly at her young tormentor, the peace of her recent quiet hour in her eyes. "I'm afraid not, I've just used it all getting dinner."

"Getting dinner!" said Hesba in a vexed tone. "But I told you I would get it! When I make a promise I always keep it, and if I can't do it one way I can another. I would have got it in time. You needn't have got worried."

"Oh, I wasn't worried about that at all, my dear," said Marget pleasantly, "I got dinner quite early this morning, that is I prepared for it. I usually do. You see, my dear, however kindly your intentions may have been in offering to get dinner, I would prefer that you don't worry yourself about the hoose. This is my home and I have always run it in my own way, and prefer to do so. When I need help I will ask it, but while you remain here you are my guest. The hoose and its arrangements are mine."

"But I should not feel right not to help with the work. That's what I promised Aunt I would do."

"But *I* should not feel right if you did, lassie, so we'll talk no more aboot it. And noo, whilse we're speaking of it, I may as weel tell you that I've been thinking it over, and I feel it's best for you to go back to your home after you've had a good rest from your journey, for this is not place for a young thing like you, and I can't see my way clear to keeping you. I'm a home buddy, and not used tae having young things around."

"Oh, you'll find I'm not much of a young thing," said Hesba looking firmly at Marget through her round rims. "I've got serious work to do. Look at all my books! I'm to go in town three days in the week, so I'll have plenty of time to help you around the house in what ever you want done. You ought to begin to learn to let someone else do some of the work. You're getting old you know, and you'll have to give up pretty soon."

The color flamed softly in Marget Macdonald's cheeks, but she kept her tone steady and even smiled a bit as she said:

"Well, when it coomes it coomes; but it's na coom yet, and I'll bide as I am whiles I can. There's nothing I want doone for me."

"You'll find I can do things exactly as well as you can—" argued Hesba crossly, "I'm quite capable."

"I've ne'er thought ye were not capable." answered Marget, "ye might be able to do things better than I, but it's my work, and I likit to do it myself. So that's settled."

"Well, I could take more classes by going in *every* morning," said Hesba practically, "if you really don't need me."

"I dinna need ye," said Marget firmly, "but I think, my girl, ye better return to yer ain schule. Our winters are bitter up here, and it'll be hard gaeing to the train some morns. Besides, as I said, I prefer you should go. I have other arrangements. After of coorse ye've had a proper resting space before you take the big trip again."

"It's quite impossible now," said Hesba just as firmly, "I've paid my tuition in advance. You should have thought of this before you telephoned my aunt. I came on in good faith, and I spent the money for the trip, and for my school, and I've made all arrangements to be transferred. I couldn't go back of course. And I should miss the whole term and be behind."

"That'll be too bad," said Marget with a troubled look, wavering. "It's been a mistake, a great mistake, but I'd no idea of coorse your aunt would send a young person. It doesn't suit me at all."

"Well, the tuition is paid and I'm under promise to stay. I guess you'll have to make the best of it," said the girl. "I really wouldn't know what to do if you didn't. I couldn't afford to pay my board. The tuition is almost twice as much at this school as it was at home."

"Tuition?" said Marget puzzled, "why it doesn't cost anything for tuition at those Bible schools. You should have asked me aboot it before ye started oot. You see my son taught at the Institute all last winter."

"The Institute!" laughed Hesba half scornfully, "Oh, I wouldn't go to a school like that! I've heard about that! They were laughing about it in the office this morning when I registered. They say those schools don't teach you anything but the chapter and verse of a scripture reference. It's not to a school like that I'm going. It's a *Training* School. You get a lot more than the Bible. You get Training, and other Cultural branches, pedagogy, and social science and things like that. We have Bible interpretation of course, and Critical Study, and all that, and it's very interesting, but we get a lot more than just Bible."

"Most Bible students find that they have their hands pretty full with juist the auld Buik," said Marget dryly, and then remembered suddenly her resolve and sheathed her sharp tongue.

"We'll speak na more aboot it," she said. "Ye may bide a few days at least, till we see. It may be that my son will return within the week."

"I should have been told that then, and not made all these arrangements," said Hesba crossly, as if she had been greatly wronged.

"There are several things that should have been told," said Marget with a sigh, "but it's too late for that now, my friend. We'll juist have to bear with things as they air till the Father changes it!"

Hesba laughed harshly.

"You're awful funny, Grandma, thinking God attends to things like that. I think it's our own look out when we get into scrapes. It's somebody's fault and ought to be set straight."

"You'd be in a sairer strait yet, I'm thinking, if the Father didn't attend to a' things. That's where you make your mistake. And I'm thinking it doesn't matter sa mooch what you or I or onyboody *thinks* aboot it, the Father attends to it, juist the same. For He says so in the Buik. Noo, if ye'll wash oop and be ready, I'll pit the dinner on."

And with dignity Marget walked out to her kitchen and began to dish up the dinner.

Chapter 15

Letters from Thurly, two of them, came promptly, one to announce his safe arrival, the second to describe his first impressions. He spoke enthusiastically of the work, his colleagues, and his classes, described his pleasant location, and the first dinner he had eaten in his new quarters. His mother sighed and wiped away a tear. Here was she, far away, having to cook for this little huzzy of an alien, who debated everything she touched from the way to draw tea, to the meaning of a text of scripture; while Thurly, her own son, ate dishes prepared by strangers, and got the indigestion from sour bread and heavy pancakes. Ah, Thurly! Why had she not accepted his invitation, just closed the house and gone with him for awhile? What joy it would have been to see Chicago under his guidance!

But of course that was all foolish. They couldn't have afforded to close the house and pay her board, not until Thurly had a church of his own and a regular salary. She must just bide and do the Lord's will, and Thurly would come back by and by. Pain did not last forever. Who was it said, "This too shall pass?" But ah, there was a better saying than that: "He knoweth the way that I take: when He hath tried me, I shall come forth as gold!"

Having taken her stand on three things that lay closest to her heart, the matter of Biblical interpretation, Thurly's room, and the conducting of her own household, Marget determined to bear with all the rest, wherever the unwelcome guest's ideas did not verge on vital matters. But there was no end to the way in which Hesba Hamilton tormented the soul of Marget Macdonald.

Marget was glad that the sessions of the school began early and lasted late in the afternoon, glad that Hesba was a perfect shark for study, and spent many hours in her room, growing wiser, more round eyed, and critical, as the days dragged by. But at least Marget had the better part of the day to herself, and she managed by much Bible reading and prayer to keep sweet the rest of the time.

It was late one afternoon that the postman brought a parcel. Hesba happened to be home that afternoon on account of a half holiday at school. Of course she took it upon herself to go to the door, and to demand that the postman account for being so late.

"He *says* the train was late," she said, returning primly with the mail, "but he's probably lying. They all do. He just got lazy and didn't pep up! Just look at this big thin package, Grandma! What is it, do you suppose? It looks like a photograph, and it's from Florida. 'Palm Beach,' it says. Mercy, do you have friends rich enough to go there? I thought they were all multimillionaires!"

"Palm Beach!"

Marget's heart took a sudden leap, and a light flashed up in her eyes. She even forgot to notice that Hesba called her "Grandma" again. She wiped her hands on the immaculate roller towel and came forward quickly, but Hesba was too quick for her.

"I'll open it for you," she said like a mother to a little child. "It's one of those patent envelopes for photographs and you won't know how. Zip! the envelope was ripped open and photograph brought forth and opened up, its protecting tissue paper front floating lazily off into the dining-room carpet where it lay unheeded while Hesba gazed in amazed contempt at the lovely face of a girl about her own age with a string of pears about her slim neck, "Anastasia" was written in a careless but characterful scrawl across one corner, and beneath in very tiny script "Just to help you remember me."

"Who on earth is that?" said Hesba contemptuously. "She looks like a movie star!"

Marget was vexed beyond words. She had a childish impulse to cry with indignation, but she managed to control herself and say nothing. She stooped to pick up the tissue cover, and when she lifted her head was able to answer Hesba's exclamation quite pleasantly.

"Oh, that is just a little friend of mine, Miss Endicott."

"Mercy!" said Hesba again, eyeing the other girl enviously, "she puts on a great deal of style, doesn't she? Does she live down in Palm Beach all the time? I suppose there are some regular all-year-round residents."

"No," said Marget composedly putting a few of the dishes on the sideboard straight, "no, she lives in the city. She's down there for the winter—that is—" remembering what she had gleaned from the society notes she had been reading lately—"The Endicotts have a winter home in Palm Beach!"

"Mercy! You don't mean it!" said Hesba still studying the picture though Marget had not as yet been able to give more than a casual glance, "then I suppose those must be real pearls she has around her neck. Are they very rich people?"

"Well, I suppose they are comfortably off," said Marget. "They have a very handsome home in the city."

"Do you visit there?" she asked, giving Marget one of her round searching glances.

"Well, no—" said Marget uneasily, feeling that she was getting into deep water. "You know I don't go out much. I'm a real hoome buddy."

"Well, how do you know it's handsome then?"

There she was, put in a corner again. That direct huzzy was always delighting to get someone in a tight place!

"Oh, my son has been there, of course," she admitted. "He has told me about it."

"Oh! Is she a friend of Thurly's?"

Hesba had taken quite easily to calling the absent son by his first name as if she had the right. Marget had never been able to quite understand why this should annoy her, but it did.

"Why—yes—" she answered slowly with somewhat heightened color, "I suppose she is," and wondered if she were quite telling the truth, and whether she ought to admit it even if it was the truth, to this prying creature.

"Are they engaged?" came the next thrust.

Marget's hands trembled so that she dropped the fluttering tissue paper again, and was glad to have the opportunity to bend down and hide her startled face.

When she had picked up the paper she turned quite away from her questioner and opening the sideboard drawer began to rearrange the napkins as if it were a work of immediate necessity, trying to make her tone quite casual as she answered:

"Why, no—not that I know of." And then was filled with compunction at the impression she must have conveyed. Yet she knew not how to change it without making it ten times worse, so she changed the subject.

"If you'd like me to turn up that hem on your new dress for you I can do it now, Hesba," she said.

Hesba laid down the photograph quickly and hurried upstairs for the dress. But after it was on and they had decided on the length and Marget on her knees was carefully measuring with the yard stick and setting pins five inches apart, Hesba resumed just where she had left off, tone and all:

"Do you like her?"

"Like her? Like whom?" queried Marget to make time. The question seemed to stir some hidden depths of her heart that she did not understand, between joy and fear.

"Like this Anastasia?"

"Why, yes, I like her," said Marget resuming her casualness.

"Does Thurly like her?" was the next question, put bluntly.

Marget was almost at the end of her patience, but she managed a smile.

"Well, Hesba, I doubt me if my son would care to have me discuss his likes and dislikes with onybuddy," she said gently. "Turn a little to the left, won't you? It seems longer right by the seam does it not?" Hesba turned sharply but continued:

"You're funny, Grandma," she said, "you're as close mouthed as a clam. I don't see why you shouldn't discuss things with me if you choose. Anybody might ask that question. Why should he mind you telling me that?"

"Well, perhaps he wouldna," said Marget easily, "but I always think the least said aboot those absent, the better. Would you like me to sew it? I've a bit spool the color."

"Thanks, Grandma, I wish you would. I'm not keen on sewing. I always buy my things ready made and have alterations made at the store when they are needed. But they didn't seem to have that kind of service in this store, so I had to take it as it was, it was such a bargain."

When Hesba had gone upstairs to take off the dress Marget went and stood by the table and looked into the sweet picture-frame with a long anxious glance. Sometimes a photograph will bring out in a face something that is hidden in the flesh, and Marget was involuntarily searching for some flaw in the girl that her heart had gone out to; for her reason told her that Anastasia was not a girl she should take too deeply into her heart of hearts, unless she wished to face keen disappointment in the future. But Marget found nothing like that in the photograph, and with a kind of triumphant satisfaction she took up the picture and went and stood it on the mantelpiece in the little parlor, where it seemed to glorify the room just as the violets the girl had sent had done.

She would much have preferred putting the picture away where no alien eyes should look upon it, but she thought that might arouse suspicion of her mentor, so she placed it out in the open and went on about her work as if nothing out of the ordinary had entered her home with the gift of that charming pictured face. Just as if it had not also throbbed with a curious kind of fear with the instant question that came: had the girl sent it that *Thurly* might remember her also, half hoping that she had, half fearful lest she had. Oh, a curious thing was Marget's heart, and that was a fact she had begun to recognize quite clearly for herself.

Quite clearly Marget was beginning to see that she herself was beginning to be in danger of falling in love with the little worldling, and if she could not withstand her charm, how could she hope that her son would? Oh, the little gold shoe, the little bonnie shoe, with its flashing stones! What havoc had it wrought in their quiet household!

But Thurly was away for a time, safe! Why might she not enjoy the sweet face for a season, watching her from the mantel as she went about her house? If only that other girl did not have to be here too, with her eagle eye watching Marget's every glance!

There had been one or two short letters passing between Palm Beach and Stonington, during the weeks since the storm. Marget had written a characteristic letter of thanks for the violets and again more at length for the watch, after Thurly had decided she must keep it. Tasha had written back telling of the summer weather she was enjoying, of the sea bathing, and tennis, and all the gay doings. But now this picture began to look as if the little brilliant butterfly had some real attachment for the friends of a day, and wanted to keep up the friendship.

So the picture remained on the mantel, and the two girls eyed each other furtively, the one on the mantel and the one behind the shell-rimmed glasses.

For Hesba had not budged for an instant from her determination to stay and keep on with her new school. Faithfully every morning she arose and made the coffee—*her* way—leaving the coffee pot on the back of the stove, never knowing that Marget had taken to tea for her breakfast, and got immense satisfaction from emptying the coffee pot, and washing it clean. It might be a bit wasteful, but it certainly did her soul good to throw out that coffee that was made the wrong way and had a wrong flavor.

For Marget after a few mornings' protest, had succumbed to letting Hesba get her own breakfast and depart, and for the first time in her life Marget slept till after seven, partly because she wanted to cut down the points of contact with her ruthless young governor whom she could not seem to dislodge without an actual battle, and partly because she did not want to fight about how the coffee should be made. If it pleased Hesba to think she was helping a little by making the coffee, and if she liked her coffee better made that way, why surely she, Marget, did not need to be so narrow about it. Let her go on and do it.

So life in the little Stonington cottage had settled down to a routine, not without a kind of outward peace. Now and again there would be a theological brush at the evening worship, for Hesba was persistent in trying to introduce modern ideas into the reading of the scripture, and Marget waxed hot when the inspiration of the scriptures was attacked; but for the most part, there was peace because Marget was daily and almost hourly praying for a higher strength than her own wherewith to walk her difficult way.

Then, one day, there arrived a delivery car from one of the big florist's establishments in the city. It happened to be the one that

Hesba passed every morning on her way to school, and she had therefore acquired a knowledge of its importance. It was a large handsome box that was delivered to Marget, and Hesba as usual did the opening, though Marget stood back with her sweet soul boiling at the rudeness, and her fingers fairly itching to untie those ribbon knots and open her own flowers. Only a few flowers like that in her lifetime and she not allowed to open them! Hesba broke the ribbon, too, with a strong right thumb and finger, instead of untying it carefully and saving it for a treasure box.

But even Hesba was overpowered for a moment with the vision that was revealed as she lifted the lid of that box. Yellow and white and green, a perfect mass of glory and beauty! Roses and lilies and daffodils, starry narcissus, and freesias, masses of white lilacs and more roses, great yellow buds!

"Mercy!" said Hesba, "what a waste!"

"A *waste*?" said Marget starting back sharply from her first sweet breath of them with a hurt look in her eyes.

"Yes, sending all these *here*, with just us two. Not even a party or a wedding or a funeral! Mercy! Do you know what those yellow roses cost, those with the yard long stems? I priced them the other day, just for curiosity, and they are seventeen dollars a dozen! Just think of that! I say that's *wicked*! Think of the heathen!"

"The heathen?" said Marget puzzled. "What about the heathen?"

"Why, think what that might do for them!"

"What would it do for them?" asked Marget burying her face in the mass of lilacs, and wishing she might keep it there awhile and not listen to the grilling of Hesba's questions.

"What would it *do*? Why feed them, and send them to school, and put decent clothes on their back, and teach them to be respectable citizens in the world."

"Is that all?" asked Marget with her eyes half closed, looking at the flowers dreamily.

"*All*? What more do you want?" asked Hesba indignantly. "Isn't that about all one needs in life?"

"I was thinking you might be saying it would send the knowledge of the Lord Jesus to them, said Marget, lifting a stately lily and gazing into its golden heart.

"Oh, that! Of course, that goes too. But they have to *live* you know. They *have* to have food and clothes."

"You think that comes first?" said Marget, laying her lips to the soft yellow coolness of a rose bud.

"I *think* so! I *know* so! How queer you are, Grandma! You are always saying such unusual things. Of course you don't mean them. You're trying to kid me I see. But really, what was the reason for sending a great lot of flowers now? It isn't even Easter. It couldn't be your birthday because you said that was in the Fall! Mercy! I call it extravagant. I hate to see waste! That's what it is. Do you know who sent them? I'd like to tell them so. It wasn't Thurly of course."

"No, it wasn't Thurly," said Marget smiling, "though the dear lad would like to send twice as many to his mother every day in the week if he could afford it."

"Well, I should hope he's be more sensible. Who *did* send them? Was it that *girl*? nodding toward the picture on the mantel. "Because she looks as if she'd have just about that much sense!"

But Marget with her face buried again in the lilacs and her eyes closed, was breathing in deep breaths of fragrance, and trying to keep from saying what she thought.

Just one more thrust the girl gave her.

"Say, was that gold shoe hers, the one I found on Thurly's closet shelf?"

And when she got no reply from Marget she added with a calm sneer,

"You needn't tell me she isn't interested in Thurly,—and *he in her!*" With which fling she walked upstairs and left Marget with her flowers and her thoughts.

Chapter 16

The winter was broken at last. Drops began to drip from the icicles on the eaves, and little rivulets appeared in the gutters of the streets. Someone said they had heard a bird's note, and Hesba brought home some stalks of pussy willow she had bought on the street.

Marget took them pleasantly, with as much fuss as if they were roses, and put them in a vase, feeling of their silky little blossoms and cuddling them as she would have done any flowers. But she could not help thinking that these little harbingers of spring were like Hesba, hard and tight and tailor-made.

Marget was beginning to try to excuse some of Hesba's trying ways. It was almost time now, surely, for her to go back to her home, and she wanted her to leave as pleasantly as possible. She hoped against hope that she would go back for the Spring term at her home school; but Hesba had begun to talk about staying on until Commencement. She said she thought it would probably be better not to change again.

It was quite evident that she was planning to stay until Thurly returned if possible. She openly said she wanted him to take her around the city and show her some of the sights that she had not had time to see, and did not care to visit alone. In dismay Marget offered to get some neighbor to go with her at once, or even to go herself, much as she dreaded going out in bad weather; but Hesba said she hadn't time yet, that she had to study hard. She was taking two courses in one and hoped to get enough credits to finish her course in one year more.

Thurly had written that the professor for whom he was substituting was to return in ten days now, and he would probably be able to come home. He would like to know very soon whether the man could take up his work at once, but it was generally supposed that he would. His mother could read between the lines that while he was eager to get home to her, he yet was disappointed not to be able to

138

carry his students through to the logical finish of the year's work, to show what he really could do with them in a year. It would be far more to his credit, and add to his reputation more than if he but substituted for a part of a year.

Marget would not have believed that the time would ever come when she would actually be willing to have her son remain away a little longer than was necessary, but she was in a real panic now as she thought of the possibility of Thurly's returning while Hesba was there. Not that she could see anything in Hesba to attract a young man beyond the fact that she was young and strong, and supposed herself to be consecrated to a Cause with a capital C. But the longer she lived with Hesba the more she felt what a dire calamity it would be to have Thurly fall in love—No she couldn't quite fancy anybody falling in love with Hesba, but she could imagine Hesba forcing a man into the frame of mind where he thought he was doing the right and proper thing to marry her. In fact she was so persistent that it was hard to see how a gallant gentleman could well escape her clutches if she should once set out to capture him. Hesba would make herself seem so eminently fitting a match for a man who was contemplating Christian work. She was so practical and matter of fact, that she could well night make a man forget there were such things as love and romance, and think that the only qualities in the world that were worth while were practicality, and devotion to a Cause.

Marget had come to feel that Hesba was no nearer being a mate to her son in spiritual things than was the little beautiful worldling who had dropped down upon them that night in the storm. For Hesba had no Bible for a foundation, no real Christ in her heart to build upon. Hesba was building upon theories of men and science so-called, and moulding the old Bible over to suit them; consequently the ground under her feet was shifting sands, and she was acquiring more and more the habit of cutting loose from former things and finding new paths, which sadly enough did not lead to old truths. Hesba was a devotee of organizations, and uplifts, and effort of every sort to save one's self, and to save the world. Thurly was a devotee of the Lord Jesus and a believer in the old Book from cover to cover. No, they were not fit mates; and Marget, though she knew and believed that her Lord could guide her son, and was able to keep him from falling, yet she hoped he wouldn't come home while Hesba was there. She did not like the idea of Thurly and Hesba under the same roof together.

Daily she prayed for Hesba, daily besought the Most High to deliver herself from rancor and hard feeling; from being unjust to one of God's children; to give her love, like His, for the girl who had seemingly been sent to her. Daily she sought in little ways to show forth the Lord Jesus, and witness as to what he had done in her life, but Hesba only smiled, wisely, and called her "grandma" and went on her high, soulish way. It would seem that her eyes were blinded that she could not see the light. Marget groaned to herself in spirit daily that the girl could not have chosen a school from among real believers, rather than the one to which her home professor had sent her. But Hesba was never one who could be advised, and she would spend hours of time trying to convince Marget Macdonald of some trifling interpretation in scripture—an interpretation that took all the spirit from the passage, and spelled destruction and distress for Marget.

It was in vain that Marget tried to show her from the Bible that no man had a right to explain away the plain truths that were written for our instruction. In vain did she quote "No scripture is of private interpretation." Hesba would smile in her superior maddening way and say, "Oh, Grandma, you're so literal! But you know of course that the Bible would be very different if it were written to-day!"

And then Marget Macdonald would quote: "Jesus Christ, the same yesterday, to-day and forever!" and Hesba would say, "Oh, but Grandma, that's a very different matter. You don't really understand what that means. If you would take a correspondence course in our school you would learn that a lot of things you used to think were so are all changed!"

Then would Marget Macdonald look out of her window sadly toward the faraway hills and acknowledge in her heart that all her talk, and all her argument were of little avail. This girl was entrenched behind a lot of sophistries that she had been taught as if they were based on truth, and she did not want to see the right. Poor child!

And she was going out to teach others, blinder than herself! The blind leading the blind. No wonder that the world was getting topsy turvy and going after new gods, when the old ones had been dust covered in an attic of antiques, and everyone had to hunt a new god for himself.

In these days Marget Macdonald spent much time upon her knees in prayer, finding out her own follies and failures, yes, and her own weaknesses, and praying to be given the victory through Him who has vanquished our enemy, the prince of this world, once and for all, and through Whose victory we have a right to triumph too.

She would have been surprised if she could have known, however, how deep an impression her life was making on this self-centered girl. In her practical, blunt way Hesba was becoming fond of Marget Macdonald, and almost regretting the time when she must leave her. Several times she went out of her way to bring some token home with her. It was always a tailor-made tribute, like the pussy willow, but it was nevertheless a tribute, and as she went forth into her self-made future she would always remember "Grandma" as one who was wholly sincere, and lived up to her narrow beliefs with a steadfast self-forgetfulness that would always cause a little question in her mind, whether after all there had not been *some* truth in the things she believed. Hesba was one who took in all "religions" into her kingdom of love, and believed that even a false belief was better than none at all, and to be respected with equal reverence with a belief in the saving death of the Lord Jesus Christ. She had hitherto shut out what she chose to call fanatics from this broad inclusiveness, but now she began to see that even a "fanatic" might be allowed to come inside the pale if he was sincere, as "Grandma" Macdonald seemed to be. But to her credit be it said that she had no idea whatever what a trial she had been to that same sweet saint.

And through it all Marget was led to a place where she ceased to argue, ceased to protest, just held her peace. Sometimes she even prayed for Hesba at their evening worship together, bringing her so tenderly to the mercy seat that Hesba would rise with tears in her eyes. Once she stood a moment afterwards brushing away a tear, and then said in her blunt way: "I'm sure I thank you, Grandma."

Marget felt a thrill of something like pleasure at that, a kind of love for the girl's soul, even though she had not yet got to the point she could enjoy being in her company.

The day came when Tasha Endicott finished her play in Florida and came home for the tail end of the season in the city.

It was Hesba who first discovered and announced the fact. In fact all winter, if there was any particular thing that Marget would have liked to be silent and a bit private about, Hesba always managed to hale it forth and make much of it.

Hesba had gone out Sunday morning and purchased a Sunday paper the first Lord's day she was in Stonington; and because she found that a Sunday paper had not been approved at the cottage where she was staying, she considered it her God-given duty to purchase one quite ostentatiously every Sunday thereafter. It had been one of the many trials that Marget had submitted to, because she felt that she had no right to impose her conscience on another.

So this Sabbath Hesba had taken her usual Sabbath morning walk to the news stand and come home with the fat flaring sheet tucked under her arm. She sat down in the parlor to read as it was not yet time for church going, and she seldom favored Marget's church when she went, but took a train to the city to attend some noted speaker, or some gathering of a queer cult which she said she attended for "experience" whatever that was.

So Hesba read her paper.

Suddenly she turned a page and gave an exclamation:

"Mercy! That must be your friend, Grandma! Yes, it is, the very same one. Look at the picture. It's got the same string of pearls around her neck, and the very same dress, although it's not the same pose. The face is more profile. But it isn't the same name. Look, Grandma, isn't that queer!"

With a sense of portending disaster Marget looked up at the paper that was being held for her inspection, and there, sure enough was the little lassie's picture, right in the midst of the society column.

"It doesn't say the same name, that's on the picture," exclaimed Hesba gain, excitedly, as if she would draw some information from her silent hostess. "It calls her Tasha! Mercy! What a queer name.

That's worse than the other. Perhaps it's her younger sister, but I'm dead certain that's her picture. See! The nose is the same too, and that flower on the shoulder of her dress. Listen! 'Mrs. Endicott and Miss Endicott have returned from Palm Beach where they have been spending the last three months in their new villa, and have opened their home on Waverly Drive where they will be until after Easter, when they are planning to sail to Europe for the summer!' Mercy! Think of that! What's the use of having a home if you don't stay in it? I think that's wasteful. Even if you are a multimillionaire, that's wasteful! Don't you think so, Grandma?"

But Marget did not answer. She was trying to keep her thoughts steady, and her heart from excitement. So, the little lassie was back once more, and there would be the matter of the little gold shoe all over again! Thurly was away— She was both glad and sorry that Thurly was away. The matter of the shoe would devolve upon her and what should she do about it? Would she have to go to the grand home herself and take the little shoe? She shrank inexpressibly from such an experience. And there would be the great lady Mrs. Endicott that the paper spoke about. That creature that the girl had called Lucia, who had been divorced so many times and married again, or was that the husband? She could not remember, but she did not want to meet her. Oh, she did not want the peace of her heart broken up again by the nearness of that girl. That lovely worldly girl. She could not help loving her, but of course they had no part with her. She was of another universe, the pretty lassie!

So Marget was paying little heed to Hesba's questions until she asked a second time.

"Don't you feel that is awfully silly, Grandma, having all those homes? I call them snobs, don't you?"

Then Marget looked up and smiled mysteriously.

"Not just snobs," she said. "She's been in this simple little hoose, and partaken of oor plain food, and sung songs thegither with Thurly and me, and she's been a parfect little lady. She's oor friend, Hesba, and I'd rather ye didn't ca' her names. You don't know her, that's a'! And now my dear, it's full time I was getting my bonnet on for church. Will you go with me the day?"

So Hesba was silenced for the time. But Hesba was never silenced for long.

It was only at dinner that same day that she looked up from the excellent dinner she was eating and asked:

"How did she come to leave that gold slipper here with all those jewels in the buckle? You never told me."

"No?" said Marget with rising inflection. "Weel, there was nothing to tell. She juist left it. That was a'."

"But didn't she miss it? Didn't she write for it? Didn't she even know she had lost it?"

"Oh, yes, she knew she had lost it. She said however it didn't matter. She has plenty of shoes. She didn't seem to worry about it, and of course, noo she's hame she'll get it again!"

Hesba eyed Marget dissatisfied. She never was willing to leave the subject till she had poured it to the dregs, even though it might make a bitter crop for someone.

"Well, I think it was awfully queer, Thurly having it up on this shelf there. Did you know he had it? What did he say about it? What does he think?"

"Certainly I knew my son had it," answer Marget serenely, "I gave it him to put safe awa'. But what does he think? Why, what shud he think? I doobt if he ever remembers the wee bit shoe at a'. Will you have anither bit of the lamb, Hesba?"

But the very next afternoon Tasha came to call regally garbed in velvet and ermine, driving her little extravagant car, with a light of real gladness in her eyes as if she enjoyed coming.

Marget took her in her arms, and kissed the soft cheek, that was free from make-up for the occasion, or was it so subtly put on as not to show to her untaught eyes? At least she looked fresh and wholesome to Marget who was glad to get the lovely lassie in her house again, looking even lovelier than she remembered her.

Tasha was childishly happy to be in the cottage again, and moved around touching things, saying, "There is the hymn book we sang from! And oh, I have heard several of those hymns since! I've been going to church. Did you know I went to church in a queer little chapel down in Florida? And they said some of the same things you did."

She stood before her own portrait seeming pleased that Marget had cared to set it up, for she could not have failed to see how it crowned and dominated everything else in the room.

She fluttered over and sat down beside Marget on the couch with the old book of college photographs in her hand and turned the pages as she talked, lingering, Marget noticed, over some of the groups of football laddies where Thurly stood in the midst as their captain.

They did not speak of Thurly, not directly, yet. They talked of the winter, how cold it had been in the North, how lovely and summer like in the South. Tasha told of her winter sketchily, not much more than she had written, till she came to the tale of the old woman in prayer meeting, and her subsequent interest in the little sick grandson who had to have an operation. Tasha told of her visits to the child; how she had enjoyed taking him toys, picture books, flowers, how he was getting well now and beginning to walk like any little boy. Marget caught her soft little hand and held it, watched the color come and go in the pretty cheeks and the light in the stormy young eyes, and wondered.

Then, suddenly when they had only begun to speak of Thurly, and Tasha had put her hand out to rest on his violin case which stood behind the couch in the corner, in walked Hesba!

The light went out blankly in Tasha's face, and her chin went up haughtily. She gave one look at Marget, and then back at the girl again, questioningly.

Hesba looked at Tasha too, but not as one taken unaware. One never took Hesba unaware. She was always prepared for everything under the sun, and quite equal to any occasion.

"Oh,!" said Hesba, cooly walking up to the visitor, "you're Anastasia, aren't you? I've wanted to meet you to see if you looked like your pictures. You do, only you're better looking of course. You really are. I wouldn't have believed it, for they generally are not. How's Florida?"

Tasha rose, with that little tilt of chin that gave insensibly the touch of hauteur and breeding. She looked at Hesba, and then at Marget questioningly, then back to Hesba.

Marget rose quickly but Hesba burst in before she could speak.

"Oh, I'm Hesba Hamilton. You must have heard of me if you're such a friend of Grandma and Thurly. I came on to take care of Grandma while Thurly's in Chicago teaching this winter. I'm attending training school in the city, getting ready to be a social service worker or missionary or something. My school will be over pretty soon, but I intend to stay a while after Thurly gets back and have a little fun when he can run around with me. I've been doing some pretty stiff studying all winter and need relaxation to keep fit. I'm glad you've come back. I hope we see a good deal of each other."

Tasha surveyed the other girl and froze visibly. So this was the kind of girl Thurly liked to run around with! She looked her keenly through, managed a haughty smile and turned back to Marget who read the occurrence like an open book, and flew into a panic, though preserving an outward calm. She essayed to explain.

"Miss Hamilton came verra kindly in her aunt's place. Her aunt was an old neibor of years back in Scootland, and my son would na leave me alane, so he telephoned Martha who promised to coome, but the verra night before—"

Just here Hesba broke in eagerly.

"The night before she was to start she fell downstairs and broke her leg. So of course I had to come. It was all in the family you know!" and by this last sentence Hesba wiped out all possibility of Marget's delicate explanation getting across and put herself in the foreground again as an intimate of the Macdonald family. Marget looked at her guest with distressed but mute appeal and apology in her eyes, but Tasha was again looking coldly at Hesba and did not see it.

Hesba was by no means mute however. She always rushed in where the proverbial angels feared.

"You came after your gold slipper, didn't you? she offered affably. "Well, it's here all right. I haven't let any burglars get in since I've been here."

Tasha's gaze grew colder.

"My slipper?" She glanced at Marget in a half surprise, saw the

rising crimson in her cheeks, and turned sweetly back to Hesba with
scarce a second's hesitation.

"Oh, yes, my slipper. I had forgotten about its being here. Of
course. No, I did not come for the slipper. I came to see my friend.
But now I think I must be going at once. It is getting late and I have
one or two other stops to make."

"Oh, but aren't you going to stay to supper!" cried Hesba with a
determined note in her voice. "Of course you are. You sit here and
talk to Grandma while I put supper on!"

"Thank you, no, it is impossible!" said Tasha, the words like icicles.
Tasha took Marget's warm little trembling hand for farewell, and
Marget murmured a little plea in a low tone, "I'd love to have you
stay."

"I know, dear, some other time," said Tasha. "Some time when
you're all alone and need me," she added in almost a whisper."

Hesba standing jealously on the outside, studying the cut of the
Endicott garments, hurriedly, avidly, perceived that the visitor was
really going, and going too, without the golden shoe.

"Oh, you mustn't forget your slipper!" she exclaimed, as Tasha
moved swiftly toward the door, "I'll run right up and get it. Where is
it, Grandma? Did you put it back on Thurly's closet shelf? Because
if you did you'll have to tell me where to find the key. You locked the
door you know."

"Sit down, Hesba, I will get the shoe," said Marget, her voice
rising severely above her excitement with the old Scotch dominant
note.

But Tasha put up a protesting hand.

"Please don't dear," she said, "I'll get it another time. I must
hurry now. I promised to meet a train and I'm late. It really is of no
consequence at all. Good bye, dear little Mrs. Macdonald," and
Tasha caught Marget in a sudden quick hug and kissed her soft
wrinkled cheek. Then she was gone, the door shut behind her, and
Marget and Hesba were left alone, two vexed, disappointed women.

"It would be better," said Marget when she had got control of herself, and could keep the angry tremble out of her voice, "if you would
let people manage their own affairs!"

"Why, Grandma, what did I do? I'm sure I was only trying to be polite to your guest," and her voice was aggrieved.

"If your own inner sense of the fitness of things does na teach you, I'm afraid I canna explain," said Marget with dignity, and went out to her kitchen and her neglected dinner, her heart sore with the sudden termination of the pleasant call, yet warm with the thought of Tasha's kiss.

"The wee lassie!" she said, winking the mist from her eyes at the remembrance. "The wee bonnie birdie!"

Hesba stalked up to her room, but came down at the tinkle of the supper bell with a self-righteous silence upon her that made the meal anything but a pleasant one, but Marget's thoughts were in a tumult and it did not matter. She was trying to think if there was anything she could to eradicate the impressions made on the caller that afternoon, and her cheeks burned with mortification as she realized what a position her Thurly had been placed in by the thoughtless words of Hesba. Or were those words so thoughtless after all? Sometimes she wondered if Hesba did not often have intention in some of the ill-timed things she said.

Marget went early to her room that night and after much deliberation wrote a short note in her stiff little cramped hand on queer thin foreign stationery she had brought with her from Scotland years ago.

"My Dear Miss Endicott:
    I so enjoyed your visit to-day, and was sad to have you leave so suddenly. I hope you will pardon what occurred. Miss Hamilton does not understand. I will explain more when I see you again, and I hope you will come to me soon. I am always alone in the mornings.
                    Very sincerely,
                    Marget Macdonald."

The only answer to this was another large box of flowers containing Tasha's card and the word "Sometime" written across the back. It arrived in the middle of the morning, and for once Marget had the pleasure of opening the box herself, and arranging her own flowers, although she was certain that Hesba would try to rearrange them when she came home. Hesba could take the poetry out of a bunch of flowers with less effort than anyone Marget had ever met.

Chapter 17

Thurly was coming home for Easter. A telegram had arrived telling her so, and Marget stood at the window and read it and wiped a tear of joy from her eyes. Even the presence of Hesba on the scene could not quite blot out her joy in his coming.

Thurly said that the returning professor was taking his own classes, so he would remain at home, and Marget's heart sang a paean as she went excitedly about her house putting it in fine array for her son's return.

During the morning she thought up a way to get rid of Hesba, at least she hoped she had. She would offer to pay Hesba's way home to visit her family for Easter vacation. Of course if Hesba insisted on returning to finish the spring term of her school she would pay her way back again, but there was a slight chance when she once got home that she might stay there. Anyhow, Marget would have a full week of time all alone with her boy, and get to understand everything before they were interrupted by Hesba's return, and who knew what might develop in a week?

But Hesba returned from school early that day, by reason of the illness of a professor, and clipped Marget's hopes in the bud.

"No, I don't care to go home at this time. Nobody expects me, and I hate to surprise people. Besides, I couldn't anyway. I've made two dates. I'm going to a symphony concert, and a lecture with one of the young men from my class, that will be Tuesday and Thursday evenings, and I may go to a social the class is planning, I'm not sure; that will be Friday. Thank you just the same, but I think I'll stay right along till school closes."

Marget's lips drooped with disappointment; but at least Hesba would be out of the way two evenings, and perhaps three. She was glad for that. Marget had not told Hesba that Thurly was coming. She had an innate feeling that if she did Hesba would remain in spite of her. Hesba's interest in Thurly had been most marked.

150

"I hope you won't mind being alone those evenings," went on Hesba, "and I may not come home even to dinner those days; he wants me to take dinner with him. I could try to get somebody to stay with you. Who was that boy you stay nights before I got here?" "That isn't at all necessary, Hesba. Besides, I may as well tell you, I'm—rather—expecting my son soon. He—might be here the day, or the morrow—!"

"Oh!" said Hesba with a sound of almost dismay, "if I had know that I wouldn't have made those dates. You see he's here away from his folks, and he's lonely—"

"Oh, that's all right, Hesba! It's bonnie fer you to be kind to him. And I wouldna have ye stay home for Thurly. He's naething to you, nor you tae him, and he wouldna expect it. In fact, we likit tae be alane thegither after the lang separation. Juist gae tae yer pleasure, and have a good time!"

But Hesba stood for a long time looking out the window, thinking that for once she had messed her plans.

Marget, with glad heart went about preparations in the kitchen, making pies, cake, biscuit, getting ready the things that her son best loved to eat, killing the fatted calf as it were, and did not notice the dismayed look on the face of the solemn-eyed girl behind the shell-rimmed glasses. Presently Hesba turned with a sigh and marched off upstairs to her room. Afterward that sigh came back and smote Marget's consciousness, and she tried to be kinder to Hesba at dinner that night, but apparently Hesba was the same matter of fact creature again that she always had been, and Marget put away the momentary anxiety on her account and let herself rejoice in anticipation.

The next morning after Hesba had gone to school Marget opened up Thurly's room and cleaned it from top to toe. But the little gold shoe remained in her own room locked safe in her treasure box, with the key on a ribbon around Marget's neck. It would be inevitable that Thurly must know the history of that shoe since he left, so there was no point in returning it to the care of Josephus. If Thurly had taken the shoe with him, Marget would not have felt that she could open the subject between them, but since he had not, since he had cared so little about it as to actually forget to speak to her about it, her heart felt free to do with it as she thought wise, and she felt that the long absence must have caused Thurly to forget the owner of the shoe as well as the little shoe itself, therefore she had naught to be worried about from that quarter. In truth, she had come to feel very differently about the girl, Anastasia, of late.

As she went about her work she was constantly thinking of her and of her visit cut so abruptly short by Hesba's ill-timed appearance. Once as she stood by the window, pausing in the polishing of a pane of glass, she looked off to the hills across the valley which were her constant delight, thinking what the lassie had told her of her winter's experience, and she to herself aloud, rejoicing that no one was nigh to hear her:

"Anastasia. Convalescent. I doobt na she's cooming back tae health, the bonnie little lamb! Anastasia. It's a bonnie name! I like it weel!"

So, when night came, Marget had the room all sweet and fine, ready for her laddie, and she locked the door and went down to prepare the evening meal with a great joy upon her. Sometime on the morrow Thurly had said he might arrive, or it might be the next morning. He had not been sure. But the air seemed full of song, and the sunshine sparkled precious gems to her glad eyes.

Thurly Macdonald had bought a car. It was not a perfectly new one, nor very grand in its way, but it was one of the better makes with a reputation for comfort, mileage, endurance and speed. He got it at a bargain from one of the professors who was going abroad and could not take it with him. And he was driving home to surprise his mother. For he meant that car to be a great comfort to his mother as well as to himself.

Thurly would not have been human if he had not dreamed dreams sometimes, and often as he drove along through the country that was practically new to his eyes, there would come to him the thought that sometime he might find another one who would go with him on these rides, along with his mother. Someone who loved to have his mother along, and who was altogether all the wonderful things that a man dreams his mate will be, before he has ever set eyes upon the girl he finally asks to be his wife.

But the thing that troubled Thurly's dreams, and made him feel almost guilty whenever he indulged in them, was the fact that the dream face and form of the girl who was to love him, and be all these wonderful things he hoped for, seemed always like just one girl—the little worldling whom he had brought in out of the terrible blizzard; who had left her little gold shoe in his heart, the feel of her little cold silken foot in his hand, and the weight of her slender figure on his shoulder as he bore her through the storm.

Now he had told himself more times than he could count that the girl he had taken home that night was no more all the things he wanted in a wife, than he was what she wanted in a husband. She was rich and haughty and proud—although she had had courtesy enough not to show it in his home. But she was a worldling! That one word told it all. She belonged to the world, the flesh and the devil as represented by her life of frivolity and pleasure. Her very errand in that storm had been to a Framstead dance, and Framstead dances were well known in the home neighborhood as being the very height of extravagance and license. Framstead! That told it all!

He belonged body and soul to the Lord of all the earth, but she did not even know that Lord. She had shown that plainly by her walk and conversation that day.

Yet how lovely she had been! What charm the world put upon the human form! Yes, and into the human spirit!

Oh, he had put her away, out of his thoughts! Many times he had put her away, yet she always came back to tantalize him. And though he recognized her as a temptation to take his thoughts away from his work, yet he thought he had conquered her. He thought that her pretty spirit had been exorcised. Put out of his heart forever. It had always been the utmost folly anyway! As if she would have ever looked at him, a poor young minister, whose calling she likely despised.

But there was one fear that had begun to possess him, and that was that though he had succeeded in putting the thought of her so far from him that he had not even remembered about the little gold shoe—not very often—he might perhaps never be able to get the vision of her out of his eyes enough to see any beauty in the right maiden when God should send her. And daily he prayed that her face and smile and the vision of her as he had seen her at different times, might be taken away from his thoughts so that he might recognize good in other girls, if they should come his way. For that a man should love one woman, some time in his life, cling to her, protect her, and make her the companion of his years, he firmly believed. It was a principle that his mother had taught him from his youth, and he had put it off until now, feeling that there was plenty of time, and that the right one would come some day.

These thoughts were with him more or less as he drove along at a flying pace toward home.

It was almost midnight when he reached a city less than a hundred miles from home. Common sense bade him stop and rest for the night and take the last lap of his journey in the early morning. Yet the sound of familiar names, and the sight of familiar roads had set him longing inexpressibly for home, and after a bite to eat he decided to push on. He knew his mother would not mind being waked to greet him. He knew his bed would be waiting, all turned down, and his things ready. He would go and surprise her!

It was between two and three in the morning that he came to a place within thirty miles of Stonington where two main highways crossed, there were lights, and voices and confusion; two cars overturned and a third badly smashed. There had been a drizzly rain all the evening and the roads were slippery as glass with the spring frost coming out of the ground, and the spring mud beginning to ooze.

Thurly came to a halt and looked out, his own lights bringing out the scene more clearly.

One man was lying across his path in a limp heap, another had been thrown in the ditch with his head badly cut. Two others were stumbling around as if half dazed, and the sound of a woman's scream mingled with oaths from one of the overturned cars. The road was covered with splintered glass, and the voices that cried out showed that most of the party were under the influence of liquor.

Thurly got out and threw his flash light on the different faces. He went first to the car that was overturned in the dark, and managed finally to get the door open and lift out the struggling, frightened inmates. They came forth cursing and weeping, young men in evening clothes, and girls in party dresses and rich furs. They fell upon him and besought him to do something about it, and some of them even blamed him for the accident. He was forced to shake them off for there was one more person in the car and he must go to the rescue. She had crept up to the opening when he turned back, and he pulled her out and set her on her feet.

"Are you hurt?" he asked gruffly, for he was filled with disgust. This was some more of the young generation engaged in having a good time, breaking the law to do it! He had little sympathy for them in the calamity that had overtaken them. They were all headed for destruction and did not seem to care.

But the girl that stood beside him shuddering did not answer, only put out her hand gropingly and touched his arm.

"Are you drunk too, like all the rest?" he said gruffly, and turned his flash upon her face that was white to the lips with a trickle of blood from the forehead down the cheek.

Then for an instant all the strength in his body seemed to be leaving him as he gazed on that face.

"*You?*"

He uttered the word like a cry of anguish.

For an instant he longed to turn and flee from the sight of her. Then he said it again, like a wail of something dying, "*You!*"

She choked in a sob, and tried to speak.

"Take me away, please, quick! Oh, take me away!" and she shrank suddenly toward him as he saw a dark young fellow lurching toward her.

"Tashshsesh! Where you? Live'n kicking! Here I am. Here's your Barry! Close call, Tashesh! Where—are—you?"

Thurly caught the girl in his arms and dashed by the drunken youth, pushing him toward the ditch to be rid of the outstretched hands which would have prevented him, and Barry toppled backward and sat down against the muddy bank off the roadside; but Thurly had Tasha safely shut inside his car.

He went back to the others, and did what he could to help. Several of the party were badly hurt and one was probably dead. But there was need of an ambulance and doctors at once so he left the party in charge of the soberest man and went back to his car, promising to send relief from the nearest town at once.

Tasha was crouched in the corner of the seat, white and still. He almost thought she had fainted, till he touched her and she opened her eyes.

"Are you hurt?" he asked sternly.

She shook her head.

He stepped on the gas and they shot out over the dark road. He did not speak, but gave his entire attention to driving. Only once he turned toward her again and said: "You are sure you are not hurt?"

"Just bruised a little on my arm," she said with a catch in her throat like a sob.

She could see his face stern and white in the dim shadows of the car, but he said no more till the lights of a town came in sight. Then he turned again to her, though he did not slow down his pace.

"Now, suppose you tell me just what happened. We'll keep you out of this thing if we can."

"Oh, don't mind me!" said the old Tasha tone of a good sport, as she caught her breath in another smothered sob.

Thurly longed to take her in his arms, and comfort her, but he held himself firmly in check. To have found her in such company! He had needed this. He was appallingly conscious that he had been thinking of her all the time underneath the surface of his mind. Even when he thought he had conquered the thought of her, she was there! And now this!

"What happened?" Thurly asked again sharply.

"We were coming down the highway pretty fast. We had skidded several times. I saw another car coming down the crossroads at top speed. It came too fast to know just what did happen, but they struck us and we overturned. I heard the brakes screaming and felt us skid and turn, and then the jar of the car behind hitting us. After that I don't remember anything but darkness and being smothered, till someone burst open the door and let the air in, and they took the people off from me."

"Were you all drunk?" asked Thurly sternly.

"I was not drunk," said Tasha speaking with a sweet sort of dignity. "I don't drink—any more!" she added.

"You go with people who do," said Thurly still sternly.

"What else can I do?" defended Tasha in a little gasp of indignation that was pitiful. "They are the people I know, the ones I was born and brought up with."

"You need to be born again," said Thurly in a voice still sharp like a surgeon cutting an open wound.

"I ww-w-wish I could!" sobbed Tasha, her face down in her hands.

"You can!" said Thurly. "It has been done. It is up to you," and suddenly he reached out one arm and drew her sharply, bringing his car to a standstill, tilting her chin and turning his flash light full in her face.

"You are hurt!" he said, "there is blood on your face!"

"It is only a scratch!" she gasped, trying to stop her falling tears, and shuddering into the haven of his arm to stop the trembling of her body. Little hard boiled Tasha Endicott, crying like a baby, and glad of arm to steady her!

"Poor child!" he said, and there was infinite tenderness suddenly in his voice, as he looked down at her.

Never in his life had Thurly Macdonald wanted to do anything so much as to gather that child close to his heart and kiss her lovely trembling lips, her sweet misty eyes, and comfort her.

But Thurly Macdonald was built of sterner stuff than most men, and he had the fear of God ever before him. He still knew that Tasha Endicott was not one that he should kiss, and he still could feel the strength of a Power higher than his own weak flesh.

For an instant he kept his strong arm supporting her, searching her face in the light of his flash to make sure she was right about not being hurt, then gently, he sat her back in her corner, and put his hand on the wheel.

"We must push on to the rescue!" he said tersely, and started the car once more.

Two or three minutes later they came into town, and found a

policeman.

Thurly did not speak to Tasha again until they had seen the chief of
police, with two doctors in his car, and an ambulance following hard
behind, start back to the scene of the accident, with another ambulance to follow in five minutes.

"Now," said Thurly, turning to Tasha, who white-faced in the
shadow of the car, "do you want to go back to your friends?"

"Oh, no!" said Tasha. "Must we? Ought We? He could feel she
was trembling at the thought.

"Not unless there is someone there for whom you—are responsible—someone you want to be with—"

"Oh, no! I have been frightened and disgusted all the evening! I
was afraid to come home with them, but I was afraid to remain where
we were. I did not know before I started that we were to go to that
roadhouse. They said we were going to a house party. Oh, could I
go home, or would it be—would it be running away?"

"I think not," said Thurly. "We have sent help enough for them
all, and in any case you could not do anything except identify each
one."

"Ned Norton can do that," said Tasha. "He was the one walking
round the road when we left. He never quite loses his head."

"Then I shall take you home. This thing is liable to get in all the
papers, and you might as well keep out of it if possible. I fancy there
are some pretty well known people in that bunch."

"Yes," said Tasha, "but I was a part of them all the evening, perhaps I ought to go back and stand by them. They are my set, and I
don't like turning yellow. Turn back, please. I guess I must!" she
said, and dropped her head back against the cushion of the car.

"You're not going back!" said Thurly sternly. "You're not fit. I
shall not let you. See," and he stepped on the gas, "you are being
carried away by someone who came along and picked you up. It is
not your fault. You are not able to go back, and you could do nothing
if you went. I am taking you home. Will anyone be up to receive you
and look after you?"

"Yes, I can call my maid," said Tasha, with thankfulness in her
tired voice.

Thurly spoke no more till he drew up in front of the Endicott mansion.

Tasha wondered how he knew where she lived, and hid that thought away in her heart for further meditation.

"Have you a key?" he asked gravely.

Tasha produced one.

Thurly helped her out and up the steps, unlocking the door for her. "Now, are you sure you will be all right?" he asked anxiously.

He took her hand and held it for just an instant, her little trembling hand, and looked down at her gravely.

"If you should ever need me for anything will you promise to let me know?" he said, and his eyes searched her face hungrily.

Tasha promised, and with a quick handclasp he turned away.

"Good night, now, I'm going back to see if there is anything more I can do for any of those folks."

And he was gone.

Chapter 18

It was still dark when Thurly arrived at the scene of the accident once more, though the East was beginning to show a faint light at the horizon. He found the chief of police still on the job, for it had been a heavy task to identify all the people of the three cars, and get them to their several homes or hospitals.

The police eyed Thurly suspiciously.

"You back?" he said with a frown.

"Yes, I had to take the lady home who was with me, but I thought perhaps there might be something I could do."

"Well, there is. Take that fella in the car there home. He ain't hurt, that is not bad, but he's bound he won't leave till he finds one of the ladies. He says she ran away from him. I ain't had men enough to send him off yet, but ef you can see him home I'll be obliged."

It was Barry Thurston who was reclining in his car, now righted upon it wheels, but badly smashed as to running gear; Barry heavy with sleep and liquor and stubborn as a mule.

Thurly and the Chief had to fairly carry him to the other machine. Thurly drove to the address he gave, when they could rouse him enough to speak at all. But once roused Thurly had all he could do to keep the drunken man from trying to seize the wheel and run the car, for he seemed to fancy that he was still in the midst of an accident which he must do something to avert. And whenever Thurly coaxed him back in the seat, and told him to sleep he would babble about Tasha. It filled Thurly with indignation to think of the frail young girl in such company, for he learned from the drunken babblings that this was the man who had been Tasha's escort for the evening. So this was the life she had been born to! This was the kind of company she had been in the habit of keeping! His heart sank. All that he had feared about her was true and yet more. Had the Lord brought him through this evening's experience to show him once and for all how far she was out of the way, and how utterly she was unfit for a

160

companion to one who had chosen the way of the Kingdom?

Before he had Barry Thurston back to his apartment, and in the hands of his valet, he was heart sick and dog weary. It seemed to him that the world was too wicked a place to stand any longer. How did the Lord bear with me all the wickedness that must come up before Him?

The day was dawning when he at last came out to his car, free to go home. But how could he go to his mother at this hour without explaining all that he had been through in the night? It would only distress her. Also half the pleasure in taking the new car home had been to see the light in her eyes when she looked from the window and saw it standing there in front of the door, her car come home to take her riding. This was no hour to appear, anyway. He would just drive to some hotel and get a snatch of sleep before he went on to Stonington.

And so, too weary to care what he did, Thurly stopped at the first hotel he came to and went to bed.

It was broad day when he awoke, and his senses were so benumbed with sleep that it took some minutes to know where he was and what had happened, but when he came fully to himself he found that it was nearly eleven o'clock.

He dressed hastily and hurried down to his car, not even waiting for a cup of coffee. He wanted to get home, into the atmosphere that was safe and sweet and sane, with his mother's eyes, and his mother's smile, and her tender love about him. His spirit felt all bruised and bleeding.

He would have liked to call on Tasha and see if she was all right, but he felt she might still be sleeping, so he drove straight home.

Hesba had been away to her school for two or three hours when he drove up to the door of the cottage, and Marget, hovering all the morning between her work and one window or another, sighted the car at once and shaded her eyes with her hand to look.

Ah! Yes, that was her Thurly getting out of the car! What a blessing that he came while Hesba was away and she might have him all to herself for the greetings without having Hesba intrude upon every word they spoke. Marget had carefully refrained from saying much in her letters about her young companion beyond the mere fact of her presence, and that she went to a training school that Thurly wouldn't approve. But Thurly gathered much between the lines, and Thurly knew his little mother well. Ah! Thurly understood what a sore trial that young presence had been to his mother all winter, and he too was glad that they might be alone for their greeting.

So Thurly took his mother in his arms as if she had been a child, and she laid her cheek against his. The comfort and the healing of each other's love went through them both, just as it had done when Thurly was a little child, and the mother had been the strong one to lift and comfort and protect.

And then, before he told her anything, he had to wrap her in a shawl and take her out to see the car.

She exclaimed in wonder.

"And is it really your ain, laddie? Now what do you think of that! Thurly Macdonald with a real chariot! Isn't it beautiful! Every line of it! I couldn't have dreamed a better if I had been choosing from the world of cars!" Marget could not say enough. And then he had to put her in the soft cushioned seat and drive her around the block. "But are ye shure ye know how to drive her, Thurly lad? There's ower mony accidents these days. I read them in the paper. There was one bad one last evening, with a man killed and a lot of silly young folk hurt. I mind ye was always a bit venturesome, laddie; ye must have a care."

"I'll have a care, Mother dear," laughed Thurly, "never fear. I've driven all the way home from Chicago, and I can surely drive you round the block."

But when they came back from the brief ride and Marget discovered that her lad had had no breakfast, she would have no more words until she had put his lunch upon the table, and then they sat together, and drank in the joy of each other's presence, talking of bits of this and that, too eager and excited to tell at once about any one thing.

It was after lunch things had been cleared away, and Thurly had put the food in the refrigerator for her, wiped the two cups, two plates, and the silver as she washed them, and they had walked together into the little parlor and sat down upon the old couch side by side. It was not until then that Thurly saw Tasha's picture on the mantel.

Marget had thought to put it away, perhaps, before he came, yet for fear of Hesba's sharp eyes and Hesba's sharp tongue she had forborne. And there smiled Tasha, true to life, with the little string of pearls about her throat, and the little crushed rose on her shoulder.

But when Marget saw the look in her boy's eyes, those eyes she had watched from his babyhood, her heart stood still in a kind of happy consternation, and she wondered whether she had done well or ill to leave the picture out.

"How did that come here, Mother?" he asked, a sound almost of awe in his voice. Rising he went and stood where he could look at it the better.

"She sent it herself from Florida," answered the mother proudly, "and see what's she writ beneath. She's a bonnie wee thing! Thurly, I'm thinking you'll have to be taking the little gold boot into town again, now, for she's back at her home."

"And how did you know she was back in the North again, Mother?" asked the son with a twinkly smile, "have you been up to your old capers, reading the society notes in the papers again?"

"Na, laddie, I had a far better w'y of knowing this time, not but what 'twas in the papers too; but she came her own bonnie self to call."

"Here!" said Thurly startled, looking around as if somehow he expected to see some lingering radiance from her presence.

"Yes," said Marget, watching her boy yearningly, scarce understanding her own feelings.

Thurly looked about the room and back again to the picture struggling to get his thoughts arranged. Suddenly he faced his mother with a quick question:

"Then why didn't you give her the shoe, Mother? Why do you say I must take it to her?"

"Ah!" said Marget, "see I must tell it ye. But it's a lang tale, and I'm sair worried ye'll be vexed. "'Twas a the fau't of that huzzy Hesba. Ye'll mind I've not said mooch aboot her in the letters—"

"You don't have to say much, Mother," laughed Thurly suddenly as if somehow he was glad about something. "I've formed my opinion of the lady already so don't be troubled. Speak out your mind and let's get the tale over with. Come sit down, Mother, and tell it out from beginning to end. What did the huzzy do?"

"Mercy!" said a voice in the dining-room doorway, "has he come already? Now isn't that just like a man to turn up when you didn't expect him? Introduce me, can't you, Grandma? We can't stand long on ceremony in a family you know, and Thurly and I know each other pretty well already, I imagine."

Marget sat frozen with dismay, her sweet face actually white with disappointment. Now what was Hesba doing home at this hour, and how did she manage to get in without being heard? Also, how much had she heard? Now Hesba carried the key to the side door, that entered the dining room, and came in the same way she did when Tasha had called.

Thurly, annoyed to be interrupted, but courteous as ever, and conscious that some of his last words might have been overhead, rose to the occasion.

"Miss Hamilton, I presume," he said bowing distantly. "I'm sure we're indebted to you for your willingness to cheer my mother's loneliness. It's been most kind of you to remain away from your home so willingly, so long. But I'm sure you'll be glad to know that I'm home to stay now for a while, and you can have your freedom as soon as you like."

"Oh, it hasn't been a bit of trouble," smiled Hesba, "I feel that it was quite an opportunity to get a new point of view from another training school, but please call me Hesba, won't you? I have been calling you Thurly all winter."

"Have you indeed!" said Thurly, and gave the young woman a good square look with a twinkle of amusement in his eyes. His mother saw the twinkle and took heart of hope.

"Yes, and you're not rid of me yet, either," laughed Hesba gaily. "My school doesn't close for sometime, and after that I've arranged to stay for at least another week and play around with you. I haven't really had time to see the sights of your city yet. And you know it's no fun to see them alone."

"Indeed!" said Thurly with lifted brows, looking the young woman over with rising amusement. "Well, I shall be rather busy myself I'm afraid, and later even more than I am now, but if you and Mother want to go anywhere in particular that would not be safe for you to go alone, why I shall be glad to arrange to accompany you sometime when I can spare an hour. I'm not just fond of romping much myself, but perhaps you and Mother might play around a little."

Hesba stared at him with her round, shell-rimmed eyes that would have been pretty if they had not been so presumptuous, and then laughed at what she perceived must have been meant for a joke.

"Oh, you're clever!" she said. "You didn't tell me he was clever, Grandma!"

"Grandma?" said Thurly, and gave his mother a quick questioning look. "I should think aunt would be more appropriate if you must have some title. Well, Lady Mother," he said turning toward Marget, "shall we go now? Get your coat and bonnet and I'll be waiting outside for you, Mother o' Mine. Better put something warm on, the sun is beginning to go down and there's a chill in the air. You'll excuse us, Miss Hamilton, my mother and I have an errand out—"

Marget turned amazed eyes to her son's face, but got to her feet and went for her wraps. Nobody noticed that the countenance of Hesba Hamilton lost several degrees of confidence as she watched them climb into the car and drive away.

"Now, Thurly, my son, was that quite the square thing?"

"Why not?" grinned Thurly.

"We haven't really an errand, my son," reproved Marget anxiously.

"Oh, yes, we have, Mother Mine. We're going to buy—what shall we buy? I know, a yeast cake for you to make old-fashioned buckwheats for breakfast in the morning. I haven't had a buckwheat since I left. Now out with your story, Mother, for we'll not go back till it's finished."

"But I'm sair troubled, laddie, that I oughtn't to tell it at all," said Marget. "It's sure to vex you one way or the ither."

"Well, I'm vexed now, Mother, so go ahead. She's a huzzy all right, I can see that at first glance, and needs a good taking down. Leave her to me, Mother and don't worry any more."

"But, laddie, you mustn't be hurting her feelings. I'm sure she has them somewhere, and I'm not doubting that she meant to be kind."

"All right, Mother, but now for the tale. I'm growing impatient, and I'll just stop the car till you begin."

So, laughing she told her tale in her own quaint way, till Thurly saw the picture of the girl as she came to call, in her velvet and ermines, saw the tint of her cheek, and the glow of her eye, through his mother's quaintly chosen words.

But his face grew grave as he heard how Hesba entered, and fetched the little gold shoe right into the conversation.

"But how did she know about the shoe, Mother?" queried Thurly amazed. "You surely never told her!"

"No, son, I did na tell her onything. You do not need to tell her, she was uncanny w'ys wie her. So lad, I'll have to tell ye the *whole* story. And here's where ye were to blame, Thurly, by not taking heed to the wee bit slipper before ye left and teeling me wher it was hid."

So she told of Hesba's change of rooms, and how she found the slipper and brought it to the front. Thurly listened, his brow in a frown.

"You're right, Mother, she *is* a huzzy," he said at last when the story was finished. "And you needn't excuse her by saying she's stupid for she's not. She thinks, Mother, that it is smart to bring things out in the open like that and put people to shame. Well, now that's bad, isn't it, Mother? The little lady thinks you've told everything to the other girl. She probably thinks this Hesba's an intimate of the family. And what does she think of me, hiding her shoe in my room? That's bad!"

Thurly was still for several seconds, his brow drawn in thought, and his mother watching him anxiously. At last he turned with a laugh.

"Well, it can't be helped this time, little Mother, we'll just have to make the best of it. The right will come out somehow in the end I guess. And now, I suppose we'll have to get our yeast cake and go home to dinner, won't we? We're a good thirty miles away and it's getting dark."

"Thirty miles!" marveled Marget. "Just think of it!" but here was a great relief in her voice that Thurly was taking the annoyance this way. Somehow the burden was only half as heavy now that Thurly shared it with her. Surely he was right and there would be a straightening out of the thing. Hesba would not be allowed to put them to shame this way.

Hesba came down to dinner vivaciously. The grace was scarcely said before she burst forth eagerly:

"I forgot to tell you the news about your friend this afternoon," she said, "it's terribly exciting, but then I thought all along she'd be that kind of a girl. Your Tasha Endicott has been caught in an awful round up. There was a double smash-up, they say, last evening; a lot of society folks out joy-riding, and all of them gloriously drunk. They killed a man who was driving along slowly, and trying to keep out of their way, and then they all got broken arms and legs and heads and everything. I say it was a good lesson for them! They ought to get all killed off and then perhaps the world would be safe for the rest of us." She finished with a little excited laugh.

Marget looked up with her eyes full of horror, and her face white. She kept on pouring cream till it ran over into the saucer and she never knew it. She turned her frightened glance toward Thurly.

But Thurly did not seem to be so upset as she expected. He was looking sternly, it is true, at the narrator, and with a kind of amused contempt in his expression.

"Where di you hear that, Miss Hamilton? It was not in the papers." His voice was quite calm. "And how did you happen to connect a tale like that with our Miss Endicott?"

"Why, I heard it at school this morning. There's a young man studying there who has a job at the apartment house where this Tasha Endicott's fiancé lives. Thurston, his name is, Barry Thurston, and he didn't get in till almost daylight, and was all lit up. He said it was awful the way he was going on about Tasha Endicott. She must have been pretty well stewed herself, from all accounts. Say, I wish you'd remember to call me Hesba, Thurly. It sounds more friendly."

"It is a pity that any young person who is studying to make something of himself, should lend his influence to create gossip like that!" said Thurly severely. "Because you see as far as Miss Endicott is concerned the story is not true at all. She was not drunk last evening. I happen to be in a position to prove that, for I spent several hours in her company, and she was quite sane and sober. In fact I happen to know that she does not drink."

"Oh!" breathed Marget in a soft little breath, and a flood of relief came into her face as she turned amazed eyes to her son's face. It was just then that she discovered the cream running over her thumb, and had all she could do to keep it from going on the cloth.

"Oh!" exclaimed Hesba, the wind suddenly gone out of her sails. "Mercy! How on earth could you have been with her last night? I thought you didn't get home till late this morning."

"I had business in the city last night that detained me," Thurly answered coldly. "You'll oblige me by contradicting any such talk about Miss Endicott that you may happen to hear in the future. She is not that kind of girl. And the young man had better be informed that it is rather dangerous to spread such stories unless he had accurate information, which he evidently did not have. What news do you hear from your aunt, Mrs. Robertson? Is she able to walk at all yet? Has the bone knit satisfactorily?"

Hesba was most thoroughly squelched for once and retired into an amazing silence, leaving the conversation unbelievably in the hands of Marget and her son.

After Hesba had withdrawn to her room to study, Marget's eyes sought her son's face with a question written large, which she would not utter.

Thurly smiled.

"It's all right Mother Mine, you needn't worry. What I said was true. But we better not discuss it tonight. Even the walls have ears at times. I think I'll take that shoe back to-morrow and break the spell that seems to have come over this house."

"I would, laddie," smiled Marget, and was content.

But up in her room Hesba was doing some hard thinking, and before she slept she came to a great resolve, and sat down and wrote a letter which she mailed in the city the next morning on her way to school. The letter reached its destination about noon.

Chapter 19

Thurly took his mother to market next morning and while she was selecting meat he made occasion to telephone from the drug store to Tasha. He hoped to make an appointment to see her if possible that afternoon.

But Tasha, it appeared, was occupied at that moment and could not come to the telephone.

"Is she—well?" asked Thurly anxiously.

"So far as I know, she is," replied the voice of the servant.

"Will you say to her that Mr. Macdonald will call this afternoon if convenient?"

"I will, sir. Good bye, sir," and the man hung up before Thurly realized that he had not made the servant understand that he wanted to know whether Tasha would see him or not.

"Dumb!" said Thurly to himself as he hung up the received, "dumb, that's what I am. Now why do I have to get things all balled up just because I know that the man at the other end of the telephone wears a livery and would probably despise me if he knew I wore a thread-bare overcoat?"

At first Thurly was inclined to call the number again and make his wishes clear. Then he decided that he would let it go. It would be a good way to find out whether Tasha wanted to see him or not.

Marget, when she came out to the car, wondered why Thurly seemed a bit absent-minded, but she said nothing about it, and he was presently smiling and joking like his old self.

As he helped her out of the car at home he said gravely:

"Mother, if you'll get that slipper ready for me to take I think I'll drive in this afternoon and get it off my mind. I'm going over to arrange about a garage now, and I'll be back in half an hour. Will that be all right for lunch?"

She assured him it would and went happily upstairs to pack the little shoe for another trip to its owner. Somehow she felt strangely elated by what Thurly had said about the little lady last night at supper. She had been looking all the morning for him to explain it but he hadn't said a word, and she felt it better to wait for him to speak. He would likely tell her all about it when he got back from his call, and she remembered that this was the evening of Hesba's symphony concert. She would not be coming home. They could have the evening to themselves!

So Thurly had his lunch and went his way with the little slipper in a white, new, shiny box that Marget had hunted up. In due time Thurly's car drew up in front of the Endicott mansion and Thurly went up to the door with a feeling that somehow this was to be a momentous call. He was gravely happy over it, and not in the least overawed this time by the grand house and the men in livery, for he had something better to think about.

But when the door opened Thurly was met by the announcement that Miss Endicott had left town.

Left town!

Thurly looked blandly at the man as if he could not have spoken the truth.

"When did she go?" he asked crisply, feeling somehow that there must be a mistake.

"Only about an hour ago, sir," answered the man eyeing the caller disparagingly, his glance lingering for just the fraction of a second on the worn place in the young man's overcoat cuff. None but a trained eye would have noticed it, and Thurly himself was not even aware of it, but he felt the glance and it made him impatient. He was not to be put off. This was not the same servant who had opened the door at his last call.

"Did she leave a message for me?" asked Thurly, hope springing anew. "My name is Macdonald."

"Not that I know of, sir," said the servant looking into Thurly's keen brown eyes and feeling an added respect. "I'll go and see, sir. Just step in, sir."

Thurly sitting impatient in the same chair he had taken on his last visit looked about him on the garish luxury but it did not impress him as it had done before. There was more cheer in his mother's little cottage than in those lofty rooms filled with the treasures of Europe and the richness of the orient.

The servant came back to report that no message had been left.

"Did you give her my message when I telephoned this morning?" asked Thurly looking at the man sharply.

"I wasn't on duty this morning in the house, sir," answered the man. "I was out on an errand for Mrs. Endicott. I'll ask, sir."

But he was back in a moment to say that the servant who had answered the telephone was out at present and no one else knew anything about a telephone message. Neither could the man tell him when the young lady was expecting to return.

Thurly went disappointedly back to his car, the little shoe still in his hand. Not that he forgot it this time; but he had decided that having waited so long to return it, he would keep it as his excuse for coming again and making certain explanations which he felt he owed to his self-respect, on account of Hesba's rudeness.

So he drove back home again, with the little gold shoe snugged close beside him on the seat. When it came right down to it he would not care to surrender that little shoe to anyone else but its owner.

The letter that Hesba wrote reached Tasha about half past eleven that morning, a few minutes before Thurly telephoned, and read as follows:

"Dear Anastasia:
    You did not tell me I might call you that, but I like to be informal, and I hope you won't mind.
    I'm going to be married, and I'm telling you first for a very special reason, because I'm going to ask you to be my maid of honor. I hope you'll be willing, for I've set my heart upon it. You're the prettiest girl I know, besides a favorite of the family. None of my friends from home will be here at the time, so I wanted somebody that sort of belonged. Of course since you're such a good friend of Thurly's it seems about as if you were a relative already, so I thought even if you were very busy you'd be willing to put something off to help me out; for of course

it means a lot to me to have someone like you at my wedding, right in it, a part of it. I'm not very good looking myself, I know, and I've always thought it didn't matter much, but here just lately, I've begun to find out that beauty matters a lot to some people, so I thought I'd like to have someone who was really beautiful to take the attention off me. Of course, there won't be many there, only the family, and I'm not wearing orange blossoms and all the fol de rols, it wouldn't suit me. So if you just wear the dress you had on when you came out to see Grandma it'll be all right and not make you any trouble, unless it's too warm for that and you've got something else you'd rather wear.

You see, I'm writing you first, because I haven't even told the groom yet, what day I've set. I wanted to make it sure you could come before I said a thing to him, men get so set, you know. If you'll please let me know by return mail whether you are willing to serve, I'd like to tell them as soon as possible now. And I know Thurly and Grandma are going to be awfully pleased if you say yes, for I've discovered they think a lot of you and then some.

So, if it's agreeable to you, I'll set the date for Wednesday two weeks from to-day at noon. Then we'll have a wedding breakfast and everybody can get back to whatever they have to do without losing time. Of course if that isn't convenient for you I can make it either the day before, or the day after, but if it's all the same to you Wednesday would suit me better.

Hoping you'll answer right away when you get this,

Affectionately,
Hesba Hamilton."

Tasha read this letter whit a strange mingling of feelings, a mild amusement at the audacity of the request, and the frankness of the flattery, passed quickly into bewilderment and consternation. Could it be then, that it was really true that that splendid young man was going to marry a girl like this?

And suddenly she realized that she had grown to consider Thurly a splendid young man. She thought back quickly over her brief acquaintance and tried to reconcile everything she knew about him, with the fact of his engagement to this girl, rude and crude, and illbred. There was nothing of that in Thurly Macdonald. Yet of course she had known him so little, and there had been the glamour of his having saved her twice from terrible situations. She drew a deep sigh of disgust, and the world somehow looked blanker than ever to her.

When she had read the letter over the second time and perceived that it was something she must answer at once unless she wished to practically affront two people who had been most kind and lovely to her, she roused to think up an excuse.

It was just at that moment that Thurly called her on the telephone. When she heard the name of Macdonald she was positively snappish in the way she refused to answer the call. Here then, was the bridegroom, probably having discovered what his fiancee had done, and come to urge his plea that she would function at his wedding! She turned hard at the thought. It seemed to her she wanted never to hear the name of Macdonald again. The romance and joy had been torn from the memory of them by their connection with that girl. Even the holy memory of that Sabbath day was blotted out in the thought that henceforth Hesba Hamilton was to share in all that pertained to these two people. She could not quite understand why she disliked that girl so. Was it the fact of her being so forward, so intimate, even before she had been introduced? Or was it that she had dared to bring out the fact that her lost slipper had been found and was hid in Thurly Macdonald's closet? It argued a coarseness about the soul of a woman who would fling intimate things into public view. Even if she were jealous at finding the shoe, even if she wanted to show the other woman that she knew all about her, there was not excuse for what she had done. The soul of Anastasia turned from her with disgust.

So Tasha refused to go to the telephone, and she sat down quickly and dashed off an answer which nipped all hope of grandeur at Hesba's wedding.

"My Dear Miss Hamilton," [she wrote],

"I regret that my engagements are such that it will be impossible for me to serve at your wedding as maid of honor. I am leaving the city to-day for New York, to meet my father, and take a trip with him. It may be weeks before my return. My arrangements are most uncertain.

Thanking you for the honor,

> Sincerely,
> A. Endicott."

Tasha's arrangements were indeed most uncertain. She knew that her father was in New York, and that he was on a business trip which also included a fishing trip in Canada. Whether she could wheedle him into taking her along on any part of the trip was a question. At least it was worth trying, and seemed the easiest way out of a situation for which she had no relish.

Marie had a bad hour and a half packing, and then Tasha was off, only telling her stepmother that she was going up to see her father for a few days in New York. Lucia made no protest. She had plans herself, and was in no wise anxious to have a disapproving daughter watching her every moment. She left the house herself soon after for her favorite hotel at the shore, and so when Thurly arrived the great mansion was peopled only by hired retainers. Of course Tasha had left no message for him, because the man who answered the telephone had not thought fit to brave his young mistress' wrath to deliver it. If the gentleman came before she left, he would come, and what was to happen would happen. It was his afternoon off, and he would not have to worry about it. It was always easy enough to cast the blame on somebody else, even if he were discovered.

So, Tasha went on her way, and the little gold shoe remained at Stonington, with Marget as custodian.

To Marget Thurly said, when he handed it over with a wry smile: "I think we'll have to adopt that shoe. There seems to be something wrong with it. I don't understand it, because I telephoned I was coming. But they tell me she is out of town again and had left no message."

Marget held the little package carefully in her hands, as if it might break, and looked down on it, thoughtfully.

About that time, Tasha, still on the train, watching the lights spring up and flee, as the train drew nearer and nearer the great city, began to face a thought that had been trying to creep up through her consciousness all the afternoon. Was it possible that the whole reason why she hated that girl who was going to marry Thurly Macdonald was because she herself was growing to care for him? She, Tasha Endicott, who might have any one of a dozen multi-millionaires! Marry a poor minister! A religionist, a fanatic, who thought of everything in terms of heaven, and had naught in common with her world?

She swung her chair around to the window, stared into the deepening dusk, and felt the hot color mounting to her temples! She, Tasha, being caught like that, in a common little romance with a man who had never even thought of her; but was engaged all the time to a commonplace, illbred girl who wore basement bargain counter clothes, looked strong minded, and hauled everybody's faults out in the open!

Well, if that was the matter she would put an end to that quicker than it took to think. She would show the man that she had no thought of him. She would never speak to him again, nor write, nor call on his mother. She had done enough to pay for his paltry trip back from the station that stormy night. He would have done it as easily for a stray cat. He had not been looking for pay. She need have no further compunctions. His kindness the night of the smash up, well, that was no more than he would have done for anyone. It was a part of his creed to be kind. And he had been unmercifully severe with her, asking her if she were drunk too! How it had cut her, when she knew she had not tasted liquor for months all on account of what he might think! Well, she was foolish! She almost felt she would go back to it. Perhaps she would order cigarettes sent up to her room when she got to the hotel! She would cut out all this nonsense and go back to life as it had come to her. Why should she reach after things that did not belong in her world? Why should she follow the dictates of a theological bully?

She stormed on madly in her soul, longing for some revenge. But somehow, behind it all, was the dread of that vision of his eyes looking at her. Or was that exorcised by the wedding invitation? Well, time would tell. She would cut loose for a while from home and all that had to do with that night of the storm, and then perhaps when Thurly and that scream of a girl were well married, and it was all over, she would be able to look back on it and laugh. She would do as she pleased through the rest of her tiresome days till her life was spent, and blown out like a candle.

Then the train shot into the tunnel under the river, and it was time to draw her coat about her and gather her magazine and bag and get out.

Tasha found her father in his hotel. He seemed almost annoyed that she had come. He was unusually busy, too busy to show her a good time, he said, but of course she might stay in the hotel a few days till she knew where she wanted to go. Why didn't she go down to the shore with Lucia? Lucia always liked to go to the shore.

But Tasha wanted to go to Canada. She wanted to fish, and to tramp in the woods, and rough it.

Mr. Endicott did not know whether he was going to be able to get away to Canada or not. There were some queer things going on in the world of finance. He did not know how long they might hold him in New York. Besides, the men with whom he intended to go, if he got off at all, were not the kind of men who would care to have a girl of Tasha's type along—at least—and the father faced her frankly, they were not the type of men that he cared to have his daughter companion with, even when he was along.

Tasha opened her eyes wide with amusement and laughed, but her father was firm, and no amount of coaxing moved him.

So Tasha settled down to amuse herself in New York, with such scraps of his attention as he could give her. She slept late in the mornings, lunched at some favorite restaurant, walked in the park for a few minutes, spent a couple of hours shopping or reading in the Library, went back and dressed for dinner. Her father usually took her somewhere in the evening when he had not some other engagement, though he sometimes found a young man among his acquaintances who was glad to take his place.

But the days went by very slowly to Tasha, out of her usual ele-
ment, with only small portions of unsatisfactory points of contact
with her father and nothing in which she was especially interested.
The young men who called or invited her to some evening of gayety
bored her. They might have interested her if her mind had not been
full of an unnamed heaviness, but all things had begun to pall. She
seemed to be waiting for something to happen. And when she began
to analyze what it was, it narrowed down to Thurly Macdonald's
wedding. She was up here in New York being bored to death till
after Thurly Macdonald should have married Hesba Hamilton, *without* her for a maid of honor.

She went out one day and bought almost a whole bale of expensive
embroidered linen and sent it to Hesba as a wedding gift. Table
linen, bed linen, fancy linen, fine and heavy and lustrous, some of it
embroidered richly and inset with hand made lace. It was ridiculous,
it was unnecessary! But it eased something in her soul that yearned
for action. It soothed something that hurt her almost unbearably
when she thought of that linen on Thurly's table.

She reasoned with herself that it would excite comment in the
Macdonald family for her, a stranger, to do so much—that perhaps
they would be offended, in their simplicity. They would feel she
thought they could not provide their own household outfit. But then,
on the other hand of course, the honor of being asked to be part of the
bridal party demanded something out of the ordinary. Any anyhow,
Hesba would likely enjoy it. Why should she not do a little thing for
her even if she didn't like the girl Thurly was marrying. It would
likely be the last thing she could do for Thurly, anyway.

So the linen went on its way, and Tasha went on hers, and the days
dragged by, till one afternoon when a telegram came that drove all
other thoughts out of mind and made life take on an aspect horrible
and altogether new.

Chapter 20

Lucia Endicott had been secretly taking lessons in flying. Whenever her husband went away for a day or two she would slip away to the shore and fly. Oh, and there were plenty of chances when her husband was not away.

Lucia had ambition. Perhaps she cherished secretly a desire to be a lady Lindbergh of parts; or it may be she was quietly planning to slip away out of sight entirely and live a new life in a new place and fool the world out of its rightful share in her affairs.

Lucia went up in the air that afternoon with only Will Clancy along. Clancy was new at the game and known as a crazy flier. The flying instructor was away, and Lucia, with the help of cash, was able to wheedle a plane out of the hanger.

So Lucia flew, and the day was glorious!

That afternoon the papers came out with the story. Those who saw the accident said that the plane took a nose dive straight to earth. They could not even tell which had been the pilot. The man was killed, and the lady was dying! The medical attendants gave no hope! Some bystander on the field with a taste for tragedy told a reporter that the lady and the pilot had been quarreling before they went up. The telegram reached Tasha just as she was about to lie down to rest after a morning of shopping. She had purchased a lot of trifles that she didn't need, because she had nothing else to do. The lines were bald and heartless, and did not soften the awful news:

"Mrs. Endicott fatally injured in airplane wreck. She can live but a few hours. Come at once!"

The address was a hospital at the shore near the flying field.

Tasha read the words with growing horror, clasping her hand to her throat and trying to keep her senses from reeling.

Lucia! Dying! One could not think of Lucia dying. So that was

179

what Lucia had been doing on all those trips to the shore—Flying!

Tasha tried to think what to do. She dashed to the telephone and tried in vain to get her father. They told her at his Club that he was somewhere playing billiards but no one knew just where. She left a message for him, and dressed hastily, sobbing as she went about her room, dry hard sobs without tears. Sobs of fright and horror. Sobs of shrinking from what she knew she must do.

This was not her job, it was her father's. He ought to be here attending to everything. Lucia was his wife.

Tasha had never seen death. Lucia was not her mother, why did she have to go to her? She did not love her. She did not even like her. Yet she knew she was going to her.

She called up the office of the hotel and asked them to find out what train she could get, and send someone up for her bags. Between times she flew into some garments for the journey, scarcely able to that what was suitable. Then she tried the telephone again, frantically searching for her father. It was going to be terrible to go without Dad. Tasha had never had to do anything like this in her life before. Sickness and death, and horror had been shielded from her sight. Servants had attended to all details. She wondered why the telegram happened to come here to the hotel, and why it had not come to her father's name. Then, as if in answer to her thoughts another message was brought her, this time wired from home. It was from Marie.

> "A man called on the phone and wanted your address. He said Mrs. Endicott had been hurt and wanted you at once. The address was at the shore hotel. Do you want me to do anything? Marie."

The little touch of everyday life in that word from home brought the tears to Tasha's eyes. Even Marie, asking if she could help! She began to cry softly, unaccustomed tears. She didn't know exactly what she cried for. Sympathy for Lucia in her horrible condition, or sympathy for herself all alone and going to Lucia, not knowing just how things were. She might wait and telephone—but—what was that Marie's telegram had said, Lucia wanted her? Lucia wanted *her*! How strange! Lucia who had always been half jealous of her! Lucia who had wanted to marry her off to get her out of the way, and who had resented any voice of warning she had ever given.

Well, she must go.

The bell boy tapped at the door and handed in a paper with a schedule of trains, a ticket and reservation. He said the taxi was waiting. Tasha snatched up her hand bag and followed him to the elevator, feeling her knees shake under her.

It seemed miles to the train, yet she kept wishing with a great shrinking that the train would be gone when she got there. She knew herself for a coward for the first time in her life. She began to imagine things. Would Lucia be very horrible to look upon? Would she be conscious? She must be or she would not have sent for her. But maybe the report was exaggerated. Maybe she would get well after all. Yet, an aeroplane! It would be fearsome to fall, and crash!

She closed her eyes and tried to shut out the dreadful thought. Oh, if she but had some strong one to lean upon! She remembered that little old woman in the chapel at Palm Beach, the little rusty black bonnet shaking with emotion as she prayed, thanking God for sending her that money for her baby. How that woman trusted in Something. If she only had something like that to lay hold upon now! Something just to take the tremble from her lips and the weak queer feeling from her whole body. Some strong hand to hold hers, and still the quaking of her heart.

The thought of Thurly Macdonald came to her with great longing. If she only had a friend like that to whom she could cry—who would go with her down into this horrible shadow, and keep her from going utterly to pieces. Once she would have thought of him as a possible refuse, a helper, but how could she call on him now, just on the eve of his marriage? He had asked her once to promise to let him know if there was ever anything he could do for her, but she couldn't ask a bridegroom to go with her to her stepmother and watch her die. She couldn't tell him that she wanted someone near whom she could trust, like a rope to hold on to when the foundation on which she stood rocked, something sure and steadfast that would take this awful sinking feeling away! No, her pride would not let her ask for help from him now, even if there was anything reasonable he could do for her. No, this was her burden, and she must bear it somehow alone. Perhaps in some way the message would reach her father and he would manage to be there before her, riding hard in a high powered car. It was what he ought to do. But how would he even know he was needed? They had not lived together enough lately to have any feeling of family responsibility about one another. The word might not reach him until it was far too late!

Oh, if only that dear old lady were somewhere near, Mrs. Macdonald! What a tower of strength she would be. She would not be afraid of death. She would stand by, and clasp hands, and pray perhaps! If she were only near by it would not be out of place to call for her to go and stand by. But she was an old lady! Thurly would not want her troubled. She would not be able to travel so far, and anyway there would not likely be time. The telegram had made it plain that it was only a matter of hours before it would all be over.

The train dragged on its slow way and Tasha sat with her head bowed on her hand, and ached from head to foot, till it seemed that she could no longer bear it.

A young interne from the hospital met her, and tried as they drove from the station, to prepare her for what she had to meet. He said she was glad she had come, that the patient had cried for her continually, and they had hesitated to administer too strong sedation before the family could be summoned, as she might never rally. He said Mrs. Endicott was suffering and utterly unable to move, as the injuries were internal, but that her mind was clear now, and that she seemed to be in great mental distress. Then he made some vapid remarks about the beauty of the day, and how long a ride it was down from New York even on the fastest trains, and Tasha felt as if she would like to shout to him to keep still, and spare her from the agony of his voice. All the time she was wondering whether it was fear for herself, or fear for Lucia that gave her the most agony.

They took her straight to Lucia, and Tasha was startled anew by the ravages pain and horror had made in Lucia's face in a few brief hours. She stood back for an instant and gazed at the huddled form that had been Lucia, and in quick succession there passed before a vision of her stepmother as she was accustomed to be, Lucia in some expensive imported sports costume walking lightly over the golf links; Lucia in cloth of gold with a great black velvet bow at one side; Lucia in frail white with a gaudy gauze poppy at her shoulder; Lucia in her riding habit ready to follow the hounds; Lucia in her vivid orange bathing suit, dropping from the diving board slim and graceful into the pool; Lucia dancing at the country club in flaming scarlet and silver. And here she lay, white and huddled, a thing all crushed and broken, and about to be snuffed out like a candle! Oh, life was a terrible thing! Why did people have to live? But the great dark eyes were upon her, with already the strange glaze of death within them. Tasha had never seen a death, but she knew instantly that that was what it must be. The thin white lips, the lips that had been wont to be so vividly scarlet, were calling her in a high weak voice that did not sound like Lucia:

"Tasha! Oh, you have come! Why have you been so long?— Tasha, you *will* get someone to help me, won't you?—You must work fast!—Oh, can't you see? I haven't long—!" The breath came in weak gasps.

Tasha came near and tried to be sympathetic. She took the weak hand that pulled at the coverlet. She felt all the rancor and contempt vanish away before Lucia's great need.

"What do you want—*dear?* What can I do?" and the tears were raining down her cheeks as she said it.

"Don't waste time in crying!—That won't do any good,"—the weak querulous voice protested. "Get me somebody quick who knows about dying!—I've *got* to talk with *somebody, quick!*—I've waited years since they sent for you—Ohhh! *Hurry—won't* you?"

"But—who shall I get?" faltered Tasha, "the minister from the church where you go sometimes? He is so far away."

"No, no, don't get that infant!—He can play golf but he doesn't know anything about dying except to read the burial service, and I'm not ready for that yet.—Don't you know *any*body—Tash—not *any*body? In the whole wide world, is there not one who knows how to die?—I had a grandmother once who wasn't afraid!—Oh, Tasha, isn't there someone?"

"Yes," said Tasha, "there is. I'll get him if I can. Where is a telephone?" she turned to the nurse. "Is there one on this floor?"

"Don't be long," wailed the sick woman, "Oh, *hurry!*"

"I will," cheered Tasha, her strong young will putting strength of hope into her voice. "Don't fret, Loo, I'll only be a minute, if I can find him at home."

It seemed an hour to her before she got the number she had called. It was a number she had memorized months ago, so she did not have to stop to look it up in the book.

As she waited sitting in the nurse's chair beside the little glass topped table in the hall, she closed her eyes and said silently to herself, "Now if there is a God, I need Him. Oh, God, if you are there, make Thurly be at home! Oh make him be—"

"Hello!" came the voice she remembered so keenly, "Hello!" and took the very prayer from her lips.

Her voice trembled with relief as she spoke:

"Oh, is that you, Mr. Macdonald?" I'm so glad! This is Anastasia Endicott. Do you remember once you told me if ever I needed you I might let you know?"

"*I do*! came the clear ringing voice over the wire with something in it which warmed her and made her feel like crying. It was almost as if he had put his arm about her and held her up, as he had done on that night of the smash-up.

"Well, then will you come, please, quick! A terrible thing has happened! Lucia has been wrecked in an airplane and she is dying. She is wild for someone who will talk with her and tell her how to die. Can you come at once?"

"I will!" rang the voice. "Where are you? Where is she?"

She gave him the address, and made plain the necessity for haste.

"Take a taxi, or hire a fast car, anything to get here before it is too late!"

"I will be there as soon as it is humanly possible," he said, "meanwhile, tell her that Jesus Christ died to save her. Tell her to call on Him, that He will save her. Good bye. I'm coming!"

She heard the click of the receiver hung up, and drew a breath of relief. He was coming! He was coming! He had not failed her. Even though she had run away from his messages and slighted him, he had not failed her.

And God had let him be there when she needed him! That was wonderful too!

Dazedly she hung up the receiver. She must go back to Lucia! How she dreaded the white face, the staring look of the anguished eyes, the high, querulous voice. It would be an awful time to wait before he could possibly get there from the city. Would she last till he came? And how could she bear it meanwhile? What could she say to Lucia. Ah! He had told her something to say. What as it. "Tell her that Jesus Christ died to save her. Tell her to call on Him and He will save her."

Tasha went back to the room. Lucia turned her great impatient eyes on her, and Tasha shrank as she had known she would shrink from the sight of them; but she marched straight up to the bed with her quick accustomed way, and took the weak hand in hers.

"I got him," she said. He's starting at once. He'll be here in a little while."

"Who is he?" asked Lucia despairingly. "Does he know what I need? Will he tell me."

"Yes, Loo, he's a Prince. He knows all about it. I've heard him pray and he talks as if God was right beside him."

"Oh, if he were only here now!" groaned the dying woman. "I feel so weak, as if I was slipping, slipping away! There's nothing to hold on to. Oh, if he'd only told you something to do till he gets here!"

As if the minister were a doctor who could suggest a sedative for the soul!

"He did!" said Tasha, trying to recall the exact words. "He said tell you that Jesus Christ died to save you. He said tell you to call on Him and He would save you."

Lucia looked at her for an instant as if she were turning the idea over in her mind.

"Yes, that's what they used to say, long ago, when people believed things. My grandmother talked that way. But he didn't know what a sinner I've been. I can't call on Jesus Christ. I've been wicked.

Nobody knows how wicked I've been. He wouldn't have told you to
tell me that if he'd known how wicked I've been."

"Never mind," said Tasha desperately, trying to think what to say,
"he likely knows. I've heard him say that everyone was a sinner.
I've heard that said in church last winter. I've heard Mr. Macdonald
say right in his prayer *he* was a sinner, himself!"

"Oh, yes, that way," moaned Lucia, "but not a real sinner like
me!"

"Well, I'd try it," said Tasha. "He said do to it, and he knows. I
know he knows. Wait till he comes and you'll know it too. He said
'He will save you if you call'; so *call*, Lucia, *call!*"

"*You* call! Tasha," pleaded the other woman, "I can't! I don't
dare!"

Tasha stood there aghast. She could not pray! Why should she
pray? She was not the one who was dying! She did not need to be
saved! She might be a sinner too, of course, but she was not now in
such desperate situation. How could she pray for another when she
did not know God herself?

And yet, Lucia was pleading with her to do it. She could not let
Lucia slip out of life without at least trying to soothe her fears. Oh,
if Thurly would come!

But Lucia was visibly weaker even now than when she had first
come in. She could not say no to her last request. Poor broken
Lucia!

How did people do when they prayed? She thought of Thurly and
his mother on their knees in the little parlor in Stonington. She thought
of the old woman in the rusty black bonnet at Palm Beach, down on
the dusty chapel floor, with the sob in her voice; and she slip down
upon the hospital floor, and closed her eyes, with Lucia's cold damp
hand in hers.

"Oh, Jesus Christ! Save her!" she said, and stopped in fright at
her own voice.

"Do it again, oh, do it again!" said Lucia holding Tasha's hand
with a vise-like grip.

"Oh, Jesus Christ, save Lucia!" said Tasha, and said it again and
yet again.

The restless eyes on the bed were watching her.

"Do you think He heard?" asked Lucia in an awed whisper.

"Why, of course!" said Tasha, trying to make her voice sound full of assurance. "Of course He did! Listen, Lucia, I met a woman last winter who told me she prayed for money when her little grandson needed an operation, and they couldn't afford it, and *it came*! She told me it came the very next morning."

"Oh, yes, but she must have been a good woman," said Lucia. "She was not a sinner, like me."

"Well, I imagine since Mr. Macdonald says He died to save you, that there must be some way. If I were you I'd just rely on that till he comes. I don't know any more to tell you, only if I were you I'd call. I'd do it myself if I were you. It might make some difference."

Lucia looked at her thoughtfully and then she closed her eyes, and began to murmur in a low whisper: "Jesus Christ, save me! Jesus Christ, can You save me? Do You know what a sinner I am? Will You save me?"

It was a strange awesome hour. Tasha knelt and held the cold hand, that seemed to grow colder and weaker moment by moment.

How long she knelt there she did not know, with her knees trembling and like to collapse, her back and head aching sorely, alternately praying that monotonous plea, and listening to the other woman repeat it, as if it were somehow a talisman to keep her alive until help came.

"Oh! isn't he ever coming?" murmured Lucia in an interval when she had seemed to sleep and suddenly awake. Then Tasha would murmur softly, "He's coming pretty soon. Keep on calling, Loo! It's going to be all right."

But the tears were raining down Tasha's cheeks, and her heart was almost ready to fail her. The time seemed so long, so long. Would Thurly never come?

She became aware of a stir at the door. The nurse slipped in, and the doctor. He touched Lucia's wrist lightly and looked gravely at his watch. Lucia flashed a glance at him.

"Have I time, doctor! Someone is coming! I must have time! Have I time?"

"I think so," said the doctor gravely, "you have a little time. He is here. Take it calmly, sister. Your minister has come."

Tasha looked up and there was Thurly towering above her, his grave kind eyes looking down at Lucia.

Lucia looked up as if he were someone straight from God.

Tasha arose and laid her hand on Thurly's.

"Oh, you have come at last!" she said with a sob in her voice. "Lucia, this is Mr. Macdonald!"

"Do you know God?" asked Lucia, her voice sounding wearily strange as if she had traveled a long distance from this life, and had to call back to make herself heard.

"I do!" said Thurly Macdonald, clear and sure; and the ring of his tone made even the nurse and the doctor look up as if it had reached their hearts.

"Then I want everyone else to go out of the room while I tell you something. Hurry. I know there isn't much more time."

The doctor signed to the nurse, the nurse gave the patient a hypodermic, then they all went silently from the room and the doctor closed the door. But they did not go away, and the nurse and doctor listened at the door for a possible recall.

What passed within that room, what confession of sin perhaps, Tasha never knew. She sat on the chair the nurse brought for her and waited, but her heart was no longer afraid. Thurly was in there making peace with God for Lucia. He had come in time, and she had done all she could.

Tasha did not know how long it was before that door was opened again. There is no means of measuring time when life and death are standing still till a soul makes peace with God.

But she became aware that the door had opened again and that the nurse was motioning her in.

Thurly stood there by the bed, with a shining in his countenance that was like a flame of triumph, and Lucia had lost the terror from her eyes.

"It is all right, now," said Thurly looking at Tasha, and speaking so that Lucia could hear him., "She wants me to tell you that it has all been made right for her, and she is not afraid any more."

"Yes," said Lucia faintly, "He died—" Her breath seemed to come faintly now and Tasha almost thought she was gone. But she roused and looked up again.

"Forgive!" she murmured and lifted her hand feebly in a little pleading motion.

"Oh, yes!" said Tasha weeping, "there is nothing to forgive—"

"Tell your father—Tash—tell him—forgive—!"

Tasha lifted her head and promised, and as she did so she perceived that her father had entered the doorway, and that he had heard. He had bowed his head suddenly as if he had received a blow; and when they both looked up again Lucia was gone!

Chapter 21

They stood together an hour later, Thurly and Tasha, in the little hospital waiting-room, while Mr. Endicott made some arrangements for the next day.

For the moment they had the room to themselves, but there seemed suddenly a shyness upon them both.

"I can never thank you for this," said Tasha, lifting her tired face to look at him. "It seems as though I could not have got through without you. It seems as though you are always coming to help me out just when I am utterly at the limit."

"If you knew how glad I am to be able to be of assistance—" said Thurly, "and now, what can I do? Is there anything more—"

"Oh, no! Dad has come. He will look after everything now of course," said Tasha wearily. "But you—you ought to rest. You have had a hard trip. Dad will get rooms at the hotel—it's not far away—"

"No," said Thurly quickly, "I must go back to the city. That is unless there is some imperative need for me here? You see I've promised to speak to-morrow night in a place away out in Indiana and unless I leave on the midnight train to-night, I can't make it!"

"Oh, but you will be all worn out!" said Tasha appalled. "You should have told me—"

"I wouldn't have missed coming for all the preaching services in the world," said the young minister, with joy of service in his eyes, "both for your sake, and for hers. I think she found peace. I'm sure she did."

"Oh, I'm so glad for that!" said Tasha, and the tears came to her eyes again. "She was so unhappy, and I didn't know what to do. We—we did what you told me to tell her—all the time until you came. We prayed."

"Did you?" said he, and his eyes were full of a great light like a benediction. "And the answer came I'm sure. But isn't there anything

190

more I can do for you now, before I leave?" he glanced at his watch, "I can spare a few minutes yet and still make my train."

"Oh," said Tasha suddenly, "there's one thing I would like to ask you, if you've just a minute. I've often wondered about it. You said once I ought to be born again, and when I said I'd like to, you said it was possible, that it was up to me. Did you mean that, or were you—disgusted with me?"

"I meant it with all my soul, dear friend," said Thurly earnestly. "Jesus Christ says, "Ye must be born again or you cannot see the Kingdom of God.' It is all in the Bible. It is a birth of the Spirit, not of the flesh, but it brings you into a new life, just as fully and just as truly as your physical birth brought you into this life. Old things are passed away. You become a new person in Christ Jesus."

"But what would I have to do?"

"Nothing. It is all done for you. The moment you are willing to let the Lord Jesus come into your life and make it over you are born again. He does it for you. The Spirit comes into your life and changes it utterly. Oh, it is a wonderful change, and a wonderful thing to be born again. I wish I had time to stay and tell you all about it. But I wonder if you will let me leave my little book with you, and will you read it? See, I'll mark a few places."

He took a small limp Bible from his pocket and fluttered the leaves over, marking certain places with his pencil.

Tasha took the book gratefully.

"I will return it soon," she said. "I cannot thank you enough!"

"Don't, please," said Thurly quickly, "I would like you to keep it if you will, and read it often."

Then with a quick pressure of her hand he was gone out into the night and she could hear the sound of his car as it shot down the drive and was lost in the darkness.

But Tasha stood there holding the little Bible in her hand.

This was the third time now, that he had come to her in distress, and helped her back to life again. And this of course was the end. He would be married in a few days, and his wife would see that he did not go around helping other young women out of difficulties. But she had this much to remember him by, and she felt strengthened by the very feel of the soft worn leather that had been carried around in his pocket and read every day.

The day after Thurly got home from his western preaching trip Hesba came home from school early and brought several packages and a hat box with her. She slid upstairs without stopping to talk, and they could hear her going about the room.

Thurly was reading the evening paper in the parlor. Marget had just come in from looking at a pan of delicious baked beans getting themselves velvet brown in the oven. She was sitting by the window darning socks. There was a savory odor from meat simmering on the back of the stove, and a baked apple dumpling stood on the shelf over the oven.

Everything in the cottage seemed right and fit, and now that Thurly was back again, Marget thought that it wasn't going to be so hard to stand Hesba for the rest of the spring till school was out. For the last week Hesba had not troubled them so much anyway. She had come in late three nights after all day away, and just in time for dinner the other three, and was altogether comporting herself like a meek and quiet person. Perhaps they could stand it, and get her away without hurting her feelings, or making any breach between the families. Marget did love to live at peace with all men—and women, so much as in her lay.

She was just thinking these thoughts when she heard Hesba coming down stairs again. Now, probably Hesba would spring something on them. She was always doing that. Marget hoped it would not be anything disagreeable, with Thurly just home again. She wanted Thurly always to have a feeling that his home was a place of peace and joy.

Hesba came down stairs slowly, not with her usual bounce and stride, and as she entered the parlor there was something in her very approach that made Marget look up.

"Why, Hesba, lassie!" said Marget, using the name she kept for very tender occasions. "Why, what have you done to yourself, child?" Hesba laughed shamedly.

"Oh, just turned foolish like the rest of the world," she said. "Been 'plaiting my hair and adorning myself.' I got a wave this afternoon, and took off my glasses. How do you like it?"

"Fine!" said Marget taking off her own and looking at the girl critically. "Why, what a bonnie lassie you are to be sure! What call had ye to hide all that beauty beneath a bushel. But won't it hurt your eyesight to take off your glasses?"

"No, I guess not. I don't really have to wear them, only for study, you know. I got in the habit of keeping them on, it seemed so much trouble to be always hunting them up. But now I guess I won't wear them any more. I went to see an oculist yesterday and he said my eyes would be all right without them now. So I've packed them away. You see—" she hesitated and tow red spots became visible in her round cheeks, "you see, I've got a friend!"

"A friend?" said Marget, "that's nice. What will he be like? Or is it a lass?"

"It's a young man from my class," said Hesba straightforwardly. "He's been real attentive all winter in little ways, but I didn't have time for such things, and I wasn't sure I cared for his style. But here this vacation he just wouldn't take no for an answer, and we've kind of come to an agreement."

"An agreement?" said Marget, catching a gleam in Thurly's eye behind the evening paper. "And what sort of an agreement will it be? Has it to do with putting by your glasses and curling your hair?"

"Well, yes," said Hesba, "he doesn't like glasses nor straight hair, so I suppose I'll have to concede him that."

"And what is the wee mannie giving up, lass? It's always weel to have two sides to a bargain."

"Oh, he's giving up chewing gum. He used to do it for dyspepsia you know, but it makes me wild to see him chew. And he doesn't wear red neckties any more. I think red neckties are unrefined."

The corners of Marget's mouth were twitching, but she managed a smile of appreciation.

"That's fine, so far as it goes, lass, but where does it all lead to?"

"Oh, well, we've decided to get married of course. I never thought

I would really give in, but he kept at me, and I see he really needs me. He's not in the least practical, though he's perfectly devoted to his work, and he needs someone to cook for him, and make him put on his overcoat when it rains, and things like that. So it's all fixed. And I came down to see if Thurly would do the ceremony for us. You see, he's got a job. He didn't expect one right away because he isn't through his course, but a friend of his is going to the foreign field and he recommended him in his place as bookkeeper in a social settlement house out in the northwest. It's a good change and the pay is much more than most beginners get, so we thought we ought to take it. They're going to give me a job too, so it's all right if we do have to give up the rest of the term and take examinations by correspondence. We're going to be married next week, and I thought perhaps you'd let us have the wedding right here in this room. We won't make much fuss, and it would be more cheerful than going to a church we don't either of us belong to."

"Why surely, lass, surely, we'd be glad to do that, wouldn't we, Thurly? But, lass, what will your folks say? Have you told them yet? Do they know the young man? Perhaps he's not all that you think he is."

Hesba laughed.

"Oh, he's all right. The dean says he's known him for years and a steadier fellow he never saw. He's not very pushing of course, but that's why I decided to marry him. He needs me. I never really found anybody before that did need me. They all resent being helped. Yes, I wrote home yesterday that I was going to be married. They'll expect me to do my own picking and choosing. I'm that way. They won't worry, whatever I do. But we're going home that way for a wedding trip, it's only fifty miles out of the way, and we're driving of course. Edward has bought a secondhand Ford, and we expect to start right away after the ceremony. You needn't go to any trouble, Grandma, just a cup of tea and some of your nice gingerbread will be all we'll want, and when we get to a nice looking lunch place we'll stop and get a chicken dinner in the evening to celebrate. There won't be anybody we need to ask but Edward's brother, and he'll have to hurry right back to school because he's on the night shift of the elevators this week. He's working his way through school you know, and that's his job, running the elevators."

"I'm sure we'll be very glad to have him with us." said Marget simply, "and anybody else you want to ask."

"No," said Hesba, "I'm not 'specially fond of any of the rest, nor they of me. If I asked one I'd have to ask all, and we don't want to be bothered. I did ask Tasha Endicott if she would be maid of honor, but she wrote and said she had to go to New York with her father. And now I see by the papers her stepmother's dead, so it wouldn't be any use asking her again."

"You asked Miss Endicott!" exclaimed Marget in consternation, and Thurly's paper gave a quick, sharp crackle.

"Yes, I asked her last week. I sort of thought I'd like to have something pretty at the wedding, but she didn't see it that way, so of course it doesn't matter. She wrote me an awfully formal note. I suppose they get used to doing thing that way. I nearly froze while I read it. But she sent me some dandy table cloths and fancy linens. I think there's enough to last a lifetime, and some of them are pretty enough to make dresses of. I shall keep them always, and I appreciate it. But I'd kind of like to have had her too. However, that's that! Thurly, will you do the ceremony?"

Thurly drew down his paper and agreed pleasantly, taking over the details making one or two little suggestions that pleased Hesba mightily.

"You're sure you are getting right man? he questioned kindly as he might have done to a sister. "I wouldn't like to see you make a mistake."

"Oh, he's all right. I looked into that early in the winter before I got to going with him. He's not what I always thought I'd marry of course. Every girl has dreams. But supposing I'd married you. I don't know as there would have been anything for me to do. You're so kind of sufficient to yourself, and finished. You wouldn't need to ask me to help in anything. What good would my training have done then? There's really nothing to do for men like you but darn their

socks and get dinner now and then when they're not invited somewhere else. Yes, that's what it'll come to, you'll be invited a lot.
Everybody likes you. But most folks don't like me, and *he* does, so
I'm just going to be contented with such things as I have and try to
make a lot out of him. He's good if he isn't rich nor handsome."

Thurly and Marget with difficulty restrained their mirth. "Well,
we'd like to look him over, Hesba," said Thurly unbending from the
"Miss Hamilton" he had used ever since his return. "We don't want
to see you make any mistakes. Why don't you bring him out and let
us look him over."

"Oh, I will if you want me to. I'll bring him out after school tomorrow for a few minutes if you're going to be at home. He isn't
much to look at of course. He has light hair and I always liked
brown in a man," Hesba's eyes lingered half wistfully on Thurly's
crisp curls. "He has real light eyelashes too, but he's kind."

"Bring him out to dinner to-morrow, Hesba, suggested Marget,
"then you three can talk over the plans. And don't you worry about
the wedding breakfast. We'll have a nice wee set out, and I shall just
enjoy getting it ready. If there's anything special you'd like say so,
otherwise keep out and let it be a surprise."

"Well, I certainly appreciate that, Grandma. No there's nothing I
mind much about, except a wedding cake. I always did think a cake
was nice for a wedding."

"We'll have a cake!" said Marget, "black with fruit and spice and
all white crimps on top. I know how to make it. I had my great
grandmother's recipe, and I've always wanted a chance to use it. I
haven't made one of those cakes since Thurly's cousin Elspeth Blythe
was married in auld Scotland, but it turned out real bonnie then, and
I'm all in a flurry to try it again."

Hesba's eyes shone.

"It'll be almost like a real wedding then," she said. I used to wonder if I would ever have one. It's queer how I had my heart set on
that cake. I never cared for most fol de rols, but I do like a rich spicy
fruit cake! Say, would you like to see that present Tasha Endicott
sent me? It's the real thing. You can see she didn't skimp. I suppose

it's really wasteful to buy so much, and such fine stuff, but I declare I like it. I'm going to write her a letter and tell her about it. I feel as if maybe she and I'll get to be friends, even yet."

So Hesba brought down her one exquisite wedding present, and Marget handled the beautiful pieces one by one, exulting in their fineness and delicate workmanship; and even Thurly came and took up one of the embroidered pieces and gazed at the little flowers wrought so carefully. But he was only thinking how it looked like the girl, the beautiful giver.

Then Marget had to be shown the few simple things Hesba had bought for an outfit, and it was later than usual when Hesba went upstairs."

"We must show her a good time, Mother," said Thurly when she was gone. "Can't you get some flowers and candy or something? She's kind of pitiful, and not so weird without her goggles, but she's a huzzy all the same. Now what do you suppose made her invite Miss Endicott to her wedding? Do you think she really didn't know any better, or was it done to annoy us, or merely a bit of bravado?"

"Oo, maybe a bit of the one and a bit of the ither. But under it a' there's a wee bit of pride to have a rich lassie companion wie her. She ower conscious of her ain self-importance, I'm thinking, too, and she wad like to make the ither lassie admit she's as good as hersel'. But laddie, do ye think we should let this wedding go on without inquiring a bit aboot the mon? These are sair times, and I wad na hae the lassie joomp into a puckle o' trouble."

"I'll find out about him to-morrow. She need never know unless I hear something to his discredit. What did she say his name was? Edward Stebbins? But if he's the same man I saw her with in the city the other day I should say he was harmless. He looks a little like an old sheep. But if he's fallen for her, and can stick it out to be bossed as she will boss him, I should say he must be a pretty strong character. However, if she's pleased I certainly am."

Marget laughed softly, and then said, with a twinkle in her eye:

"Laddie, dinna ye think ye 'ar a bit haird on yer ain sex, sometimes? But hark, ye, Thurly, do ye mind how soon the Lord has lifted the annoyance from our hoose, since we pit it in His hands to handle?"

"I do," said Thurly with a ring of gratitude in his voice. "I certainly do. And no harm to the other party concerned either, unless the man turns out to be a fool. I'm thinking a huzzy and a fool would make a poor combination."

Chapter 22

The accident which caused the death of Lucia Endicott was quickly forgotten. It featured in the papers for a day or two, and then gave way to other more recent tragedies, and new feats of the air; and the toll of death went merrily on, as society took a careless hand in the mysteries and experiments of science.

Lucia's funeral services had been held at fashionable funeral parlors where her set usually repaired when one of their merry company was compelled to die. The officiating clergyman was from the fashionable church which Lucia had attended when she went to any at all. It was a thing of solemnity, of stately sentences, and rare music, banked in masses of expensive flowers. It was held just as soon as was at all respectable, and was all over when Thurly came back from his engagement to preach.

Life in the mansion on Waverly Drive went smoothly on from day to day, just as if Lucia were alive, only there was no Lucia and no Will Clancy coming to call and staying to dinner. The household reins had passed into Tasha's hands, but Tasha had very little to do with the actual workings. The servants were perfectly trained, and knew what was expected of them.

Now that for a small season not much would be expected of her in the social line on account of Lucia's death, Tasha had much deadly leisure on her hands, and little to occupy it.

Great restlessness took hold upon her, and sometimes she wandered from room to room in the big house, her soul crying out and beating its wings as if it were a bird in a cage.

She had taken to reading the little book that Thurly had left with her. And as she read and studied particularly the passages which Thurly had marked for her, a strange thing happened. A meaning sprang out of the printed pages into her heart, a meaning that at first reading had not seemed to be there. She was beginning to get light on some of the things she had seen and heard in the Macdonald

199

household, to grasp a little thread of the meaning of life on this earth and what it was meant to be. Not a butterfly existence, but a sort of testing time. She was beginning to understand that to be born again meant a surrendering to her Maker, a severing of all connection with the old life of the flesh, the mere physical existence, and letting a new Life come in. Gradually the meaning of it all entered into her soul, and became a new belief. She must forsake the old life with its sinfulness, and surrender to the new life as a little babe enters into the world of this life, knowing nothing, having no past contacts with a former existence, ready to make new ones in a new world to which it has been born. Why, it was all true, as Thurly Macdonald had said. One might be a new creature in Christ Jesus if one would.

Tasha went out of the house very seldom in these days. She shrank from meeting her old friends, from having them commiserate her, from having them talk about Lucia. They knew Lucia as she had been. They did not know the Lucia she had helped down through the valley of the shadow of death. They did not know how all her hardness had dropped away when she came to those last hours. They did not know that a mysterious change had passed over her with those last passing moments. They thought of her as blotted out: like a bright rocket that ascended the sky for a few brief sparkles and descended into blackness, to be no more.

Tasha used to feel that way herself about death. But now she did not want to hear others laugh and try to make her forget. She had a great loathing for all her life of the past.

Tasha's father had gone back to New York after a few restless days at home. Tasha had told him briefly of her last hours with Lucia, and he had listened gravely, had said little and gone his way. He knew she was not bereaved. He did not pretend to be greatly bereaved himself. He was quiet and respectable and conventional, but he had not been deeply stirred by his wife's tragic death for more than a day or two. It may be because his real heart had been dead years ago and had never belonged to this woman whom he had married by way of a passing amusement.

So Tasha was left alone, and she gave herself to the little book as she never would have been likely to do if she had been surrounded by friends, and the gayeties that had hitherto made up her life.

Meanwhile the cottage at Stonington was taking on a gala atmosphere. A fat pink geranium appeared in the other parlor window opposite the red one. A Boston fern, and an asparagus fern took places of honor on two little taborets. The smell of spices and citron and lemon and raisins filled the air for days while the fruit cake was in the making. Marget insisted on having the neat stair carpet taken up and turned end for end so that the worn place on the first step would be up the stair out of sight.

In all these preparations Thurly helped, cheerfully, whenever he was at home: taking down the muslin curtains from the parlor windows, putting them up again after they were washed and starched and ironed like new; dusting the glove of the ceiling electric light, to save his mother climbing on a step ladder; chopping raisins, nuts, citron and lemon peel; beating eggs, and stirring the batter with strong firm strokes in rhythm.

Hesba, goggless, and really pretty with her straight hair waved softly about her face, went about as practically as ever.

The day before the wedding she and her Edward were in the city selecting a few things for their journey. Coming out from the store in the late afternoon they came upon Tasha Endicott who had driven down to the shopping district on an errand that she did not care to trust to anyone else.

Slipping out to her car when her errand was done, hoping to avoid meeting any of her acquaintances, she came face to face with Hesba accompanied by a meek young man bearing packages, piled high almost up to his shy gray eyes.

Tasha was about to pass with merely a nod when Hesba reached out a detaining hand.

"Oh, it's you!" she cried, "Anastasia!" I'm so glad I met you. We were just talking about you. I was saying it was a pity I couldn't see you and tell you how much that linen shower meant to me. I don't expect to get any other wedding presents, and to have that one so grand, just made up for all the rest!"

"Oh, that's quite all right!" smiled Tasha, anxious only to get away from this impossible girl who was about to marry Thurly Macdonald.

She almost wished she had not sent the linen if she had to be thanked for it.

"Oh, don't go yet!" cried Hesba, as Tasha backed away, "I want to introduce you to my fiancé, Mr. Stebbins."

"I'm pleased to meet you," stammered out Hesba's Edward, with an awkward bow, and an attempt to remove his hat, which sent the packages flying in every direction, while the color mounted painfully purple in his already pink countenance.

Tasha had opportunity to recover her poise while they were picking up the packages. Mr. Stebbins was rescuing his hat which had fallen off as he stooped to get the last bundle from the gutter where a truck was about to pass over it. There was a light of eagerness in her eyes, however, as she spoke to Hesba with sudden cordiality in her tone:

"Did you say this gentleman was your fiancé?"

"Yes. Didn't I tell you his name when I wrote you? I thought I did. I intended to. Edward has wanted to meet you and thank you too for the linen. Haven't you, Edward?"

Edward ducked an embarrassed assent which bade fair to start another avalanche of bundles.

"And you can't think how sorry I was you had to refuse to be my maid of honor. Of course I understood and when you had an engagement with your father and you couldn't come. But I was disappointed. You see there's going to be nobody there but Edward's brother and the Macdonalds and I kind of wanted some other girl or someone I could sort of call my own friend. Of course, though, I know you wouldn't feel like doing it now, though you have come back unexpectedly. It wouldn't look right so soon after a funeral. I understand."

Tasha caught the childish wistfulness in the other girl's eyes, the girl who had grown strangely young without her glasses, and paused. Some impulse stirred within her, an impulse she did not in the least understand.

"Why, she said thoughtfully, "why—I suppose I could. It wouldn't be at all public of course. No outsiders there. I don't know what difference it could possibly make to anybody. If you want it so much

I'll come."

"Oh, would you?" exclaimed Hesba excitedly. "Say that would be just dandy! and her face lit up with delight.

"Very well," said Tasha, "I'll come. At noon did you say? Where is it to be?"

"Oh, at the house of course. I haven't anywhere else, and Grandma is making me a wedding cake! I certainly am pleased. Thurly is going to marry us of course. We're going to visit my home on our wedding trip and go right to his new job afterwards."

Tasha looked at the colorless young man with a wondering glance. To think of him in the light of a husband! And yet, there was kindness in the good gray eyes behind the yellow lashes, and a certain kind of shy dignity. Perhaps there might be worse lots in the world than marrying him.

"What shall I wear?" asked Tasha.

"Oh, just what you think best. Of course, I suppose you'll think you ought to wear black now."

"Oh, no," said Tasha smiling. "Lucia wouldn't have wanted that. She hated mourning things. And I never could see why a color made any difference."

"Well, that's real sensible," agreed Hesba. "Say, then—wear something bright if you don't mind. It's kind of like having the sun shine on your wedding day, sort of good luck. I'll tell you what. Wear that dress you had your picture taken in down at Palm Beach. You know, the one with the rose on the shoulder. You look sweet in that. You've got it yet, haven't you?"

A wave of color went over Tasha's cheek.

"Yes, I've got it yet but—it's rather—soiled."

"Oh, that won't make any difference. Just put it on as it is. I'd like to see how it really looks."

"All right!" said Tasha. "I'll be there about eleven. Good bye," and she got into her car and drove away.

But something was singing in Tasha Endicott's heart as she threaded her way among traffic, and planned how she would get out the little rose colored silk from its white box in her treasure chest that had been under lock and key ever since the storm.

"I'm not going to tell Thurly and Grandma she's coming," announced Hesba as they watched Tasha's car out of sight. I'll just say I'm bringing another guest and that will do. Then I can surprise them."

"They might not like it," protested Edward.

"They'll like it all rightie!" said Hesba, taking her share of the bundles and stalking away by his side.

So she told Marget Macdonald that she was having another girl come, and Marget suspected nothing, but said it was all right of course, and the morning of the wedding day dawned.

At eleven o'clock sharp Tasha drove up to the Macdonald house and parked her car. There was a pretty color in her cheeks that was not put on, and her eyes were sparkling. This was going to be more interesting than anything she had done in a long time!

Thurly had gone out for some salted nuts for the feast, for Marget had overheard Hesba saying that people had them nowadays at all functions. Hesba had sent Edward after a bouquet for the maid of honor and one for herself. She had not intended bothering as much as that, but now that Tasha was really coming she wanted to do things right.

Marget was in the kitchen doing last things to the creamed chicken on the stove; the stuffed potatoes, the pan of puffy little white biscuits; and opening a glass of ruby jelly. The wedding cake stood on the dining room table wreathed in myrtle from the side yard, and two tall pink candles in quaint glass candle sticks stood on either side. Marget had been studying the magazine pictures and this was the result.

Tasha seeing no one about, came round to the side door and let herself into the dining room cautiously. She could hear Marget around the stove, and she stepped out to the kitchen, the sunshine from the window reaching sudden fingers and laying them on her cheek. She appeared to Marget like an angel.

"Well, I've come!" she announced joyously. "Can you lend me the little room off the dining room to slip into my dress. I'm to be bridesmaid and maid of honor all in one, did you know it?"

Marget turned from her cooking and her face was full of great welcome.

"Oh, the bonnie wee lassie!" she exclaimed. "You have come to help us! What a fine, kind thing to do. Yes, go into the wee room and change your dress, and mayhap ye'll pit a wee tooch to the table. Ye kne how, finer than I."

So Tasha set the table for the wedding breakfast and then she slipped in and put on the little rose silk.

Marie had been fixing it all the evening before, cutting off the draggle draperies, fastening on a wisp more pink gauze, and sewing the rose on more firmly. Now the lovely color flowed round the girl and made her look like a flower.

She heard Thurly come into the kitchen with the nuts as she finished arranging her draperies, and casting a rosy gauze scarf about her shoulders, out she stepped in her gay attire, with one gold shoe, and one silken foot just touching the clean kitchen floor.

"I'm Cinderella," she said, "and I've only one shoe. Could you find me the other, do you think, Mr. Macdonald?"

Thurly suddenly wheeled about and faced her, his eyes full of wonder and joy.

"I can," said he. "I will."

"It's in the strong box, laddie. Ye aye ken where the key is keppit," called Marget.

Tasha leaned against the door and balanced herself on the one little tarnished gold shoe, touching just the tip of her silken stocking to the floor, and watched Marget happily.

"It's good to get back," she breathed with a happy sigh."

"And it's good to have ye back the day," said Marget beaming on her.

Then Thurly was back, and down like any gallant upon his knees putting on the little gold shoe, fastening its glittering buckle around the silken ankle. Marget watched them furtively out of the tail of her eye and was glad, glad, glad! Hesba was being married the day and she *wasn't* marrying Thurly! Sing! Sing! Sing!

"I thought that would be about the way it would be," said a sudden sharp voice behind them, and there stood the bride, as if she had done it all, practical and plain-spoken as ever, arrayed in her sensible dark blue crepe de chine, with a three dollar string of pearls that the groom had bought for her wedding gift.

Thurly looked up from his task, his face wreathed in smiles, and his color high. But he held on to the little foot till the slipper was fastened good and tight around the silken ankle.

Then his brother, a mere boy, shyer than himself, the bridegroom entered the picture too, beaming over the flowers he had brought. He had got white sweet peas for the bride with a few blue forget-me-nots scattered among them, and a tight hard bunch of pink sweet peas for the attending lady. He fairly shone with pleasure in his purchase.

Tasha took the flowers, and somehow under her touch they spread themselves and became two bouquets worthy of the occasion. A little loosening here, a flower standing up there, the cord that held them cut, and a wide white ribbon produced from her belongings somewhere to tie around the bride's handful. It was a different thing altogether. Then she took her own, and transformed them, slung them over one arm as if they had been a great sheaf, and all the four stood round and laughed and looked at her.

"Come," said Thurly, letting go the little gold shoe at last and leaving it finally on the owner's foot. "Mother, aren't you ready? Take off that apron, and let's get on with this wedding. What's the use of standing around in the kitchen when there's all this grandeur in the parlor and dining room waiting for us?"

So the wedding procession formed, Thurly escorting his mother ahead, and seating her in the big chair at one side as had been arranged, the shy brother as best man following next, then Tasha, gorgeous as a flower plucked from some other world garden. With measured step in her little gold shoes she walked, her sweet peas held like a sheaf of wheat over her left arm. After her came Edward and Hesba arm in arm till they stood opposite to Thurly, with his small black book, and his fine black coat, looking as if the world had suddenly come all right for him.

Tasha listened to the solemn ceremony in Thurly's reverent tones, and wondered that in this world of disappointing people there had been yet left a man so fine as Thurly Macdonald. "Oh, Thurly, Thurly, Thurly!" her heart sang. And he was *not* marrying Hesba Hamilton after all!

But after the ceremony was over, and the groom turned and kissed his bride, Tasha caught a glimpse in those shy gray eyes that told what love might mean, even for a plain little shy commonplace man, and a round blunt little person like Hesba.

They ate the wonderful wedding breakfast, from chicken to wedding cake, all the way through, and then Mr. and Mrs. Edward Stebbins, amid a shower of good wishes, climbed into their Ford and started for their new life.

Thurly came back from bidding them farewell and, laughing, said to his mother:

"I still maintain that she's a huzzy! But perhaps that's the kind he needs."

Then he turned to Tasha, standing there in her pretty frock and her gold shoes.

"Now, Princess," said he, his eyes devouring her, "can you and I have a real talk?"

He took her over to the old couch and they sat down together.

"Now, tell me about it," he said, his eyes earnestly upon her, "you came back to us. Why did you do it, little Anastasia? Did you know what your coming would mean to me?"

Tasha was silent for a moment, letting her hands lie in the big clasp his had taken of hers. Then she lifted her eyes to his.

"I think," she said softly, "I think it's because I've been born again as you said I needed to be; and now I belong to your world!"

He gathered her close in his arms then and laid his lips against her hair. "Thank the Lord!" he breathed softly, with closed eyes. "Thank the Lord."

Marget, coming to find them, saw the lassie's face hid in her Thurly's coat, her fine gold hair against his cheek, and a little gold shoe resting confidently on the top of a big well polished black one. She trotted away with shining eyes.

"Now let the Lord be thankit!" she praised, as she put the rest of the wedding cake away in the cake box, wound the clock for the night, and did all the noisy little things she could think of to show she had no thought of such a thing as intruding into the parlor.

"Bless the bonnie lassie, she's come into her own at last!" she said aloud to the shining kitchen. "She's come back to health. She's *Anastasia!* Our little Anastasia in her fairy gold shoes."

Time of the Singing of Birds

Chapter 1

The birds were singing madly in the old orchard around the house when Barney Vance woke up that first morning back in the old house where he was born and brought up, and where, two years before he had kissed his mother good-by to go across the seas and fight. Now he was Lieutenant Vance and had been invalided out of the army and sent home to recuperate, with little probability that he would be called back. His strong young body had taken a terrible beating during his last engagement with the enemy, and the doctor had thought there was grave doubt whether it would ever get back to the old vigor where he could hope to go on and continue fighting. And he had been tired. So tired! And glad to rest a bit, though in his heart of hearts he had the determination to be back on the job again as soon as he recovered his normal strength. But now he was here, and it was good to rest. It was like crawling into a foxhole when the enemy got too strenuous, and he was temporarily out of ammunition. It was good to find a real haven. That was how he had felt as he swung off the midnight train last night at the little flag station where he knew he would have to walk over a mile, to make the old home. He was none too ready for that dark lonely walk, but it was home, and it was where he had a right to be, and he wanted to get there, so he had walked. He had stumbled up to the porch seat after sounding the knocker, and dropped down with his head leaning against the chip-boards of the old house, his eyes closed.

Of course he knew that his mother was gone. Word of her death had come to him while he was still in the hospital, recovering from his desperate wounds, and had much delayed his thoughts of restoration to health. But he had fought that long battle out, and recognized it as one of the inevitable chances of war he had taken when he bade his mother good-by. She herself had seen it, and reminded him that she might not be there when he returned, reminded him that she would be watching for him in Heaven. He had known that she would not be in the old farmhouse to meet him. He had reminded himself of that fact again and again during the long journey. And yet he had wanted to come.

There would be nobody at the old home to meet him but the two old servants, old Joel Babbit, and his wife Roxy, who had been in charge of the house and the farm since ever he could remember. That is, he hoped they were still there. For after his mother was gone there had been no one to write to him about things but old Roxy, and she wasn't much of a correspondent. Still he had hoped. Roxy used to love him, and next to his mother would be more like home-folks than anybody he knew. And so he had kept on hoping through every hard step of that mile and a half he had walked from the station.

And Roxy had come to answer that knock. He had known she would if she was alive. And if she wasn't, what did it matter? That was how he felt as he slumped to the porch seat and waited.

And then there was her step, in the old felt bedroom slippers, down at the heel, shuffling along, a candle in her hand, to supplement the electricity that she had turned on at the head of the stairs.

Roxy had brought him in and crooned over him, called him her dear boy, and drawn him into the old front room, where she had always kept a fire laid ready for lighting should he ever return.

"I promised yer mommie, ye know," she said as she knelt and touched her candle to the kindling and whipped up a fire in no time.

Of course it wasn't cold weather, for those birds wouldn't have been singing so joyously now this morning if it were, but he remembered the fire had felt good to his stiff joints and aching muscles last night, and the crackling of the flames as they snapped the dry old twigs had sounded cheerily as if they were welcoming him, even though there were only two very humble retainers besides themselves to do it.

Those were the first impressions he had as he gradually came awake. Something cheery, in spite of the fact that it was all sad, because his mother was gone; and wouldn't be back there any more—wouldn't be there to ask him all about his experiences, nor to mourn over his wounds, nor worry lest there might be aftereffects. She had gone to another world, where wounds down here didn't matter any more. Oh, she would be sympathetic with his worries even now, up in Heaven, where he was sure she had gone! But they wouldn't pierce her own soul the way his bumps and bruises used to do even when he was just a little child and fell down on the old doorstone at the kitchen steps, and skinned his knee. He always knew those bruises of his hurt his mother even more than they did him. He came to know that at a very early age when he watched the slow tears travel down her smooth cheek; as she bathed the blood away and put on the lotion, wincing herself because it smarted him. He remembered asking her then, "Does it hurt your fingers when you put it on my cut?" And she had smiled and shaken away the tears, and said, "No, it doesn't hurt mother."

"Then why does you cwy?" And she had answered tenderly, "Oh, I guess I was feeling how it hurt you, little boy. That's what made the tears come. I didn't like anything to hurt my brave boy."

He remembered puzzling over that, and then asking, "Is I your brave boy, muvver?"

She had looked at the lingering tears on his cheeks, and then smiled a bit sadly, "Well, perhaps not just yet, dear. But you're going to be brave by-and-by. Brave people don't cry for hurts you know. They bear a hurt quietly. With beautiful courage. When you grow up you will grow courageous I hope."

He could remember every word she had said about being brave. Dear mother! He remembered her tender smile. Somehow it almost comforted him for her absence now. It was the greatest hurt he had, that she was gone. Was he being brave about it? And would she think, was she thinking now, where she was in Heaven; was she feeling satisfied that he had been brave in the war he had been fighting? There was a time to which he could look back, when his very soul had been torn with pain, and he had remembered her words then, of how a real man would be brave, even when suffering great pain.

Over on the other side of the room lay his uniform, a purple heart and a silver star adorned its somberness, but what were they to him now? Would his mother think he had won the silver star? Would she have been pleased? Oh, yes, she would! But he must not think about that now. He had come home and she was not here. He had a new life to live, though he had little heart for it, now, when it suddenly dawned upon him that he was here. Here in the old house, where he had so longed to be! Here with the old apple trees around him in full bloom, and the birds singing their tumultuous songs, just as if there had been no war. Just as if there were no death, and no more war going on even now, where some of his former comrades were going bravely into fire. Birds singing. Almost as if it might be Heaven and he was hovering on the edge of it, as if there were no sorrow, and only peace and joy. Glad birds! How could they? How could they sing when there was still sorrow in the world?

But this couldn't last forever, this wrenching of hearts, and pain in the midst of joy. Someday there would dawn glory, and joy forever, and he must live for that time. It sounded almost like a sermon he was preaching to himself these first dawning thoughts of home coming.

But there were sweet things to think about too. Perhaps they were some of the themes of the songs those little birds were singing out there among the apple blossoms.

And there had been old Roxy, coming to the door to let him in, her old arms about him, a tenderness in their touch that reminded him of his mother's touch. She had been his nurse and comforter long ago while his mother was still there. Now she would go on comforting him, just with a gentle hand, the kindliness in her voice, the look in her old eyes, the good things with which she would feed him.

Even last night she had brought him hot broth, and fed him as if he had been that little child she had loved from his babyhood. He had been so tired, and so nearly overcome with exhaustion from his long walk after weeks in the hospital, that he had scarcely thanked her. It had been good to him to be fed. Then she had called old Joel, and together they had got him upstairs to his old room, with the sweet-smelling sheets fresh from their hiding among lavender blossoms, the cool pillows under his head with their breath of lavender. How homelike it had all been, as if his mother had ordered it for him, as if she had arranged it and left it ready when she had to go off to Heaven!

So he lay and came slowly back to waking again on a new day. A day where he must be brave. Even though he bitterly missed the past, he must be brave.

He must stop this kind of reminiscing. It was glooming the first morning of his day at home. He must not let that be. What was it he had anticipated so keenly, beyond the mere getting here and feeling the old home about him? He had known his mother was gone, and yet he had wanted to come. What else was there in the life he had left behind those two long years ago?

Friends? Yes, there were a lot of friends of course. But the fellows were all off in the service somewhere. Two who had been very close, he had left lying on the battlefield that last night he was in action and was carried off himself, waking up in a hospital a long time afterward. Girls? Yes, there had been girls, a lot of attractive ones, but he hadn't wanted to marry any one of them. He had been very young when he went away to college. He hadn't begun to think about marrying yet. Some of them had been rather sweet. One he had heard was married now, and another had died in an accident. But there had been others. Where were they now? Probably off doing war nursing, or working in some war plant, though he didn't know of such a place in this vicinity. There might be, of course. He would presently have to look up some of those old contacts. They could have changed some with the years, probably, and world happenings. He must have changed, too. But it would be pleasant to get together with someone he used to know and talk over old times, find out what had become of this one and that one of whom he had lost track.

There had been Hank Bristow and Casper Withrow. They were probably in the war somewhere. Maybe someone knew. He must get Roxy to talking. She would have heard. Roxy never used to miss a trick in the old days, and she loved to talk when she was in the mood.

There had been Hortense Revenal. What had become of her? She and her mother had come to board over at the next farm a couple of summers before the war. She had been in high school with him, and much in evidence at all the school parties and activities. And because of their living in the same neighborhood it had often fallen to his lot to see her home from gatherings. As she grew older she developed a possessiveness that had not pleased his mother. What was it about her that mother had criticized? She said she was bold and was much too sophisticated for her age. This was after Hortense had returned from a summer with her father, who was estranged from his wife, and lived in New York. It was rumored there was a divorce in the offing. Hortense's mother was a giddy person who paid very little attention to her child, and had many weekend visitors from a distance. His own mother used always to have a troubled look in her eyes whenever Hortense had been much in his company.

But it had been no wonder that Hortense was often coming over to see him on one pretense or another, a problem she could not solve, or a Latin sentence she could not translate, and then would stay for a few games. Poor kid! She had nothing at home to attract her. He had felt sorry for her. And mother had been very kind to her of course. She would always bring her sewing and sit in the room, sometimes playing games with them, taking part in their talk, occasionally reading aloud to them. But he had a strong feeling that his mother had been much relieved when Hortense went to visit her father, or went away to see her grandmother or one of her aunts. His mother definitely had objected to Hortense. Well now why? That was a question he would have to take out and examine and sift, in case Hortense should turn up again. Just why hadn't mother felt easy in having her come over so often? It couldn't be just that mother was old-fashioned and didn't like the way Hortense was dressed, too elaborately, or something of that sort.

Hortense had large appealing black eyes, a dominating personality, and a way of ignoring questions of right and wrong, truth and falsehood, mine and thine. He could look back and see that now. Was it just because his mother had called his attention to it or had he known it all the time and had he excused it because Hortense had a sort of personal fascination for him?

Well, she had been only a kid then, and he hadn't been much more himself. If mother were here now she might not have the same objection, and of course his mother wouldn't want him to be biased by her judgments of several years ago. Still, he was not deeply anxious to see Hortense. If she came in his way well and good. If not, well, that was that. It was only childhood stuff, anyway. Of course if he found she was still living in the old place he would have to go and call, after awhile, when he got strong enough to feel like visiting. Then he could judge if he wanted to see her any more. He could ask Roxy about her. But of course Roxy had never liked her either.

And there had been Lucy Anne Salter, and the Wrexall twins, Madge and Martha, and Janet Harper. But hadn't he heard that Janet had gone overseas, in some capacity, a WAC or a WAVE or one of those things? He wasn't sure. Somehow in those two terrible years of his absence the things he had left behind had grown so unimportant. Well, perhaps it wouldn't have been that way if his mother had lived and kept on writing her wonderful letters to him. How he used to envy the other fellows after she was gone when they got a letter from their mothers! Well, there! He must stop that. That kind of a memory would bring smarting tears to his eyes, and a soldier did not wear tears. Even if he had been in bed for weeks and weeks, and was all unnerved. He must brace up. Listen to those birds. They were screaming their joy of the morning, and he must be glad too, for he was at home, where he had wanted for so long to be. He was here, and the morning sounded good, and the breath of apple blossoms was born on the soft April air. "The time of the singing of birds" had come. He had liked that verse when he was a kid.

But home without mother wasn't all he had hoped it would be. Out there in a foreign land in a hospital, home had seemed just Heaven, even with his mother gone. Her presence would sort of be lingering around. And it was. Yes, he could remember when she would come into the room in the morning and pull his shades down, to let him sleep a little longer. But there! He mustn't remember. It would get him all stirred up.

It was early yet, and he was still weary. He would just turn over and go to sleep again.

So the birds sang on and lulled him into a dream of his mother, who seemed to come and soothe his forehead, and tell him to lie still and rest yet a little while, as she used to do. And so he slept again.

Chapter 2

The journey home had been precarious, and wearisome. There were so many changes, and he scarcely got over the excitement of one stage of it until another was thrust upon him. Change of scene, conditions, environment, and personnel of his companions.

From the first suggestion of it, the doctor and the nurses had been opposed to letting him go. They felt it was too soon to move him. He had so recently been considered one who would not recover from that last terrible engagement.

"It's all wrong," said the doctor. "Lieutenant Vance should not be moved for at least another month. If they insist upon it I will not answer for the consequences. He is too valuable a man to be taking any chances with his life."

"Yes, I agree with you," said Barney Vance's captain. "He is too valuable a man."

But when they asked Barney himself they found him strangely indifferent—just that pleasant grin, and a quiet lifting of his eyebrows. "It's all right with me, Doc," he said. "It feels good to rest for awhile." The eyes of the doctor and the captain met with that negative glance that was decisive.

"He doesn't seem to care," said the puzzled captain, back in the shack he called his headquarters. "I thought he'd be all on fire to get home."

A waiting private looked up, saluted respectfully, and said:

"Beg pardon, sir, but perhaps you don't know that guy has just recently received word from home that his mother's dead. He wouldn't be so keen about anything just now. He banked a lot on his mother."

"Oh," said the captain, "I didn't know! How unfortunate he should have got the message yet. He is in no state of health to bear any more shocks. They should have had a care how they gave him letters."

"Oh, he's taking it all right! He's that kind of a guy!"

"Yes, I know," said the captain, "he would. A fellow who could do what he's just got done doing to the enemy, and manage to get back

10

alive, and *live*, wouldn't fall down on any of the other attacks of life. He's *real*, that man!"

The young private's eyes were filled with agreement.

"He sure is!" he answered, lifting a look like the raising of a banner.

But definitely, the idea of sending Barney Vance home on furlough was postponed.

Then suddenly an order came through to evacuate the position, abandon the hospital and equipment, except such as could be gathered in haste, and depart. Warning had come that the enemy was on the way.

By night, in a shackly old ambulance they hastily bundled Barney Vance over rough roads, or no roads at all. They jolted frightfully, bringing all the pain of the past weeks back into the weakened body that had been bearing so much—bumping into looming trees in the pathway, not even stars to light them. There was distant booming of enemy fire, frightening rumors brought by stealthy scouts, whispered orders, hurrying feet, muted motors, and then an open sky. Careful, anxious hands carried the patients hurriedly across a stubbly field, and deposited them in haste in an airplane. A jerk, a roar, a dash, and they were soaring up, somehow like the eventualities of battle that had been so much a part of his life and thoughts for the past months, that he was plunged backward and roused to a tense alertness, wondering if he was responsible again to help quell what was going on. Then the whir of wings overhead, around, everywhere! Was the enemy pursuing? He looked up with a strange apathy, as he felt that they were mounting. Would they escape? Or was this the end, in a decrepit airplane, unable to escape? Shot down at the last, ignominiously, after two years of noble fighting! At least they all called the work he had done noble. But there didn't seem much nobility to an end like this. Crippled, weak, sick, and no chance for escape!

Still they were mounting. Were they going up to God now? Well the enemy wouldn't come that far, at least. Enemies would have to stop before they reached God's throne. That was one refuge they would not dare to face.

He drew a weary relaxed breath as he felt their altitude. Clouds about, below! He raised up on one elbow to get a glimpse out the

window. There didn't seem to be an enemy in sight. Had they lost
them? But there was still the sound of bombs far below. Would the
clouds keep their secret, or part and give the enemy another view to
follow?

He dropped wearily back on the roughly improvised pillow and
closed his eyes. What did it matter? He *had* to go to sleep. Even in
such straits, he *had* to go to sleep.

When he awoke it was night, and they were coming down silently
in the darkness. There was some trouble about refueling, but it didn't
have to concern him, though he was comfortably relieved when he
felt the lift of wings again. They were going high now, but he did not
look out to see if they were followed. He did not care. Perhaps they
were really going to God, and that was all right with him if they did.
He knew God. He had got acquainted with Him out there on the
battlefield in all that stress. Of course his mother had tried to teach
him from the time he was a mere babe, but it hadn't somehow meant
anything to him till he got out there facing danger. Danger and a
battlefield. That was a great place to have God, the great God, come
walking toward you with welcome on His face. A hand held out to
help and lift. No, he wasn't afraid of God.

When he woke again he was being carried on a stretcher to a dim
building where was a hospital of sorts. But it didn't matter. He was
glad of any anchorage for the time.

There followed an indeterminate period of dullness. Waiting for
orders. Waiting for transportation. And then more journeying. A ship
at last. But it was all hazy. He hadn't even then quite aroused to the
consciousness of the moment enough to ask just where in the great
world he was, or perhaps no one talked about those things. He hadn't
entirely come out of the stress of war far enough to care much. There
were only two places that mattered any more. Where he was, and
home. And perhaps home was only a great wistfulness now, since he
had had the word that his mother was gone It was all just a great
weariness, and wanting to get where he might have the say of what
he should do and when he should eat and sleep. Rest was a great
need.

Then the rough truck journey to the ship, his first attempts to walk
about by himself, without much desire to do so. Was it always going

to be like this? This great aversion of his body to take the initiative in any movement? Would this continue? Was he half dead already? He wasn't afraid of death outright, but this deadness of senses, this apathy of mind, this terrible weakness, it was intolerable. Sinking into a deck chair and closing his eyes brought momentary relief. Gradually the quiet of the sea, the invigorating salt air, cleared his brain. Hours came when he could walk with almost a spring in his step, when he could look off over the blue of the sea. Such peace of blue with sunlight on its billows. So wide so quiet, so far from tumult and war! He was sailing, sailing! It was better than sailing up among the clouds. It was quieter. It rested him. This might go on forever.

In the night the scene of peace changed. An ominous sound. Was it wind? Or wings? Motors? Hurrying footsteps, voices, shouts, sudden lights, startling words hurled hissingly through long whispers. And again the old tumult back, a pounding heart, presaging disaster. The enemy again? He must get up and fight for victory. He could not lie here and rest when the enemy was rampant again.

Explosions! Yes, that must be a submarine! He sprang from his berth to investigate. A sudden long shudder through the ship. More explosions! He shook the sleep from his eyes and tried to think. He was back on the alert again now, dropping into the old training, thinking quickly, working fast, back among the crew taking a hand, his weakness forgotten, his mind racing ahead. Long hours of activity, anxiety, readiness for what might come, no time to think of where he was going, nor how it was going to be when he got there. No time to rest, or even to sleep or eat. No one with time enough to prepare meals. Putting out fires, saving their ship. There was plenty to be done, and not even a doctor with time enough to notice whether he was fit for the work he was doing.

He told himself that perhaps it was as well, that is, when he had a split second to think about it. He had been getting lazy. That apathy was gone. It took an enemy, and threat of disaster, to bring him back to normal again. Oh, perhaps there might be a reaction afterwards, and the apathy return. What he was doing now might retard his final recovery. Oh, well, what matter? This was the job at hand and it must be done. Something that future generations might need for their well-being. This was what he was set to do. His business in life was to help win the war, not to humor his physical needs.

So, the hours went by, and the ship was saved, the submarine vanquished. The anxiety lessened and a great impatience followed, a gradual lethargy stealing on again, as native skies drew nearer. Strange ships dimly on the horizon, airplanes at night!

Would they never reach the land, the place of peace?

He had thought when he left his home that he would not return until every enemy was vanquished, yet here he was, almost at home, and the war not won yet! A rising shame engloomed him. What had he not done that he might have done to save his world? He had wrought his best, and here he was almost back among a people that had expected so much of him and his companions, and now they had had to send him home without them. It was ridiculous. He went over there to *die*, didn't he? Why didn't they let him stay and die then? He could have sent a *few* more deadly shots, couldn't he, before he was done? What matter if he died doing it, after he had done his best? Why hold him to recover? Just his few last shots might have helped the deciding battle.

Those were his last thoughts before he dropped out of consciousness.

The birds sang on. And off in the distance there came the sound of a cooing dove, bringing dimly to mind the rest of that verse. "The time of the singing of birds is come, and the voice of the turtle (dove) is heard in our land."

Chapter 3

Three boys were wheeling by the old Vance house on bicycles that rattled and clattered, and showed their age gaily and nonchalantly. They looked toward the old house with something of a possessiveness in their eyes.

"What's become of the guy that usedta live here?" asked Jimmy Holzer. "He get killed er somepin'?"

"Naw," said Billy Lang, "I heard it was worse'n that. I guess he got took prisoner, by the Japs, I guess it was, ur else the other fellas."

"Naw! You're wrong!" said Boog Tiller importantly. "He got took by the Japs, all righty, after he'd brought down seventeen of those mosquito things, ur mebbe it was twenty-six, I ferget which. An' then they got him, and tuk him to n'nterment camp, I guess it was, but he escaped, see? And he had all kinds of a time gettin' back to his outfit, an' mos' died on the way, only some pal of his found him and carried him back to his own company, an' he's been in the hospital an awful long time. He was hurt bad, y'know. But they say now he's gonta get well after all, an' he's gonta be sent home fer rest, sometime, mebbe soon."

"You mean he's gonta come back here to Vance's Point? You mean we can see him again sometime, Boog?"

"Could be," said Boog, speculatively.

"Oh, gee! Wouldn't that be great? Mebbe they'll have a celebration with a procession an' eats an' things, an' we can be there!"

"Could be," said Boog again, contemplating the possibility of giving out such information as a fact, and whether it might have any bad reactions for the giver of such news, provided it didn't turn out to be exactly true. However, one could always qualify it by prefacing such information by the words: "I heard—"

But the subject of all this speculation was sweetly sleeping behind the apple blossom screen. And didn't hear. Even though the voices of the boys were by no means hushed, but rang out clearly as if they wanted to make an audience hear. So they wheeled on around the

15

bend of the road, and could be heard no more.

Two old men and their hired helper sitting in the back of a truck steadying a plow, were the next to pass by.

"I see that young Vance has been doing great things over there across the water," said Ezekiel Summers, as he drove down the road gripping the wheel of his car with his gnarled old hands, and nodding toward the old house. "Pity his ma ain't alive to know about it. They tell me where they read in the papers how he got a star and a purple something for honorable bravery—ain't that what they call it? Yes, it certainly is a pity his ma can't know about it. It would have done her heart good. She certainly did think a heap of that boy o' hers, an' rightly too. She done a good job, bringing him up, all alone as it were. Without any dad ta he'p. He ain't no sis, neither, even ef he has got a collidge eddication, an' wasted a lotta time playin' ball, an' got his picter in the papers. But I guess we can rightly be proud of him in our town in spite of all that, after all them enemy planes he done for."

"Yeah," said the tough young plowman, Sam Gillers, "bet they do say he's been wounded bad. Some say he may not get well. He might not even come home at all. There's thousands of them boys just die, and their folks don't know fer a long time."

"Aw, yes, their folks get notices," said Ike Peterson. "The Gov'n'ment's been real nice about sendin' their folks word about what's happened to 'em, afore they tell it to the papers, Zeke!'

"Well, yes, I guess they hev been kinda careful about sech things," said Zeke. "But you know it ain't sa easy ta attend ta sech little trifels when you've got a hull army ta look out fer. B'sides, they don't waste many words tellin' their folks. There was the Barrowses only just got word their Joe was missin' in action, an' got tuk pris'ner an' they haven't heard one word since, An' that was two years, lackin' a month, ago, an' Miz Barrows she's pretty near went crazy about that boy of hers they oughtn't ta wait that long, I don't think."

Well, in this case," spoke up the young plowman, "thur ain't nobody ta let know, since Miz Vance passed on. There ain't none of his folks left around here."

"Wal, I guess Roxy an' Joel think a lot o' that Barney fella. Roxy's took care o' him since he was a babe in arms," said Summers.

"Yes, I guess she has," said Peterson.

Their echoing voices clanged among the apple blooms and seemed to hit the very clapboards of the old house as they passed, but they did not reach the sleeper whose dreams were sweet and deep.

A little later, when the morning sun was mounting higher, a smart car drove by with two dashing girls talking hilariously above their motor's noise.

"Oh *Boy*! I wish this war would end!" yawned one daintily. "I'm fed up with all the things we do these days, and all the things we can't do. It's too ridiculous, telling us we can't have things we like to eat, and not giving us all the gas we want. Why I've heard there's *plenty* of gas, stored up somewhere. What right have they got to tell us we can't take pleasure rides I'd like to know? Look at all their spending, sending tanks around the world. That must cost a lot! I don't really think I believe in war, anyway," said Irma Watts. "They act like they were playing a game trying to see which could kill the most. For my part, I don't see why the good people have to go out and endanger their lives just because some crazy people over the ocean want to fight. Look at Mary Forbes having to go to work, and let her young husband go off for no telling how long, and maybe never come back. And Janet Waters with three babies to take care of. And her husband has to get called. He goes next Monday. I don't think it's fair, do you, Hortense? I don't see why somebody doesn't do something about it. I think it's time for this war to be over, don't you?"

"Yes," yawned Hortense, "I think it's an awful *bore*!"

"Say, Hortense, isn't this the old Vance house? Didn't you used to have a crush on the handsome boy they called Barney? Seems to me they told me that when I got back from visiting my grandmother. What became of him?"

"Oh, he's gone to war of course, like everybody else," said Hortense. "There's hardly any men left in town worth speaking about. But they say some of them are coming back on furloughs pretty soon. I shouldn't wonder if Barney Vance would be coming home. Nobody seems to know. Yes, I used to go with him a lot. We were practically engaged before he went to war, but of course he was pretty much under his mother's thumb, and she had a terrible religious complex.

She didn't want him to do this and that, and he had to go with her to church. Even after he grew up she hung onto him, and she and I never would have hit it off. But now, she's out of the way, I might be interested in him again. Well see! He was a nice kid, and awfully handsome of course."

"He's mebbe changed a lot himself," said Irma.

"Well, yes, probably. He wouldn't have stood for lipstick and rouge, not in the old days. But he's likely come in touch with little European sophistication, and learned how girls ought to look. Anyhow, why should I care? If I want him I'll risk but what I can get him back, especially now that his mother is gone," and Hortense tossed her dark curls back from her forehead, and tilted her ridiculous little trifle of a hat down over one eye with anticipatory assurance, while her laugh rang out noisily and startled a wood robin that was practicing a love song on a tree by Barney's window. Perhaps it was the cessation of that love song that made Barney wake up, and then the next sound that he heard was the shuffling of Roxy's old felt slippers as she scuffed along the hall that led to his room. The footsteps paused, and there came the subdued tinkle of glass against silver. Roxy was bringing his breakfast, the way she used to bring it when he was a kid and had been sick for a few days, measles or mumps or something. He half smiled and opened his eyes. Softly he heard the doorknob turn, and Roxy's gray head and the gleam of her steel-rimmed spectacles appeared cautiously.

"Hello Roxy!" he called with his old grin. "Top of the morning to you! What are you stealing in so carefully for? I don't have to go to school this morning, do I?"

Roxy almost cried at the familiar greeting, and her sweet old lips parted in her well-remembered merry smile.

"Bless you, dear boy!" she said. "No, you don't have to go to school any more. Leastways, not to the old village school. Mayhap you'll find a few more lessons in the school of life for you to learn yet, but this morning you're home, and you have the whole day before you. Ready for breakfast, are you?"

"You betcher life, Roxy. Real home breakfast! That's something I haven't had for two long years. Whatcha got, Roxy? Is it bacon I smell? And eggs? Pancakes? Oh, *Boy!* Honey? From our bees? Say,

Roxy! That's swell! I was afraid honey might be rationed, or perhaps the bees had gone to war."

Roxy laughed happily.

"No, the bees ain't gone yet. They're using mosquitoes instead in the war, I heard. I read something about that in the papers."

Roxy twinkled one of her amusing winks, and the young soldier laughed aloud, a good old-fashioned boy-laugh that greatly cheered the heart of the old nurse.

"Say, Roxy. You still have your fine old sense of humor, haven't you? That's good. You said you were getting old, Roxy, but you're mistaken. You couldn't twinkle like that if you were old."

"Oh, go way with you, child!" said Roxy happily.

"Say, this is a swell breakfast, Roxy, and I see you've started to spoil me just the way you always did. Didn't you know I'm graduated from having my breakfast in bed? They wouldn't have let me come home if I hadn't. You can't baby a big soldier like that Roxy. The government will get after you if you do."

Roxy dropped into a straight chair with her arm over the back and sat there beaming on her adored nursling as he ate his breakfast and joked with her, till she was convinced that he had not lost any of his old spirit by going to war, grim as it must have been. And when he had eaten the last crumb she arose to take the tray.

"Want some more of anything?" she asked anxiously.

"Not on your life, Roxy," he said with a grin. "You know it doesn't do to feed a starving person too much at the first meal, and I'm sure I've already eaten twice as much as I should have eaten for the first meal at home. Now, Roxy, sit down again and tell me all about everybody. Where are all the fellows and the girls I used to run around with? Are any of them here yet?"

Roxy sighed.

"Well, no, only a couple of them. Cy Baxter is still in the bank. You know he has flat feet, and he's tried several things and they won't take him. Of course his mother's glad, but she keeps it to herself, though you can't blame her. She's almost blind, and he's all she's got."

"No, I suppose war is hard for mothers. It must have been hard for mine, although she urged me to go, said she was glad I wanted to.

She always taught me to be loyal to my country, and brave to do the right thing, even if it meant fighting and dying, for a principle."

"Yes, that she would, lad. Your mother was a brave lady to the end, and I thank the Lord she didn't have to suffer too long. She was always so quiet and so brave. And she was that pleased when the piece came out in the paper saying how brave her boy was. She held the paper in her hand all that first day. She wouldn't let it go out of her sight, and she read it over till she knew it by heart. And then she'd say, 'Roxy, I knew he'd be like that. I knew he'd be brave, because his father was. I used to tell him about his father in the last war, and I knew he'd be like that! I'm glad I lived long enough to know that; though if I hadn't, doubtless my Lord would have told me about it after I get home."

There were tears dropping down the boy's face before she was done.

"Oh, Roxy, I'm glad you told me that!" he said. "I'm glad she lived to know about the nice things they said. But oh, if she could have lived a little longer till I got home!"

"Yes, I know, laddie!" soothed the old woman, coming over beside the bed.

The young man had buried his face in the pillow, and his shoulders were shaking with dry soundless sobs. Only the back of his head was visible, and one arm, with his hand gripping the bedclothes. Then old Roxy bent over and patted the thick dark hair that curled over his handsome head.

"But she said for you not to grieve, you know, laddie," continued the sweet old voice. "She said for you to live out your life and be happy till it was time for you to come Home, and She'd be waiting there to welcome you."

The shaking shoulders were suddenly still, and presently the soldier turned over and brushed the tears away, with a semblance of his old grin.

"Yes, I know," he said. "Now, let's go on from here. We'll talk about mother again, sometime, but now, tell me about the rest of the boys. What became of the Nezbit twins, Dave and Donnie? And where did they finally get away to? And where is Will Glegg?"

"Well, let me see. Dave an' Donnie, why they're over in Iceland,

and homesick as they can be fer a sight of home. Donnie wrote back
last fall some other fella got an autumn leaf in a letter from a girl, an'
it made them all envious, wantin' ta get back. An' Willy Glegg, he's
somewheres in Africa. They certainly do think up the most heathen-
ish places to send our boys to, seem's if they might have gone where
they wouldn't have to learn a new language."

The forlorn soldier began to laugh, and Roxy, was pleased, and
rattled on.

"Then there was Gene Tolland, he got hisself a nice fat office job
with plenty of gold stripes he hadn't earned fighting. Came back
here and strutted around like he owned the earth. And Phelps Larue
was missing in action. He would be you know. He was always everywhere when he was needed, and he had plenty honors to his credit.
And Taffy Rolland is out somewhere underseas in a submarine. That
don't seem right either, nice quiet boy like Taffy, never did anybody
any harm, and hasta go off undersea. How could he ever expect to do
anything for the war undersea? And Bill Brower, he got killed at
Guadalcanal they say, and that's about all the boys."

"And the girls?" asked the soldier. "Are they doing anything?"

"I should say they are," said Roxy. "Arta Perry and Franny Forsythe
went in training for nurses. They're off on a big transport somewhere. And Betty Price is a WAC, and the Bowman girls and Lula
Fritz are WAVES, or some of those A.B.C.'s, I forget what. And the
Grady, and Baker, and Watson girls went into a defense plant and
are welders. I must say I'm not sure I like nice girls going around
doing men's work, but I suppose that's what war is, and we can't
help it. Though in my day it wouldn't have been considered nice."

The young man on the bed laughed, and then after a moment He
asked:

"And whatever became of Hortense? Is she around here anywhere?"

"Oh, she got herself married soon after you left," announced Roxy
triumphantly.

"*Married?*" There was a shade of surprise in the voice of the soldier. Then after an instant, "Who did she marry?"

"Oh, she married some rich good-looking lieutenant, and then when
he got himself sent away off somewhere she tried to insist he refuse
to go, and when he wouldn't do as she wanted she got herself di-

vorced. Oh, she had some other trumped up excuse, but when it came to alimony they found he wasn't so rich after all, and she sort of lost out! And now I understand she's trotting around to camps and the places they call 'Centers,' entertaining soldiers. Though it never struck me she was very entertaining. Kind of coarse and loud I thought she was."

"You never liked Hortense, did you Roxy?"

"Oh, I wasn't so keen on her of course, but I did own she used to be pretty after a fashion. But she's changed a lot. She's all painted up fit to kill, got a mouth as big as a hollyhock, all greasy red stuff. I don't know why they paint 'em so thickly if they must paint 'em. But anyhow she's a sight. However, she's got plenty fellas to run after her where she is now, though I don't know what good it'll do her, when they're all going overseas all the time."

"No, you never did like Hortense," laughed the young man. "I always knew that."

"Well, neither did your mother," said Roxy belligerently, looking grim and sober. "Say, would you like another batch of pancakes? The griddle is still on. It won't take a minute."

"No, oh, no! I've eaten a big breakfast already, and I ought to be getting up sometime pretty soon."

"Oh, why not lie still and get a good rest? You had a long journey and you need to really sleep a lot to make up your strength There won't be anybody around today. They don't know you're home yet you know. You just keep quiet a day or two, till you really feel like going out. I won't let on you've come till you're ready to see people, and I'll tell Joel to keep mum too."

"All right," grinned the soldier, "maybe I will. This bed still feels pretty good to me," and he turned over and settled down for another nap.

Then out in the hall he heard the telephone ring, and heard the felt slippers shuffle to answer it. His senses were already drowsy with the thought that there was no need for him to rouse yet, but he heard a raucous voice, a girl's voice, asking a question about himself.

"When is Barney coming back?" it said.

Then his senses came alive a little. That was Hortense's voice, wasn't it? Sharper, more nasal, more possessive than it used to be?

And then Roxy, disapproving, reproving, quite final:
"Why, I really couldn't say!"
Barney grinned silently.
Then the other voice, murmuring sharply again. But something had happened to the telephone now. He couldn't hear the annoyed questions that were being asked next, for it seemed that Roxy's capable hand was being laid firmly over some part of the mechanism of the instrument so that the sound would not penetrate to the other end of the hall, and he could vision Roxy standing there with her thin lips firmly set in a grim line. Then he heard Roxy's voice again: "No, I really couldn't say No, I couldn't say!" That last with finality, and then the click of the receiver as Roxy hung up.

The young man on the pillow grinned to himself again. Foiled! Hortense was foiled, effectively. And yet apparently Roxy hadn't told any lies. Just reiterated that she couldn't say. And he knew her of old, that her grim conscience would not hold her to account for that statement, even though it was not made with the meaning that it might be understood to have. Roxy had a clever way of protecting her beloved ones when she felt they needed protection. And still grinning, the young man closed his eyes and surrendered himself to the luxury of going on with the rest he had been definitely ordered to take every day when he got home. Oh, it was good to be at home!

When next he came awake, some hours later, it was the clear sweet notes of a whistle that brought him back to his senses. It was a peculiar whistle, one that was all his own, and nobody else had ever seemed to be able to imitate, though many had tried. Its sweetness swept across his heart like a skillful hand on the strings of a harp, bringing back old days when home had been the place he loved best, and there was no grim specter of war anywhere. It was a sound of heartening cheer and it almost seemed to him that it came out of his dreams, so sweet and perfect it had been. Not just one note, but several tones, like a bit of a message. It was that peculiar trill that was not easy to imitate. He must have dreamed it! But no, there it was again, and now he was hearing the crunch of bicycle wheels on the gravel of the drive. Someone was coming to the house and giving that clarion call of his.

He sprang from the bed and stole to the window, peering from behind the curtain. Had some other boy succeeded in getting that whistle?

But now he could see, it was not a boy. It was a girl, riding a bicycle, carrying a small parcel in the rack before her. A girl with a cloud of golden hair.

He stepped back so he would not be seen, but kept her in view. Who could she be?

Then she called.

"Roxy! Oh, Roxy! Where are you? Mother sent you a pat of her new butter."

The girl stepped from her wheel, and lifted her face to scan the windows of the house. She was very lovely. A flash of shy blue eyes, wide and sweet, a beautiful face framed in apple blossoms. Then he heard Roxy's voice as she opened the kitchen door, and the vision vanished. There was only the bicycle lying on its side against the grassy terrace, and the sound of the closing kitchen door. She had gone inside. Who was she?

Yet that whistle still seemed to linger on the air hauntingly. Was she someone to whom he had tried to teach it?

Then a robin came noisily back to the branch by the window, looked down at the wheel on the ground, and turned a beady, wondering eye on Barney as he stirred behind the curtain.

Chapter 4

He waited breathlessly behind the screening curtain, and presently he heard the kitchen door open again, low voices, just a few words, then the girl came out, flinging backward to Roxy a kiss from her finger tips, and the single word: "Bye!" as she mounted her wheel and rode away. Out the gravel drive, down the road, a slender graceful figure in a soft gray suit with a rosy collar, a bright blue sweater, and gold hair flying back from her shoulders. She made a picture that toned well into the background of apple blossoms and tender new leaves. Barney stood and watched her as she flashed out into the sunlight and on down the road. Almost she might have been a bird, so swiftly and easily she rode.

When she disappeared from sight down toward the village the bird unfurled his wings and sailed into the spring sunshine, and the young man turned and picked up his garments to make a swift toilet. He had no desire any longer to lie and sleep. He wanted to get back into life and find out who that girl was, and how she happened to be able to give that whistle, which he had always supposed was his own private property.

Barney appeared down in the kitchen very soon.

"Roxy, wasn't there someone here a few minutes ago?" he asked, after he had greeted her. "Who was it?"

"Oh," said Roxy with distress in her tone, "did we waken you? I tried to be very quiet."

"No, you didn't waken me," laughed Barney. "It was the whistle wakened me. Roxy, who can whistle like that? I didn't know anybody but myself had that trick."

"Well, it was yourself that taught her to whistle. You've nobody else to blame."

"*I* taught her?" exclaimed the young man amazed. "But I don't remember ever teaching any of the *girls* to whistle. I didn't think they could. I tried to teach a couple of children now and then, but they couldn't seem to get it."

25

"Well, *one* of 'em did!" said Roxy firmly. "And it wasn't one of them silly girls that used to swarm around here, either. It was one of the little ones. Think back, boy, and see if you can't figure out who it was. You took a lot of pains teaching her, and she never forgot. She practiced and practiced after you went away, and once in a while she would come over to me and say, "Roxy, do I sound all right now? Do I do it at all the way Barney did?" And I would tell her how it sounded to me. But she said she wouldn't be satisfied till I couldn't tell the difference. Till she could make me think it was you come back again. So one morning she came early while I was getting breakfast for Joel, and I heard her whistling, and I went quick to the door with my heart all a-twitter, for I really thought it was you, come back somehow! Yes, I did! And when I saw her pert little face all a-twinkle, I knew she had reached her ambition and she could whistle as well as you did. So—that's the story! And to think you should hear her your first day when she didn't even know you were home!"

"Roxy, you don't mean that was Sunny Roselle? Not little Sunny! The little girl I used to play ball with?"

"The very same, Mr. Barney. She hasn't changed a mite, only grown up a little bit."

"But, I don't understand. The last time I saw her I'm sure she was only a child. Where has she been all this time? I haven't seen her since I went away to college. I thought the family had moved away. Didn't someone say so?"

"Children do grow up, you know," laughed Roxy. "And you remember there were two summers when you went out to the Warren farm to work as soon as you came back from college. You didn't see much of her then. And the next year she went off to stay with her grandmother who was getting old and sick and needed her. She was out there three years, off and on, her mother, too, part of the time, till her grandmother died, and then she came home again. No, the family didn't move away. They are right on their little farm just where they were. They still have the best garden in town, and make their own butter. Of course two of her brothers went away to the service, and there's only her youngest brother Frank left to help his father on the farm."

"Well, that's interesting," said Barney. "And I suppose Sunny is in high school by this time."

Roxy laughed.

"Yes, she's in high school all right, but she's a teacher, not a scholar. Why, boy, she must be all of nineteen by now, and they do say she's about the best teacher they ever had in that school, barring none."

"Sunny a *teacher!*" exclaimed Barney. "Why, I can't believe it. Little Sunny!"

"Wait till you see her!" said Roxy with satisfaction.

"Tell me about her," said the young man, settling back in the old kitchen chair, and clasping his hands behind his head with comfortable informality. "Is she as pretty as she used to be?"

"Prettier," said Roxy without reservation. "And she don't have to put a lot of paint and powder on to make herself look attractive either. She's as sweet and unspoiled as she was when she was a baby, and I don't believe you'll find another like her the whole country round."

"Well, that's great! I've often wondered what became of her. And you say it was she who was whistling when she came in? You say I taught her to whistle like that! Well I certainly am proud to know of it. That child! To think she's remembered it all these years!"

"Oh, yes, she remembered it. She never forgot anything you taught her. She adored the very ground you walked on in those days!"

"Yes we were pretty good pals," said Barney with a reminiscent grin. "But I suppose she's forgotten all about me by this time. Does she know I've come home?"

Roxy shook her head.

"No, I didn't tell her yet. I thought you wanted a few days to rest in before you began to see people."

"Oh, well, that goes for the others, but somehow I'd like to see Sunny. She's different. When will she come again?"

"Well, she's pretty busy with her school, and she helps her mother around the house too, since Miranda went down to the factory to do welding. They thought they ought to help the war that much by letting her go, and she was keen for it herself, though I guess it was hard for her to leave the Roselles, too."

"Well, then I suppose I ought to go and see Sunny, instead of expecting her to come over here the way she used to do when she was a

kid," said Barney thoughtfully. "I can't make it seem real that she is
grown up and rates being treated like a young woman."

"Oh, she's still a kid," smiled Roxy, "I'm sure she will be to you
anyway. Yet she seldom speaks of you except to ask now and then if
anything has been heard from you, and whether you're all right. She's
pretty much of a lady you know. Quiet like, and eyes like two stars.
She's grown up, but yes, she's still a kid," said Roxy happily. "And
the sweetest kid you ever saw. She may not be fashionable, but I
think she's a sight better looking than those other girls all painted up
and their fingernails like birds' claws. Oh, I can't abide the way they
fix their nails now!"

"Well I can't say I admire them either," said Barney with a shrug.
"I wonder what they do it for? It can't be pleasant to live with clattery claws like that on their hands, and surely they're not good-looking. It gives me the shivers just to see them."

"Oh, they think it's smart!" snapped Roxy with a disapproving
toss of her head. "That's all they live for nowadays, 'to be smaht!' "
and she imitated a silly girl's tone so exactly that it set Barney off
laughing again.

Roxy had to go out and look after her chickens then, and Barney
sauntered slowly into the other part of the house. Somehow he wanted
to take his first look around when he was by himself. There was
something sacred in the blessed places where he remembered his
mother's presence, and he wanted to take it for the first time, tenderly and alone.

Awhile he lingered in the library where she had always spent so
much time. The walls were almost lined with books, dear old books
that he had cherished, and his mother had loved.

Roxy, with a careful thought to Barney's tastes had built up a delightful fire in the old fireplace, and drawn up the big chair that had
always been his favorite seat, to tempt him to a pleasant rest. And it
was there she found him when she came in, deep in the old chair,
with a book, one of his old-time favorites, his long limbs stretched
out to the pleasant warmth of the kindly blaze, comfort and peace all
about him, the vague consciousness of his mother's desk there almost beside him. It seemed just as she had left it, neat papers and
letters in orderly fashion, tucked into their compartments as if she

had been there just that morning.

After awhile, maybe not today, but some day pretty soon, when he could bear it, he would go and sit where she had sat and look through all those papers, and perhaps read some of her last thoughts through their medium. But not now, not just this first morning. He did not want to brush aside the veil of make-believe and definitely feel that she was really gone forever— not just away. He would wait a few hours perhaps, or it might be a day or so, till he felt strong enough to stand it. But just now it was enough to sit here quietly, as if he were waiting for her to come in and talk with him. That was blessed, at least for the moment. And since he had been in the hospital he found that he had to take things of the heart slowly, adjust his mind and thoughts to the new order, and take it like a man. And that was the reason that he was so glad that Roxy was willing he should keep quietly out of sight for a little till he was used to the new way of his broken world. So he read an old book that he had loved in the past, and now and again he closed his eyes and prayed in his heart for strength to go on into the future that was before him.

His choice of course, after his resting time was done and when he felt fit again, would be to go back into war and do his part till the whole job was finished up and Right established once more in this seething world. Till Evil was vanquished, and the world safe for everybody. But that was dependent upon how quickly his strength came back, and what the doctors said. Well, he must take it a day at a time, and be ready for whatever was planned ahead for him of course. His mother had taught him that, and his war experience had taught him too. But the waiting was not an easy thing to do when his impatient soul was daily growing more eager to be back and into the great fray again. Just to lie by, and be an invalid, that was never an easy role for Barney Vance to play.

So as he reclined in the old easy chair and tried to read a book he used to love, these thoughts drifted in a background across his mind to reassure him. This was the important thing to do first. Just let the atmosphere of home and the past saturate his weary spirit, and hearten him, before he must meet life again and go on.

Into this quiet brooding atmosphere breezed Roxy, with her kindly smile and a brimming glass of milk.

"It's time you had a sip of milk, laddie," she said, "and a cooky or two? You used to like them for a snack when you were a child."

"Oh, Roxy, you're going to spoil me completely. I can see I'll have to get away from here in a hurry or I'll not be fit to get back into war when I'm called again."

"Oh, but we'll not talk about that now," said the old nurse. "Time enough for that when the call comes. Meantime it's good to see you sit there like you used to do. The fire on one side and your mommie's desk on the other."

Roxy dropped down on a straight chair for a minute watching the soldier boy drink the milk, so evidently enjoying it.

"Have you been over to her desk?" she asked, after a minute. "I've kept it just as she left it. I thought you would enjoy going through it. Indeed I think she thought you would want to do that, too. For the very last time she was downstairs she sat at her desk working away at the bit papers, and writing a line here and there. She sat there far too long that last day, I thought, for her own good, and when I urged her to let me help her back to her bed she would shake her head, and say, No, Roxy, I must finish here. You know I may not be well enough to come down again perhaps, and I want to get it all in order for my boy, if he comes home after I'm gone. So I thought you might feel it was something she left for you to go through. She might even have written a few words on something just for you, you know."

The young man caught his breath, and turned his face away toward the desk, that she might not see the mist in his eyes.

"I must go through it," he said. "I was working up to that but I wasn't sure I was up to bearing it yet." His voice was husky and he tried to give a pitiful little grin for Roxy's sake.

Wise Roxy rose, with no sign that she saw how much he was stirred by her words, and true to her old habit of keeping cheerful in an issue, put on a matter-of-fact tone:

"That's good, of course. You don't want to get yourself all worked up. She wouldn't have wanted that. She just wanted you to be comforted. And now, don't you think you've been up long enough and you ought to get back to your bed and take another long sleep? Tomorrow or the next day will be time enough for you to look into any business papers. She said they were not important, but you would want to look them over some time, and so she got them ready for you. Now, get you upstairs and take your nap, and after a while I'll be bringing your tray up. A bit of chicken cooked the way you used to like it. With dumplings? How is that?"

"Sounds swell," he said, slowly getting up from his chair and putting down his book on the table. "But you needn't bring it up. I can come down." Then after a minute, wistfully, "And will there be apple sauce?"

"Oh yes, surely," said Roxy smiling and winking back a recalcitrant tear of her own.

So she shooed him off to his rest, and went out to see how the chicken was getting on, and prepare her dumplings.

Barney did not get back to the library until late the next afternoon, though the thought of that precious desk was hovering in his mind. His heart cried out to go through it at once, but he wanted to do it alone. He did not want even Roxy watching him, not even her cheery voice commenting upon whatever he might find. The contents of that desk was too sacred for others to intrude upon him while he examined it.

So he slept late, waking only to hear the morning matins of the birds among the apple blossoms, and then drifting off to sleep again, taking the real rest that the doctor had hoped he would get when he once reached home.

He came down to the kitchen while Roxy was preparing lunch and talked with her, asking about some of his mother's old friends, discovering that some had moved away and a few had died, but quite a number were still living in their old homes, and often asked after him.

There had been no sweet piercing whistle that morning to turn his thoughts toward his young friend Sunny, and perhaps a feeling of self-consciousness prevented his speaking of her again. At least she was not mentioned.

Barney ate heartily of the delightful homemade soup compounded of meat and vegetables with plenty of light fluffy potatoes generously floating among the carrots and onions. He said how good it tasted. Told her that nobody else knew how to make soup like that, took a second helping, and then equally praised the apple and nut salad that came after, and declared that nobody could cook like Roxy, anyway.

He helped to dry the dishes and when the kitchen and dining room were in spic-and-span order he drifted into the library again and took some time selecting a book to read, waiting till Roxy should go up-stairs for her afternoon nap.

But Roxy sensed that he wanted to be entirely alone for a little, and so she put her head in at the door and said:

"Would you mind if I just run out for a wee while? I promised old lady Sanborne I would run over and write a bit of a letter for her to her daughter. She can't see so good any more, and she finds it hard to write. You won't feel lonesome, will you?"

"No, of course not. I'll be all right. It's very restful here you know, Roxy. I'm just luxuriating in the quiet. Stay as long as you like. There are plenty of books around for me to enjoy."

So Roxy took off her apron and put on her little shoulder cape and hurried away down the road, promising to be back soon. And Barney laid down his book where he could easily assume it again if need be, and went to the window, watching her away down the road until she turned off toward the Sanborne cottage. Then with a sigh of relief he went quickly over to his mother's desk and sat down, as if he were keeping a rendezvous with her.

Tenderly he looked over the whole front of the familiar desk. It seemed so much as usual. Dear mother! Yet he sensed that it was in more than its accustomed tidy order. His mother had prepared it for him to go over.

And so he began at the right-hand cubby hole, and went slowly, steadily through them all. Neat packets of letters from friends and distant relatives, some since now dead, but letters that were notably friendly and newsy. Barney found himself fancying that his mother had retained these thinking he might enjoy reading them. A few from a favorite and ancient great aunt who had a keen sense of humor and could make the simplest remarks in droll and original language, with grotesque pen sketches illustrating her news. He read them through, and had a feeling that his mother was there, enjoying them with him. What a beautiful thing it was for her to have done, to arrange this little getting-together with her for his homecoming! More than once this thought brought tender tears to his eyes, as slowly he read on from one neat packet to the next, folding them back when he had read them, into their confining bands as he had found them.

Then he came to more recent letters, showing sympathy for her in her illness, cheering her up, speaking of her boy who was fighting overseas. He hurried through those. It wasn't pleasant to him to realize how hard his mother's lonely part had been in this terrible war, sickness and pain, and anxiety for her beloved son!

Then there was a compartment of business letters, clear statements of transactions made since he had left, receipts in full of all bills, so that he might understand what she had done.

He found that she had put all her business into a joint account of herself and her son, so that he would have no trouble, and there would be no delay in his taking over when he came back. It seemed that she had thought of everything. There was even a little book of notes, telling where certain important papers, and keys would be found and just what had been put into the safety deposit box in the bank.

He went rapidly through all these business matters, knowing that their time would come in later when he felt strong enough to go into everything with his mother's lawyer, and finally he came to a single letter, bearing his name, his mother's handwriting, a letter from the dead!

With a quick sore breath of a sigh almost like a sob he drew it out and began to read.

> My precious Barney:
> This is probably the last letter I will write you on this earth—

His eyes were blurred with tears so that the precious words were almost dimmed by them, and he had to brush them away before he could go on reading. And then he sat back and looked at those words again as if there were glimpses of her beloved face in the written lines. His dear mother, gone from him, but thinking of him at the last minute and leaving him a message—!

Then suddenly there was a sound at the side door, rushing noisy feet, sharp heels clicking across the linoleum of the hall, coming straight and inexorably toward his hiding place. Who could it be? Not Roxy. No! Some intruder!

Instinctively he gripped the precious letter and stared toward the door, which he had taken the precaution to close before he sat down at the desk, but now it was suddenly burst open, tempestuously, as if the intruder would brook no resistance, and a girl with black hair, great dark bold eyes, and a painted face flung herself arrogantly into the room. A girl with sharp red fingernails like claws on her lily white fingers, and a number of noisy clattery rings and bracelets jingling as she moved.

"Well, there you are at last, Barney Vance! I knew I could find you in spite of that old hag of a nurse of yours. I knew she was lying when she wouldn't tell me when you were coming. So I went to the postmaster and found out you were getting letters in the mail, so I just watched my chance when your keeper was out and stole a march on her. And here you are! Darling you look *grand*! And I've come to drag you out of your shell and help you to have some good times and make you forget war. But say, you look wonderful in your uniform! And won't I put it all over the other girls to think I've seen you first! Look up and smile, can't you? I'm Hortense. Your old friend. Your almost fiancée. We were almost engaged before you left, weren't we, Barney? And if it hadn't been for a snooping prowler of a nurse, and a prissy mother, we probably would have been married before you left, too, wouldn't we dolling?"

And Barney Vance sat there by his mother's desk, with her precious last letter, still unread, gripped fiercely in his fingers, and his knees shaking like any girl's—was it with weakness or anger?—and glared sternly at the unwelcome visitor.

Chapter 5

There was a long moment of silence while the two took stock of one another, and the young man's glare did not change. The girl was almost taken aback at his silence.

"What's the matter with you, Barney Vance, don't you know me? I haven't changed so much have I? You needn't put on that far-away superior army air. You and I *were* practically engaged you know before you went away to war."

"We were *what?*" asked the young soldier fiercely, hastily wrapping his long fingers protectively about the letter he held, slowly, carefully laying it in its original folds, placing it definitely, in an inner pocket, as if he would shield it from contact with the very air this arrogant person breathed.

"Why engaged. Or practically so, don't you know? We would have been openly engaged if you hadn't been so much afraid of your fussy old mother. In fact I think we would have been married before you left if she hadn't interfered with her puritanical ideas, so I went away. It seems funny, doesn't it, that we let people with such funny old-fashioned ideas manage us that way? Sometimes it is easy to see why we needed a war, to wake us up and make us understand that we didn't have to be tied down by such fantastic obedience to our elders. My word! I sometimes wonder how we existed in those days. You certainly must have enjoyed the freedom when you got away from home and in the army among real men, didn't you? But you certainly remember we were practically engaged once."

Barney lifted a haughty chin. The weakness in his knees was beginning to go away now, and anger was surging over him. What right had this girl to barge in here without being asked, as if she belonged, and insult his mother, and the way he had been brought up? He roused to answer coldly:

"Not that I remember," he said brusquely.

"Now Barney, don't be so obtuse."

"It certainly never entered my head that we were anything more than schoolmates. You and I were practically only kids when we last saw each other, too young to give even a thought to engagement or marriage. You must have got your memories mixed." He ended with a distant grin that practically put the whole idea out of the running.

"Now Barney, you horrid thing! What are you trying to do? Take all the romance out of our friendship? And here I've been missing you all this long time, and trying my best to forget you, and I just couldn't do it. I keep thinking back to the time when we were playing games in your dining room and hall and you caught me under the stairs and almost kissed me once, only your snooping old mother came along and stopped you just in time."

The young man arose suddenly, haughtily.

"You will leave my mother out of the conversation, Hortense. She is too precious to me to allow you to insult her."

"But I wasn't insulting her," laughed the young woman. "I talk the same way about my mother. They couldn't help it that they were born in the Victorian age. But I'm glad I'm out from under, and free to do as I please. And your mother is gone now, and you are free to act yourself. I don't see why you want to be so stuffy about it."

To do Hortense justice she had been to a luncheon and then a tea that afternoon and had partaken of altogether too many cocktails to be quite her normal self, and by this time Barney had begun to recognize that fact, and take the situation in hand.

"Suppose we go out to the porch," he suggested stiffly. "It seems close in here," and he led the way to the side door.

"By the way, how did you say you knew I was in town?" he asked in a formal tone as they went out. "I came at night, and I didn't know anybody knew I was here yet. You see I'm supposed to be under orders to keep very quiet for a while and not see people."

"Oh, *really*? Now Barney that sounds ridiculous! You look just as well as ever, and everybody knows that what a returned soldier needs is a lot of company and a lot of cheering up. That's what I came for, to cheer you up."

"You don't say so!" said the young man with a sardonic grin, though there was still an angry note in his voice. "Well, if you did, please lay off that bunk about our being engaged, for it wasn't true and you know it. Now, come out and see my apple trees in blossom. They're a lovely sight. And don't let's talk about me any more. Tell me about yourself. What have you been doing?"

Barney drew a long breath as the out-of-door air, sweet with the breath of blossoms, reached him. This was a healthier atmosphere. Somehow it didn't seem as if she *could* quite be so unpleasant out here.

He drew out one of the big rockers tidily tied into white linen covers in Roxy's best style.

"Sit down," he said politely. "Now tell me about yourself. What has happened to you? You know I haven't been home long enough to get any of the gossip. What are you doing with yourself? You're not in uniform, so I judge you didn't join any of the army organizations. I suppose you must be doing defense work of some sort."

Barney was struggling for his best polite manner, in order to awe this terrible girl. If she got interested in talking about herself she might forget to insult his mother, or to claim an undue intimacy for their past. She must be a little drunk or she would never go to such lengths. She was grown up now, and surely she would not insult his mother who had often given her hospitality in the days that were gone.

He drew up another chair, not too near, and settled back wearily dropping his eyelids down for just an instant and taking a deep breath.

"You'll have to excuse me if I don't talk much," he said. "I've been in the hospital for a number of weeks, and I'm just home after a long hard journey you know. You do the talking. What are you? A defense worker, or a nurse?"

"Yes, well, suppose you and I have a little smoke to begin with," said the girl. "This isn't going to be easy for me either, you know. Give me a cigarette. I've used mine all up this afternoon."

"Sorry," said Barney haughtily. "I don't have any. Had you forgotten I'm not a smoker?"

"Now Barney Vance. You don't mean to tell me that you've been away to war and haven't learned to smoke yet?"

"Oh, does one have to *learn* to smoke?" said the young man amusedly.

"But I thought the army made real men out of boys," said Hortense contemptuously. "I thought surely when you got away from your mother's apron strings you'd turn out to be a real man."

"Oh," said Barney with quizzical lifted brows, "does smoking make a real man out of a boy?"

"Don't be silly," said Hortense. "You know all men in the service smoke and drink."

"Oh no," said the young soldier, "I know quite a number who don't. But don't let's argue about that. You were going to tell me about yourself."

Hortense flung him a sullen furious look.

"Well, get me a drink then and I'll go on. I've got to have something to hearten me."

"A drink? Why certainly," said the young man rising, "come back with me to the old pump. Roxy always keeps some nice clean glasses on the shelf by the door, and the water is ice cold, you remember."

He rose and led her back to the old pump where they used to drink as children.

"*Water?*" said Hortense contemptuously, "I want something stronger than that. Get me some brandy or wine or something real. It isn't easy for me to tell my story."

"Sorry," said Barney genially. "You'd better try the water. You'll find it good and cold and quite heartening. I'm quite sure there isn't any other kind of liquor in the house, unless you'd like a glass of milk, or I could make you a cup of tea."

"Heavens! No," said the girl in contempt.

She took a small sip of the clear cold water and flung the rest on the ground. He took the glass from her, and led the way back to the chairs where they had been sitting.

"But Heavens! Barney! You aren't going to stand for that sort of thing are you, now your mother is gone? Of course I knew she was always a terrific temperance woman, but surely now you can have a mind of your own. You don't have to live on her ideas after you are a man do you? Don't you realize that there is nobody left in this world that you have to *obey* any more? Nobody who can force their ideas and doctrines upon you, nobody to say you have to do anything? I know your mother dominated you, but now you can do as you please."

"And did you think I had no convictions of my own?"

"Of your *own*? Why of course not. You never were allowed to do the things the rest of us did."

"I beg your pardon. That is not true," said the young man gravely. "I was taught to think things out for myself, and decide what was wise and right, after I had looked into the subject carefully. And I have not found that the army life has changed many of those convictions thus formed. But we are getting away from our subject. I believe when we came out here you were going to tell me of yourself. We did not come out here to talk about me and my principles, or convictions of right and wrong. Here's a cushion in this other chair. Perhaps that will make you a little more comfortable. Now, sit down and begin. You do the talking. What are you? A defense worker? A nurse?"

Hortense laughed derisively.

"Me? A defense worker! Not on your life!" she drawled. "You couldn't drag me into a thing like that. I couldn't be bothered. I m just myself, out to have a good time!"

Barney's annoyed eyes studied her derisively for a moment and suddenly he knew what it was in this girl that his mother had disliked. Mother had been keen. She had seen deep into the character of Hortense Revenal even when she was but a child, and had done her best to guard her son from contact with her.

And yet she was beautiful, after a bold coarse fashion. She had the faculty for taking her own native prettiness and developing it to its fullest extent, even when it meant bringing out her worst traits. She well knew how to lift her lashes and bring an appeal to her great black eyes. She was an adept in all the arts of a woman who wants to appeal to men. And Barney saw now that Hortense was bringing to bear all her arts upon him.

She dropped gracefully into the chair that Barney had brought for her and gave him a ravishing smile.

"Yes?" said the young man. "Well, did you find the good time?"

He watched her as one would watch and study a forward child, although there was nothing at all about Hortense that was childlike. But she quickly snatched the role offered her and began to act it out.

So," she said dolefully. "I didn't! I did the best I could, but the fates were against me."

"Oh, how is that?" asked the soldier with a quizzical lifting of his brows.

"Well, you see Barney, I got married," she confessed with down-drooping lashes, and an upward quick glance to see what effect that fact would have upon him.

But Barney, not by so much as the flicker of an eyelash let it be known that this was no news to him. He took it quite calmly as if he had not heard it before, and as if it made no difference in the world to him.

"Yes?" he said in a matter-of-fact tone, "well surely that gave you happiness, a good time, didn't it? That is something that is generally supposed to make people very happy."

The black lashes continued to droop, the cheeks were deeply flushed—or was that just the paint? Had they been as red as that before they came out to the porch? Barney wasn't sure.

Then the pouting lips spoke, reluctantly, drawlingly:

"That is what I thought, too," said Hortense dramatically. "But I found it makes all the difference in the world who you marry."

"Well, yes, of course," said the young soldier amusedly, "but I would have supposed that you would have looked out for that little matter before you married."

"Well, I thought I did," the girl drawled. She wasn't so good in the role of humility, shameful shyness, but she was attempting it artfully. "He was a rather swell person. At least I thought he was. And reported to be very wealthy in his own right. I couldn't see anything the matter with him, except that he wasn't the man I was in love with. But he had gone off to war, and there wasn't anything I could do about that, so I thought I would take the next best thing that offered. You see, Barney, it was really you I cared for, but when you went off that way without making me marry you, I was terribly hurt, and I felt I must do something else. Life was simply unbearable without you, and I thought if I could go places and do things and have a good time I would forget you."

"Well, now that's too bad, Hortense. I didn't know that I had had such an unfortunate effect upon you. It never entered my mind that you and I were more than mere acquaintances, sort of playmates, schoolmates, neighbors. But I think you were very wise if you found someone else who was worthy, who might take your mind off of one who wasn't interested in you, you were very wise to marry. Where is he now? Overseas? Is that why your marriage didn't bring you happiness?"

"I'm sure I don't know where he is now," said Hortense sullenly. "That was the first difference we had. I found he was determined to go in the service, and I did simply everything to stop him, but he wouldn't give it up."

"But of course," said the soldier, "anybody that was worth anything would feel that way."

"Oh, of course you would *have* to say that. You're a soldier yourself. But look at you. You came home as quick as they would let you, didn't you?"

"No," said Barney steadily, "I was sent home because I wasn't able to do the job for awhile, and much against my will I was ordered home to recuperate. I'm only anxious to get back and help finish my job as soon as they will let me. But we're not talking about me now. Go on with your story. So he went, did he?"

"Yes, he went. But before he went I found out that he wasn't the wealthy person I had been told he was at all, and he couldn't settle hardly anything on me, and I was about as badly off as I was before. So before he went I got a divorce, but that didn't help me either. It didn't bring me any money at all. And now I'm up a tree, and I thought I'd come to you and see if you wouldn't help me. You were always kind, Barney, and I knew I had to have some real man, someone I could really trust. Will you help me, Barney?" She gave him a languishing, pleading look. "Will you?"

Barney drew a deep breath. What kind of a situation was this going to be for him to get into? What was this girl aiming for anyway? Did she want to borrow money?

Then suddenly he heard a step in the hall, coming from the way of the back door and Roxy marched out on the porch and stood like a Nemesis looking at the drooping girl.

"And what is all this," asked Roxy sternly. "How did you come here?"

Hortense looked up, brushed a few false tears from her big, black eyes, and gave Roxy a casual glance, as if she were scarcely worth noticing.

"Oh, hello, Roxy," she said unconcernedly. "What are you? A special kind of a watch dog? You lied to me, didn't you, when I asked you when you expected Barney, but I was too smart for you, and you'll find out I can always outsmart you Roxy. Run along now. We were right in the middle of a confidential talk that's very important. I've been asking for some advice. Hurry along and leave us to ourselves, won't you?"

This interlude was just long enough to give the young soldier a

chance to think just what he should do, and when Hortense dismissed
Roxy so summarily, and she grimly stood there looking at him questioningly, he turned toward her pleasantly with his old smile.

"Yes, Roxy, I know that I'm off my schedule a bit, but I'm going to
lie down right away. I just want to give Hortense an address and then
I'll go right upstairs, and perhaps you will give the young lady a bit
of your lovely cake and a cup of tea after I'm gone."

Roxy stood there grimly looking as if she would like to say: "I'll
do nothing of the kind," but Barney took out his pencil and a card
and wrote an address on the card, handing it over to the girl with
another smile.

"I'm sorry, Hortense, I'm afraid I'm not up to giving you any advice or help this time, but here is the address of an old friend of mine
who is a very wise man, and kindly. Just tell him I sent you to him,
and I know he will do all he can for you. Now good afternoon, and
we'll probably be meeting again before I go back overseas. So nice
to have seen you. I know you'll excuse me under the circumstances!"
The tall young soldier made his way quickly upstairs, quietly locking his door when he reached the haven of his own room.

And Hortense stood looking at the card he had given her and then
she looked up at Roxy and made a face at her.

"So! You think you won this time, don't you? But you can't always tell. I got here first, and after this I'll thank you to keep out of
my affairs. You certainly can't think you're still Barney Vance's nurse,
can you? Surely you know he's grown up, and his mother isn't here
any more to back you up."

Roxy held her head high and said in her grimmest tone, "Will you
have your tea with lemon or cream?"

"Neither!" said Hortense with a lofty look, "I'm going where I can
get something stronger than I can find in this antique dwelling, but
you needn't think you can keep that young man under your thumb
any longer. He's grown up, and I have my plans for the future."

Then she pranced across the porch, and down the steps to her car,
and Barney, watching out the window above, to his great relief saw
her drive away.

And Roxy, down on the porch where Hortense had left her, stood
and shook a menacing fist at the back of the car as it disappeared in
the distance.

Chapter 6

When the car was out of sight down the road Barney suddenly found himself greatly shaken. It wasn't alone that this girl had barged in on him when he was just about to get a message from the dead, although that of course was the beginning of it. But by this time he was so outraged at what had followed that he had almost forgotten that precious letter which he had managed to thrust inside his coat before she saw it, but it was the whole affair. To think that one of his former associates had turned into such a girl—That she had actually dared to disparage his precious mother's memory, that she had declared herself in love with him, and claimed a former engagement. He was enraged by the whole matter.

He went and sat down in the big easy chair and closed his eyes. He drew a deep breath, and then another, and realized that he was more shaken than he liked to own even to himself.

This was no way for a soldier to feel, just because a silly girl, who was really half drunk had said a few foolish things. He should be above caring about things like this. The doctor must have been right after all about his physical condition. If he wanted to get ready to go back to the front he must be able to meet such trifling emergencies, and vanquish them. And it was not a victory just to excuse himself and say he must take a nap because it was in his schedule. He didn't do that when the submarine attacked the ship and for a time they were all in danger of going to the bottom of the sea. Why should he fall before a silly unscrupulous girl? He must get over this. He must go to his stronghold and get strength.

And there in his quiet room, he leaned his head on his uplifted hand and prayed in his heart for a way to meet this situation. For somehow he sensed that this was not just a brief attack by a person outside of his serious world. It was the beginning of a siege, and his experience as a soldier had taught him not to go into combat with *any* enemy, no matter how harmless he seemed, without orders from his commanding officer. So now Barney was asking for orders.

43

Back in those last few weeks of his strenuous war-life, those weeks during which he had done all that "noble work" in battle that the world over here was beginning to prate about and plan to lift him up as a hero, there had been a comrade, one who though he wore the insignia of high rank, went by the endearing name to his comrades, of "Stormy" Applegate.

Almost at once when Stormy came among their company he and Barney had become friends, had also recognized that both gave allegiance to a higher power than any on earth, had often held brief sweet converse of heavenly ways in the midst of an earthly tumult, to the great heartening of both their spirits! Barney thought of him now as he bent his head to ask for orders, for it was Stormy who had first brought this idea to mind.

"For you know, fella', there are spiritual enemies that come on us unawares, snipers and sharpshooters, hiding behind ever tree and shadow, and we're almost apt to think they are one of our own number sometimes, unless we always have our eyes to the Captain. We've just *got* to ask for orders, and then rest it there, knowing we'll be guided right."

Barney half smiled with a tender curve to his lips as he thought of this, and rested his soul about the whole matter. He wished with all his heart that Stormy were there now to talk with him.

For it was Stormy who had been there the night he got his worst wound, that almost finished him and left him lying in the dark among a nest of enemies, dying he thought, and unable to get to his knees and creep away to safety. It was Stormy, who, just back from a noteworthy mission of his own, weary and hungry and all in, Stormy who had gone out to hunt him. Against odds almost impossible he went, and *found* him, quite unconscious, all but dead, and putting him on his shoulder, went toiling back to camp. Stormy had saved his life. Yet when he came back to consciousness Stormy was gone again, out on a secret mission of great danger. For Stormy was a special man, detailed for mysterious missions, seldom expected to return when he went among the enemy. Yet time and time again he had come back, quietly, stepping in among them, greeting them as if he had only been out for a walk, and ready to go again whenever he was sent. When they asked their chaplain how it was he was able to come back, he smiled quietly and said: "Because he goes in the strength of the Lord."

Barney had not seen Stormy now for months. For Stormy had gone away while Barney was still unconscious, on the most dangerous mission of all. Barney had not even been able to thank him for saving his life. And this time he had not come back! It was generally supposed that he had been captured by the enemy, or even killed, or he might be languishing in a concentration camp, or even tortured by the enemy. If they found out in what capacity he had served they would surely wreak vengeance upon him.

"But I don't believe it," Barney had said when they told him about it afterward. And when they asked him why he didn't believe it, he answered with a confident smile: "Because he went in the strength of the Lord."

"Yes, but," said a doubtful listener, "suppose the Lord had something else for Stormy to do this time instead of coming back?" and Barney had answered thoughtfully, "That might be so. But sometime I believe he will come back. I wish it could be before I start for home. I want to thank him for bringing me back to camp. You'll tell him, boys?" And they had promised. Yes, they would tell him.

Barney was wishing for him now. He longed for his understanding companionship, in this new world to which he had come back, where people did not all seem to know there *was* a war, and that life was real. And more than anything he longed to be well enough and allowed to go back to search for Stormy, who had searched for him and brought him back from almost certain death. Now if he might only find his friend, and bring him back!

Of course it had been long days since he had left the place from which Stormy had gone out on his mission. And it had been some time that he had been on the way home, and had had no word. There would be no way perhaps that he could find out if Stormy had come back until he got back overseas again. Or would there? He must look into that. But oh, if he only might go and find Stormy!

These thoughts helped to turn Barney's mind away from his afternoon caller, until his spirit was quieted, and his muscles and emotions had ceased to tremble. Little by little, he went back over the happenings of the afternoon. It was then he remembered his mother's letter, the letter he had not read. His hand went quickly to its hiding place, within the breast of his coat, suddenly anxious lest he might have dropped it in coming up the stairs. No, it was there safely.

He took it out and smoothed the rumpled pages, tenderly, thrilled to hold it now, and to know that he was at last free to read it.

My precious Barney:

This is probably the last letter I will write you on this earth. I know from what the doctor told me, and the way I feel, that I am almost at the end of this life, and ready to walk into the presence of the Lord. Our Lord, Barney! You don't know how it thrills me to know that He is truly your Lord as well as mine. It is what I have hoped and prayed for all these years. But although you outwardly acquiesced I was never quite sure that you really knew Him.

So, your last letter, in which you said you had met Him out on the battlefield, and taken Him for your own Saviour, has given me joy beyond any I had hoped to know on this earth. Dear boy, it was worth all the dread and agony and suffering of parting from you, of having you so far away, your location a mystery sometimes, danger and death around you constantly. It was worth all that to have this knowledge now, while I am still on this earth, and to be able to thank you for writing it to me at once.

So dear son, I'm rejoicing that you are born again, and that I am sure we shall meet in Heaven. It just might be, you know, that the Lord Jesus may come for His own while you are still on this earth, in which case I'll be coming with Him, and we'll meet in the air. But in any case I'll likely be there first. I'll be waiting for you at the gate when you come. And I'm expecting to meet your father there too.

So now dear child, a last bit of warning. Don't let your enemy, the devil, deceive you into getting separated from your Lord. He knows his time is short, and he'll be trying to get you in the subtlest way he has.

And one more thing. Be careful who you marry, Barney! Be sure she knows your Lord. It can make a lot of sorrow for you if she isn't a true believer. And blessings on you both dear lad, when you find the right girl.

Now don't grieve for me, dear. There isn't time. You've a job to do for the Lord. You've witnessing to do in the world. Let your life speak louder than words, and your words be always guided by Him.

And it won't be long, dear lad. It just might be that I may even be allowed to watch you as you come on your way to join me. So good-by till then.

Your loving mother,
Mary Graham Vance.

Barney sat a long time with the finished letter in his hands the slow tears streaming down his cheeks. Yes, she had told him not to grieve for her, but he was not aware of the tears. His heart seemed welded to hers, his precious mother! To have this letter seemed a dearer treasure than any gift she could have left him. Her memory had always been dear to him whenever he had been away even for a little while, for he had loved her deeply from babyhood. But now she seemed to be more his than ever in their lives before, for now their love was bound about with the love of Christ who died for them, and in Whom they both believed. It seemed to the young man as he sat there alone in the darkening room, that he grew up in that brief hour, more than in all his years before, even more than he had grown up during the terrible revelations of war, with death and hate stalking the way on every hand. Just to know his mother's God had been as real to her as He had been years ago when she first taught his baby lips to pray, was satisfaction for all his doubts of the past, assurance for the future, even if that future contained more sorrow and disappointment, more war, and sudden death. It would not be long. He had her word for it, that it would not be long. Tenderly he bowed his head and laid his lips on the precious letter, and there in the darkness he prayed:

"Dear God! Keep me faithful. Keep me close. Make my life a true witness. Guard me in *any* temptation, and give me Thy righteousness and Thy strength."

It almost seemed as he lingered with bowed head, that he felt his mother's presence there beside him, her dear hand upon his head, as in the old days. And her Lord's presence filled the room with unspeakable joy and promise.

Then he heard Roxy come slowly, hesitantly up the stairs, and linger outside his door, listening. She would be thinking he was asleep perhaps, and doubtless she had prepared a nice dinner. He must not disappoint her. She would be bringing up a tray pretty soon.

"Coming, Roxy!" he called. "Do you want me?"

"I thought you might be wanting a bite to eat," she said wistfully. "It's all ready. I'll be bringing you a tray."

"No, Roxy! I'm coming down. I've had a good rest, and now I'm coming down to supper. Coming right away!" and his voice had that old hearty ring that cheered her heart.

She eyed him anxiously as he entered the dining room. It couldn't be that his pleasant manner came from any memory of that hussy, Hortense's visit could it? If that was it she had far rather see him glower.

But he looked her straight in the eye, seeming to read her thought, and beamed out his old grin to reassure her. "She's some terrific brat, isn't she, Roxy? That's what you think, don't you? And I agree with you."

Roxy's face relaxed into smiles.

"Well, I thought if you didn't see I didn't know what I should do. Your mom would be terrible worried."

"Yes, I know, Roxy. Mother never trusted her, and I guess she wasn't far wrong in her reading of that girl, even when she was a kid. But, poor kid! How did she get that way? What was her mother doing? Why didn't she bring her up right?"

"Well, laddie, her mom was a fool, that's why. Your mom knew that when she invited her over here and tried to get acquainted with her, but she never come but once. All she wanted to do when she got here was fool with them bits of playin' cards and eat cakes, and when she found your mom wasn't interested, she went off visitin' where they had big parties and danced a lot. And she had lots of callers, men callers, an' a tough-lookin' lot they was too. That was her life, and that poor child had to suffer for it. Of course it wasn't the child's fault in the first place perhaps, but she certainly has growed up to be a menace to the community. That's what I heard the minister's wife say about her the other day at the Ladies' Aid. She didn't know I heard her, she was talkin' confidential like to the senior elder's wife, and she said, low-like, 'that girl's a menace to the community. She certainly is. I wish she would get to work doing something worthwhile. But I don't know where it would be that she couldn't do all sorts of harm to the people she worked with.' That's exactly what she said. But of course I wouldn't repeat it, only to you. Because I want you to know it's not just because I don't like the girl."

"I understand, Roxy," grinned Barney. "You're only repeating it to me because you want me to understand that I'm in danger from her. Is that it, Roxy? Come now. 'Fess-up?"

Roxy giggled, unable to retain her serious poise of gravity, and her anxious expression relaxed.

"Well, yes, I 'spose there's lots to say to excuse her from the little bringin' up she had, but still—well, she's a menace all the same. Every last boy she can get her hands on she winds right around her little red-clawed finger. Hardly a one of them has the nerve to turn her down. It's curious. They all see what she is, and yet they fall for her."

Well, Roxy, I expect she'll bear praying for, won't she?"

Roxy, looked embarrassed.

"Well, now,—that sounds like your mom. It certainly does. But all the same I'd say it was safer for the prayin' ones to be women. I just wouldn't trust most of the men I know to get even that close to her, as prayin' would be. I tell you, boy, she's got the devil in league with her, an' no mistake."

Barney looked gravely back.

"I expect she has, Roxy. Most wrong people have, when you come to consider it, haven't they? The only sure way is for the people who are doing the praying to get in league with the Lord isn't it?"

A surprised light rose in old Roxy's eyes. She almost choked on a bread crumb, and sudden tears came in her kind old eyes. Glad eyes they were now, and no mistake, but embarrassed.

"You—sound—like your little—mom—boy!" she stammered out.

"I guess if you talk like that I needn't worry about you any more."

"Oh," said Barney with a twinkle. "Were you worrying about me? Well, that's good of you Roxy, but I'm with the Lord now, Roxy, so suppose you find somebody else to worry about. Say, Roxy, this is swell soup. It tastes like the old times. I shall get well so quick on such fare as you are giving me, that I'll have to be getting my bags packed pretty soon to go back."

"No chance!" said Roxy with a new look of alarm on her kindly features. "You promised me you wouldn't go till the doctor said it was all right for you to go."

There was so much alarm and pleading in her voice that Barney began to laugh.

"Now Roxy, don't you go and get excited. I have no intention of leaving your tender ministry until it is quite all right for me to go, and you'll find the army is pretty rigid about their restrictions. I suspect they'll keep me here far longer than I feel I should stay. However, we haven't come to that question yet awhile. What we've got to concern ourselves about is what we are going to do about these old friends. Are any more of them as far out of the way as Hortense?"

"Well, there's a-plenty of them need prayin' for, if that's what you mean. I reckon prayin' is about as good a way to deal with them as there is, and not quite so dangerous as some other ways. Yes, there's a few girls are followin' in Hortense's ways just as fast as they can. They've got a start kickin' at the traces, an' they think it's smart. You'll see when you get around."

"That's too bad, Roxy. How about Sunny? Is there any danger of her getting the disease? I'd hate to see her growing up to drink and smoke, and talk the way Hortense did today."

Roxy's face beamed into a smile.

"No, Sunny's not like that. She hasn't the time, and wouldn't have the interest if she did have the time. Besides they don't have anything to do with her. They think she's only a stuffy old school teacher. A 'working girl' they call her. They couldn't be bothered with keeping children still and trying to teach them anything."

"That's good!" said the young man. "One less thing to worry about. But say, when is Sunny coming to see us? Does she know I'm here?"

"Well, if she doesn't I suppose somebody'll tell her pretty soon, but I think likely that would be the very reason she wouldn't come. She may have heard you're here, and she's not one to call on a young man, especially when he's a soldier who has been advertised as a hero. Sunny realizes that she was a little child when you knew her, and she's not one to force herself to the front, even to claim an old playmate."

"Oh, so that's it, is it? Well then I see *I'll* have to go call on her. Just find out for me what day and hour would be most agreeable for her to receive me, and I'll lose no time. I want to see how she looks, and make her whistle for me. You don't suppose she'd come over and play ball with me some evening, do you? I think I'll be fit enough for that in a few days. And couldn't we have a tea party out on the terrace? The side away from the road you know, where there couldn't be any intruders barging in on us? I think that would be great!"

Roxy smiled, and entered into the plan eagerly, then hurried away to hand Joel the pail of chicken feed, and to pour the new milk he brought into the shining old pans standing ready for it. Barney finished his meal thoughtfully with some of Roxy's wonderful chocolate cake and peach preserves, and finally went up to his room, feeling quite ready for rest. Also he had some praying to do tonight. That was like getting ready for a battle. His heart must be prepared for whatever the Lord was planning ahead. He felt as if his Christian life had taken a new lease after he had lain dormant so long in the hospital. His mother's letter had given him the impetus, and now he felt he had a job here at home to do, before the Lord would send him back to war again. There was a foe here he could see now, as well as across the water.

And over in the town a couple of miles away, in an ornate boardinghouse, Hortense was laying plans and smiling in anticipation of the way she meant to snare Barney.

Chapter 7

About that same time in a bleak detention camp in a far land almost the other side of the world, Stormy Applegate was stealing cautiously in the dead of night out from the surveillance of the enemy. He had done his deadly work that he had come over there to do, had obtained information, and left misleading papers in code behind him in such a way that they would bewilder the enemy, and now he had but to make his getaway. But it was by far the most hopeless looking situation from which he had ever attempted to escape. Only a dummy hastily devised from a log and some of his own garments which he could ill afford to spare on that bitter cold night had made it possible, and even now that might at any minute be found out.

The location was bleak and with little if any spot that might be a shelter. Twice he had almost been discovered, but lying like a log the sleepy guard had not noticed him and had passed on. And now there was barely a brief interval before he would come again. Could he cross that wide stretch of open ground before he arrived? And having crossed it safely would there be another guard more vigilant beyond? Even the stars seemed to have withdrawn their light, and he could not be sure of his direction, although he thought it was ingrained into his very being. Every inch he rolled, every foot he crawled was but an experiment in a great venture for his life.

Wide away toward the homeland somewhere was Barney Vance. Barney had known he was to try this venture sometime in the near future. If Barney were still alive he would be thinking of him now and then, and would lift a real prayer for him. He was almost sure of that.

"Oh God," he prayed under his held breath, "You are here! You'll show me where to go, what to do!"

There! There were the steps of the guard again! Or was that God stepping gently to let him know that He was there?

He rolled another inch or two, tuning his turning with a wind that was blowing. Now was he out of range of the guard's path?

But rolled as he was to resemble a log, he lay in a sort of gully where even a quickly flashed light would scarcely recognize him as alive. On and on he persisted, stretched horizontal, stiff with the cold, too stiff to even shudder when he heard the distant clang of steel upon stone, as a guard passed the great rock that loomed behind.

On, on he crept, almost too numb to move cautiously, but not too numb to pray.

"God, if it's Your will, let me get back!"

A single star winked out behind a ragged cloud, and gave him his bearings again. There was another wide expanse of open ground before him to cross. Could he reach a shelter before the dawning?

"Oh God! Do what You want to do with me! It's just Your Stormy, asking to be guided!"

And now ahead was the guard fence. Barbed wire. Plenty of it. Could he manage to separate the strands enough to get through? Were his hands too numb to work them apart?

"God, are You there?"

And now!

There was no sound of guard's steps yet. Perhaps the guard was asleep. Listening cautiously Stormy worked, wrapping the wires together with his blouse. Could he get through before a guard arrived?

At last the final wire was cut, the opening large enough to creep through, and with his heart thumping wildly again as when he first set out, he came nearer, put a cautious arm through the opening, his head and shoulders, then worked his whole body slowly through!

He looked around. No shadow even in sight yet, it was still very dark. There seemed a hill just below him. Dared he try rolling? Would it make too much noise? He listened again. Was that a step? He must not risk getting caught now.

Carefully he crept ahead, over the little hillock, so slowly that there was scarcely the sound a rubber step would make in the sand. On, on he went, and now and then a star winked briefly to blaze his way.

Off in the distance he could hear a sound. One man calling to another. Had they discovered his absence already? But surely not, for this was the time when the camp was always quiet, the sleepy guards longing to be relieved. He had gone too far and stayed too long not to know the ways of the enemy world into which he had come for the sake of righteousness. A little farther on there were trees and some bushes. If he could make their shelter.

"God, are you there? I'm depending on You. I can't see ahead You know."

His silent thoughts took grotesque turnings. It seemed that he was thinking over his situation, almost aloud, though that couldn't be true, for he was going most guardedly.

"Traveling with God!" he said to himself. "That's what I'm doing. I wonder if any soldier ever thought of that before? Stormy Applegate, if you ever get back to the world, you'll have to tell other soldiers how it is. How safe it is travelling with God. You'll have to tell the world how they forgot to calculate on God, and what He will do for them if they take Him for their Saviour. And I shall certainly tell Barney Vance about this if he is still on this earth and I can find him."

It was almost morning when at last he came within sight of a few forlorn straggling houses. And now, was he far enough away from the camp to dare to risk being seen? And if he should approach one of those ramshackle dwellings, was there anyone there who would dare to hide him? There in an enemy-occupied country? No, there wouldn't be, of course.

On and on he hurried now, in the gathering dawn, making toward what looked like the ruins of a shed at some distance from a shackly barn. If he could get within the shelter of even a few boards, perhaps he could reconstruct his outfit so that he would dare to walk on into daylight for he remembered he was wearing portions of an enemy uniform that he had bargained for from among his fellow-prisoners. Could he pass as one of the enemy? He, an escaped prisoner?

Weary and weak for lack of food, and exhausted with the terrible cold, he plodded on in the lessening gloom of dawn.

He knew enough about the location. He had studied deeply into that. He knew where and when there would be great dangers, he knew of some hazards that were incalculable, he knew his stars when there were any stars to guide him, and he knew how to be exceedingly cautious. But there were things he did not know, and then he could only trust to his Guide. So some of those who knew him well, and had watched for him these weeks since his departure, had said he might come back because he went "in the strength of the Lord!"

Barney, safe at home, thought about it that night before he fell asleep. He thought of every step that friend of his might have to travel, he thought of the ventures of the way, because he had been in that land himself at one time and had escaped. He knew what there might be to pass through, and so he began to pray about Stormy, until before he slept it came to seem that the way he had envisioned Stormy's path of escape, was a sort of a picture of the way his life might have to go. Even over here in his own land of freedom—supposed freedom—where there were no actual prisoners' camps that might entrap him, no sharpshooters, no enemy guards, no spies and informers to bring him into danger. But yet there was an enemy. The great enemy of his Lord, and he had his scouts out to trap unwary soldiers of a heavenly allegiance. His mother's letter from the dead had warned him of that, had made him see that he must be aware of danger everywhere, and so be watching, and so be trusting in a higher power where he could not see the way clearly himself.

Fantastic thinking. That was what Hortense would call such ideas. But yet, was there real danger for him in that girl? No, he could not think it. Yet he knew of old that she had had powers to enmesh one's sympathies, one's lower nature. Perhaps this was one of the temptations that his mother meant when she said the Bible taught that there were some temptations from which one must *flee*.

It had sounded to him as a young boy when his mother taught him, that "fleeing" was what the fellows called "yellow." The idea had not commended itself to him as a child, but now he was beginning to see. His youthful trust had been in his own strength, but he had seen enough of life now to know that there were temptations that one had no right to enter into if there was a way to escape them, and that it wasn't yellow for a soldier, unarmed, to stand around in battle. He must get ready to protect himself if he was to go to war. He must have his armor on at all times, and if he didn't have it on he was to flee from the danger. Well, he was beginning to see. And what was the next direction his mother had taught him about what to do when temptation came? Oh, yes, "Resist." He wasn't to give in weakly. He was to resist. That was what all right-minded people should do in battle.

He was thinking all this out as sleep came down upon him and he dreamed on, tracing Stormy's possible way through danger. He woke up longing to see him. Determined, too, to make his own spiritual walk from day to day with as much caution as if he were Stormy trying to wend his way back in the strength of the Lord, from the power of the enemy where he had gone in his service for the war.

But his last waking thought was a resolve that in the morning he would try to get in touch with Washington and find out if they had any information yet about Stormy. Perhaps he had been heard from, and he felt as if he must know.

Then he knew nothing more, through the long hours of the lovely quiet night, till he woke to another spring morning, gay with the singing of birds.

His first waking thought was of thankfulness that there was still a place where birds could sing, where war had not scarred the earth, where little birds, and even people, could be glad. And then he remembered Stormy. Where was Stormy? Was he still alive? Was he somewhere under torture. God grant it might not be that. He were better dead than under some of the tortures that other soldiers had endured. Would Stormy ever come back? Would he be able to get to a place where the birds were singing and people were really glad? Would the world ever come to a place again where sun could shine without the thought of the gloom of sorrow and bitterness? Would the war be over sometime soon? Oh, if he might but go back now, this morning, and help to bring the end of the war! He felt such a good-for-nothing lying here and luxuriating in the singing of birds when his comrades were over there dying, and Stormy was somewhere doing his part, and he ought to be over there finding Stormy and bringing him back. If he only could find him now, this morning, and bring him here to this place of song. Would the world *ever* come back to peace, and the singing of birds again?

Then he thought of what Stormy would say if he could ask him that. "God is not dead," Stormy would say, with that great wide trusting smile of his. Yes, if Stormy wasn't already in Heaven with the Lord, Stormy was surely saying that somewhere, even if only to himself. Stormy was the trustingness man Barney had ever known, the man who walked continually in the strength of the Lord.

Then he sprang up with almost his old vigor and got ready for the day. There were two definite things he meant to do that day, and somehow the thought of them heartened him. He was going to do his best to get information about Stormy, and he was going to manage somehow to see his little girl friend of past years, Sunny Roselle, and get acquainted with her again. He had a feeling that she would not be as disappointing as Hortense had been. And oh, of course, there were other girls, his old schoolmates. He ought to look them all up pretty soon. Maybe he'd have a party or something, just for the sake of the old days. He would talk to Roxy about that.

But meantime a party for Barney was being arranged with speed and determination by Hortense, and its plan was anything but along the lines in which Barney had been thinking. Hortense meant to make it the smartest gathering that had ever ventured to show its head in the town of Farmdale. But of that Barney knew nothing of course, and was not intended to know, as it was to be a surprise, to welcome him back from the war, and the speedy preparations were carried on behind whispers and a wink or two.

"But don't you think you ought to consult Roxy about this, Hortense?" asked Amelia Haskell, one of the more sensible of the group that traveled after Hortense.

"Consult Roxy? For Pete's sake, *why?*"

"Well, because I've heard that Barney has been terribly wounded, and that he's home on a stiff schedule and has to rest a lot. Roxy would know if it is all right to have a party," finished Amelia lamely.

"Rot!" said Hortense angrily. "Consult that old hag? Not I! Ridiculous nonsense! As if she knew what was good for a down-and-out-soldier! What he needs is a little cheering up. He needs to see his old friends, and realize that they are all proud of him and care for him a lot. He needs to laugh and grow merry, and that's what I'm planning for him. Let that old harridan know about our party? Not on yer life! She would put the quietus on it at the start. She wants to keep that young hero all for herself. She wants to put him right back under the thumb his mother tried to fasten on him for life. But I'm setting him free, see? He's a man now and an old nurse can't keep him back and make him walk a chalk line any more. And if any of you so-called 'friends' let her get an inkling of what we're planning,

I'm off you for life, and I don't mean mebbe!"

Amelia subsided meekly and no more was dared by anybody else, although several of the girls remembered Barney's decided ideas of right and wrong in his school days. But then, maybe the war *had* changed him, the way Hortense had said. They whispered it over together, but not when Hortense was about.

But Hortense, as a result of these suggestions, merely hastened her plans, and set the time for her surprise party a day sooner. It was necessary that this thing get definitely started before it could possibly be suspected by the victim or else she was practically sure it would never be permitted to come off at all.

So Hortense got busy, and gave her orders, and the very next evening three carloads of young people turned noisily into the driveway of the old Vance house, and after barely waiting long enough to park their cars burst wildly into the house with gay laughter and an improvised number of what they called singing, to make the occasion more definitely a celebration.

And when there was no immediate response from the house, when instead there seemed to be a breathless silence, they looked wildly about and then sang their song over again:

> Happy welcome to you,
>   Happy welcome to you,
>   Happy welcome, dear Barney,
>   Happy welcome to you!"

But, in the meantime, Barney was having a little private party of his own, out on the side terrace, quite away from the road side of the house. Roxy had given Joel his supper early before he went to his fire company business meeting, and had set a little table on the terrace for Barney and Sunny. They had just finished their dessert when the cavalcade arrived. Barney did not at first recognize what all this other disturbance was about. Not till he looked up and saw the dismay on the face of his guest, and the frown on the face of old Roxy. And just about the time his uninvited onslaught of old acquaintances began to sing their song for the third time, still louder, and more pointedly than before, he began to listen and to recognize what was happening inside the house.

Aghast he started to his feet flinging down his napkin and giving a startled look, first at Sunny's sweet face suddenly grown grave, and then questioningly at Roxy, to whom he had been so accustomed for years to looking in any time of stress.

It was Sunny who gained her poise first, with her sweet smile dominating the situation.

"I think," she said in a very low voice, "that you are about to have a surprise party, and the best thing for me to do is to vanish. Go in there quickly, Barney, before they swarm out here and spoil everything."

Then Barney came to himself.

"Vanish? Not much you won't vanish! Come on in with me and help me through this situation."

He put out his hand to take hers, and lead her in, but she stepped back and eluded him quickly.

"No, I mustn't, Barney. I wouldn't fit with them, and I would be much misunderstood. Really! Go quickly! They mustn't know about this you know," and she swept her hand toward the table. "Good-by, I've had a lovely time!" and suddenly she was gone! Vanished! Just like a little pink and golden wraith in the mist of the evening.

Barney gave a despairing motion toward her, started to call but Roxy shook her head.

"Hush! Go in there quick! She's right! They mustn't know about this!" and she caught up the trayful of dishes that was standing on a chair and vanished into the kitchen.

Chapter 8

To say that Barney was annoyed at the sudden turn of events was putting it mildly. He had been looking forward to a pleasant evening getting acquainted all over again with the little girl, Sunny, and trying to reconcile her with the charming grown-up Sunny who seemed so fittingly to be called "Margaret" as Roxy had been calling her that evening. And now she had to disappear and he must go in and be gracious to a lot of nitwits in the other room who had come to do a little hero-worshipping and look him over, at the instigation of that brat of a Hortense. For he at once jumped to the conclusion that Hortense was at the bottom of this.

Well, he would go into the other room and greet them for half an hour perhaps, and then, afterwards, they *might* leave in time for him to run down to Sunny's house and apologize for letting her go home in that unattended way. And he meant also to find out just why she hadn't stayed.

Ah, but he was reckoning without the present-day knowledge of Hortense and her ways.

So he put on his dignity in haste and stalked into the side door, that opened into the back hall from the terrace. He reflected as he passed their supper table that it was well they had finished the strawberries and ice cream they had been eating for dessert, and there were very few dishes for Roxy to get out of sight, since she had taken the tray in with her.

So he entered the hall as they finished the last line of that awful song again, and assumed a surprised attitude, looking at them curiously, identifying a few of the men, and recognizing some of the others, Hortense, right in the forefront, in a very scant and sophisticated evening frock. For an instant he was so angry at her that she should have pulled off a thing like this without warning, he could scarcely trust his voice to speak. But he quickly controlled himself and went forward, a distant smile upon his face.

"Well," he said formally, "look who we have here! Old friends,

60

come to call! Say, that's kind of you. Come in and sit down, won't you? This really isn't my birthday though, you know, so you needn't overwork that poor old song any longer. Now, let me see, do I know you all? Some of you have changed a lot, haven't you? Grown up, isn't that it? This one is Amelia Haskell, isn't it? Yes, I thought I knew those big gray eyes. And the Wrexall twins! Yes, I'd know you anywhere. And—say, don't tell me you are Hortense Revenal? Why, I'd hardly know you in that glad rag. Isn't that one of those they call a 'smaht fwock'? And here is Lucy Anne, and Jan Harper! Why, I'm doing pretty well identifying my old friends, don't you think? And my word! There's Cap Withrow. How'd you get here? I thought I heard you were in Africa, or somewhere overseas. And Hank! Good night! how many feet do you grow a month? What size of shoes do you wear? You've grown so tall I have to look up to you, now."

So he went on down the line, cheerily, a word for everybody, and for the moment in perfect control of the situation, as they all stood watching him, studying him, recognizing the changes that had come to him, in gravity, in assurance, in experience. Yes, he was different. Even Hortense could recognize that.

Yet Hortense wasn't quite satisfied with the state of things. She wanted to be the center of the show, right from the start, in fact the whole show, in her new and expensive gown that wasn't paid for yet, and had cost her more than she could afford. She wanted to dominate the evening, and here she was only one of the whole bunch, and she could see by Barney's manner that he intended to keep her so. She was not to be allowed to exercise her possessive powers, not if he had anything to say about it. But she was only the more determined to show him. He couldn't put her off like that when she had got this whole thing up to honor him. She would show him!

"Won't you all sit down? I guess there are chairs enough in here, aren't there?" said Barney. "It looks like we ought to have a regular old time talk-fest, doesn't it? Hank, you and Cap bring some of the dining-room chairs in here, won't you? You remember where the old dining room is, don't you? Same room where we used to play blindman's-buff in the past ages. Amelia, you take the piano stool. We'll be wanting to sing some of the old songs pretty soon, and you'll be handy there to play for us. Martha take the big chair next."

He was certainly taking things in his own hands, and doing it very thoroughly. Hortense realized that she must get busy and take control.

"Hi, Hank!" she called, making a picturesque trumpet of her pretty white hands with their gleaming red claws, and flashing jewels. "Get busy and bring the gramophone in. We want to get started on our evening. We came to have a good time you know. This is no church social. We want to dance."

"Oh, we don't need a gramophone," said Barney coolly with one of his old-time grins. "Don't try to be so sophisticated. We're all just hungering and thirsting to do some of the old-time things we used to do. How about playing 'I have a rooster for sale,' and 'Drop the handkerchief,' and 'Here we go round the barberry bush,' and a few of those. Nothing like the old-time childish games to take off the stiffness. And then, pretty soon we ought to sit down and really get acquainted over again. Call the roll and find out where everybody is and what you all have been doing. Suppose we do that first. I'll call the roll as far as I can, and then somebody else take over and finish, till we've got around. When you answer tell where you are, where you've been, what you've been doing and what's likely ahead of you, and when we get done I'll be caught up on my home history. Hank, we'll begin with you!"

Hank grinned and answered briskly, "Working in a defense plant, got called, had my physical, they found I had a bad heart and turned me down, so now I'm a riveter."

"Next! Cap. What of you?" asked Barney quickly.

"Oh, I wanted to be a flier the worst way, but they found I had something the matter with one eye, so now I'm a machinist. Over at Tennally's, fiddling with screws for airplanes, when I wanted to fly the planes." He grinned comfortably and somewhat ruefully, and one of the girls called out "Lucky boy!" That was Rowena Lake. Barney gave her one quick withering glance and passed on to the next.

"Arta Perry, what of you?"

"I joined the Army Nurses. I'm leaving tomorrow morning for my new location."

Barney gave her a keen once-over, decided the uniform was becoming, and turned to Hortense who stood next to her.

"And you, Hortense?" He asked the question casually, making her just one of many, instead of a special one, and Hortense resented it. She tossed her head indifferently.

"Oh, I'm an entertainer for the boys at the center," she said, quite as if it bored her to even think of it. "But say, for heaven's sake, Barney, how long are your going to keep this up? We came here to show you a good time, and you're just spoiling it all."

"Oh, I'm sorry," said Barney gravely. "I was under the impression I was the host to my guests and ought to do my best to entertain them. I think we ought to get acquainted all over again, though, don't you? It won't take long and then we can go on from there."

"Oh, well, make it snappy then," said Hortense. "We've got a program of our own, you know."

"Oh, I see. Well, we'll hurry this up. Who's the next one?" Two dimpling grinning girls in nurse's uniforms were next, and they answered the roll call interspersed with giggles.

They went down the line rapidly, crisply, each telling a bit about himself, briefly, sometimes half in the spirit of fun, and some more gravely, and when the last guest had answered the roll call, Barney called out, "That's good. Now we can go on from here and enjoy ourselves more intelligently. How about it, Hortense, will you take over and let me sit down?"

"Oh, but we haven't heard from you, Barney!" called out one of the Wrexall twins. "It's time for you to give an account of yourself now!" and a chorus of the others called out, "Yes, yes! A speech from Barney. Where have you been, and what have you done?"

"Oh," said Barney, "I suppose I *am* still one of the old crowd, but it hadn't occurred to me I would have to give account of myself. Well, here goes. I'll make it brief. The most notable thing that has happened to me since I went away was that one dark night on a lonely shore, a smashed plane on the ground behind me, crouching enemies behind every tree, and nothing before but a big lonely stretch of sea, not even a foxhole to hide in, out there in a place like that I met God, and got to know Him. It was the greatest thrill that ever came to me, and still is. Sometime I'll tell you all about it, if you care to hear, but it's too long a story for tonight. Now, fellows who's going to take over? Shall we sing some of the old songs?"

"Oh, for heaven's sake!" said Hortense angrily, "Hank you and Cap go get the eats and drinks. I'm near dead for a drink myself, and I guess you're all pretty well fed up with this gruesome start. Now Barney, you sit down and try to realize we came to welcome you home again, and give you the honor due to a hero of war."

"Oh," grinned Barney, "don't bother about that hero stuff, just be yourselves, my old friends! But excuse me a minute, I'll go out and help. Fellas, hold up a minute, I'm coming!"

Amid the immediate protests of the girls, he flashed out into the kitchen, hoping to find Roxy.

There she was, getting out glasses, trays and napkins.

"Roxy, can you get us some coffee, or lemonade or something?" he called in a quick, low voice as he vanished out the side door and streaked it across the lawn, arriving at the line of parked cars almost as soon as the committee Hortense had sent out.

Two large baskets of cakes and sandwiches were deposited on the lawn beside the gramophone and Hank was just reaching farther into the car, and edging out the case of liquor they had brought along.

Barney gave it a scrutinizing glance, and put out a protesting hand.

"It won't be necessary to bring that in, fellas. Roxy's getting something for us. Come, take your gramophone and your eats, and let's get back." Barney's hope of getting to see Sunny again that night was fast vanishing.

Hank paused and looked at his host.

"Sorry, Barney, but I guess I have to take this in. Hortie'll have all kinds of a fit if I don't. She was very particular about this."

"Well, I guess we can stand a few fits, if it comes to that. Hortense knows how I feel about that. You see we just don't serve that here, so you needn't bring it in. Come on fellows!"

So the three went in together, silently. Hank had it in mind to tell Barney what a fuss Hortense had made to get that liquor, and how she had made everyone contribute to it, but then he decided not to say anything, and they walked along for the most part in silence, only Barney now and then making a cheerful remark, and so they arrived in the house.

They put the four baskets of cakes and sandwiches in the kitchen where Roxy took grim possession, Barney seized the trayful of brimming glasses of fruit punch fragrant and luscious, and assigning Hank and Cap to the other two trays, marched into the living room and straight over to Hortense. She looked up hopefully, and he bent and tendered her a glass.

"You were thirsty, lady?" he said mischievously, and Hortense looked up in surprise.

She reached an eager hand to the glass, then caught the fragrance of well-blended fruit, and frowned.

"Why, what's this?" she asked, drawing back her hand. "This isn't what I sent you for, Hank. What are you trying to put over on us?"

"Try it, lady," urged Barney with his old-time grin, "I think you'll find it quite drinkable. Or, if you prefer coffee, I think that some is on the way."

"But I brought. . ." burst forth Hortense in a vexed tone. "Hank, I told you to bring. . ."

"Yes, I know," said Barney. "But don't blame Hank. I told him we don't serve that here, and I thought you would understand."

Barney flashed her a pleasant confident smile, and went on passing the tray to the other girls. They seized eagerly upon the glasses for everyone knew that anything Roxy had concocted would be something extra, and so it was.

Several of the girls had slipped into the kitchen as the boys came in with the trays, and now they began to march in with plates and napkins and platters of sandwiches, and it was presently a happy young crowd that chattered away, and ate up every sandwich and crumb of cake, and drank the seemingly inexhaustible cups of coffee, and glasses of fruit lemonade, until, before long, no one thought any more about that liquor except the girl who had schemed to bring it just for the sake of forcing Barney to drink. She knew how Barney's mother had felt on that subject, and it was her great desire to bring the young man to the place where he would go against those queer old-fashioned principles of the women who had so annoyingly dominated him all his life, and who now even in her death was holding him from things that Hortense loved. Things she knew if she could just break down there would be some hope of bringing him to her feet.

But the evening wore on, and the gay young crowd grew cheerful in the memory of the dear old days, and forgot the glum Hortense who had retired disapprovingly into a corner and taken little part in the merriment of the rest.

Only once she came out of her corner and started that gramophone noisily on its way, and then made the boys move back the chairs, and started dancing with one of them. Soon a few others joined her, but for the most part they were interested in a story Barney was telling, and the dancing, being rather forced just then, languished for lack of participants. Somehow Barney was having a queer effect upon that young crowd, who of late had most of them followed Hortense in everything she did. To have one come in who definitely ignored her lead and openly, pleasantly defied her; Hortense herself could not believe that this was really happening. And yet with it all, Barney was his old merry engaging self, not long-faced nor self-righteous, not goody-goody, nor conceited, not mamma's-little-boy, still tied to her apron strings, though she was gone to another world. Certainly he was not a sissy, but a strong man who had ideas, and what he called principles of his own; who had made his mark in the war and won trophies, and honorable mentions, and been unafraid in danger, done deeds of daring, and had outranked many who seemed harder and tougher than he when he was a lad. And yet now even Hortense saw this, although she could not explain it. What was it made him so quietly firm in certain matters? And why had he so deliberately foiled her attempts to put on the kind of party that she knew his mother would not have enjoyed having in her home? Had it been just for hatefulness? No, somehow he did not seem that way, for there was in his manner a gentleness and strength that she did not remember to have noticed in his childhood. And yet she was frantic that her plans had been spoiled, and everyone could see that she had failed in putting over this worldy kind of a party in a house where the whole atmosphere had always been what she called, even in her childhood, "old fogy."

Hortense watched the young man as the evening went on, and saw his continued pleasantness and courtesy under what she sensed must be trying circumstances for him. She didn't care for that of course, but she couldn't understand what kept him strong and sweet through it all.

They began to sing after a time, Amelia, seeing Hortense defied, dared to start a little something on her own initiative, and sitting at the piano let her fingers run into several old-time songs that caught the whim of the crowd and made them hum together, and finally pour out their voices in a big peppy chorus.

> School days! School days!
> Dear old golden rule days!
> Reading and writing and 'rithmetic,
> Taught to the tune of a hickory stick!

How it rang out and stirred the heart of Roxy and Joel, disapprovingly cleaning up in the kitchen.

Then came *Put on Your Old Gray Bonnet*. They were such very old songs that Roxy marveled those young things should know the words, even though the radio had been reviving them now and again. And there was *Juanita* and *Annie Laurie* and *Old Black Joe* and *Swanee River*. Sometimes Amelia's nimble fingers would tinkle out the beginning of another and all would take it up, sometimes a girl's voice would be ready with a new one, ere the last one was finished. It was a gay bright ending to a queer evening, and Barney, as he sang, looked about upon them all and wondered why Sunny hadn't stayed. As he continued to think about it he realized how far superior she was to most of the girls there. Even the few minutes they had been together this evening at supper had told him that. Yet some of those girls had good faces, though some were vapid, some conceited, and some just idle pleasure-loving kittens who merely wanted a good time out of life. The boys were not much. That is, the ones who were here. They were the henchmen of such girls as Hortense, who went their errands and were satisfied to be their humble escorts when more desirables were not at hand. And yet, if those same boys had gone off to war, nine out of ten of them would have learned the serious side of life, and be ready to do some purposeful thinking.

Somebody suddenly started *The Old Rugged Cross*, and strange to say, even in that crowd, everybody seemed to know the words and rather like to sing it, although he could see Hortense's lips curl in scorn. He felt sure that if she were a singer she certainly would have chimed in with some modern jazz just in contrast. Then, as the last notes of the hymn died away Barney struck up in his clear beautiful baritone:

> Abide with me: fast falls the even tide;
>   The darkness deepens; Lord with me abide!

It was a song he had sung often when overseas, when he was about to go into a dangerous engagement. It seemed to him now as he sang it that his song, as it had often been before, was a prayer. He had a passing thought that he was perhaps in as much need of help now as he had ever been in battle.

A strange dark look came into Hortense's eyes as she watched his face while he sang, but he was not looking at her and did not notice, and so he sang the verses as he remembered them from childhood, till at the last line when the final word died away.

It was very still in the room for an instant, and then the silence was suddenly broken with as distinct a snap as if the quietness had been as brittle as a glass tube, that fairly broke at the new sound. It was Hortense, of course. She make a restless impatient movement, shoving her chair back sharply to the bare floor beyond the rug, and arose with decision and a disagreeable sneer on her lips.

"I'm going home!" she announced sharply. "I'm just fed up with this sob stuff, and I have to run up to New York in the morning for a shopping trip so I want to save my strength. Good night! Are any of you coming with me?" and she sailed out of the room toward the front door with her head high.

"Oh, cut it out, Hortie," shouted one of the young men who had come with her "we're just getting into the fun. You said you were going to stay late."

"Sorry," said Barney, "have I been monopolizing the program too much? Suppose I sit back and rest awhile and you take over, Hortense. How about your giving us a solo yourself? Seems to me I remember you had a good voice when you were a kid. What numbers have you got? I'd like to hear you sing again, and then meantime you can be thinking up what you want to do next. Come on, be a good sport and sing us some songs, Hortense."

Hortense paused in the doorway, and surveyed the young soldier, good-looking and courteous in his well-fitting uniform. Was it really worth while? Then Barney turned on his winning smile, and she suddenly resolved to try again. She simply *had* to conquer him now, or they would all see that she had failed. And besides, she was flattered to be asked to sing. She was proud of her voice, So she fixed her languishing gaze on Barney's eyes for a moment, and then drawled:

"Oh, well, I don't mind waiting long enough to sing for you, since you ask it," she said it with the air of conferring a great favor. Hortense was exceedingly fond of herself. She would do almost anything to glorify herself.

Amelia arose from the piano stool as if she felt she ought to be apologizing for having been there, and Hortense sat down with an air, entirely aware of the lovely lines of her expensive evening dress, glad that there was really an opportunity at last to display it to advantage. She had been showing off, either herself or her possessions, ever since she was born.

Hortense's white fingers fell daintily upon the keys, as if she idly searched among the notes to find what she would sing.

At last she looked up.

"Just what do you want me to sing?" she asked Barney loftily, as if her repertoire included anything he could possibly ask, but Barney only smiled:

"I'd like to hear the song you like best to sing," he said graciously, and Hortense settled down to work with a look of satisfaction on her sharp, hard young face.

Hortense had a thin shallow voice, with a distinct whine to it, and moreover was inclined to the mournful desolate self-pitying tone that so many of the current crooners affect. Barney, as he watched her wondered why she did not know that her voice was unpleasant. Then he put on an attentive attitude and let his thoughts wonder off to other things.

The other girls in the room sat about politely, and he studied each face. Amelia's was quiet and humble, not much sparkle there, some of the others were very pretty, but yet didn't seem to have much behind the prettiness. Or was it because he had another face in his thoughts with which he was comparing them? Well, that was silly. He hadn't been seeing Sunny but a very few minutes, and that while they were eating their supper out on the terrace, and at such close range that he could not stare at her and really know how she did look. Just a lovely, rose and golden look, with a glance in here eyes that one could not help trusting. Well, this was silly, only he wished this party would get itself over and let him go to sleep and wake up to a new day when he might perhaps get a chance to go and see Sunny and study her a little more.

Chapter 9

From that time on the party became quite gay, to Barney's utter weariness.

But in spite of that fact he was up early next morning and down to breakfast much to the surprise of Roxy who had expected him to sleep late, and was meditating an especially tempting breakfast, later, when he woke up.

But he told her all he wanted was just what she and Joel had, some of that nice looking oatmeal, with real cream, and a cup of her coffee.

"Would I embarrass Sunny if I went down there this early?" he asked suddenly, while he was enjoying the scrambled eggs she heaped upon his plate, and the crisp buttered toast she produced after the oatmeal and orange juice she insisted upon. "I can't seem to settle to anything," he went on, "not even resting, till I apologize for the way I let her run off alone in the dark."

"Oh, she didn't mind that," laughed Roxy, "she's used to running around alone. And it didn't seem to me you had much choice about the matter. It was Sunny ran away from you."

"Yes, but I should have stopped her somehow. Why did she do it, Roxy?"

"She was right, Barney boy. You don't realize. If she had stayed here that crowd would have made her feel very uncomfortable. They would either have taken it for granted she was here as a sort of servant, helping me out, or else they would have judged her by themselves and made it appear that she was running after you. I thought it quite sensible of her to go."

"But why should they treat her that way, Roxy? They're no better than she is. They're none of them anything great. I'm sure teaching school is just as honorable and necessary in these times, as riveting, or going around entertaining soldiers home on leave, or any of the other things those girls are doing."

"Wouldn't you think so?" assented Roxy. "But would you believe it, those other girls almost ignore her. You wouldn't think she was brought up in the same town. And it's just because she hasn't forged ahead and forced herself into all their silly parties. She doesn't drink nor smoke nor dance the night away. She has too much real work to do. Of course there's a few others wouldn't care so much to be frivolous, if they didn't feel they had to copy that poor simp of a Hortense. And why, I can't understand. She hasn't got any money, and she isn't good-looking. I believe it's just because she's dared to do things and take the lead and laugh at them if they don't follow her. She dared to get married in a hurry, and then she dared to get divorced, and she's sort of made herself the fashion although she calls it 'smaht'. And there's Sunny with her sweet delicate lips clean and smiling, without any paint on them but her own healthy skin the way God made them, and they won't speak to her, unless they want her to do something for them that they can't do themselves. And they go around with their great wide thick lips all staring bright red and horrid, and disgusting. I've often wondered why they paint them up so thick and wide. They look as if they were swollen and bleeding."

"Yes, they do, don't they?" laughed Barney. "It isn't a bit attractive. A good many fellows I know laugh at the way the girls are painted, just to attract attention. But you didn't answer my question. Do you think it's too early for me to run over to Sunny's house? Would I be interrupting some work she ought to do? This is Saturday. She wouldn't be teaching school today would she?"

"No, there's no school today, and I don't think she'd mind your being there even if she was busy. She'd probably let you help her if it was anything important she couldn't leave till another time. Run along and see Sunny, and if you want to bring her back here to a meal any time just feel free to do it. Sunny's a dear child, and I'm fond of her."

So Barney finished his breakfast and started out eagerly, reflecting with satisfaction that he was glad his guests of the night before wouldn't have waked up yet, at least not many of them, and would therefore not be on hand to see where he was going.

As he walked along the sunlit road he heard the birds singing high in the sky, some far in the distance, and in spite of himself his heart was filled with a grave delight. The quiet air filled with sunshine, the birds everywhere. Oh, it was good to be at home again where there were no sounds of bombing, no tenseness in the air, no fear of what was going to develop during a day, or what would happen on the morrow! No feeling of desperation, when comrades and fiends moved out of sight for an engagement from which some would, in all probability, never return. Oh, it was good to be in a land of peace for a little while! Though somehow last night's gaiety did not appeal to him as good. It had seemed that all his former friends were just children yet, where he had left them when he went away, seeking fun and more fun, thrills, and greater thrills. They had not yet reached the place where they cared much about anything that did not affect them personally, that would bring them a better time, a forgetfulness of life. It didn't occur to them that there might be disappointment in the world, and that there were grave serious things to think about. It was a sense of the nearness of death that brought that; and while they were eager about doing things in an important way, especially if they could wear a uniform, they did not in the least recognize what war was like. To them war was just a big game, to win at all odds, and to tell tales about afterwards of their own prowess.

He looked across to the soft green hills. Off there, just, beyond the woods, gleamed the white stones of the little cemetery where his mother's body had been laid, and a tender look came into his eyes. He hadn't been up there yet. Some day he must go, pretty soon. But he had been better taught than to do honor to a mere human body from which the spirit was gone. He did not think of that spot up there on the hill as being sacred for his mother's sake. It was only her tired-out body that lay there. Her spirit was with her Lord. She had taught him that. Yet he looked toward the white stones that gleamed in the morning sunshine, and realized that he would want to mark the place where they had laid her with a stone bearing record of her birth and Home-Going, and some verse from God's word that could be a testimony for a chance reader who might be unsaved. Yes, even though he knew it was but her tired body that lay there waiting, like old garments that were no longer needed, it brought tender thoughts.

And then he came in sight of the Roselle farm. A pleasant, wide, rambling white house, gleaming in the sun, nestling in its tall setting of old elms. It had such a homey, prosperous look, as if it had just newly been finished, although he knew it had been there many years. How well they had kept it up, even in these hard wartimes. And Sunny's father must have been the only one to do the work, since Sunny's brother went into the service.

He was almost to the hedge-bordered lane that led to the house when he saw a lithe young figure flash out of the kitchen door carrying a clothesbasket. She put it down on the stone pavement by the pump and stooping, took out a roll of cloth and shook it out till it filmed into a curtain, thin and white. With firm brisk fingers she fastened it to the clothesline just a step away. Then she stooped and took out another roll and treated it the same way, till the row of curtains were blowing gaily in the morning breeze.

Barney was walking slowly, watching her. Apparently she had not noticed him yet, and most of the time her back was toward the road. It seemed that she was too busy to be watching what went on in the world about her.

He had not reached the turning of the lane before she had the basket empty and all those curtains blowing on the line. Then she swung around and hurried up the steps to the kitchen door, and in out of sight without even looking down toward the road. Had she seen him or not? He didn't think she had. And yet, she wasn't a girl who was always trying to attract attention to herself. Besides she wouldn't likely be expecting him to call so very early.

With quickened step he turned up the lane and hurried to the house, tapping at the door where he had seen her vanish, and calling, "Sunny! Sunny! Where are you?" Then he heard her mother's voice calling from an inner room.

"Margaret, someone is calling you at the kitchen door. Won't you answer the knock? I'm not fit to be seen. I've just spilled some milk down the front of my dress."

And then he heard Sunny's quick step hurrying to the door.

"Oh!" she said, a glad light coming into her face. "Barney! It's you! And out so early! I thought you were supposed to be an invalid who had to sleep late."

Barney grinned.

"Not when I have something more important to do," he said. "Did I come too early? Will I be in the way? If I am just tell me the truth and I'll go outside and sit in the sun till you have time for me, but I simply couldn't stand it until I came to apologize for letting you go home that way last night."

The twinkle came into the girl's eyes, just as when she was a tiny child.

"Oh, but you couldn't help it," she laughed, and her laughter was like a string of silver bells. "I know how to vanish. And then it was getting dark. Besides, it wouldn't have been good."

"Yes? Well, as soon as you get done what you're doing you've got to sit down for at least five minutes and tell me just why it wouldn't have been good. I thought it would, and I still think so, but out of deference to you I have tried to be reconciled till I could get here and have it explained."

The girl laughed brightly again.

"Well, you see, I'm not in their crowd. Those girls have no use for me, and I'm afraid maybe I haven't felt very friendly toward them. They are not at all in my class. We just don't fit, that's all. But—they are *your* friends. I don't want to say anything against them. We just don't fit.

Barney was studying her sweet face as she talked. He saw she was trying to be nice about it and not to say too much. Trying to be polite, and not to seem self-righteous. He watched her gravely till she stopped and gave him a grave questioning look.

Barney grinned.

"Having spent an entire evening with that crowd I can well understand that you don't fit," he said fervently. "And I'm *glad* you don't! I would be disappointed in you if you did. Oh, there are two of three of those girls who aren't so bad, might be all right if they were in the right company, but just now they aren't. Yet all the same I'm sorry I had to let you go off that way unattended. It was not in my plan to have my own party end up that way."

Sunny's eyes lighted.

"Oh, that was all right," she said demurely, "but—thank you. It is nice you cared."

"Cared?" he said. "Why of course I cared, and I still care. Aren't you my little pal, Sunny? Did you suppose I could forget that? Only they call you Margaret, now, don't they? I heard you called after I knocked. Was that your mother's voice? *Margaret!* It fits you. I like it. I've always liked that name, only I'm afraid I shall always think of you as Sunny! Little Sunny!"

He gave her a clear admiring steady look, that seemed to be searching her through and through, and held her own glance for the moment, while the rosy color swept up into her lovely face, and then her eyes went down.

How lovely she was, he thought as he watched her for another long minute in a sweet silence, and then he spoke:

"And now, what were you going to do, and may I help? Were you going to hang those curtains? They have to be ironed first, don't they? I can iron. My mother taught me, and then we often had to do some of that in training. And how about the windows? Don't they have to be washed? I could do that! I used to be good at it."

"Oh, but those things can all wait," said Sunny with a golden look. "You have come to call on me, and I'm going to have a nice time. I'll do the work when this is over. I'm just going to enjoy your company now."

"Oh yes?" he asked comically, "not if the court knows herself. We'll do the work first and then we'll have earned a good time. We might even take a long walk to the woods and have a picnic. But the work must be done first. Where do I find the rags and brushes to clean the windows?"

"But no!" said Sunny with a troubled look. "You with a lovely uniform and all those wonderful decorations, washing windows! You'd get all messed up."

"No," said Barney decidedly, "I'll not get messed up. The army taught me to do work and not get messed up. And besides, young lady you had your way last night, cutting my party short and running away in the dark, and now it's my turn! I say we're going to work first, and then play, and I mean it! May I take off my coat?"

"But—" said Sunny, with still that troubled look.

"What are you two arguing about?" said Mrs. Roselle, suddenly appearing at the door of the dining room. "Isn't this our old friend Barney, Margaret? Why do you sound so dictatorial?"

"But mother, he is insisting on helping me. He wants to wash windows! Imagine it. With that handsome uniform on."

"Mrs. Roselle, I am only offering to help Sunny,—Margaret. We'll get the work out of the way and then we'll go and play, have a picnic maybe. Isn't that fair?"

"Splendid!" said the mother with a smile. "I'll get him an apron, and he can roll up his sleeves. You'll have fun working. There isn't so much to be done. I've started the ironing machine, and you'll have the curtains up in a jiffy. Barney will be a lot happier that way, I know, for I know how his mother brought him up," and she trotted away and brought him a big apron that enveloped him. He tied it on and went around admiring himself in the crisp blue gingham folds, so that the whole argument ended in a good laugh, and then they went to work with a will.

"But I thought you were an invalid, sent home to get well, and here you are working as hard as if you were fighting a battle," said Sunny, still troubled.

"I'm afraid, madam, your education has been neglected. I'm afraid you haven't a very good idea of what a battle would be like as compared with a little job of washing a few windows with the garden hose and all these brushes to help."

So, with laughter and song they went to work. For the ironing machine was close at hand where the windows had to be washed and they had a lot of time to talk. And then they got to the subject of whistling, and Barney asked her all about that, and demanded to hear her whistle, and Sunny began to whistle.

Barney was amazed. He had always felt no girl could really whistle, but Sunny could whistle as well as he had ever been able to do it.

"I'm proud of you," he said. "I never found a boy that could do it that well, and I've tried to teach several of them. But you do it like a bird."

She looked at him with a quick flush, surprise and pleasure in her gaze.

"I never expected you to say that," she said quietly. "I practiced, and I never could get Roxy to say I did it as well as you did but once. You can't think what that used to mean to me when I was a child. I thought your whistle was the sweetest music I had ever heard anywhere. It seemed to me better than the bird's singing."

"You certainly were a cute little trick," said Barney with quick appreciation. "And how have they kept you so unspoiled? All the other girls are so illuminated that you can scarcely recognize your old acquaintances."

Sunny smiled.

"I guess I'm just old-fashioned," she said. "I don't admire faces that are not natural. I like God's plan best."

"So do I," said Barney with vehemence. "I can't see why anyone can like it. Well, I certainly like you as you are. You seem so much as you were, and not as if you were trying to be 'smaht' as Roxy says." And then they laughed, and presently Mrs. Roselle came back into the room.

"Come, children, you've worked enough for one lovely spring day. Enough for a soldier home on sick leave, and a busy little schoolma'am. Besides I've got your lunch all put up and if you're going on a picnic it's high time you got started. It's April you know, and you're liable to run into a shower or two by afternoon. Come now, put your work away and hurry off."

"Oh, but we're almost done, dear," said Barney in his old familiar way. "I've just one more window curtain to hang, and then the room is done."

"Why, so it is! And how beautiful it seems! My, that's wonderful to get these windows all cleaned so early in the season. Soldiers are great workers, aren't they, Margaret?"

It seemed a happy thing to Barney to be there with those two, his mother's old friend and her little girl, in the simple home life doing honest work, and being happy together. It comforted a lonely spot in his heart that had been reaching out for something like a home ever since he arrived. Roxy was good and dear, but she wasn't his mother, and there was an emptiness in his own home with mother gone. He watched wistfully the companionship between this mother and daughter. It warmed his heart to know there was still such a mother and such a daughter.

So with a generous basket of lunch, they started off to the woods. April it was, but a warm sunny day, and the birds were singing all about, through the meadow, and trilling through the air, as if they were just crazy-happy at the return of spring. As if they were glad this soldier was home too, and this girl and he were going off to their out-of-doors to be happy together.

They climbed the hill over the meadow, enjoying every step of the way, and when they came to a fence they climbed it and went on, Barney catching Margaret's hand as they swung along together in the sunshine, like two children. Barney hadn't been so happy since his mother died. Somehow it had seemed to him those first few hours that he never would be happy again. That perhaps when people grew up they never were happy. Though when he thought back he realized that his own mother and father had been very happy together, until the war came along and separated them, and even after his father died his mother and he had always had glad times together.

They sat down on a mossy slope at last when they reached the top of the hill. It was warm and dry with the sunshine all the morning, and they were glad to rest.

"I wonder what's in that basket," said Barney eying it wistfully. "I'm hungry, aren't you?"

Margaret smiled warmly.

"Wild strawberry tarts for one thing, I think. Mother made some yesterday. And there'll likely be chicken sandwiches. Are you as tired of chicken as everybody is these rationing days?"

"Me? Tired of *chicken*? Not on your life! We didn't always have all the chicken we could use over there in the hospital where I took my recovery. And I know your mother's chicken sandwiches will be something to boast about. And those dear little sharp pickles I just love. I think they must be peculiar to this part of the world for somehow I don't seem to remember having them anywhere else."

Just little nothings they talked about while they were eating, glad little nothing, that signified that they were happy to be together and having a grand time. And when they had finished everything in the basket, and drank the milk from the thermos bottle, they shook out the napkins, and closed the basket and settled down for a good talk.

"Now," said Barney, "we've got to get acquainted. You see you are not at all the same little child you were when I went away, and we have a lot to catch up on. You begin first and tell me all about you."

So Sunny told, pleasant little sketches from her sweet young life, and Barney watched her, impressing her lovely face like a picture on his heart. This was a girl worth cultivating. This was a girl in a thousand.

She told about the finish of her school days, about her brief year at college, before she was called home to teach. About her father and mother and the little intimate things of the farm life. She told of her school, and then of her Sunday school class, and the church choir and how she was having to play the organ because the man who used to play it had to go to war.

"May I go to church with you tomorrow?" he asked suddenly, interrupting her story.

"Oh, *will* you? And would you be able to sing a solo? Our soloist is gone into the Navy, and I don't know anyone else to get on such short notice."

"Why, yes, I'll do my best, if you want me, but I'm really not much on singing any more. I've been in a war you know, and then in a hospital, and my voice is all shot to pieces. But I'll try."

Then he suddenly reached out and took her hand in his.

"You're cold," he charged. "I saw you shiver! Yes, I did. Your fingers are like little icicles." He took both her hands in his own and rubbed them softly.

"Such little bits of hands to do so many things," he said gently, looking down at them, smiling as if she was still the little child she used to be when he went away.

"Now come, we must walk around and get warm," he said suddenly, "In fact I'm afraid it's time for me to go home, I've got some important letters to write and a phone call to make to Washington. But I've had such a nice time. May I come again?" Then he sprang up and drew her to her feet and they started on their way down the meadow.

It was on the way down the quiet meadow that Sunny suddenly looked up with a question.

"Do you have to go back to war, Barney?"

He gave her a quick glance and hesitated before he answered. Then he spoke earnestly.

"I sincerely hope so," he said. "I wouldn't have come away now if I could have had my way. But it seemed that at the time I had no strength to go on. I was just tired out. But now, the last few days, I feel rested, and I *want* to go back. I want to get this war done. That's what I'm telephoning Washington about. That, and trying to find my friend Stormy. I've got a friend down there, an admiral, with a pretty big pull among the powers that be, and I'm going to see if I can't get them to send me back sooner than the stated time they gave me. I feel like a slacker staying home and resting day after day. It was wonderful at first of course, hearing birds sing instead of bombs falling, getting the sound and smell of spring in the world that has not yet been desolated by war. And yet, since I've got around some and seen how little our people over here really understand what war is, I feel as if I must hurry back and do all I can. Oh, the people over here, some of them, many of them, think they know all about war because they take a little time out of amusing themselves to entertain soldiers waiting to be sent overseas, or to roll a few bandages occasionally in the Red Cross. If you had stayed with us last night and heard them talk you would have understood what I mean."

"I know," said the girl earnestly. "I don't wonder you feel that way. But I'm sorry you feel you must go back so soon. It's been so great to have you home again. And it does seem as if you really ought to stay until the doctor thinks it is right for you to return, if you must go. Of course, I understand how you must feel to be taken out of it before it is over, but it doesn't seem as if it was right that you should be allowed to go back into such strenuous action until you've really got rested. I should think they would insist on your taking your full leave."

"Perhaps they will," said Barney with a sigh, "but I'm hoping they'll see it the way I do. You see I have a reason. I have a buddy out there somewhere, perhaps among the enemy, who saved my life once when I was near death. He was wounded himself, and had been doing hard duty for hours, and he came across me wounded, unconscious, in the dark, and strung me across his big splendid shoulders, even though he was badly wounded himself, and carried me back to my outfit. He carried me through enemy fire safely, I owe him my life. And now he is missing in action himself somewhere, or was when I came away, and I can't get him out of my mind. It may be he has been heard from, but I doubt it. They had about given up hope for him when I was sent home. But I've got it on my heart that I want to get permission to go back and hunt for him, save him from whatever mess he's in, if I can. I owe him that. He did as much for me, and after all he's a valuable man. He's done a lot in his special line. It may be I can make them see it my way."

"But—aren't *you* a valuable man too?" asked Sunny shyly.

"I wouldn't say so," smiled Barney, "not in comparison with Stormy Applegate. And what's my life if I can't give it for one who would have done the same for me?"

"I see," said the girl with sweet understanding in her eyes. "It's beautiful of you. And I can see why you want to go. Will they let you, do you think?"

"I'm not sure, I'm going to do my best to make them see it my way. But there's always a lot of delay and red tape about changes of this sort. I'm glad you can understand. It's nice to have a real friend. One who is in sympathy and can see why I must go, and soon, if I can get the chance."

"Yes," said the girl gravely, "I can see. But I could wish it didn't have to be."

With a tender understanding smile he took her hand in a quick grateful clasp.

"Thank you," he said, looking down at her gravely, "I'll remember that. It will help me. And you'll be praying, won't you?"

"Oh yes," said Sunny. "I've been doing that for you all the way through."

They had come to the highway. He helped her across the fence, took her up to the house, and then hurried home, and to the telephone.

Chapter 10

Meantime the gang that had swarmed down upon him with a surprise party the night before had no intention of letting Barney get out of their clutches. They promptly organized their forces, and inaugurated a series of parties and dinners, calculated not only to keep his time rather full, but with the object in view of changing his whole point of view. They felt it was for his good that they should instruct him in the ways of this new and present world that war had brought to his home town. He simply must not be allowed to go around acting "pious" as they simply called it, just because he was in the old town where his mother brought him up that way.

To that end the gang took their way to the Vance home early on Sunday evening, carrying with them several large boxes of candy, feeling that this offering certainly would not start any antagonism, and could be passed around so casually that all would go smoothly.

The plan was to bring invitations to various parties, gatherings, and entertainments. They called themselves "The Community Cheer Association." Their professed object was to bring a degree of comfort and cheer to lonely mothers and wives and sweethearts of soldiers who were far away in peril on land or sea or air. The statement had been drawn up by Hortense, and she was clever at that sort of thing. There was ample opportunity for eloquence, and Hortense felt that if she knew anything at all about Barney Vance such an object would appeal to him at once, for she could see that Barney was still keen about his mother, so perhaps that would be the best appeal for a start. Later, when sentiment failed, a more worldly appeal would surely have a better chance. Of course Hortense did not tell all her satellites this. They thought they were merely assisting in a clever plan to divert Barney from a war obsession that threatened to make him prematurely grave and depressed, and they entered into the scheme with all their giddy young hearts. That is all of them who were not already pledged to some defense outfit and about to leave for their assignments.

The Association arrived at the Vance home in the early gloaming while the church bells were still ringing far and near, and, a few birds were still chirping anxiously about the problems of the next day, involving the cat that had taken up a sniper's position behind the lilac bush and menaced every crumb that fell outside the kitchen door.

Roxy and Joel were sitting in the big rockers on the front porch enjoying the lovely night, for the moon was rising and there were many stars in sight. It wasn't often they got to enjoy a Sunday night rest on the porch, for they were regular attendants at church and never stayed at home for trifles. But Joel had stepped on a nail and had a very sore foot, so they had decided they ought to stay at home that night.

But when those noisy girls and boys drew up in the driveway by the end of the front porch, Joel groaned aloud.

"There come those termagants again," he said angrily, and began to swing his sick foot down from the pillow on the chair that Roxy had arranged so comfortably for him. " It seems we're not to have any peace any more. Get your duds on, Roxy. I'm going to church!"

"No!" said Roxy sharply. "Sit still. Don't take your foot down! You're not going to church and neither am I. Leave this to me. I'll settle this thing."

Roxy got up and walked to the end of the porch, her hands folded neatly over the stomach of her Sunday dress.

"Yes?" she said in her most severe formal tone. "Did you want something?"

"We sure did," said Hortense defiantly. "We want Barney. Call Barney won't you, right away? We've come to see him."

"Sorry," said Roxy loftily. "He isn't here!" She told herself in her heart that that wasn't quite true. She *wasn't* sorry. She was *glad* that Barney wasn't there. But she had been hearing the young people talk so much that that word "Sorry" had become common parlance, like a formal apology. Well, perhaps it was allowable in that sense. Then she called back her attention to what the hated Hortense was saying.

"Not here? Where is he?" she demanded.

"He didn't say where he was going," said Roxy severely.

"Well, when is he coming back?" she asked imperiously.

"Well, I wouldn't be able to say," said Roxy affably. "He doesn't consult me about his plans. He comes and goes as he want to, you know."

Hortense gave her an unbelieving look.

"Well, that's ridiculous!" said the girl curling her lip. "You probably know all about it. You're his old nurse and you always used to snoop around and find out. I'm sure you know perfectly well. So spit it out! We're in a hurry!"

Roxy stood there, her arms folded, looking at Hortense calmly. At last she asked:

"Would you like to leave a message?"

The other girls looked at their leader thoughtfully. Where would such a course get them?

But Hortense closed he lips firmly and shook her head:

"No," she said. "We wish to talk with Barney himself. We don't want any of your twisted reports carried back to him. Maybe we'll come in and wait for him. We could sing. We've got somebody here who can play for dancing. We could have a little dance and just wait for Barney to come back." She looked at them all for their assent.

"No!" said Roxy firmly. "You won't do that! This is Sunday and we don't have things like that going on in this house on Sunday."

"Well, this doesn't happen to be your house," said Hortense haughtily. "You really have nothing to say about it."

"It happens that we are in charge," said old Joel suddenly hobbling over to the end of the porch, his voice gruff and dictatorial: "We're in charge of this house," he repeated firmly, and the young would-be guests looked at him in amazement. In all the years they had been coming to this house Joel had never put forth such a determined personality. He really looked threatening, standing there with one stocking foot wrapped about with bandages.

"Aw, c'mon Hortie," said Hank scowling at the girl whose willing henchman he usually was glad to be. He well remembered a vigorous spanking administered in his youth by Joel after he was found picking raspberries from the Vance bushes.

"Yes, c'mon," echoed the girls. "Let's drive around a little while and see if we won't meet Barney."

"Yes, c'mon Hortie," said Cap uneasily. "It's a nice night to drive around, and we don't wanta have an argument with that old guy. He looks unpleasant. I'd sorta hate ta have ta knock him out. C'mon, we can come back after a while!"

And suddenly Hortense decided he was right. Clamorously they drove away, shouting appropriate remarks to the old couple who had so effectually foiled their plans.

When they were out of sight in the moonlight, and out of sound down the road, Joel hobbled back and stood looking down at the chair where he had sat so comfortably a few minutes ago.

"That's what we got for staying home from church, Roxy," he remarked grimly. "If it wasn't so late I'd go yet. But seeing it is late and everybody would turn around and watch us hobble into the back seat in the middle of the sermon, suppose we go to bed Roxy. I hate to give up sitting out here in the moonlight, but I can't stand having that gang coming back here, for I just know if they did come back I'd go out in spite of this ding-busted foot and wallop each one of them. I swear I would."

Roxy set her lips firmly and said, "Yes, let's go to bed. We'll lock all the doors, and turn out all the lights and then they can go hang. Barney has his key. And anyway, wherever he is, he may be pretty late coming in."

"Yes? I thought they said he had to rest? Didn't he have doctor's orders? He don't seem to be keeping any orders very well," said Joel.

"Well, I guess there isn't anything we can do about it, is there?" drawled Roxy indifferently.

"Seems like," assented Joel, climbing into bed with a gingerly care for his sick foot. "But then Barney always was a good boy. I don't fancy he'll do anything to really upset his health. I heard him say he was keen to get back to war, and the quicker he gets okay, the quicker he can go, more's the pity. Although I can't help being glad he wasn't home tonight when those banshees arrived. I wonder what his mother would have done if she'd been here when they arrived?"

"Well, I'm glad she wasn't for her sake, but I'm sure if she had been she would have had some gentle very natural way of stopping the things she didn't approve. She always could, even when Barney was a mere baby. She never let the neighbor-children's gang get ahead of her. And yet she was friendly with them all, and always spoke gently to them. That's a real lady for you. Always speak gentle, but never let wrong things go on. They all knew that when she was alive, and they never tried any of their high shines on her. If I don't miss my guess her son's got the same gift, and they'll presently find out. Not till then will they let him alone."

Meantime Barney had gone to see Sunny, late that afternoon, in answer to a telephone invitation from Mrs. Roselle to come to Sunday night supper, and to have time to run over his solo before they went to church, and Barney accepted the invitation eagerly.

Ever since he had left Sunny at her home and hurried back to his unwritten letters, he had been thinking about her. Perhaps it was not conscious thinking, but nevertheless in the back of his mind her face had been hovering, and when he was reminded of her, of anything she said, of the way she looked when she said it, there was a kind of satisfaction in his mind about her. She had grown up just as her sweet little child personality had promised, and he was thankful that in the world there was one girl who was like that.

Barney had not been giving much thought to girls in the last two years. A few girls, friends of his college days, had written him several times each when he was overseas and in constant action, and he had answered them gaily as he had opportunity, and that had been the end of it. Some of the home young people had written occasionally, too, at first, and then dropped out of his knowledge. And now he had come home and found to his disappointment that so many of them seemed to have changed, grown coarse, hard, giddy and selfish. He wondered if that could all be laid to the account of war and the changing world. And then when he spent a few hours with Sunny he had been so relieved to find that she was not like the rest.

So as he walked down the sunlit meadow that Sunday afternoon and up the hill toward her home he found his heart quickened with pleasant anticipation of going to meet one who had the same moral background as himself. The kind of living and thinking that had formed the background of home in his mind during those terrible days of war. The home to which he would go back, where living was sane, people had right ideas, men believed in God and at least tried to keep up a semblance of serving Him. He didn't think this all out in words, but it was a kind of atmosphere surrounding his thought and made him pleasant company in his walk in the sunshine.

So the afternoon had been a congenial one, exchanging thoughts

with one who was in sympathy with the convictions he felt were
most vital.

Sitting under the trees in the old rustic chairs where he remembered sitting long ago when he had come over on some errand for his
mother, they had a long talk. Only instead of the little girl whose
name was Sunny, who used to beg him to swing her, or to play ball
with her, there was this slim lovely girl just as sweet-faced, with just
as bright hair, who went by the name of Margaret. And seemed to
know all the answers to the questions he asked, and was deeply interested in every topic he introduced. She wanted to know about his
thoughts and feelings when he went into battle. Things he had never
expected to tell anyone, now that his mother was gone. But he found
himself telling this girl his innermost experiences.

All too soon the delightful talk was over, as they were called to the
pleasant dining room, and the delicious supper. Hot muffins and
strawberry jam, hot chocolate with whipped cream. Tempting slices
of cold chicken, crisp celery, a luscious maple-walnut cake, and canned
peaches from the peach orchard back of the house.

Then suddenly it was getting late. There was scarcely time to go
over the solo before they started for church.

"You know I really haven't any business singing a solo," said
Barney as he folded up his music.

"Why not, I should like to know?" asked Margaret. "Your voice is
even better than I remember it, and I used to think it was the most
wonderful voice I had ever heard."

"Oh, you were just a kid you know. But I really haven't done any
singing for two years, except as a crowd of fellows always sing in
their leisure time when they get together."

"Well, your voice is as good as ever," said the girl earnestly, "and
I know. I really do. We had a very noted singer staying in the neighborhood all last summer, and he used to ask me to play his accompa-
niments sometimes. I used to think his voice was like yours. It was
very beautiful."

"You're very flattering," smiled Barney, "but I'm afraid you're
prejudiced. And I do hope you will not be disillusioned about my
voice when I sing tonight."

"No," said Margaret, "I'm sure I shall not. I am entirely satisfied
at the way you have just been singing. Now, let's forget it. I don't

want you to get self-conscious. Look at that sunset. Isn't it glorious? It makes my heart thrill the way it thrilled me while you were singing,

> 'And the glory, the glory of the Lord, shall be revealed,
> And all flesh shall see it together.' "

"It's rather presumptive in me to attempt such a big thing when I'm practically off a battlefield and a hospital bed."

"Never mind. You're not to think of that. Remember your audience has not been hearing many oratorios and masterpieces of music, and it will be the words that you will get across to them. Certainly you can put over words with music better than anyone I ever heard."

They walked slowly down the road together into the glory of the evening, as the sunset lit their way. It seemed to them both that it was the end of one of those perfect days that only come now and then, like resting places on the way to Heaven.

Mercifully they were spared meeting that cavalcade of would-be callers who had come out searching for Barney, for they had gone in the opposite direction, and there was nothing to spoil the beauty of their walk to church, with the church bells now ringing out in the sweet air, now near, now far, and now and again a sleepy bird giving a flutelike call, and with happiness in their hearts.

Then they were at the church, his mother's church, and all the old friends sitting in their accustomed seats, some of them — sweet old faces, his mother's friends, old men and old women, carrying on at home, very few younger men in the audience, just a few in uniform. He could recognize the grin on a few of those uniformed young faces. They had been little boys sitting around the sidelines when he was playing baseball.

The old minister in the pulpit, with a kindly voice that trembled a little and white hair that had grown scant, was the same minister who had been in the pulpit for years. He had been retired, and the pulpit had been filled by a younger man. But he had gone into the service as a chaplain, and the old minister was back carrying on. Barney was glad of that. It seemed more natural with old Mr. Copeland there. He gave a tender glance toward the old-fashioned pew where his mother used to sit, and where for years he had sat beside her, finding the hymns for her, and the place in the Bible; and looking over with her.

Barney had taken a retired seat in the choir, at one side of the organ, most of the choir in front of him, and he had the advantage of being able to see everybody in the house, without himself being conspicuous. Also, when the young organist took her place at the organ he found himself where he could watch her sweet face with its earnest changing expression. It gave him opportunity to study her without seeming to stare. He was glad to find her face just as flawless, just as sweet and unworldly at such close range as he had judged it to be when he was talking with her, across the room, and he continued to be amazed that she, so young in a world at war, had been able to mature so beautifully, and without the hardness of so many of the current age.

Then he grew interested in the music, and marveled that she played so well. Not that he was a connoisseur in music, though during his college days he had managed to hear some of the best, and to enjoy it greatly.

When it came time for his solo he found himself so in tune with the whole sweet simple service that he felt none of the reluctance to sing that he had had when Sunny first asked him. He let the song roll forth with its message, till the audience hushed into breathlessness, listening. And there were tears even in some old eyes as the listeners remembered Barney's mother, wondering if in Heaven she could know, and hear.

Some of his old playmates, who had been deferred because of some physical ailment, sat in wonder at him, and drank in the message of his song as something they seemed to have missed out on so far. For Barney sang as if the words of his song had taken deep hold upon his life, and he were urging them to accept what he had. There was one fellow, Cy Baxter by name, a little older than Barney, who had been morbid for months because he couldn't get in anywhere, army or navy, and had to stay quietly in the bank and be looked down upon by the others as a slacker. The bank was all right of course in peacetime but it made him feel like an old man now, and all because of a little physical defect.

But when he heard Barney singing he caught some message from that song that pointed his heart above. Somehow Barney got it across to him that God wanted him right where he was, and because it had been ordered by God that was the highest honor he could have had. Afterward he wondered what it was, what had been the words Barney had sung that had made him willing to yield to God's will and do what he was doing with a smiling face and a satisfied soul, even if he would have been so much better pleased if he might have gone out and done some of the brave hazardous deeds that Barney was reported to have done.

Did the angels somehow convey the message to Barney that he was not just entertaining old friends and neighbors who were curious about him for his mother's sake, but that he was singing to souls who needed a message? For that was the way he sang. And to his own astonishment, that was the way he felt.

It seemed, when the benediction was pronounced, that it had been a blessed service and he was glad he had gone.

Afterwards, they swarmed around him and thanked him, those old friends of his childhood, friends of his mother's, and some few who remembered his father. They told him how much they had enjoyed his singing, and how proud they were of all he had done in the service, and proud that afterward he had cared enough to come back to the old church. And Cy Baxter had lingered indifferently in the back of the church until most of the others were gone, and then he came up and gripped Barney's hand and said fervently: "Say, Barn, that was swell!" Barney looked in his eyes, saw a hint of tears, and gripped Cy's hand warmly.

"Thanks, pard!" he said. "Glad you liked it." But there was a message warmer than just those words in Barney's eyes, almost tears behind his own glance, as his hands held the other young man's hand with a lingering pressure. Somehow, there seemed to be a bond forged right there that linked a chain to Heaven.

The young organist's cheeks were rosy as she watched the reaction to Barney's song, and she was more pleased than at any praise that had ever been given to her.

It was on the way home that she told him how his singing had stirred her, and how she had seen the effect on different ones in the audience.

"Oh, Barney!" she said. "I wish you were going to stay here and help in that choir! Of course I know that's not to be compared with the work you are doing in service for the country, but oh, I believe you could reach *souls* with your voice!"

"Thank you, Margaret," he said, laying his hand for an instant on the little hand that rested on his arm. "I had never thought of that as a calling, but I'd be glad if I might help people some times that way."

They were walking slowly, too much stirred by the service, and the warm reception of the people, to be willing to have it over soon.

Then suddenly the girl looked up.

"How did you make out with your Washington call yesterday, Barney?"

"Oh, Washington. Yes. Why, I found my man, the admiral, was out of the city. I'm to see him at eleven o'clock tomorrow."

"Oh," said she with a tight little catch in her breath. "Well — I'll be praying for you."

"Thank you," he said, "I'll be remembering that," and he laid his hand on hers again with another quick pressure. "But," he said, after a minute, looking down at her almost mischievously, "which way will you be praying? That I'm to go, or stay?"

Margaret was still for a minute and then she looked up confidently and answered:

"I'll be praying for *God's* way."

"That's great!" said Barney thoughtfully. "That puts it up to God, doesn't it? And after all I wouldn't want it otherwise. I don't want to impose my wishes in this. I'll make my offer to Washington, but I can't really do anything else about it but that. God knows where Stormy is, and if He needs me to go after him. I'll just ask Him too, to take over, and have it His way. Thank you for making me see that."

Walking home alone in the moonlight afterwards, he thought again what an unusual girl Sunny had developed into, and rejoiced. He was glad he had come home to get to know her again as she was now. What a girl to have for a friend!

Chapter 11

Roxy, wearing an old dressing gown that had done duty almost ever since she had been in service, and her front hair in curlers, appeared at the door with a speck of a flashlight in her hand while Barney was trying to find the keyhole.

"Oh, is that you, Roxy?" he said, somewhat startled to find the house in darkness. "What's the matter? Something gone wrong with the electricity?"

"No," said Roxy ruefully, "it's just that we've had callers, and they said as how they might be coming back when you got home. They said it was important they see you tonight."

Barney slid inside the door, shut it firmly, and locked it before he spoke. Then he stood with his back against it and said:

"Who was it, Roxy? Not that gang again?"

"Yes, the very same. Joel and I were sitting on the front porch and I had his bad foot all fixed comfortable on a cushion, and we was enjoying the moonlight, when they come roistering into the drive and ordered me to call you. And when I said you weren't here they wanted to know where you was, and I said you hadn't told me. And they wanted to know when you'd be back, and I said I hadn't any idea. And first they was going to come in and play the pianna and dance, but Joel he got up and ordered them out. I never saw Joel so riled up, not before folks. They tole him this wasn't his house, but he said he was in charge of it, and they hadta *go*. He said it was Sunday night and we didn't have such goings on here Sunday night. So they decided to go, but they said they'd drive around and find you, and they'd come back later. And I wouldn't put it past 'em to come, no matter how late it was, so Joel and I locked all the doors and turned out the lights and went to bed. We thought that might discourage 'em a little if they found it dark. But now you've come, if you want the light you do as you please. You could hang some blankets over your windows if you want to sit up and read or anything, but I thought I'd wait and tell you."

"No, of course not, Roxy. I can get to bed in the dark. I've done it many a time in my life, especially since I've been in service. I'm sorry I kept you up so late, but I certainly don't want a visitation tonight again. Can you find your way with that flashlight? All right, I'll come up behind you. Is this all the doors to lock? Okay, I think they'll be disappointed if they come back again tonight. No, I don't need the flashlight. I know every inch of this house from garret to cellar, dark or light. Don't worry about me. Wasn't I born and brought up in this house? There, find your way to bed, Roxy. Good night!" and Barney went to his own room, took off his shoes, and lost no time in getting undressed and into bed. He was sound asleep when the gang returned, and drove up to the house.

He might have heard them, discussing whether he had come home yet, if he had been awake, but he was tired after the pleasurable excitement of the day and evening, and he always slept soundly, so he did not waken. But Roxy, over on her side of the house was crouching down by the window sill and she heard them.

"He probably hasn't come home yet," said Hortense. "Soldiers generally stay out late when they go to see a girl. I wonder who she is? I wonder if he took the train or not?"

"Aw, you forgot he's under orders and s'posed to go to bed at a certain time, don't you remember?" drawled Hank. It was evident that he had no relish for another encounter with Joel. He remembered that Joel wielded a heavy hand, and Hank was no fighter.

"Oh you poor simp, didn't you know that that talk about orders and rest was all bunk?" said Hortense. "You don't catch Barney Vance doing anything he doesn't want to do, not with his army orders several thousand miles away over a lot of ocean. What I'm aiming to do is make Barney *want* to break orders, and do what we want him to do, and I mean to win out, too! Well, let's drive around a little more, and come back past here again, to see if there's any light. It isn't midnight yet."

"Mebbe he's gone down to Washington," volunteered Amelia. "I heard him say he might have to go down pretty soon to report to some doctor or something."

"Well, if that's the case we might meet the midnight train and bring him home. How about it Hank? Drive over to the highway and let's meet the Washington train. The local one, too. He may have been visiting some friend of his mother's, or some girl he met somewhere. But we can't afford to let too much time go by before we get our plans started."

So with much hilarity they drove away again, and Roxy crept thankfully into her bed hoping the home enemy was subdued for the night at least.

But Barney was sound asleep, dreaming of Stormy Applegate who had saved his life.

And over in another white farm house about a mile or so away, where the lights were out and the family slept, the girl that used to be little Sunny, knelt beside her bed and prayed earnestly that such things as she desired might go God's way. And afterward when she lay down to rest, her heart kept thrilling over the notes that Barney Vance had sung in church that night, and she went to sleep praying: "Oh, God, bless Barney Vance, and make him into what You want him to be. And oh, take care of him, for Your name's sake."

The next morning's mail brought a number of letters for Barney, and among them were several invitations, for those girls had lost no time in getting their invitations into the early morning mail.

Barney opened two from overseas first, gay messages from his buddies who were still with the company, one from a nurse in the hospital where he had been recuperating, enclosing one of his handkerchiefs he had left behind him. He was glad to get that for it was the last little thing his mother had sent him, and he prized it very highly. He had left it under his pillow in the hospital, and she had found it when she put fresh linen on the bed.

She was a nice little nurse, and had served him well. It was kind of her to take so much trouble for him. He would have to write and thank her, of course.

Then he came to the three little notes. The first one from Amelia, asking him to come over prepared to stay the evening and take dinner with her family. She said they wanted to hear all about his experiences in the war. He frowned, flung down the letter and picked up the next. That was from Lucy Anne Salter. She was inviting him to take lunch with her and her mother on Tuesday noon, and divulging cleverly that she had borrowed her grandmother's car for the after-

noon and they were going to take a drive over to the neighboring
navy camp that wasn't too far away. They would return in time for
dinner at the inn and see a movie for the close of the evening.

Barney tossed the letter after the other one and began to laugh.

"What is this, Roxy, a conspiracy? Or is it a social club? Wait!
Here's another! From Martha and Madge Wrexall, as I live! They
want me for an all-day picnic at Hunter's Park, dancing in the evening
in the pavilion. Special war music for the soldiers! Can you beat it
Roxy? What do they think I am? Why a *strong* man couldn't stand
all that program, and here I am *invalided* home!"

Roxy sat grimly disapproving with anxiety written across her loving face.

"I could tell we weren't done with that crowd yet," she said with a
sigh. "What are you going to do, lad? You couldn't stand all that
froth. I could tell by your eyes after their first raid on you. You
better take to your bed for awhile and let me tell them you are sick."

"Not on your life, Roxy! Let that gang drive me to bed? Not if the
court knows itself, and she thinks she does. No, I'll just write a nice
little note to each one and tell them I'm having to run down to Washington on business, and when I get back I shall be much too busy to
accept social engagements. How will that do? Of course I hate to
hurt some of those people, but I just can't take it. They aren't my
kind, Roxy."

"I should say not," said Roxy indignantly. "But they think just
because you wear a uniform you ought to be willing to go the whole
way and have a regular riot-act while you're here."

"Well, they'll find out they're mistaken," said Barney striding over
to his mother's desk and opening a drawer where he knew she always kept writing paper.

He sat for a few minutes scratching away with his fountain pen,
and presently presented Roxy with appropriate answers declining all
his invitations.

"There! See how they sound will you? And then will you kindly
give them to the postman when he comes, so he can get them around
before the evening? Especially that one for tonight, Amelia's. And
meantime I'm taking the train right now for Washington, see? You
don't know how long I have to stay. Tell them I have an appointment

with an admiral down there, and I'm not sure when I shall get back, so you can't make any promises for me. I shall be very busy when I come. Maybe by and by I'll have a party myself, and invite them all, but if I do I'll set the program my way, and I don't mean maybe. See?"

"Yes, I see," said Roxy with a troubled look. "And I'll do my best, even if Joel and I have to go to bed to get rid of them. But boy, there's something else. This morning Mrs. Kimberly telephoned that she was having a guest some day this week who was going to stay a few days with her, her niece, Cornelia Mayberry, and she was crazy to see you. She said her brother was overseas with you and he had written her to come on and get acquainted with you. Now what shall I say to her? I told her I'd tell you and I thought you'd be glad to see her sometime, but now I better tell her you're going away and not say anything more about it, hadn't I?"

Barney looked up startled.

"What do you say her name is? Mayberry? Cornelia Mayberry? Why sure, I'll *have* to see her. Her brother was one of my closest buddies through all our engagements over there. He used to talk a lot about her. He thought she was tops. You fix it up, can't you Roxy? Just because I don't want to go carousing around with that other gang is no sign I can't have any friends. And anyway, they don't need to know everything I do. You know how to be polite and get out of things I know, Roxy, because you always sent the people home that mother didn't want here without making them mad either. You'd give them each a cooky or something, and they never got mad."

"Of course," said Roxy with a smile.

Then suddenly Barney looked at his watch, and sprang to his feet. "For Pete's sake! I'm gonta miss my train if I don't hurry. Bye, Roxy! Be a good girl, and don't worry about me if I don't come back right away. I'll be all right, and you know I have to stay as long as they say."

Then Barney went striding down the road at a good military pace, arrived at the station just two minutes before the train came in, and missed by half a second a contact with two of his would-be hostesses. He saw them from the car window and hid behind his morning paper so they wouldn't see him. In the name of all conscience,

why did girls want to make such fools of themselves? Running after
a fellow until he wished he had never seen them. Not even giving
him a chance to look them over and see if he liked them yet. Then he
fell to wondering what Cornelia Mayberry would be like. Would
she resemble her brother? He was a good guy, and he was crazy
about his sister. He would just have to show her a little attention.
How would she fit with Margaret Roselle? Would Margaret like
her?

And there was another question. If it turned out that Miss Mayberry
was to be in town long and he would be expected to pay her a little
attention, what other fellows and girls could he get together? There
was Sunny, of course, in case she would be willing to help him, but
what fellows were home whom he could call upon? If only Stormy
were here he would jump right in and help. Stormy was that way.
Good old Stormy! Would he ever see him again?

And then his thoughts merged into a plan for what he would say to
the admiral in case he succeeded in seeing him. Oh, if he could only
be allowed to go and hunt for Stormy! At least to make sure if he
was dead or alive. Praise God he was in Heaven if he had died, but
if he was still alive, if only he might rescue him somehow from any
unpleasant experience he might be undergoing!

Back in his home town of Farmdale a little school teacher with
bright hair and earnest eyes was praying for him, all day long. Always in between what she was doing she was crying out in her heart
to God to keep him, and to help him to get his friend back if he was
still in need of help.

Barney sat for awhile staring out the window, scarcely seeing the
quick rushing landscape, thinking what it would probably be like
when the war was finally over, and the boys came back. What it
would be like to have Stormy living over here perhaps. He remembered that Stormy had once said longingly that he wished he could
go back home to America and live an old-fashioned normal life again.
Good old Stormy! Would that ever be? Or had he already begun a
heavenly life?

Then suddenly he noticed that the train was coming into Washington. There was the dome of the Capitol, the sharp point of the monu-
ment, and the distant outlines of the lovely Lincoln Memorial. He

would be in time to see the cherry blossoms. He had seen them once, long ago, when he was a boy in high school and went with the high school crowd on that memorable trip to see his nation's capitol.

He caught up his bag and hurried out. Would his admiral have arrived yet? Would he be able to see him today, or would there be a lot of tiresome waiting around, and then more waiting, and then maybe disappointment at last?

Meantime, back at his home in Farmdale Roxy was having troubles of her own. She simply couldn't get any work at all done because she was continually being called to the telephone.

Amelia, first, in great dismay.

"Roxy, isn't Barney there? Won't you let me speak to him right away? He hasn't gone anywhere *yet*, has he?"

"Yes, Miss Amelia," answered Roxy pleasantly. "He went on the early train this morning."

"Oh, do you mean he's just gone to the *city*?"

"No, Miss Amelia, he's gone to Washington." There was satisfaction in Roxy's tone as she announced this importantly.

"To *Washington*! My goodness! I thought he was invalided home and had to rest. Did he go sight-seeing? I shouldn't think that was very restful."

"No, Miss Amelia, I'm sure he's not gone sight-seeing. I think he was under some sort of orders. You know he has to report to the government from time to time." Roxy didn't know this. She merely *assumed* it. She thought it would make her answers have more weight if they seemed to be official.

"Well, but—isn't he coming back *tonight*?"

"He didn't know when he would be back. He took a suitcase with him."

"Oh, for Pete's sake!" exclaimed the dismayed Amelia, "I was having a party especially for him tonight, and I've got all the other people invited."

"That's too bad," said Roxy sympathetically, "but he wouldn't want you to stop on that. He said something about some invitations, but I thought he wrote notes to explain why he couldn't be there."

"Yes, I got a note, but I thought if he was coming back tonight I'd just tell him to come over anyway, no matter how late he was."

"Yes?" said Roxy. "That's kind of you. But I don't think he is likely to come tonight. If he comes of course I'll tell him, but I don't think he expected to be back tonight."

"Oh, how perfectly *horrid*!" said Amelia. "We certainly are having bad luck with Barney."

"Well, you can't count on service men you know, these war times," said Roxy sympathetically. "The government isn't thinking about parties when they give orders. You have to expect things like that."

"Mercy! You don't suppose they're going to send him back overseas right away, do you?"

"Well, I really wouldn't know," said Roxy serenely. "He hasn't said anything about it, but then perhaps he wouldn't know himself."

"Heavenly days!" said the disappointed Amelia. "What are we coming to? Life isn't really worth living any more, is it Roxy?"

"Well, that depends on what you think is really worth-while, I guess, doesn't it?"

"Worth-while?" queried Amelia bewilderedly, and suddenly hung up.

From then on all day Roxy was kept busy running to the telephone, always with a grin on her face. She really was enjoying this. It was one time when she had the situation well in hand and those "pesky young ones," as she called the young people, couldn't get the better of her.

And it wasn't only the young would-be hostesses of the week that did the calling up. Several of the rest of the young gang called up in dismay to verify the rumor that was going around that Barney might have been ordered overseas right away again. So Roxy quite enjoyed her day. It was a chance to make that crowd of good-for-nothings understand that they weren't the whole show in this world. She really was glad to see that crowd get their comeuppance once. The very idea of their getting up parties enough to fill Barney's whole time, when they knew he didn't hold with a lot of their wild goings on! Perhaps they couldn't understand that a person could keep his principles, even when he was off with a whole army who could do as they pleased about such little matters as principles.

But there was one girl who did not call up, and perhaps she was the one girl who had known that Barney was going away. But Roxy

wasn't even sure of that, for Sunny Roselle was a very quiet man-
nered girl who didn't go around running after boyfriends, even if
they had been friends from very long ago. And even if he had taken
her to church, and sung a solo for her in the service! This bit of news
she had learned from more than one of her loquacious telephone callers that day. They hadn't been there themselves but others had told
them about that song, and they were calling up to make sure it was
true. But all they succeeded in doing was to make Roxy sorry she
hadn't been present, and she and Joel had a little time of mourning
over it that evening when they again sat on the porch to enjoy the
twilight.

"He mighta told us about it," grumbled Joel.

"He *wouldn't*," said Roxy. "Did you ever hear him boast about
anything yet?"

"Well, no, but Sunny mighta told us."

"She didn't have a chance," said Roxy. "Besides she probably
thought we'd be at church."

"Yes, I s'pose so," mourned Joel.

"Well, we'll likely have other chances. They'll ask him again
from all I hear, and if I don't miss my guess there'll be an increase in
the attendance of young people at next Sunday night's service."

"Yes, if he ain't gone overseas by that time," mourned Joel. "Come
on, let's go to bed. I gotta sow that south meadow in the morning,
and I gotta get up early."

Chapter 12

Stormy Applegate, escaped a pitifully short distance from the camp where he had been interned by the enemy for several weeks, half-starved and ill-treated, had found refuge in a broken shed in the rear of a decrepit dwelling that might have been at one time the remnants of someone's home. It was isolated and desolate now, with outlying buildings and occasional other remains of houses for several miles around, as a result of being in occupied territory.

Watching stealthily for some hours, Stormy decided there was no one anywhere near. He could not even see a lagging guard, so far was he from the surrounding fence of the camp.

Toward evening, hungry and thirsty, weak with long fasting, he ventured forth toward what was left of an old garden back of the house. He was sure he had sighted a sickly looking leaf that might mean a possible vegetable or two. Even a frozen leaf might be edible, sickly looking though it was. It might serve to still the awful gnawing in the region of his stomach, and enable him to keep on. Perhaps that woodland a mile or two away might shelter a stream where he could get water to hearten him for his adventurous journey.

The landscape was a blank desert. Not even a dog in sight. No birds even in the distance except a hovering hawk, circling, identifying prey from the sky, which might mean some prisoner had died and been cast forth for the elements to do their worst and save the trouble of burying him.

Stormy in his weak state shuddered, and crept forward cautiously. Even if one had been watching with binoculars from a distance he could scarcely have been seen to move, so slow and steady was his progress. He was so nearly the color of the earth about him, so burned with the sun and rain to which he had been continuously exposed, that he was practically invisible, a neutral that would never be notice. At least he hoped that might be so.

Lying thus in the old garden ruts he found a few frozen roots that he could gnaw on. There was not much sustenance to be had from them, but at least it helped the awful craving for food.

When the shadows were growing longer on the wide sullen ground, and he was satisfied that there were no more roots to be found in that location, he crept on, keeping the old barn between himself and the camp from which he had come. And once he came to a sedgy place where tall grasses stood grimly in marshland, and when he went he went close enough he was able to reach down and wet a corner of his grimy rag of a handkerchief, his one remaining remnant of a civilized life.

He was so weak that he lay for sometime near this source of water, realizing that he ought to wash out that dirty handkerchief, for it might be a long time before he came near any water again, and to have one clean rag would be a comfort in all his squalor. But at last he roused himself and washed the rag as best he could, wiping his face with its wetness, licking his parched lips, washing the rag again and again, gaining new strength from the few drops of filthy water he was able to suck from the rag.

Dusk was coming down over the land again, and with it more comparative safety. He put his head down in the coolness among the tall grasses, and prayed.

"Oh God, I'm going on now. You said you would go with me. Show me where and how to move. I am still Yours, but I'm very tired and weak. Do with me what you will for Christ's sake. I'm Stormy, you know. Trusting to the end. Don't let me fall before the enemy."

Then he crept on.

As evening began to come down, and there were no lights whatever to be seen except very far ahead, and no sounds of a living human being, nor even animal, no birds' cries in the gray deserted sky, as if it were made of brass, Stormy steadied himself to his feet and managed to walk a few steps. It was a rest from the continual creeping and rolling he had been subjected to all day. But still he found he was very weary, for the weakness was growing upon him, and his hands and head felt hot. Was it fever coming on? Could it be poison from the stream where he had drunk? But no, there would have been no reason for even an enemy to poison a bit of sedge water so far from human habitation.

On and on he went, realizing that the night would be short at most for him to get away, counting up the mileage as he had calculated it, and what he had yet to go.

As the night progressed and his weary footsteps lagged, he began to wonder if perhaps God meant him to die here, on the way, without ever a chance to get the information he had bought at such a price, back to his outfit. Was it all going to be of no avail? Had he taken this last trip for nothing after all? True, he had downed planes, he had done his part at driving the enemy back, but that needed information about conditions, that he had volunteered to get at all hazards, was still in his own mind. Even if he dared to write it, he would not dare to send it, here from an enemy-infested land. Here where every move of contact with his own world would be watched alertly, and worse than death would be the retaliation.

As he lay down midway between midnight and dawning, the dizziness overcame him so that he almost lost consciousness for a little moment, and then, his partly waking soul dazedly wondered if this was the end. The weakness and utter weariness seemed to submerge him again, strong man though he had been. Of course he had been for weeks on very short rations, and knew he was half starved, but strange visions began to swim across his rousing consciousness. A vision of a face—was that a girl he had seen sometime? Or could it be an angel come to conduct him Home? Was this then the end of his struggle? The end of his service to his country? Had he done all that God expected him to do in this great crisis?

The sweet face was smiling down at him. It seemed a girl who knew him. Was that what angels were like? Or if it were a girl, how did she get here, on the edge of a forest in a land he did not know?

As he came back to life again after that brief rest he tried to clear his mind and think. Her face was clearer now, and she was somehow connected with his company. Some member of his company. Who was it? Surely he could remember! Mayberry, that was the name. Lieutenant Mayberry's sister. She has visited her brother once at camp, and Mayberry had introduced her to him. A lovely girl! Gray eyes and dark hair, softly curled about her face. He looked again at the vision above him there in the edge of the forest. And now her name was coming. Cornelia! That was it. Cornelia Mayberry! A lovely name, and her brother had called her Cornie. She had a beautiful smile too. She has smiled at him when he said good night to her before she left on the evening train. He hadn't known her before that night, though he had seen her several times in the distance, and admired her, she seemed so unspoiled. He had seen her picture too in her brother's barracks. A face untarnished by the make-up of the world. She had made a deep impression upon him. Sometime when the war was over, if he came through alive, he would like to get to know a girl like that. That was what he had thought the night of the day he had met her, and then put the memory of her aside. Some day he might find a girl like that for himself. Would that ever happen? Or was he just dreaming of Heaven? "God, are you there? And is that vision one of Your angels, or was it that Cornelia-girl come out of my heart to smile at me? Was it really that girl? And did You tell her to come? She doesn't belong to me, You know. Her people belong to the rich of the earth, and I'm just plain Stormy Applegate, but I'm Your child! Oh, God is there something wrong with my head? Things seem so queer! Help me! Don't let me play out before I can get back and make my report."

It was almost dawn when he awoke again with a start. His head was clearer, but when he tried to sit up he was still very dizzy and he had to wait a few minutes before he dared to struggle to his feet again. Even then he had to grope ahead with his hands from tree to tree, almost ready to topple over. Unsteady from now on he was going to be, and yet he must go on as long as there was breath in his body. This was the job he had undertaken to do, and he must get back with his information or the whole expedition was a failure. He must not climax his life by failure at the end. If he could only find something edible.

Finally he heard the babbling of a little brook, and he slid down to his knees and drank deeply.

Somewhat refreshed he crept along through the rough ground of the woods, crawling on hands and knees, stopping now and again to lay his head down on his big dirty hands and close his eyes. It seemed to make it more possible for him to get a deeper breath again. If he could only get plenty of deep breaths he could go on.

But at last he came to the edge of the woods, and a wide lonely hillside stretched down before him. No gardens anywhere. Or was that a little patch farther on? He strained his eyes to see, and then struggled on. Finally, when a smooth stretch of hillside developed he lay down and tried his old trick of rolling. But when presently he came to a rise in the ground, that stopped his progress. Then he was quite dizzy again, and wondered how he was to go on, but lying still awhile he took a new lease of life and looked around carefully, searching for something green he might dare to eat. If only there were a stream that might have fish, yet how could he catch fish? No line, no hook. Only his bare hands, no longer strong enough to be deft, alert. If only there were hens somewhere that might leave an egg about in this stark land. If only there were a cow he could try to milk. But there seemed to be no living inhabitants in the few dilapidated houses that dotted the bleak landscape ahead of him.

It was growing dark again. If he only could walk, really walk, there was no reason why he couldn't make time now, with no danger of being seen.

The thought gave him a new spurt of courage. He drew a deep breath, and tried to pretend that he was only a few rods from his destination, although he well knew that was far from true.

It was more than the middle of the night when he came to a group of rough houses.

Cautiously he stole from one to the other, peering into the dusty windows, studying the closed doors. Somehow those houses looked uninhabited, yet he dared not presume. He was only thankful that his mind was still keen enough to realize that he must be careful. Yet he bungled on slowly, from one building to another, and at the very last one he found the door an inch ajar.

Carefully listening, peering into every side of the small sordid edifice, revealed no inhabitant.

With fear and trembling he ventured to shove the door wider open and look inside. Nobody about. Utter silence in the small dim precincts. He crept within and let his trembling hands feel his way. If he only had a match, or a flashlight, but he had been a long time away from such amenities. He began to feel his way again cautiously, slowly. It was evident that there were no householders here, for surely if there were he would at least hear the sound of breathing.

His sensibilities seemed to have grown keener since he had entered a place with four walls. He must be very careful! If he could only find something to eat, or a drink of water! Would there perhaps be two dry sticks he could rub together to make a light? But no, he must not dare do that. There might be a dweller somewhere about, or approaching. They would see and come. Or the enemy might be hidden watching. There were so many things to be thought of on this strange journey.

Then his hand came into contact with a tin basin. He felt cautiously inside. Something was rolling around in there. Two smooth round objects. Eggs. There were eggs! Could that be true? Or were his senses deceiving him?

He was sure now that this little group of buildings must be a place from which the dwellers had departed in haste before the approach of the enemy. That might explain the open door. They had hurried away, and left those two eggs. How long ago? How old were those two eggs? Would even a rotten egg keep life in his body? He slipped them in the pockets of his ragged blouse, and moved on. He must not venture to stay here too long. The owner could be returning. After daylight he could tell more about things. What was that on the floor that his foot had touched? He stooped to feel. A pair of shoes, and a tin can, still unopened. There might be something eatable there. Then he came upon a few more cans, some on a shelf above his head, three on the floor as if dropped in a hurry. Surely this spoke of sudden flight. Wasn't that right reasoning?

He stuffed the cans inside his blouse, and groped on. There was a crude chair. He almost fell over it, and there was a garment of some king lying across it. It felt like a coat. It had pockets. He deposited the next can he found in one of the pockets. Then it came to him that he was rifling somebody's house. But he had to do it to save his own life, if he would get away. His mission was important. He must not stop for anything. And if he lived he could some day come back and pay the man for what he had taken, provided he could find the man, and the place. Oh God, are You here?

The late moon was peeping over the rim of the world, and suddenly looking into the high dusty window, revealing a clutter of other articles.

Now, if he could only find some water, or a can opener, or something that he might drink. He felt as if he could not stand up another second, and to lie down there, with perhaps the owner, or worse still the enemy, not far away, was certainly sure death.

He groped again and his hand came into touch with a pail half filled with water. He lifted a handful to his face, put his lips to it. Even the thought of it was refreshing.

Then suddenly, feeling along the shelf above the water pail he found a tin box with three matches in it. Dared he light one? No, better not venture. He stepped over to the door. He must go. Far in the distance he heard a sound. He must get out and into shadow.

Outside the moon had slipped behind a cloud. It was heavily dark, and he had three matches, but he dared not use them. He crept on hurriedly, his heart palpitating until it almost choked him. It occurred to him that he was probably following those who had earlier found escape down this same path he was taking. Would he find them later, in case he was able to go on?

After a little he crept within a group of stunted bushes, back from the path he had been going, and tried one of the eggs, breaking the end open against a stone he found by the wayside. He smelled it. It wasn't bad. Not too bad. He was not in a condition to be squeamish anyway. And he sucked the eggs as if they were the very breath of life, as indeed they were to him. Then he dropped his head down on his arms and closed his eyes for a few minutes. He mustn't go to sleep. No, he must get away from here as soon as possible while it was still dark.

He opened his eyes and attempted to go on. He was lame and sore in every joint and sinew, but he felt new vigor from the eggs he had sucked, and now before he started out again he ventured to knock a hole in one of the cans he was carrying. What if it should be tomatoes, or some kind of fruit juice?

A sharp stone was not hard to find, another blunt one for a hammer, and soon he had a hole in the top of that can. He applied his nose and got the smell of tomato juice. He tipped up the can and drank, long deep quaffs of the life-giving liquid. It seemed to go through his starved veins, and to put new vigor into his faint heart. And after he had drunk the juice, he started on again.

Still a great empty country, no town or even distant visions of a town. What had those cabins been where he had found the cans? Were they hastily built to harbor refugees as the enemy came into the land, and then abandoned as the internment camp was placed so near them? It was as if he were looking back and trying to read the story of what had happened along that way.

But even with the refreshment he had found in the cabin, his limbs were still very shaky, and it did not seem to him he could go on any farther.

But the stars were coming out again, and reminded him that he must keep on while they would guide him where he wanted to go. So he compelled himself step by step, making scarcely any progress, yet persisting.

At last he dropped down. Just a minute. He must sleep a minute. And so he slept, on and on, and the night grew old, and the dawn crept on stealthily.

The baying of a distant hound burst suddenly upon the air, and though it was very far away it startled the weary man into quick frenzy.

He sat up sharply. He looked around him, and up. The stars were gone. Clouds had obscured them. But the hound kept on, and he came to himself and his caution.

There was no time to stop to consider. He must get on.

So he struggled to his feet and straggled on.

Of the three cans he still had with him two of them were canned milk, and the third was another can of tomatoes. In the morning he drank a can of milk, and lay down in a shadowed place in the woods to sleep once more. When he woke again his hands and head were burning and he was shivering as with an ague.

"H'm! Trying to get sick!" he murmured to himself. "Can't afford to do that. Got to get on while the getting is good. When is this blamed desert going to be done?"

But he blundered up and stumbled on, more because his body was accustomed to the motion perhaps, than because he quite knew what he was doing. Only with that one steady idea behind it all that he had a job to do, to get his information back to the right sources in spite of anything, live or die, before it was too late. The same spirit with which he would have fought if he had been out on the battle-field, obeying combat orders from his officer.

There came a time when he finally fell, stumbling over some root or stone of which his fagged senses had not warned him, and when he fell he lay still. Perhaps he had struck his head. He was never quite sure afterwards, and when he came to semiconsciousness and wondered where he was, and how much longer this thing was going on, all he could really think about was the terrible burning heat of his head and body. His hands were like red hot furnaces as he lifted them to touch his face. He still gave a passing thought to his job, but he had to do something about this awful heat of his body before he could go on. So he lay and slept again at odd intervals.

And the next he knew he opened his eyes in a little wooden shack, on a bed of pine boughs, and a gruff man with hair on his face was bending over him and giving him water to drink. He couldn't quite make out what this meant, for he didn't recognize the man as one of his own outfit, so he hadn't reached his destination yet.

"Oh God, are You there?" he cried out at intervals. "If You're still there it's all right with me."

But the man who was attending him said nothing. Perhaps he spoke a foreign tongue. The fever and the dim light made it impossible to tell of what nationality the man came. He seemed only present as a vague shadow, perhaps one of those angels God sent sometimes. Certainly there could be no relation between him and the girl whose face had haunted him earlier in his journey. But sometimes this at-tendant brought him water to drink, and at times there was broth. Queer broth. He wasn't sure what it tasted of, but its warmth in his stomach, and its filling quality brought a little relief from the gnaw-ing pain that had gripped his vitals.

Once in the night he looked about him to try to identify something, but all was strange. Just a blank wooden wall. The semblance of a small window, a door beyond. There was a fitful fire burning on an infinitesimal hearth, and there was smoke in the room. He was cold, and he was hot, yet once the old man bathed his face with an ill-smelling rag, and that seemed to help, till he got to shivering again.

"Oh, God, are You going to take me Home now?" he cried out once, as if the old man were not there. "But couldn't I first go by way of my own outfit and give the message I went over the line for? They need it Lord. But You know that. And if I don't take it, and You want them to have it, You've other ways of getting it to them. I'll just stay here till You tell me what to do."

Weird talking for the old foreigner to hear.

The old man went out one day for several hours and Stormy thought he was deserted. But then he came back with some herbs, and began to brew a concoction on the hearth, using a tin can for a cooking vessel. Later he administered it, a vile bitter mixture, and the sick man drank it because he could not help himself. Then he slept again, and when he woke there was more of the bitter medicine to swallow, and he too weak to resist.

He had no means of measuring time. He had long ago sold his wrist watch to a fellow prisoner in return for a garment he needed. But as time went on he felt a decided change. Some of the heat in his body was gone, the chills had stopped. He could swallow the taste-less broth because it appeased the terrible emptiness. And then he became aware the old man was speaking to him in a foreign tongue. He wasn't just sure what nationality it was, but there were parts of words that conveyed a vague meaning, and as he roused to the world again, and his need to go on living became more urgent he began to try to utter words himself. He tried a number of tongues of which he knew a smattering, and at last struck a few words the old man seemed to understand. Simple, basic terms, but with feeble gestures he could ask for drink, and food.

As the hours passed they talked a good deal, these two, so strangely brought together. They talked each in his own tongue, and under-stood but little.

But now and again when the sick man would cry out to God and look above, the old man would seem to understand that he was pray-ing and would pause, whatever he was doing, and stand, head bowed, his hands crossed upon his breast. And afterwards he would point up and jabber a lingo, of which now and then Stormy thought he could cipher out a bit of meaning. He concluded at last that it was some queer dialect the man spoke, but his brain was too tired to try to figure out what it was. So with a method of his own, pointing to an object and saying a word over and over he managed to make the other man understand a few primitive ideas.

He had lost all sense of time, but one morning he woke, knowing he must get up that day, and must go on as soon as possible.

The old man looked sad when he pointed that he must go, and shook his head, but the next morning they separated. He could not make the old man go with him. He gathered from their meager communication that he was waiting for someone to come for him, and must not go away till his friend came.

So, with a bit of hard bread in his blouse and his one remaining can of condensed milk he started out alone, both pointing up, and waving quiet hands. After he had thanked his old nurse with a warm grasp of his hand, he started off down a hill in a softly gray morning, before the sun had quite decided what to do about shining that day, and now Stormy was out on his own, a little rested from his hours on the resinous bed of pine boughs, and much weakened by the fever that had taken its toll from his already weakened system.

He knew when he started that he would not be able to go far, and he must stop and rest shortly, but before he turned into a woodland stretch where there would be hiding, he turned and looked back and saw the dim figure of the old man standing where he had left him in the gray of the morning. So he lifted up his hand and pointed to Heaven and the old man lifted his arm and looked up.

"Oh God, You take care of him, and keep him safely till his folks come, please. This is Stormy asking, for Christ's sake."

The old man must have understood that he was praying for him for when Stormy looked back he saw the old man still standing with bowed head and hands crossed on his breast.

Chapter 13

How frantic Barney Vance would have been if he could have known that even as he took the elevator up to the office where he was hoping to meet his friend the admiral in behalf of a scheme to find Stormy Applegate, that Stormy at that very moment was toiling, wary and footsore, and nigh unto despair along an unknown way. For Stormy was entering the first smart-looking village he had seen on his journeying from the detention camp, and he had just seen signs that it was enemy-occupied.

But Barney had thought so long about this desire of his to find Stormy that it had come to seem almost a dream, that might take years to accomplish. It was something he was working out to satisfy his own desire, and which everybody else seemed to think was utterly foolish and not worth the attempt, because they felt that Stormy was out of the running. He was either dead, or so hopelessly a prisoner that no one but God could save him, and Barney met so few in his questionings that even counted on God to do anything about such things that sometimes he questioned whether he might not be losing some of his own faith too. But still he felt he must make some attempt. If he found the admiral inclined to take this discouraging attitude and say it was out of the question, he didn't know what other earthly help he could try for. Perhaps it was all wishful thinking, this belief of his that Stormy was still alive. Perhaps he was just being foolishly sentimental, as several men and more than one girl had already told him frankly. Well, time would tell.

"Oh God," he prayed in his heart, "won't You work this thing out for me? This is the only thing I know to do. If it fails I won't know what to do next. I'll just have to let it rest with You. But please, if that's the way You want it, if I should make no further effort, please make me know somehow. Help me to be rid of this tormenting urge to go after him."

Then the elevator stopped at the floor he had named, and he got out and walked down the corridor to the door where he had been told to

113

find the admiral.

And back in the schoolhouse where she presided over a restless throng of various-aged children, a golden-haired girl was earnestly praying in her heart as she listened to Skinny Wilson stumbling over his reading lesson. And while he read:

"A soldier of the lee-*gy*-on lay adying in Al-*gy*-ers—"

"That is leegion, Tommy," corrected the gentle voice. "And it is Aljeers, not Al-gy-ers. Read it again Tommy."

Tommy read it again rapidly before he should forget the accent:

"A soldier of the leegion lay dying in Aljeers—

There was a lack of woman's kindness, there was dearth of woman's tears,"

But Sunny was praying in her heart:

"Oh God, please don't let him have to go. Anyway not now before he is strong again. But if he *has* to go, please go with him. Guide him, bring him safely back again, and *please* help him to find Stormy—if he *has* to go."

Tommy was reading on:

"But a comrade stood beside him, as he took that comrade's hand,

Said he, 'I never more shall reach my own my native land.

Take a message and a token of some distant friend of mine,

For I was born—for I was born'"

He paused, but the teacher was praying frantically, "Oh Father, please bring him back to his native land. If he has to go don't let anything happen to him."

But Tommy's hand was raised:

"Miss Roselle, how do you say the name of that place? I can't pernounce it. That there R-H-I-N-E. Is it Ro-hi-nie? Wasn't that guy one of our enemies? It sounds to me like the name of an enemy town."

Sunny suddenly roused to her job, and set the young student straight both on his geography and his pronunciation as well.

And over in a distant city another sweet girl named Cornelia was reading a letter from her brother "somewhere overseas." She paused and looked troubled over one paragraph and reread it:

'Our whole company is worried over Stormy Applegate.

You remember I told you he was with us several months

ago. I guess you met him once at home before we left, didn't you? Well he was sent off on some very special mission among the enemy somewhere, a very dangerous errand. Perhaps to get information. But he's long time overdue now. The guess is that he's either a prisoner among those worse than fiends, or else he's dead. We don't know which, but they've about given up hope he'll ever be heard from. One thing is sure, no information has come from him and everyone is sure if he's alive he'd find some way to send us word. He's one who's never failed so far."

Then another girl bent her head and prayed for Stormy Applegate.

"Oh God, couldn't You find him?" she prayed. "You ought to know where he is. You could set him free if he's a prisoner, couldn't You?"

She wasn't a girl who was very used to praying, not for definite things like that. Not for lost soldiers whom she'd only met once and that casually. So, instead of the formal "Amen" that another might have added, she spoke the one word "*Please!*"

It was about then Stormy Applegate came in touch with a man from an "underground" outfit. Like a shadow he grew out of the darkness one night, and suddenly seemed to have been there a long time before Stormy was even aware there was a man.

Deadly weary, Stormy had been trying to forge ahead, hoping against hope that he could get around this occupied town, by the determined method of pushing on and trying to make it appear he belonged in that region, hoping nobody would notice him. But suddenly he heard harsh footsteps ringing on the smooth road, loud voices, arguments, unmistakable accents of the enemy. Raucous laughter. Without doubt if he were seen he would be hauled to the authorities, and instantly his game would be over, the long hours of his weary journey traveled for naught, his mission lost. True, the information he carried was all in his memory. He carried nothing convicting on his person. Even if he languished in prison, or died, the enemy would never know what deadly knowledge he carried against them. But neither would his own outfit know the thing that would mean so much to the cause of righteousness if it could once be told them. Ah! He could not stay here. Less than a minute now and they would be upon him.

Quickly he turned, took a step to the left, across a ditch and dropped flat to the earth in the dark, holding his breath until the noisy enemy passed by, and lay wondering which way he might turn for safety. Having seen those arrogant men who dared to take another's country from them and march around assuming to rule it he knew now that it was useless for him to try to go alone through that town. He must somehow go around. And yet so confused, so weary he was, that he would fain have lain right where he was and called it the end. He could not drag himself up and try to keep going on.

It was then he felt the presence of that shadowy person who had been watching him for some time from a little distance.

He looked up and the shadowy figure seemed to draw nearer. It wasn't God. The man wore rough garments, like a laborer. Reaching out he touched the rough shoe and then drew back. It was after that the stranger drew close and dropped upon one knee beside him.

"Can I help you?" he asked in a low tone.

The tone was friendly. Did he dare to trust this shadowy stranger?

"I have come a long journey," he answered evasively. "I am very tired. I must rest a few minutes."

"Come, I will show you where you can rest safely."

He helped Stormy to his feet.

Stormy followed him, aside from the road. They came to a shanty built of boughs, behind a group of bushes, a pile of straw covered with tow bags was there. The stranger pointed.

"Lie down. No one will disturb you. And when you leave take the upper road." Again he pointed, and turning away, "God's blessing," he said, and vanished into the darkness.

Stormy hesitated, "And on you too, stranger," he said half under his breath.

He lay on that pallet of bag-covered straw, pondering. Had this been a real man, or one of the shadowy figments of his imagination? Rather, had it not been a vision that God sent to hearten him? He was too weary to think it through. Of course if this was someone sent from the camp to track him down, it might be only a trick to get him asleep and kill him for escaping from their clutches. It might

well be that. The enemy seemed to enjoy such tricks. But if it was a
trick he could not help it. He could not keep on much longer tonight,
and if he tried to he would fall somewhere else and be tracked down
the sooner. He must get some sleep if it were only a few minutes. He
would not sleep long. Besides he was not alone. God was his guide
and help. And there came to him a verse from his childhood: "My
help cometh from the Lord, which made heaven and earth. He will
not suffer thy foot to be moved: He that keepeth thee will not slum-
ber."

He closed his eyes, and lifted his heart:

"Oh Lord, I'm in Your care. I'm trusting You to keep watch while
I sleep. This is Your Stormy."

And in the morning when he woke, there beside him on the ground
was food. Coarse bread and a tin of water, and on his eyelids lingered the memory of a frail hand touching him.

Of course that was the way God fed Elijah, but such miracles did
not come today without a human instrument. Surely not an angel.
Not that girl of his dreams for she was far away. His guess was that
the shadowy man who had directed him to a resting place had done it
and he thanked God. He ate his breakfast gratefully, puzzling meantime about the kindly stranger in the shadows last night. Was he one
of God's men?

But he must not linger. The sun was over the rim of the world and
light was growing brighter. He must get on. The upper road the man
had said. "God, shall I take it? I'm trusting *You!*" he murmured in
his soul.

He put the last morsel of bread in his pocket for another time of
need and crept softly out from under the boughs. He wished he might
thank whoever had brought him comfort, but he would thank God
instead. The man would understand.

He looked about him, followed the path, an obscure one, that had
been pointed out, and found himself mounting above the town, yet
almost hidden from the world below. The way was not smooth, but
he did not have to be so furtive about his going, and so could make
progress. His limbs were stiff and still painful from the long journey
of the days before, but he felt definitely rested, and much more cheerful. He no longer felt so alone. Surely some of God's messengers

must be about somewhere. Surely sometime soon there would be someone whom he could dare to ask his location. And yet, he must not be impulsive. The enemy still had tricks to play. He must keep his eyes on his Guide.

He had been walking for what seemed hours when he suddenly rounded a tree, larger than most, and saw ahead of him down the leafy way, a figure of a man. Startled he watched him. The man walked steadily on ahead, and did not seem to see him. It made him uneasy, but he knew he must not show uneasiness. He must walk on as if he had a perfect right there. It would only lay him open to suspicion to seem uneasy. So he walked on. But when he rounded a little turn in the dim path he was treading, lo, the man ahead had disappeared! Now, what did that mean? Was it possible that he could hear quick footsteps farther ahead running? Oh, what did this mean? Was someone else hiding? And was there some way that he too could disappear before this person ahead could bring someone else to help seize him?

He looked around, but there was no sign of a way anywhere near him for him to hide. To the right, just beyond the bushes that made a wall at his side, he could see a bluff, with a sheer fall down into what looked like an old quarry, no trees nor foliage to hide behind. Just the rough open side of the blank mountainside.

He hastened his own steps, hoping perhaps to come within sight again of the stranger, but a swift survey at each turn of the way revealed only a lonely empty landscape, desolate, even in spite of the scraggly foliage that was a far healthier growth than any he had seen the day before. But as the day began to wane the way ahead seemed more and more desolate, filled with thick undergrowth that only seemed to him to be leading away from the direction he had hoped to take. Was this intention, this detour that had apparently been mapped out for his unwary feet by that shadowy stranger who had seemed so kind?

He paused and sat down by the wayside to think it over before he would decide what to do, and to bow his head and consult his Guide.

Should he turn about and go back? Lose all that time? Or should he go on a little farther, and perhaps run into a nest of enemies who might take him captive again? Still, why should enemies take the trouble to lead him so far out of the way? They must know, if they knew anything about him at all, that he had come a long weary way, and must be weak and sick, almost starved. They would understand of course that he was in a state to be easily taken, without much force, or strategy. So why would enemies take all this trouble to mislead him?

And while he thought upon these things he took out the dry crust which he had saved, from the food the stranger had left for him that morning, and slowly ate it, trying to savor every crumb and make it taste to his sick imagination like a whole meal.

Suddenly he looked up and the shadowy stranger was before him again, looking down at him curiously, with almost a smile on his face.

"You found the way?" the stranger said.

"Yes," assented Stormy. "At least so far, I've you to thank for that. Or at least—I'm wondering?"

The stranger smiled vaguely, and looked at him keenly.

"You mean you do not know whether to trust me?" asked the man almost amusedly.

Stormy met his gaze across the dusk and smiled back.

"Well, something like that," he said, and smiled himself. "I was just questioning whether I was right. I am inclined to trust you. You certainly have been kind."

"Not very kind," said the man. "The bed on which you slept last night was not luxurious. The food left by your side was not very palatable. You see I wasn't sure if *you* were to be trusted," and the man smiled outright.

"Yes, well we don't know much about each other," said Stormy, "I was just asking God what to do."

The face of the other man softened.

"Yes?" said the man with a new tone in his voice. "Well, I take my orders from Him too. Suppose we have a little talk. I'm not an enemy at least. Can you tell me anything about yourself? I don't want to pry into your secrets. What do you want? Where do you want to go? How could I help you, if I find that I can help you?"

Stormy grinned wearily.

"All right," he said, "I guess I owe you a little information. You've certainly been kind to me. The very fact that you can talk my language is an asset. Well, I'll tell you. I'm tired and I'm sick and I want to get home. If you can show me how to get there alive I'll be grateful."

"And home is America? Is that right?"

"That is right," said Stormy wearily. "How did you know?"

"Not because you are wearing an enemy coat," said the stranger pointedly. "You are from the internment camp."

"And you want to turn me back?" said Stormy wearily, his tired lips trembling. Then he gave a quick look at the other man, a man who was almost frail in his build, and yet there was about him a certain ruggedness. Still if he himself was up to his normal strength he could knock him out quickly enough and escape. But he was astonished to see a look of pity on that other face. Or was it just the shadows of the dusk that made it look that way?

"No, I have no desire to turn you back to that hell of existence," said the man in a kindly voice. "That is what we are here for, to bring help to any who are trying to get away. But it is not always easy, nor always possible. You will understand there must be great care, great caution. No impulsive moves."

"Of course not," said Stormy. "I think I have learned that."

"Perhaps," said the man, studying him carefully. "We shall see. But it may take some time. Arrangements have to be made. We are a long way from boats and air fields. But there are ways, at times. Then there have to be permits. Have you any identification papers?"

"Naturally not. They took those all away from me at that camp. Though I went with very little. It was a part of my job not to be recognized."

"I see," said the man. "Be careful not to tell that to everybody. We have a few with us who are not yet tried out. We cannot trust everybody."

"Of course not, " said Stormy, "but see! I am trusting you."

The man smiled.

"And I you, or I should not have told you some of these things. I am warning you to be as cautious as if you knew we were all enemies. Something might be overheard even when you are talking with one you trust."

"I understand," said Stormy. "And I think I begin to see that you belong to some kind of underground, loyal to your country, but in an enemy-occupied territory. France, perhaps? Am I right?"

"We do not put those things into words, my friend," said the man gravely, "we wait and see."

"I beg your pardon. I think I understand," said Stormy as gravely, "and if I transgress in any way I beg that you will let me know."

"I will, my friend. Now come. You need some food, and you need to sleep. It will be plain food and a humble bed, but you need have no fear. Come!"

Stormy followed him down a hidden path to an entrance. Inside there was a rough corridor cavelike in its structure, with several turnings, and at last a hollowed-out room furnished with a cot and blanket, a wooden table and a bench of rough boards.

"There!" said his guide. "Can you be comfortable here awhile?"

"*Comfortable?*" said Stormy. "It is like Heaven in comparison with the place from which I came."

"Yes, I know," said the older man. "I have heard others tell. Stay here now. They will bring you food, but I must go. I have other business to attend to. Stay here till I come back, or till I send you word. They will call me Pierre. Good night. God rest you!"

There was a quick handclasp, as between old friends, and the man was gone.

Almost at once a boy entered with a tray and food upon it. A bowl of steaming soup whose fragrance was most heartening, a plate of coarse bread, a pitcher of water and a tin cup.

The boy showed him where to wash, and then left him. Stormy sat down and ate every drop, and every crumb they had brought him. Then he washed and lay down on the cot drawing the blanket up around his shoulders. "God, I'm trusting You," he murmured, half aloud, as if God were standing there close beside him within that refuge. Then he closed his eyes and was immediately lost to the world in a deep profound sleep, such as he had not dared to take since he stole from that awful camp.

Chapter 14

Milk and a kind of porridge in the morning for breakfast. Good milk, and good porridge! God be thanked! Stormy was grateful. Later he lay down and slept again, not even bothering to wonder how long he would be kept prisoner in this semidarkness. He was storing up new strength, replenishing the life that had almost failed him once or twice on the way here.

For three days Stormy rested a great deal, slept much, ate all they brought him, found his way to the shower bath and was refreshed. But when a fourth day came without the return of his guide, Pierre, who had brought him here, he grew exceedingly restless. Occasionally, when he was sure there would be no one by to see him he would put himself through some bodily exercises. He did not wish to grow so soft he could not keep on with his journey, in case all the promises Pierre had suggested should fail him. He trusted the man, was sure he was genuine, but by this time he had decided that probably Pierre had promised more than he was able to fulfill, and in the meantime he should get ready to break away and fend for himself.

It seemed as he thought it over, that it might be an easy enough thing to do, to break away. The room he was occupying was, as he remembered his coming, but a few rods from the entrance door, and surely he could retrace the way by which he had come, after he was once out of this labyrinth of cavelike corridors. Yet he hesitated to make the break. Suppose Pierre should return and find him gone! It would be construed by him as breaking faith with him. It would show him that he had not fully trusted him.

And after all, even if he had to wait even twice as long as he had already waited, did he know any other method of hoping to get away from this dangerous location? It seemed sometimes that he was building hope upon a mighty frail foundation, but still he knew no other substitute for what had been promised.

So, on the fourth morning when they brought his breakfast, he asked the lad who fetched it if there wasn't some work that he could do, something to help in the scheme of the things out of which he was getting his living.

The lad looked at him speculatively, and said: "I'll ask." Later he returned and said: "Can you scrub and keep the washroom clean?"

Stormy agreed readily enough, and was promptly set to work, albeit he noticed that there were very few people around when he did it. Were they keeping him separated from all others until they should prove him out? Well, that was fair enough. So far he had not had access to much space beyond his own little room and the washroom. But somehow, though it gave him a queer feeling not to be trusted, he recognized the necessity and was content. But the scrubbing they gave him to do occupied but very little of the time that began to hang heavy on his hands, for he was getting slept out and really refreshed in body, and continually his rejuvenated mind grew more active. He tried to imagine what it would be like if he ever got back to his outfit. What he would say first and how the others would react to his coming. He began to count up the ones who had still been alive when he left, and found the fellow named Mayberry was outstanding as a friend he prized. Oh, he hoped no mishap had befallen Mayberry. He was good in his line and was responsible for the destruction of a number of enemy planes. But sooner or later everyone, even of the best, fell, or was wounded or killed or taken prisoner, and even Mayberry might be among the list of casualties.

And then it came to him that not alone for his own sake would this man's loss be a catastrophe. There was that lovely girl, his sister Cornelia, the girl whose face had appeared to him in his own distress, with the appearance of an angel. If anything happened to her brother Cornelia would suffer. He did not want that. He found himself more than once praying that that would not be.

Then suddenly he told himself he was getting sentimental. He must snap out of this and turn his thoughts another way. There were others in his company whose friendship he prized. There was Barney Vance. He loved Barney. They were buddies. Even before he had brought Barney back from the battlefield in a dying condition, and hovered over him in the hospital while he was recovering from his own wounds, they had been like brothers.

Barney had still been in the hospital when he left on this expeditions, still too gravely ill to be allowed to be sent home yet. Did Barney get well, or did he die? Where was he now? Boy! How he wished he might see him and talk with him for a little while! How they could talk about their Lord now, and he could tell his friend how again and again the Bible promises had been verified for him. How wonderful it would be if he had recovered enough to be able to go home. Supposing he had, and was even now back in their own land, if he should ever get back and be allowed a furlough he would go straight back to good old United States of America and hunt out Barney Vance. They would have a good old talk together. Yes, sir, that was a *plan*, and some day, if it pleased the Lord to let him go home, he would carry out that plan.

So he whiled away the hours, when there was nothing else to do, trying to keep his mind in a wholesome attitude toward the world in general, his world from which he had come.

And then one day, just as the long rays of the dying sun that reached a sharp brilliancy were slanting into the corridor beyond his doorway, where it shone every pleasant day for about ten minutes, he heard a sound. Soft footsteps along the stone floor, and then suddenly Pierre stood before him.

Stormy looked up with quick relief, an exclamation of welcome in his voice and eyes.

"You have come back!" he said with deep relief. "I was fearful that something had happened to you. I thought there must be danger to you whenever you went abroad."

"Yes, perhaps there is," smiled Pierre. "But then, isn't that the case with everyone, everywhere, even out in the world when there *is no* war?"

"I suppose it is," said Stormy. "And no one can die until God gets ready to call him. Yet humanly speaking we feel that we must care for our lives, unless duty demands otherwise."

"Yes," said Pierre with a smile. "Well, friend, this was duty demanding."

Stormy flashed him a look.

"I would not want to be the cause of anything happening to you, my good sir."

"Friend, those things are so tied up together that we have to trust our God while we are doing our best. That, I think, is what He wants us to do. And now come, I must tell you what I have accomplished. Come sit down beside me and I will show you."

Stormy sat down.

"These are your papers, and I have prepared this little wallet that you can strap beneath your garments where they will be safe. Now, listen, and set it all down clearly in your mind, for it should not be written lest it fall into enemy hands and do harm, either for yourself, or for our cause."

"I understand," said Stormy gravely.

"Tomorrow night you go out from here under escort. You will be taken to a certain point on the river where you will be met by a man in a boat, who is supposedly fishing. You will wait till the dark of the moon when he will draw up to the bank, and you will get into the boat and lie down. He will cover you with a dark piece of cloth, and will take you down the river to an airport where you will present this first set of papers, and you will be hired as an assistant radio operator. Did you ever do anything in the radio line?"

"Yes, I've fooled around with radio quite a good deal when I was a kid."

"Good! That will help! And then in due time you will be assigned to radio work on an airplane. When this plane reaches its second landing airport you will get off and take the train, and you will find all the data for that trip in this second little envelope. If anything happens that you fall into the hands of the enemy, you must quickly destroy all these papers, tickets and so on, and from that time you'll be on your own. But I have tried to forestall any trouble of that sort, except for some unforeseen occurrence. Try to hang on to your passport if possible of course. Now that was as far as I was able to arrange for you but that will carry you entirely out of enemy occupied territory, if all goes well. Can you make out from there, either to your fighting outfit, or to your homeland?"

"Oh, I'm sure I can. Yes," said Stormy. "But this is wonderful. I have God to thank for this as well as you, for I could never have worked all this out. Every step would have had to be an adventure, an experiment, and an exceedingly doubtful one."

"I hope that this will not be that now, not in any stage of the trip.

But—will you let me know when you reach a place of safety?"

"I sure will, " said Stormy, relapsing into his army dialect.

"You'll have to write in code," said Pierre, "else it might do us harm. We must not be found out for others' sakes. But I have written down an address to which you can write, which will be forwarded to me, and you must memorize it. Will you do that?"

"I will do that, my friend," promised Stormy solemnly. "And if in the days or the years to come there should be a time when I might do something for you to repay you for this great thing you have done for me, will you write to me? I will give you an address that will always reach me sooner or later."

"I will promise," said the man. And so with a "God keep you" they parted for the night, Pierre promising to see him the next day before he left.

Next evening when it had grown quite dark, and even the stars were hidden behind clouds, Stormy prepared to leave, and sat waiting for his escort.

Out across the world his friend Barney Vance fairly haunted the office of the admiral, seeking permission to look for him, and his own regiment solemnly prayed in secret that he might be found. And over in America two girls, one golden-haired and one dark-haired with a face like an angel, were praying for him. So in a little while Stormy Applegate went out of the cavelike maze of corridors into the night, and an untraveled way, trusting in the strength of the Lord.

He went out, not having seen very far into that underground maze, not knowing its exact location, nor hardly any of its inhabitants, and unable to make known its deepest secrets even if he wanted to, which he did not of course. But he went out with a profound reverence and admiration for the beleaguered brave people who would not yield, and who were brave enough and strong enough to stand out against the enemy, against all odds.

He thought about that underground company a great deal during that first adventurous night, and it definitely registered in his mind as one more great reason why he ought to go back to his own outfit and help fight the rest of that war to the finish, just for those brave valiant men who were defending their rights and the rights of poor captive prisoners at the risk of their own lives. Always he could feel that

Pierre was one of his most valued friends.

There might be perils on his way back, doubtless would be, but he felt that he was not trying to save his own hide, but seeking to convey vitally needed information to his officers that in the end would save lives and principles and promote peace in the future world.

So Stormy Applegate was once more on his way to unoccupied territory, and a great thankfulness grew within his heart. God had saved him once again, and he must go on feeling that every step of the way was directed by an unseen hand.

Chapter 15

Who is the female snob at Kimberly's?" asked Hortense as she slammed into Amelia's hall and frowned at the girl who was usually so willing to lie down and let her walk over her. Therefore when Hortense was in an ill-humor she betook her self to Amelia's house and took it out on her.

"Oh," said Amelia with a sparkling face, "that's Mrs. Kimberly's niece from New York! She's come to visit her aunt. Isn't she lovely? I thought we might run in there and get acquainted and invite her to join our crowd."

"Not on your life!" said Hortense contemptuously. "She's not my type. Any girl who can afford to wear a mink coat like the one she had on her arm when she got off the bus this morning, and is so stingy or so unsophisticated that she doesn't buy lipstick is definitely not my type."

"Oh!" said Amelia with a sudden gloom over her pleasant morning smile. "But—Hortense, I read somewhere that it's going to be fashionable pretty soon to wear your face natural, and likely she knows it and started doing it. They probably don't use lipstick in New York any more now, not among the very high class people."

"What do you mean, you little ignoramus? Where did you get all that stuff. On the radio I'll bet with some old maid crank talking that wants to make all pretty girls look as drab as she does. I can't abide people like that."

"Well," said Amelia thoughtfully, "she seemed awfully nice. I think maybe you'd like her if you'd meet her. Mrs. Kimberly introduced me this morning when I was passing the house. I wish you'd go over there with me to call."

"Not I!" said Hortense fiercely. "I want nothing to do with that type of person. And can't you see that we should be undoing all our plans if we got in a girl like that? She would make straight for Barney and absorb him. Literally *absorb* him, if you know what I mean, and then where would we be? As few young men as there are in town any more we can't afford to do that."

"Oh, well, I suppose you're right," said Amelia ruefully. "I said practically that to Jan Harper yesterday when she suggested asking that Roselle girl."

"What do you mean? That little school-ma'am? The perfect idea! As if *we* would mix with her. Besides she's years younger, isn't she? Just a mere baby. Jan must be crazy!"

"Well, she says she had Barney over singing at church Sunday night. You know she's playing the organ over at the Old First now. And they say he can sing. Really *sing!*"

"Do you mean he sang a solo?"

"Yes, Jan said so. She said everybody was crazy about it."

"Well, he used to have a good voice when he was a kid, but if they get him roped in with that church crowd it will spoil all our plans. They're awfully straight-laced, almost as bad as Barney's mother used to be. They don't approve of anything that's any fun. They call it 'worldly'! Can you imagine it? We've got to get to work as quick as Barney gets back and put a stop to that church business. Did you call up Roxy this morning? When did she say he was coming back?"

"She didn't know. She said he had to see somebody in the service about when he might have to go back overseas, or something."

"Oh, for Pete's sake! Are they going to send him back again so soon?"

"She didn't know. She said he wanted to go hunt for a buddy of his that was missing."

"What folly. Barney *would* do a thing like that. That's the way his mother brought him up. We've got to get to work in a hurry. Although I don't believe the army would allow him to go off on a fool errand like that. If a fellow is missing it means he's *missing*, that's all, and they better give him up and concentrate on somebody else. Just suppose everybody who has somebody over there they admire should take it into their heads to run over after their friends. Why there wouldn't be any room left for war! *Imagine* it! But no, we certainly don't want that little school-teacher-child, nor that other important looking Kimberly girl either. Forget it, Amelia, and let's call up our guests and postpone our parties till Barney comes, and then we've got to get going without delay. Now I'm going around to that Roxy person and get it out of her where Barney is, and how long before he is coming back. This is all bunk that she doesn't know. I'll *make* her tell." Hortense gave her henchwoman a contemptuous look and marched out of the house.

On her way down the street she passed the Kimberly house and there was Cornelia Mayberry out in the yard picking white violets. Hortense studied the cut of her handsome frock and resolved to get one like it if she could. She hurried on her way, not even glancing again toward the beautiful girl who looked up as she passed.

Hortense found Roxy out gathering eggs from her chickens giving her a bad half hour, but getting not one atom of information from her. Roxy was canny, and Roxy certainly did not like Hortense.

"It's a pity you didn't have several children to look after," was Roxy's parting shot as Hortense swung indignantly off toward the gate. "If you had some children you wouldn't have half so much time to run around after young men." But Hortense strode on pretending not to hear, and Roxy, enjoying the scene, especially as she saw two women approaching down the road within earshot grinned mischievously.

"Hortense!" she called clearly, as if she had forgotten to tell her something, and Hortense paused and looked around haughtily.

"Do you know what you ought to do? You ought to go around to the Community Center and look after some of those refugee children they've undertaken to care for. That would be a real heartwarming task and give you good practice for the time when you have some children of your own. I'll speak to the committee about you if you'd like the job."

"Oh, shut up!" said Hortense in her most disagreeable tone, and swung around to open the gate and march on.

"Still," continued Roxy to herself, grinning amusedly, "I'd be sorry for the children if *you* had charge of 'em."

Hortense as she pranced on her way was thinking bitter frustrated thoughts. An old playmate, a returned soldier, highly spoken of for his bravery, had returned for a furlough and *she* was being kept entirely in the background. Her frantic efforts for his notice had been futile. She hadn't been able to get him to do anything she planned for him, and that little light-haired schoolteacher had carried him off to church in triumph. Made him sing for her. For of course *she* had been the one who had done it. "Sunny" he used to call her, just a *child*! And *she* was presuming upon that old acquaintance when she was a mere baby! Bah. She had to get even with that girl. Teach her where to get off. Show her that she wasn't even in the picture with *her* and her group of friends. A public reception in the town hall would be a good idea. She would start that going right away. Barney could be made to sing at that too, some army song. And a speech about his experiences could be demanded by the whole crowd. That would be popular enough. Everybody liked Barney, and those that didn't know him had loved his mother anyway. It wouldn't be hard to get up such a thing. And really the town ought to recognize what he had done in the war of course. She had heard some of the women of the women's club suggest it, but why shouldn't *she* get ahead of them and start it herself, thereby getting all the glory?

She walked on well pleased with herself, and decided that she would begin by putting that Margaret Roselle in her place.

To that end she mounted the steps of the schoolhouse when she came to it, clattered down the bare hall on her high spindly heels, opened first one door and then another, slamming them resoundingly behind her when she found them empty, until she came to the big sunny room where Margaret Roselle was hearing the history class recite.

Without knocking she flung the door wide open and stepped into the room, and all the pupils turned and looked at her wonderingly.

The teacher looked up in surprise.

"Oh, did you want something?" she asked in her gentle voice.

"Yes, I did," said Hortense. "I came to find *you*. I'm giving a dinner at my house Saturday night of this week. I expect to have several service men and some girls, and I wanted to know if I could hire you to wait on the table. You'll be well paid of course."

Sunny looked at Hortense, astonished, and then she laughed.

"Oh, I'm sorry," she said, "I'm afraid you've been misinformed about me. I don't do that sort of thing."

"Oh, *really*? I thought you would do *any*thing to earn a little money," she said disagreeably. "But surely you would do it for the cause of patriotism. There are to be some service men there."

Sunny gave her a distant smile and answered firmly: "That would be quite impossible."

Then turning her back to her class she said: "Now, Mabel, you may recite. What was the great question that came up before Congress at that time?"

And to Hortense's amazement the young teacher went calmly on with her work, ignoring the outsider in the room, and all the children astonishingly did the same. Were they trained to such utter concentration on their work, or were they simply indignant at the insult given a teacher who was evidently a great favorite of theirs? Hortense was not so dense that she could not sense this feeling of the children through her own chagrin. She had even failed in mortifying the girl she disliked so much. Disliked without any reason too, except that she was younger and prettier than herself.

The end of the matter was that Hortense finally went home and retired behind locked doors to have one of her terrific sick headaches.

Amelia, calling up later to ask some trifling question, and being told that Hortense had a headache and was gone to bed, got herself together and went over to call on the interesting Miss Mayberry, taking care that this visit should not come to the ears of her erstwhile mentor. But she did not invite Cornelia Mayberry to join their group. She wouldn't have dared, not after what Hortense said. But she did admire Miss Mayberry, and somehow she felt that Hortense was getting a trifle too much what the more conservative people called "ultra." Somehow Amelia's natural bent was toward things more quietly conventional.

Amelia went home very thoughtful, and even much more intrigued by Cornelia Mayberry.

High on the fifth floor of the office building where he spent a great deal of his time, the admiral sat in his comfortable desk chair across from Barney Vance whom he had just welcomed warmly.

Out the open window they could look off down the silver winding of the river, and see a busy steamer puffing on its way. Down below there somewhere was the beautiful whiteness of the lovely Lincoln Memorial, and across from it the ethereal beauty of the famed cherry-blossom walk not so far away but that they seemed somehow related, as if like lovely funeral blossoms they marked the passing of a great, white, powerful soul.

Barney had waited some time for this interview, and now that he was within the presence of this, his father's old friend, he almost shrank from making known his request. For suddenly it had become to him something presumptuous that he should ask permission to go on a special search for the one for whom doubtless the army had already made all the search that was necessary. And yet it was Stormy, *his* Stormy who had saved his life, and therefore Stormy could in no wise be so important to anyone else as to himself. Even though Stormy had rendered notable service to his country.

But now the time had come and he must speak.

"I'm here in behalf of a buddy of mine who saved my life and brought me on his own wounded shoulder, back to my outfit. If he hadn't done it I would have died six months ago. The doctors all said so. And while I was still in the hospital he got well and was sent on another special important assignment to get facts about the enemy that were needed. Well, he didn't come back before I left, and I have reason to think he hasn't come back yet. Meantime, I'm invalid home somewhat indefinitely, under doctor's order. But Admiral, I want to go back *now* and search for my friend. Or at least to find out somehow whether he is alive, and I can save him. Admiral, I wonder if you could tell me whether what I want to do is at all permissible, or possible, while I am still in the army; and if it is, whether you can help me to pull the right ropes to get permission? I'm still in the army you know."

The admiral sat staring at Barney with his heavy white eyebrows lifted, and his eyes keen and earnest, studying the young soldier before him. He sat with his elbows on the arms of his mahogany chair and his long white fingers just touching their tips. And then he began to ask questions.

"I suppose you know that this is a very unusual and irregular thing you are asking?" he said gravely.

"Yes, I was afraid so," said Barney, "but somehow I had to come. I knew you could advise me. You were the only one I knew to turn to, and I feel this very much on my heart. I must know whether my buddie is alive, and needs help. I must give it if I can."

At last the admiral spoke:

"Well, my dear fellow, that is very commendable, of course. I do appreciate your feeling for your friend, and especially as he helped to save your life, but I'm not just sure whether what you want *can* be done or not. It is quite out of the ordinary of course. I should think, as you are still of the army, it is your duty of course to ask about the ruling in such a case. I understand you did some very commendable work yourself. You seem to be wearing a good many ribbons and medals of honor, and your present proposition is quite within the character you seem to have established while in the service. But now, I will not say what can be done. I will of course be glad to help you in any way allowable I can, but I should say that the very first thing would be to ascertain, if possible, just how much is absolutely known of your friend, and whether he is still missing. There are ways of course to get that fact established beyond a doubt and it is well to do so before the question of your going after him is gone into, also to find out your own status with regard to health. I will make it my business of course to find that out. If you can be around here for the next twenty-four hours I *may* be able to tell you just what the prospects are, and by that time I shall have looked into the ruling about what you want to do, and *perhaps* can then let you know what is possible. But there is one question I would like to ask just for my own curiosity. Just why did you think *you* would be able to find your friend when the whole army has failed in doing so? Have you any inside information that you could not pass on to another? It seems a pity for you to have to use up your leave time and strength going on a long journey like that, that could be more economically accomplished by one nearer to the place where he disappeared. Had you a special reason beyond your own obligation for what he did for you?"

Barney looked troubled.

"Yes," he said earnestly. "You see I have been to the same place myself where we thought he was being sent, and we talked together a little about what one could do if he got stuck there. I thought—perhaps it's only a hunch,—but I know the region pretty well, and I think I'd know where he would hide out, if he didn't get caught in an internment camp they've got up there."

"I see. But suppose he is in the camp? You couldn't do anything."

"I figured that a man outside could help better than the man who was inside," said Barney, "and I know what Stormy would do under such circumstances."

"Yes, that might be," said the older man, "but you must bear in mind that you would probably be shot by the guards while you were trying to save your friend."

"I'd rather be shot to save a life like Stormy's, than to be shot just in a battle," said Barney fiercely. "Excuse me, but you don't know Stormy yet," said Barney. "Some day maybe I'll bring him here to see you, and then you'll understand."

The older man smiled:

"You're very sure he's alive, aren't you?"

"I am," said Barney.

"Very well then, we'll get to work. Suppose you write down all the names in the case, and the location, your company, your engagements, and the address where I can contact you when I get information."

Barney handed out a folded paper.

"It's all written here," he said, "everything you need to know. Now, I'll thank you for giving me your attention and time, and get out of your way. And I'll be praying."

"*What?*" said the admiral. "What did you say?"

Barney smiled half shyly.

"I said I'd be *praying*."

"Oh," said the admiral, studying the young man, "in other words, since you didn't get quite what you hoped from me, you intend to take this to a higher court. Is that it?"

Barney's smile was very reverent and engaging.

"I took it to a higher court before I came here, sir."

"Oh, I see!" said the surprised admiral. "Then it's rather up to me to find out what the higher court would have me do," he said thoughtfully, as if an entirely new idea had been presented to him. "Well, I'll have to look into that."

Then Barney, saluting, went out, and the admiral walked to his window and stood staring toward the ribbon of silver river shining in the distance, and the dome of marble that honored a great man who was not afraid.

Presently he turned and touching a button on his desk that called his secretary, directed her to start an investigation to find out what was definitely known of the whereabouts of one William Applegate, more familiarly known as "Stormy."

Then he went to this desk and wrote two or three brief notes to personal friends in the service, called up a few more on the telephone, and all in the matter of what could be done to find Stormy Applegate. But Barney Vance had wandered out under the great pink and white row of cherry trees to look up and talk to God, as he had promised the admiral he would do.

Chapter 16

Barney came back to Farmdale at the end of the week, having sent two postcards back to explain his absence. One to Sunny, promising to return in time to help her with the choir Sunday; the other to Roxy ordering buckwheat cakes for breakfast Sunday morning. Both cards bore beautiful pictures of the famed cherry blossoms. But not a world of all this leaked out to the gang that was chasing in vain after Barney Vance.

But it was only Sunny who carried in her heart an ache because she was fearful that Barney might be going back overseas before he was physically able, and so she prayed the more.

About the middle of that week Mrs. Kimberly sent for Margaret Roselle to come to supper and get acquainted with her niece Cornelia Mayberry. And Margaret came, pleased that Mrs. Kimberly had selected her to meet her niece instead of the other crowd, although Mrs. Kimberly was a friend of Margaret's mother and *would* do that. But the fact that she was asked perhaps prejudiced her in favor of the niece beforehand.

The two girls studied each other politely while the introductions were going on, and then smiled and sat down to talk.

"It is your brother who was in Barney Vance's company overseas, wasn't it?" asked Margaret. "Barney told me about him, how fine he was."

"Yes," said Cornelia cordially, "and Jim wrote me that I must be sure to see Barney, and he sent a lot of messages to him. There was a message about Stormy Applegate. He said I was to tell Barney that they have heard nothing further from Stormy. The outfit is sure now that he was taken prisoner, and there seems no hope they will ever see him again. He knew Barney was anxious about him when he left for home."

"Yes," said Margaret anxiously, "I've heard about Stormy. But Barney doesn't believe he was killed. He says that he went in the strength of the Lord, and he believes he will come back."

The other girl gave her a quick appreciative look that was almost embarrassed. Cornelia Mayberry was not used to speaking of things religious in ordinary conversation. She hardly knew how to answer, and yet she realized that this other girl was something fine and un-usual. She wondered if her brother knew of her. He had never men-tioned a girl named Margaret, nor even a girl named Sunny, which was what her aunt Mrs. Kimberly called her. She would have a lot of things to ask Jim when next she wrote him. Meanwhile, she was here to stay a few days at least, surely until Barney came back and she could deliver her messages from Jim. If she liked it here, and this girl proved as pleasant as she seemed to be at first sight, she might stay longer, instead of joining here cousins at the resort where they usu-ally spent the summer together.

Cornelia's young cousin Sam Kimberly had come into the house now and was in the next room turning on the radio, hastily, as if he were hunting for some special station. The girls were talking and not noticing the radio, till suddenly Barney's voice spoke out clearly and came into the living room as if he had just walked in at the door.

"Friends, I'm glad to greet you, and to say hello to all in my native land."

Margaret looked up and caught her breath, exclaiming:

"Why! There's Barney now! Listen! That's *Barney* talking!"

Her eyes were bright with joy, and her cheeks a lovely shy pink. Cornelia looked up interested and began to listen, and also to watch this other girl whom she was just beginning to know.

But almost at once Cornelia Mayberry knew she was listening to a very unusual voice, and did not wonder that her brother had written so enthusiastically of Barney.

"Friends, I don't like to talk about myself, nor what happened to me over there in the war, but they have asked me to tell you about the most thrilling experience I had while I was serving, and though I shrink from talking about it, yet I guess you have a right to know. For it was your war I was fighting, and I was glad to be able to do what I could to attain the victory for which we are all waiting so anx-iously."

"Oh!" said Cornelia. "This is what I wanted to hear!"

But Margaret said nothing, only listened with her heart in her eyes, and her breath bated, as if she feared to lose a single syllable.

Barney's clear ringing voice went on, describing vividly in a few words the day and the command that sent him out on that most thrilling experience of his life, till the listeners almost felt they heard the bursting bombs, the heavy firing, and seemed to see the thick smoke that filled the air, the strain and excitement of the moment when the enemy was met. Oh, they had heard other returned soldiers tell on the radio about such experience, but this was different, hearing somebody they knew, or knew of intimately, talk! And Barney's way of telling was different from any other they had heard.

Out across the road in Amelia's home somebody yelled over from the Harper house. "Amelia is Hortense there? Tell her to turn on Washington. Tell her Barney Vance is speaking on the radio!"

The girls in the Kimberly house did not hear that outcry, but Amelia did, and there was immediate action. Then the radio spoke out, and the girls who had assembled at Amelia's house to arrange for that public reception they were planning to put on for Barney as soon as he came home, stopped talking to listen. But all plans ceased while Barney's voice held the audience breathless.

"It was that last plane shot that got me," went on Barney. "I was just thanking God that the attack was over and I could go back again to my outfit and feel that I had done my duty and both myself and my plane were without injury, when I got the warning. There was another plane coming, and coming fast. I had only time to cry to God for help. I somehow knew this was going to be worse than all the others. But I worked fast and my best till just at the end when I felt that sharp burning pain strike my shoulder and run down my arm, and I knew I was helpless so far as further fighting was concerned."

Margaret sat there gripping her small hands together, her lips pressed, her eyes like great dark pools of horror, Cornelia, watching her, said to herself "How very much she cares! And no wonder! A man like that!"

But Barney's voice went on:

"Somehow I got my plane down, for the other plane had gone on after it had done its deadly worst, and just there, there was no more enemy in sight. Afterwards I was weak with the pain and loss of blood, and probably unconscious for a long time. But later, when the sun went down I came back to myself. I knew when I saw my plane that I couldn't fly back. I knew there was an injury to my pipe line, and that I must start at once and try to get back under my own power, So I just cried out to God, and told Him how I was fixed, and asked Him to help me back. I crept out and crawled along the ground till I got to a woods, and knew I was on the right way, but every foot I went was agony, and I did not know how long I could hold out. I found a brook, and drank, but it was hard for me to reach. That helped a little and I got to my feet and went on a little way, but I was faint and dizzy from loss of blood and soon I ran against a tree in the dark and fell, striking my head on a stone perhaps. I must have been unconscious for a long time, but finally I came to again and tried to creep on, but I couldn't make it. I went out like a light and lay there, with my last conscious thought that this was the end. Then, what seemed a long time after that I felt a hand touch my face gently, I felt a light strike my eyelids, a flashlight perhaps, and then I felt myself lifted to a shoulder, and carried on over the rough ground, slowly, among the trees, stumbling but still going on. And I found out afterward that the man who was carrying me was my old buddy, Stormy Applegate, and that he was badly wounded himself when he picked me up. But yet he carried me back to my outfit all the way back. And friends, I'm glad to tell you of that great thing my friend did for me. I wouldn't have been living today if he hadn't brought me in spite of his own injury and pain.

"I was a long time getting well. At first they thought I never would. But my buddy, Stormy, got well before I did, and they sent him out again on a special assignment involving great risk, and calling for much skill and cleverness. He said good-bye to me, knowing we might never again meet on earth, and he has never yet come back! They think he was either killed or taken prisoner by the enemy, and they say there is nothing more that they can do. But I believe that he is still alive, because he told me he was going in the strength of the Lord. I would ask no greater privilege than if I might go myself out there in the enemy land to find him. But since I have not obtained permission yet to do that, friends, I'm asking *you* if you will pray for Stormy Applegate, for I believe he is still alive! I thank you for listening to me."

A storm of applause followed the silence that fell as Barney ceased to speak. And over at Amelia's house Hortense's voice came out sharp and clear:

"For the love of Mike! Can you beat that! He certainly has got it bad! We'll have to get him over that religious complex quick or he won't be any good at all in *our* world. Imagine all that sob stuff about another soldier! That's his mother coming out in him."

But over at the Kimberly's the two girls had tears on their cheeks, and the young brother appeared in the doorway with an excited face. "Wasn't that great, cousin Cornie?" he said, his voice all husky with feeling. "Imagine him wanting to go back! But that's Barney for you. He was always that way."

"I should say it was great!" said Cornelia. "Was he always that way, Margaret, or is it the war that has made him so?"

"No, he was always a good deal that way. He was a Christian you know. He had a wonderful Christian mother. But still, I think the war has done a good deal, too. And you ought to hear him sing! He sang a solo in church last Sunday night. I think he'll sing again next Sunday. He has a beautiful voice, but it's the way he gets the words across that is so great. It's just like a sermon preached when he gets done."

"I should like to hear him," said Cornelia gravely. "I think I'll stay and hear him. That will be something to tell Jim about."

Margaret looked at the beautiful girl before her, and a sudden qualm of jealousy shot through her. It had been hard to see Barney taken over by the set that went with Hortense, hard worldly girls, that was different. They weren't his kind. But here was a girl that was worthy of him, a girl so beautiful that she could not hope to compete.

It was only an instant that such a thought flashed through her mind, and then Margaret, being who she was, put it instantly from her. Why, she could love this girl herself, and why shouldn't Barney like to meet her, and to take her for a very special friend? And who was *she* to feel badly about it? If this was what God was planning for Barney why she must be glad for him. She must not think of herself. Both she and Barney were God's children, pledged to His service. And after all Barney did not belong to her. He was just an old friend, and would be, of course, all her days, no matter what else came to him. So quickly she smiled cordially.

"Yes, do stay and hear him. I know you'll think he is fine," she said. "He really has a very unusual voice, and it will be nice to tell your brother about it of course."

"I could see he had an unusual voice just from his speaking," said Cornelia. "I will stay. My aunt was hoping I would stay longer, and since I know you, and like you so much, perhaps I will."

"Oh, that will be wonderful!" said Margaret smiling.

Then suddenly Cornelia spoke again:

"Say, tell me about Stormy. Have you met him? Do you know him?"

"No," said Margaret, "only by hearing Barney tell about him."

"Then you wouldn't know much about his life, would you? I was wondering . . . is he . . . a religious man?"

"Oh yes," said Margaret positively. "He is a Christian. Barney told me about his experience. I think he was just a church member before he went to war. But afterward he became quite changed. When he first went across the sea and came into the region of actual war, where he saw death in all its ugly realities, and the terrible possibilities of going out to do his duty, he said he met God. It was one night when he was flying through the sky, going into his first engagement, and he realized that he might be going straight into death. But he felt he didn't know God well enough to stand in His presence with his life just as it had been on the *old* earth, living for *himself*. It was then that he felt God came to him. Of course he had heard the way of salvation preached all his life, but had never really accepted it, nor even fully understood how great God's love had been to let Christ take his sins upon Himself and die for his soul. And he said that night in the clouds as he went forth to meet the enemy, God met him in the way, and talked it all out with him, *made* him understand it, in just those few minutes. It didn't take long, because one needed only to get that one glimpse of the Lord Jesus to understand it all. Just to *know* Him. And Barney says that Stormy always tells people that if you've never known Jesus you can't understand, or you can't be ready to face death without Him. After that all fear is going, and it makes all the difference in the world. That is why he is so eager and anxious to make other people know his Lord."

"That sounds very wonderful," said Cornelia. "I didn't know he was like that. You see I met Stormy once myself. It was before my brother went across. They were in the same training camp. I went to camp to see my brother before he was being sent away, and Stormy was there. Only they didn't call him Stormy then. It was Bill

Applegate, and they hadn't known each other very long. I don't suppose they had talked about such things then. They were almost new acquaintances, but they liked each other from the start, and he was one of the first fellows Jim wanted me to meet. He said he liked him a lot. I liked him too. He's a very interesting fellow, and awfully good-looking, a strong fine face. One you can't forget, even if you've never seen it much. I've never forgotten him. You haven't ever seen him you say?"

"No," said Margaret, "only a snapshot Barney carries around with him. He says he owes his life to him, you know. But Stormy *is* very handsome I think, with a great wide lovely smile. Of course *I've* been praying for him too, ever since Barney told me about him. But didn't your brother tell you about his being a Christian?"

"Not exactly," said the girl with a puzzled look. "Only one thing he said. When he wrote us about Stormy's being lost he said, 'Some of us fellows can't believe that Stormy is gone. We think he'll turn up, yet, because when he went away he waved his hand and said good-bye, and he said he knew he'd be all right, because he was "going in the strength of the Lord."' You see, my brother and I were not brought up to talk freely about religious things. It wasn't done in our family, and Jim would think he was saying a great deal to tell me even that. But I've wondered. You think that Stormy is definitely a Christian now, do you? And that when he went away on this mission that phrase he used that he was 'going in the strength of the Lord' was something real, not just an empty phrase he used, like good-bye or good luck or something of that sort?"

"Oh, no," said Margaret with a smile, "I *know* it was real. You see just before he left he came to the hospital where Barney was and they prayed together. That is Stormy prayed, mostly, for Barney was still very weak. And Barney says it was a wonderful prayer, full of utter trust. Barney seems very sure he is still alive."

"Well, I don't know as I have any right to pray, for I'm not a very good Christian, but I've been praying too, ever since Jim's letter came telling about his being missing in action, I've been praying every night. I can't somehow seem to forget him. I don't know him really well, you know. Oh, you'll think I'm a sap, I suppose, but somehow I wanted to find out if you knew."

"No, of course you're not a sap," laughed Margaret. "I'm glad you are a praying girl. That makes me feel as if you and I could be real friends. We love the same Lord, and speak the same language."

Cornelia looked a bit hesitant.

"I don't know if you would think I'd qualify for that honor if you knew me better. I'm not so sure about loving the Lord. I don't really know Him well enough to be sure I love Him. And I'm quite sure I can't speak many sentences in your language, for I've never learned. Perhaps you can teach me.

"*Teach* you? Oh, I'll be glad to *tell* you what I've learned, but you know it is the Holy Spirit that must really do the teaching."

"I'm afraid I don't know much about the Holy Spirit," said Cornelia, filled with awe. "You know I've never read the Bible much. I tried once or twice, but I just couldn't understand it, and got discouraged and gave it up."

"Oh, I'll take you to our Bible class," said Margaret. "It's wonderful. And we're all so interested the people never want to leave and go home. It meets one evening a week, and we have one of the best teachers in the city, so clear and interesting. I know you will enjoy it."

"It sounds good," said the formal city girl, a bit bewildered to find there was so much to this matter of being a Christian.

So the two girls sat and talked. Finally, Margaret took out the little Testament she always carried in her handbag and began to explain the lesson on John that they had had last week, and both were so absorbed in it that they were surprised when Mrs. Kimberly called them to dinner.

Mrs. Kimberly, listening to their pleasant talk at the table, and watching their animated faces, felt that she had done well in selecting this girl to companion with her niece.

But over across the street the plans were going forward for that reception that Hortense was getting up for Barney. And Mrs. Kimberly would have been surprised indeed if she could have heard them plotting just as if the young war hero was the special property of Hortense, and would do exactly as she told him to do.

Chapter 17

Barney Vance came back from Washington late Saturday afternoon, after having received from his friend the admiral that he had found that he could do nothing in the matter of Barney's request until the authorities had cabled overseas and received a report from his company, both concerning Stormy, and about Barney's state of health when he was sent home. And it might be some time before that matter was cleared up and it was definitely established that Stormy was still counted missing.

Much disheartened Barney came back and went at once to Margaret Roselle's home. Somehow it seemed the natural thing for him to talk it over with his old friend.

Margaret's face glowed with pleasure when she saw him turning in to the lane, and her eyes were shining happily as she ran down the lane to meet him halfway. But she had no idea how that little act of welcoming him back thrilled Barney.

He hurried up the lane, watching her as she came, so graceful, lithe and lovely. She seemed like something of his own, and yet he told himself he must not think that. He did not know but that she was promised already to someone else. Yet that thought appalled him, for he found that he had really been thinking of her all the time he had been away, counting on telling her about his experiences, counting on coming back to her. He had seen many good-looking girls while he was in Washington, for the admiral had introduced him to a number of them who were near his mansion, and they were all interesting girls, yet none so sweet nor beautiful as this dear girl. How was it that she had grown up so unspoiled, as lovely of heart as she was of face?

His heart quickened as her feet hurried toward him and he saw the welcome in her eyes. She was glad to see him. He had a sudden wish that he might take her in his arms and hold her close, but he put it from him. He was not a young man who had been used to going around making love to girls. His mother's teaching had gone deep on that subject, and he had an utmost reverence for womanhood. But he did not remember to have felt like this before about any other girl. Was it this brief absence that had made this girl Margaret seem so much more desirable that she had, even when he first saw her that morning among the apple blossoms?

But these were foolish thoughts. She would think him crazy if she knew. It must be just that he was tired and excited, and had been through a heavy strain in Washington, with all the noise and bustle, and the anxiety about getting his wishes across to the right authorities, who *might* permit him to go after Stormy. Yet oh, it was good to get back to this girl and her sweet sympathy! And she was as much interested to pray for Stormy as he was. He had felt lonely while away.

And now she stood before him, her hands out in eager welcome, and he reached out and took both her hands in a close clasp, and felt the thrill of a great joy sweep over him. The sweetest thing he had ever experienced. Why he wanted to fold her in his arms and hold her close! What was the matter with him? Was he falling in love? No, of course not, and he must not frighten her. She would think he was crazy! Besides, it was broad daylight, and there were three men in the neighboring field, and her mother might be looking out the window. "I'm—so—glad to get back!" he murmured, shamefacedly, but kept on holding both her hands.

"And I'm so glad you've come!" said Margaret shyly. "It has seemed you have been gone a long time. And I am so anxious to know what you did." She added quickly, "Do you have to go away soon again?" and she almost held her breath waiting for the answer.

He smiled down into her face. He was still holding her hands in his warm clasp. He pressed them closer, and her own nestled in his happily.

"Not yet," he said half ruefully. "It seems anything like this takes a long time. One would have time to die before rescue came. But it looks at present as though there wasn't much chance of my getting to help Stormy, not yet anyway."

She drew a breath as if of relief.

"I'm glad," she said softly. "I was so afraid for you. Yet I do think God will send him back. I have been praying so very hard."

He was watching the changing eagerness on her sweet face, the look of joy in her beautiful eyes, and suddenly forgetful of the watching eyes about that farm, he murmured softly:

"You *dear!*" And then without warning, and certainly without a definite intention beforehand, he stooped quickly and kissed her! A fervent earnest kiss. And her warm lips responded, lingering with a thrill of joy upon his own, and brought that desire to fold her in his arms again. Only now there was the consciousness of that wide world of three men, and a mother, perhaps in observation. He was astonished at what he had done almost impulsively, for his whole life training had been along the lines of careful deliberation before acting. But this time his heart had taken the lead, and he was glad.

Suddenly Margaret drew back a little, looked up at him with question in her eyes, then dropped her face against his shoulder.

"Oh—Barney—" she breathed fearsomely, and there were quick tears upon her lashes.

It was then that Barney forgot any possible audience and drew her close within his arms, bringing his face down to hers again.

"Forgive me dearest," he murmured to her little pink ear that he found beneath his lips. "I ought not to have done this out here in plain sight. I ought to have waited. But oh, *darling!* Sunny! *I love you!* I love you, and I couldn't wait! I felt as if I had got home and you were mine. Maybe I am presuming. Maybe you belong to someone else." He held her off and looked deeply into her eyes, but she laughed back at him with a joyous happy lilt.

"No," she said with a sweet little tremble in her voice. "No, I don't belong to anyone else. I've—*always*—belonged—to you!"

And then he had to fold her close again.

"Oh, my darling!" he said.

The sharp ringing of a scythe against a whetstone brought them both back to consciousness, and they looked around. Suddenly, from a tall tree near by a wood thrush thrilled out a silver note of exultancy, and their two hands clasped again joyfully.

But the men in the field were very busy trying to get done a swath before the set of sun, and the mother in her kitchen was just putting a pan of puffy rolls in the oven for supper. Nobody saw the little love scene but Margaret's twelve-year-old cousin, who had come over to pick berries for supper; and he, canny before his time, looked on with eager pleasure.

"For Pete's sake! Now ain't that something?" he murmured to himself. "I didn't think they'd have that much sense to pick each other out. But I'm mighty glad before that Hortense got her finger in the pie. I *like* Barney a lot. He's *swell*!"

Needless to say there was no reception for Barney Vance *that* night, because the plotters had not been able to find out just when Barney was to be at home. And they didn't find out that he was home until the next day, for Margaret and Barney took a walk in the woods after supper, and came back to the house under the soft moonlight, Barney's arm about her, her hand in his, with no workmen, nor twelve-year-old cousin around to watch. They were going back to the house to tell Mother Roselle what had happened to them.

And there was no fear in their going, for they were quite sure of the welcome that awaited them. Mother Roselle was very fond of Barney, and had been one of his mother's dearest friends.

Hand-in-hand they made their way slowly, and now and again Barney would draw her closer to his side and bend to kiss her softly.

"Oh, Sunny, my darling Sunny! To think you are mine!" he whispered in a glad voice.

"Oh, but I haven't told you everything that's happened since you went away!" said Margaret suddenly remembering, as they went up the path to the house. "A new girl has come!"

"Oh, what a nuisance!" said Barney. "There's only *one* girl for me, and I have her right here beside me."

A sweet solemnity of joy swept over the young girl's face. She needn't fear to present the other girl, since she had such dear words of Barney's to hide in her heart.

"But she's very lovely," said Margaret.

"Not so lovely as my girl," insisted Barney.

"Oh, but she *is*," said Margaret eagerly. "She's much *much* better looking than I am."

"Oh, no, she isn't. She couldn't be," said Barney. "I have never seen a girl as lovely as you are. That's true. I've never looked at girls at all. They didn't attract me. Not till I saw you."

"But wait until you see her," said Margaret laughing. "She really is lovely."

"*Must* I see her?" said Barney, putting on a martyrlike look.

"Oh, yes, you must *see* her. That's what she's here for. To see you. Her brother was in your outfit overseas, and he wrote and told her to see you. She is Mrs. Kimberly's niece."

"Oh," said Barney suddenly remembering, and looking bored, "I remember now! I was to go and call on her. Mrs. Kimberly called up Roxy and asked her to send me. She's Jim Mayberry's sister. But seeing you put her completely out of my mind. You've met her? What's she like?"

"Yes, I've met her and I think she's lovely! We're friends already. Mrs. Kimberly invited me over to see her. And Barney, she knows your Stormy. That is she met him once at camp. And she and I have been praying for him. She has some messages from her brother for you, and one is that Stormy has not been heard from yet, and most of the men think he is dead, for they say if he were alive he would never have let them go so long without some kind of a message. She says her brother said, 'Because he went in the strength of the Lord,' she thinks that means that maybe her brother is saved too."

"He *is*," said Barney with conviction. "We had a talk before I left. But he's not much used to talking about such things. He's a nice kid, a bit younger than Stormy and myself. Well, then, dearest, we'll go and see her together, shall we? But not tonight. I want you all to myself tonight."

"Of course," said Margaret, nestling close to him as they reached the door and must now go in.

And then the door was opened by Mrs. Roselle, and she gave one quick glance at their faces, their clasped hands, and a great joy came into her own face to welcome them.

"Oh, mother," Margaret said, "you don't know what has happened to me!"

The mother turned a searching glance to the smiling soldier's face, and Barney rose to the occasion:

"I *love* her, mother, do you mind?"

"Mind?" said Mrs. Roselle, beaming at them. "Do I *mind*, did you say? Why yes, I mind very much, dear boy. I couldn't ask anything better for my child than her to be loved by you," and she put up her arms and gave Barney a warm motherly hug and kiss.

"And I know your own mother would be very glad about this too, dear son," she said, standing back and looking at them happily.

"Yes," said Barney fervently, "I know she would. I know she *is*, for somehow I can't help feeling she knows all about it, and has perhaps been watching us."

"Of course," said Margaret's mother. "And now come in at once. The chicken and waffles are all ready to be served, and I know you must be hungry, even if you have found you love each other. Come."

So they went in to a happy supper. And Sam the young cousin came to supper too, and sat and stared and grinned at the two. He could hardly eat his own share of the waffles and chicken, so awed he was by the thing that had happened within his sight. For every time he remembered what he had seen down the lane, he grinned to himself about it, till his face was a study in growing up.

After supper they all went into the kitchen and washed the dishes, and Barney dried them. Then the two young people went to the piano and sang a little while, selecting the music for the next day's services.

So Barney stood by the piano while Margaret played, and exulted in the fact that he was now privileged to put his hands possessively on the dear girl's shoulders, and know that she was his.

Outside down the highway went Hortense's shiny car, with a gang of loud-voiced revelers, bound for a roadhouse wherewith to pass the time, till they could get hold of Barney and complete their plans for a public reception.

And back at Mrs. Kimberly's Cornelia sat and talked with her aunt for a while, listened to the war news on the radio, and then took some books from the library and went up to her room to read. Somehow this Saturday night was the lonesomest day yet, for Margaret hadn't been over all day, and she didn't even know whether Barney had come back yet. She almost wondered why she was staying in Farmdale. Yet when she got up to her room the book she actually picked up to read was the Bible that her aunt had loaned her. For she thought she would make another try at reading it and see if there was anything in it she could understand, now in the light of some things this new girlfriend had said.

She tried several places to read, but somehow they didn't seem to mean anything to her, till at last she opened by chance to the book of

John, and then remembered that Margaret had said that was a good book to begin with. So she read on, becoming more and more interested as she went deeper into the story, for she saw it was a story, and an interesting one. And when at last she laid down the book and prepared to go to her rest, she turned out her light and knelt down by her bed and prayed. Yes, she had been praying every night of late for the lost soldier called Stormy, but this time she ended her prayer with a petition for herself:

"Oh Lord, I think I need to be born again, like that man Nicodemus I've been reading about. Won't You please show me how, and make me able to pray acceptable for Stormy Applegate? Because I want him to come home. I want to see him again, and understand what You can have made of a strong splendid man like that."

Then she got into her bed and closed her eyes, but somehow she kept seeing the strong handsome face of the young soldier who had been with her brother in the camp the day when she was there. And she kept imagining him a prisoner, hungry, suffering, unable to help himself, and yet cheerful, and full of faith in God in spite of it all.

Of course her idea of Stormy was partly the product of hearsay, things her brother and Barney and Margaret had said of him, with a little background of her own memory of Stormy's handsome sparkling face as he had talked to her at camp. But her thoughts had hovered over the memory of him so much that he seemed very real to her. What would she have said could she have known that it was her face that had come to Stormy Applegate in his weariness and fever and utter discouragement, and that he had thought she was God's angel sent to help him?

Where was Stormy now, tonight? Now while she had been praying for him? Could it be possible that he was still alive? Why was she so certain he was? Was it just because his believing friends thought he was, or because God had put the thought in her heart? And why should she care so much? He was practically a stranger to her.

At last she fell asleep, dreaming her way across the clouds to see a plane in the distance, with dangers and fogs and enemies to hinder, and only a hidden passport and some trifling papers to see him across the border of a land that was enemy-infested. Would Stormy ever come back? And would their faith be justified?

While Cornelia slept the Holy Spirit was working a change in her heart, a conviction that she needed to be save, to be born again. That she must accept what Christ had done for her to make good in the scheme of His plan of salvation. Though she had had so little teaching and so little understanding of the Scripture that she wouldn't have understood what part the Holy Spirit had in calling her to accept Christ as her own Saviour, nor have comprehended what this change meant that was coming upon her, making her so dissatisfied with the self she had been, the self she had hitherto felt was rather to be admired. Popular, that was what she had always been in the circle in which she moved. But now, was she popular with God? Could she claim any request from Him and hope to have it granted? Not perhaps if she had not accepted His offer of salvation, the kind of salvation that Margaret Roselle believed in. The kind that Stormy, and his friend Barney believed in. Yes, and her own brother Jim. Life wasn't just a round of pleasant things as she had always believed, with her stage set with luxury. There was war, and death, and separation; and a God with a place in Heaven to which one might go through accepting the gift of salvation. And there was a devil, and a hell, and a death that was not just the body dying, but the soul being separated forever from God and good and all righteousness! It was all very terrible, and she must find out how to understand it.

These things had begun to dawn upon Cornelia's soul since she started to pray for Stormy Applegate.

Chapter 18

Cornelia went to church the next morning with her aunt, and watched the choir file in, the sweet young organist at the organ, playing exquisitely. There was something about Margaret Roselle that intrigued her greatly.

Then she took to studying the faces of the choir, especially the tall young man who came in last and took a seat at the end next to the organ, rather out of sight. Could that be Barney? He wasn't quite so good-looking as she remembered Stormy to have been. Or was he? He *was* good-looking. And he was in uniform. Of course that must be Barney. If he sang a solo she would know. Or would she? There might be other young soldiers who sang solos, and Barney might still be in Washington of course. But this one certainly *was* good-looking whoever he was. Though probably the uniform made all of them look rather well. She knew her own brother was quite impressive in his uniform.

As the service progressed she was impressed by the reverence and dignity and quiet interest of all. She noticed, too, the quick look that passed between Margaret and this soldier by her side. It was an intimate smile, as of people who had known one another long, and were very fond of each other.

Then came the solo, and Cornelia was sure it was Barney. Somehow he was so like the man her brother had described. And there was something about his face that seemed so in keeping with his wish to go back into the region of war to find his friend and bring him back.

It was a most unusual song, not a regular solo. Just a hymn, but it was sung almost as if it were spoken, and yet the voice was very beautiful, mellow, tender.

> I see a Man at God's right hand,
>   Upon the throne of God,
> And there in sevenfold light I see
>   The sevenfold sprinkled blood.

153

I look upon that glorious Man,
  On that blood-sprinkled throne;
I know that He sits there for me,
  That glory is my own.

The heart of God flows forth in love,
  A deep eternal stream;
Through that beloved Son it flows
  To me as unto Him.
And looking on his face, I know—
  Weak, worthless, though I be—
How deep, how measureless, how sweet,
  That love of God to me.

He sang as if it were so real to him, as if that love of God he was singing about was the most precious thing to his soul. And that blood that was sprinkled was the most priceless coin that could be paid for a sinful soul. Cornelia found herself with tears slipping down her cheeks, and she was aghast at herself. She hurriedly flicked her wisp of a handkerchief over her cheeks, and Hortense and her crowd sitting staring in the back seat, studied her and saw the tears. What was the idea, that high-hat crying in church? Had she recently lost her lover, or some close relative? There didn't seem to be anything in that solo to make anybody cry. It didn't make good sense anyway. What was it all about and why didn't Barney use his head selecting a song, and get something really peppy, something that would show off his voice if he had such a fine voice? But what was that poor sap crying about, anyway? Then they turned and gave attention to the singing again, and they decided that Barney hadn't picked the song at all. That girl Margaret must have picked it and she was a regular sob sister. But what on earth did it mean anyway and who was a man on God's throne whose glory Barney was claiming for his own. Well, he probably didn't understand it himself. Then they turned their attention to the beautiful girl who was sitting with Mrs. Kimberly and listening with her heart in her eyes. Did she know Barney? Was he one of her long lost lovers, or what?

But there was one girl in that audience who had got something out of that song, one girl who listened afterward to the dear old preacher, telling in such simple terms what the story of the blood meant, and who was the Man of the song, the Man Christ, sitting on God's throne, presenting His blood to pay for our sin. Bringing it right down to souls, so that they couldn't help understanding what it all meant.

But the hymn at the close of the sermon was more in the language Hortense's crowd could understand. Barney sang the verses and the choir softly came in on the chorus.

> On Calva'ry's brow my Saviour died,
> 'Twas there my Lord was crucified,
> 'Twas on the cross He bled for me
> And purchased there my pardon free.

And then the choir came softly in on the chorus:

> Oh, Calvary! Dark Calvary,
> Where Jesus shed His blood for me . . .

"For Pete's sake," whispered Hortense quite audibly, "why don't they sing something cheerful? I should think a returned soldier would want to talk about something besides death and blood, or do you suppose they've got so used to it all that they don't know the difference? That's the reason I never to go church. They are always so gloomy, harping about sin and dying. As far as I'm concerned I want to have a good time while I do live, and then when I die that'll likely be the end of me, so what?"

But Amelia who sat next to her was listening to the last words of the song and made no response, so Hortense turned her attention to the very smart hat that Cornelia was wearing. She might be from New York and be very snooty, but she certainly could pick out the clothes, and Hortense prided herself that she knew good clothes when she saw them.

When the service was over those girls in that back seat pranced promptly up to the choir platform and greeted Barney as if he had been away for a year. They congratulated him on his *wonderful* singing, and his *marvelous* voice. And they simple raved over him so that the rest of the people in the church hung back and looked askance. Then Barney began to see what was going on, and smilingly sought to dismiss his would-be intimates.

"Well, that's awfully good of you, friends," said Barney smiling, "but suppose we cut out this flattery. I see somebody down there whom I must speak to, and you'll excuse me I know," and he courteously slipped past Hortense and stepped down from the choir platform.

But Hortense was not to be sidetracked so summarily. She had come to church for one purpose only and she did not intend to go home without accomplishing it.

"But Barney, there's something I must tell you," she shouted at him. "You are in for a surprise and we felt that you should know about it beforehand, so there won't be any mistakes."

"A surprise," said Barney turning with almost a frown. "Tell me quickly, please. I am really in a hurry." For Barney could see that Mrs. Kimberly and her young guest were starting down the aisle toward the door.

"Why, yes of course, but when you hear what it is you'll see I can't be hurried about it. It is quite important. We have planned . . ."

Barney saw by her tone that she was going to absorb a good deal of time with her important surprise.

"Well, then if you can't tell it quickly, perhaps you'll excuse me please, for a few minutes. There is someone I must see before they leave," and he slid out past Hortense and hurried down the aisle toward the Kimberly pew.

"Oh! *Indeed!*" said Hortense in that cold offended tone she could assume so disagreeably on occasion.

But Barney was not listening to her tone, and there was nothing for Hortense to do but stand and frown at him, as she watched him go down and speak to Mrs. Kimberly and be introduced to "that obnoxious snob" as she had come to call Cornelia.

She saw the cordial greeting between Barney and Cornelia, and watched the interested smiles that each face held. She saw that there must be some special bond of interest between those two, and little by little she edged her crowd down the aisle till she was fairly standing in on their conversation.

She heard Barney say:

"Why, I don't know. I'll ask Margaret just what she has planned for tomorrow," and then he looked toward the organ.

Margaret had but just stopped playing and was picking up her music and getting ready to leave, and Barney called, across the heads of those girls who had tracked him down:

"Margaret! Margaret! Can you come down here a minute? Mrs. Kimberly wants to ask you something."

Margaret gave her beautiful smile and hurried down toward them, but Hortense leaned forward and spoke:

"But Barney, we've simply *got* to speak to you a minute at once. It's *quite* important. I am sure these people will excuse you. We've arranged for tomorrow night to give you a reception in the Woman's Club House, and there are some arrangements about publicity that simply won't wait another hour, or we shall be too late to carry out our plans."

Barney lifted his head toward Hortense with raised eyebrows and a sudden sharp note of dissent in his voice.

"What was that you said, Hortense? A reception? To *me*? Not on your life you don't! No, lady. You'll simply have to change your plans, for I won't appear at any reception, and that's flat! I'm here for just a little while, and I don't want to be held up for admiration. I haven't done anything more than all the boys did who went out there to fight. I've just done my duty, and you folks over here don't need to waste your time plastering admiration on me. I just want to meet my friends in the ordinary everyday walk of life. And I want you folks to go on fighting on the home front the way you were when I got home. There isn't time for parties and frills."

His voice was almost genial as he finished, though it was still very firm, and he did not look at Hortense as he grinned to them all in general, but turned smilingly back to Mrs. Kimberly.

"But Barney," protested Hortense, "you can't *possibly* mean that! All our plans are made and we've hired the hall and got the invitations out. You *can't* do that to us!"

"Sorry, girls, but I'm afraid I can. I'll just have to return the compliment and say *you can't do that to me*! I'm just Barney Vance and not a little tin god, so please don't get any more of these things going.

If you've got your plans made so you can't stop them, turn your show into a war bond sale. That'll please me better than anything else."

"And will you *speak* to us?" called out one of the girls, realizing that Hortense was not getting on so well.

"And *sing*?" asked Amelia.

"Why?" asked Barney smiling.

"Don't you think you owe this to your own townspeople?" spoke up Hortense bitterly.

"*Owe* this to you? How? Haven't I been out fighting for you? Why do I have to get up and show off before you? Oh, of course I'll be glad to say a few words of greeting, and tell everybody to buy all the war bonds they can, if that will do you any good! That is I'll do that if I'm not in Washington. I'm liable to be sent for any minute so I can't really *promise* anything. When did you say this was? Tomorrow night? Okay. Come if I can. Now Margaret, shall we walk over with Mrs. Kimberly?"

"But you'll sing for us too, won't you?" pleaded Amelia.

He gave her a quick look. Poor Amelia! She didn't often have the nerve to plead, or hardly *speak* when Hortense was there.

"Why, yes, I'll sing if you'll let me sing what I want to."

"Oh, but we want some of the popular songs you sing overseas! We don't want your long-faced hymns," wailed out Hortense.

"Sorry," said Barney, "I'll have to do the picking. I can't sing everything you know," and he gave her a mischievous grin.

"Come on Margaret, let's go," he said, and slipping his hand in her arm he led the way after Mrs. Kimberly. The gang hung back disconsolate, with Hortense mad as a hatter.

Margaret and Cornelia were smiling amusedly.

"I suppose they planned it to please you, didn't they Barney?" said Mrs. Kimberly in a kindly tone.

"Well, perhaps. We'll give them the benefit of a doubt," said Barney, "but if you ask *me* I'd say they planned it to please *themselves*," and he gave his twinkling grin. It made them laugh outright.

So they walked home with the Kimberly's and went in for a few minutes while Cornelia and Barney talked of her brother Jim, and of Stormy Applegate who had not come back yet. Then Barney and Margaret walked back to her house. Hortense, meantime, behind the window curtain, watched them enviously. There went Barney, just as he always had done, going with somebody else, when she had tried with all her might to get him for herself. Why was it that she failed? Well, at least he would come to the reception for a little while, and he would speak about war bonds. That wouldn't give him any room to drag in religion. And she'd see that he sang some of the popular music too, even if she had to ask somebody else to call for something. But all the rest of that Sunday she was bitter and disagreeable to everybody around her, and at last Amelia in despair said:

"Oh, for Pete's sake, Hortie, why do you have to be so jealous? You can't be *it* all the time, you know."

"What do you mean *jealous*? Do you suppose I'd stoop to be jealous of that little colorless mouse of a Sunny? She, going around posing as 'Margaret' now, as if she were some great personage. She was always called Sunny! And what's Barney being so sweet to her for? Just because she plays the organ in the church? What's the church, anyway, nobody that's very important goes to *that* church. As far as I'm concerned I don't intend ever to enter the door of that church again, after the way I was treated this morning. The *idea*! When I told him we had got up this reception to *honor* him!"

"Oh, you're too sensitive, Hortie," said Janet Harper. "Barney was only half joking all the time. But I don't believe, really, that he honestly likes parties and speeches and things. Boys never do, don't you know that?"

"No, I don't!" responded Hortense snappily. "The general run of men *like* to be flattered, and be called 'it,' and praised, and all that. If you ask my opinion of *men*, they're all a conceited lot, and the only way you can get anything out of them is either to praise them or else *feed* them."

"Oh, Hortie, that's not so! I don't believe men are like that!" said Janet Harper again.

"Well, *really*. I don't suppose it matters what *you* believe! You never had any brothers, and you don't have much to do with any other men, so you wouldn't be supposed to know."

Janet sat back subdued and kept out of the conversation for a whole hour, while Hortense raved on about the church, and the way they had been treated that morning.

Nevertheless, as evening drew on, they all planned to go to church that night, to hear Barney sing again.

Hortense did her best to get Amelia to write Barney a note, asking to sing that lovely little gem of a song called "My Prayer."

"That'll keep him off those dismal religious things he delights in," she said, "and he certainly can't object to that. It sounds real ethical to me. It's about doing good to others, or something on that order, 'making some heart glad' I believe is one line isn't it? I remember I sang it for a Christian Endeavor prayer meeting one night when I was quite a little girl."

But while those girls knew that song pretty well by heart, none of them ventured to quote the words, and Amelia refused point blank to make any request of Barney for *any* song.

But they all went to church.

The song that Barney sang that evening was "Ye Must Be Born Again."

This time it was Cornelia who sat as one hypnotized as she listened to the words, so clearly telling over the story she had read in the Bible the night before, and she wondered if she would have any opportunity while she was here to ask Barney about being born again and how she could get it for herself.

The sermon hat night was very stirring, given by a young chaplain from the nearby camp, who was a man after God's own heart, and knew his Bible better than most. Even Hortense's hardened, contemptuous, empty little heart must have been searched by it, as she sat for a time staring fiercely at the young preacher, her eyes wide and almost frightened. Then, in the midst of it, she turned utterly away and putting her elbow on the back of the seat and her head down on her hand, yawned openly, and closed her eyes, pretending to be asleep. Margaret, watching her from the little mirror over the organ, decided that she was greatly stirred by that simple earnest sermon; but if she was, she certainly did not intend that anybody should know it.

But when the service was over, Barney, after talking with the young minister for a few minutes, suddenly disappeared, nobody knew where, and Margaret after her organ stopped, slipped out the back door and somehow nobody could find either of them after that. "Queer, wasn't it?" said the girls who had been hanging around hoping to have another talk with Barney.

"Well, I'm not surprised," said Amelia to a group of them. "I wouldn't think he'd stick around after the way you treated him this morning, Hortense."

"*Treated* him?" said Hortense. "How did we treat him? I don't know what you mean. I certainly don't think he's being very courteous tonight, do you?" But nobody answered her.

Barney and Margaret had gone out the back driveway of the church and were sprinting rapidly in the direction of Margaret's home.

"I wonder what he sees in that little washed-out schoolteacher!" said Hortense angrily as she lingered for a moment at Amelia's door to say good night and suggest what to do about collecting the sandwiches that had been promised for the reception Monday night.

"Well," said Amelia thoughtfully, trying to speak the truth and yet avoid angering Hortense any further, "I suppose it all depends on one's point of view. I don't think most men admire much make-up, do you?"

"Meaning that you think *I* wear too much?" snapped Hortense.

"I didn't say that," said Amelia. "I suppose it all depends on the type you admire."

"Well, good night. I think I've taken plenty for one evening. I'll go home and gather up a little strength to try and get through tomorrow night. And after this I'm *done* with homecoming soldiers, no matter how popular they are. I wonder what this Stormy fellow is like? I'd like to see him. He sounds interesting to me. I'll bet that religious complex is a figment of Barney's imagination. Makes a nice sob-stuff story. Ten to one he's having the time of his life somewhere among so-called enemies, while Barney goes around posing as his would-be rescuer."

"Why, Hortense! I thought you *liked* Barney."

"Well, I thought I did too, but I've taken as much off him as I'll take from now on."

Chapter 19

On the way home Barney and Margaret discussed the reception of the next evening.

"It's a doggone nuisance," said Barney disgustedly. "I just knew those fool girls would do something unpleasant. Of course I can't refuse to go, because of the rest of my old friends, but I jut hate to go through a thing like that. We can come away early, though, can't we? It wouldn't be necessary for us to stay till the last cat is hung, would it? I wouldn't want anybody's feelings to be hurt of course. My mother's old friends! And after all it is nice of people to want to say hello to me. But couldn't we say we had another engagement, and get away?"

"*We!*" said Margaret with a troubled look, "why I don't think they would expect *me* to come. I never went with their crowd."

"Say, look here! You don't mean to say this isn't a community affair, do you? Isn't *every*body invited?"

"Well, I'm sure I don't know," laughed Margaret. "Nobody's told *me* anything about it."

"Well, you *better* be told! If you don't go *I'm* not going, that's definite!"

"Well, of course I *could* go I suppose. I could get mother to go with me. But really, I don't believe they expect *every*body. Not the older people. Or maybe they do, but I haven't seen any notices, and it wasn't in the paper. Besides, how could they tell people? They didn't know whether you would be here."

"Well, we'll go over, you and your mother and I, and if we find there is only that crowd of highfliers there, we'll only stay about ten minutes, and then we'll have another important engagement. I'll fix that up. I certainly am not going to waste a whole evening on that crowd. Besides, you and I have a lot of time to catch up on, and we can't afford to waste it."

Margaret slid her hand into his, they walked happily along together and soon forgot the reception, and everything else but their love for each other, and their joy in being together.

"Oh, Barney," said Margaret. "You don't know how wonderful this all is for me. To have you singing in our dear old church, to have you here again, even if there is the dreadful possibility that you may have to go away again. It will be something to remember I have had. To know it is me you love, and I'm not left outside, the way I have so often been. No, I ought not to have said that, for I really never cared that I was left out by those other girls. I never could have enjoyed being with *them*. They do not love the things that I love. They delight to snub me, and jeer at anything they understand I like. But there! I should not talk that way. Some of those girls could be very nice, if only they wouldn't listen to Hortense so much. But say, Barney did you watch her face during the sermon? I do believe she was listening."

"I thought she'd gone to sleep the one time I saw her."

"No, I think that was only a pose. I saw her in the little organ mirror. Before she leaned her head on her arm and closed her eyes they were wide open and she positively looked frightened! She always tries to pose as being one who isn't afraid of anything, but somehow I had the feeling that that sermon got under her skin. I think she saw for a minute or two what it would mean to get sent away from the presence of God forever. I don't think it ever occurred to her before that hell was like that. An absence of all righteousness, all that was good, separation from God forever. I think it really frightened her. And when you sang that last song about the blood she looked frightened again. I don't believe that after all one could hear a sermon like that and not mind the thought of spending all eternity in the company of devils in hell. I suppose maybe nobody has ever tried to make her understand, before."

"Yes," said Barney thoughtfully. "I suppose she has a soul that needs saving. Somehow I never realized that with regard to her. She has always been so self-sufficient, so sure of herself. Still, of course, Christ died for her, as well as for all other unsaved souls, and probably we ought to pray for such people the more. Make our lives a better witness before them, rather than to be sarcastic and try to shy away from them. But they don't want our prayers and witnessing I'm afraid."

"No, I suppose they don't," said Margaret earnestly. "But I guess we can't go up to God's throne and expect to meet Him with unburdened souls, if we haven't at least told them about our so great salvation."

"That's right, dear. And I guess I'm glad I said I'd go to their reception. It wouldn't have been Christian to be selfish about it. But we'll go, and we'll do our best to witness, even if Hortense did try to stipulate we shouldn't have any long-faced hymns. Well, perhaps there is some way of getting a bit of truth across in a bright and cheerful way that will make them want to find our Lord. That's the business of Christians, of course, to be witnessing everywhere, even when we can't just really like the people. They certainly need the truth even more than attractive ones."

"Oh Barney dear!" said Margaret softly. "How wonderful that you turned out to be like this! And how happy your mother must be to know about it! I'm sure she knows."

"Yes, so am I," said the young soldier, folding his girl's hand close in his clasp. "But there's something else that is wonderful to me, and that is the fact that God kept you so sweet and dear and fine, brought you up in His love and strength, taught you to serve Him; and then let you love me. That seems to me the crowning joy, that you love me, and that someday if God lets me live, you can be my wife. I don't think there is anything else that is so sweet on this earth as for God to have given me the love of a girl like you."

"Oh, Barney! That's such a wonderful thing for you to say. And just a few days ago I was almost afraid to have you meet Cornelia Mayberry because I was afraid you would fall in love with her. Just think of my being jealous and selfish like that!"

"Dear!" said Barney, laying his other hand on hers that rested on his arm. "You dear! That you should care like that! But, my darling why should you think I would ever turn from you to that other girl? She's a sweet attractive girl, I own, and I think she'd make a very nice friend for—well, somebody else—but I could never choose her instead of you, my little Sunny girl! She's a lovely girl, and she's asking a lot of interesting questions about the Lord, and the Bible, but you needn't ever think that anybody can possibly be to me what *you* are, and I hope will always be, my precious!"

So they walked slowly along the moonlit road, and talked of things of Heaven and things of earth, and rejoiced more and more in their love for each other. It was characteristic of Barney that he did not think of that reception that was to be tendered him but once and that was to be glad that his best uniform was cleaned and pressed and in order. He would have nothing to do to get ready for the affair except to put it on. He went to sleep pondering what he could say in the few words he had promised, that would not only sell war bonds, but would also be helpful to some soul in the dark of a war-torn world. Not too much. Just to go on record and show what he stood for.

As Margaret was busy with her teaching the next morning Barney had arranged to call on Cornelia and answer some of her questions about the Bible over which she seemed deeply troubled. But his going did not escape the young gang who were undertaking to establish an espionage over him.

"There! Look out there! There goes Barney into the Kimberly house," announced Janet Harper who had just arrived at Amelia's with a basket of sandwiches she had been collecting for the evening festivity. "You see you were wrong, Hortense! He's caught on to the new girl now. I guess he's not so keen on Sunny after all."

"Oh, that's nothing!" sniffed Hortense, who was there to borrow more teaspoons and cups. "He's got to go somewhere, hasn't he, just to pass the time? And Sunny is a schoolteacher, so he can't go around with her weekdays. Evenings maybe, but not daytime."

"Did you invite Sunny and her mother?" asked Amelia's mother.

"No, I didn't," said Hortense. "I thought it wasn't any business of theirs, and anyway it's been announced now. There's a notice on the post office bulletin board. I simply don't care for that silly Sunny, and I resent Barney's trotting her around everywhere, so why should I invite them? And I didn't ask the Kimberly's either. If anybody else wants to they can, but I'm not going ton."

"Well, I think that was very rude," said Amelia's mother. "They are lovely people, and dear friends of Barney's."

"Not any dearer than we are," sneered Hortense, "and not half so interesting. They are awfully full to have around I think, and always trying to run everything their way, if you ask me. We don't hit it off well together at all," and Hortense got up and went to the front door. She had known she would meet with opposition if this subject came up but she wasn't afraid of Mrs. Hassle anyway. She was just like Amelia, hadn't the backbone even to make a fuss. So the subject died down and was forgotten.

Mrs. Kimberly invited Barney to stay to lunch, but he excused himself, saying he had telephone calls to make and letters to write, and must go home. The truth was he wanted a little time to himself to rest and think over the coming affair that evening, and he had promised Margaret to meet her at the schoolhouse and take a long walk, and he did not intend to allow anything to break up that plan.

So Cornelia and Barney sat down with the Bible and went over a few verses that Cornelia had been puzzling over, and then she began to ask questions about Stormy. She listened intently as Barney told of Stormy's religious experience, meeting God out on his way to die as he supposed, and how he had been serving Him ever since.

When Barney went back at noon Cornelia sat with the Bible in her lap and her eyes far away. Then she took out a little snapshot of Stormy that her brother had sent her, and she had treasured ever since. She studied the tiny picture, trying to read into that handsome laughing face all the beautiful experience about which Barney had been telling her. And that afternoon, out on their long lovely walk Barney said to Margaret:

"Do you know, dear, I wouldn't be surprised if your friend Cornelia is more than half in love with our Stormy. She says she's only seen him that one time that she visited the camp. But of course he is very stunning looking, and has a great way with him. But she seemed to want to know more than anything else if Stormy was really saved, and did I think one could always be sure that a dead Christian *always* went to be with the Lord when he died. I wonder if she thinks Stormy is dead?"

"Well, I'm afraid she does, Barney. You see everybody has been telling her that he must have been killed or he would have sent some word. That he never let his regiment go uninformed if there was any possible way to let them get a message. Her brother wrote her that just yesterday."

"And yet she is praying for him to come back."

"Yes, but she thinks it is only wishful thinking that makes us say we are sure he is alive. And perhaps she wants to be sure that she can meet him in Heaven, and it seems so unlikely she will ever see him again on earth."

"Poor child!" said Barney. "And poor Stormy! What a girl she would be for him! He deserves somebody like that who would love him a great deal. But he would never presume to ask her to marry him I'm afraid. He knows she belongs to a rich family, and while he hasn't and inferiority complex, he would feel it was presuming when he has no fortune to offer he."

"Oh, but that would be foolish! She is not at all like that. She doesn't think of money."

"Well, no, I don't believe she does, but *he* might."

"He'd better not meet her then," said Margaret with a troubled look. "That would be an awful thing, to love a man and not have him ask her to marry him just because she has a little money even though he loves her. How utterly silly. A nice girl couldn't ask him, and will she have to go alone all her life because he has such an idea?"

"Well, I don't know if Stormy would feel that way. Perhaps he's got more sense now. I think he has come so close to bigger things than any on this earth that he might not think of such things anymore. He *might* only ask her if she was saved. And now I think of it and remember how he talked when last I saw him, I believe if he loved her, that would be the only thing that might hinder him from asking her to be his wife. He would ask first, 'does she love my Lord? Is she saved?'"

"Oh," said Margaret earnestly, "I'm so glad he is like that! I do wish he might come back. It would be so great to have those two come together. I believe Cornelia's brother wishes it too, from some things she read to me from her brother's letter yesterday. Was he a Christian too when you knew him?"

"Well, kind of a shy one I guess. I never was just sure where he stood. But it must be talking with Stormy has made a difference in him. Or else meeting death out on the battlefield so familiarly. She read that letter to me too this morning, and I wondered. He wasn't like that with me, the last time I talked with him. But then I had been very low myself, and they wouldn't let us talk long."

Margaret reached over and slipped her hand in Barney's, pressing her fingers close.

"Dear," she said softly, looking up into his face, "I'm so continually thankful to God for saving your life and bringing you back to me. I keep thinking how dreadful it would have been if you had never come back and I had never known you loved me."

The look that passed between them then was one to be remembered.

They came back when the sun was going down, and the long sweet spring twilight was beginning, hurrying at the last, because they remembered that they must really be dressed up tonight. "Oh, I forgot to tell you. I asked Mrs. Kimberly and Cornelia to go with us tonight," said Barney. "I knew your mother wouldn't mind, and I found they hadn't had any invitation. So as I am the one who is being recepted, I thought I had the right. You don't mind do you, dear?"

"Mind! Why of course not. I was going to suggest it myself, only I forgot. We can stop for them as we go down. Mother will be delighted. She loves Mrs. Kimberly. And you must remember neither mother nor I were invited, either. There will be strength in numbers. And especially as we are in the company of the guest of honor."

"Why, yes, of course," laughed Barney. "It would be a pity if I didn't have any rights at my own party. Come, I think we had better hurry."

"For the love of Mike! Will you look at what's coming!" exclaimed Hortense to Amelia, as the guest of honor entered with the four ladies. "He would do something like that, wouldn't he? Bring a lot of snobs and chaperones. But my word! Look at their clothes! Even that little mouse of a Sunny has a new frock I never saw her wear before. It isn't half bad, is it? One of those new shades of blue I've read about. You don't suppose she borrowed it from the New York girl, do you?"

"Of course not," said Amelia sharply, "that Mayberry girl is a foot taller and several inches wider in her shoulders than Sunny. And why should Sunny have to borrow clothes? She's making plenty teaching school, isn't she? Besides, I heard Mr. Werner say the other day in the bank that Mrs. Roselle is wealthy herself. She gives a lot to the church they say."

"How foolish!" said Hortense. "I wonder what she gets out of doing a thing like that."

Then she roused herself to gather her reception committee together, stand in line, herself at the head, and introduce the incoming guests, though most of them had known one another all their lives.

But the pleasant friendship of the evening didn't depend upon Hortense, although she had hoped it would seem that way. The people were all glad to be there, for they loved Barney, and they had also loved his precious mother. So they just took over the evening themselves and didn't bother in the least about Hortense and her gang. So Hortense found that she and her henchwomen were becoming nothing but young waitresses to pass around the delectable sandwiches and cake that had come pouring in all day, much of it from people who hadn't been solicited at all. Hortense discovered that she had finally hit on something in the town that was really popular, yet nobody seemed to think that she had been the instigator. One elderly woman who had a wide smile and a pleasant sort of purr, came up to Hortense and said:

"Wasn't this a lovely idea, getting up this reception for Barney? Was it the Woman's Club did it, or the church? I suppose it must have been the church, because they all loved his mother so much. Though probably they all worked together."

Hortense was speechless with rage.

But finally the time came for the program, and Hortense assayed to take over. She got up on the platform, and patted her sparkling white hands with their many bright rings and their sharp crimson nails. She shouted as loud as her inadequate voice could be forced into shouting:

"Won't you all please come to order!" Then she patted her hands again, and fairly screamed at them. "Won't you all please come *to order.*"

Failing to get the attention of the noisy crowd she began to talk in a cross between a scream and a whine, until someone noticed her standing there, and said "Ssh!" and it hissed all over the room. There followed a lull in conversation. Then Hortense plunged in and tried to recite the speech she had prepared, but she suddenly forgot her lines, and stumbled and blundered around till the conversation began to buzz wildly around her again. Finally the young minister who had preached the night before, got up beside her, and with a voice that boomed out like a lovely trumpet he said:

"Friends, one of the committee is trying to call you to order and make an announcement."

There was instant silence, and he turned to Hortense for further facts, but Hortense was not going to surrender her rights so easily, and she began again to recite her piece:

"Friends, we are met together tonight to honor one of our number who has been out to fight for us, and has won great honors and come back to us with laurels on his brow. We have asked him to tell us about some of his great deeds, and how he won the purple heart and the silver star, and some of the other decorations he is wearing. We have also asked him to sing for us. I am turning over the program to our old friend and fellow-citizen Lieutenant Barney Vance. Lieutenant Vance."

Hortense's voice lisped along like a little chipping bird, and what she said wasn't heard over half the room at least, but when the end of the speech was reached, she made a sweeping bow toward Barney, and there was a tremendous cheer that shook the room till it seemed the roof would surely come down on them.

Then Barney, with a running jump, ascended the platform informally, grinning.

"Dear friends of my hometown," he began, when the cheering had slowed down so he could be heard, "I do appreciate the welcome you have given me, and I do feel honored by your presence here. But as for the announcement about my speech, that was a mistake. I was asked to speak, yes, but I said no, until they told me I might sell war bonds. So, here goes. Who'll buy the first bond and start the ball a-rolling? What I did overseas was my part of the war. You don't need to know about that. Now this is the home front, and we want to sell a lot of bonds tonight to do our part *here*. Who takes the first bond? That you, Mr. Haskell? How many? Miss Haskell, will you get a pencil and paper and sit right down here by the platform and make a record. Cy, you're from the bank, you take the money, and let's do this thing in an orderly way. Come, get to work, good people. Who's next? Ezekiel Summers, did I see your hand? One or two? Two? Put him down for two, Amelia."

The room grew very still listening to Barney Vance selling war bonds, and then it grew very enthusiastic as the sale went on and the sum of the bonds mounted up. They were really doing something big in Farmdale. They were really doing something big, weren't they? Something great for the war. And it was going over without the least assistance from Hortense, or without her being even recognized in connection with it. She was too vexed to take the frown off her brow and try to let on that she had done it all.

When the buying had reached the limit—a sum higher than any that had ever been subscribed in Farmdale before, for any cause— suddenly a prominent businessman went up on the platform and looking straight at the handsome young soldier selling war bonds, called out: "Barney Vance, we were promised a song from you and we want to hear it now. My wife wasn't out to church Sunday morning but I told her all about that song you sung, the one about the Man on the throne of God offering His blood for the sins of us all, and I promised her if she could come tonight I'd ask you to sing it over again for her. Come on now, sing it, won't you? This will be a good time. Won't you sing it for my wife?"

Barney's grew suddenly sober. He gave a quick look at the man, Mr. Harper, and then he glanced at the frowning Hortense, knowing that she wouldn't like it. But Hortense stood haughtily silent, as if she had not heard, and Barney turned back to Mr. Harper.

"Do you want that special song or would you like another?"

"I want that special song," said the man. "I thought that was *great*."

"Very well," said Barney, gravely, "Margaret, where are you? Can you play it without the music?"

"Oh yes," she said, and went and sat down at the piano.

"The nerve of her!" whispered Hortense contemptuously.

Margaret's fingers touched the keys, quietly, almost reverently, and then Barney sang, with the instant attention a voice like his will always get.

> I see a Man at God's right hand,
> Upon the throne of God,
> And there in sevenfold light I see

> The sevenfold sprinkled blood.
> I look upon that glorious Man,
>   On that blood-sprinkled throne;
> I know that He sits there for me,
>   That glory is my own.

The room was very still now. The words were going straight into hearts more even than they had done in the church, and it seemed that they were being understood. And then in the back of the room where Hortense had taken refuge when he began to sing, there was a movement. Quick, flashing, angry eyes brimming with frightened tears, and Hortense made a dive for the dressing room and disappeared from view. She fastened the door, too and no one saw the tears that pelted down over her make-up. Angry tears.

It may have been that Barney saw her go, sensed how disappointed she was, and felt somehow he ought to make it up to her in some way. He had prayed a little for her, but somehow he didn't seem to feel very genuine in his prayers. Too many years he had been growing in his distrust of her. Yet the Lord could forgive her, and love her, even though she was so silly and superficial. And if that was so he ought to be able to pray for her at least. Hadn't he seen tears in her eyes? Maybe somehow, a message had got across to her soul. The Lord was able to reach any soul.

But Hortense was not weeping for her sins, she was weeping for her*self*, and her own mortification in failing to get the admiration and acclaim from the whole community. She had wanted to show Barney what she could do, and to show those two upstarts of girls, and they had all simply been witnesses to her humiliation.

But Barney had little further time for thought about the silly girl, for he was surrounded by the old inhabitants of the hometown, and he found that a reception could be a very pleasant affair when one knew the people well.

Hortense did not remain in the dressing room long to weep. She heard Barney's voice singing again, and knew that the song he was singing had been requested. That was a relief. She got out her make-up and repaired the damage done to her face, and then she went loftily out to resume her duties as hostess, and act exactly as if everybody knew that she had been responsible for this great social success. But she watched jealously the two girls who were so at home among these people, and the young man who was not giving her the attention that she felt he owed her now, since she had given him this reception.

But Barney was having a good time, and stayed willingly beyond the hour he had set as the time for his little company to retire from the social scene and go home. And when finally the company really began to break up, Barney went smilingly up to Hortense, shook her hand cordially, and thanked her for the pleasant evening she had planned for him. At least Hortense felt that she had been treated with outward respect, now at the end, even though Barney did frustrate every part of the program she had planned. Well, at least he had come, and done the courteous thing, and everybody had seen him do it. That somewhat salved her hurt feelings.

Chapter 20

It was the next morning that the telegram arrived from the admiral. Roxy brought it up to him reluctantly, because he had been up so late the night before and she thought he needed to sleep. But a telegram had always been an alarming thing to Roxy, so she finally decided it was her duty to let Barney be the judge. A telegram? Barney was instantly wide awake and all attention. Yes, it was from the admiral. He blinked at it and began to read.

> If still interested in proposition be ready to start, awaiting telegram to come at once. You would have to be in Washington for medical examination first, and then await orders. Let me know your plans immediately.

Barney waited only a minute and then he sprang from his bed and went to the telephone, called up Western Union and sent his answer.

> Still eager to go. Will be ready when you call. Gratefully yours,
> Barney Vance.

After he had hung up the telephone it came to him that this was going to make a radical change in his program of the days. And first, he had to tell Margaret.

He knew that she was hoping against hope that her beloved would not have to go yet, on account of his health. He knew that she felt it was all wrong for him to have offered. If Stormy must be gone after, someone else surely ought to go, not Barney, who was himself but just out of the hospital, and not at all strong yet. And yet, she had been praying for Stormy's return, and he knew she was ready to give him a smiling farewell if he felt he must go. Yes, he must tell Margaret now.

No, he couldn't tell her right away. She was in school. He couldn't disturb her until noon. Of course if he had to leave at once he wouldn't stop on that, but he didn't want a lot of curious children around when

174

he told her. Of course he could call her on the telephone, but that would be hard on her. She would have to go back to her classes. No, there was no hurry yet. He would go down to the schoolhouse and be there when she came out to her lunch. They could walk a few steps together. Yet why was he making such a perplexity of this, for Margaret knew he wanted to go? She understood. And in a way she would be glad that he was getting his wish. Yet he knew what a trial it was going to be for her. And for himself too.

He drew a deep quivering sigh as he hurried with his dressing. Would this mean a long separation? Going after Stormy might not be quick work. It might be a long-drawn-out affair. And when he found him, *if* he did, would it perhaps involve imprisonment or even death for himself? Yes, he had counted the possibility of that when he first said he would go, but then he hadn't found Margaret yet. Now he had, and he saw that it was sorrow for her if that happened. He could well sacrifice himself for the man who had once saved his life, but to bring sorrow on his beloved was another matter. And yet he knew he could not back out, could not go back on his offer. Margaret knew about it and Margaret would not have him stay safely here when duty and loyalty called. Yes, it was going to be hard, but he *had* to go! Yes and be *glad* over it, too. He must not be sad. That was no way to sacrifice, to do it sadly. No, he must trust God to bring it all out right.

But he went about his packing with a heavy heart. He had to own that it was not *going* to be easy to tell Margaret that he had practically received his summons. The admiral would not have sent that telegram if he hadn't been pretty sure that he had been able to put this thing across, and Barney was almost trembling at the thought of the trust that was being put in him. It seemed almost audacious in him to have suggested that he was fitted to go, and yet he had been so confident that he could find Stormy if he were allowed to try.

Very humble about it all he knelt down and talked to his Lord about it, and when he arose there was a new peace on his brow, also a certain assurance in his heart that Margaret would understand. It would be a sorrow they would have to bear together, but perhaps a special joy would come through that sorrow.

So it was with a grave face that he went downstairs and sought out Roxy, who had been filled with quiet forebodings ever since that telegram came.

"Well, Roxy," he said as he entered the kitchen and saw the anxious face of his old nurse, "I guess I'm going to have my wish and be allowed to go after my lost friend."

"Oh, Mr. Barney! Now ain't that *awful*! They would never be letting you go if they knew how white you were still looking. I'm a mind to go myself down to Washington and *tell* them, so I am."

Barney grinned.

"No, Roxy, you mustn't think of that. They would only laugh at you and think you were an old mollycoddler. Besides, if they let me go I'll have to pass the doctor's test, so don't you worry. They won't let me go if I'm not able. And now see here, Roxy, you can't go around looking and acting like that. Don't you know God is managing this thing, and it can't go through unless He says so. We've done a lot of praying about this trip, and if I go I must go in the strength of the Lord, not my own strength. Besides, this isn't any worse than my going to war the first time, is it? And I came back, didn't I?"

"Well, there just doesn't seem any sense to it at all, you going through all that war, and being so sick and then getting back home, and having the temerity to go back again before you have to. It seems to me like tempting Providence."

"Oh, no, Roxy. It's not like that. I'm going of my own free will to try and find and bring back my friend who saved my life when he was wounded himself. You don't want me to be a coward, do you, Roxy?"

He talked for sometime to try and make her understand. All the time she was getting his breakfast and sitting around while he ate it, and then she was not more than half convinced that this was something his mother would have wanted him to do. Something that God wanted him to do or He would not have made it possible.

"Well, you aren't gone yet," she said at last. "Maybe God'll stop it yet somehow. I think we need a bit more praying."

"Now Roxy," charged Barney, with a grin, "you wouldn't go and pray *against* me, would you?"

"No, not against you," said Roxy with a grim set of her lips. "I'll just pray that God will see to it that you behave till you get strong enough to go out saving people again."

Barney laughed and then went upstairs to put last things in his suitcase. If he should be called to go suddenly he must be ready. The admiral had asked that he do that. And it was getting almost time to go and meet Margaret. He mustn't miss that, and he would feel easier in his mind if the suitcase was ready to go whenever he left the house for a few minutes.

So he packed his things, for he had thought it all out in the night just what things would have to go to make him ready for any contingency he might have to meet. Then he went downstairs and smelled the cinnamon buns that Roxy was baking.

"Give me a couple, Roxy," he begged. "I'm going to meet Sunny at her lunch hour, and I thought if we had a couple of those nice hot cinnamon buns we could stay out a little longer, and she wouldn't have to go to the lunch room."

"Why of course," said Roxy brightening. "Here! I'll fix them in a little box for you."

In a trice she whisked four lovely candied buns rich with raisins into a box, with plenty of paper napkins to wipe off the stickiness afterwards.

Barney took the box and started away, trying to plan just how he would break the news to Margaret.

And then he didn't have to break it at all. Margaret understood at once. It seemed almost uncanny. She saw him as she came down the steps of the schoolhouse, and her eyes got wide with trouble.

"It's *come*," she said breathlessly as she hurried to his side. "Hasn't it? Your summons has come, and they are going to let you go. Isn't that right? Please tell me quickly and get it over with."

"You dear child!" was all Barney said, looking down at her with deep compassion in his eyes. "Perhaps I ought not to have suggested it. I didn't want *you* to have to suffer."

"No, it's all right, Barney! Truly it is! I want it to be God's way of course. But I've just been expecting this all day and when I saw you walking along with your shoulders over and your head bent I knew it must have come, and that you were realizing what it is going to be to us. But we're not the only people who have to suffer for this awful war, and of course we'll be brave and keep on praying."

"You dear child!" said Barney again, feeling sharp tears stinging into his eyes.

"Well, there!" said Margaret, giving a quick rub across her eyes. "That's over. Now tell me about it. What did they say? Were they pleased or not?"

"Here is the telegram," said Barney in a husky voice.

They stopped on the walk while Margaret read it, then she handed it back to him and looked up with a pale little watery smile.

"Well, I'm glad they didn't turn you down utterly. It shows they must have had good reports of you, and they must think a lot of Stormy. Of you both of course. And I'm proud of you. It hurts, but I'm proud of you!"

Margaret's quiet sensible acceptation of the fact did a lot toward taking away the sting of the separation that was to come, the thought that perhaps he would never come back to her on this earth, when they had just found one another. But after they had walked quite a distance, and it was only a half hour before the school bell would sound for the afternoon session, they were calm enough to eat their cinnamon buns.

"Mmmm!" said Margaret eating the last crumb of hers. "They are good. I'm glad you brought them along. I'll thank Roxy for them myself the next time I see her."

"But think of all the time we wasted last night in that fool reception," said Barney. "When we might have been alone together."

"No!" said the girl cheerfully, "it wasn't wasted. I'm glad you had that reception, and glad I was in on it with you. It is something to remember while you are gone. Something beautiful. I shall always hear you singing to my heart, until you come back to sing to me again."

"Dearest!" said Barney, and stooped right on the public highway and kissed her.

"But Barney, dear, you *mustn't*! Can't you remember I'm the schoolma'am. They'll perhaps have me expelled for carrying on in public this way with a soldier! And there might be some of my bad boys around watching. And old lady Cramer lives in that little house up the road. They say she can see a mile away, and talk as if she had seven tongues."

And so they talked lightly, as if there were no anxieties and burdens in the world for them, and Barney went home almost cheered. What a wonderful girl she was! But he did not know that back in her little cloak room where she stored unused school books and boxes of chalk, and piles of old examination papers, Sunny was down on her knees behind an old blackboard asking for keeping for Barney, and strength for them both to go through this trial.

Chapter 21

Stormy going down the dark river in a little open boat with a man who was supposedly fishing, lay under the great piece of sailcloth that was thrown carelessly over him, and now and again looked out furtively between the folds. He way trying to identify the places he was passing, cities he must have known well at one time. Yet some cities were so much alike at night it was hard to tell them apart. He feared even to think of names of places he knew, lest somehow the enemy might sense his thought. He knew nothing of the man in whose boat he traveled. He trusted nobody. He was only trying to follow orders. And lying still beneath that cover in the night he fell asleep.

Sometimes he wakened, but the cover was still upon him, and he lay as still as possible. He somehow felt he must not call the attention ever of his fisherman.

He had carefully memorized all the papers he carried. If any enemies appeared he could destroy them and be little worse off than he was before when he had been in the underground.

He began to wonder about that radio, and if it would be some new type that would make them suspect him. He tried to remember all he knew of such instruments that might be used on planes. He whiled away the long journey in that little boat by repeating over in his mind the names and number of the papers he carried. He must have these all at his tongue's end. There must be no hesitation in his answers if any questions were asked.

In the dimness of the dawning they reached the airport, a bleak place with no lights, and hazy ships like giant shadowy insects hovered about in most unexpected places.

The oarsman who had been strangely silent all the way drew up to land, pointed to a distant building dimly outlined against the dawn and uttered one single word, "Hangar." Then he took away the covering cloth and helped his passenger to get out, which was not an easy job after such a long time of lying in one cramped position. His feet on solid ground again he watched his conductor turn his boat

179

and sweep away into the dimness from which they had come. Just like that, without a word! Twelve hours at least he must have been in the company of that man, and they had not spoken to each other, save that one word. Stormy would not know him if he were to see him in the daylight. Would he ever see him again? Was he a saved man or an enemy perhaps? That might of course be possible. For it would not have been easy to get a native to bring him here.

But now he had no time to think. His orders were to go at once to the office and report. He took out his identification papers and walked with as firm a step as he could muster with the stiffness in his legs. It was well that it was still dark or his gait might be noticeable.

The man in the office was asleep, his head down on his folder arms upon the desk, and Stormy had to pound on the door to waken him and gain admittance, and attention.

He stood waiting while the official read his papers with sleepy eyes, and then looked him over, saying a few words in French, to the effect that he was the new radio operator to take the place of the man who had been taken sick. It was well for Stormy that he had been well taught in languages and could converse easily in several, so he had no trouble in answering the few questions.

The official showed him where to go, and what would be required of him, told him it was uncertain when the plane would leave, assigned him temporary quarters where he could rest till the day officer would arrive who would give him further orders. Then he departed, and Stormy lay down on the hard cot in the bare little room and shivered. The broken rest, the bleakness of the airport, the dismal outlook into a day in which a fine drizzle of rain was obscuring the surroundings, combined to make him feel half sick. But he was a soldier and not expecting luxury. And he was on his way. A few mouthfuls of dry bread he had brought with him, and a swallow or two of water from a pitcher on the shelf, a bit of a prayer, and he felt better, and went off into a refreshing sleep.

The day officer seemed more indifferent than the night officer had been, and it struck Stormy that all the people he saw coming and going about that airport, looked unhappy, and suspicious, as if they trusted nobody. But he did not venture to talk with any except when he had to ask a question about his duties. He judged that as this was enemy occupied territory none dared to trust any, so he did not do so himself. He was glad that nobody asked him questions. They did not seem to care whence he came, or whither he was going. Each went his way with sodden indifference.

He was clothed as inconspicuously as possible, having got rid of the ragged enemy-uniform he had worn when he escaped from the camp. The little parking room where they had put him when he came contained a coat and cap evidently worn by the former radio operator, now sick. Stormy appropriated them. They were a bit too small, but what did that matter? They seemed clean and gave him a more self-respecting look.

The three days of waiting went hard with Stormy, and as he began to experiment with the radio he wished he dared send some message to his outfit, but the friend who had helped him at the underground had warned him not to try anything like that. He must remember that he was still in enemy-occupied territory.

At last the time of waiting was over, and the plane appeared. Then there was work to do, messages to be sent, and by this time he was fairly well acquainted with his instrument. He was filled with excitement to think that in a little while now he would be out of enemy-occupied land and free to go on where he would. But he had been trained in a hard school and well knew that he must not count on anything ahead. Almost anything might happen yet to hold him up. And he prayed that it might not be too long for the information of which he was possessed to be of value.

That last night before the plane came he slept but fitfully and often in his dreams he saw that vision again that had been that girl he had seen at camp back in his home land. The girl whose tiny snapshot collected from among her brother's pictures the last time he was back with the outfit had gone with him everywhere so far, hidden inside the pocket of his blouse, where happily no sneering guard had yet discovered it. It was only a tiny one, and now soiled and crumpled in spite of his care, but somehow that face had cheered him when he felt utterly without human friends. Could it be that he would see that girl herself some day? That there was hope he might yet go home and see her? Her brother Jim had been his friend. There might be an opportunity. It was a pleasant hope to ponder on as he watched the great plane come sailing into the airport. Only a figment of his imagination, perhaps, but it helped to pass the time away.

Then things began to happen. He was given many messages to send, some that contained facts that he knew his officers back at the outfit would be glad to get. Some that he would fain have withheld from sending to the enemy. Dared he do a bit of editing? He wished he could, but he must run no risks for the sake not only of himself but for the sake of those good people who had taken their lives in their hands to help to set him free. He had been warned.

As he set sail at last out into the gloomy world a great exultation filled him. He was *going.*

How he wished he were free to replace that pilot up there, and drive that plane where he would. For he was a pilot himself of course and felt at home in the air. If only there had been nobody but himself and the pilot on board, he could easily have overpowered the pilot and taken over. But there were a lot of people on board, soldiers of course, and sturdy men. And anyway he should not think such crazy thoughts. For while under certain circumstances he might have gotten away with it, it would certainly have reacted on those blessed people of the underground who had helped him away, and were living to help others who might escape, and he could think of nothing more despicable than to be disloyal to them.

Still there was exhilaration in being among the clouds again and daring to hope that in the not far distance he might be seeing his buddies of the outfit, and be perhaps hearing from home. Again he wondered about Barney Vance. Were was he? Was he living yet, and did he get well and go home, or was he still in a hospital bed, as he had left him.

And that was the morning that Barney received that first telegram from the admiral.

The first airport was passed at last. The next one was still many miles ahead. Stormy's heart was pounding in his breast as they went on. Soon, soon though they would pass out of enemy jurisdiction. The second airport! There the new radio man was to take over and he would be free to edge along into unoccupied territory.

It was only a little while after that that he noticed something queer about the way they were flying, something quite out of the ordinary.

He wished he dared go over to that pilot and suggest something. He wished he dared take over to run them into safety. He felt fairly certain he knew what was the matter with that plane, but that wasn't his business, and might of course lay him open to suspicion. He must not do that. If he should be taken prisoner, here, now, before they had crossed the border into free land what would become of all the valuable information he carried in his mind. It would be lost to his side, he would probably be taken prisoner again, too. No, he must be quiet and calm.

"Oh, God, take over, please!" he prayed.

And now the plane was definitely out of hand, and going down swiftly, a forced landing was inevitable. Stormy looked down. Was that water beneath those clouds, or mountains, or what? He couldn't see for the rain and mist that surrounded the swiftly falling ship. The passengers were in a panic. He could easily have been in one himself, to have to come down among the enemy when he had been almost out into freedom. Was God going to let this happen to him again? Was this what He had planned? But if it was going to happen of course it was in the eternal plan, and Stormy must yield in contentment.

"Oh God, take over for me. I can do nothing myself," he prayed.

And then the crash came!

Chapter 22

Barney had waited five days for another message from the admiral before it came. A day letter sent that morning making an appointment in Washington.

Barney was all ready to go, although he had about lost hope that he would hear anything more of his request. He took only time for a brief telephone conversation with Margaret, and hurried on his way to Washington, leaving a deeply disappointed Roxy, weeping salt tears into her dishpan, and a bright-haired girl who had already shed her tears, and had prayed her way through to peace, trying to smile through her day of hard work in school.

Meanwhile Barney was on the train, trying to forget the sad little lilt of his dear girl's voice as she bade him Godspeed and told him how she would be praying all the time for him.

They hadn't had much time to talk, for he knew he should catch the first train possible, and he knew also that she had duties which he must not interrupt. Besides, they had said good-by last night, with always the thought every night that perhaps he might have to go before she saw him again.

But presently he was able to turn his attention to what might be just before him.

He got out his telegram and read it over carefully. Oh, it was all uncertain business. He wished he could have gone straight from his hospital before he came home. That would have been the way to find Stormy. All this endless delay! And now, he would scarcely know which direction to take, unless the outfit had since received more definite knowledge of where Stormy had been taken prisoner.

He put his head back on the seat and closed his eyes, trying to pray. He was in God's hands, why should he be so upset by a simple change of plans? God was in Washington. He was across the seas. He knew whether it was in the plan for Barney to go after Stormy or not. Why should he fret? And so, laying down his burden, peace came to his heart and he slept.

One of the hardest things in life to Barney to do was to wait
184

patiently for something he wasn't in the least sure of, and he found
that there was a good deal of that in store for him for the next two
days. Then suddenly things began to happen.

The admiral's secretary came to him in the office where she had
parked him the day before, and sent him off to the doctor to have a
through physical examination.

Barney saw in that only another way to hinder him for he knew he
was not up to his normal strength yet, and he did not want that held
up against him. He knew that he *could* go out and fight again if he
was back with his companions and that was his duty. He knew that
he had strength enough to do what he had set out to do under ordinary circumstances, or even under extraordinary ones. And even if
it was not the way to recover normal strength now, yet we were at
war, weren't we? And soldiers were not expected to consider themselves. Still he felt he was fit enough and would be all right, and if
the Lord wanted him to go he was going. That is if the army would
let him. And of course if he was allowed to go that would be a sign
that it was the Lord's will. But he went to the doctor as he was
ordered, waited an unconscionable time for his turn, answered innu-
merable questions, and got very little personal satisfaction out of the
interview, save that he was advised that he still needed to take as
much rest as possible. Then he went back to the admiral's secretary,
and was told that the admiral would see him the next morning, and
hoped to have definite information for him.

Meanwhile Barney had taken all this waiting time to write a letter
to Margaret, a real love letter, the first he had ever written, pouring
out all the precious thoughts of his heart for her, trying to make up
for the brief time they had had together since they had found out their
love.

Dear Sunny:
    You will not mind If I use the dear name I knew first,
will you, my darling, in this my first love letter to you? It
somehow seems right that I should bridge the years in
this way. My precious love, you cannot know how hard
it is has been to leave you this way, when we have but
just found each other. And yet I think you understood
that it meant an obligation which could not be ignored. I

think, too, that you agreed with me that it was right for
me to go. But that is something we have talked over,
something we have left in the Lord's hands, and both of
us are trusting that He will bring it out in His own way.

But now I want to go back to the first morning when I
returned from overseas, and saw you standing down
among the apple blossoms, your sweet face looking up to
the bird singing by my window.

I am astonished at myself that I haven't told you this
before, but we had so little time along you know, and
there were so many important things to say. I wanted
this to be a very special time, this telling you the lovely
picture you made there among the apple blossoms, when
you didn't even know I was there watching you. So I'm
going to take this first minute by myself, when I've nothing to do but think about you, and this seems the best
way to feel near to you, by bringing out that dear picture
I have in my very recent memory. When I woke this
morning I took a look at it as I always do every morning
since I first saw you and I feel guilty that I have not told
you about it before.

But now, I am wondering if I can find words to paint
the picture of you as I saw you that morning when the
birds were singing, and I was at home again after war
and horror, and pain and desolation.

It was the time of the singing of birds, you know, and
they were fairly whooping it up out there in the apple
tree, that was all pink and white blossoms, with sunshine
glinting through the perfumed air.

And then I heard the soft crunch of wheels on the gravel
of the drive, blending into my dreams, but scarcely noticed it as anything out of harmony with the waking world,
till suddenly I heard a silver sweet whistle, high and clear,
a whistle that I had though for years was practically my
personal property. Astonished I listened, and there it came
again. This I have told you before, briefly, of course, and
have since heard you give a demonstration of what you
can do in that line. But that night was so suddenly inter-

rupted that I did not tell you what was in my heart, and somehow there has never been a time since when I could return to it, because there were so many other important things to say.

Barney took time and much comfort in describing the thrill that came to him with the silver sound of Sunny's whistle, and smiled as he set down the lovely words of description, almost as if he were writing notes in a musical score.

And then he came to the picture as he went to the window and saw her.

He was like an artist taking out his tubes of paint and arranging them on his palette, mixing and blending them to express just the right shade of meaning as he gathered out the words and set them in order in his mind, till it resolved itself into a delight to put them into the picture.

So the letter grew and went on to almost a volume.

Oh, it wasn't all a love letter! There were bits of incidents he had met by the way as he walked about the streets of Washington. There were notable people to mention and describe, some he had even met, and there were items of war news that perhaps hadn't yet got on the radio. He described some of the great buildings he had visited to pass the time away, told of the lovely flowers in the parks. And then he went back to his love for Margaret and began to tell her all over again how happy it made him that she loved him, so happy that he couldn't rightly think about the serious mission he was expecting presently to go out on. A mission that would probably be filled with peril and danger and toil and weariness before he could even hope to come back to her, if he *ever* came. But he did not want to make her suffer as he was suffering every time he thought of that possibility.

Two or three times Barney came on lovely little things that he could send back to his dear girl. A charming bracelet, delicately wrought. A few pictures of the city. Other souvenirs. He wanted to get her a ring as soon as there was time. As soon as he could get back to her, and put in on her hand himself. It was too sacred a thing for him to do by "absent treatment," he told himself.

But thinking about that matter of a ring brought back the memory of the day when his mother took off her engagement ring. It was getting too tight for her, and she had to work for some time before she could slip it off. He remembered that he had finally gone and helped her.

"I shall likely never wear it again," she had said, with a sigh and the quick flashing of a smile at the end that he knew was put there for him. She was studying these days to leave no sad memories for him. He had had flashes of understanding of this at times, in those days, but he had been so filled with eagerness over his own approaching entrance into the army that he didn't fully realize. Now, however, it came to him fully, to understand and realize what that scene with the ring had meant to his mother. She was saying good-by to him forever. That is, so far as this earth was concerned.

Now he felt that he must review it thoroughly and understand everything, come nearer to his mother in knowing what this all had meant to her. She must have know that she would not be here when he came back.

It had been a bright lovely day, almost the first of May, and the birds were singing then, just as they were singing now. As he thought of it their shrill sweet voices seemed hopelessly tangled with that look of pain on his mother's face. That sweet quiet sacrifice of all that she counted dear because she knew that the cause for which he was going forth to fight was a cause of righteousness, and loyalty to his country. Freedom and Right were calling him. It was God's cause and God would car for him. That was the way his mother had felt.

And she had taken off that old blue ring, a sapphire it was, and *old* sapphire, as if she were giving up the self she had been through the years. She had told him about the ring again that day, although he remembered she had often spoken of its history before. She had said it was worth a great deal of money. He wondered if that could possibly be true. Valuable? Why would a simple blue stone be valuable? It wasn't even a star sapphire was it? Just a blue stone. A sapphire. Was that a precious stone, or just a semi-precious one? But his mother had always spoken of it as something very unusual. Would she know about such things? Her grandfather had brought it home with him from some far land, he couldn't remember the story, but it was written down somewhere. His mother had put the story in the box with the ring, and told him that he was to get it reset and give it to his bride some day.

He had laughed when she gave it to him, and said that he hadn't any idea of getting married, and it would be a long time before he did if he went to war, before he had time to get acquainted with any girls. She had kissed him as she put the ring box in his hand and told him she hoped he would find the right girls, and never give her ring into the keeping of a girl who was not worthy of him. He wondered as he remembered this if possibly his mother hadn't been thinking of Hortense when she said this. How she had always dreaded Hortense's coming! He had not then understood that in his sweet gentle loving mother—to be so set against one girl that she couldn't *see* anything good in her at all. But now, since he had been at home and had seen more of Hortense's machinations, he could understand. Mother had looked into the girl's character when she was quite young and had seen what she was. Wise dear mother! Oh, could mother see dear Sunny, his precious lovely Margaret now? Surely if she knew, she was happy over his having found her. He seemed to feel that he had his mother's blessing on this union he hoped would come about some day—if he lived to come home.

He thought about the blue ring again. Would Margaret like it? He must find out whether she liked it or not before he gave it to her. Or rather could he offer it as a substitute for a diamond, until he could get home and really pick out the stone she liked best? Why hadn't he done something about that ring before he left home? She could have been wearing it while he was away, a sort of bond between them till he returned. It was too late to do it now of course, for the blue ring was in the bank with all his valuable papers. And there was another thing he ought to have done. He should have made a will and left everything to Margaret. That was what should be of course, and perhaps he could find a lawyer here in Washington and arrange that, having the paper sent to the bank afterward. Yes, he must look after that. He could even arrange that by telephone, probably. No, he would have to sign papers of course. But he just must not forget that. One couldn't be too careful when one was going into a dangerous zone, and while money of course was not greatly important, still he would like to have his go to his dear girl, if anything happened to him.

But if he did get back home soon he must go and get that ring and examine it carefully, have it appraised, and then ask Margaret if she liked it. If she knew the story of its being his mother's she would be likely to ask to have it in place of any other ring, for she loved his mother, and would be prejudiced in its favor, but he would not speak of what his mother had said until he really found out if she liked it. He would not condemn her to wear something the rest of her days that she perhaps had disliked.

So he planned, and filled his time of waiting with pleasant thoughts.

He had a little snapshot of Margaret that he had begged last Sunday night, and kept it in a little leather case in his pocket over his heart. Often he would take it out and look into that sweet face, and remember how beautiful she was, and how wonderful it was that God had kept such a lovely girl safe for him until he could get home to find her. Surely God would let him come back again to her. "Oh my Father, keep her safely!" he prayed in his heart again and again as he went about through those days of waiting before he expected to leave.

And so he lay down to rest that last night before he was to meet the admiral and get some definite answer about his request, he was thinking of Margaret—Sunny as he still called her in his most intimate thoughts—and feeling that she was very near. She was probably kneeling now to pray for him, for they had arranged a trysting hour for prayer which he meant to keep whenever possible, even if it meant amid battle or danger. So was somewhat dispelled the anxiety which he had been feeling about the outcome of the morrow.

About a half hour before it was time to go to the admiral's office Barney was ready, and sat glancing over the morning paper, noting the headlines and what had been happening over night in the war zones, when he heard footsteps coming along the hall. Could it be the bell boy bringing up another telegram? Oh, he hoped there was not going to be another long delay. Well, it there was to be, and he had to back home, he would at least try to do something about that ring, so that Margaret would have something to help her feel he was hers.

And then the footsteps paused outside his door!

But instead of knocking a hand took hold of the knob and turned it, the door opened, and there stood Stormy Applegate!

Chapter 23

Barney took a deep breath and passed his hand over his eyes. Was he seeing things? He must have high blood pressure or something. This couldn't be real. This tall soldier who looked so much like Story, only somehow thinner, and tired-looking, who stood there in his doorway grinning at him.. He *couldn't* be Stormy. Why they didn't even know for certain that Stormy was alive yet, and if he was he must be on the other side of the world!

"Stormy!" he gasped. "My word, man, is it really you? How did you manage to get here? Why—we thought you were *lost*! We didn't even know whether you were alive or not. They all said you weren't, but I wasn't letting it go at that. I was sure you were alive, and I have been doing my best to get permission to go out and hunt you up."

"I know," grinned Stormy. "I heard about that, but I *beat you to it!* I didn't want you to take all that trouble when I *was* having to come anyway you see, so I just caught the next plane after I'd imparted the information I was sent for, and here I am! Glad to see me, old man?"

"Glad to see you?" said Barney springing to his feet and grasping Stormy's hand. "Glad to see you? *I'll say* I am! Bless the Lord for bringing you through!"

"Amen!" said Stormy heartily.

And then suddenly Barney felt weak in the knees and as if all the happenings of the last two weeks had got him down.

"Sit down," he said grasping Stormy's arm and pressing him into the big chair by the window. "Tell me all about it. Where have you been and how did you get here?"

"Well, that's a pretty big order, Barn," said the other man, "but I imagine I can sketch out a kind of an outline of my doings if I take the rest of the day. God plenty of time?"

"Oh," said Barney, suddenly remembering the admiral and his engagement. "No, I forgot. I've got an engagement in two minutes now with the admiral and I'll have to run. Come with me, won't you? He's the one who has been arranging for me to go over after you, and he told me he would give me a definite answer this morning."

"That's all right," grinned Stormy, waving Barney off as he tried to draw him to his feet, "*I'm* the definite answer. I just came from your admiral, and he sent me over to tell you, you needn't come till five o'clock this afternoon, and we are to take dinner with him at his house tonight, so settle down and relax and I'll begin my story."

"But—did the admiral know all the time that you were coming?"

"Well, no, not *all* the time. But he knew day before yesterday. He's been cabling like mad to the outfit, and when they got my first contact, which was as soon as I could get to a telephone in unoccupied territory after the crash—"

"*Crash*?" asked Barney excitedly. "Were you back in combat?"

"No, I was on my way out of occupied territory, and we had a crash a few miles before we escaped from there. It was just a mere trifle of something like fifty or a hundred miles, and no way to get over the line but to *walk*, and dodge bombs and incidental snipers, but at last I got to a friendly town and found a telephone, and let them know I was alive. I couldn't give them much information of course. Too important, but I called my officer and told him number two question of our list was as he hoped, and that was the most important question I was sent to find out. Then I said I'd get there as soon as I could get transportation, for walking was almost too slow, not while I had valuable information to impart. So they maneuvered a plane after me, and I got there at last and gave my report. Then they told me you were out after me, and had been keeping the wires hot in pursuit, so they sent me through a medical exam and then got me a plane over here, so here I am!"

"Praise the Lord!" said Barney, his face shining. "But—tell me about the crash. How did it happen? Where was it? Were you hurt? Was anybody hurt?"

"Not so fast. You know I've been though a nervous shock and I can't answer everything at once. The crash was pretty bad, and I don't know how long I was unconscious, but pretty soon I felt it getting pretty hot and I woke to consciousness, and found the plane was on fire. Then I got busy. A good many were killed, and only a few of the passengers were able to crawl out. I managed to get out. But it was a long time before I got to anywhere, and I guess some of the men that escaped the fire died before help came. But you know how such things are. You've been through enough yourself."

"Indeed I have."

"Well, Jim Mayberry wanted to take a plane back to look up the people that were saved in the crash, but he was needed in another direction and went by himself to get some more information. He's beginning to do some notable things along that line now. Bright kid he is."

"Yes," said Barney. "I though that when I was there, but he's a quiet fellow. It wasn't easy to know him well, but I got to like him a lot. And by the way I think he has accepted the Lord."

"He *has*? That's wonderful! I hoped he would come to see it. You know you can't go around in the face of death continually and not see yourself, and see what the Lord can do, and how much everybody needs Him."

"That's right," said Barney. "I had several quiet talks with Jim while I was still in the hospital. He's never had much teaching along those lines, and has had to think things out for himself, but it seems to me that one meets God out there among flying bombs and learns directly from Him, and perhaps that's the best way to know God, and to see oneself."

The two young men were silent for a moment, enjoying the quiet agreement of fellowship they were having. Then Barney said:

"Did you know Jim's sister was over her, in Farmdale visiting her aunt? She's been much interested in you, by the way, been one of our group who were praying that you might be found."

Stormy looked up with quick interest:

"She *has*?" he said, greatly stirred. "I met her once in camp before we left this country. I didn't suppose she'd remember me."

"She *does*," said Barney. "She asked me one day if you were a Christian. She is greatly interested in the subject. She seemed to feel that it would be very terrible if you had died without knowing the Lord. You see everybody had told her that you were probably killed. Even Jim wrote her that was the general opinion of the outfit. And she was greatly concerned to know if you were saved. Things of the kingdom have become very real to her these days. She has told us that she knows you."

Stormy was silent searching the face of his friend. At last he asked slowly, quietly, "*You* are then interested in her?"

"Me? Interested in Cornelia Mayberry? No, not specially, except that I have tried to tell her more about the Lord in answer to her questions now and then, but our conversation has been mainly about you. It seems that she remembers you very vividly."

"That's strange," said Stormy, "we had scarcely any opportunity to talk together, just a little fun now and then when everybody was by. But I have thought often of her, and wished I knew if she had ever found the Lord. She was a most interesting girl."

"Yes," said Barney. "She is intimate with a dear friend of mine, and so I have seen her rather often since I have been at home. But that hasn't been so long you know."

"No, it hasn't been long as the world counts time, since you and I parted and went out way to meet death, yet here we are and it seems that years must have passed. What has the time brought to you, fella? Changes? I remember they said you mother had died. That will have made it hard for your homecoming."

"Yes, it has," said Barney, "but she expected it and wrote me a farewell letter left in her desk. It gave me courage to go on. I had time to write her before she went how I had come to know the Lord intimately, and she was so glad of that. She has left me the feeling that she's just over at the gate of Heaven waiting for me till I get done my work here, and that we must not either of us mourn, because we're meeting soon."

"How precious to have a heritage like that!" said Stormy, and then he sighed. "I never really knew my mother at all. She died when I was just a little chap, and my father didn't live much longer. He was killed in the last war. I was raised by a lot of relatives who didn't quite understand me, and now think I am a fanatic. It doesn't matter of course, but it would have been pleasant to have had a mother and a father. Barney, how has it seemed, getting back to real living again? Or is it real living? Sometimes I have thought the real part was over there where we see the stark side of life and everybody is on a level before God."

"It is, isn't it!" said Barney. "I thing we didn't understand what life was for before we went into battle."

"That's right," said Stormy. "But how has it seemed, coming back? Have you been happy, fella?"

Then suddenly Barney looked up and his face was illuminated by a great smile, the smile that Sunny called his "golden look."

"Why yes, Stormy, I've been happy! Very happy! I was coming to that. God has given me a great joy. The love of the most wonderful girl I have ever known. I never knew there was any earthly joy like that! Of course we've only known this a comparatively few days, but I've practically known her all my life. She was just a little kid when I went away to college, but now she'd grown into a beautiful woman, as lovely of soul as she is of face, but wait till you see her. Her name is Margaret Roselle, and he mother was one of my mother's dearest friends. She and I have been praying for you that you might come home. Stormy, I only hope some day you'll know a love like this."

Stormy was silent again, but his face had a glorified interest in it.

"I'm glad for you," he said. "I thought there was something new about you, something that was making you very glad. I thought perhaps at first when you said you had found a girl that it might be Jim's sister. Jim talked a good deal about her."

"Well, she's a very wonderful girl," said Barney. "Margaret enjoys her a lot. They are awfully good friends. They seem to be most congenial. But wait till we get home and you'll see."

"Yes," said Stormy eagerly, "I'm looking forward to that. I'm looking forward to meeting your girl, too. She's got to be something very special to satisfy me for you, Barney."

"She *is*," said Barney with his glorified smile again. "And then," he added, "you'll like Cornelia, I'm sure you will. And you've got to remember that she's *very much* interested in you. In fact, she has a picture of you that she cherishes. It's a snapshot her brother gave her I think, but she showed it to me and asked if you had change any."

Stormy listened eagerly, thoughtfully.

"Do you know," said he slowly, "I'm interested in her too. And I have a picture of her. I made Jim give it to me just before I went away that last time. I've carried it with me wherever I've gone. It's been a sort of mascot. I don't know what she would think if she knew I had it, but sometimes I've taken it out and looked at it, and it has helped me over hard places. Queer, isn't it, to take over an almost stranger and let her be a help in loneliness, because one didn't have any folks of one's own. But it has really meant a lot to me.

Sometime perhaps I'll know her well enough to apologize for having taken the liberty, but anyway it's been good. I hope she won't be angry with me for presuming—if I ever tell her."

Barney looked at Stormy joyously.

"She won't be angry," he said, "and *you'll tell her* of course. Wait till we get to Farmdale. Why did the admiral want to see us? Why invite us to dinner? I'd rather get home and tell Margaret what's happened. And tell Cornelia, too."

"Yes?" said Stormy, "I would too, but your admiral was so insistent that we come, and he said there were some of the people who had been assisting him about your request who wanted to see us. I think we should go. He said they wanted to ask some questions. You know, the old dope that you have to give over the radio every little while, perhaps. Anyhow he's been so kind to us both we'll have to go of course."

"Of course," said Barney, "but I wish we could hurry away right off. I want to see Margaret, and I want you to see Cornelia."

Stormy sat for a moment in silence, thoughtfully. Then he spoke, as if it was something he must explain.

"I have had the strangest experience about Cornelia," he said. "Sometimes I wonder if I was out of my head when it happened. I guess perhaps I was at one time at least. I had been going for days with scarcely anything to eat, chewing a little dried grass, once a raw egg I found in a deserted shack, and once a can of tomatoes. Then so long a time with nothing, not even any clean water to drink. I had a fever I know, and couldn't think very straight. I thought I had reached the end and I was dying, and then there came a spot of moonlight and I saw her face, like an angel, up by the clouds. I wasn't rational enough to work it out the first time who she was, just an angel that God had sent to cheer me, to help me to Heaven perhaps. And looking at her face I fell asleep. I saw her face several times after that, and when I began to come to myself I took out her picture and looked at it. I saw they were the same."

He took out the little picture, looked at it earnestly, and then handed it over to Barney.

"Does she look like that now?" he asked.

"Yes," said Barney taking the picture. "Exactly."

There came a satisfied look in Stormy's eyes, and then he met

Barney's glance with a grin."

"You think I'm a *nut*, don't you?" he said.

But Barney grinned back.

"No," said Barney, "I don't! Besides, you see, I'm in love myself, and I know what it is to be lonely and long for someone to act like homefolks."

"Yes, I guess that's it," said Stormy half sheepishly. "But I'll be glad to get to Farmdale. Of course she'll think I'm a fool I suppose. She's from a swell family, all kinds of money and social training and all that, but I want to see her, anyway. Maybe I won't feel this way when I see her in the flesh again, but I've got to get this idea out of my system before I'll be much good anywhere."

"Oh, *sure!* You've got it *bad*," grinned Barney. "I know the symptoms. I haven't got over them yet myself. After all I've had such a few days with Margaret."

"Well, come on you old bomber, it's time we went and got some lunch. I'll own I'm hungry as a bear. I've not been in the land of plenty so long but that I get hungry now and then. And after lunch, two o'clock to be more accurate, I promised that you and I would appear at that radio station and give a broadcast of our life together in service. Something about the camp life and how I was supposed to have saved your life, and how you tried to save mine or something along those lines. Though of course we won't. We'll just shy off politely and sneak out. But we've got to appear once for I promised. It was all the fault of that doggone admiral. If he hadn't been right there on tiptoe, smiling, I would have got out of it somehow, but he seems to think he's running mamma's two little boys, and we have to do whatever he chooses to order next."

So they went to lunch, then to the radio station, then walked a little about the city seeing a few things they hadn't seen before. They brought up at the admiral's stately mansion and were ushered into the presence of the entire body of powers who had under their control such matters as the request of Barney that he might go out and hunt for Stormy.

It was an august body, and most impressive, and Stormy grinned to himself to think that these dignified gentlemen could have any conception of what it had been like to get lost out there. To roll out of an internment camp between barbed wires, to go hungry for days. And not knowing that, how could they presume to order whether a lost one should be searched for, or allowed to stay lost? Also he thought how good it was to know that God Himself was able to order matters over the heads of all the notables in any country, and work out the need of every living soul.

But the men were interesting and pleasant. They took a personal interest in the two young men who had made such attainments in war service. The dinner was good, the conversation a bit thrilling because it smacked of political problems, and deadly differences of opinion, and it gave Barney and Stormy an opportunity to get the pulse of their country at first hand, as it was represented by a few of the powerful men who had the affairs of the country in their hands, at least for the time being.

After dinner they went into a great luxurious library and sat around a costly table. They answered a lot of questions, that at first seemed utterly pointless, but afterward it developed that these two young men were to be appointed heads of a new groups which should function for the furtherance of an understanding of the enemy, what enemy plans were likely to be and how to frustrate them.

It appeared that these two because of their valor in bombing enemy planes, and in searching in dangerous places for valuable information, were to be awarded notable honors. They were told to return to Washington on a certain day in the near future to publicly receive these awards. They were also informed that after their furloughs were ended they would be assigned to new work which likely would keep them in Washington, or vicinity at least for some time.

Dazed, almost bewildered the two young men went back to their hotel room at last and sat down to discuss the matter for awhile, and then side by side they knelt and committed it all to their heavenly Father. And then as it was definite orders and not anything that they had a choice about, they went to bed. They were still in the army and what the army said, they must do.

"Well," said Barney, "I can't help thinking there may be good in it. I'm not anxious to go on killing, or even spying, but I'm entirely willing to teach others the methods by which I gained my honorable mentions."

"Yes," said Stormy, "this war isn't going on forever of course, and I guess it's our turn to have a little look at peace before we leave and go up higher."

So the next morning they went home to Farmdale, having first telephoned Roxy to have a good dinner ready, and told her to please invite Margaret and Cornelia to dinner that night.

"It's a surprise," said Barney, "Roxy won't tell, but she'll see that the girls are there and that there is plenty to eat, but they won't know a thing yet about you being home, nor our new status in the army."

So like two little boys planning mischief, these two tall handsome soldiers plotted to relax and have a little fun.

Meantime the two girls back in Farmdale prayed most earnestly, wondering if Barney had started for overseas yet, and how many weeks it would be before they would hear from him and know what he had been able to do.

Hortense and her crowd were wondering what was going to happen next and how they could manage to reap a little benefit from that reception they had put over on the unsuspecting Barney. Wondering what they should do next to separate him from those two obnoxious girls who seemed to have absorbed him.

"We might have a religious service in the public square," said Hortense. "Sunday afternoon would be a good time and get an enormous crowd. And we could get up a glee club and sing choruses and songs. We could decorate the plat form in the park with flags, and get a band, and let them play softly all through the prayer,—I suppose we'd *have* to have a prayer, wouldn't we? We couldn't get by without that, could we, not with Barney in it, for if we didn't have in on the program he'd drag one in somehow. I never saw what a religious complex that fellow has! I declare it's a shame. He simply spoils everything we try to get up."

"Well, what I don't understand is, why you insist upon working Barney into everything," said Janet Harper. "He isn't our kind, you *know* he isn't, and you can't make him over, no matter how hard you try. If I were you I'd go down to the camp and get some soldiers who *aren't* that kind, soldiers who'll be real peppy and ready for any devilment you want to get up, and they you can have some real fun."

"Well, to tell you the truth," said Hortense wearily, "there aren't hardly any of that other kind left. They seem to all have got soft and religious. I can't understand it. Just as soon as they get into real fighting they seem to get awfully religious. Do you know, the other night at the canteen, where I was helping to entertain soldiers, a kid walked in and the hostess asked him it he would like to dance. He said no, he didn't know how to dance. And she said: Oh, that's all right. You go right up those stairs and you'll find a woman up there who will *teach* you to dance, and you can come back down here and have a real good time. It doesn't take her long to teach you a few steps. And do you know that fellow fairly glared at her, and he was only a kid, too. But he said 'Lady, I didn't come in here to learn how to dance. I've got to go out tomorrow morning into battle and be ready to *die* perhaps, and I came in here to find somebody who could teach me how to die.' Did you ever hear of such talk? Can you imagine it? Talking like that to really nice people who were trying to help him have a little good time? Why it made me positively *sick* when I heard it. I didn't want to stay there any longer where a thing like that could happen. I hate all this talk about dying. Everybody has to die sometime I suppose of course, but I certainly don't want to hear about it till my time comes."

"Well, Hortense, if you wait till your time comes," spoke up Hand suddenly, "it will certainly be too late to get ready to die. But perhaps you don't care. Probably you think you can get by without getting ready."

"Oh, shut up," said Hortense. "Are you getting religious too? I declare, if you are, I'm off you for life!"

"Well, I wouldn't be losing so much at that," said Hand sourly. "All I get out of this is a chance to do your heavy work. If I'd quit you I might have a little time left on my hands, and I'd stand some chance of learning myself how to die. They tell me I'm in line to be called to war pretty soon, and I might need to know."

"It's a pity you wouldn't try a little religion yourself, Hortense," said Janet Harper. "You might be able to get hold of Barney that way. You've tried everything else on him and it doesn't work, but I think he'd be caught that way."

"Oh, for Pete's sake! What's the matter with you all?" said Hortense angrily, and walked off with her chin up and her eyes flashing angrily.

Chapter 24

The two girls were surprised at Roxy's telephoned invitation, but because they were both unsettled and anxious to get news, and thought perhaps Barney would telephone to Roxy or she might have had a letter, they went. Margaret, mainly because she loved to be where Barney had been, and also because she had known and loved Roxy for years. And Cornelia because she was lonely, just didn't know what to do; and she liked to be with Margaret.

Roxy had told them to come early, but they reached there a little before dinner time, and as they stepped up to the door Barney swung it open, and stood smiling to greet them.

"Oh!" they exclaimed in delight. "You've *come back*! How *grand*! But wouldn't they let you go? *What* has happened?"

A flame of lovely rose swept up into Margaret's cheeks, and her eyes shone with delight.

"Welcome!" said Barney joyously, and turned to the other tall soldier just behind him. "And let me introduce my friend Stormy Applegate!" He grabbed Stormy's arm and brought him forward. And then, and not till then, he turned and took his Margaret in his arms and kissed her. Right there before them all, when nobody had been told yet that they belonged to each other. Margaret's cheeks grew flame-color, but she gasped and returned the kiss eagerly, and then hid her face on Barney's shoulder.

But she needn't have minded, for when she at last ventured to peek out from those enfolding arms that held her close and still more closely, she saw that the other two were not looking at her at all, they were just standing there holding hands, both pairs of hands and looking into one another's faces, with a look of great wonder and delight, as if they were getting to know one another all in a minute, in place of the years of acquaintance they wished they might have had. As if no one else were by and they had nothing to think of but one another.

So Margaret relaxed and just stayed there in Barney's arms, that drew her close and then Barney bent his head and kissed her again quite thoroughly.

201

Suddenly Stormy caught on to what had been happening, and he said in his droll way:

"Oh, is *that* the order of the day? You should have told me. Do you mind, Cornelia? Because you see I've known you for a very long time, even though you may not remember," and quickly he drew her to him and kissed her, almost shyly, if Stormy could do anything shyly—certainly reverently. And then those two were for the moment oblivious to everything but their two selves.

A moment more and a little silver bell tinkled and they looked up to see a puzzled but delighted Roxy standing in the doorway ringing the table bell for attention.

"Children, you dinner is ready," she called. "Would you like to have it hot or would you prefer to eat it cold?"

Laughingly they drew apart, and the two couples, hand in hand went out to the dining room, where was a table loaded with good things. Hot chicken with dumplings sending forth a savory salad, crisp celery, and on the sideboard a great glass dish heaped with luscious strawberries, flanked by a pitcher of rich golden cream. *Real* cream from a pampered cow who wouldn't have known what a ration stamp was if she'd been offered one.

"Oh, boy!" said Stormy as he held out Cornelia's chair, "gaze on that! And to think that I once was glad to get an ancient raw egg, and cried for more when it was gone!"

Amid the laughter they sat down and Barney bowed his head:

"Lord, our Father, we thank Thee for this food, and we thank Thee most of all that Thou hast answered our prayers and brought our Stormy back to us safely. We thank Thee that Thou are our Saviour who hast saved us, all of us, and taught us to know Thee and to love Thee better than anything else in life. We all of us thank Thee today. For Christ's sake, Amen."

Roxy stood by with folded hands and unspeakable joy in her face, he eyes closed and a smile on her lips. She was felling how glad Barney's mother would be about this.

It was a wonderful dinner, every crumb appreciated, every bit of it eaten, after they had made sure that Roxy had saved enough for Joel and herself. And then they went back into the living room for a few minutes and stood beaming at one another.

"I'll tell you what," said Stormy. "Let's go out and take a walk in the lovely twilight. I want to tell Cornelia something." Cornelia looked up and smiled assent.

"Well," said Barney, "I was just wishing we would because I want to tell a lot of things to Margaret."

So, into the twilight they went, holding hands again, and walking very close to one another.

"We're going to see Margaret's mother first," announced Barney. "We want to show Stormy off to her. She's been praying as hard as any of us for his return."

"Why sure," said Stormy, "I like to be shown off to nice people who've been praying me home again. How about it Cornelia?"

"Oh, of course," said Cornelia. "She's very nice. You'll like her, Stormy."

"Of course I will," said Stormy drolly. "Look who she has for a daughter."

And then amid laughter and joy they started on, Barney and Sunny taking the lead, the other two coming more and more slowly, and talking in low tones.

"I've known you a long time, Cornelia only you didn't know me."

"Oh, yes, I did. My brother has told me so much about you that I feel as if we almost might have grown up together."

Stormy smiled and slipped her hand in his other one, putting the nearest arm about her shoulders.

"But you see, I've been loving you a long long time, too."

"Well," said Cornelia quietly, "maybe it just wasn't very formal of me, but I'm afraid I've almost been loving you too. Of course I haven't any right to be loving you, only Jim told me so much about you, and he adored you so thoroughly that I somehow couldn't help loving everything you did. And I've cherished a little picture of you I stole from my brother. I don't think he knows I have it but I wouldn't give it up for anything."

"Yes?" said Stormy. "But, my dear, I have carried a picture of you close to my heart all through this war. It has helped me a lot over hard places, and it got so thoroughly into my soul that once when I was ill and hungry and burning with fever, I though it was you who came into the shack where I was lying on a bunch of old potato bags and hay, and laid your cool little hand on my forehead. And I have seen you often when I looked up to the clouds and I thought you were an angel smiling down at me. Sometimes it seemed that if it hadn't been for you I never would have got through to come home. And then after the crash—I know you haven't heard about that yet, but I'm coming to it. After the crash you came alongside and wakened me, when otherwise I would have burned to death. And when I got out at last safely, and there was a long way to walk to safety, you walked with me sometimes in the night, and I held your hand this way. Of course I had no right to let myself think all that out, and dream of you, but I'm asking you for the right now, Cornelia. Will you let me love you? And will you marry me, and be with me always?"

And Cornelia lifted a lovely face and said softly, "Yes, Stormy, darling!"

And a couple of steps ahead came Barney's voice.

"Oh, I say, you two, come up to the surface and look around you. This is where we turn in to the farm, and it's worth seeing. You might not recognize it next time you come this way unless you look around now."

At first they didn't near at all, but the third time he called they came to themselves with a start, and quickened their steps.

"Yes, it's beautiful, especially in the soft dusk," said Cornelia. "And you'll just love Margaret's mother, Stormy."

"Well, if I have any love left over from loving you I might try," said Stormy. "Come on, let's go in. Say, isn't that a thrush singing at evening? I haven't heard a thrush sing for years, but I never forget those silver spoons against cut glass they use for accompaniment. Say, isn't that some song?"

They marched into the house with arms about one another.

Barney went calling through the house:

"Where are you, Sunny's mother? Where are you Mother Roselle?" and they could hear her running from upstairs:

"Yes, I'm here, Barney dear. Coming at once!"

"Well we've come to get your blessing for another couple, Mother. That is, I *think* we have? There seemed to be signs that way as we cam over. How about it, Stormy? Put it over yet, or am I butting in too soon?"

"You're butting in, Barn, but I guess it's all right with me? How about it Cornelia?"

Cornelia lifted lovely dark eyes and smiled, her face scarlet from all this publicity, but very joyous, and twinkled her consent.

"Okay, company, let's all kneel right here and get that mother-blessing. We'll need it plenty I'm sure as the years go by," said Barney.

It was Stormy who led the way. They came and stood in line before her, and at his slightly lifted hand they all knelt and bowed their heads.

Mother Roselle always knew how to fit right into anything, and she came close to them, pushed their heads close together, and laid one hand on Barney's and Margaret's heads, and the other hand on Cornelia's and Stormy's heads.

"May the dear Lord bless you, my children," she said softly, and then after an instant they arose and each of them kissed her tenderly.

"Now," said Barney, "we're going back to my house and arrange about these weddings. They ought to come off soon you know for we don't know just when we may be called to move on. We don't want a thing like this hanging fire. We've got to decide whether it will be two weddings or one double one. We've got to decide where it will be, and who shall officiate, and what we shall wear. If I'm not mistaken there's a wedding veil somewhere in my house among the heirlooms. I might wear that. Do you all think it would be becoming over my uniform?"

Hortense and her crowd happened to be driving by the Roselle farm just then and they heard peals of laughter coming from the front windows which were open.

"Mercy! What do you suppose they find to laugh about like that in there?" said Hortense.

"Well, if I'm not greatly mistaken I think you'll find that Barney is home, and he's probably down there."

"Yes," said Amelia in a kind of triumphant voice, "I saw him arrive, and he had the best-looking soldier with him, even a little taller than Barney, and just stunningly handsome. He's probably there. I saw Sunny go down and get that Cornelia girl just before dinner time. They're probably all there!"

"Oh!" said Hortense, and was very quiet for the rest of the evening.

But in the old white farmhouse there was much joy. Sunny's mother looked up with a smile.

"You would all be very welcome to have the weddings here of course," she said with a smile.

"And I know my aunt would say that too, of course," said Cornelia, "and perhaps feel hurt if I went somewhere else."

"You better come to my house," said Barney. "After all, I'm the one who started all these weddings."

Sunny gave him a radiant smile, but then she spoke in a quiet voice:

"I think that I would like to be married in the church," she said. "Then we could feel that Barney's mother was there, sitting right in the middle of the church in the same pew where she sat ever since she was married."

The look that Barney gave her then was one she would remember always, and so would the others.

"I think that would be nice," said Cornelia, "then nobody could be hurt. And it certainly would be nice to have the two weddings together. Barney and Stormy have always been so much to one another. How I wish my brother Jim could be here."

"Of course," said Stormy, "I'll see if we can't arrange for that. How about it Barn? Don't you suppose we can do that over the phone or would we have to go down to Washington to have it fixed?" He was grinning, but the two young men gave a twinkling promise to one another of what they were going to try to do.

"Well, it will be great to have some uniforms anyway," said Cornelia. "And if it is in a church you can just invite anybody who wants to come, and not have to bother about invitations. You couldn't get them engraved now, very likely anyway not if we have it in a hurry."

"And about what we'll wear," said Margaret, looking toward her mother, "would your wedding dress be all right?"

"Why of course," said her mother. "I've always kept it for you and it fits you nicely. People are not getting a lot of new finery these wartimes."

"Well, I can wear my mother's wedding dress. It's in storage, but I can have it sent at once. And the veils. Shall we wear veils?"

"Yes," said Mrs. Roselle. "Veils are always lovely to remember. I think mine is still good. It has some real lace on it. Of course it will be somewhat yellow, but that will make it all the more worth-while."

"Why, this is great," said Cornelia, "getting a wedding all arranged in a few minutes like this. But then that is the way everything has to be done in wartimes, and after all, when the war is over we may learn not to spend so much time on trifles and nonsense. But I think this is going to be pretty, too. There'll be a few friends we'll want to ask down. There's a hotel not too far away for them to come to, isn't there? And as for a reception we can just stand at the back of the church after the ceremony and shake hands."

"Great!" said Sunny. "I was afraid you would want a big reception."

"Not on your life!" said Stormy with a sigh of relief.

"Here neither," said Barney with satisfaction. "But I just want to state here and now that I think Stormy and I have found the two best girls on all the face of the earth. They've settled their weddings without a squabble, and they care more about their Lord, and their men than they do about style or what the world thinks. Come on now and let's go home and think it over. There's another day coming, and Storm, you and I have a few things to arrange. When did they say we had to come down to Washington and be decorated? I'd like to have that over so I could wear my decorations at the wedding, for I don't much think I'll flaunt them any other time, except to show them to my grandchildren. Come on now, let's go down and tell Auntie Kimberly and see how she likes it, and then everybody's happy from now on."

So they presently took up their march down the road, and the gang of pleasure-seekers came driving glumly down behind them and passed them.

"There they are," said Janet Harper.

"Heavens! Isn't he tall," said Hortense. "But they didn't speak. I don't think that was very nice of them."

"They didn't even see us," said Amelia. "They didn't see anybody but each other. They were holding hands."

"I thought your pattern Barney never did things like that," said Janet Harper.

"Oh, shut up, can't you, Janet, I have a terrible headache!" said Hortense.

But it presently got around that the wedding was coming off soon, and everybody in town who wanted to come was invited.

"I don't suppose they knew any better than to think that is good form," said Hortense with her nose in the air. But she arranged to buy a new dress to wear to the wedding to dazzle that New York girl.

Barney and Stormy were called to Washington to receive their decorations and to speak over the radio just three days before the day they had set for the wedding. And the girls arranged to go along. The whole thing was on the radio of course, and the gang at home furtively and jealously listened to it.

And then the day of the weddings came, and in the morning Jim Mayberry arrived!

It appeared that the two bridegrooms had arranged the whole matter with their superior officers, and Jim was back from his mission and due for a furlough anyway. So he came in a plane, and Jim was to be best man for both of his old buddies.

And there were other uniforms in the audience besides those three. A lot of the old friends and fellow-soldiers from the army, a few sailors. Even the admiral came with a few of his fellow-officers who wanted to do honor to the young men who had served so wonderfully in the service.

It was both the young minister and the old one who had the service together, and the whole plan of it had been carefully arranged so that the service would be a testimony to the world, of how Christ could save from sin, what true marriage should be, and how a Christian home should be carried on. It was only a few words, bits of Bible quotations, that carried these great lessons, but they were there, and the gang in the back seat stopped whispering and listened, and more than one besides Amelia Haskell said, "Heavens! If I thought I could have a marriage like that it would be worth-while trying to be a Christian, and find a fellow who believed such things."

As they came out from the church, the sun was beginning to set, and the birds were singing their evening songs. Wood thrushes spilling out their silver notes, a lot of other birds.

"I'm glad they are singing," said Margaret.

"Yes," said Cornelia as she paused by the car and looked up to the trees by the church, "Isn't it wonderful?"

"Yes," said Barney solemnly, a beautiful light in his face, "The Time of the Singing of Birds is come."